CW00971022

ALAN E. NOURSE SUPER PACK

ALAN E. NOURSE SUPER PACK

by Alan E. Nourse

TABLE OF CONTENTS

STAR SURGEON

TABLE OF CONTENTS

THE INTRUDER

The shuttle plane from the port of Philadelphia to Hospital Seattle had already gone when Dal Timgar arrived at the loading platform, even though he had taken great pains to be at least thirty minutes early for the boarding.

"You'll just have to wait for the next one," the clerk at the dispatcher's desk told him unsympathetically. "There's nothing else you can do."

"But I *can't* wait," Dal said. "I have to be in Hospital Seattle by morning." He pulled out the flight schedule and held it under the clerk's nose. "Look there! The shuttle wasn't supposed to leave for another forty-five minutes!"

The clerk blinked at the schedule, and shrugged. "The seats were full, so it left," he said. "Graduation time, you know. Everybody has to be somewhere else, right away. The next shuttle goes in three hours."

"But I had a reservation on this one," Dal insisted.

"Don't be silly," the clerk said sharply. "Only graduates can get reservations this time of year—" He broke off to stare at Dal Timgar, a puzzled frown on his face. "Let me see that reservation."

Dal fumbled in his pants pocket for the yellow reservation slip. He was wishing now that he'd kept his mouth shut. He was acutely conscious of the clerk's suspicious stare, and suddenly he felt extremely awkward. The Earth-cut trousers had never really fit Dal very well; his legs were too long and spindly, and his hips too narrow to hold the pants up properly. The tailor in the Philadelphia shop had tried three times to make a jacket fit across Dal's narrow shoulders, and finally had given up in despair. Now, as he handed the reservation slip across the counter, Dal saw the clerk staring at the fine gray fur that coated the back of his hand and arm. "Here it is," he said angrily. "See for yourself."

The clerk looked at the slip and handed it back indifferently. "It's a valid reservation, all right, but there won't be another shuttle to Hospital Seattle for three hours," he said, "unless you have a priority card, of course."

"No, I'm afraid I don't," Dal said. It was a ridiculous suggestion, and the clerk knew it. Only physicians in the Black Service of Pathology and a few

Four-star Surgeons had the power to commandeer public aircraft whenever they wished. "Can I get on the next shuttle?"

"You can try," the clerk said, "but you'd better be ready when they start loading. You can wait up on the ramp if you want to."

Dal turned and started across the main concourse of the great airport. He felt a stir of motion at his side, and looked down at the small pink fuzz-ball sitting in the crook of his arm. "Looks like we're out of luck, pal," he said gloomily. "If we don't get on the next plane, we'll miss the hearing altogether. Not that it's going to do us much good to be there anyway."

The little pink fuzz-ball on his arm opened a pair of black shoe-button eyes and blinked up at him, and Dal absently stroked the tiny creature with a finger. The fuzz-ball quivered happily and clung closer to Dal's side as he started up the long ramp to the observation platform. Automatic doors swung open as he reached the top, and Dal shivered in the damp night air. He could feel the gray fur that coated his back and neck rising to protect him from the coldness and dampness that his body was never intended by nature to endure.

Below him the bright lights of the landing fields and terminal buildings of the port of Philadelphia spread out in panorama, and he thought with a sudden pang of the great space-port in his native city, so very different from this one and so unthinkably far away. The field below was teeming with activity, alive with men and vehicles. Moments before, one of Earth's great hospital ships had landed, returning from a cruise deep into the heart of the galaxy, bringing in the gravely ill from a dozen star systems for care in one of Earth's hospitals. Dal watched as the long line of stretchers poured from the ship's hold with white-clad orderlies in nervous attendance. Some of the stretchers were encased in special atmosphere tanks; a siren wailed across the field as an emergency truck raced up with fresh gas bottles for a chlorine-breather from the Betelgeuse system, and a derrick crew spent fifteen minutes lifting down the special liquid ammonia tank housing a native of Aldebaran's massive sixteenth planet.

All about the field were physicians supervising the process of disembarcation, resplendent in the colors that signified their medical specialties. At the foot of the landing crane a Three-star Internist in the green cape of the Medical Service—obviously the commander of the ship—was talking with the welcoming dignitaries of Hospital Earth. Half a dozen doctors in the Blue Service of Diagnosis were checking new lab supplies ready to be loaded aboard. Three young Star Surgeons swung by just below Dal with their bright scarlet capes fluttering in the breeze, headed for customs and their first Earthside liberty in months. Dal watched them go by, and felt the sick, bitter feeling in the pit of his stomach that he had felt so often in recent months.

He had dreamed, once, of wearing the scarlet cape of the Red Service of Surgery too, with the silver star of the Star Surgeon on his collar. That had been a long time ago, over eight Earth years ago; the dream had faded slowly, but now the last vestige of hope was almost gone. He thought of the long years of intensive training he had just completed in the medical school of Hospital Philadelphia, the long nights of studying for exams, the long days spent in the laboratories and clinics in order to become a physician of Hospital Earth, and a wave of bitterness swept through his mind.

A dream, he thought hopelessly, *a foolish idea and nothing more. They knew before I started that they would never let me finish. They had no intention of doing so, it just amused them to watch me beat my head on a stone wall for these eight years.* But then he shook his head and felt a little ashamed of the thought. It wasn't quite true, and he knew it. He had known that it was a gamble from the very first. Black Doctor Arnquist had warned him the day he received his notice of admission to the medical school. "I can promise you nothing," the old man had said, "except a slender chance. There are those who will fight to the very end to prevent you from succeeding, and when it's all over, you may not win. But if you are willing to take that risk, at least you have a chance."

Dal had accepted the risk with his eyes wide open. He had done the best he could do, and now he had lost. True, he had not received the final, irrevocable word that he had been expelled from the medical service of Hospital Earth, but he was certain now that it was waiting for him when he arrived at Hospital Seattle the following morning.

The loading ramp was beginning to fill up, and Dal saw half a dozen of his classmates from the medical school burst through the door from the station below, shifting their day packs from their shoulders and chattering among themselves. Several of them saw him, standing by himself against the guard rail. One or two nodded coolly and turned away; the others just ignored him. Nobody greeted him, nor even smiled. Dal turned away and stared down once again at the busy activity on the field below.

"Why so gloomy, friend?" a voice behind him said. "You look as though the ship left without you."

Dal looked up at the tall, dark-haired young man, towering at his side, and smiled ruefully. "Hello, Tiger! As a matter of fact, it *did* leave. I'm waiting for the next one."

"Where to?" Frank Martin frowned down at Dal. Known as "Tiger" to everyone but the professors, the young man's nickname fit him well. He was big, even for an Earthman, and his massive shoulders and stubborn jaw only served to emphasize his bigness. Like the other recent graduates on the platform, he was wearing the colored cuff and collar of the probationary physician, in the bright green of the Green Service of Medicine. He reached out a huge hand and gently rubbed the pink fuzz-ball sitting on Dal's arm. "What's the trouble, Dal? Even Fuzzy looks worried. Where's your cuff and collar?"

"I didn't get any cuff and collar," Dal said.

"Didn't you get an assignment?" Tiger stared at him. "Or are you just taking a leave first?"

Dal shook his head. "A permanent leave, I guess," he said bitterly. "There's not going to be any assignment for me. Let's face it, Tiger. I'm washed out."

"Oh, now look here—"

"I mean it. I've been booted, and that's all there is to it."

"But you've been in the top ten in the class right through!" Tiger protested. "You know you passed your finals. What is this, anyway?"

Dal reached into his jacket and handed Tiger a blue paper envelope. "I should have expected it from the first. They sent me this instead of my cuff and collar."

Tiger opened the envelope. "From Doctor Tanner," he grunted. "The Black Plague himself. But what is it?"

"Read it," Dal said.

"'You are hereby directed to appear before the medical training council in the council chambers in Hospital Seattle at 10:00 A.M., Friday, June 24, 2375, in order that your application for assignment to a General Practice Patrol ship may be reviewed. Insignia will not be worn. Signed,

Hugo Tanner, Physician, Black Service of Pathology.'" Tiger blinked at the notice and handed it back to Dal. "I don't get it," he said finally. "You applied, you're as qualified as any of us—"

"Except in one way," Dal said, "and that's the way that counts. They don't want me, Tiger. They have never wanted me. They only let me go through school because Black Doctor Arnquist made an issue of it, and they didn't quite dare to veto him. But they never intended to let me finish, not for a minute."

For a moment the two were silent, staring down at the busy landing procedures below. A warning light was flickering across the field, signaling the landing of an incoming shuttle ship, and the supply cars broke from their positions in center of the field and fled like beetles for the security of the garages. A loudspeaker blared, announcing the incoming craft. Dal Timgar turned, lifting Fuzzy gently from his arm into a side jacket pocket and shouldering his day pack. "I guess this is my flight, Tiger. I'd better get in line."

Tiger Martin gripped Dal's slender four-fingered hand tightly. "Look," he said intensely, "this is some sort of mistake that the training council will straighten out. I'm sure of it. Lots of guys have their applications reviewed. It happens all the time, but they still get their assignments."

"Do you know of any others in this class? Or the last class?"

"Maybe not," Tiger said. "But if they were washing you out, why would the council be reviewing it? Somebody must be fighting for you."

"But Black Doctor Tanner is on the council," Dal said.

"He's not the only one on the council. It's going to work out. You'll see."

"I hope so," Dal said without conviction. He started for the loading line, then turned. "But where are *you* going to be? What ship?"

Tiger hesitated. "Not assigned yet. I'm taking a leave. But you'll be hearing from me."

The loading call blared from the loudspeaker. The tall Earthman seemed about to say something more, but Dal turned away and headed across toward the line for the shuttle plane. Ten minutes later, he was aloft as the tiny plane speared up through the black night sky and turned its needle nose toward the west.

*

He tried to sleep, but couldn't. The shuttle trip from the Port of Philadelphia to Hospital Seattle was almost two hours long because of passenger stops at Hospital Cleveland, Eisenhower City, New Chicago, and Hospital Billings. In spite of the help of the pneumatic seats and a sleep-cap, Dal could not even doze. It was one of the perfect clear nights that often occurred in midsummer now that weather control could modify Earth's air currents so well; the stars glittered against the black velvet backdrop above, and the North American continent was free of clouds. Dal stared down at the patchwork of lights that flickered up at him from the ground below.

Passing below him were some of the great cities, the hospitals, the research and training centers, the residential zones and supply centers of Hospital Earth, medical center to the powerful Galactic Confederation, physician in charge of the health of a thousand intelligent races on a thousand planets of a thousand distant star systems. Here, he knew, was the ivory tower of galactic medicine, the hub from which the medical care of the confederation arose. From the huge hospitals, research centers, and medical schools here, the physicians of Hospital Earth went out to all corners of the galaxy. In the permanent outpost clinics, in the gigantic hospital ships that served great sectors of the galaxy, and in the General Practice Patrol ships that roved from star system to star system, they answered the calls for medical assistance from a multitude of planets and races, wherever and whenever they were needed.

Dal Timgar had been on Hospital Earth for eight years, and still he was a stranger here. To him this was an alien planet, different in a thousand ways from the world where he was born and grew to manhood. For a moment now he thought of his native home, the second planet of a hot yellow star which Earthmen called "Garv" because they couldn't pronounce its full name in the Garvian tongue. Unthinkably distant, yet only days away with the power of the star-drive motors that its people had developed thousands of years before, Garv II was a warm planet, teeming with activity, the trading center of the galaxy and the governmental headquarters of the powerful Galactic Confederation of Worlds. Dal could remember the days before he had come to Hospital Earth, and the many times he had longed desperately to be home again.

He drew his fuzzy pink friend out of his pocket and rested him on his shoulder, felt the tiny silent creature rub happily against his neck. It had been his own decision to come here, Dal knew; there was no one else to blame. His people were not physicians. Their instincts and interests lay in trading and politics, not in the life sciences, and plague after plague had swept across his home planet in the centuries before Hospital Earth had been admitted as a probationary member of the Galactic Confederation.

But as long as Dal could remember, he had wanted to be a doctor. From the first time he had seen a General Practice Patrol ship landing in his home city to fight the plague that was killing his people by the thousands, he had known that this was what he wanted more than anything else: to be a physician of Hospital Earth, to join the ranks of the doctors who were serving the galaxy.

Many on Earth had tried to stop him from the first. He was a Garvian, alien to Earth's climate and Earth's people. The physical differences between Earthmen and Garvians were small, but just enough to set him apart and make him easily identifiable as an alien. He had one too few digits on his hands; his body was small and spindly, weighing a bare ninety pounds, and the coating of fine gray fur that covered all but his face and palms annoyingly grew longer and thicker as soon as he came to the comparatively cold climate of Hospital Earth to live. The bone structure of his face gave his cheeks and nose a flattened appearance, and his pale gray eyes seemed abnormally large and wistful. And even though it had long been known that Earthmen and Garvians were equal in range of intelligence, his classmates still assumed just from his appearance that he was either unusually clever or unusually stupid.

The gulf that lay between him and the men of Earth went beyond mere physical differences, however. Earthmen had differences of skin color, facial contour and physical size among them, yet made no sign of distinction. Dal's alienness went deeper. His classmates had been civil enough, yet with one or two exceptions, they had avoided him carefully. Clearly they resented his presence in their lecture rooms and laboratories. Clearly they felt that he did not belong there, studying medicine.

From the first they had let him know unmistakably that he was unwelcome, an intruder in their midst, the first member of an alien race ever to try to earn the insignia of a physician of Hospital Earth.

And now, Dal knew he had failed after all. He had been allowed to try only because a powerful physician in the Black Service of Pathology had befriended him. If it had not been for the friendship and support of another Earthman in the class, Tiger Martin, the eight years of study would have been unbearably lonely.

But now, he thought, it would have been far easier never to have started than to have his goal snatched away at the last minute. The notice of the council meeting left no doubt in his mind. He had failed. There would be lots of talk, some perfunctory debate for the sake of the record, and the medical council would wash their hands of him once and for all. The decision, he was certain, was already made. It was just a matter of going through the formal motions.

Dal felt the motors change in pitch, and the needle-nosed shuttle plane began to dip once more toward the horizon. Ahead he could see the sprawling lights of Hospital Seattle, stretching from the Cascade Mountains to the sea and beyond, north to Alaska and south toward the great California metropolitan centers. Somewhere down there was a council room where a dozen of the most powerful physicians on Hospital Earth, now sleeping soundly, would be meeting tomorrow for a trial that was already over, to pass a judgment that was already decided.

He slipped Fuzzy back into his pocket, shouldered his pack, and waited for the ship to come down for its landing. It would be nice, he thought wryly, if his reservations for sleeping quarters in the students' barracks might at least be honored, but now he wasn't even sure of that.

In the port of Seattle he went through the customary baggage check. He saw the clerk frown at his ill-fitting clothes and not-quite-human face, and then read his passage permit carefully before brushing him on through. Then he joined the crowd of travelers heading for the city subways. He didn't hear the loudspeaker blaring until the announcer had stumbled over his name half a dozen times.

"Doctor Dal Timgar, please report to the information booth."

He hurried back to central information. "You were paging me. What is it?"

"Telephone message, sir," the announcer said, his voice surprisingly respectful. "A top priority call. Just a minute."

Moments later he had handed Dal the yellow telephone message sheet, and Dal was studying the words with a puzzled frown:

CALL AT MY QUARTERS ON ARRIVAL REGARDLESS OF HOUR STOP URGENT THAT I SEE YOU STOP REPEAT URGENT

The message was signed THORVOLD ARNQUIST, BLACK SERVICE and carried the priority seal of the Four-star Pathologist. Dal read it again, shifted his pack, and started once more for the subway ramp. He thrust the message into his pocket, and his step quickened as he heard the whistle of the pressure-tube trains up ahead.

Black Doctor Arnquist, the man who had first defended his right to study medicine on Hospital Earth, now wanted to see him before the council meeting took place.

For the first time in days, Dal Timgar felt a new flicker of hope.

HOSPITAL SEATTLE

It was a long way from the students' barracks to the pathology sector where Black Doctor Arnquist lived. Dal Timgar decided not to try to go to the barracks first. It was after midnight, and even though the message had said "regardless of hour," Dal shrank from the thought of awakening a physician of the Black Service at two o'clock in the morning. He was already later arriving at Hospital Seattle than he had expected to be, and quite possibly Black Doctor Arnquist would be retiring. It seemed better to go there without delay.

But one thing took priority. He found a quiet spot in the waiting room near the subway entrance and dug into his day pack for the pressed biscuit and the canister of water he had there. He broke off a piece of the biscuit and held it up for Fuzzy to see.

Fuzzy wriggled down onto his hand, and a tiny mouth appeared just below the shoe-button eyes. Bit by bit Dal fed his friend the biscuit, with squirts of water in between bites. Finally, when the biscuit was gone, Dal squirted the rest of the water into Fuzzy's mouth and rubbed him between the eyes. "Feel better now?" he asked.

The creature seemed to understand; he wriggled in Dal's hand and blinked his eyes sleepily. "All right, then," Dal said. "Off to sleep."

Dal started to tuck him back into his jacket pocket, but Fuzzy abruptly sprouted a pair of forelegs and began struggling fiercely to get out again. Dal grinned and replaced the little creature in the crook of his arm. "Don't like that idea so well, eh? Okay, friend. If you want to watch, that suits me."

He found a map of the city at the subway entrance, and studied it carefully. Like other hospital cities on Earth, Seattle was primarily a center for patient care and treatment rather than a supply or administrative center. Here in Seattle special facilities existed for the care of the intelligent marine races that required specialized hospital care. The depths of Puget Sound served as a vast aquatic ward system where creatures which normally lived in salt-water oceans on their native planets could be cared for, and the specialty physicians who worked with marine races had facilities here for research and teaching in their specialty. The dry-land sectors of the hospital were organized to support the aquatic wards; the surgeries, the laboratories, the pharmacies and living quarters all were arranged on the periphery of the salt-water basin, and rapid-transit tubes carried medical workers, orderlies, nurses and physicians to the widespread areas of the hospital city.

The pathology sector lay to the north of the city, and Black Doctor Arnquist was the chief pathologist of Hospital Seattle. Dal found a northbound express tube, climbed into an empty capsule, and pressed the buttons for the pathology sector. Presently the capsule was shifted automatically into the pressure tube that would carry him thirty miles north to his destination.

It was the first time Dal had ever visited a Black Doctor in his quarters, and the idea made him a little nervous. Of all the medical services on Hospital Earth, none had the power of the Black Service of Pathology. Traditionally in Earth medicine, the pathologists had always occupied a position of power and discipline. The autopsy rooms had always been the "Temples of Truth" where the final, inarguable answers in medicine were ultimately found, and for centuries pathologists had been the judges and inspectors of the profession of medicine.

And when Earth had become Hospital Earth, with status as a probationary member of the Galactic Confederation of Worlds, it was natural that the Black Service of Pathology had become the governors and policy-makers, regimenting every aspect of the medical services provided by Earth physicians.

Dal knew that the medical training council, which would be reviewing his application in just a few hours, was made up of physicians from all the services—the Green Service of Medicine, the Blue Service of Diagnosis, the Red Service of Surgery, as well as the Auxiliary Services—but the Black Doctors who sat on the council would have the final say, the final veto power.

He wondered now why Black Doctor Arnquist wanted to see him. At first he had thought there might be special news for him, word perhaps that his assignment had come through after all, that the interview tomorrow would not be held. But on reflection, he realized that didn't make sense. If that were the case, Doctor Arnquist would have said so, and directed him to report to a ship. More likely, he thought, the Black Doctor wanted to see him only to soften the blow, to help him face the decision that seemed inevitable.

He left the pneumatic tube and climbed on the jitney that wound its way through the corridors of the pathology sector and into the quiet, austere quarters of the resident pathologists. He found the proper concourse, and moments later he was pressing his thumb against the identification plate outside the Black Doctor's personal quarters.

*

Black Doctor Thorvold Arnquist looked older now than when Dal had last seen him. His silvery gray hair was thinning, and there were tired lines around his eyes and mouth that Dal did not remember from before. The old man's body seemed more wispy and frail than ever, and the black cloak across his shoulders rustled as he led Dal back into a book-lined study.

The Black Doctor had not yet gone to bed. On a desk in the corner of the study several books lay open, and a roll of paper was inserted in the dicto-typer. "I knew you would get the message when you arrived," he said as he took Dal's pack, "and I thought you might be later than you planned. A good trip, I trust. And your friend here? He enjoys shuttle travel?" He smiled and stroked Fuzzy with a gnarled finger. "I suppose you wonder why I wanted to see you."

Dal Timgar nodded slowly. "About the interview tomorrow?"

"Ah, yes. The interview." The Black Doctor made a sour face and shook his head. "A bad business for you, that interview. How do you feel about it?"

Dal spread his hands helplessly. As always, the Black Doctor's questions cut through the trimming to the heart of things. They were always difficult questions to answer.

"I ... I suppose it's something that's necessary," he said finally.

"Oh?" the Black Doctor frowned. "But why necessary for you if not for the others? How many were there in your class, including all the services? Three hundred? And out of the three hundred only one was refused assignment." He looked up sharply at Dal, his pale blue eyes very alert in his aged face. "Right?"

"Yes, sir."

"And you really feel it's just normal procedure that your application is being challenged?"

"No, sir."

"How *do* you feel about it, Dal? Angry, maybe?"

Dal squirmed. "Yes, sir. You might say that."

"Perhaps even bitter," the Black Doctor said.

"I did as good work as anyone else in my class," Dal said hotly. "I did my part as well as anyone could, I didn't let up once all the way through. Bitter! Wouldn't you feel bitter?"

The Black Doctor nodded slowly. "Yes, I imagine I would," he said, sinking down into the chair behind the desk with a sigh. "As a matter of fact, I do feel a little bitter about it, even though I was afraid that it might come to this in the end. I can't blame you for your feelings." He took a deep breath. "I wish I could promise you that everything would be all right tomorrow, but I'm afraid I can't. The council has a right to review your qualifications, and it holds the power to assign you to a patrol ship on the spot, if it sees fit. Conceivably, a Black Doctor might force the council's approval, if he were the only representative of the Black service there. But I will not be the only Black Doctor sitting on the council tomorrow."

"I know that," Dal said.

Doctor Arnquist looked up at Dal for a long moment. "Why do you want to be a doctor in the first place, Dal? This isn't the calling of your people. You must be the one Garvian out of millions with the patience and peculiar mental make-up to permit you to master the scientific disciplines involved in studying medicine. Either you are different from the rest of your people—which I doubt—or else you are driven to force yourself into a pattern foreign to your nature for very compelling reasons. What are they? Why do you want medicine?"

It was the hardest question of all, the question Dal had dreaded. He knew the answer, just as he had known for most of his life that he wanted to be a doctor above all else. But he had never found a way to put the reasons into words. "I can't say," he said slowly. "I *know*, but I can't express it, and whenever I try, it just sounds silly."

"Maybe your reasons don't make reasonable sense," the old man said gently.

"But they do! At least to me, they do," Dal said. "I've always wanted to be a doctor. There's nothing else I want to do. To work at home, among my people."

"There was a plague on Garv II, wasn't there?" Doctor Arnquist said. "A cyclic thing that came back again and again. The cycle was broken just a few years ago, when the virus that caused it was finally isolated and destroyed."

"By the physicians of Hospital Earth," Dal said.

"It's happened again and again," the Black Doctor said. "We've seen the same pattern repeated a thousand times across the galaxy, and it has always puzzled us, just a little." He smiled. "You see, our knowledge and understanding of the life sciences here on Earth have always grown hand in hand with the physical sciences. We had always assumed that the same thing would happen on *any* planet where a race has developed intelligence and scientific methods of study. We were wrong, of course, which is the reason for the existence of Hospital Earth and her physicians today, but it still amazes us that with all the technology and civilization in the galaxy, we Earthmen are the only people yet discovered who have developed a broad knowledge of the processes of life and illness and death."

The old man looked up at his visitor, and Dal felt his pale blue eyes searching his face. "How badly do you want to be a doctor, Dal?"

"More than anything else I know," Dal said.

"Badly enough to do anything to achieve your goal?"

Dal hesitated, and stroked Fuzzy's head gently. "Well ... almost anything."

The Black Doctor nodded. "And that, of course, is the reason I had to see you before this interview, my friend. I know you've played the game straight right from the beginning, up to this point. Now I beg of you not to do the thing that you are thinking of doing."

For a moment Dal just stared at the little old man in black, and felt the fur on his arms and back rise up. A wave of panic flooded his mind. *He knows*! he thought frantically. *He must be able to read minds*! But he thrust the idea away. There was no way that the Black Doctor could know. No race of creatures in the galaxy had *that* power. And yet there was no doubt that Black Doctor Arnquist knew what Dal had been thinking, just as surely as if he had said it aloud.

Dal shook his head helplessly. "I ... I don't know what you mean."

"I think you do," Doctor Arnquist said. "Please, Dal. Trust me. This is not the time to lie. The thing that you were planning to do at the interview would be disastrous, even if it won you an assignment. It would be dishonest and unworthy."

Then he does know! Dal thought. *But how? I couldn't have told him, or given him any hint*. He felt Fuzzy give a frightened shiver on his arm, and then words were tumbling out of his mouth. "I don't know what you're talking about, there wasn't anything I was thinking of. I mean, what could I do? If the council wants to assign me to a ship, they will, and if they don't, they won't. I don't know what you're thinking of."

"Please." Black Doctor Arnquist held up his hand. "Naturally you defend yourself," he said. "I can't blame you for that, and I suppose this is an unforgivable breach of diplomacy even to mention it to you, but I think it must be done. Remember that we have been studying and observing your people very carefully over the past two hundred years, Dal. It is no accident that you have such a warm attachment to your little pink friend here, and it is no accident that wherever a Garvian is found, his Fuzzy is with him, isn't that so? And it is no accident that your people are such excellent tradesmen, that you are so remarkably skillful in driving bargains favorable to yourselves ... that you are in fact the most powerful single race of creatures in the whole Galactic Confederation."

The old man walked to the bookshelves behind him and brought down a thick, bound manuscript. He handed it across the desk as Dal watched him. "You may read this if you like, at your leisure. Don't worry, it's not for publication, just a private study which I have never mentioned before to anyone, but the pattern is unmistakable. This peculiar talent of your people is difficult to describe: not really telepathy, but an ability to create the emotional responses in others that will be most favorable to you. Just what part your Fuzzies play in this ability of your people I am not sure, but I'm quite certain that without them you would not have it."

He smiled at Dal's stricken face. "A forbidden topic, eh? And yet perfectly true. You know right now that if you wanted to you could virtually paralyze me with fright, render me helpless to do anything but stand here and shiver, couldn't you? Or if I were hostile to your wishes, you could suddenly force me to sympathize with you and like you enormously, until I was ready to agree to anything you wanted—"

"No," Dal broke in. "Please, you don't understand! I've never done it, not once since I came to Hospital Earth."

"I know that. I've been watching you."

"And I wouldn't think of doing it."

"Not even at the council interview?"

"Never!"

"Then let me have Fuzzy now. He is the key to this special talent of your people. Give him to me now, and go to the interview without him."

Dal drew back, trembling, trying to fight down panic. He brought his hand around to the soft fur of the little pink fuzz-ball. "I ... can't do that," he said weakly.

"Not even if it meant your assignment to a patrol ship?"

Dal hesitated, then shook his head. "Not even then. But I won't do what you're saying, I promise you."

For a long moment Black Doctor Arnquist stared at him. Then he smiled. "Will you give me your word?

"Yes, I promise."

"Then I wish you good luck. I will do what I can at the interview. But now there is a bed for you here. You will need sleep if you are to present your best appearance."

THE INQUISITION

The interview was held in the main council chambers of Hospital Seattle, and Dal could feel the tension the moment he stepped into the room. He looked at the long semicircular table, and studied the impassive faces of the four-star Physicians across the table from him.

Each of the major medical services was represented this morning. In the center, presiding over the council, was a physician of the White Service, a Four-star Radiologist whose insignia gleamed on his shoulders. There were two physicians each, representing the Red Service of Surgery, the Green Service of Medicine, the Blue Service of Diagnosis, and finally, seated at either end of the table, the representatives of the Black Service of Pathology. Black Doctor Thorvold Arnquist sat to Dal's left; he smiled faintly as the young Garvian stepped forward, then busied himself among the papers on the desk before him. To Dal's right sat another Black Doctor who was not smiling.

Dal had seen him before—the chief co-ordinator of medical education on Hospital Earth, the "Black Plague" of the medical school jokes. Black Doctor Hugo Tanner was large and florid of face, blinking owlishly at Dal over his heavy horn-rimmed glasses. The glasses were purely decorative; with modern eye-cultures and transplant techniques, no Earthman had really needed glasses to correct his vision for the past two hundred years, but on Hugo Tanner's angry face they added a look of gravity and solemnity that the Black Doctor could not achieve without them. Still glaring at Dal, Doctor Tanner leaned over to speak to the Blue Doctor on his right, and they nodded and laughed unpleasantly at some private joke.

There was no place for him to sit, so Dal stood before the table, as straight as his five-foot height would allow him. He had placed Fuzzy almost defiantly on his shoulder, and from time to time he could feel the little creature quiver and huddle against his neck as though to hide from sight under his collar.

The White Doctor opened the proceedings, and at first the questions were entirely medical. "We are meeting to consider this student's application for assignment to a General Practice Patrol ship, as a probationary physician in the Red Service of Surgery. I believe you are all acquainted with his educational qualifications?"

There was an impatient murmur around the table. The White Doctor looked up at Dal. "Your name, please?"

"Dal Timgar, sir."

"Your *full* name," Black Doctor Tanner rumbled from the right-hand end of the table.

Dal took a deep breath and began to give his full Garvian name. It was untranslatable and unpronounceable to Earthmen, who could not reproduce the sequence of pops and whistles that made up the Garvian tongue. The doctors listened, blinking, as the complex family structure and ancestry which entered into every Garvian's full name continued to roll from Dal's lips. He was entering into the third generation removed of his father's lineage when Doctor Tanner held up his hand.

"All right, all right! We will accept the abbreviated name you have used on Hospital Earth. Let it be clear on the record that the applicant is a native of the second planet of the Garv system." The Black Doctor settled back in his chair and began whispering again to the Blue Doctor next to him.

A Green Doctor cleared his throat. "Doctor Timgar, what do you consider to be the basic principle that underlies the work and services of physicians of Hospital Earth?"

It was an old question, a favorite on freshman medical school examinations. "The principle that environments and life forms in the universe may be dissimilar, but that biochemical reactions are universal throughout creation," Dal said slowly.

"Well memorized," Black Doctor Tanner said sourly. "What does it mean?"

"It means that the principles of chemistry, physiology, pathology and the other life sciences, once understood, can be applied to any living creature in the universe, and will be found valid," Dal said. "As different as the various life forms may be, the basic life processes in one life form are the same, under different conditions, as the life processes in any other life form, just as hydrogen and oxygen will combine to form water anywhere in the universe where the proper physical conditions prevail."

"Very good, very good," the Green Doctor said. "But tell me this: what in your opinion is the place of surgery in a Galactic practice of medicine?"

A more difficult question, but one that Dal's training had prepared him well to answer. He answered it, and faced another question, and another. One by one, the doctors interrogated him, Black Doctor Arnquist among them. The questions came faster and faster; some were exceedingly difficult. Once or twice Dal was stopped cold, and forced to admit that he did not know the answer. Other questions which he knew would stop other students happened to fall in fields he understood better than most, and his answers were full and succinct.

But finally the questioning tapered off, and the White Doctor shuffled his papers impatiently. "If there are no further medical questions, we can move on to another aspect of this student's application. Certain questions of policy have been raised. Black Doctor Tanner had some things to say, I believe, as co-ordinator of medical education."

The Black Doctor rose ponderously to his feet. "I have some things to say, you can be sure of that," he said, "but they have nothing to do with this Dal Timgar's educational qualifications for assignment to a General Practice Patrol ship." Black Doctor Tanner paused to glare in Dal's direction. "He has been trained in a medical school on Hospital Earth, and apparently has passed his final qualifying examinations for the Red Service of Surgery. I can't argue about that."

Black Doctor Arnquist's voice came across the room. "Then why are we having his review, Hugo? Dal Timgar's classmates all received their assignments automatically."

"Because there are other things to consider here than educational qualifications," Hugo Tanner said. "Gentlemen, consider our position for a moment. We have thousands of probationary physicians abroad in the galaxy at the present time, fine young men and women who have been trained in medical schools on Hospital Earth, and now are gaining experience and judgment while fulfilling our medical service contracts in every part of the confederation. They are probationers, but we must not forget that we physicians of Hospital Earth are also probationers. We are seeking a permanent place in this great Galactic Confederation, which was in existence many thousands of years before we even knew of its existence. It was not until our own scientists discovered the Koenig star-drive, enabling us to break free of our own solar system, that we were met face to face with a confederation of intelligent races inhabiting the galaxy—among others, the people from whom this same Dal Timgar has come."

"The history is interesting," Black Doctor Arnquist broke in, "but really, Hugo, I think most of us know it already."

"Maybe we do," Doctor Tanner said, flushing a little. "But the history is significant. Permanent membership in the confederation is contingent on two qualifications. First, we must have developed a star-drive of our own, a qualification of intelligence, if you will. The confederation has ruled that only races having a certain level of intelligence can become members. A star-drive could only be developed with a far-reaching understanding of the physical sciences, so this is a valid criterion of intelligence. But the second qualification for confederation membership is nothing more nor less than a question of usefulness."

The presiding White Doctor looked up, frowning. "Usefulness?"

"Exactly. The Galactic Confederation, with its exchange of ideas and talents, and all the wealth of civilization it has to offer, is based on a division of labor. Every member must have something to contribute, some special talent. For Earthmen, the talent was obvious very early. Our technology was primitive, our manufacturing skills mediocre, our transport and communications systems impossible. But in our understanding of the life sciences, we have far outstripped any other race in the galaxy. We had already solved the major problems of disease and longevity among our own people, while some of the most advanced races in the confederation were being reduced to helplessness by cyclic plagues which slaughtered their populations, and were caused by nothing more complex than a simple parasitic virus. Garv II is an excellent example."

One of the Red Doctors cleared his throat. "I'm afraid I don't quite see the connection. Nobody is arguing about our skill as doctors."

"Of course not," Black Doctor Tanner said. "The point is that in all the galaxy, Earthmen are by their very nature the *best* doctors, outstripping the most advanced physicians on any other planet. And this, gentlemen, is our bargaining point. We are useful to the Galactic Confederation only as physicians. The confederation needed us badly enough to admit us to probational membership, but if we ever hope to become full members of the confederation, we must demonstrate our usefulness, our unique skill, as physicians. We have worked hard to prove ourselves. We have made

Hospital Earth the galactic center of study and treatment of diseases of many races. Earthmen on the General Practice Patrol ships visit planets in the remotest sections, and their reputation as physicians has grown. Every year new planets are writing full medical service contracts with us … as Earthmen serving the galaxy—"

"As *physicians* serving the galaxy," Black Doctor Arnquist's voice shot across the room.

"As far as the confederation has been concerned, the two have been synonymous," Hugo Tanner roared. "*Until now.* But now we have an alien among us. We have allowed a non-Earthman to train in our medical schools. He has completed the required work, his qualifications are acceptable, and now he proposes to go out on a patrol ship as a physician of the Red Service of Surgery. But think of what you are doing if you permit him to go! You will be proving to every planet in the confederation that they don't really need Earthmen after all, that any race from any planet might produce physicians just as capable as Earthmen."

The Black Doctor turned slowly to face Dal, his mouth set in a grim line. As he talked, his face had grown dark with anger. "Understand that I have nothing against this creature as an individual. Perhaps he would prove to be a competent physician, although I cannot believe it. Perhaps he would carry on the traditions of medical service we have worked so long to establish, although I doubt it. But I do know that if we permit him to become a qualified physician, it will be the beginning of the end for Hospital Earth. We will be selling out our sole bargaining position. We can forget our hopes for membership in the confederation, because one like him this year will mean two next year, and ten the next, and there will be no end to it. We should have stopped it eight years ago, but certain ones prevailed to admit Dal Timgar to training. If we do not stop it now, for all time, we will never be able to stop it."

Slowly the Black Doctor sat down, motioning to an orderly at the rear of the room. The orderly brought a glass of water and a small capsule which Black Doctor Tanner gulped down. The other doctors were talking heatedly among themselves as Black Doctor Arnquist rose to his feet. "Then you are claiming that our highest calling is to keep medicine in the hands of Earthmen alone?" he asked softly.

Doctor Tanner flushed. "Our highest calling is to provide good medical care for our patients," he said.

"The best possible medical care?"

"I never said otherwise."

"And yet you deny the ancient tradition that a physician's duty is to help his patients help themselves," Black Doctor Arnquist said.

"I said no such thing!" Hugo Tanner cried, jumping to his feet. "But we must protect ourselves. We have no other power, nothing else to sell."

"And I say that if we must sell our medical skill for our own benefit first, then we are not worthy to be physicians to anyone," Doctor Arnquist snapped. "You make a very convincing case, but if we examine it closely, we see that it amounts to nothing but fear and selfishness."

"Fear?" Doctor Tanner cried. "What do we have to fear if we can maintain our position? But if we must yield to a Garvian who has no business in medicine in the first place, what can we have left but fear?"

"If I were really convinced that Earthmen were the best physicians in the galaxy," Black Doctor Arnquist replied, "I don't think I'd have to be afraid."

The Black Doctor at the end of the table stood up, shaking with rage. "Listen to him!" he cried to the others. "Once again he is defending this creature and turning his back on common sense. All I ask is that we keep our skills among our own people and avoid the contamination that will surely result—"

Doctor Tanner broke off, his face suddenly white. He coughed, clutching at his chest, and sank down groping for his medicine box and the water glass. After a moment he caught his breath and shook his head. "There's nothing more I can say," he said weakly. "I have done what I could, and the decision is up to the rest of you." He coughed again, and slowly the color came back into his face. The Blue Doctor had risen to help him, but Tanner waved him aside. "No, no, it's nothing. I allowed myself to become angry."

Black Doctor Arnquist spread his hands. "Under the circumstances, I won't belabor the point," he said, "although I think it would be good if Doctor Tanner would pause in his activities long enough for the surgery that would make his anger less dangerous to his own life. But he represents a view, and his right to state it is beyond reproach." Doctor Arnquist looked from face to face along the council table. "The decision is yours, gentlemen, I would ask only that you consider what our highest calling as physicians really is—a duty that overrides fear and selfishness. I believe Dal Timgar would be a good physician, and that this is more important than the planet of his origin. I think he would uphold the honor of Hospital Earth wherever he went, and give us his loyalty as well as his service. I will vote to accept his application, and thus cancel out my colleague's negative vote. The deciding votes will be cast by the rest of you."

He sat down, and the White Doctor looked at Dal Timgar. "It would be good if you would wait outside," he said. "We will call you as soon as a decision is reached."

*

Dal waited in an anteroom, feeding Fuzzy and trying to put out of his mind for a moment the heated argument still raging in the council chamber. Fuzzy was quivering with fright; unable to speak, the tiny creature nevertheless clearly experienced emotions, even though Dal himself did not know how he received impressions, nor why.

But Dal knew that there was a connection between the tiny pink creature's emotions and the peculiar talent that Black Doctor Arnquist had spoken of the night before. It was not a telepathic power that Dal and his people possessed. Just *what* it was, was difficult to define, yet Dal knew that every Garvian depended upon it to some extent in dealing with people around him. He knew that when Fuzzy was sitting on his arm he could sense the emotions of those around him—the anger, the fear, the happiness, the suspicion—and he knew that under certain circumstances, in a way he did not clearly understand, he could wilfully change the feelings of others toward himself. Not a great deal, perhaps, nor in any specific way, but just enough to make them look upon him and his wishes more favorably than they otherwise might.

Throughout his years on Hospital Earth he had vigilantly avoided using this strange talent. Already he was different enough from Earthmen in appearance, in ways of thinking, in likes and dislikes. But these differences were not advantages, and he had realized that if his classmates had ever dreamed of the advantage that he had, minor as it was, his hopes of becoming a physician would have been destroyed completely.

And in the council room he had kept his word to Doctor Arnquist. He had felt Fuzzy quivering on his shoulder; he had sensed the bitter anger in Black Doctor Tanner's mind, and the temptation deliberately to mellow that anger had been almost overwhelming, but he had turned it aside. He had answered questions that were asked him, and listened to the debate with a growing sense of hopelessness.

And now the chance was gone. The decision was being made.

He paced the floor, trying to remember the expressions of the other doctors, trying to remember what had been said, how many had seemed friendly and how many hostile, but he knew that only intensified the torture. There was nothing he could do now but wait.

At last the door opened, and an orderly nodded to him. Dal felt his legs tremble as he walked into the room and faced the semi-circle of doctors. He tried to read the answer on their faces, but even Black Doctor Arnquist sat impassively, doodling on the pad before him, refusing to meet Dal's eyes.

The White Doctor took up a sheet of paper. "We have considered your application, and have reached a decision. You will be happy to know that your application for assignment has been tentatively accepted."

Dal heard the words, and it seemed as though the room were spinning around him. He wanted to shout for joy and throw his arms around Black Doctor Arnquist, but he stood perfectly still, and suddenly he noticed that Fuzzy was very quiet on his shoulder.

"You will understand that this acceptance is not irrevocable," the White Doctor went on. "We are not willing to guarantee your ultimate acceptance as a fully qualified Star Surgeon at this point. You will be allowed to wear a collar and cuff, uniform and insignia of a probationary physician, in the Red Service, and will be assigned aboard the General Practice Patrol ship *Lancet*, leaving from Hospital Seattle next Tuesday. If you prove your ability in that post, your performance will once again be reviewed by this board, but you alone will determine our decision then. Your final acceptance as a Star Surgeon will depend entirely upon your conduct as a member of the patrol ship's crew." He smiled at Dal, and set the paper down. "The council wishes you well. Do you have any questions?"

"Just one," Dal managed to say. "Who will my crewmates be?"

"As is customary, a probationer from the Green Service of Medicine and one from the Blue Service of Diagnosis. Both have been specially selected by this council. Your Blue Doctor will be Jack Alvarez, who has shown great promise in his training in diagnostic medicine."

"And the Green Doctor?"

"A young man named Frank Martin," the White Doctor said. "Known to his friends, I believe, as 'Tiger.'"

THE GALACTIC PILL PEDDLERS

The ship stood tall and straight on her launching pad, with the afternoon sunlight glinting on her hull. Half a dozen crews of check-out men were swarming about her, inspecting her engine and fuel supplies, riding up the gantry crane to her entrance lock, and guiding the great cargo nets from the loading crane into her afterhold. High up on her hull Dal Timgar could see a golden caduceus emblazoned, the symbol of the General Practice Patrol, and beneath it the ship's official name:

GPPS 238 *LANCET*

Dal shifted his day pack down from his shoulders, ridiculously pleased with the gleaming scarlet braid on the collar and cuff of his uniform, and lifted Fuzzy up on his shoulder to see. It seemed to Dal that everyone he had passed in the terminal had been looking at the colorful insignia; it was all he could do to keep from holding his arm up and waving it like a banner.

"You'll get used to it," Tiger Martin chuckled as they waited for the jitney to take them across to the launching pad. "At first you think everybody is impressed by the colors, until you see some guy go past with the braid all faded and frazzled at the edges, and then you realize that you're just the latest greenhorn in a squad of two hundred thousand men."

"It's still good to be wearing it," Dal said. "I couldn't really believe it until Black Doctor Arnquist turned the collar and cuff over to me." He looked suspiciously at Tiger. "You must have known a lot more about that interview than you let on. Or, was it just coincidence that we were assigned together?"

"Not coincidence, exactly." Tiger grinned. "I didn't know what was going to happen. I'd requested assignment with you on my application, and then when yours was held up, Doctor Arnquist asked me if I'd be willing to wait for assignment until the interview was over. So I said okay. He seemed to think you had a pretty good chance."

"I'd never have made it without his backing," Dal said.

"Well, anyway, he figured that if you *were* assigned, it would be a good idea to have a friend on the patrol ship team."

"I won't argue about *that*," Dal said. "But who is the Blue Service man?"

Tiger's face darkened. "I don't know much about him," he said. "He trained in California, and I met him just once, at a diagnosis and therapy conference. He's supposed to be plenty smart, according to the grapevine. I guess he'd have to be, to pass Diagnostic Service finals." Tiger chuckled. "Any dope can make it in the Medical or Surgical Services, but diagnosis is something else again."

"Will he be in command?"

"On the *Lancet*? Why should he? We'll share command, just like any patrol ship crew. If we run into problems we can't agree on, we holler for help. But if he acts like most of the Blue Doctors I know, he'll *think* he's in command."

A jitney stopped for them, and then zoomed out across the field toward the ship. The gantry platform was just clanging to the ground, unloading three technicians and a Four-bar Electronics Engineer. Tiger and Dal rode the platform up again and moments later stepped through the entrance lock of the ship that would be their home base for months and perhaps years.

They found the bunk room to the rear of the control and lab sections. A duffel bag was already lodged on one of the bunks; one of the foot lockers was already occupied, and a small but expensive camera and a huge pair of field glasses were hanging from one of the wall brackets.

"Looks like our man has already arrived," Tiger said, tossing down his own duffel bag and looking around the cramped quarters. "Not exactly a luxury suite, I'd say. Wonder where he is?"

"Let's look up forward," Dal said. "We've plenty to do before we take off. Maybe he's just getting an early start."

They explored the ship, working their way up the central corridor past the communications and computer rooms and the laboratory into the main control and observation room. Here they found a thin, dark-haired young man in a bright blue collar and cuff, sitting engrossed with a tape-reader.

For a moment they thought he hadn't heard them. Then, as though reluctant to tear himself away, the Blue Doctor sighed, snapped off the reader, and turned on the swivel stool.

"So!" he said. "I was beginning to wonder if you were ever going to get here."

"We ran into some delays," Tiger said. He grinned and held out his hand. "Jack Alvarez? Tiger Martin. We met each other at that conference in Chicago last year."

"Yes, I remember," the Blue Doctor said. "You found some holes in a paper I gave. Matter of fact, I've plugged them up very nicely since then. You'd have trouble finding fault with the work now." Jack Alvarez turned his eyes to Dal. "And I suppose this is the Garvian I've been hearing about, complete with his little pink stooge."

The moment they had walked in the door, Dal had felt Fuzzy crouch down tight against his shoulder. Now a wave of hostility struck his mind like a shower of ice water. He had never seen this thin, dark-haired youth before, or even heard of him, but he recognized this sharp impression of hatred and anger unmistakably. He had felt it a thousand times among his medical school classmates during the past eight years, and just hours before he had felt it in the council room when Black Doctor Tanner had turned on him.

"It's really a lucky break that we have Dal for a Red Doctor," Tiger said. "We almost didn't get him."

"Yes, I heard all about how lucky we are," Jack Alvarez said sourly. He looked Dal over from the gray fur on the top of his head to the spindly legs in the ill-fitting trousers. Then the Blue Doctor shrugged in disgust and turned back to the tape-reader. "A Garvian and his Fuzzy!" he muttered. "Let's hope one or the other knows something about surgery."

"I think we'll do all right," Dal said slowly.

"I think you'd better," Jack Alvarez replied.

Dal and Tiger looked at each other, and Tiger shrugged. "It's all right," he said. "We know our jobs, and we'll manage."

Dal nodded, and started back for the bunk room. No doubt, he thought, they would manage.

But if he had thought before that the assignment on the *Lancet* was going to be easy, he knew now that he was wrong.

Tiger Martin may have been Doctor Arnquist's selection as a crewmate for him, but there was no question in his mind that the Blue Doctor on the *Lancet*'s crew was Black Doctor Hugo Tanner's choice.

*

The first meeting with Jack Alvarez hardly seemed promising to either Dal or Tiger, but if there was trouble coming, it was postponed for the moment by common consent. In the few days before blast-off there was no time for conflict, or even for much talk. Each of the three crewmen had two full weeks of work to accomplish in two days; each knew his job and buried himself in it with a will.

The ship's medical and surgical supplies had to be inventoried, and missing or required supplies ordered up. New supplies coming in had to be checked, tested, and stored in the ship's limited hold space. It was like preparing for an extended pack trip into wilderness country; once the *Lancet* left its home base on Hospital Earth it was a world to itself, equipped to support its physician-crew and provide the necessary equipment and data they would need to deal with the problems they would face. Like all patrol ships, the *Lancet* was equipped with automatic launching, navigation and drive mechanisms; no crew other than the three doctors was required, and in the event of mechanical failures, maintenance ships were on continual call.

The ship was responsible for patrolling an enormous area, including hundreds of stars and their planetary systems—yet its territory was only a tiny segment of the galaxy. Landings were to be made at various specified planets maintaining permanent clinic outposts of Hospital Earth; certain staple supplies were carried for each of these check points. Aside from these lonely clinic contacts, the nearest port of call for the *Lancet* was one of the hospital ships that continuously worked slow orbits through the star systems of the confederation.

But a hospital ship, with its staff of Two-star and Three-star Physicians, was not to be called except in cases of extreme need. The probationers on the patrol ships were expected to be self-sufficient. Their job was to handle diagnosis and care of all but the most difficult problems that arose in their travels. They were the first to answer the medical calls from any planet with a medical service contract with Hospital Earth.

It was an enormous responsibility for doctors-in-training to assume, but over the years it had proven the best way to train and weed out new doctors for the greater responsibilities of hospital ship and Hospital Earth assignments. There was no set period of duty on the patrol ships; how long a young doctor remained in the General Practice Patrol depended to a large extent upon how well he handled the problems and responsibilities that faced him; and since the first years of Hospital Earth, the fledgling doctors in the General Practice Patrol—the self-styled "Galactic Pill Peddlers"—had lived up to their responsibilities. The reputation of Hospital Earth rested on their shoulders, and they never forgot it.

As he worked on his inventories, Dal Timgar thought of Doctor Arnquist's words to him after the council had handed down its decision. "Remember that judgment and skill are two different things," he had said. "Without skill in the basic principles of diagnosis and treatment, medical judgment isn't much help, but skill without the judgment to know how and when to use it can be downright dangerous. You'll be judged both on the judgment you use in deciding the right thing to do, and on the skill you use in doing it." He had given Dal the box with the coveted collar and cuff. "The colors are pretty, but never forget what they stand for. Until you can convince the council that you have both the skill and the judgment of a good physician, you will never get your Star. And you will be watched closely; Black Doctor Tanner and certain others will be waiting for the slightest excuse to recall you from the *Lancet*. If you give them the opportunity, nothing I can do will stop it."

And now, as they worked to prepare the ship for service, Dal was determined that the opportunity would not arise. When he was not working in the storerooms, he was in the computer room, reviewing the thousands of tapes that carried the basic information about the contract planets where they would be visiting, and the races that inhabited them. If errors and fumbles and mistakes were made by the crew of the *Lancet*, he thought grimly, it would not be Dal Timgar who made them.

The first night they met in the control room to divide the many extracurricular jobs involved in maintaining a patrol ship.

Tiger's interest in electronics and communications made him the best man to handle the radio; he accepted the post without comment. "Jack, you should be in charge of the computer," he said, "because you'll be the one who'll need the information first. The lab is probably your field too. Dal can be responsible for stores and supplies as well as his own surgical instruments."

Jack shrugged. "I'd just as soon handle supplies, too," he said.

"Well, there's no need to overload one man," Tiger said.

"I wouldn't mind that. But when there's something I need, I want to be sure it's going to be there without any goof-ups," Jack said.

"I can handle it all right," Dal said.

Jack just scowled. "What about the contact man when we make landings?" he asked Tiger.

"Seems to me Dal would be the one for that, too," Tiger said. "His people are traders and bargainers; right, Dal? And first contact with the people on unfamiliar planets can be important."

"It sure can," Jack said. "Too important to take chances with. Look, this is a ship from Hospital Earth. When somebody calls for help, they expect to see an Earthman turn up in response. What are they going to think when a patrol ship lands and *he* walks out?"

Tiger's face darkened. "They'll be able to see his collar and cuff, won't they?"

"Maybe. But they may wonder what he's doing wearing them."

"Well, they'll just have to learn," Tiger snapped. "And you'll have to learn, too, I guess."

Dal had been sitting silently. Now he shook his head. "I think Jack is right on this one," he said. "It would be better for one of you to be contact man."

"Why?" Tiger said angrily. "You're as much of a doctor from Hospital Earth as we are, and the sooner we get your position here straight, the better. We aren't going to have any ugly ducklings on this ship, and we aren't going to hide you in the hold every time we land on a planet. If we want to make anything but a mess of this cruise, we've got to work as a team, and that means everybody shares the important jobs."

"That's fine," Dal said, "but I still think Jack is right on this point. If we are walking into a medical problem on a planet where the patrol isn't too well known, the contact man by rights ought to be an Earthman."

Tiger started to say something, and then spread his hands helplessly. "Okay," he said. "If you're satisfied with it, let's get on to these other things." But obviously he wasn't satisfied, and when Jack disappeared toward the storeroom, Tiger turned to Dal. "You shouldn't have given in," he said. "If you give that guy as much as an inch, you're just asking for trouble."

"It isn't a matter of giving in," Dal insisted. "I think he was right, that's all. Don't let's start a fight where we don't have to."

Tiger yielded the point, but when Jack returned, Tiger avoided him, keeping to himself the rest of the evening. And later, as he tried to get to sleep, Dal wondered for a moment. Maybe Tiger was right. Maybe he was just dodging a head-on clash with the Blue Doctor now and setting the stage for a real collision later.

Next day the argument was forgotten in the air of rising excitement as embarkation orders for the *Lancet* came through. Preparations were completed, and only last-minute double-checks were required before blast-off.

But an hour before count-down began, a jitney buzzed across the field, and a Two-star Pathologist climbed aboard with his three black-cloaked orderlies. "Shakedown inspection," he said curtly. "Just a matter of routine." And with that he stalked slowly through the ship, checking the storage holds, the inventories, the lab, the computer with its information banks, and the control room. As he went along he kept firing medical questions at Dal and Tiger, hardly pausing long enough for the answers, and ignoring Jack Alvarez completely. "What's the normal range of serum cholesterol in a vegetarian race with Terran environment? How would you run a Wenberg electrophoresis? How do you determine individual radiation tolerance? How would you prepare a heart culture for cardiac transplant on board this ship?" The questions went on until Tiger and Dal were breathless, as count-down time grew closer and closer. Finally the Black Doctor turned back toward the entrance lock. He seemed vaguely disappointed as he checked the record sheets the orderlies had been keeping. With an odd look at Dal, he shrugged. "All right, here are your clearance papers," he said to Jack. "Your supply of serum globulin fractions is up to black-book requirements, but you'll run short if you happen to hit a virus epidemic; better take on a couple of more cases. And check central information just before leaving. We've signed two new contracts in the past week, and the co-ordinator's office has some advance information on both of them."

When the inspector had gone, Tiger wiped his forehead and sighed. "That was no routine shakedown!" he said. "What *is* a Wenberg electrophoresis?"

"A method of separating serum proteins," Jack Alvarez said. "You ran them in third year biochemistry. And if we *do* hit a virus epidemic, you'd better know how, too."

He gave Tiger an unpleasant smile, and started back down the corridor as the count-down signal began to buzz.

But for all the advance arrangements they had made to divide the ship's work, it was Dal Timgar who took complete control of the *Lancet* for the first two weeks of its cruise. Neither Tiger nor Jack challenged his command; not a word was raised in protest. The Earthmen were too sick to talk, much less complain about anything.

For Dal the blast-off from the port of Seattle and the conversion into Koenig star-drive was nothing new. His father owned a fleet of Garvian trading ships that traveled to the far corners of the galaxy by means of a star-drive so similar to the Koenig engines that only an electronic engineer could tell them apart. All his life Dal had traveled on the outgoing freighters with his father; star-drive conversion was no surprise to him.

But for Jack and Tiger, it was their first experience in a star-drive ship. The *Lancet*'s piloting and navigation were entirely automatic; its destination was simply coded into the drive computers, and the ship was ready to leap across light years of space in a matter of hours. But the conversion to star-drive, as the *Lancet* was wrenched, crew and all, out of the normal space-time continuum, was far outside of normal human experience. The physical and emotional shock of the conversion hit Jack and Tiger like a sledge hammer, and during the long hours while the ship was traveling through the time-less, distance-less universe of the drive to the pre-set co-ordinates where it materialized again into conventional space-time, the Earthmen were retching violently, too sick to budge from the bunk room. It took over two weeks, with stops at half a dozen contract planets, before Jack and Tiger began to adjust themselves to the frightening and confusing sensations of conversion to star-drive. During this time Dal carried the load of the ship's work alone, while the others lay gasping and exhausted in their bunks, trying to rally strength for the next shift.

To his horror, Dal discovered that the first planetary stop-over was traditionally a hazing stop. It had been a well-kept patrol secret; the outpost clinic on Tempera VI was waiting eagerly for the arrival of the new "green" crew, knowing full well that the doctors aboard would hardly be able to stumble out of their bunks, much less to cope with medical problems. The outpost men had concocted a medical "crisis" of staggering proportions to present to the *Lancet*'s crew; they were so clearly disappointed to find the ship's Red Doctor in full command of himself that Dal obligingly became violently ill too, and did his best to mimick Jack and Tiger's floundering efforts to pull themselves together and do *something* about the "problem" that suddenly descended upon them.

Later, there was a party and celebration, with music and food, as the clinic staff welcomed the pale and shaken doctors into the joke. The outpost men plied Dal for the latest news from Hospital Earth. They were surprised to see a Garvian aboard the *Lancet*, but no one at the outpost showed any sign of resentment at the scarlet braid on Dal's collar and cuff.

Slowly Jack and Tiger got used to the peculiarities of popping in and out of hyperspace. It was said that immunity to star-drive sickness was hard to acquire, but lasted a lifetime, and would never again bother them once it was achieved. Bit by bit the Earthmen crept out of their shells, to find the ship in order and a busy Dal Timgar relieved and happy to have them aboard again.

Fortunately, the medical problems that came to the *Lancet* in the first few weeks were largely routine. The ship stopped at the specified contact points—some far out near the rim of the galactic constellation, others in closer to the densely star-populated center. At each outpost clinic the *Lancet* was welcomed with open arms. The outpost men were hungry for news from home, and happy to see fresh supplies; but they were also glad to review the current medical problems on their planets with the new doctors, exchanging opinions and arguing diagnosis and therapy into the small hours of the night.

Occasionally calls came in to the ship from contract planets in need of help. Usually the problems were easy to handle. On Singall III, a tiny planet of a cooling giant star, help was needed to deal with a new outbreak of a smallpox-like plague that had once decimated the population; the disease had finally been controlled after a Hospital Earth research team had identified the organism that caused it, determined its molecular structure, and synthesized an antibiotic that could destroy it without damaging the body of the host. But now a flareup had occurred. The *Lancet* brought in supplies of the antibiotic, and Tiger Martin spent two days showing

Singallese physicians how to control further outbreaks with modern methods of immunization and antisepsis.

Another planet called for a patrol ship when a bridge-building disaster occurred; one of the beetle-like workmen had been badly crushed under a massive steel girder. Dal spent over eighteen hours straight with the patient in the *Lancet*'s surgery, carefully repairing the creature's damaged exoskeleton and grafting new segments of bone for regeneration of the hopelessly ruined parts, with Tiger administering anaesthesia and Jack preparing the grafts from the freezer.

On another planet Jack faced his first real diagnostic challenge and met the test with flying colors. Here a new cancer-like degenerative disease had been appearing among the natives of the planet. It had never before been noted. Initial attempts to find a causative agent had all three of the *Lancet*'s crew spending sleepless nights for a week, but Jack's careful study of the pattern of the disease and the biochemical reactions that accompanied it brought out the answer: the disease was caused by a rare form of genetic change which made crippling alterations in an essential enzyme system. Knowing this, Tiger quickly found a drug which could be substituted for the damaged enzyme, and the problem was solved. They left the planet, assuring the planetary government that laboratories on Hospital Earth would begin working at once to find a way actually to rebuild the damaged genes in the embryonic cells, and thus put a permanent end to the disease.

These were routine calls, the kind of ordinary general medical work that the patrol ships were expected to handle. But the visits to the various planets were welcome breaks in the pattern of patrol ship life. The *Lancet* was fully equipped, but her crew's quarters and living space were cramped. Under the best conditions, the crewmen on patrol ships got on each other's nerves; on the *Lancet* there was an additional focus of tension that grew worse with every passing hour.

From the first Jack Alvarez had made no pretense of pleasure at Dal's company, but now it seemed that he deliberately sought opportunities to annoy him. The thin Blue Doctor's face set into an angry mold whenever Dal was around. He would get up and leave when Dal entered the control room, and complained loudly and bitterly at minor flaws in Dal's shipboard work. Nothing Dal did seemed to please him.

But Tiger had a worse time controlling himself at the Blue Doctor's digs and slights than Dal did. "It's like living in an armed camp," he complained one night when Jack had stalked angrily out of the bunk room. "Can't even open your mouth without having him jump down your throat."

"I know," Dal said.

"And he's doing it on purpose."

"Maybe so. But it won't help to lose your temper."

Tiger clenched a huge fist and slammed it into his palm. "He's just deliberately picking at you and picking at you," he said. "You can't take that forever. Something's got to break."

"It's all right," Dal assured him. "I just ignore it."

But when Jack began to shift his attack to Fuzzy, Dal could ignore it no longer.

One night in the control room Jack threw down the report he was writing and turned angrily on Dal. "Tell your friend there to turn the other way before I lose my temper and splatter him all over the wall," he said, pointing to Fuzzy. "All he does is sit there and stare at me and I'm getting fed up with it."

Fuzzy drew himself up tightly, shivering on Dal's shoulder. Dal reached up and stroked the tiny creature, and Fuzzy's shoe-button eyes disappeared completely. "There," Dal said. "Is that better?"

Jack stared at the place the eyes had been, and his face darkened suspiciously. "Well, what happened to them?" he demanded.

"What happened to what?"

"To his eyes, you idiot!"

Dal looked down at Fuzzy. "I don't see any eyes."

Jack jumped up from the stool. He scowled at Fuzzy as if commanding the eyes to come back again. All he saw was a small ball of pink fur. "Look, he's been blinking them at me for a week," he snarled. "I thought all along there was something funny about him. Sometimes he's got legs and sometimes he hasn't. Sometimes he looks fuzzy, and other times he hasn't got any hair at all."

"He's a pleomorph," Dal said. "No cellular structure at all, just a protein-colloid matrix."

Jack glowered at the inert little pink lump. "Don't be silly," he said, curious in spite of himself. "What holds him together?"

"Who knows? I don't. Some kind of electro-chemical cohesive force. The only reason he has 'eyes' is because he thinks I want him to have eyes. If you don't like it, he won't have them any more."

"Well, that's very obliging," Jack said. "But why do you keep him around? What good does he do you, anyhow? All he does is eat and drink and sleep."

"Does he have to do something?" Dal said evasively. "He isn't bothering you. Why pick on him?"

"He just seems to worry you an awful lot," Jack said unpleasantly. "Let's see him a minute." He reached out for Fuzzy, then jerked his finger back with a yelp. Blood dripped from the finger tip.

Jack's face slowly went white. "Why, he—he *bit* me!"

"Yes, and you're lucky he didn't take a finger off," Dal said, trembling with anger. "He doesn't like you any more than I do, and you'll get bit every time you come near him, so you'd better keep your hands to yourself."

"Don't worry," Jack Alvarez said, "he won't get another chance. You can just get rid of him."

"Not a chance," Dal said. "You leave him alone and he won't bother you, that's all. And the same thing goes for me."

"If he isn't out of here in twelve hours, I'll get a warrant," Jack said tightly. "There are laws against keeping dangerous pets on patrol ships."

Somewhere in the main corridor an alarm bell began buzzing. For a moment Dal and Jack stood frozen, glaring at each other. Then the door burst open and Tiger Martin's head appeared. "Hey, you two, let's get moving! We've got a call coming in, and it looks like a tough one. Come on back here!"

They headed back toward the radio room. The signal was coming through frantically as Tiger reached for the pile of punched tape running out on the floor. But as they crowded into the radio room, Dal felt Jack's hand on his arm. "If you think I was fooling, you're wrong," the Blue Doctor said through his teeth. "You've got twelve hours to get rid of him."

CRISIS ON MORUA VIII

The three doctors huddled around the teletype, watching as the decoded message was punched out on the tape. "It started coming in just now," Tiger said. "And they've been beaming the signal in a spherical pattern, apparently trying to pick up the nearest ship they could get. There's certainly some sort of trouble going on."

The message was brief, repeated over and over: REQUIRE MEDICAL AID URGENT REPLY AT ONCE. This was followed by the code letters that designated the planet, its location, and the number of its medical service contract.

Jack glanced at the code. "Morua VIII," he said. "I think that's a grade I contract." He began punching buttons on the reference panel, and several screening cards came down the slot from the information bank. "Yes. The eighth planet of a large Sol-type star, the only inhabited planet in the system with a single intelligent race, ursine evolutionary pattern." He handed the cards to Tiger. "Teddy-bears, yet!"

"Mammals?" Tiger said.

"Looks like it. And they even hibernate."

"What about the contract?" Dal asked.

"Grade I," said Tiger. "And they've had a thorough survey. Moderately advanced in their own medical care, but they have full medical coverage any time they think they need it. We'd better get an acknowledgment back to them. Jack, get the ship ready to star-jump while Dal starts digging information out of the bank. If this race has its own doctors, they'd only be hollering for help if they're up against a tough one."

Tiger settled down with earphones and transmitter to try to make contact with the Moruan planet, while Jack went forward to control and Dal started to work with the tape reader. There was no argument now, and no dissension. The procedure to be followed was a well-established routine: acknowledge the call, estimate arrival time, relay the call and response to the programmers on Hospital Earth, prepare for star-drive, and start gathering data fast. With no hint of the nature of the trouble, their job was to get there, equipped with as much information about the planet and its people as time allowed.

The Moruan system was not distant from the *Lancet*'s present location. Tiger calculated that two hours in Koenig drive would put the ship in the vicinity of the planet, with another hour required for landing procedures. He passed the word on to the others, and Dal began digging through the mass of information in the tape library on Morua VIII and its people.

There was a wealth of data. Morua VIII had signed one of the first medical service contracts with Hospital Earth, and a thorough medical, biochemical, social and psychological survey had been made on the people of that world. Since the original survey, much additional information had been amassed, based on patrol ship reports and dozens of specialty studies that had been done there.

And out of this data, a picture of Morua VIII and its inhabitants began to emerge.

The Moruans were moderately intelligent creatures, warm-blooded air breathers with an oxygen-based metabolism. Their planet was cold, with 17 per cent oxygen and much water vapor in its atmosphere. With its vast snow-fields and great mountain ranges, the planet was a popular resort area for oxygen-breathing creatures; most of the natives were engaged in some work related to winter sports. They were well fitted anatomically for their climate, with thick black fur, broad flat hind feet and a four-inch layer of fat between their skin and their vital organs.

Swiftly Dal reviewed the emergency file, checking for common drugs and chemicals that were poisonous to Moruans, accidents that were common to the race, and special problems that had been met by previous patrol ships. The deeper he dug into the mass of data, the more worried he became. Where should he begin? Searching in the dark, there was no way to guess what information would be necessary and what part totally useless.

He buzzed Tiger. "Any word on the nature of the trouble?" he asked.

"Just got through to them," Tiger said. "Not too much to go on, but they're really in an uproar. Sounds like they've started some kind of organ-transplant surgery and their native surgeon got cold feet halfway through and wants us to bail him out." Tiger paused. "I think this is going to be your show, Dal. Better check up on Moruan anatomy."

It was better than no information, but not much better. Fuzzy huddled on Dal's shoulder as if he could sense his master's excitement. Very few races under contract with Hospital Earth ever attempted their own major surgery. If a Moruan surgeon had walked into a tight spot in the operating room, it could be a real test of skill to get him—and his patient—out of it, even on a relatively simple procedure. But organ-transplantation, with the delicate vascular surgery and micro-surgery that it entailed, was never simple. In incompetent hands, it could turn into a nightmare.

Dal took a deep breath and began running the anatomical atlas tapes through the reader, checking the critical points of Moruan anatomy. Oxygen-transfer system, circulatory system, renal filtration system—at first glance, there was little resemblance to any of the "typical" oxygen-breathing mammals Dal had studied in medical school. But then something struck a familiar note, and he remembered studying the peculiar Moruan renal system, in which the creature's chemical waste products were filtered from the bloodstream in a series of tubules passing across the peritoneum, and re-absorbed into the intestine for excretion. Bit by bit other points of the anatomy came clear, and in half an hour of intense study Dal began to see how the inhabitants of Morua VIII were put together.

Satisfied for the moment, he then pulled the tapes that described the Moruans' own medical advancement. What were they doing attempting organ-transplantation, anyway? That was the kind of surgery that even experienced Star Surgeons preferred to take aboard the hospital ships, or back to Hospital Earth, where the finest equipment and the most skilled assistants were available.

There was a signal buzzer, the two-minute warning before the Koenig drive took over. Dal tossed the tape spools back into the bin for refiling, and went forward to the control room.

Just short of two hours later, the *Lancet* shifted back to normal space drive, and the cold yellow sun of the Moruan system swam into sight in the viewscreen. Far below, the tiny eighth planet glistened like a snowball in the reflection of the sun, with only occasional rents in the cloud blanket revealing the ragged surface below. The doctors watched as the ship went into descending orbit, skimming the outer atmosphere and settling into a landing pattern.

Beneath the cloud blanket, the frigid surface of the planet spread out before them. Great snow-covered mountain ranges rose up on either side.

A forty-mile gale howled across the landing field, sweeping clouds of powdery snow before it.

A huge gawky vehicle seemed to be waiting for the ship to land; it shot out from the huddle of gray buildings almost the moment they touched down. Jack slipped into the furs that he had pulled from stores, and went out through the entrance lock and down the ladder to meet the dark furry creatures that were bundling out of the vehicle below. The electronic language translator was strapped to his chest.

Five minutes later he reappeared, frost forming on his blue collar, his face white as he looked at Dal. "You'd better get down there right away," he said, "and take your micro-surgical instruments. Tiger, give me a hand with the anaesthesia tanks. They're keeping a patient alive with a heart-lung machine right now, and they can't finish the job. It looks like it might be bad."

*

The Moruan who escorted them across the city to the hospital was a huge shaggy creature who left no question of the evolutionary line of his people. Except for the flattened nose, the high forehead and the fur-less hand with opposing thumb, he looked for all the world like a mammoth edition of the Kodiak bears Dal had seen displayed at the natural history museum in Hospital Philadelphia. Like all creatures with oxygen-and-water based metabolisms, the Moruans could trace their evolutionary line to minute one-celled salt-water creatures; but with the bitter cold of the planet, the first land-creatures to emerge from the primeval swamp of Morua VIII had developed the heavy furs and the hibernation characteristics of bear-like mammals. They towered over Dal, and even Tiger seemed dwarfed by their immense chest girth and powerful shoulders.

As the surface car hurried toward the hospital, Dal probed for more information. The Moruan's voice was a hoarse growl which nearly deafened the Earthmen in the confined quarters of the car but Dal with the aid of the translator could piece together what had happened.

More sophisticated in medical knowledge than most races in the galaxy, the Moruans had learned a great deal from their contact with Hospital Earth physicians. They actually did have a remarkable grasp of physiology and biochemistry, and constantly sought to learn more. They had already found ways to grow replacement organs from embryonic grafts, the Moruan said, and by copying the techniques used by the surgeons of Hospital Earth, their own surgeons had attempted the delicate job of replacing a diseased organ with a new, healthy one in a young male afflicted with cancer.

Dal looked up at the Moruan doctor. "What organ were you replacing?" he asked suspiciously.

"Oh, not the entire organ, just a segment," the Moruan said. "The tumor had caused an obstructive pneumonia—"

"Are you talking about a segment of *lung*?" Dal said, almost choking.

"Of course. That's where the tumor was."

Dal swallowed hard. "So you just decided to replace a segment."

"Yes. But something has gone wrong, we don't know what."

"I see." It was all Dal could do to keep from shouting at the huge creature. The Moruans had no duplication of organs, such as Earthmen and certain other races had. A tumor of the lung would mean death ... but the technique of grafting a culture-grown lung segment to a portion of natural lung required enormous surgical skill, and the finest microscopic instruments that could be made in order to suture together the tiny capillary walls and air tubules. And if one lung were destroyed, a Moruan had no other to take its place. "Do you have any micro-surgical instruments at all?"

"Oh, yes," the Moruan rumbled proudly. "We made them ourselves, just for this case."

"You mean you've never attempted this procedure before?"

"This was the first time. We don't know where we went wrong."

"You went wrong when you thought about trying it," Dal muttered. "What anaesthesia?"

"Oxygen and alcohol vapor."

This was no surprise. With many species, alcohol vapor was more effective and less toxic than other anaesthetic gases. "And you have a heart-lung machine?"

"The finest available, on lease from Hospital Earth."

All the way through the city Dal continued the questioning, and by the time they reached the hospital he had an idea of the task that was facing him. He knew now that it was going to be bad; he didn't realize just how bad until he walked into the operating room.

The patient was barely alive. Recognizing too late that they were in water too deep for them, the Moruan surgeons had gone into panic, and neglected the very fundamentals of physiological support for the creature on the table. Dal had to climb up on a platform just to see the operating field; the faithful wheeze of the heart-lung machine that was sustaining the creature continued in Dal's ears as he examined the work already done, first with the naked eye, then scanning the operative field with the crude microscopic eyepiece.

"How long has he been anaesthetized?" he asked the shaggy operating surgeon.

"Over eighteen hours already."

"And how much blood has he received?"

"A dozen liters."

"Any more on hand?"

"Perhaps six more."

"Well, you'd better get it into him. He's in shock right now."

The surgeon scurried away while Dal took another look at the micro field. The situation was bad; the anaesthesia had already gone on too long, and the blood chemistry record showed progressive failure.

He stepped down from the platform, trying to clear his head and decide the right thing to do.

He had done micro-surgery before, plenty of it, and he knew the techniques necessary to complete the job, but the thought of attempting it chilled him. At best, he was on unfamiliar ground, with a dozen factors that could go wrong. By now the patient was a dreadful risk for any surgeon. If he were to step in now, and the patient died, how would he explain not calling for help?

He stepped out to the scrub room where Tiger was waiting. "Where's Jack?" he said.

"Went back to the ship for the rest of the surgical pack."

Dal shook his head. "I don't know what to do. I think we should get him to a hospital ship."

"Is it more than you can handle?" Tiger said.

"I could probably do it all right—but I could lose him, too."

A frown creased Tiger's face. "Dal, it would take six hours for a hospital ship to get here."

"I know that. But on the other hand...." Dal spread his hands. He felt Fuzzy crouching in a tight frightened lump in his pocket. He thought again of the delicate, painstaking microscopic work that remained to be done to bring the new section of lung into position to function, and he shook his head. "Look, these creatures hibernate," he said. "If we could get him cooled down enough, we could lighten the anaesthesia and maintain him as is, indefinitely."

"This is up to you," Tiger said. "I don't know anything about surgery. If you think we should just hold tight, that's what we'll do."

"All right. I think we'd better. Have them notify Jack to signal for a hospital ship. We'll just try to stick it out."

Tiger left to pass the word, and Dal went back into the operating room. Suddenly he felt as if a great weight had been lifted from his shoulders. There would be Three-star Surgeons on a Hospital Ship to handle this; it seemed an enormous relief to have the task out of his hands. Yet something was wriggling uncomfortably in the back of his mind, a quiet little voice saying *this isn't right, you should be doing this yourself right now instead of wasting precious time....*

He thrust the thought away angrily and ordered the Moruan physicians to bring in ice packs to cool the patient's huge hulk down to hibernation temperatures. "We're going to send for help," Dal told the Moruan surgeon who had met them at the ship. "This man needs specialized care, and we'd be taking too much chance to try to do it this way."

"You mean you're sending for a hospital ship?"

"That's right," Dal said.

This news seemed to upset the Moruans enormously. They began growling among themselves, moving back from the operating table.

"Then you can't save him?" the operating surgeon said.

"I think he can be saved, certainly!"

"But we thought you could just step in—"

"I could, but that would be taking chances that we don't need to take. We can maintain him until the hospital ship arrives."

The Moruans continued to growl ominously, but Dal brushed past them, checking the vital signs of the patient as his body temperature slowly dropped. Tiger had taken over the anaesthesia, keeping the patient under as light a dosage of medication as was possible.

"What's eating them?" he asked Dal quietly.

"They don't want a hospital ship here very much," Dal said. "Afraid they'll look like fools all over the Confederation if the word gets out. But that's their worry. Ours is to keep this bruiser alive until the ship gets here."

They settled back to wait.

It was an agonizing time for Dal. Even Fuzzy didn't seem to be much comfort. The patient was clearly not doing well, even with the low body temperatures Dal had induced. His blood pressure was sagging, and at one time Tiger sat up sharply, staring at his anaesthesia dials and frowning in alarm as the nervous-system reactions flagged. The Moruan physicians hovered about, increasingly uneasy as they saw the doctors from Hospital Earth waiting and doing nothing. One of them, unable to control himself any longer, tore off his sterile gown and stalked angrily out of the operating suite.

A dozen times Dal was on the verge of stepping in. It was beginning to look now like a race with time, and precious minutes were passing by. He cursed himself inwardly for not taking the bit in his teeth at the beginning and going ahead the best he could; it had been a mistake in judgment to wait. Now, as minutes passed into hours it looked more and more like a mistake that was going to cost the life of a patient.

Then there was a murmur of excitement outside the operating room, and word came in that another ship had been sighted making landing maneuvers. Dal clenched his fists, praying that the patient would last until the hospital ship crew arrived.

But the ship that was landing was not a hospital ship. Someone turned on a TV scanner and picked up the image of a small ship hardly larger than a patrol ship, with just two passengers stepping down the ladder to the ground. Then the camera went close-up. Dal saw the faces of the two men, and his heart sank.

One was a Four-star Surgeon, resplendent in flowing red cape and glistening silver insignia. Dal did not recognize the man, but the four stars meant that he was a top-ranking physician in the Red Service of Surgery.

The other passenger, gathering his black cloak and hood around him as he faced the blistering wind on the landing field, was Black Doctor Hugo Tanner.

*

Moments after the Four-star Surgeon arrived at the hospital, he was fully and unmistakably in command of the situation. He gave Dal an icy stare, then turned to the Moruan operating surgeon, whom he seemed to know very well. After a short barrage of questions and answers, he scrubbed and gowned, and stalked past Dal to the crude Moruan micro-surgical control table.

It took him exactly fifteen seconds to scan the entire operating field through the viewer, discussing the anatomy as the Moruan surgeon watched on a connecting screen. Then, without hesitation, he began manipulating the micro-instruments. Once or twice he murmured something to Tiger at the anaesthesia controls, and occasionally he nodded reassurance to the Moruan surgeon. He did not even invite Dal to observe.

Ten minutes later he rose from the control table and threw the switch to stop the heart-lung machine. The patient took a gasping breath on his own, then another and another. The Four-star Surgeon stripped off his gown and gloves with a flourish. "It will be all right," he said to the Moruan physician. "An excellent job, Doctor, excellent!" he said. "Your technique was flawless, except for the tiny matter you have just observed."

It was not until they were outside the operating room and beyond earshot of the Moruan doctors that the Four-star surgeon turned furiously to Dal. "Didn't you even bother to examine the operating field, Doctor? Where did you study surgery? Couldn't you tell that the fools had practically finished the job themselves? All that was needed was a simple great-vessel graft, which an untrained idiot could have done blindfolded. And for this you call me clear from Hospital Earth!"

The surgeon threw down his mask in disgust and stalked away, leaving Dal and Tiger staring at each other in dismay.

TIGER MAKES A PROMISE

"I think," Black Doctor Hugo Tanner said ominously, "that an explanation is in order. I would now like to hear it. And believe me, gentlemen, it had better be a very sensible explanation, too."

The pathologist was sitting in the control room of the *Lancet*, his glasses slightly askew on his florid face. He had climbed through the entrance lock ten minutes before, shaking snow off his cloak and wheezing like a boiler about to explode; now he faced the patrol ship's crew like a small but ominous black thundercloud. Across the room, Jack Alvarez was staring through the viewscreen at the blizzard howling across the landing field below, a small satisfied smile on his face, while Tiger sulked with his hands jammed into his trousers. Dal sat by himself feeling very much alone, with Fuzzy peering discreetly out of his jacket pocket.

He knew the Black Doctor was speaking to him, but he didn't try to reply. He had known from the moment the surgeon came out of the operating room that he was in trouble. It was just a matter of time before he would have to answer for his decision here, and it was even something of a relief that the moment came sooner rather than later.

And the more Dal considered his position, the more indefensible it appeared. Time after time he had thought of Dr. Arnquist's words about judgment and skill. Without one the other was of little value to a doctor, and whatever his skill as a surgeon might have been in the Moruan operating room, he now realized that his judgment had been poor. He had allowed himself to panic at a critical moment, and had failed to see how far the surgery had really progressed. By deciding to wait for help to arrive instead of taking over at once, he had placed the patient in even greater jeopardy than before. In looking back, Dal could see clearly that it would have been far better judgment to proceed on his own.

But that was how it looked *now*, not *then*, and there was an old saying that the "retrospectoscope" was the only infallible instrument in all medicine.

In any event, the thing was done, and couldn't be changed, and Dal knew that he could only stand on what he had done, right or wrong.

"Well, I'm waiting," Black Doctor Tanner said, scowling at Dal through his thick-rimmed glasses. "I want to know who was responsible for this fiasco, and why it occurred in the first place."

Dal spread his hands hopelessly. "What do you want me to say?" he asked. "I took a careful history of the situation as soon as we arrived here, and then I examined the patient in the operating room. I thought the surgery might be over my head, and couldn't see attempting it if a hospital ship could be reached in time. I thought the patient could be maintained safely long enough for us to call for help."

"I see," the Black Doctor said. "You've done micro-surgery before?"

"Yes, sir."

"And organ transplant work?"

"Yes, sir."

The Black Doctor opened a folder and peered at it over his glasses. "As a matter of fact, you spent two solid years in micro-surgical training in Hospital Philadelphia, with all sorts of glowing reports from your preceptors about what a flair you had for the work."

Dal shook his head. "I—I did some work in the field, yes, but not on critical cases under field conditions."

"You mean that this case required some different kind of technique than the cases you've worked on before?"

"No, not really, but—"

"But you just couldn't quite shoulder the responsibility the job involved when you got into a pinch without any help around," the Black Doctor growled.

"I just thought it would be safer to wait," Dal said helplessly.

"A good conservative approach," Dr. Tanner sneered. "Of course, you realized that prolonged anaesthesia in itself could threaten that patient's life?"

"Yes, sir."

"And you saw the patient's condition steadily deteriorating while you waited, did you not?"

"It was too late to change my mind then," Dal said desperately. "We'd sent for you. We knew that it would be only a matter of hours before you arrived."

"Indeed," the Black Doctor said. "Unfortunately, it takes only seconds for a patient to cross the line between life and death, not hours. And I suppose you would have stood there quietly and allowed him to expire if we had not arrived at the time we did?"

Dal shook his head miserably. There was nothing he could answer to that, and he realized it. What could he say? That the situation seemed quite different now than it had under pressure in the Moruan operating room? That he would have been blamed just as much if he had gone ahead, and then lost the case? His fingers stole down to Fuzzy's soft warm body for comfort, and he felt the little creature cling closer to his side.

The Black Doctor looked up at the others. "Well? What do the rest of you have to say?"

Jack Alvarez shrugged his shoulders. "I'm not a surgeon," he said, "but even I could see that *something* should be done without delay."

"And what does the Green Doctor think?"

Tiger shrugged. "We misjudged the situation, that's all. It came out fortunately for the patient, why make all this fuss about it?"

"Because there are other things at stake than just medical considerations," the Black Doctor shot back. "This planet has a grade I contract with Hospital Earth. We guarantee them full medical coverage of all situations and promise them immediate response to any call for medical help that they may send us. It is the most favorable kind of contract we have; when Morua VIII calls for help they expect their call to be answered by expert medical attention, not by inept bungling."

The Black Doctor leafed through the folder in his hands. "We have built our reputation in the Galactic Confederation on this kind of contract, and our admission to full membership in the Confederation will ultimately depend upon how we fulfill our promises. Poor medical judgment cannot be condoned under any circumstances—but above all, we cannot afford to jeopardize a contract."

Dal stared at him. "I—I had no intention of jeopardizing a contract," he faltered.

"Perhaps not," the Black Doctor said. "But you were the doctor on the spot, and you were so obviously incompetent to handle the situation that even these clumsy Moruan surgeons could see it. Their faith in the doctors from Hospital Earth has been severely shaken. They are even talking of letting their contract lapse at the end of this term."

Tiger Martin jumped to his feet. "Doctor Tanner, even Four-star Surgeons lose patients sometimes. These people should be glad that the doctor they call has sense enough to call for help if he needs it."

"But no help was needed," the Black Doctor said angrily. "Any half-decent surgeon would have handled the case. If the Moruans see a patrol ship bring in one incompetent doctor, what are they going to expect the next time they have need for help? How can they feel sure that their medical needs are well taken care of?" He shook his head grimly. "This is the sort of responsibility that doctors on the patrol ships are expected to assume. If you call for help where there is need for help, no one will ever complain; but when you turn and run the moment things get tough, you are not fit for patrol ship service."

The Black Doctor turned to Dal Timgar. "You had ample warning," he said. "It was clearly understood that your assignment on this ship depended upon the fulfillment of the duties of Red Doctor here, and now at the first real test you turn and run instead of doing your job. All right. You had your opportunity. You can't complain that we haven't given you a chance. According to the conduct code of the General Practice Patrol, section XIV, paragraph 2, any physician in the patrol on probationary status who is found delinquent in executing his duties may be relieved of his assignment at the order of any Black Doctor, or any other physician of four-star rank." Doctor Tanner closed the folder with a snap of finality. "It seems to me that the case is clear. Dal Timgar, on the authority of the Code, I am now relieving you of duty—"

"Just a minute," Tiger Martin burst out.

The Black Doctor looked up at him. "Well?"

"This is ridiculous," Tiger said. "Why are you picking on *him*? Or do you mean that you're relieving all three of us?"

"Of course I'm not relieving all three of you," the Black Doctor snapped. "You and Dr. Alvarez will remain on duty and conduct the ship's program without a Red Doctor until a man is sent to replace this bungler. That also is provided for in the code."

"But I understood that we were operating as a diagnostic and therapeutic team," Tiger protested. "And I seem to remember something in the code about fixing responsibility before a man can be relieved."

"There's no question where the responsibility lies," the Black Doctor said, his face darkening. "This was a surgical problem, and Dal Timgar made the decisions. I don't see anything to argue."

"There's plenty to argue," Tiger said. "Dal, don't you see what he's trying to do?"

Across the room Dal shook his head wearily. "You'd better keep out of it, Tiger," he said.

"Why should I keep out of it and let you be drummed out of the patrol for something that wasn't even your fault?" Tiger said. He turned angrily to the Black Doctor. "Dal wasn't the one that wanted the hospital ship called," he said. "I was. If you're going to relieve somebody, you'd better make it me."

The Black Doctor pulled off his glasses and glared at Tiger. "Whatever are you talking about?" he said.

"Just what I said. We had a conference after he'd examined the patient in the operating room, and I insisted that we call the hospital ship. Why, Dal—Dal wanted to go ahead and try to finish the case right then, and I wouldn't let him," Tiger blundered on. "I didn't think the patient could take it. I thought that it would be too great a risk with the facilities we had here."

Dal was staring at Tiger, and he felt Fuzzy suddenly shivering violently in his pocket. "Tiger, don't be foolish—"

The Black Doctor slammed the file down on the table again. "Is this true, what he's saying?" he asked Dal.

"No, not a word of it," Dal said. "I wanted to call the hospital ship."

"Of course he won't admit it," Tiger said angrily. "He's afraid you'll kick me out too, but it's true just the same in spite of what he says."

"And what do *you* say?" the Black Doctor said, turning to Jack Alvarez.

"I say it's carrying this big brother act too far," Jack said. "I didn't notice any conferences going on."

"You were back at the ship getting the surgical pack," Tiger said. "You didn't know anything about it. You didn't hear us talking, and we didn't see any reason to consult you about it."

The Black Doctor stared from Dal to Tiger, his face growing angrier by the minute. He jerked to his feet, and stalked back and forth across the control room, glaring at them. Then he took a capsule from his pocket, gulped it down with some water, and sat back down. "I ought to throw you both out on your ears," he snarled. "But I am forced to control myself. I mustn't allow myself to get angry—" He crashed his fist down on the control panel. "I suppose that you would swear to this statement of yours if it came to that?" he asked Tiger.

Tiger nodded and swallowed hard. "Yes, sir, I certainly would."

"All right," the Black Doctor said tightly. "Then you win this one. The code says that two opinions can properly decide any course of action. If you insist that two of you agreed on this decision, then I am forced to support you officially. I will make a report of the incident to patrol headquarters, and it will go on the permanent records of all three of this ship's crew—including my personal opinion of the decision." He looked up at Dal. "But be very careful, my young friend. Next time you may not have a technicality to back you up, and I'll be watching for the first plausible excuse to break you, and your Green Doctor friend as well. One misstep, and you're through. And I assure you that is not just an idle threat. I mean every word of it."

And trembling with rage, the Black Doctor picked up the folder, wrapped his cape around him, and marched out of the control room.

*

"Well, you put on a great show," Jack Alvarez said later as they prepared the ship for launching from the snow-swept landing field on Morua VIII. An hour before the ground had trembled as the Black Doctor's ship took off with Dr. Tanner and the Four-star Surgeon aboard; now Jack broke the dark silence in the *Lancet*'s control room for the first time. "A really great show. You missed your calling, Tiger. You should have been on the stage. If you think you fooled Dr. Tanner with that story for half a second, you're crazy, but I guess you got what you wanted. You kept your pal's cuff and collar for him, and you put a black mark on all of our records, including mine. I hope you're satisfied."

Tiger Martin took off his earphones and set them carefully on the control panel. "You know," he said to Jack, "you're lucky."

"Really?"

"You're lucky I don't wipe that sneer off your face and scrub the walls with it. And you'd better not crowd your luck, because all I need right now is an invitation." He stood up, towering over the dark-haired Blue Doctor. "You bet I'm satisfied. And if you got a black mark along with the rest of us, you earned it all the way."

"That still doesn't make it right," Dal said from across the room.

"You just keep out of this for a minute," Tiger said. "Jack has got to get a couple of things straight, and this is the time for it right now."

Dal shook his head. "I can't keep out of it," he said. "You got me off the hook by shifting the blame, but you put yourself in trouble doing it. Dr. Tanner could just as well have thrown us both out of the service as not."

Tiger snorted. "On what grounds? For a petty little error like this? He wouldn't dare! You ought to read the log books of some of the other GPP ships some time and see the kind of bloopers they pull without even a reprimand. Don't worry, he was mad enough to throw us both out if he thought he could make it stick, but he knew he couldn't. He knew the council would just review the case and reverse his decision."

"It was still my error, not yours," Dal protested. "I should have gone ahead and finished the case on the spot. I knew it at the time, and I just didn't quite dare."

"So you made a mistake," Tiger said. "You'll make a dozen more before you get your Star, and if none of them amount to any more than this one, you can be very happy." He scowled at Jack. "It's only thanks to our friend here that the Black Doctor heard about this at all. A hospital ship would have come to take the patient aboard, and the local doctors would have been quieted down and that would have been all there was to it. This business about losing a contract is a lot of nonsense."

"Then you think this thing was just used as an excuse to get at me?"

"Ask him," Tiger said, looking at Jack again. "Ask him why a Black Doctor and a Four-star Surgeon turned up when we just called for a hospital ship."

"I called the hospital ship," Jack said sullenly.

"But you called Dr. Tanner too," said Tiger. "Your nose has been out of joint ever since Dal came aboard this ship. You've made things as miserable for him as you could, and you just couldn't wait for a chance to come along to try to scuttle him."

"All right," Jack said, "but he was making a mistake. Anybody could see that. What if the patient had died while he was standing around waiting? Isn't that important?"

Tiger started to answer, and then threw up his hands in disgust. "It's important—but something else is more important. We've got a job to do on this ship, and we can't do it fighting each other. Dal misjudged a case and got in trouble. Fine, he won't make that mistake again. It could just as well have been you, or me. We'll all make mistakes, but if we can't work as a team, we're sunk. We'll all be drummed out of the patrol before a year is out." Tiger stopped to catch his breath, his face flushed with anger. "Well, I'm fed up with this back-stabbing business. I don't want a fight any more than Dal does, but if I have to fight, I'll fight to get it over with, and you'd better be careful. If you pull any more sly ones, you'd better include me in the deal, because if Dal goes, I go too. And that's a promise."

There was silence for a moment as Jack stared up at Tiger's angry face. He shook his head and blinked, as though he couldn't quite believe what he was hearing. He looked across at Dal, and then back at Tiger again. "You mean you'd turn in your collar and cuff?" he said.

"If it came to that."

"I see." Jack sat down at the control panel, still shaking his head. "I think you really mean it," he said soberly. "This isn't just a big brother act. You really like the guy, don't you?"

"Maybe I do," Tiger said, "but I don't like to watch anybody get kicked around just because somebody else doesn't happen to like him."

The control room was very quiet. Then somewhere below a motor clicked on, and the ventilation fan made a quiet whirring sound. The teletype clicked sporadically down the corridor in the communications room. Dal sat silently, rubbing Fuzzy between the eyes and watching the two Earthmen. It seemed suddenly as if they were talking about somebody a million miles away, as if he were not even in the room.

Then the Blue Doctor shrugged and rose to his feet. "All right," he said to Tiger. "I guess I just didn't understand where you stood, and I suppose it wasn't my job to let the Black Doctor know about the situation here. I don't plan to be making all the mistakes you think we're going to make, and I won't take the blame for anybody else's, but I guess we've got to work together in the tight spots." He gave Dal a lop-sided grin. "Welcome aboard," he said. "We'd better get this crate airborne before the people here come and cart it away."

They moved then, and the subject was dropped. Half an hour later the *Lancet* lifted through the atmospheric pull of the Moruan planet and moved on toward the next contact point, leaving the recovering patient in the hands of the native physicians. It was not until hours later that Dal noticed that Fuzzy had stopped quivering, and was resting happily and securely on his shoulder even when the Blue Doctor was near.

ALARUMS AND EXCURSIONS

Once more the crew of the *Lancet* settled down to routine, and the incident on Morua VIII seemed almost forgotten.

But a change had come about in the relations between the three doctors, and in every way the change was for the better. If Jack Alvarez was not exactly cordial to Dal Timgar, at least he had dropped the open antagonism that he had shown before. Apparently Tiger's angry outburst had startled Jack, as though he had never really considered that the big Earthman might honestly be attached to his friend from Garv II, and the Blue Doctor seemed sincere in his agreement to work with Dal and Tiger as a team.

But bit by bit Dal could sense that the change in Jack's attitude went deeper than the surface. "You know, I really think he was *scared* of me," Dal said one night when he and Tiger were alone. "Sounds silly, but I think it's true. He pretends to be so sure of himself, but I think he's as worried about doing things wrong as we are, and just won't admit it. And he really thought I was a threat when I came aboard."

"He probably had a good thorough briefing from Black Doctor Tanner before he got the assignment," Tiger said grimly.

"Maybe—but somehow I don't think he cares for the Black Doctor much more than we do."

But whatever the reason, much of the tension was gone when the *Lancet* had left the Moruan system behind. A great weight seemed to have been lifted, and if there was not quite peace on board, at least there was an uneasy truce. Tiger and Jack were almost friendly, talking together more often and getting to know each other better. Jack still avoided Dal and seldom included him in conversations, but the open contempt of the first few weeks on the ship now seemed tempered somewhat.

Once again the *Lancet*'s calls fell into a pattern. Landings on the outpost planets became routine, bright spots in a lonely and wandering existence. The calls that came in represented few real problems. The ship stopped at one contract planet to organize a mass inoculation program against a parasitic infestation resembling malaria. They paused at another place to teach the native doctors the use of some new surgical instruments that had been developed in Hospital Earth laboratories just for them. Frantic emergency calls usually proved to involve trivial problems, but once or twice potentially serious situations were spotted early, before they could develop into real trouble.

And as the three doctors got used to the responsibilities of a patrol ship's rounds, and grew more confident of their ability to handle the problems thrust upon them, they found themselves working more and more efficiently as a team.

This was the way the General Practice Patrol was supposed to function. Each doctor had unsuspected skills that came to light. There was no questioning Jack Alvarez's skill as a diagnostician, but it seemed uncanny to Dal the way the slender, dark-haired Earthman could listen carefully to a medical problem of an alien race on a remote planet, and then seem to know exactly which questions to ask to draw out the significant information about the situation. Tiger was not nearly as quick and clever as Jack; he needed more time to ponder a question of medical treatment, and he would often spend long hours poring over the data tapes before deciding what to do in a given case—but he always seemed to come up with an answer, and his answers usually worked. Above all, Tiger's relations with the odd life-forms they encountered were invariably good; the creatures seemed to like him, and would follow his instructions faithfully.

Dal, too, had opportunities to demonstrate that his surgical skill and judgment was not universally faulty in spite of the trouble on Morua VIII. More than once he succeeded in almost impossible surgical cases where there was no time to call for help, and little by little he could sense Jack's growing confidence in his abilities, grudging though it might be.

Dal had ample time to mull over the thing that had happened on Morua VIII and to think about the interview with Black Doctor Tanner afterward. He knew he was glad that Tiger had intervened even on the basis of a falsehood; until Tiger had spoken up Dal had been certain that the Black Doctor fully intended to use the incident as an excuse to discharge him from the General Practice Patrol. There was no question in his mind that the Black Doctor's charges had been exaggerated into a trumped-up case against him, and there was no question that Tiger's insistence on taking the blame had saved him; he could not help being thankful.

Yet there was something about it that disturbed Dal, nibbling away persistently at his mind. He couldn't throw off the feeling that his own acceptance of Tiger's help had been wrong.

Part of it, he knew, was his native, inbred loathing for falsehood. Fair or unfair, Dal had always disliked lying. Among his people, the truth might be bent occasionally, but frank lying was considered a deep disgrace, and there was a Garvian saying that "a false tongue wins no true friends." Garvian traders were known throughout the Galaxy as much for their rigid adherence to their word as they were for the hard bargains they could drive; Dal had been enormously confused during his first months on Hospital Earth by the way Earthmen seemed to accept lying as part of their daily life, unconcerned about it as long as the falsehood could not be proven.

But something else about Tiger's defense of him bothered Dal far more than the falsehood—something that had vaguely disturbed him ever since he had known the big Earthman, and that now seemed to elude him every time he tried to pinpoint it. Lying in his bunk during a sleep period, Dal remembered vividly the first time he had met Tiger, early in the second year of medical school. Dal had almost despaired by then of making friends with his hostile and resentful classmates and had begun more and more to avoid contact with them, building up a protective shell and relying on Fuzzy for company or comfort. Then Tiger had found him eating lunch by himself in the medical school lounge one day and flopped down in the seat beside him and began talking as if Dal were just another classmate. Tiger's open friendliness had been like a spring breeze to Dal who was desperately lonely in this world of strangers; their friendship had grown rapidly, and gradually others in the class had begun to thaw enough at least to be civil when Dal was around. Dal had sensed that this change of heart was largely because of Tiger and not because of him, yet he had welcomed it as a change from the previous intolerable coldness even though it left him feeling vaguely uneasy. Tiger was well liked by the others in the class; Dal had been grateful more than once when Tiger had risen in hot defense of the Garvian's right to be studying medicine among Earthmen in the school on Hospital Earth.

But that had been in medical school, among classmates. Somehow that had been different from the incident that occurred on Morua VIII, and

Dal's uneasiness grew stronger than ever the more he thought of it. Talking to Tiger about it was no help; Tiger just grinned and told him to forget it, but even in the rush of shipboard activity it stubbornly refused to be forgotten.

One minor matter also helped to ease the tension between the doctors as they made their daily rounds. Tiger brought a pink dispatch sheet in to Dal one day, grinning happily. "This is from the weekly news capsule," he said. "It ought to cheer you up."

It was a brief news note, listed under "incidental items." "The Black Service of Pathology," it said, "has announced that Black Doctor Hugo Tanner will enter Hospital Philadelphia within the next week for prophylactic heart surgery. In keeping with usual Hospital Earth administrative policy, the Four-star Black Doctor will undergo a total cardiac transplant to halt the Medical education administrator's progressively disabling heart disease." The note went on to name the surgeons who would officiate at the procedure.

Dal smiled and handed back the dispatch. "Maybe it will improve his temper," he said, "even if it does give him another fifty years of active life."

"Well, at least it will take him out of *our* hair for a while," Tiger said. "He won't have time to keep us under too close scrutiny."

Which, Dal was forced to admit, did not make him too unhappy.

Shipboard rounds kept all three doctors busy. Often, with contact landings, calls, and studying, it seemed only a brief time from sleep period to sleep period, but still they had some time for minor luxuries. Dal was almost continuously shivering, with the ship kept at a temperature that was comfortable for Tiger and Jack; he missed the tropical heat of his home planet, and sometimes it seemed that he was chilled down to the marrow of his bones in spite of his coat of gray fur. With a little home-made plumbing and ingenuity, he finally managed to convert one of the ship's shower units into a steam bath. Once or twice each day he would retire for a blissful half hour warming himself up to Garv II normal temperatures.

Fuzzy also became a part of shipboard routine. Once he grew accustomed to Tiger and Jack and the surroundings aboard the ship, the little creature grew bored sitting on Dal's shoulder and wanted to be in the middle of things. Since the early tension had eased, he was willing to be apart from his master from time to time, so Dal and Tiger built him a platform that hung from the ceiling of the control room. There Fuzzy would sit and swing by the hour, blinking happily at the activity going on all around him.

But for all the appearance of peace and agreement, there was still an undercurrent of tension on board the *Lancet* which flared up from time to time when it was least expected, between Dal and Jack. It was on one such occasion that a major crisis almost developed, and once again Fuzzy was the center of the contention.

Dal Timgar knew that disaster had struck at the very moment it happened, but he could not tell exactly what was wrong. All he knew was that something fearful had happened to Fuzzy.

There was a small sound-proof cubicle in the computer room, with a chair, desk and a tape-reader for the doctors when they had odd moments to spend reading up on recent medical bulletins or reviewing their textbooks. Dal spent more time here than the other two; the temperature of the room could be turned up, and he had developed a certain fondness for the place with its warm gray walls and its soft relaxing light. Here on the tapes were things that he could grapple with, things that he could understand. If a problem here eluded him, he could study it out until he had mastered it. The hours he spent here were a welcome retreat from the confusing complexities of getting along with Jack and Tiger.

These long study periods were boring for Fuzzy who wasn't much interested in the oxygen-exchange mechanism of the intelligent beetles of Aldebaran VI. Frequently Dal would leave him to swing on his platform or explore about the control cabin while he spent an hour or two at the tape-reader. Today Dal had been working for over an hour, deeply immersed in a review of the intermediary metabolism of chlorine-breathing mammals, when something abruptly wrenched his attention from the tape.

It was as though a light had snapped off in his mind, or a door slammed shut. There was no sound, no warning; yet, suddenly, he felt dreadfully, frighteningly alone, as if in a split second something inside him had been torn away. He sat bolt upright, staring, and he felt his skin crawl and his fingers tremble as he listened, trying to spot the source of the trouble.

And then, almost instinctively, he knew what was wrong. He leaped to his feet, tore open the door to the cubicle and dashed down the hallway toward the control room. "Fuzzy!" he shouted. "Fuzzy, *where are you?*"

Tiger and Jack were both at the control panel dictating records for filing. They looked up in surprise as the Red Doctor burst into the room. Fuzzy's platform was hanging empty, gently swaying back and forth. Dal peered frantically around the room. There was no sign of the small pink creature.

"Where is he?" he demanded. "What's happened to Fuzzy?"

Jack shrugged in disgust. "He's up on his perch. Where else?"

"He's not either! Where is he?"

Jack blinked at the empty perch. "He was there just a minute ago. I saw him."

"Well, he's not there now, and something's wrong!" In a panic, Dal began searching the room, knocking over stools, scattering piles of paper, peering in every corner where Fuzzy might be concealed.

For a moment the others sat frozen, watching him. Then Tiger jumped to his feet. "Hold it, hold it! He probably just wandered off for a minute. He does that all the time."

"No, it's something worse than that." Dal was almost choking on the words. "Something terrible has happened. I know it."

Jack Alvarez tossed the recorder down in disgust. "You and your miserable pet!" he said. "I knew we shouldn't have kept him on board."

Dal stared at Jack. Suddenly all the anger and bitterness of the past few weeks could no longer be held in. Without warning he hurled himself at the Blue Doctor's throat. "Where is he?" he cried. "What have you done with him? What have you done to Fuzzy? You've done something to him! You've hated him every minute just like you hate me, only he's easier to pick on. Now where is he? What have you done to him?"

Jack staggered back, trying to push the furious little Garvian away. "Wait a minute! Get away from me! I didn't do anything!"

"You did too! Where is he?"

"I don't know." Jack struggled to break free, but there was powerful strength in Dal's fingers for all his slight body build. "I tell you, he was here just a minute ago."

Dal felt a hand grip his collar then, and Tiger was dragging them apart like two dogs in a fight. "Now stop this!" he roared, holding them both at arm's length. "I said *stop it*! Jack didn't do anything to Fuzzy, he's been sitting here with me ever since you went back to the cubicle. He hasn't even budged."

"But he's *gone*," Dal panted. "Something's happened to him. I *know* it."

"How do you know?"

"I—I just know. I can feel it."

"All right, then let's find him," Tiger said. "He's got to be somewhere on the ship. If he's in trouble, we're wasting time fighting."

Tiger let go, and Jack brushed off his shirt, his face very white. "I saw him just a little while ago," he said. "He was sitting up on that silly perch watching us, and then swinging back and forth and swinging over to that cabinet and back."

"Well, let's get started looking," Tiger said.

They fanned out, with Jack still muttering to himself, and searched the control room inch by inch. There was no sign of Fuzzy. Dal had control of himself now, but he searched with a frantic intensity. "He's not in here," he said at last, "he must have gone out somewhere."

"There was only one door open," Tiger said. "The one you just came through, from the rear corridor. Dal, you search the computer room. Jack, check the lab and I'll go back to the reactors."

They started searching the compartments off the rear corridor. For ten minutes there was no sound in the ship but the occasional slamming of a hatch, the grate of a desk drawer, the bang of a cabinet door. Dal worked through the maze of cubby-holes in the computer room with growing hopelessness. The frightening sense of loneliness and loss in his mind was overwhelming; he was almost physically ill. The warm, comfortable feeling of *contact* that he had always had before with Fuzzy was gone. As the minutes passed, hopelessness gave way to despair.

Then Jack gave a hoarse cry from the lab. Dal tripped and stumbled in his haste to get down the corridor, and almost collided with Tiger at the lab door.

"I think we're too late," Jack said. "He's gotten into the formalin."

He lifted one of the glass beakers down from the shelf to the work bench. It was obvious what had happened. Fuzzy had gone exploring and had found the laboratory a fascinating place. Several of the reagents bottles had been knocked over as if he had been sampling them. The glass lid to the beaker of formalin which was kept for tissue specimens had been pushed aside just enough to admit the little creature's two-inch girth. Now Fuzzy lay in the bottom of the beaker, immersed in formalin, a formless, shapeless blob of sickly gray jelly.

"Are you sure it's formalin?" Dal asked.

Jack poured off the fluid, and the acrid smell of formaldehyde that filled the room answered the question. "It's no good, Dal," he said, almost gently. "The stuff destroys protein, and that's about all he was. I'm sorry—I was beginning to like the little punk, even if he did get on my nerves. But he picked the one thing to fall into that could kill him. Unless he had some way to set up a protective barrier...."

Dal took the beaker. "Get me some saline," he said tightly. "And some nutrient broth."

Jack pulled out two jugs and poured their contents into an empty beaker. Dal popped the tiny limp form into the beaker and began massaging it. Layers of damaged tissue peeled off in his hand, but he continued massaging and changing the solutions, first saline, then nutrient broth. "Get me some sponges and a blade."

Tiger brought them in. Carefully Dal began debriding the damaged outer layers. Jack and Tiger watched; then Jack said, "Look, there's a tinge of pink in the middle."

Slowly the faint pink in the center grew more ruddy. Dal changed solutions again, and sank down on a stool. "I think he'll make it," he said. "He has enormous regenerative powers as long as any fragment of him is left." He looked up at Jack who was still watching the creature in the beaker almost solicitously. "I guess I made a fool of myself back there when I jumped you."

Jack's face hardened, as though he had been caught off guard. "I guess you did, all right."

"Well, I'm sorry. I just couldn't think straight. It was the first time I'd ever been—apart from him."

"I still say he doesn't belong aboard," Jack said. "This is a medical ship, not a menagerie. And if you ever lay your hands on me again, you'll wish you hadn't."

"I said I was sorry," Dal said.

"I heard you," Jack said. "I just don't believe you, that's all."

He gave Fuzzy a final glance, and then headed back to the control room.

*

Fuzzy recovered, a much abashed and subdued Fuzzy, clinging timorously to Dal's shoulder and refusing to budge for three days, but apparently basically unharmed by his inadvertent swim in the deadly formalin bath. Presently he seemed to forget the experience altogether, and once again took his perch on the platform in the control room.

But Dal did not forget. He said little to Tiger and Jack, but the incident had shaken him severely. For as long as he could remember, he had always had Fuzzy close at hand. He had never before in his life experienced the dreadful feeling of emptiness and desertion, the almost paralyzing fear and helplessness that he had felt when Fuzzy had lost contact with him. It had seemed as though a vital part of him had suddenly been torn away, and the memory of the panic that followed sent chills down his back and woke him up trembling from his sleep. He was ashamed of his unwarranted attack on Jack, yet even this seemed insignificant in comparison to the powerful fear that had been driving him.

Happily, the Blue Doctor chose to let the matter rest where it was, and if anything, seemed more willing than before to be friendly. For the first time he seemed to take an active interest in Fuzzy, "chatting" with him when he thought no one was around, and bringing him occasional tid-bits of food after meals were over.

Once more life on the *Lancet* settled back to routine, only to have it shattered by an incident of quite a different nature. It was just after they had left a small planet in the Procyon system, one of the routine check-in points, that they made contact with the Garvian trading ship.

Dal recognized the ship's design and insignia even before the signals came in, and could hardly contain his excitement. He had not seen a fellow countryman for years except for an occasional dull luncheon with the Garvian ambassador to Hospital Earth during medical school days. The thought of walking the corridors of a Garvian trading ship again brought an overwhelming wave of homesickness. He was so excited he could hardly wait for Jack to complete the radio-sighting formalities. "What ship is she?" he wanted to know. "What house?"

Jack handed him the message transcript. "The ship is the *Teegar*," he said. "Flagship of the SinSin trading fleet. They want permission to approach us."

Dal let out a whoop. "Then it's a space trader, and a big one. You've never seen ships like these before."

Tiger joined them, staring at the message transcript. "A SinSin ship! Send them the word, Jack, and be quick, before they get disgusted and move on."

Jack sent out the approach authorization, and they watched with growing excitement as the great trading vessel began its close-approach maneuvers.

The name of the house of SinSin was famous throughout the galaxy. It was one of the oldest and largest of the great trading firms that had built Garv II into its position of leadership in the Confederation, and the SinSin ships had penetrated to every corner of the galaxy, to every known planet harboring an intelligent life-form.

Tiger and Jack had seen the multitudes of exotic products in the Hospital Earth stores that came from the great Garvian ships on their frequent visits. But this was more than a planetary trader loaded with a few items for a single planet. The space traders roamed from star system to star system, their holds filled with treasures beyond number. Such ships as these might be out from Garv II for decades at a time, tempting any ship they met with the magnificent variety of wares they carried.

Slowly the trader approached, and Dal took the speaker, addressing the commander of the *Teegar* in Garvian. "This is the General Practice Patrol Ship *Lancet*," he said, "out from Hospital Earth with three physicians aboard, including a countryman of yours."

"Is that Dal Timgar?" the reply came back. "By the Seven Moons! We'd heard that there was now a Garvian physician, and couldn't believe our ears. Come aboard, all of you, you'll be welcome. We'll send over a lifeboat!"

The *Teegar* was near now, a great gleaming ship with the sign of the house of SinSin on her hull. A lifeboat sprang from a launching rack and speared across to the *Lancet*. Moments later the three doctors were climbing into the sleek little vessel and moving across the void of space to the huge Garvian ship.

It was like stepping from a jungle outpost village into a magnificent, glittering city. The Garvian ship was enormous; she carried a crew of several hundred, and the wealth and luxury of the ship took the Earthmen's breath away. The cabins and lounges were paneled with expensive fabrics and rare woods, the furniture inlaid with precious metals. Down the long corridors goods of the traders were laid out in resplendent display, surpassing the richest show cases in the shops on Hospital Earth.

They received a royal welcome from the commander of the *Teegar*, an aged, smiling little Garvian with a pink fuzz-ball on his shoulder that could have been Fuzzy's twin. He bowed low to Tiger and Jack, leading them into the reception lounge where a great table was spread with foods and pastries of all varieties. Then he turned to Dal and embraced him like a long-lost brother. "Your father Jai Timgar has long been an honored friend of the house of SinSin, and anyone of the house of Timgar is the same as my own son and my son's son! But this collar! This cuff! Is it really possible that a man of Garv has become a physician of Hospital Earth?"

Dal touched Fuzzy to the commander's fuzz-ball in the ancient Garvian greeting. "It's possible, and true," he said. "I studied there. I am the Red Doctor on this patrol ship."

"Ah, but this is good," the commander said. "What better way to draw our worlds together, eh? But come, you must look and see what we have in our storerooms, feast your eyes on the splendors we carry. For all of you, a thousand wonders are to be found here."

Jack hesitated as the commander led them back toward the display corridors. "We'd be glad to see the ship, but you should know that patrol ship physicians have little money to spend."

"Who speaks of money?" the commander cried. "Did I speak of it? Come and look! Money is nothing. The Garvian traders are not mere money-changers. Look and enjoy; if there is something that strikes your eye, something that would fulfill the desires of your heart, it will be yours." He gave Dal a smile and a sly wink. "Surely our brother here has told you many times of the wonders to be seen in a space trader, and terms can be arranged that will make any small purchase a painless pleasure."

He led them off, like a head of state conducting visiting dignitaries on a tour, with a retinue of Garvian underlings trailing behind them. For two delirious hours they wandered the corridors of the great ship, staring hungrily at the dazzling displays. They had been away from Hospital Earth and its shops and stores for months; now it seemed they were walking through an incredible treasure-trove stocked with everything that they could possibly have wanted.

For Jack there was a dress uniform, specially tailored for a physician in the Blue Service of Diagnosis, the insignia woven into the cloth with gold and platinum thread. Reluctantly he turned away from it, a luxury he could never dream of affording. For Tiger, who had been muttering for weeks about getting out of condition in the sedentary life of the ship, there was a set of bar bells and gymnasium equipment ingeniously designed to collapse into a unit no larger than one foot square, yet opening out into a completely equipped gym. Dal's eyes glittered at the new sets of surgical instruments, designed to the most rigid Hospital Earth specifications, which appeared almost without his asking to see them. There were clothes and games, precious stones and exotic rings, watches set with Arcturian dream-stones, and boots inlaid with silver.

They made their way through the corridors, reluctant to leave one display for the next. Whenever something caught their eyes, the commander snapped his fingers excitedly, and the item was unobtrusively noted down by one of the underlings. Finally, exhausted and glutted just from looking, they turned back toward the reception room.

"The things are beautiful," Tiger said wistfully, "but impossible. Still, you were very kind to take your time—"

"Time? I have nothing but time." The commander smiled again at Dal. "And there is an old Garvian proverb that to the wise man 'impossible' has no meaning. Wait, you will see!"

They came out into the lounge, and the doctors stopped short in amazement. Spread out before them were all of the items that had captured their interest earlier.

"But this is ridiculous," Jack said staring at the dress uniform. "We couldn't possibly buy these things, it would take our salaries for twenty years to pay for them."

"Have we mentioned price even once?" the commander protested. "You are the crewmates of one of our own people! We would not dream of setting prices that we would normally set for such trifles as these. And as for terms, you have no worry. Take the goods aboard your ship, they are already yours. We have drawn up contracts for you which require no payment whatever for five years, and then payments of only a fiftieth of the value for each successive year. And for each of you, with the compliments of the house of SinSin, a special gift at no charge whatever."

He placed in Jack's hands a small box with the lid tipped back. Against a black velvet lining lay a silver star, and the official insignia of a Star Physician in the Blue Service. "You cannot wear it yet, of course," the commander said. "But one day you will need it."

Jack blinked at the jewel-like star. "You are very kind," he said. "I—I mean perhaps—" He looked at Tiger, and then at the display of goods on the table. "Perhaps there are *some* things—"

Already two of the Garvian crewmen were opening the lock to the lifeboat, preparing to move the goods aboard. Then Dal Timgar spoke up sharply. "I think you'd better wait a moment," he said.

"And for you," the commander continued, turning to Dal so smoothly that there seemed no break in his voice at all, "as one of our own people, and an honored son of Jai Timgar, who has been kind to the house of SinSin for many years, I have something out of the ordinary. I'm sure your crewmates would not object to a special gift at my personal expense."

The commander lifted a scarf from the table and revealed the glittering set of surgical instruments, neatly displayed in a velvet-lined carrying case. The commander took it up from the table and thrust it into Dal's hands. "It is yours, my friend. And for this, there will be no contract whatever."

Dal stared down at the instruments. They were beautiful. He longed just to touch them, to hold them in his hands, but he shook his head and set the case back on the table. He looked up at Tiger and Jack. "You should be warned that the prices on these goods are four times what they ought to be, and the deferred-payment contracts he wants you to sign will permit as much as 24 per cent interest on the unpaid balance, with no closing-out clause. That means you would be paying many times the stated price for the goods before the contract is closed. You can go ahead and sign if you want but understand what you're signing."

The Garvian commander stared at him, and then shook his head, laughing. "Of course your friend is not serious," he said. "These prices can be compared on any planet and you will see their fairness. Here, read the contracts, see what they say and decide for yourselves." He held out a sheaf of papers.

"The contracts may sound well enough," Dal said, "but I'm telling you what they actually say."

Jack looked stricken. "But surely just one or two things—"

Tiger shook his head. "Dal knows what he's talking about. I don't think we'd better buy anything at all."

The Garvian commander turned to Dal angrily. "What are you telling them? There is nothing false in these contracts!"

"I didn't say there was. I just can't see them taking a beating with their eyes shut, that's all. Your contracts are legal enough, but the prices and terms are piracy, and you know it."

The commander glared at him for a moment. Then he turned away scornfully. "So what I have heard is true, after all," he said. "You really have thrown in your lot with these pill-peddlers, these idiots from Earth who can't even wipe their noses without losing in a trade." He signaled the lifeboat pilot. "Take them back to their ship, we're wasting our time. There are better things to do than to deal with traitors."

The trip back to the *Lancet* was made in silence. Dal could sense the pilot's scorn as he dumped them off in their entrance lock, and dashed back to the *Teegar* with the lifeboat. Gloomily Jack and Tiger followed Dal into the control room, a drab little cubby-hole compared to the *Teegar*'s lounge.

"Well, it was fun while it lasted," Jack said finally, looking up at Dal. "But the way that guy slammed you, I wish we'd never gone."

"I know," Dal said. "The commander just thought he saw a perfect setup. He figured you'd never question the contracts if I backed him up."

"It would have been easy enough. Why didn't you?"

Dal looked at the Blue Doctor. "Maybe I just don't like people who give away surgical sets," he said. "Remember, I'm not a Garvian trader any more. I'm a doctor from Hospital Earth."

Moments later, the great Garvian ship was gone, and the red light was blinking on the call board. Tiger started tracking down the call while Jack went back to work on the daily log book and Dal set up food for dinner. The pleasant dreams were over; they were back in the harness of patrol ship doctors once again.

Jack and Dal were finishing dinner when Tiger came back with a puzzled frown on his face. "Finally traced that call. At least I think I did. Anybody ever hear of a star called 31 Brucker?"

"Brucker?" Jack said. "It isn't on the list of contracts. What's the trouble?"

"I'm not sure," Tiger said. "I'm not even certain if it's a call or not. Come on up front and see what you think."

PLAGUE!

In the control room the interstellar radio and teletype-translator were silent. The red light on the call board was still blinking; Tiger turned it off with a snap. "Here's the message that just came in, as near as I can make out," he said, "and if you can make sense of it, you're way ahead of me."

The message was a single word, teletyped in the center of a blue dispatch sheet:

GREETINGS

"This is all?" Jack said.

"That's every bit of it. They repeated it half a dozen times, just like that."

"*Who* repeated it?" Dal asked. "Where are the identification symbols?"

"There weren't any," said Tiger. "Our own computer designated 31 Brucker from the direction and intensity of the signal. The question is, what do we do?"

The message stared up at them cryptically. Dal shook his head. "Doesn't give us much to go on, that's certain. Even the location could be wrong if the signal came in on an odd frequency or from a long distance. Let's beam back at the same direction and intensity and see what happens."

Tiger took the earphones and speaker, and turned the signal beam to coincide with the direction of the incoming message.

"We have your contact. Can you hear me? Who are you and what do you want?"

There was a long delay and they thought the contact was lost. Then a voice came whispering through the static. "Where is your ship now? Are you near to us?"

"We need your co-ordinates in order to tell," Tiger said. "Who are you?"

Again a long pause and a howl of static. Then: "If you are far away it will be too late. We have no time left, we are dying...."

Abruptly the voice message broke off and co-ordinates began coming through between bursts of static. Tiger scribbled them down, piecing them together through several repetitions. "Check these out fast," he told Jack. "This sounds like real trouble." He tossed Dal another pair of earphones and turned back to the speaker. "Are you a contract planet?" he signaled. "Do we have a survey on you?"

There was a much longer pause. Then the voice came back, "No, we have no contract. We are all dying, but if you must have a contract to come...."

"Not at all," Tiger sent back. "We're coming. Keep your frequency open. We will contact again when we are closer."

He tossed down the earphones and looked excitedly at Dal. "Did you hear that? A planet calling for help, with no Hospital Earth contract!"

"They sound desperate," Dal said. "We'd better go there, contract or no contract."

"Of course we'll go there, you idiot. See if Jack has those co-ordinates charted, and start digging up information on them, everything you can find. We need all of the dope we can get and we need it fast. This is our golden chance to seal a contract with a new planet."

All three of the doctors fell to work trying to identify the mysterious caller. Dal began searching the information file for data on 31 Brucker, punching all the reference tags he could think of, as well as the galactic co-ordinates of the planet. He could hardly control his fingers as the tapes with possible references began plopping down into the slots. Tiger was right; this was almost too good to be true. When a planet without a medical service contract called a GPP Ship for help, there was always hope that a brand new contract might be signed if the call was successful. And no greater honor could come to a patrol craft crew than to be the originators of a new contract for Hospital Earth.

But there were problems in dealing with uncontacted planets. Many star systems had never been explored by ships of the Confederation. Many races, like Earthmen at the time their star-drive was discovered, had no inkling of the existence of a Galactic Confederation of worlds. There might be no information whatever about the special anatomical and physiological characteristics of the inhabitants of an uncontacted planet, and often a patrol crew faced insurmountable difficulties, coming in blind to solve a medical problem.

Dal had his information gathered first—a disappointingly small amount indeed. Among the billions of notes on file in the *Lancet*'s data bank, there were only two scraps of data available on the 31 Brucker system.

"Is this all you could find?" Tiger said, staring at the information slips.

"There's just nothing else there," Dal said. "This one is a description and classification of the star, and it doesn't sound like the one who wrote it had even been near it."

"He hadn't," Tiger said. "This is a routine radio-telescopic survey report. The star is a red giant. Big and cold, with three—possibly four—planets inside the outer envelope of the star itself, and only one outside it. Nothing about satellites. None of the planets thought to be habitable by man. What's the other item?"

"An exploratory report on the outer planet, done eight hundred years ago. Says it's an Earth-type planet, and not much else. Gives reference to the full report in the Confederation files. Not a word about an intelligent race living there."

"Well, maybe Jack's got a bit more for us," Tiger said. "If the place has been explored, there must be *some* information about the inhabitants."

But Jack also came up with a blank. Central Records on Hospital Earth sent back a physical description of a tiny outer planet of the star, with a thin oxygen-nitrogen atmosphere, very little water, and enough methane mixed in to make the atmosphere deadly to Earthmen.

"Then there's never been a medical service contract?" Tiger asked.

"Contract!" Jack said. "It doesn't even say there are any people there. Not a word about any kind of life form."

"Well, that's ridiculous," Dal said. "If we're getting messages from there, somebody must be sending them. But if a Confederation ship explored there, there's a way to find out. How soon can we convert to star-drive?"

"As soon as we can get strapped down," Tiger said.

"Then send our reconversion co-ordinates to the Confederation headquarters on Garv II and request the Confederation records on the place."

Jack stared at him. "You mean just ask to see Confederation records? We can't do that, they'd skin us alive. Those records are closed to everyone except full members of the Confederation."

"Tell them it's an emergency," Dal said. "If they want to be legal about it, give them my Confederation serial number. Garv II is a member of the Confederation, and I'm a native-born citizen."

Tiger got the request off while Jack and Dal strapped down for the conversion to Koenig drive. Five minutes later Tiger joined them, grinning from ear to ear. "Didn't even have to pull rank," he said. "When they started to argue, I just told them it was an emergency, and if they didn't let us see any records they had, we would file their refusal against claims that might come up later. They quit arguing. We'll have the records as soon as we reconvert."

*

The star that they were seeking was a long distance from the current location of the *Lancet*. The ship was in Koenig drive for hours before it reconverted, and even Dal was beginning to feel the first pangs of drive-sickness before they felt the customary jolting vibration of the change to normal space, and saw bright stars again in the viewscreen.

The star called 31 Brucker was close then. It was indeed a red giant; long tenuous plumes of gas spread out for hundreds of millions of miles on all sides of its glowing red core. This mammoth star did not look so cold now, as they stared at it in the viewscreen, yet among the family of stars it was a cold, dying giant with only a few moments of life left on the astronomical time scale. From the *Lancet*'s position, no planets at all were visible to the naked eye, but with the telescope Jack soon found two inside the star's envelope of gas and one tiny one outside. They would have to be searched for, and the one that they were hoping to reach located before centering and landing maneuvers could be begun.

Already the radio was chattering with two powerful signals coming in. One came from the Galactic Confederation headquarters on Garv II; the other was a good clear signal from very close range, unquestionably beamed to them from the planet in distress.

They watched as the Confederation report came clacking off the teletype, and they stared at it unbelieving.

"It just doesn't make sense," Jack said. "There *must* be intelligent creatures down there. They're sending radio signals."

"Then why a report like this?" Tiger said. "This was filed by a routine exploratory ship that came here eight hundred years ago. You can't tell me that any intelligent race could develop from scratch in less than eight centuries' time."

Dal picked up the report and read it again. "This red giant star," he read, "was studied in the usual fashion. It was found to have seven planets, all but one lying within the tenuous outer gas envelope of the star itself. The seventh planet has an atmosphere of its own, and travels an orbit well outside the star surface. This planet was selected for landing and exploration."

Following this was a long, detailed and exceedingly dull description of the step-by-step procedure followed by a Confederation exploratory ship making a first landing on a barren planet. There was a description of the atmosphere, the soil surface, the land masses and major water bodies. Physically, the planet was a desert, hot and dry, and barren of vegetation excepting in two or three areas of jungle along the equator. "The planet is inhabited by numerous small unintelligent animal species which seem well-adapted to the semi-arid conditions. Of higher animals and mammals only two species were discovered, and of these the most highly developed was an erect biped with an integrated central nervous system and the intelligence level of a Garvian *drachma*."

"How small is that?" Jack said.

"Idiot-level," Dal said glumly. "I.Q. of about 20 on the human scale. I guess the explorers weren't much impressed; they didn't even put the planet down for a routine colonization survey."

"Well, *something* has happened down there since then. Idiots can't build interstellar radios." Jack turned to Tiger. "Are you getting them?"

Tiger nodded. A voice was coming over the speaker, hesitant and apologetic, using the common tongue of the Galactic Confederation. "How soon can you come?" the voice was asking clearly, still with the sound of great reticence. "There is not much time."

"But who are you?" Tiger asked. "What's wrong down there?"

"We are sick, dying, thousands of us. But if you have other work that is more pressing, we would not want to delay you—"

Jack shook his head, frowning. "I don't get this," he said. "What are they afraid of?"

Tiger spoke into the microphone again. "We will be glad to help, but we need information about you. You have our position—can you send up a spokesman to tell us your problem?"

A long pause, and then the voice came back wearily. "It will be done. Stand by to receive him."

Tiger snapped off the radio receiver and looked up triumphantly at the others. "Now we're getting somewhere. If the people down there can send a ship out with a spokesman to tell us about their troubles, we've got a chance to sew up a contract, and that could mean a Star for every one of us."

"Yes, but who are they?" Dal said. "And where were they when the Confederation ship was here?"

"I don't know," Jack said, "but I'll bet you both that we have quite a time finding out."

"Why?" Tiger said. "What do you mean?"

"I mean we'd better be very careful here," Jack said darkly. "I don't know about you, but I think this whole business has a very strange smell."

*

There was nothing strange about the Bruckian ship when it finally came into view. It was a standard design, surface-launching interplanetary craft, with separated segments on either side suggesting atomic engines. They saw the side jets flare as the ship maneuvered to come in alongside the *Lancet*.

Grapplers were thrown out to bind the emissary ship to the *Lancet*'s hull, and Jack threw the switches to open the entrance lock and decontamination chambers. They had taken pains to describe the interior atmosphere of the patrol ship and warn the spokesman to keep himself in a sealed pressure suit. On the intercom viewscreens they saw the small suited figure cross from his ship into the *Lancet*'s lock, and watched as the sprays of formalin washed down the outside of the suit.

Moments later the creature stepped out of the decontamination chamber. He was small and humanoid, with tiny fragile bones and pale, hairless skin. He stood no more than four feet high. More than anything else, he looked like a very intelligent monkey with a diminutive space suit fitting his fragile body. When he spoke the words came through the translator in English; but Dal recognized the flowing syllables of the universal language of the Galactic Confederation.

"How do you know the common tongue?" he said. "There is no record of your people in our Confederation, yet you use our own universal language."

The Bruckian nodded. "We know the language well. My people dread outside contact—it is a racial characteristic—but we hear the Confederation broadcasts and have learned to understand the common tongue." The space-suited stranger looked at the doctors one by one. "We also know of the good works of the ships from Hospital Earth, and now we appeal to you."

"Why?" Jack said. "You gave us no information, nothing to go on."

"There was no time," the creature said. "Death is stalking our land, and the people are falling at their plows. Thousands of us are dying, tens of thousands. Even I am infected and soon will be dead. Unless you can find a way to help us quickly, it will be too late, and my people will be wiped from the face of the planet."

Jack looked grimly at Tiger and Dal. "Well," he said, "I guess that answers our question, all right. It looks as if we have a plague planet on our hands, whether we like it or not."

THE INCREDIBLE PEOPLE

Slowly and patiently they drew the story from the emissary from the seventh planet of 31 Brucker.

The small, monkey-like creature was painfully shy; he required constant reassurance that the doctors did not mind being called, that they wanted to help, and that a contract was not necessary in an emergency. Even at that the spokesman was reluctant to give details about the plague and about his stricken people. Every bit of information had to be extracted with patient questioning.

By tacit consent the doctors did not even mention the strange fact that this very planet had been explored by a Confederation ship eight hundred years before and no sign of intelligent life had been found. The little creature before them seemed ready to turn and bolt at the first hint of attack or accusation. But bit by bit, a picture of the current situation on the planet developed.

Whoever they were and wherever they had been when the Confederation ship had landed, there was unquestionably an intelligent race now inhabiting this lonely planet in the outer reaches of the solar system of 31 Brucker. There was no doubt of their advancement; a few well-selected questions revealed that they had control of atomic power, a working understanding of the nature and properties of contra-terrene matter, and a workable star drive operating on the same basic principle as Earth's Koenig drive but which the Bruckians had never really used because of their shyness and fear of contact with other races. They also had an excellent understanding, thanks to their eavesdropping on Confederation interstellar radio chatter, of the existence and functions of the Galactic Confederation of worlds, and of Hospital Earth's work as physician to the galaxy.

But about Bruckian anatomy, physiology or biochemistry, the little emissary would tell them nothing. He seemed genuinely frightened when they pressed him about the physical make-up of his people, as though their questions were somehow scraping a raw nerve. He insisted that his people knew nothing about the nature of the plague that had stricken them, and the doctors could not budge him an inch from his stand.

But a plague had certainly struck.

It had begun six months before, striking great masses of the people. It had walked the streets of the cities and the hills and valleys of the countryside. First three out of ten had been stricken, then four, then five. The course of the disease, once started, was invariably the same: first illness, weakness, loss of energy and interest, then gradually a fading away of intelligent responses, leaving thousands of creatures walking blank-faced and idiot-like about the streets and countryside. Ultimately even the ability to take food was lost, and after an interval of a week or so, death invariably ensued.

Finally the doctors retired to the control room for a puzzled conference. "It's got to be an organism of some sort that's doing it," Dal said. "There couldn't be an illness like this that wasn't caused by some kind of a parasitic germ or virus."

"But how do we know?" Jack said. "We know nothing about these people except what we can see. We're going to have to do a complete biochemical and medical survey before we can hope to do anything."

"But we aren't equipped for a real survey," Tiger protested.

"We've got to do it anyway," Jack said. "If we can just learn enough to be sure it's an infectious illness, we might stand a chance of finding a drug that will cure it. Or at least a way to immunize the ones that aren't infected yet. If this is a virus infection, we might only need to find an antibody for inoculation to stop it in its tracks. But first we need a good look at the planet and some more of the people—both infected and healthy ones. We'd better make arrangements as fast as we can."

An hour later they had reached an agreement with the Bruckian emissary. The *Lancet* would be permitted to land on the planet's surface as soon as the doctors were satisfied that it was safe. For the time being the initial landings would be made in the patrol ship's lifeboats, with the *Lancet* in orbit a thousand miles above the surface. Unquestionably the first job was diagnosis, discovering the exact nature of the illness and studying the afflicted people. This responsibility rested squarely on Jack's shoulders; he was the diagnostician, and Dal and Tiger willingly yielded to him in organizing the program.

It was decided that Jack and Tiger would visit the planet's surface at once, while Dal stayed on the ship and set up the reagents and examining techniques that would be needed to measure the basic physical and biochemical characteristics of the Bruckians.

Yet in all the excitement of planning, Dal could not throw off the lingering shadow of doubt in his mind, some instinctive voice of caution that seemed to say *watch out, be careful, go slowly! This may not be what it seems to be; you may be walking into a trap....*

But it was only a faint voice, and easy to thrust aside as the planning went ahead full speed.

*

It did not take very long for the crew of the *Lancet* to realize that there was something very odd indeed about the small, self-effacing inhabitants of 31 Brucker VII.

In fact, "odd" was not really quite the proper word for these creatures at all. No one knew better than the doctors of Hospital Earth that oddness was the rule among the various members of the galactic civilization. All sorts and varieties of life-forms had been discovered, described and studied, each with its singular differences, each with certain similarities, and each quite "odd" in reference to any of the others.

In Dal this awareness of the oddness and difference of other races was particularly acute. He knew that to Tiger and Jack he himself seemed odd, both anatomically and in other ways. His fine gray fur and his four-fingered hands set him apart from them—he would never be mistaken for an Earthman, even in the densest fog. But these were comprehensible differences. His close attachment to Fuzzy was something else, and still seemed beyond their ability to understand.

He had spent one whole evening patiently trying to make Jack understand just how his attachment to the little pink creature was more than just the fondness of a man for his dog.

"Well, what would you call it, then?"

"Symbiosis is probably the best word for it," Dal had replied. "Two life-forms live together, and each one helps the other—that's all symbiosis is. Together each one is better off than either one would be alone. We all of us live in symbiosis with the bacteria in our digestive tracts, don't we? We provide them with a place to live and grow, and they help us digest our food. It's a kind of a partnership—and Fuzzy and I are partners in the same sort of way."

Jack had argued, and then lost his temper, and finally grudgingly agreed that he supposed he would have to tolerate it even if it didn't make sense to him.

But the creatures on 31 Brucker VII were "odd" far beyond the reasonable limits of oddness—so far beyond it that the doctors could not believe the things that their eyes and their instruments were telling them.

When Tiger and Jack came back to the *Lancet* after their first trip to the planet's surface, they were visibly shaken. Geographically, they had found it just as it had been described in the exploratory reports—a barren, desert land with only a few large islands of vegetation in the equatorial regions.

"But the people!" Jack said. "They don't fit into *any* kind of pattern. They've got houses—at least I guess you'd call them houses—but every one of them is like every other one, and they're all crammed together in tight little bunches, with nothing for miles in between. They've got an advanced technology, a good communications system, manufacturing techniques and everything, but they just don't use them."

"It's more than that," Tiger said. "They don't seem to *want* to use them."

"Well, it doesn't add up, to me," Jack said. "There are thousands of towns and cities down there, all of them miles apart, and yet they had to go dig an old rusty jet scooter out of storage and get the motor rebuilt just specially to take us from one place to another. I know things can get disorganized with a plague in the land, but this plague just hasn't been going on that long."

"What about the sickness?" Dal asked. "Is it as bad as it sounded?"

"Worse, if anything," Tiger said gloomily. "They're dying by the thousands, and I hope we got those suits of ours decontaminated, because I don't want any part of this disease."

Graphically, he described the conditions they had found among the stricken people. There was no question that a plague was stalking the land. In the rutted mud roads of the villages and towns the dead were piled in gutters, and in all of the cities a deathly stillness hung over the streets. Those who had not yet succumbed to the illness were nursing and feeding the sick ones, but these unaffected ones were growing scarcer and scarcer. The whole living population seemed resigned to hopelessness, hardly noticing the strangers from the patrol ship.

But worst of all were those in the final stages of the disease, wandering vaguely about the street, their faces blank and their jaws slack as though they were living in a silent world of their own, cut off from contact with the rest. "One of them almost ran into me," Jack said. "I was right in front of him, and he didn't see me or hear me."

"But don't they have *any* knowledge of antisepsis or isolation?" Dal asked.

Tiger shook his head. "Not that we could see. They don't know what's causing this sickness. They think that it's some kind of curse, and they never dreamed that it might be kept from spreading."

Already Tiger and Jack had taken the first routine steps to deal with the sickness. They gave orders to move the unaffected people in every town and village into isolated barracks and stockades. For half a day Tiger tried to explain ways to prevent the spread of a bacteria or virus-borne disease. The people had stared at him as if he were talking gibberish; finally he gave up trying to explain, and just laid down rules which the people were instructed to follow. Together they had collected standard testing specimens of body fluids and tissue from both healthy and afflicted Bruckians, and come back to the *Lancet* for a breather.

Now all three doctors began work on the specimens. Cultures were inoculated with specimens from respiratory tract, blood and tissue taken from both sick and well. Half a dozen fatal cases were brought to the ship under specially controlled conditions for autopsy examination, to reveal both the normal anatomical characteristics of this strange race of people and the damage the disease was doing. Down on the surface Tiger had already inoculated a dozen of the healthy ones with various radioactive isotopes to help outline the normal metabolism and biochemistry of the people. After a short sleep period on the *Lancet*, he went back down alone to follow up on these, leaving Dal and Jack to carry on the survey work in the ship's lab.

It was a gargantuan task that faced them. They knew that in any race of creatures they could not hope to recognize the abnormal unless they knew what the normal was. That was the sole reason for the extensive biomedical surveys that were done on new contract planets. Under normal conditions, a survey crew with specialists in physiology, biochemistry, anatomy, radiology, pharmacology and pathology might spend months or even years on a new planet gathering base-line information. But here there was neither time nor facilities for such a study. Even in the twenty-four hours since the patrol ship arrived, the number of dead had increased alarmingly.

Alone on the ship, Dal and Jack found themselves working as a well organized team. There was no time here for argument or duplicated efforts; everything the two doctors did was closely co-ordinated. Jack seemed to have forgotten his previous antagonism completely. There was a crisis here, and more work than three men could possibly do in the time available. "You handle anatomy and pathology," Jack told Dal at the beginning. "You can get the picture five times as fast as I can, and your pathology slides are better than most commercial ones. I can do the best job on the cultures, once I get the growth media all set up."

Bit by bit they divided the labor, checking in with Tiger by radio on the results of the isotopes studies he was running on the planet's surface. Bit by bit the data was collected, and Earthman and Garvian worked more closely than ever before as the task that faced them appeared more and more formidable.

But the results of their tests made no sense whatever. Tiger returned to the ship after forty-eight hours with circles under his eyes, looking as though he had been trampled in a crowd. "No sleep, that's all," he said breathlessly as he crawled out of his decontaminated pressure suit. "No time for it. I swear I ran those tests a dozen times and I still didn't get any answers that made sense."

"The results you were sending up sounded plenty strange," Jack said. "What was the trouble?"

"I don't know," Tiger said, "but if we're looking for a biological pattern here, we haven't found it yet as far as I can see."

"No, we certainly haven't," Dal exploded. "I thought I was doing something wrong somehow, because these blood chemistries I've been doing have been ridiculous. I can't even find a normal level for blood sugar, and as for the enzyme systems...." He tossed a sheaf of notes down on the counter in disgust. "I don't see how these people could even be alive, with a botched-up metabolism like this! I've never heard of anything like it."

"What kind of pathology did you find?" Tiger wanted to know.

"Nothing," Dal said. "Nothing at all. I did autopsies on the six that you brought up here and made slides of every different kind of tissue I could find. The anatomy is perfectly clear cut, no objections there. These people are very similar to Earth-type monkeys in structure, with heart and lungs and vocal cords and all. But I can't find any reason why they should be dying. Any luck with the cultures?"

Jack shook his head glumly. "No growth on any of the plates. At first I thought I had something going, but if I did, it died, and I can't find any sign of it in the filtrates."

"But we've got to have *something* to work on," Tiger said desperately. "Look, there are some things that always measure out the same in *any* intelligent creature no matter where he comes from. That's the whole basis of galactic medicine. Creatures may develop and adapt in different ways, but the basic biochemical reactions are the same."

"Not here, they aren't," Dal said. "Take a look at these tests!"

They carried the heap of notes they had collected out into the control room and began sifting and organizing the data, just as a survey team would do, trying to match it with the pattern of a thousand other living creatures that had previously been studied. Hours passed, and they were farther from an answer than when they began.

Because this data did not fit a pattern. It was *different*. No two individuals showed the same reactions. In every test the results were either flatly impossible or completely the opposite of what was expected.

Carefully they retraced their steps, trying to pinpoint what could be going wrong.

"There's *got* to be a laboratory error," Dal said wearily. "We must have slipped up somewhere."

"But I don't see where," Jack said. "Let's see those culture tubes again. And put on a pot of coffee. I can't even think straight any more."

Of the three of them, Jack was beginning to show the strain the most. This was his special field, the place where he was supposed to excel, and nothing was happening. Reports coming up from the planet were discouraging; the isolation techniques they had tried to institute did not seem to be working, and the spread of the plague was accelerating. The communiqués from the Bruckians were taking on a note of desperation.

Jack watched each report with growing apprehension. He moved restlessly from lab to control room, checking and rechecking things, trying to find some sign of order in the chaos.

"Try to get some sleep," Dal urged him. "A couple of hours will freshen you up a hundred per cent."

"I can't, I've already tried it," Jack said.

"Go ahead. Tiger and I can keep working on these things for a while."

"No, no, it's not that," Jack said. "Without a diagnosis, we can't do a thing. Until we have that, our hands are tied, and we aren't even getting close to it. We don't even know whether this is a bacteria, or a virus, or what. Maybe the Bruckians are right. Maybe it's a curse."

"I don't think the Black Service of Pathology would buy that for a diagnosis," Tiger said sourly.

"The Black Service would choke on it—but what other answer do we have? You two have been doing all you can, but diagnosis is *my* job. I'm supposed to be good at it, but the more we dig into this, the farther away we seem to get."

"Do you want to call for help?" Tiger said.

Jack shook his head helplessly. "I'm beginning to think we should have called for help a long time ago," he said. "We're into this over our heads now and we're still going down. At the rate those people are dying down there, we don't have time to call for help now." He stared at the piles of notes on the desk and his face was very white. "I don't know, I just don't know," he said. "The diagnosis on this thing should have been duck soup. I thought it was going to be a real feather in my cap, just walking in and nailing it down in a few hours. Well, I'm whipped. I don't know what to do. If either of you can think of an answer, it's all yours, and I'll admit it to Black Doctor Tanner himself."

*

It was bitter medicine for Blue Doctor Jack Alvarez to swallow, but that fact gave no pleasure to Dal or Tiger now. They were as baffled as Jack was, and would have welcomed help from anyone who could offer it.

And, ironically, the first glimpse of the truth came from the direction they least expected.

From the very beginning Fuzzy had been watching the proceedings from his perch on the swinging platform in the control room. If he sensed that

Dal Timgar was ignoring him and leaving him to his own devices much of the time, he showed no sign of resentment. The tiny creature seemed to realize that something important was consuming his master's energy and attention, and contented himself with an affectionate pat now and then as Dal went through the control room. Everyone assumed without much thought that Fuzzy was merely being tolerant of the situation. It was not until they had finally given up in desperation and Tiger was trying to contact a Hospital Ship for help, that Dal stared up at his little pink friend with a puzzled frown.

Tiger put the transmitter down for a moment. "What's wrong?" he said to Dal. "You look as though you just bit into a rotten apple."

"I just remembered that I haven't fed him for twenty-four hours," Dal said.

"Who? Fuzzy?" Tiger shrugged. "He could see you were busy."

Dal shook his head. "That wouldn't make any difference to Fuzzy. When he gets hungry, he gets hungry, and he's pretty self-centered. It wouldn't matter what I was doing, he should have been screaming for food hours ago."

Dal walked over to the platform and peered down at his pink friend in alarm. He took him up and rested him on his shoulder, a move that invariably sent Fuzzy into raptures of delight. Now the little creature just sat there, trembling and rubbing half-heartedly against Dal's neck.

Dal held him out at arm's length. "Fuzzy, *what's the matter with you?*"

"Do you think something's wrong with him?" Jack said, looking up suddenly. "Looks like he's having trouble keeping his eyes open."

"His color isn't right, either," Tiger said. "He looks kind of blue."

Quite suddenly the little black eyes closed and Fuzzy began to tremble violently. He drew himself up into a tight pink globule as the fuzz-like hair disappeared from view.

Something was unmistakably wrong. As he held the shivering creature, Dal was suddenly aware that something had been nibbling at the back of his mind for hours. Not a clear-cut thought, merely an impression of pain and anguish and sickness, and now as he looked at Fuzzy the impression grew so strong it almost made him cry out.

Abruptly, Dal knew what he had to do. Where the thought came from he didn't know, but it was crystal clear in his mind. "Jack, where is our biggest virus filter?" he asked quietly.

Jack stared at him. "Virus filter? I just took it out of the autoclave an hour ago."

"Get it," Dal said, "and the suction machine too. *Quickly*!"

Jack went down the corridor like a shot, and reappeared a moment later with the big porcelain virus filter and the suction tubing attached to it. Swiftly Dal dumped the limp little creature in his hand into the top of the filter jar, poured in some sterile saline, and started the suction.

Tiger and Jack watched him in amazement. "What are you doing?" Tiger said.

"Filtering him," Dal said. "He's infected. He must have been exposed to the plague somehow, maybe when our little Bruckian visitor came on board the other day. And if it's a virus that's causing this plague, the virus filter ought to hold it back and still let Fuzzy's molecular structure through."

They watched and sure enough a bluish-pink fluid began moving down through the porcelain filter, and dripping through the funnel into the beaker below. Each drop coalesced in the beaker as it fell until Fuzzy's whole body had been sucked through the filter and into the jar below. He was still not quite his normal pink color, but as the filter went dry, a pair of frightened shoe-button eyes appeared and he poked up a pair of ears. Presently the fuzz began appearing on his body again.

And on the top of the filter lay a faint gray film. "Don't touch it!" Dal said. "That's real poison." He slipped on a mask and gloves, and scraped a bit of the film from the filter with a spatula. "I think we have it," he said. "The virus that's causing the plague on this planet."

It was a virus, beyond doubt. The electron microscope told them that, now that they had the substance isolated and could examine it. In the culture tubes in the *Lancet*'s incubators, it would begin to grow nicely, and then falter and die, but when guinea pigs were inoculated in the ship's laboratory, the substance proved its virulence. The animals injected with tiny bits of the substance grew sick within hours and very quickly died.

The call to the Hospital Ship was canceled as the three doctors worked in feverish excitement. Here at last was something they could grapple with, something so common among the races of the galaxy that the doctors felt certain that they could cope with it. Very few, if any, higher life forms existed that did not have some sort of submicroscopic parasite afflicting them. Bacterial infection was a threat on every inhabited world, and the viruses—the tiniest of all submicroscopic organisms—were the most difficult and dangerous of them all.

And yet virus plagues had been stopped before, and they could be stopped again.

Jack radioed down to the planet's surface that the diagnosis had been made; as soon as the proper medications could be prepared, the doctors would land to begin treatment. There was a new flicker of hopefulness in the Bruckian's response, and an appeal to hurry. With renewed energy the doctors went back to the lab to start working on the new data.

But trouble continued to dog them. This was no ordinary virus. It proved resistant to every one of the antibiotics and antiviral agents in the *Lancet*'s stockroom. No drug seemed to affect it, and its molecular structure was different from any virus that had ever been recorded before.

"If one of the drugs would only just slow it up a little, we'd be ahead," Tiger said in perplexity. "We don't have anything that even touches it, not even the purified globulins."

"What about antibodies from the infected people?" Jack suggested. "In every virus disease I've ever heard of, the victim's own body starts making antibodies against the invading virus. If enough antibodies are made fast enough, the virus dies and the patient is immune from then on."

"Well, these people don't seem to be making any antibodies at all," Tiger said. "At least not as far as I can see. If they were, at least some of them would be recovering from the disease. So far not a single one has recovered once the thing started. They all just go ahead and die."

"I wonder," Dal said, "if Fuzzy had any defense."

Jack looked up. "How do you mean?"

"Well, Fuzzy was infected, we know that. He might have died too, if we hadn't caught it in time—but as it worked out, he didn't. In fact, he looks pretty healthy right now."

"That's fine for Fuzzy," Jack said impatiently, "but I don't see how we can push the whole population of 31 Brucker VII through a virus filter. They're flesh-and-blood creatures."

"That's not what I mean," Dal said. "Maybe Fuzzy's body developed antibodies against the virus while he was infected. Remember, he doesn't have a rigid body structure like we do. He's mostly just basic protein, and he can synthesize pretty much anything he wants to or needs to."

Jack blinked. "It's an idea, at least. Is there any way we can get some of his body fluid away from him? Without getting bit, I mean?"

"No problem there," Dal said. "He can regenerate pretty fast if he has enough of the right kind of food. He won't miss an ounce or two of excess tissue."

He took a beaker over to Fuzzy's platform and began squeezing off a little blob of pink material. Fuzzy seemed to sense what Dal wanted; obligingly he thrust out a little pseudopod which Dal pinched off into the beaker. With the addition of a small amount of saline solution, the tissue dissolved into thin, pink suspension.

In the laboratory they found two or three of the guinea pigs in the last stages of the infection, and injected them with a tiny bit of the pink solution. The effect was almost unbelievable. Within twenty minutes all of the injected animals began to perk up, their eyes brighter, nibbling at the food in their cages, while the ones that had not been injected got sicker and sicker.

"Well, there's our answer," Jack said eagerly. "If we can get some of this stuff injected into our friends down below, we may be able to protect the healthy ones from getting the plague, and cure the sick ones as well. If we still have enough time, that is."

They had landing permission from the Bruckian spokesman within minutes, and an hour later the *Lancet* made an orderly landing on a newly-repaved landing field near one of the central cities on the seventh planet of 31 Brucker.

Tiger and Jack had obviously not exaggerated the strange appearance of the towns and cities on this plague-ridden planet, and Dal was appalled at the ravages of the disease that they had come to fight. Only one out of ten of the Bruckians was still uninfected, and another three out of the ten were clearly in the late stages of the disease, walking about blankly and blindly, stumbling into things in their paths, falling to the ground and lying mute and helpless until death came to release them. Under the glaring red sun, weary parties of stretcher bearers went about the silent streets, moving their grim cargo out to the mass graves at the edge of the city.

The original spokesman who had come up to the *Lancet* was dead, but another had taken his place as negotiator with the doctors—an older, thinner Bruckian who looked as if he carried the total burden of his people on his shoulders. He greeted them eagerly at the landing field. "You have found a solution!" he cried. "You have found a way to turn the tide—but hurry! Every moment now is precious."

During the landing procedures, Dal had worked to prepare enough of the precious antibody suspension, with Fuzzy's co-operation, to handle a large number of inoculations. By the time the ship touched down he had a dozen flasks and several hundred syringes ready. Hundreds of the unafflicted people were crowding around the ship, staring in open wonder as Dal, Jack and Tiger came down the ladder and went into close conference with the spokesman.

It took some time to explain to the spokesman why they could not begin then and there with the mass inoculations against the plague. First, they needed test cases, in order to make certain that what they thought would work in theory actually produced the desired results. Controls were needed, to be certain that the antibody suspension alone was bringing about the changes seen and not something else. At last, orders went out from the spokesman. Two hundred uninfected Bruckians were admitted to a large roped-off area near the ship, and another two hundred in late stages of the disease were led stumbling into another closed area. Preliminary skin-tests of the antibody suspension showed no sign of untoward reaction. Dal began filling syringes while Tiger and Jack started inoculating the two groups.

"If it works with these cases, it will be simple to immunize the whole population," Tiger said. "From the amounts we used on the guinea pigs, it looks as if only tiny amounts are needed. We may even be able to train the Bruckians to give the injections themselves."

"And if it works we ought to have a brand new medical service contract ready for signature with Hospital Earth," Jack added eagerly. "It won't be long before we have those Stars, you wait and see! If we can only get this done fast enough."

They worked feverishly, particularly with the group of terminal cases. Many were dying even as the shots were being given, while the first symptoms of the disease were appearing in some of the unafflicted ones. Swiftly Tiger and Jack went from patient to patient while Dal kept check of the names, numbers and locations of those that were inoculated.

And even before they were finished with the inoculations, it was apparent that they were taking effect. Not one of the infected patients died after inoculation was completed. The series took three hours, and by the time the four hundred doses were administered, one thing seemed certain: that the antibody was checking the deadly march of the disease in some way.

The Bruckian spokesman was so excited he could hardly contain himself; he wanted to start bringing in the rest of the population at once. "We've almost exhausted this first batch of the material," Dal told him. "We will have to prepare more—but we will waste time trying to move a whole planet's population here. Get a dozen aircraft ready, and a dozen healthy, intelligent workers to help us. We can show them how to use the material, and let them go out to the other population centers all at once."

Back aboard the ship they started preparing a larger quantity of the antibody suspension. Fuzzy had regenerated back to normal weight again, and much to Dal's delight had been splitting off small segments of pink protoplasm in a circle all around him, as though anticipating further demands on his resources. A quick test-run showed that the antibody was also being regenerated. Fuzzy was voraciously hungry, but the material in the second batch was still as powerful as in the first.

The doctors were almost ready to go back down, loaded with enough inoculum and syringes to equip themselves and a dozen field workers when

Jack suddenly stopped what he was doing and cocked an ear toward the entrance lock.

"What's wrong?" Dal said.

"Listen a minute."

They stopped to listen. "I don't hear anything," Tiger said.

Jack nodded. "I know. That's what I mean. They were hollering their heads off when we came back aboard. Why so quiet now?"

He crossed over to the viewscreen scanning the field below, and flipped on the switch. For a moment he just stared. Then he said: "Come here a minute. I don't like the looks of this at all."

Dal and Tiger crowded up to the screen. "What's the matter?" Tiger said. "I don't see ... *wait a minute*!"

"Yes, you'd better look again," Jack said. "What do you think, Dal?"

"We'd better get down there fast," Dal said, "and see what's going on. It looks to me like we've got a tiger by the tail...."

*

They climbed down the ladder once again, with the antibody flasks and sterile syringes strapped to their backs. But this time the greeting was different from before.

The Bruckian spokesman and the others who had not yet been inoculated drew back from them in terror as they stepped to the ground. Before, the people on the field had crowded in eagerly around the ship; now they were standing in silent groups staring at the doctors fearfully and muttering among themselves.

But the doctors could see only the inoculated people in the two roped-off areas. Off to the right among the infected Bruckians who had received the antibody there were no new dead—but there was no change for the better, either. The sick creatures drifted about aimlessly, milling like animals in a cage, their faces blank, their jaws slack, hands wandering foolishly. Not one of them had begun reacting normally, not one showed any sign of recognition or recovery.

But the real horror was on the other side of the field. Here were the healthy ones, the uninfected ones who had received preventative inoculations. A few hours before they had been left standing in quiet, happy groups, talking among themselves, laughing and joking....

But now they weren't talking any more. They stared across at the doctors with slack faces and dazed eyes, their feet shuffling aimlessly in the dust. All were alive, but only half-alive. The intelligence and alertness were gone from their faces; they were like the empty shells of the creatures they had been a few hours before, indistinguishable from the infected creatures in the other compound.

Jack turned to the Bruckian spokesman in alarm. "What's happened here?" he asked. "What's become of the ones we inoculated? Where have you taken them?"

The spokesman shrank back as though afraid Jack might reach out to touch him. "Taken them!" he cried. "We have moved none of them! Those are the ones you poisoned with your needles. What have you done to make them like this?"

"It—it must be some sort of temporary reaction to the injection," Jack faltered. "There was nothing that we used that could possibly have given them the disease, we only used a substance to help them fight it off."

The Bruckian was shaking his fist angrily. "It's no reaction, it is the plague itself! What kind of evil are you doing? You came here to help us, and instead you bring us more misery. Do we not have enough of that to please you?"

Swiftly the doctors began examining the patients in both enclosures, and on each side they found the same picture. One by one they checked the ones that had previously been untouched by the plague, and found only the sagging jaws and idiot stares.

"There's no sense examining every one," Tiger said finally. "They're all the same, every one."

"But this is impossible," Jack said, glancing apprehensively at the growing mob of angry Bruckians outside the stockades. "What could have happened? What have we done?"

"I don't know," Tiger said. "But whatever we've done has turned into a boomerang. We knew that the antibody might not work, and the disease might just go right ahead, but we didn't anticipate anything like this."

"Maybe some foreign protein got into the batch," Dal said.

Tiger shook his head. "It wouldn't behave like *this*. And we were careful getting it ready. All we've done was inject an antibody against a specific virus. All it could have done was to kill the virus, but these people act as though they're infected now."

"But they're not dying," Dal said. "And the sick ones we injected stopped dying, too."

"So what do we do now?" Jack said.

"Get one of these that changed like this aboard ship and go over him with a fine-toothed comb. We've got to find out what's happened."

He led one of the stricken Bruckians by the hand like a mindless dummy across the field toward the little group where the spokesman and his party stood. The crowd on the field were moving in closer; an angry cry went up when Dal touched the sick creature.

"You'll have to keep this crowd under control," Dal said to the spokesman. "We're going to take this one aboard the ship and examine him to see what this reaction could be, but this mob is beginning to sound dangerous."

"They're afraid," the spokesman said. "They want to know what you've done to them, what this new curse is that you bring in your syringes."

"It's not a curse, but something has gone wrong. We need to learn what, in order to deal with it."

"The people are afraid and angry," the spokesman said. "I don't know how long I can control them."

And indeed, the attitude of the crowd around the ship was very strange. They were not just fearful; they were terrified. As the doctors walked back to the ship leading the stricken Bruckian behind them, the people shrank back with dreadful cries, holding up their hands as if to ward off some monstrous evil. Before, in the worst throes of the plague, there had been no sign of this kind of reaction. The people had seemed apathetic and miserable, resigned hopelessly to their fate, but now they were reacting in abject terror. It almost seemed that they were more afraid of these walking shells of their former selves than they were of the disease itself.

But as the doctors started up the ladder toward the entrance lock the crowd surged in toward them with fists raised in anger. "We'd better get help, and fast," Jack said as he slammed the entrance lock closed behind them. "I don't like the looks of this a bit. Dal, we'd better see what we can learn from this poor creature here."

As Tiger headed for the earphones, Dal and Jack went to work once again, checking the blood and other body fluids from the stricken Bruckian. But now, incredibly, the results of their tests were quite different from those they had obtained before. The blood sugar and protein determinations fell into the pattern they had originally expected for a creature of this type. Even more surprising, the level of the antibody against the plague virus was high—far higher than it could have been from the tiny amount that was injected into the creature.

"They must have been making it themselves," Dal said, "and our inoculation was just the straw that broke the camel's back. All of those people must have been on the brink of symptoms of the infection, and all we did was add to the natural defenses they were already making."

"Then why did the symptoms appear?" Jack said. "If that's true, we should have been *helping* them, and look at them now!"

Tiger appeared at the door, scowling. "We've got real trouble, now," he said. "I can't get through to a hospital ship. In fact, I can't get a message out at all. These people are jamming our radios."

"But why?" Dal said.

"I don't know, but take a look outside there."

Through the viewscreen it seemed as though the whole field around the ship had filled up with the crowd. The first reaction of terror now seemed to have given way to blind fury; the people were shouting angrily, waving their clenched fists at the ship as the spokesman tried to hold them back.

Then there was a resounding crash from somewhere below, and the ship lurched, throwing the doctors to the floor. They staggered to their feet as another blow jolted the ship, and another.

"Let's get a screen up," Tiger shouted. "Jack, get the engines going. They're trying to board us, and I don't think it'll be much fun if they ever break in."

In the control room they threw the switches that activated a powerful protective energy screen around the ship. It was a device that was carried by all GPP Ships as a means of protection against physical attack. When activated, an energy screen was virtually impregnable, but it could only be used briefly; the power it required placed an enormous drain on a ship's energy resources, and a year's nuclear fuel could be consumed in a few hours.

Now the screen served its purpose. The ship steadied, still vibrating from the last assault, and the noise from below ceased abruptly. But when Jack threw the switches to start the engines, nothing happened at all.

"Look at that!" he cried, staring at the motionless dials. "They're jamming our electrical system somehow. I can't get any turn-over."

"Try it again," Tiger said. "We've got to get out of here. If they break in, we're done for."

"They can't break through the screen," Dal said.

"Not as long as it lasts. But we can't keep it up indefinitely."

Once again they tried the radio equipment. There was no response but the harsh static of the jamming signal from the ground below. "It's no good," Tiger said finally. "We're stuck here, and we can't even call for help. You'd think if they were so scared of us they'd be glad to see us go."

"I think there's more to it than that," Dal said thoughtfully. "This whole business has been crazy from the start. This just fits in with all the rest." He picked Fuzzy off his perch and set him on his shoulder as if to protect him from some unsuspected threat. "Maybe they're afraid of us, I don't know. But I think they're afraid of something else a whole lot worse."

*

There was nothing to be done but wait and stare hopelessly at the mass of notes and records that they had collected on the people of 31 Brucker VII and the plague that afflicted them.

Until now, the *Lancet*'s crew had been too busy to stop and piece the data together, to try to see the picture as a whole. But now there was ample time, and the realization of what had been happening here began to dawn on them.

They had followed the well-established principles step by step in studying these incredible people, and nothing had come out as it should. In theory, the steps they had taken should have yielded the answer. They had come to a planet where an entire population was threatened with a dreadful disease. They had identified the disease, found and isolated the virus that caused it, and then developed an antibody that effectively destroyed the virus—in the laboratory. But when they had tried to apply the antibody in the afflicted patients, the response had been totally unexpected. They had stopped the march of death among those they had inoculated, and had produced instead a condition that the people seemed to dread far more than death.

"Let's face it," Dal said, "we bungled it somehow. We should have had help here right from the start. I don't know where we went wrong, but we've done something."

"Well, it wasn't your fault," Jack said gloomily. "If we had the right diagnosis, this wouldn't have happened. And I *still* can't see the diagnosis. All I've been able to come up with is a nice mess."

"We're missing something, that's all," Dal said. "The information is all here. We just aren't reading it right, somehow. Somewhere in here is a key to the whole thing, and we just can't see it."

They went back to the data again, going through it step by step. This was Jack Alvarez's specialty—the technique of diagnosis, the ability to take all the available information about a race and about its illness and piece it together into a pattern that made sense. Dal could see that Jack was now bitterly angry with himself, yet at every turn he seemed to strike another obstacle—some fact that didn't jibe, a missing fragment here, a wrong answer there. With Dal and Tiger helping he started back over the sequence of events, trying to make sense out of them, and came up squarely against a blank wall.

The things they had done should have worked; instead, they had failed. A specific antibody used against a specific virus should have destroyed the virus or slowed its progress, and there seemed to be no rational explanation for the dreadful response of the uninfected ones who had been inoculated for protection.

And as the doctors sifted through the data, the Bruckian they had brought up from the enclosure sat staring off into space, making small noises with his mouth and moving his arms aimlessly. After a while they led him back to a bunk, gave him a medicine for sleep and left him snoring gently. Another hour passed as they pored over their notes, with Tiger stopping from time to time to mop perspiration from his forehead. All three were aware of the moving clock hands, marking off the minutes that the force screen could hold out.

And then Dal Timgar was digging into the pile of papers, searching frantically for something he could not find. "That first report we got," he said hoarsely. "There was something in the very first information we ever saw on this planet...."

"You mean the Confederation's data? It's in the radio log." Tiger pulled open the thick log book. "But what...."

"It's there, plain as day, I'm sure of it," Dal said. He read through the report swiftly, until he came to the last paragraph—a two-line description of the largest creatures the original Exploration Ship had found on the planet, described by them as totally unintelligent and only observed on a few occasions in the course of the exploration. Dal read it, and his hands were trembling as he handed the report to Jack. "I knew the answer was there!" he said. "Take a look at that again and think about it for a minute."

Jack read it through. "I don't see what you mean," he said.

"I mean that I think we've made a horrible mistake," Dal said, "and I think I see now what it was. We've had this whole thing exactly 100 per cent backward from the start, and that explains everything that's happened here!"

Tiger peered over Jack's shoulder at the report. "Backward?"

"As backward as we could get it," Dal said. "We've assumed all along that these flesh-and-blood creatures down there were the ones that were calling us for help because of a virus plague that was attacking and killing them. All right, look at it the other way. Just suppose that the intelligent creature that called us for help was the *virus*, and that those flesh-and-blood creatures down there with the blank, stupid faces are the *real* plague we ought to have been fighting all along!"

DAL BREAKS A PROMISE

For a moment the others just stared at their Garvian crewmate. Then Jack Alvarez snorted. "You'd better go back and get some rest," he said. "This has been a tougher grind than I thought. You're beginning to show the strain."

"No, I mean it," Dal said earnestly. "I think that is exactly what's been happening."

Tiger looked at him with concern. "Dal, this is no time for double talk and nonsense."

"It's not nonsense," Dal said. "It's the answer, if you'll only stop and think."

"An intelligent *virus?*" Jack said. "Who ever heard of such a thing? There's never been a life-form like that reported since the beginning of the galactic exploration."

"But that doesn't mean there couldn't be one," Dal said. "And how would an exploratory crew ever identify it, if it existed? How would they ever even suspect it? They'd miss it completely—unless it happened to get into trouble itself and try to call for help!" Dal jumped up in excitement.

"Look, I've seen a dozen articles showing how such a thing was theoretically possible ... a virus life-form with billions of submicroscopic parts acting together to form an intelligent colony. The only thing a virus-creature would need that other intelligent creatures don't need would be some kind of a host, some sort of animal body to live in so that it could use its intelligence."

"It's impossible," Jack said scornfully. "Why don't you give it up and get some rest? Here we sit with our feet in the fire, and all you can do is dream up foolishness like this."

"I'm not so sure it's foolishness," Tiger Martin said slowly. "Jack, maybe he's got something. A couple of things would fit that don't make sense at all."

"All sorts of things would fit," Dal said. "The viruses we know have to have a host—some other life-form to live in. Usually they are parasites, damaging or destroying their hosts and giving nothing in return, but some set up real partnership housekeeping with their hosts so that both are better off."

"You mean a symbiotic relationship," Jack said.

"Of course," Dal said. "Now suppose these virus-creatures were intelligent, and came from some other place looking for a new host they could live with. They wouldn't look for an intelligent creature, they would look for some *unintelligent* creature with a good strong body that would be capable of doing all sorts of things if it only had an intelligence to guide it. Suppose these virus-creatures found a simple-minded, unintelligent race on this planet and tried to set up a symbiotic relationship with it. The virus-creatures would need a host to provide a home and a food supply. Maybe they in turn could supply the intelligence to raise the host to a civilized level of life and performance. Wouldn't that be a fair basis for a sound partnership?"

Jack scratched his head doubtfully. "And you're saying that these virus-creatures came here after the exploratory ship had come and gone?"

"They must have! Maybe they only came a few years ago, maybe only months ago. But when they tried to invade the unintelligent creatures the exploratory ship found here, they discovered that the new host's body couldn't tolerate them. His body reacted as if they were parasitic invaders, and built up antibodies against them. And those body defenses were more than the virus could cope with."

Dal pointed to the piles of notes on the desk. "Don't you see how it adds up? Right from the beginning we've been assuming that these monkey-like creatures here on this planet were the dominant, intelligent life-forms. Anatomically they were ordinary cellular creatures like you and me, and when we examined them we expected to find the same sort of biochemical reactions we'd find with any such creatures. And all our results came out wrong, because we were dealing with a combination of two creatures—the host and a virus. Maybe the creatures on 31 Brucker VII were naturally blank-faced idiots before the virus came, or maybe the virus was forced to damage some vital part just in order to fight back—but it was the *virus* that was being killed by its own host, not the other way around."

Jack studied the idea, no longer scornful. "So you think the virus-creatures called for help, hoping we could find some way to free them from the hosts that were killing them. And when Fuzzy developed a powerful antibody against them, and we started using the stuff—" Jack broke off, shaking his head in horror. "Dal, if you're right, we were literally *slaughtering our own patients* when we gave those injections down there!"

"Exactly," Dal said. "Is it any wonder they're so scared of us now? It must have looked like a deliberate attempt to wipe them out, and now they're afraid that we'll go get help and *really* move in against them."

Tiger nodded. "Which was precisely what we were planning, if you stop to think about it. Maybe that was why they were so reluctant to tell us anything about themselves. Maybe they've already been mistaken for parasitic invaders before, wherever in the universe they came from."

"But if this is true, then we're really in a jam," Jack said. "What can we possibly do for them? We can't even repair the damage that we've already done. What sort of treatment can we use?"

Dal shook his head. "I don't know the answer to that one, but I do know we've got to find out if we're right. An intelligent virus-creature has as much right to life as any other intelligent life-form. If we've guessed right, then there's a lot that our intelligent friends down there haven't told us. Maybe there'll be some clue there. We've just got to face them with it, and see what they say."

Jack looked at the viewscreen, at the angry mob milling around on the ground, held back from the ship by the energy screen. "You mean just go out there and say, 'Look fellows, it was all a mistake, we didn't really mean to do it?'" He shook his head. "Maybe you want to tell them. Not me!"

"Dal's right, though," Tiger said. "We've got to contact them somehow. They aren't even responding to radio communication, and they've scrambled our outside radio and fouled our drive mechanism somehow. We've got to settle this while we still have an energy screen."

There was a long silence as the three doctors looked at each other. Then Dal stood up and walked over to the swinging platform. He lifted Fuzzy down onto his shoulder. "It'll be all right," he said to Jack and Tiger. "I'll go out."

"They'll tear you to ribbons!" Tiger protested.

Dal shook his head. "I don't think so," he said quietly. "I don't think they'll touch me. They'll greet me with open arms when I go down there, and they'll be eager to talk to me."

"Are you crazy?" Jack cried, leaping to his feet. "We can't let you go out there."

"Don't worry," Dal said. "I know exactly what I'm doing. I'll be able to handle the situation, believe me."

He hesitated a moment, and gave Fuzzy a last nervous pat, settling him more firmly on his shoulder. Then he started down the corridor for the entrance lock.

*

He had promised himself long before ... many years before ... that he would never do what he planned to do now, but now he knew that there was no alternative. The only other choice was to wait helplessly until the power failed and the protective screen vanished and the creatures on the ground outside tore the ship to pieces.

As he stood in the airlock waiting for the pressure to shift to outside normal, he lifted Fuzzy down into the crook of his arm and rubbed the little creature between the shoe-button eyes. "You've got to back me up now," he whispered softly. "It's been a long time, I know that, but I need help now. It's going to be up to you."

Dal knew the subtle strength of his people's peculiar talent. From the moment he had stepped down to the ground the second time with Tiger and Jack, even with Fuzzy waiting back on the ship, he had felt the powerful wave of horror and fear and anger rising up from the Bruckians, and he had glimpsed the awful idiot vacancy of the minds of the creatures in the enclosure, in whom the intelligent virus was already dead. This had required no effort; it just came naturally into his mind, and he had known instantly that something terrible had gone wrong.

In the years on Hospital Earth, he had carefully forced himself never to think in terms of his special talent. He had diligently screened off the impressions and emotions that struck at him constantly from his classmates and from others that he came in contact with. Above all, he had fought down the temptation to turn his power the other way, to use it to his own advantage.

But now, as the lock opened and he started down the ladder, he closed his mind to everything else. Hugging Fuzzy close to his side, he turned his mind into a single tight channel. He drove the thought out at the Bruckians with all the power he could muster: *I come in peace. I mean you no harm. I have good news, joyful news. You must be happy to see me, eager to welcome me....*

He could feel the wave of anger and fear strike him like a physical blow as soon as he appeared in the entrance lock. The cries rose up in a wave, and the crowd surged in toward the ship. With the energy field released, there was nothing to stop them; they were tripping over each other to reach the bottom of the ladder first, shouting threats and waving angry fists, reaching up to grab at Dal's ankles as he came down....

And then as if by magic the cries died in the throats of the ones closest to the ladder. The angry fists unclenched, and extended into outstretched hands to help him down to the ground. As though an ever-widening wave was spreading out around him, the aura of peace and good will struck the people in the crowd. And as it spread, the anger faded from the faces; the hard lines gave way to puzzled frowns, then to smiles. Dal channeled his thoughts more rigidly, and watched the effect spread out from him like ripples in a pond, as anger and suspicion and fear melted away to be replaced by confidence and trust.

Dal had seen it occur a thousand times before. He could remember his trips on Garvian trading ships with his father, when the traders with their fuzzy pink friends on their shoulders faced cold, hostile, suspicious buyers. It had seemed almost miraculous the way the suspicions melted away and the hostile faces became friendly as the buyers' minds became receptive to bargaining and trading. He had even seen it happen on the *Teegar* with Tiger and Jack, and it was no coincidence that throughout the galaxy the Garvians—always accompanied by their fuzzy friends—had assumed the position of power and wealth and leadership that they had.

And now once again the pattern was being repeated. The Bruckians who surrounded Dal were smiling and talking eagerly; they made no move to touch him or harm him.

The spokesman they had talked to before was there at his elbow, and Dal heard himself saying, "We have found the answer to your problem. We know now the true nature of your race, and the nature of your intelligence. You were afraid that we would find out, but your fears were groundless. We will not turn our knowledge against you. We only want to help you."

An expression almost like despair had crossed the spokesman's face as Dal spoke. Now he said, "It would be good—if we could believe you. But how can we? We have been driven for so long and come so far, and now you would seek to wipe us out as parasites and disease-carriers."

Dal saw the Bruckian creature's eyes upon him, saw the frail body tremble and the lips move, but he knew now that the intelligence that formed the words and the thoughts behind them, the intelligence that made the lips speak the words, was the intelligence of a creature far different from the one he was looking at—a creature formed of billions of submicroscopic units, imbedded in every one of the Bruckian's body cells, trapped there now and helpless against the antibody reaction that sought to destroy them. This was the intelligence that had called for help in its desperate plight, but had not quite dared to trust its rescuers with the whole truth.

But was this strange virus-creature good or evil, hostile or friendly? Dal's hand lay on Fuzzy's tiny body, but he felt no quiver, no vibration of fear. He looked across the face of the crowd, trying with all his strength to open his mind to the feelings and emotions of these people. Often enough, with Fuzzy nearby, he had felt the harsh impact of hostile, cruel, brutal minds, even when the owners of those minds had tried to conceal their feelings behind smiles and pleasant words. But here there was no sign of the sickening feeling that kind of mind produced, no hint of hostility or evil.

He shook his head. "Why should we want to destroy you?" he said. "You are good, and peaceful. We know that; why should we harm you? All you want is a place to live, and a host to join with you in a mutually valuable partnership. But you did not tell us everything you could about yourselves, and as a result we have destroyed some of you in our clumsy attempts to learn your true nature."

They talked then, and bit by bit the story came out. The life-form was indeed a virus, unimaginably ancient, and intelligent throughout millions of years of its history. Driven by over-population, a pure culture of the virus-creatures had long ago departed from their original native hosts, and traveled like encapsulated spores across space from a distant galaxy. The trip had been long and exhausting; the virus-creatures had retained only the minimum strength necessary to establish themselves in a new host, some unintelligent creature living on an uninhabited planet, a creature that could benefit by the great intelligence of the virus-creatures, and provide food and shelter for both. Finally, after thousands of years of searching, they had found this planet with its dull-minded, fruit-gathering inhabitants. These creatures had seemed perfect as hosts, and the virus-creatures had thought their long search for a perfect partner was finally at an end.

It was not until they had expended the last dregs of their energy in anchoring themselves into the cells and tissues of their new hosts that they discovered to their horror that the host-creatures could not tolerate them. Unlike their original hosts, the bodies of these creatures began developing deadly antibodies that attacked the virus invaders. In their desperate attempts to hold on and fight back, the virus-creatures had destroyed vital centers in the new hosts, and one by one they had begun to die. There was not enough energy left for the virus-creatures to detach themselves and move on; without some way to stem the onslaught of the antibodies, they were doomed to total destruction.

"We were afraid to tell you doctors the truth," the spokesman said. "As we wandered and searched we discovered that creatures like ourselves were extreme rarities in the universe, that most creatures similar to us were mindless, unintelligent parasites that struck down their hosts and destroyed them. Wherever we went, life-forms of your kind regarded us as disease-bearers, and their doctors taught them ways to destroy us. We had hoped that from you we might find a way to save ourselves—then you unleashed on us the one weapon we could not fight."

"But not maliciously," Dal said. "Only because we did not understand. And now that we do, there may be a way to help. A difficult way, but at least a way. The antibodies themselves can be neutralized, but it may take our biochemists and virologists and all their equipment months or even years to develop and synthesize the proper antidote."

The spokesman looked at Dal, and turned away with a hopeless gesture. "Then it is too late, after all," he said. "We are dying too fast. Even those of us who have not been affected so far are beginning to feel the early symptoms of the antibody attack." He smiled sadly and reached out to stroke the small pink creature on Dal's arm. "Your people too have a partner, I see. We envy you."

Dal felt a movement on his arm and looked down at Fuzzy. He had always taken his little friend for granted, but now he thought of the feeling of emptiness and loss that had come across him when Fuzzy had been almost killed. He had often wondered just what Fuzzy might be like if his almost-fluid, infinitely adaptable physical body had only been endowed with intelligence. He had wondered what kind of a creature Fuzzy might be if he were able to use his remarkable structure with the guidance of an intelligent mind behind it....

He felt another movement on his arm, and his eyes widened as he stared down at his little friend.

A moment before, there had been a single three-inch pink creature on his elbow. But now there were two, each just one-half the size of the original. As Dal watched, one of the two drew away from the other, creeping in to snuggle closer to Dal's side, and a pair of shoe-button eyes appeared and blinked up at him trustingly. But the other creature was moving down his arm, straining out toward the Bruckian spokesman....

Dal realized instantly what was happening. He started to draw back, but something stopped him. Deep in his mind he could sense a gentle voice reassuring him, saying, *It's all right, there is nothing to fear, no harm will come to me. These creatures need help, and this is the way to help them.*

He saw the Bruckian reach out a trembling hand. The tiny pink creature that had separated from Fuzzy seemed almost to leap across to the outstretched hand. And then the spokesman held him close, and the new Fuzzy shivered happily.

The virus-creatures had found a host. Here was the ideal kind of body for their intelligence to work with and mold, a host where antibody-formation could be perfectly controlled. Dal knew now that the problem had almost been solved once before, when the virus-creature had reached Fuzzy on the ship; if they had only waited a little longer they would have seen Fuzzy recover from his illness a different creature entirely than before.

Already the new creature was dividing again, with half going on to the next of the Bruckians. To a submicroscopic virus, the body of the host would not have to be large; soon there would be a sufficient number of hosts to serve the virus-creatures' needs forever. As he started back up the ladder to the ship, Dal knew that the problem on 31 Brucker VII had found a happy and permanent solution.

*

Back in the control room Dal related what had happened from beginning to end. There was only one detail that he concealed. He could not bring himself to tell Tiger and Jack of the true nature of his relationship with Fuzzy, of the odd power over the emotions of others that Fuzzy's presence gave him. He could tell by their faces that they realized that he was leaving something out; they had watched him go down to face a blood-thirsty mob, and had seen that mob become docile as lambs as though by magic. Clearly they could not understand what had happened, yet they did not ask him.

"So it was Fuzzy's idea to volunteer as a new host for the creatures," Jack said.

Dal nodded. "I knew that he could reproduce, of course," he said. "Every Garvian has a Fuzzy, and whenever a new Garvian is born, the father's Fuzzy always splits so that half can join the new-born child. It's like the division of a cell; within hours the Fuzzy that stayed down there will have divided to provide enough protoplasm for every one of the surviving intelligent Bruckians."

"And your diagnosis was the right one," Jack said.

"We'll see," Dal said. "Tomorrow we'll know better."

But clearly the problem had been solved. The next day there was an excited conference between the spokesman and the doctors on the *Lancet*. The Bruckians had elected to maintain the same host body as before. They had gotten used to it; with the small pink creatures serving as a shelter to protect them against the deadly antibodies, they could live in peace and security. But they were eager, before the *Lancet* disembarked, to sign a full medical service contract with the doctors from Hospital Earth. A contract was signed, subject only to final acceptance and ratification by the Hospital Earth officials.

Now that their radio was free again, the three doctors jubilantly prepared a full account of the problem of 31 Brucker and its solution, and dispatched the news of the new contract to the first relay station on its way back to Hospital Earth. Then, weary to the point of collapse, they retired for the first good sleep in days, eagerly awaiting an official response from Hospital Earth on the completed case and the contract.

"It ought to wipe out any black mark Dr. Tanner has against any of us," Jack said happily. "And especially in Dal's case." He grinned at the Red Doctor. "This one has been yours, all the way. You pulled it out of the fire after I flubbed it completely, and you're going to get the credit, if I have anything to say about it."

"We should all get credit," Dal said. "A new contract isn't signed every day of the year. But the way we all fumbled our way into it, Hospital Earth shouldn't pay much attention to it anyway."

But Dal knew that he was only throwing up his habitual shield to guard against disappointment. Traditionally, a new contract meant a Star rating for each of the crew that brought it in. All through medical school Dal had read the reports of other patrol ships that had secured new contracts with uncontacted planets, and he had seen the fanfare and honor that were heaped on the doctors from those ships. And for the first time since he had entered medical school years before, Dal now allowed himself to hope that his goal was in sight.

He wanted to be a Star Surgeon more than anything else. It was the one thing that he had wanted and worked for since the cruel days when the plague had swept his homeland, destroying his mother and leaving his father an ailing cripple. And since his assignment aboard the *Lancet*, one thought had filled his mind: to turn in the scarlet collar and cuff in return for the cape and silver star of the full-fledged physician in the Red Service of Surgery.

Always before there had been the half-conscious dread that something would happen, that in the end, after all the work, the silver star would still remain just out of reach, that somehow he would never quite get it.

But now there could be no question. Even Black Doctor Tanner could not deny a new contract. The crew of the *Lancet* would be called back to Hospital Earth for a full report on the newly contacted race, and their days as probationary doctors in the General Practice patrol would be over.

After they had slept themselves out, the doctors prepared the ship for launching, and made their farewells to the Bruckian spokesman.

"When the contract is ratified," Jack said, "a survey ship will come here. They will have all of the information that we have gathered, and they will spend many months gathering more. Tell them everything they want to know. Don't conceal anything, because once they have completed their survey, any General Practice Patrol ship in the galaxy will be able to answer a call for help and have the information they need to serve you."

They delayed launching hour by hour waiting for a response from Hospital Earth, but the radio was silent. They thought of a dozen reasons why the message might have been delayed, but the radio silence continued.

Finally they strapped down and lifted the ship from the planet, still waiting for a response.

When it finally came, there was no message of congratulations, nor even any acknowledgment of the new contract. Instead, there was only a terse message:

PROCEED TO REFERENCE POINT 43621 SECTION XIX AND STAND BY FOR INSPECTION PARTY

Tiger took the message and read it in silence, then handed it to Dal.

"What do they say?" Jack said.

"Read it," Dal said. "They don't mention the contract, just an inspection party."

"Inspection party! Is that the best they can do for us?"

"They don't sound too enthusiastic," Tiger said. "At least you'd think they could acknowledge receipt of our report."

"It's probably just part of the routine," Dal said. "Maybe they want to confirm our reports from our own records before they commit themselves."

But he knew that he was only whistling in the dark. The moment he saw the terse message, he knew something had gone wrong with the contract. There would be no notes of congratulation, no returning in triumph and honor to Hospital Earth.

Whatever the reason for the inspection party, Dal felt certain who the inspector was going to be.

It had been exciting to dream, but the scarlet cape and the silver star were still a long way out of reach.

THE SHOWDOWN

It was hours later when their ship reached the contact point co-ordinates. There had been little talk during the transit; each of them knew already what the other was thinking, and there wasn't much to be said. The message had said it for them.

Dal's worst fears were realized when the inspection ship appeared, converting from Koenig drive within a few miles of the *Lancet*. He had seen the ship before—a sleek, handsomely outfitted patrol class ship with the insignia of the Black Service of Pathology emblazoned on its hull, the private ship of a Four-star Black Doctor.

But none of them anticipated the action taken by the inspection ship as it drew within lifeboat range of the *Lancet*.

A scooter shot away from its storage rack on the black ship, and a crew of black-garbed technicians piled into the *Lancet*'s entrance lock, dressed in the special decontamination suits worn when a ship was returning from a plague spot into uninfected territory.

"What is this?" Tiger demanded as the technicians started unloading decontamination gear into the lock. "What are you doing with that stuff?"

The squad leader looked at him sourly. "You're in quarantine, Doc," he said. "Class I, all precautions, contact with unidentified pestilence. If you don't like it, argue with the Black Doctor, I've just got a job to do."

He started shouting orders to his men, and they scattered throughout the ship, with blowers and disinfectants, driving antiseptic sprays into every crack and cranny of the ship's interior, scouring the hull outside in the rigid pattern prescribed for plague ships. They herded the doctors into the decontamination lock, stripped them of their clothes, scrubbed them down and tossed them special sterilized fatigues to wear with masks and gloves.

"This is idiotic," Jack protested. "We aren't carrying any dangerous organisms!"

The squad leader shrugged indifferently. "Tell it to the Black Doctor, not me. All I know is that this ship is under quarantine until it's officially released, and from what I hear, it's not going to be released for quite some time."

At last the job was done, and the scooter departed back to the inspection ship. A few moments later they saw it returning, this time carrying just three men. In addition to the pilot and one technician, there was a single passenger: a portly figure dressed in a black robe, horn-rimmed glasses and cowl.

The scooter grappled the *Lancet*'s side, and Black Doctor Hugo Tanner climbed wheezing into the entrance lock, followed by the technician. He stopped halfway into the lock to get his breath, and paused again as the lock swung closed behind him. Dal was shocked at the physical change in the man in the few short weeks since he had seen him last. The Black Doctor's face was gray; every effort of movement brought on paroxysms of coughing. He looked sick, and he looked tired, yet his jaw was still set in angry determination.

The doctors stood at attention as he stepped into the control room, hardly able to conceal their surprise at seeing him. "Well?" the Black Doctor snapped at them. "What's the trouble with you? You act like you've seen a ghost or something."

"We—we'd heard that you were in the hospital, sir."

"Did you, now!" the Black Doctor snorted. "Hospital! Bah! I had to tell the press something to get the hounds off me for a while. These young puppies seem to think that a Black Doctor can just walk away from his duties any time he chooses to undergo their fancy surgical procedures. And you know who's been screaming the loudest to get their hands on me. The Red Service of Surgery, that's who!"

The Black Doctor glared at Dal Timgar. "Well, I dare say the Red Doctors will have their chance at me, all in good time. But first there are certain things which must be taken care of." He looked up at the attendant. "You're quite certain that the ship has been decontaminated?"

The attendant nodded. "Yes, sir."

"And the crewmen?"

"It's safe to talk to them, sir, as long as you avoid physical contact."

The Black Doctor grunted and wheezed and settled himself down in a seat. "All right now, gentlemen," he said to the three, "let's have your story of this affair in the Brucker system, right from the start."

"But we sent in a full report," Tiger said.

"I'm aware of that, you idiot. I have waded through your report, all thirty-five pages of it, and I only wish you hadn't been so long-winded. Now I want to hear what happened directly from you. Well?"

The three doctors looked at each other. Then Jack began the story, starting with the first hesitant "greeting" that had come through to them. He told everything that had happened without embellishments: their first analysis of the nature of the problem, the biochemical and medical survey that they ran on the afflicted people, his own failure to make the diagnosis, the incident of Fuzzy's sudden affliction, and the strange solution that had finally come from it. As he talked the Black Doctor sat back with his eyes half closed, his face blank, listening and nodding from time to time as the story proceeded.

And Jack was carefully honest and fair in his account. "We were all of us lost, until Dal Timgar saw the significance of what had happened to Fuzzy," he said. "His idea of putting the creature through the filter gave us our first specimen of the isolated virus, and showed us how to obtain the antibody. Then after we saw what happened with our initial series of injections, we were really at sea, and by then we couldn't reach a hospital ship for help of any kind." He went on to relate Dal's idea that the virus itself might be the intelligent creature, and recounted the things that happened after Dal went down to talk to the spokesman again with Fuzzy on his shoulder.

Through it all the Black Doctor listened sourly, glancing occasionally at Dal and saying nothing. "So is that all?" he said when Jack had finished.

"Not quite," Jack said. "I want it to be on the record that it was my failure in diagnosis that got us into trouble. I don't want any misunderstanding about that. If I'd had the wit to think beyond the end of my nose, there wouldn't have been any problem."

"I see," the Black Doctor said. He pointed to Dal. "So it was this one who really came up with the answers and directed the whole program on this problem, is that right?"

"That's right," Jack said firmly. "He should get all the credit."

Something stirred in Dal's mind and he felt Fuzzy snuggling in tightly to his side. He could feel the cold hostility in the Black Doctor's mind, and he started to say something, but the Black Doctor cut him off. "Do you agree to that also, Dr. Martin?" he asked Tiger.

"I certainly do," Tiger said. "I'll back up the Blue Doctor right down the line."

The Black Doctor smiled unpleasantly and nodded. "Well, I'm certainly happy to hear you say that, gentlemen. I might say that it is a very great relief to me to hear it from your own testimony. Because this time there shouldn't be any argument from either of you as to just where the responsibility lies, and I'm relieved to know that I can completely exonerate you two, at any rate."

Jack Alvarez's jaw went slack and he stared at the Black Doctor as though he hadn't heard him properly. "Exonerate us?" he said. "Exonerate us from what?"

"From the charges of incompetence, malpractice and conduct unbecoming to a physician which I am lodging against your colleague in the Red Service here," the Black Doctor said angrily. "Of course, I was confident that neither of you two could have contributed very much to this bungling mess, but it is reassuring to have your own statements of that fact on the record. They should carry more weight in a Council hearing than any plea I might make in your behalf."

"But—but what do you mean by a Council hearing?" Tiger stammered. "I don't understand you! This—this problem is *solved*. We solved it as a patrol team, all of us. We sent in a brand new medical service contract from those people...."

"Oh, yes. *That*!" The Black Doctor drew a long pink dispatch sheet from an inner pocket and opened it out. The doctors could see the photo reproductions of their signatures at the bottom. "Fortunately—for you two—this bit of nonsense was brought to my attention at the first relay station that received it. I personally accepted it and withdrew it from the circuit before it could reach Hospital Earth for filing."

Slowly, as they watched him, he ripped the pink dispatch sheet into a dozen pieces and tossed it into the disposal vent. "So much for that," he said slowly. "I can choose to overlook your foolishness in trying to cloud the important issues with a so-called 'contract' to divert attention, but I'm afraid I can't pay much attention to it, nor allow it to appear in the general report. And of course I am forced to classify the *Lancet* as a plague ship until a bacteriological and virological examination has been completed on both ship and crew. The planet itself will be considered a galactic plague spot until proper measures have been taken to insure its decontamination."

The Black Doctor drew some papers from another pocket and turned to Dal Timgar. "As for you, the charges are clear enough. You have broken the most fundamental rules of good judgment and good medicine in handling the 31 Brucker affair. You have permitted a General Practice Patrol ship to approach a potentially dangerous plague spot without any notification of higher authorities. You have undertaken a biochemical and medical survey for which you had neither the proper equipment nor the training qualifications, and you exposed your ship and your crewmates to an incredible risk in landing on such a planet. You are responsible for untold—possibly fatal—damage to over two hundred individuals of the race that called on you for help. You have even subjected the creature that depends upon your own race for its life and support to virtual slavery and possible destruction; and finally, you had the audacity to try to cover up your bungling with claims of arranging a medical service contract with an uninvestigated race."

The Black Doctor broke off as an attendant came in the door and whispered something in his ear. Doctor Tanner shook his head angrily, "I can't be bothered now!"

"They say it's urgent, sir."

"Yes, it's always urgent." The Black Doctor heaved to his feet. "If it weren't for this miserable incompetent here, I wouldn't have to be taking precious time away from my more important duties." He scowled at the *Lancet* crewmen. "You will excuse me for a moment," he said, and disappeared into the communications room.

The moment he was gone from the room, Jack and Tiger were talking at once. "He couldn't really be serious," Tiger said. "It's impossible! Not one of those charges would hold up under investigation."

"Well, I think it's a frame-up," Jack said, his voice tight with anger. "I knew that some people on Hospital Earth were out to get you, but I don't see how a Four-star Black Doctor could be a party to such a thing. Either someone has been misinforming him, or he just doesn't understand what happened."

Dal shook his head. "He understands, all right, and he's the one who's determined to get me out of medicine. This is a flimsy excuse, but he has to use it, because it's now or never. He knows that if we bring in a contract with a new planet, and it's formally ratified, we'll all get our Stars and he'd never be able to block me again. And Black Doctor Tanner is going to be certain that I don't get that Star, or die trying."

"But this is completely unfair," Jack protested. "He's turning our own words against you! You can bet that he'll have a survey crew down on that planet in no time, bringing home a contract just the same as the one we wrote, and there won't be any questions asked about it."

"Except that I'll be out of the service," Dal said. "Don't worry. You'll get the credit in the long run. When all the dust settles, he'll be sure that you two are named as agents for the contract. He doesn't want to hurt you, it's me that he's out to get."

"Well, he won't get away with it," Tiger said. "We can see to that. It's not too late to retract our stories. If he thinks he can get rid of you with something that wasn't your fault, he's going to find out that he has to get rid of a lot more than just you."

But Dal was shaking his head. "Not this time, Tiger. This time you keep out of it."

"What do you mean, keep out of it?" Tiger cried. "Do you think I'm going to stand by quietly and watch him cut you down?"

"That's exactly what you're going to do," Dal said sharply. "I meant what I said. I want you to keep your mouth shut. Don't say anything more at all, just let it be."

"But I can't stand by and do nothing! When a friend of mine needs help—"

"Can't you get it through your thick skull that this time I don't want your help?" Dal said. "Do me a favor this time. *Leave me alone.* Don't stick your thumb in the pie."

Tiger just stared at the little Garvian. "Look, Dal, all I'm trying to do—"

"I know what you're trying to do," Dal snapped, "and I don't want any part of it. I don't need your help, I don't *want* it. Why do you have to force it down my throat?"

There was a long silence. Then Tiger spread his hands helplessly. "Okay," he said, "if that's the way you want it." He turned away from Dal, his big shoulders slumping. "I've only been trying to make up for some of the dirty breaks you've been handed since you came to Hospital Earth."

"I know that," Dal said, "and I've appreciated it. Sometimes it's been the only thing that's kept me going. But that doesn't mean that you own me. Friendship is one thing; proprietorship is something else. I'm not your private property."

He saw the look on Tiger's face, as though he had suddenly turned and slapped him viciously across the face. "Look, I know it sounds awful, but I can't help it. I don't want to hurt you, and I don't want to change things with us, but *I'm a person just like you are.* I can't go on leaning on you any longer. Everybody has to stand on his own somewhere along the line. You do, and I do, too. And that goes for Jack, too."

They heard the door to the communications shack open, and the Black Doctor was back in the room. "Well?" he said. "Am I interrupting something?" He glanced sharply at the tight-lipped doctors. "The call was from the survey section," he went on blandly. "A survey crew is on its way to 31 Brucker to start gathering some useful information on the situation. But that is neither here nor there. You have heard the charges against the Red Doctor here. Is there anything any of you want to say?"

Tiger and Jack looked at each other. The silence in the room was profound.

The Black Doctor turned to Dal. "And what about you?"

"I have something to say, but I'd like to talk to you alone."

"As you wish. You two will return to your quarters and stay there."

"The attendant, too," Dal said.

The Black Doctor's eyes glinted and met Dal's for a moment. Then he shrugged and nodded to his attendant. "Step outside, please. We have a private matter to discuss."

The Black Doctor turned his attention to the papers on the desk as Dal stood before him with Fuzzy sitting in the crook of his arm. From the moment that the notice of the inspection ship's approach had come to the *Lancet*, Dal had known what was coming. He had been certain what the purpose of the detainment was, and who the inspector would be, yet he had not really been worried. In the back of his mind, a small, comfortable thought had been sustaining him.

It didn't really matter how hostile or angry Black Doctor Tanner might be; he knew that in a last-ditch stand there was one way the Black Doctor could be handled.

He remembered the dramatic shift from hostility to friendliness among the Bruckians when he had come down from the ship with Fuzzy on his shoulder. Before then, he had never considered using his curious power to protect himself and gain an end; but since then, without even consciously bringing it to mind, he had known that the next time would be easier. If it ever came to a showdown with Black Doctor Tanner, a trap from which he couldn't free himself, there was still this way. *The Black Doctor would never know what happened*, he thought. *It would just seem to him, suddenly, that he had been looking at things the wrong way. No one would ever know.*

But he knew, even as the thought came to mind, that this was not so. Now, face to face with the showdown, he knew that it was no good. One person would know what had happened: himself. On 31 Brucker, he had convinced himself that the end justified the means; here it was different.

For a moment, as Black Doctor Tanner stared up at him through the horn-rimmed glasses, Dal wavered. Why should he hesitate to protect himself? he thought angrily. This attack against him was false and unfair, trumped up for the sole purpose of destroying his hopes and driving him out of the Service. Why shouldn't he grasp at any means, fair or unfair, to fight it?

But he could hear the echo of Black Doctor Arnquist's words in his mind: *I beg of you not to use it. No matter what happens, don't use it.* Of course, Doctor Arnquist would never know, for sure, that he had broken faith ... but *he* would know....

"Well," Black Doctor Tanner was saying, "speak up. I can't waste much more time dealing with you. If you have something to say, say it."

Dal sighed. He lifted Fuzzy down and slipped him gently into his jacket pocket. "These charges against me are not true," he said.

The Black Doctor shrugged. "Your own crewmates support them with their statements."

"That's not the point. They're not true, and you know it as well as I do. You've deliberately rigged them up to build a case against me."

The Black Doctor's face turned dark and his hands clenched on the papers on the desk. "Are you suggesting that I have nothing better to do than to rig false charges against one probationer out of seventy-five thousand traveling the galaxy?"

"I'm suggesting that we are alone here," Dal said. "Nobody else is listening. Just for once, right now, we can be honest. We both know what you're trying to do to me. I'd just like to hear you admit it once."

The Black Doctor slammed his fist down on the table. "I don't have to listen to insolence like this," he roared.

"Yes, you do," Dal said. "Just this once. Then I'll be through." Suddenly Dal's words were tumbling out of control, and his whole body was trembling with anger. "You have been determined from the very beginning that I should never finish the medical training that I started. You've tried to block me time after time, in every way you could think of. You've almost succeeded, but never quite made it until this time. But now you *have* to make it. If that contract were to go through I'd get my Star, and you'd never again be able to do anything about it. So it's now or never if you're going to break me."

"Nonsense!" the Black Doctor stormed. "I wouldn't lower myself to meddle with your kind. The charges speak for themselves."

"Not if you look at them carefully. You claim I failed to notify Hospital Earth that we had entered a plague area—but our records of our contact with the planet prove that we did only what any patrol ship would have done when the call came in. We didn't have enough information to know that there was a plague there, and when we finally did know the truth we could no longer make contact with Hospital Earth. You claim that I brought harm to two hundred of the natives there, yet if you study our notes and records, you will see that our errors there were unavoidable. We couldn't have done anything else under the circumstances, and if we hadn't done what we did, we would have been ignoring the basic principles of diagnosis and treatment which we've been taught. And your charges don't mention that by possibly harming two hundred of the Bruckians, we found a way to save two million of them from absolute destruction."

The Black Doctor glared at him. "The charges will stand up, I'll see to that."

"Oh, I'm sure you will! You can ram them through and make them stick before anybody ever has a chance to examine them carefully. You have the power to do it. And by the time an impartial judge could review all the records, your survey ship will have been there and gathered so much more data and muddied up the field so thoroughly that no one will ever be certain that the charges aren't true. But you and I know that they wouldn't really hold up under inspection. We know that they're false right down the line and that you're the one who is responsible for them."

The Black Doctor grew darker, and he trembled with rage as he drew himself to his feet. Dal could feel his hatred almost like a physical blow and his voice was almost a shriek.

"All right," he said, "if you insist, then the charges are lies, made up specifically to break you, and I'm going to push them through if I have to jeopardize my reputation to do it. You could have bowed out gracefully at any time along the way and saved yourself dishonor and disgrace, but you wouldn't do it. Now, I'm going to force you to. I've worked my lifetime long to build the reputation of Hospital Earth and of the Earthmen that go out to all the planets as representatives. I've worked to make the Confederation respect Hospital Earth and the Earthmen who are her doctors. You don't belong here with us. You forced yourself in, you aren't an Earthman and you don't have the means or resources to be a doctor from Hospital Earth. If you succeed, a thousand others will follow in your footsteps, chipping away at the reputation that we have worked to build, and I'm not going to allow one incompetent alien bungler pretending to be a surgeon to walk in and destroy the thing I've fought to build—"

The Black Doctor's voice had grown shrill, almost out of control. But now suddenly he broke off, his mouth still working, and his face went deathly white. The finger he was pointing at Dal wavered and fell. He clutched at his chest, his breath coming in great gasps and staggered back into the chair. "Something's happened," his voice croaked. "I can't breathe."

Dal stared at him in horror for a moment, then leaped across the room and jammed his thumb against the alarm bell.

THE TRIAL

Red Doctor Dal Timgar knew at once that there would be no problem in diagnosis here. The Black Doctor slumped back in his seat, gasping for air, his face twisted in pain as he labored just to keep on breathing. Tiger and Jack burst into the room, and Dal could tell that they knew instantly what had happened.

"Coronary," Jack said grimly.

Dal nodded. "The question is, just how bad."

"Get the cardiograph in here. We'll soon see."

But the electrocardiograph was not needed to diagnose the nature of the trouble. All three doctors had seen the picture often enough—the sudden, massive blockage of circulation to the heart that was so common to creatures with central circulatory pumps, the sort of catastrophic accident which could cause irreparable crippling or sudden death within a matter of minutes.

Tiger injected some medicine to ease the pain, and started oxygen to help the labored breathing, but the old man's color did not improve. He was too weak to talk; he just lay helplessly gasping for air as they lifted him up onto a bed. Then Jack took an electrocardiograph tracing and shook his head.

"We'd better get word back to Hospital Earth, and fast," he said quietly. "He just waited a little too long for that cardiac transplant, that's all. This is a bad one. Tell them we need a surgeon out here just as fast as they can move, or the Black Service is going to have a dead physician on its hands."

There was a sound across the room, and the Black Doctor motioned feebly to Tiger. "The cardiogram," he gasped. "Let me see it."

"There's nothing for you to see," Tiger said. "You mustn't do anything to excite yourself."

"Let me see it." Dr. Tanner took the thin strip of paper and ran it quickly through his fingers. Then he dropped it on the bed and lay his head back hopelessly. "Too late," he said, so softly they could hardly hear him. "Too late for help now."

Tiger checked his blood pressure and listened to his heart. "It will only take a few hours to get help," he said. "You rest and sleep now. There's plenty of time."

He joined Dal and Jack in the corridor. "I'm afraid he's right, this time," he said. "The damage is severe, and he hasn't the strength to hold out very long. He might last long enough for a surgeon and operating team to get here, but I doubt it. We'd better get the word off."

A few moments later he put the earphones aside. "It'll take six hours for the nearest help to get here," he said. "Maybe five and a half if they really crowd it. But when they get a look at that cardiogram on the screen they'll just throw up their hands. He's got to have a transplant, nothing less, and even if we can keep him alive until a surgical team gets here the odds are a thousand to one against his surviving the surgery."

"Well, he's been asking for it," Jack said. "They've been trying to get him into the hospital for a cardiac transplant for years. Everybody's known that one of those towering rages would get him sooner or later."

"Maybe he'll hold on better than we think," Dal said. "Let's watch and wait."

But the Black Doctor was not doing well. Moment by moment he grew weaker, laboring harder for air as his blood pressure crept slowly down. Half an hour later the pain returned; Tiger took another tracing while Dal checked his venous pressure and shock level.

As he finished, Dal felt the Black Doctor's eyes on him. "It's going to be all right," he said. "There'll be time for help to come."

Feebly the Black Doctor shook his head. "No time," he said. "Can't wait that long." Dal could see the fear in the old man's eyes. His lips began to move again as though there were something more he wanted to say; but then his face hardened, and he turned his head away helplessly.

Dal walked around the bed and looked down at the tracing, comparing it with the first one that was taken. "What do you think, Tiger?"

"It's no good. He'll never make it for five more hours."

"What about right now?"

Tiger shook his head. "It's a terrible surgical risk."

"But every minute of waiting makes it worse, right?"

"That's right."

"Then I think we'll stop waiting," Dal said. "We have a prosthetic heart in condition for use, don't we?"

"Of course."

"Good. Get it ready now." It seemed as though someone else were talking. "You'll have to be first assistant, Tiger. We'll get him onto the heart-lung machine, and if we don't have help available by then, we'll have to try to complete the transplant. Jack, you'll give anaesthesia, and it will be a tricky job. Try to use local blocks as much as you can, and have the heart-lung machine ready well in advance. We'll only have a few seconds to make the shift. Now let's get moving."

Tiger stared at him. "Are you sure that you want to do this?"

"I never wanted anything less in my life," Dal said fervently. "But do you think he can survive until a Hospital Ship arrives?"

"No."

"Then it seems to me that I don't have any choice. You two don't need to worry. This is a surgical problem now, and I'll take full responsibility."

The Black Doctor was watching him, and Dal knew he had heard the conversation. Now the old man lay helplessly as they moved about getting the surgical room into preparation. Jack prepared the anaesthetics, checked and rechecked the complex heart-lung machine which could artificially support circulation and respiration at the time that the damaged heart was separated from its great vessels. The transplant prosthetic heart had been grown in the laboratories on Hospital Earth from embryonic tissue; Tiger removed it from the frozen specimen locker and brought it to normal body temperature in the special warm saline bath designed for the purpose.

Throughout the preparations the Black Doctor lay watching, still conscious enough to recognize what was going on, attempting from time to time to shake his head in protest but not quite succeeding. Finally Dal came to the bedside. "Don't be afraid," he said gently to the old man. "It isn't safe to try to delay until the ship from Hospital Earth can get here. Every minute we wait is counting against you. I think I can manage the transplant if I start now. I know you don't like it, but I am the Red Doctor in authority on this ship. If I have to order you, I will."

The Black Doctor lay silent for a moment, staring at Dal. Then the fear seemed to fade from his face, and the anger disappeared. With a great effort he moved his head to nod. "All right, son," he said softly. "Do the best you know how."

*

Dal knew from the moment he made the decision to go ahead that the thing he was undertaking was all but hopeless.

There was little or no talk as the three doctors worked at the operating table. The overhead light in the ship's tiny surgery glowed brightly; the only sound in the room was the wheeze of the anaesthesia apparatus, the snap of clamps and the doctors' own quiet breathing as they worked desperately against time.

Dal felt as if he were in a dream, working like an automaton, going through mechanical motions that seemed completely unrelated to the living patient that lay on the operating table. In his training he had assisted at hundreds of organ transplant operations; he himself had done dozens of cardiac transplants, with experienced surgeons assisting and guiding him until the steps of the procedure had become almost second nature. On Hospital Earth, with the unparalleled medical facilities available there, and with well-trained teams of doctors, anaesthetists and nurses the technique of replacing an old worn-out damaged heart with a new and healthy one had become commonplace. It posed no more threat to a patient than a simple appendectomy had posed three centuries before.

But here in the patrol ship's operating room under emergency conditions there seemed little hope of success. Already the Black Doctor had suffered violent shock from the damage that had occurred in his heart. Already he was clinging to life by a fragile thread; the additional shock of the surgery, of the anaesthesia and the necessary conversion to the heart-lung machine while the delicate tissues of the new heart were fitted and sutured into place vessel by vessel was more than any patient could be expected to survive.

Yet Dal had known when he saw the second cardiogram that the attempt would have to be made. Now he worked swiftly, his frail body engulfed in the voluminous surgical gown, his thin fingers working carefully with the polished instruments. Speed and skill were all that could save the Black Doctor now, to offer him the one chance in a thousand that he had for survival.

But the speed and skill had to be Dal's. Dal knew that, and the knowledge was like a lead weight strapped to his shoulders. If Black Doctor Hugo Tanner was fighting for his life now, Dal knew that he too was fighting for his life—the only kind of life that he wanted, the life of a physician.

Black Doctor Tanner's antagonism to him as an alien, as an incompetent, as one who was unworthy to wear the collar and cuff of a physician from Hospital Earth, was common knowledge. Dal realized with perfect clarity that if he failed now, his career as a physician would be over; no one, not even himself, would ever be entirely certain that he had not somehow, in some dim corner of his mind, allowed himself to fail.

Yet if he had not made the attempt and the Black Doctor had died before help had come, there would always be those who would accuse him of delaying on purpose.

His mouth was dry; he longed for a drink of water, even though he knew that no water could quench this kind of thirst. His fingers grew numb as he worked, and moment by moment the sense of utter hopelessness grew stronger in his mind. Tiger worked stolidly across the table from him, inexpert help at best because of the sketchy surgical training he had had. Even his solid presence in support here did not lighten the burden for Dal. There was nothing that Tiger could do or say that would help things or change things now. Even Fuzzy, waiting alone on his perch in the control room, could not help him now. Nothing could help now but his own individual skill as a surgeon, and his bitter determination that he must not and would not fail.

But his fingers faltered as a thousand questions welled up in his mind. Was he doing this right? This vessel here ... clamp it and tie it? Or dissect it out and try to preserve it? This nerve plexus ... which one was it? How important? How were the blood pressure and respirations doing? Was the Black Doctor holding his own under the assault of the surgery?

The more Dal tried to hurry the more he seemed to be wading through waist-deep mud, unable to make his fingers do what he wanted them to do. How could he save ten seconds, twenty seconds, a half a minute? That half a minute might make the difference between success or failure, yet the seconds ticked by swiftly and the procedure was going slowly.

Too slowly. He reached a point where he thought he could not go on. His mind was searching desperately for help—any kind of help, something to lean on, something to brace him and give him support. And then quite suddenly he understood something clearly that had been nibbling at the corners of his mind for a long time. It was as if someone had snapped on a floodlight in a darkened room, and he saw something he had never seen before.

He saw that from the first day he had stepped down from the Garvian ship that had brought him to Hospital Earth to begin his medical training, he had been relying upon crutches to help him.

Black Doctor Arnquist had been a crutch upon whom he could lean. Tiger, for all his clumsy good-heartedness and for all the help and protection he had offered, had been a crutch. Fuzzy, who had been by his side since the day he was born, was still another kind of crutch to fall back on, a way out, a port of haven in the storm. They were crutches, every one, and he had leaned on them heavily.

But now there was no crutch to lean on. He had a quick mind with good training. He had two nimble hands that knew their job, and two legs that were capable of supporting his weight, frail as they were. He knew now that he had to stand on them squarely, for the first time in his life.

And suddenly he realized that this was as it should be. It seemed so clear, so obvious and unmistakable that he wondered how he could have failed to recognize it for so long. If he could not depend on himself, then Black Doctor Hugo Tanner would have been right all along. If he could not do this job that was before him on his own strength, standing on his own two legs without crutches to lean on, how could he claim to be a competent physician? What right did he have to the goal he sought if he had to earn it on the strength of the help of others? It was *he* who wanted to be a Star Surgeon—not Fuzzy, not Tiger, nor anyone else.

He felt his heart thudding in his chest, and he saw the operation before him as if he were standing in an amphitheater peering down over some other surgeon's shoulder. Suddenly everything else was gone from his mind but the immediate task at hand. His fingers began to move more swiftly, with a confidence he had never felt before. The decisions to be made arose, and he made them without hesitation, and knew as he made them that they were right.

And for the first time the procedure began to move. He murmured instructions to Jack from time to time, and placed Tiger's clumsy hands in the places he wanted them for retraction. "Not there, back a little," he said. "That's right. Now hold this clamp and release it slowly while I tie, then reclamp it. Slowly now ... that's the way! Jack, check that pressure again."

It seemed as though someone else were doing the surgery, directing his hands step by step in the critical work that had to be done. Dal placed the connections to the heart-lung machine perfectly, and moved with new swiftness and confidence as the great blood vessels were clamped off and the damaged heart removed. A quick check of vital signs, chemistries, oxygenation, a sharp instruction to Jack, a caution to Tiger, and the new prosthetic heart was in place. He worked now with painstaking care, manipulating the micro-sutures that would secure the new vessels to the old so firmly that they were almost indistinguishable from a healed wound, and he knew that it was going *right* now, that whether the patient ultimately survived or not, he had made the right decision and had carried it through with all the skill at his command.

And then the heart-lung machine fell silent again, and the carefully applied nodal stimulator flicked on and off, and slowly, at first hesitantly, then firmly and vigorously, the new heart began its endless pumping chore. The Black Doctor's blood pressure moved up to a healthy level and stabilized; the gray flesh of his face slowly became suffused with healthy pink. It was over, and Dal was walking out of the surgery, his hands trembling so violently that he could hardly get his gown off. He wanted to laugh and cry at the same time, and he could see the silent pride in the others' faces as they joined him in the dressing room to change clothes.

He knew then that no matter what happened he had vindicated himself. Half an hour later, back in the sickbay, the Black Doctor was awake, breathing slowly and easily without need of supplemental oxygen. Only the fine sweat standing out on his forehead gave indication of the ordeal he had been through.

Swiftly and clinically Dal checked the vital signs as the old man watched him. He was about to turn the pressure cuff over to Jack and leave when the Black Doctor said, "Wait."

Dal turned to him. "Yes, sir?"

"You did it?" the Black Doctor said softly.

"Yes, sir."

"It's finished? The transplant is done?"

"Yes," Dal said. "It went well, and you can rest now. You were a good patient."

For the first time Dal saw a smile cross the old man's face. "A foolish patient, perhaps," he said, so softly that no one but Dal could hear, "but not so foolish now, not so foolish that I cannot recognize a good doctor when I see one."

And with a smile he closed his eyes and went to sleep.

STAR SURGEON

It was amazing to Dal Timgar just how good it seemed to be back on Hospital Earth again.

In the time he had been away as a crewman of the *Lancet*, the seasons had changed, and the port of Philadelphia lay under the steaming summer sun. As Dal stepped off the shuttle ship to join the hurrying crowds in the great space-port, it seemed almost as though he were coming home.

He thought for a moment of the night not so long before when he had waited here for the shuttle to Hospital Seattle, to attend the meeting of the medical training council. He had worn no uniform then, not even the collar and cuff of the probationary physician, and he remembered his despair that night when he had thought that his career as a physician from Hospital Earth was at an end.

Now he was returning by shuttle from Hospital Seattle to the port of Philadelphia again, completing the cycle that had been started many months before. But things were different now. The scarlet cape of the Red Service of Surgery hung from his slender shoulders now, and the light of the station room caught the polished silver emblem on his collar. It was a tiny bit of metal, but its significance was enormous. It announced to the world Dal Timgar's final and permanent acceptance as a physician; but more, it symbolized the far-reaching distances he had already traveled, and would travel again, in the service of Hospital Earth.

It was the silver star of the Star Surgeon.

The week just past had been both exciting and confusing. The hospital ship had arrived five hours after Black Doctor Hugo Tanner had recovered from his anaesthesia, moving in on the *Lancet* in frantic haste and starting the shipment of special surgical supplies, anaesthetics and maintenance equipment across in lifeboats almost before contact had been stabilized. A large passenger boat hurtled away from the hospital ship's side, carrying a pair of Four-star surgeons, half a dozen Three-star Surgeons, two Radiologists, two Internists, a dozen nurses and another Four-star Black Doctor across to the *Lancet*; and when they arrived at the patrol ship's entrance lock, they discovered that their haste had been in vain.

It was like Grand Rounds in the general wards of Hospital Philadelphia, with the Four-star Surgeons in the lead as they tramped aboard the patrol ship. They found Black Doctor Tanner sitting quietly at his bedside reading a journal of pathology and taking notes. He glared up at them when they burst in the door without even knocking.

"But are you feeling well, sir?" the chief surgeon asked him for the third time.

"Of course I'm feeling well. Do you think I'd be sitting here if I weren't?" the Black Doctor growled. "Dr. Timgar is my surgeon and the physician in charge of this case. Talk to him. He can give you all the details of the matter."

"You mean you permitted a probationary physician to perform this kind of surgery?" The Four-star Surgeon cried incredulously.

"I did not!" the Black Doctor snapped. "He had to drag me kicking and screaming into the operating room. But fortunately for me, this particular probationary physician had the courage of his convictions, as well as wit enough to realize that I would not survive if he waited for you to gather your army together. But I think you will find the surgery was handled with excellent skill. Again, I must refer you to Dr. Timgar for the details. I was not paying attention to the technique of the surgery, I assure you."

"But sir," the chief surgeon broke in, "how could there have been surgery of any sort here? The dispatch that came to us listed the *Lancet* as a plague ship—"

"*Plague ship*!" the Black Doctor exploded. "Oh, yes. Egad! I—hum!—imagine that the dispatcher must have gotten his signals mixed somehow. Well, I suppose you want to examine me. Let's have it over with."

The doctors examined him within an inch of his life. They exhausted every means of physical, laboratory and radiological examination short of re-opening his chest and looking in, and at last the chief surgeon was forced reluctantly to admit that there was nothing left for him to do but provide post-operative follow-up care for the irascible old man.

And by the time the examination was over and the Black Doctor was moved aboard the hospital ship, word had come through official channels to the *Lancet* announcing that the quarantine order had been a dispatcher's unfortunate error, and directing the ship to return at once to Hospital Earth with the new contract that had been signed on 31 Brucker VII. The crewmen of the *Lancet* had special orders to report immediately to the medical training council at Hospital Seattle upon arrival, in order to give their formal General Practice Patrol reports and to receive their appointments respectively as Star Physician, Star Diagnostician and Star Surgeon. The orders were signed with the personal mark of Hugo Tanner, Physician of the Black Service of Pathology.

Now the ceremony and celebration in Hospital Seattle were over, and Dal had another appointment to keep. He lifted Fuzzy from his elbow and tucked him safely into an inner jacket pocket to protect him from the crowd in the station, and moved swiftly through to the subway tubes.

He had expected to see Black Doctor Arnquist at the investment ceremonies, but there had been neither sign nor word from him. Dal tried to reach him after the ceremonies were over; all he could learn was that the Black Doctor was unavailable. And then a message had come through to Dal under the official Hospital Earth headquarters priority, requesting him to present himself at once at the grand council building at Hospital Philadelphia for an interview of the utmost importance.

He followed the directions on the dispatch now, and reached the grand council building well ahead of the appointed time. He followed corridors and rode elevators until he reached the twenty-second story office suite where he had been directed to report. The whole building seemed alive with bustle, as though something of enormous importance was going on; high-ranking physicians of all the services were hurrying about, gathering in little groups at the elevators and talking among themselves in hushed voices. Even more strange, Dal saw delegation after delegation of alien creatures moving through the building, some in the special atmosphere-maintaining devices necessary for their survival on Earth, some characteristically alone and unaccompanied, others in the company of great retinues of underlings. Dal paused in the main concourse of the building as he saw two such delegations arrive by special car from the port of Philadelphia.

"Odd," he said quietly, reaching in to stroke Fuzzy's head. "Quite a gathering of the clans, eh? What do you think? Last time I saw a gathering like this was back at home during one of the centennial conclaves of the Galactic Confederation."

On the twenty-second floor, a secretary ushered him into an inner office. There he found Black Doctor Thorvold Arnquist, in busy conference with a Blue Doctor, a Green Doctor and a surgeon. The Black Doctor looked up, and beamed. "That will be all right now, gentlemen," he said. "I'll be in touch with you directly."

He waited until the others had departed. Then he crossed the room and practically hugged Dal in delight. "It's good to see you, boy," he said, "and above all, it's good to see that silver star at last. You and your little pink friend have done a good job, a far better job than I thought you would do, I must admit."

Dal perched Fuzzy on his shoulder. "But what is this about an interview? Why did you want to see me, and what are all these people doing here?"

Dr. Arnquist laughed. "Don't worry," he said. "You won't have to stay for the council meeting. It will be a long boring session, I fear. Doubtless every single one of these delegates at some time in the next few days will be standing up to give us a three hour oration, and it is my ill fortune as a Four-star Black Doctor to have to sit and listen and smile through it all. But in the end, it will be worth it, and I thought that you should at least know that your name will be mentioned many times during these sessions."

"My name?"

"You didn't know that you were a guinea pig, did you?" the Black Doctor said.

"I ... I'm afraid I didn't."

"An unwitting tool, so to speak," the Black Doctor chuckled. "You know, of course, that the Galactic Confederation has been delaying and stalling any action on Hospital Earth's application for full status as one of the Confederation powers and for a seat on the council. We had fulfilled two criteria for admission without difficulty—we had resolved our problems at home so that we were free from war on our own planet, and we had a talent that is much needed and badly in demand in the galaxy, a job to do that would fit into the Confederation's organization. But the Confederation has always had a third criterion for its membership, a criterion that Hospital Earth could not so easily prove or demonstrate."

The Black Doctor smiled. "After all, there could be no place in a true Confederation of worlds for any one race of people that considered itself superior to all the rest. No race can be admitted to the Confederation until its members have demonstrated that they are capable of tolerance, willing to accept the members of other races on an equal footing. And it has always been the nature of Earthmen to be intolerant, to assume that one who looks strange and behaves differently must somehow be inferior."

The Black Doctor crossed the room and opened a folder on the desk. "You can read the details some other time, if you like. You were selected by the Galactic Confederation from a thousand possible applicants, to serve as a test case, to see if a place could be made for you on Hospital Earth. No one here was told of your position—not even you—although certain of us suspected the truth. The Confederation wanted to see if a well-qualified, likeable and intelligent creature from another world would be accepted and elevated to equal rank as a physician with Earthmen."

Dal stared at him. "And I was the one?"

"You were the one. It was a struggle, all right, but Hospital Earth has finally satisfied the Confederation. At the end of this conclave we will be admitted to full membership and given a permanent seat and vote in the galactic council. Our probationary period will be over. But enough of that. What about you? What are your plans? What do you propose to do now that you have that star on your collar?"

They talked then about the future. Tiger Martin had been appointed to the survey crew returning to 31 Brucker VII, at his own request, while Jack was accepting a temporary teaching post in the great diagnostic clinic at Hospital Philadelphia. There were a dozen things that Dal had considered, but for the moment he wanted only to travel from medical center to medical center on Hospital Earth, observing and studying in order to decide how he would best like to use his abilities and his position as a Physician from Hospital Earth. "It will be in surgery, of course," he said. "Just where in surgery, or what kind, I don't know just yet. But there will be time enough to decide that."

"Then go along," Dr. Arnquist said, "with my congratulations and blessing. You have taught us a great deal, and perhaps you have learned some things at the same time."

Dal hesitated for a moment. Then he nodded. "I've learned some things," he said, "but there's still one thing that I want to do before I go."

He lifted his little pink friend gently down from his shoulder and rested him in the crook of his arm. Fuzzy looked up at him, blinking his shoe-button eyes happily. "You asked me once to leave Fuzzy with you, and

I refused. I couldn't see then how I could possibly do without him; even the thought was frightening. But now I think I've changed my mind."

He reached out and placed Fuzzy gently in the Black Doctor's hand. "I want you to keep him," he said. "I don't think I'll need him any more. I'll miss him, but I think it would be better if I don't have him now. Be good to him, and let me visit him once in a while."

The Black Doctor looked at Dal, and then lifted Fuzzy up to his own shoulder. For a moment the little creature shivered as if afraid. Then he blinked twice at Dal, trustingly, and snuggled in comfortably against the Black Doctor's neck.

Without a word Dal turned and walked out of the office. As he stepped down the corridor, he waited fearfully for the wave of desolation and loneliness he had felt before when Fuzzy was away from him.

But there was no hint of those desolate feelings in his mind now. And after all, he thought, why should there be? He was not a Garvian any longer. He was a Star Surgeon from Hospital Earth.

He smiled as he stepped from the elevator into the main lobby and crossed through the crowd to the street doors. He pulled his scarlet cape tightly around his throat. Drawing himself up to the full height of which he was capable, he walked out of the building and strode down onto the street.

AN OUNCE OF CURE

The doctor's office was shiny and modern. Behind the desk the doctor smiled down at James Wheatley through thick glasses. "Now, then! What seems to be the trouble?"

Wheatley had been palpitating for five days straight at the prospect of coming here. "I know it's silly," he said. "But I've been having a pain in my toe."

"Indeed!" said the doctor. "Well, now! How long have you had this pain, my man?"

"About six months now, I'd say. Just now and then, you know. It's never really been bad. Until last week. You see—"

"I see," said the doctor. "Getting worse all the time, you say."

Wheatley wiggled the painful toe reflectively. "Well—you might say that. You see, when I first—"

"How old did you say you were, Mr. Wheatley?"

"Fifty-five."

"Fifty-*five*!" The doctor leafed through the medical record on his desk. "But this is incredible. You haven't had a checkup in almost ten years!"

"I guess I haven't," said Wheatley, apologetically. "I'd been feeling pretty well until—"

"*Feeling* well!" The doctor stared in horror. "But my dear fellow, no checkup since January 1963! We aren't in the Middle Ages, you know. This is 1972."

"Well, of course—"

"Of course you may be *feeling* well enough, but that doesn't mean everything is just the way it should be. And now, you see, you're having pains in your toes!"

"One toe," said Wheatley. "The little one on the right. It seemed to me—"

"One toe *today*, perhaps," said the doctor heavily. "But *tomorrow*—" He heaved a sigh. "How about your breathing lately? Been growing short of breath when you hurry upstairs?"

"Well—I *have* been bothered a little."

"I thought so! Heart pound when you run for the subway? Feel tired all day? Pains in your calves when you walk fast?"

"Uh—yes, occasionally, I—" Wheatley looked worried and rubbed his toe on the chair leg.

"You know that fifty-five is a dangerous age," said the doctor gravely. "Do you have a cough? Heartburn after dinner? Prop up on pillows at night? Just as I thought! And no checkup for ten years!" He sighed again.

"I suppose I should have seen to it," Wheatley admitted. "But you see, it's just that my toe—"

"My dear fellow! Your toe is *part* of you. It doesn't just exist down there all by itself. If your *toe* hurts, there must be a *reason*."

Wheatley looked more worried than ever. "There must? I thought—perhaps you could just give me a little something—"

"To stop the pain?" The doctor looked shocked. "Well, of course I could *do* that, but that's not getting at the root of the trouble, is it? That's just treating symptoms. Medieval quackery. Medicine has advanced a long way since your last checkup, my friend. And even treatment has its dangers. Did you know that more people died last year of *aspirin* poisoning than of *cyanide* poisoning?"

Wheatley wiped his forehead. "I—dear me! I never realized—"

"We have to *think* about those things," said the doctor. "Now, the problem here is to find out *why* you have the pain in your toe. It could be inflammatory. Maybe a tumor. Perhaps it could be, uh, functional . . . or maybe vascular!"

"Perhaps you could take my blood pressure, or something," Wheatley offered.

"Well, of course I *could*. But that isn't really my field, you know. It wouldn't really *mean* anything, if I did it. But there's nothing to worry about. We have a fine Hypertensive man at the Diagnostic Clinic." The doctor checked the appointment book on his desk. "Now, if we could see you there next Monday morning at nine—"

*

"Very interesting X rays," said the young doctor with the red hair. "*Very* interesting. See this shadow in the duodenal cap? See the prolonged emptying time? And I've never seen such beautiful pylorospasm!"

"This is my toe?" asked Wheatley, edging toward the doctors. It seemed he had been waiting for a very long time.

"Toe! Oh, no," said the red-headed doctor. "No, that's the Orthopedic Radiologist's job. I'm a Gastro-Intestinal man, myself. Upper. Dr. Schultz here is Lower." The red-headed doctor turned back to his consultation with Dr. Schultz. Mr. Wheatley rubbed his toe and waited.

Presently another doctor came by. He looked very grave as he sat down beside Wheatley. "Tell me, Mr. Wheatley, have you had an orthodiagram recently?"

"No."

"An EKG?"

"No."

"Fluoroaortogram?"

"I—don't *think* so."

The doctor looked even graver, and walked away, muttering to himself. In a few moments he came back with two more doctors. "—no question in *my* mind that it's cardiomegaly," he was saying, "but Haddonfield should know. He's the best Left Ventricle man in the city. Excellent paper in the AMA Journal last July: 'The Inadequacies of Modern Orthodiagramatic Techniques in Demonstrating Minimal Left Ventricular Hypertrophy.' A brilliant study, simply brilliant! Now *this* patient—" He glanced toward Wheatley, and his voice dropped to a mumble.

Presently two of the men nodded, and one walked over to Wheatley, cautiously, as though afraid he might suddenly vanish. "Now, there's nothing to be worried about, Mr. Wheatley," he said. "We're going to have you fixed up in just no time at all. Just a few more studies. Now, if you could see me in Valve Clinic tomorrow afternoon at three—"

Wheatley nodded. "Nothing serious, I hope?"

"Serious? Oh, no! Dear me, you *mustn't* worry. Everything is going to be all right," the doctor said.

"Well—I—that is, my toe is still bothering me some. It's not nearly as bad, but I wondered if maybe you—"

Dawn broke on the doctor's face. "Give you something for it? Well now, we aren't Therapeutic men, you understand. Always best to let the expert handle the problem in his own field." He paused, stroking his chin for a moment. "Tell you what we'll do. Dr. Epstein is one of the finest Therapeutic men in the city. He could take care of you in a jiffy. We'll see if we can't arrange an appointment with him after you've seen me tomorrow."

Mr. Wheatley was late to Mitral Valve Clinic the next day because he had gone to Aortic Valve Clinic by mistake, but finally he found the right waiting room. A few hours later he was being thumped, photographed, and listened to. Substances were popped into his right arm, and withdrawn from his left arm as he marveled at the brilliance of modern medical techniques. Before they were finished he had been seen by both the Mitral men and the Aortic men, as well as the Great Arteries man and the Peripheral Capillary Bed man.

The Therapeutic man happened to be in Atlantic City at a convention and the Rheumatologist was on vacation, so Wheatley was sent to Functional Clinic instead. "Always have to rule out these things," the doctors agreed. "Wouldn't do much good to give you medicine if your trouble isn't organic, now, would it?" The Psychoneuroticist studied his sex life, while the Psychosociologist examined his social milieu. Then they conferred for a long time.

Three days later he was waiting in the hallway downstairs again. Heads met in a huddle; words and phrases slipped out from time to time as the discussion grew heated.

"—no doubt in my mind that it's a—"

"But we can't ignore the endocrine implications, doctor—"

"You're perfectly right there, of course. Bittenbender at the University might be able to answer the question. No better Pituitary Osmoreceptorologist in the city—"

"—a Tubular Function man should look at those kidneys first. He's fifty-five, you know."

"—has anyone studied his filtration fraction?"

"—might be a peripheral vascular spasticity factor—"

After a while James Wheatley rose from the bench and slipped out the door, limping slightly as he went.

*

The room was small and dusky, with heavy Turkish drapes obscuring the dark hallway beyond. A suggestion of incense hung in the air.

In due course a gaunt, swarthy man in mustache and turban appeared through the curtains and bowed solemnly. "You come with a problem?" he asked, in a slight accent.

"As a matter of fact, yes," James Wheatley said hesitantly. "You see, I've been having a pain in my right little toe . . . ."

"Just suppose," said Morgan, "that I *did* believe you. Just for argument." He glanced up at the man across the restaurant table. "Where would we go from here?"

The man shifted uneasily in his seat. He was silent, staring down at his plate. Not a strange-looking man, Morgan thought. Rather ordinary, in fact. A plain face, nose a little too long, fingers a little too dainty, a suit that doesn't quite seem to fit, but all in all, a perfectly ordinary looking man.

Maybe *too* ordinary, Morgan thought.

Finally the man looked up. His eyes were dark, with a hunted look in their depths that chilled Morgan a little. "Where do we go? I don't know. I've tried to think it out, and I get nowhere. But you've *got* to believe me, Morgan. I'm lost, I mean it. If I can't get help, I don't know where it's going to end."

"I'll tell you where it's going to end," said Morgan. "It's going to end in a hospital. A mental hospital. They'll lock you up and they'll lose the key somewhere." He poured himself another cup of coffee and sipped it, scalding hot. "And that," he added, "will be that."

*

The place was dark and almost empty. Overhead, a rotary fan swished patiently. The man across from Morgan ran a hand through his dark hair. "There must be some other way," he said. "There has to be."

"All right, let's start from the beginning again," Morgan said. "Maybe we can pin something down a little better. You say your name is Parks—right?"

The man nodded. "Jefferson Haldeman Parks, if that helps any. Haldeman was my mother's maiden name."

"All right. And you got into town on Friday—right?"

Parks nodded.

"Fine. Now go through the whole story again. What happened first?"

The man thought for a minute. "As I said, first there was a fall. About twenty feet. I didn't break any bones, but I was shaken up and limping. The fall was near the highway going to the George Washington Bridge. I got over to the highway and tried to flag down a ride."

"How did you feel? I mean, was there anything strange that you noticed?"

"*Strange!*" Parks' eyes widened. "I—I was speechless. At first I hadn't noticed too much—I was concerned with the fall, and whether I was hurt or not. I didn't really think about much else until I hobbled up to that highway and saw those cars coming. Then I could hardly believe my eyes. I thought I was crazy. But a car stopped and asked me if I was going into the city, and I knew I wasn't crazy."

Morgan's mouth took a grim line. "You understood the language?"

"Oh, yes. I don't see how I could have, but I did. We talked all the way into New York—nothing very important, but we understood each other. His speech had an odd sound, but—"

Morgan nodded. "I know, I noticed. What did you do when you got to New York?"

"Well, obviously, I needed money. I had gold coin. There had been no way of knowing if it would be useful, but I'd taken it on chance. I tried to use it at a newsstand first, and the man wouldn't touch it. Asked me if I thought I was the U.S. Treasury or something. When he saw that I was serious, he sent me to a money lender, a hock shop, I think he called it. So I found a place—"

"Let me see the coins."

Parks dropped two small gold discs on the table. They were perfectly smooth and perfectly round, tapered by wear to a thin blunt edge. There was no design on them, and no printing. Morgan looked up at the man sharply. "What did you get for these?"

Parks shrugged. "Too little, I suspect. Two dollars for the small one, five for the larger."

"You should have gone to a bank."

"I know that now. I didn't then. Naturally, I assumed that with everything else so similar, principles of business would also be similar."

Morgan sighed and leaned back in his chair. "Well, then what?"

Parks poured some more coffee. His face was very pale, Morgan thought, and his hands trembled as he raised the cup to his lips. Fright? Maybe. Hard to tell. The man put down the cup and rubbed his forehead with the back of his hand. "First, I went to the mayor's office," he said. "I kept trying to think what anyone at home would do in my place. That seemed a good bet. I asked a policeman where it was, and then I went there."

"But you didn't get to see him."

"No. I saw a secretary. She said the mayor was in conference, and that I would have to have an appointment. She let me speak to another man, one of the mayor's assistants."

"And you told him?"

"No. I wanted to see the mayor himself. I thought that was the best thing to do. I waited for a couple of hours, until another assistant came along and told me flatly that the mayor wouldn't see me unless I stated my business first." He drew in a deep breath. "So I stated it. And then I was gently but firmly ushered back into the street again."

"They didn't believe you," said Morgan.

"Not for a minute. They laughed in my face."

Morgan nodded. "I'm beginning to get the pattern. So what did you do next?"

"Next I tried the police. I got the same treatment there, only they weren't so gentle. They wouldn't listen either. They muttered something about cranks and their crazy notions, and when they asked me where I lived, they thought I was—what did they call it?—a wise guy! Told me to get out and not come back with any more wild stories."

"I see," said Morgan.

Jefferson Parks finished his last bite of pie and pushed the plate away. "By then I didn't know quite what to do. I'd been prepared for almost anything excepting this. It was frightening. I tried to rationalize it, and then I quit trying. It wasn't that I attracted attention, or anything like that, quite the contrary. Nobody even looked at me, unless I said something to them. I began to look for things that were *different*, things that I could show them, and say, see, this proves that I'm telling the truth, look at it—" He looked up helplessly.

"And what did you find?"

"Nothing. Oh, little things, insignificant little things. Your calendars, for instance. Naturally, I couldn't understand your frame of reference. And the coinage, you stamp your coins; we don't. And cigarettes. We don't have any such thing as tobacco." The man gave a short laugh. "And your house dogs! We have little animals that look more like rabbits than poodles. But there was nothing any more significant than that. Absolutely nothing."

"Except yourself," Morgan said.

"Ah, yes. I thought that over carefully. I looked for differences, obvious ones. I couldn't find any. You can see that, just looking at me. So I searched for more subtle things. Skin texture, fingerprints, bone structure, body proportion. I still couldn't find anything. Then I went to a doctor."

Morgan's eyebrows lifted. "Good," he said.

Parks shrugged tiredly. "Not really. He examined me. He practically took me apart. I carefully refrained from saying anything about who I was or where I came from; just said I wanted a complete physical examination, and let him go to it. He was thorough, and when he finished he patted me on the back and said, 'Parks, you've got nothing to worry about. You're as fine, strapping a specimen of a healthy human being as I've ever seen.' And that was that." Parks laughed bitterly. "I guess I was supposed to be happy with the verdict, and instead I was ready to knock him down. It was idiotic, it defied reason, it was infuriating."

Morgan nodded sourly. "Because you're not a human being," he said.

"That's right. I'm not a human being at all."

* * * * *

"How did you happen to pick this planet, or this sun?" Morgan asked curiously. "There must have been a million others to choose from."

Parks unbuttoned his collar and rubbed his stubbled chin unhappily. "I didn't make the choice. Neither did anyone else. Travel by warp is a little different from travel by the rocket you fiction writers make so much of. With a rocket vehicle you pick your destination, make your calculations, and off you go. The warp is blind flying, strictly blind. We send an unmanned scanner ahead. It probes around more or less hit-or-miss until it locates something, somewhere, that looks habitable. When it spots a likely looking place, we keep a tight beam on it and send through a manned scout." He grinned sourly. "Like me. If it looks good to the scout, he signals back, and they leave the warp anchored for a sort of permanent gateway until we can get a transport beam built. But we can't control the directional and dimensional scope of the warp. There are an infinity of ways it can go, until we have a guide beam transmitting from the other side. Then we can just scan a segment of space with the warp, and the scanner picks up the beam."

He shook his head wearily. "We're new at it, Morgan. We've only tried a few dozen runs. We're not too far ahead of you in technology. We've been using rocket vehicles just like yours for over a century. That's fine for a solar system, but it's not much good for the stars. When the warp principle was discovered, it looked like the answer. But something went wrong, the scanner picked up this planet, and I was coming through, and then something blew. Next thing I knew I was falling. When I tried to make contact again, the scanner was gone!"

"And you found things here the same as back home," said Morgan.

"The same! Your planet and mine are practically twins. Similar cities, similar technology, everything. The people are the same, with precisely the same anatomy and physiology, the same sort of laws, the same institutions, even compatible languages. Can't you see the importance of it? This planet is on the other side of the universe from mine, with the first intelligent life we've yet encountered anywhere. But when I try to tell your people that I'm a native of another star system, *they won't believe me*!"

"Why should they?" asked Morgan. "You look like a human being. You talk like one. You eat like one. You act like one. What you're asking them to believe is utterly incredible."

"*But it's true.*"

Morgan shrugged. "So it's true. I won't argue with you. But as I asked before, even if I *did* believe you, what do you expect *me* to do about it? Why pick *me*, of all the people you've seen?"

There was a desperate light in Parks' eyes. "I was tired, tired of being laughed at, tired of having people looking at me as though I'd lost my wits when I tried to tell them the truth. You were here, you were alone, so I started talking. And then I found out you wrote stories." He looked up eagerly. "I've got to get back, Morgan, somehow. My life is there, my family. And think what it would mean to both of our worlds—contact with another intelligent race! Combine our knowledges, our technologies, and we could explore the galaxy!"

He leaned forward, his thin face intense. "I need money and I need help. I know some of the mathematics of the warp principle, know some of the design, some of the power and wiring principles. You have engineers here, technologists, physicists. They could fill in what I don't know and build a guide beam. But they won't do it if they don't believe me. Your government won't listen to me, they won't appropriate any money."

"Of course they won't. They've got a war or two on their hands, they have public welfare, and atomic bombs, and rockets to the moon to sink their money into." Morgan stared at the man. "But what can *I* do?"

"You can *write*! That's what you can do. You can tell the world about me, you can tell exactly what has happened. I know how public interest can be aroused in my world. It must be the same in yours."

Morgan didn't move. He just stared. "How many people have you talked to?" he asked.

"A dozen, a hundred, maybe a thousand."

"And how many believed you?"

"None."

"You mean *nobody* would believe you?"

"*Not one soul.* Until I talked to you."

And then Morgan was laughing, laughing bitterly, tears rolling down his cheeks. "And I'm the one man who couldn't help you if my life depended on it," he gasped.

"You believe me?"

Morgan nodded sadly. "I believe you. Yes. I think your warp brought you through to a parallel universe of your own planet, not to another star, but I think you're telling the truth."

"Then you *can* help me."

"I'm afraid not."

"Why not?"

"Because I'd be worse than no help at all."

Jefferson Parks gripped the table, his knuckles white. "Why?" he cried hoarsely. "If you believe me, why can't you help me?"

Morgan pointed to the magazine lying on the table. "I write, yes," he said sadly. "Ever read stories like this before?"

Parks picked up the magazine, glanced at the bright cover. "I barely looked at it."

"You should look more closely. I have a story in this issue. The readers thought it was very interesting," Morgan grinned. "Go ahead, look at it."

The stranger from the stars leafed through the magazine, stopped at a page that carried Roger Morgan's name. His eyes caught the first paragraph and he turned white. He set the magazine down with a trembling hand. "I see," he said, and the life was gone out of his voice. He spread the pages viciously, read the lines again.

The paragraph said:

"Just suppose," said Martin, "that I *did* believe you.

Just for argument." He glanced up at the man across the table.

"Where do we go from here?"

MY FRIEND BOBBY

My name is Jimmy and I am five years old, and my friend Bobby is five years old too but he says he thinks he's really more than five years old because he's already grown up and I'm just a little boy. We live out in the country because that's where mommy and daddy live, and every morning daddy takes the car out of the barn and rides into the city to work, and every night he comes back to eat supper and to see mommy and Bobby and me. One time I asked daddy why we don't live in the city like some people do and he laughed and said you wouldn't really want to live in the city would you? After all he said you couldn't have Bobby in the city, so I guess it's better to live in the country after all.

Anyway daddy says that the city is no place to raise kids these days. I asked Bobby if I am a kid and he said he guessed so but I don't think he really knows because Bobby isn't very smart. But Bobby is my friend even if he doesn't know much and I like him more than anybody else.

Mommy doesn't like Bobby very much and when I am bad she makes Bobby go outdoors even when it's cold outside. Mommy says I shouldn't play with Bobby so much because after all Bobby is only a dog but I like Bobby. Everyone else is so big, and when mommy and daddy are home all I can see is their legs unless I look way up high, and when I do something bad I'm scared because they're so big and strong. Bobby is strong too but he isn't any bigger than I am, and he is always nice to me. He has a long shaggy brown coat and a long pointed nose, and a nice collar of white fur and people sometimes say to daddy what a nice collie that is and daddy says yes isn't he and he takes to the boy so. I don't know what a collie is but I have fun with Bobby all the time. Sometimes he lets me ride on his back and we talk to each other and have secrets even though I don't think he is very smart. I don't know why mommy and daddy don't understand me when I talk to them the way I talk to Bobby but maybe they just pretend they can't hear me talk that way.

I am always sorry when daddy goes to work in the morning. Daddy is nice to me most times and takes me and Bobby for walks. But mommy never takes me for walks and when we are alone she is busy and she isn't nice to me. Sometimes she says I am a bad boy and makes me stay in my room even when I haven't done anything bad and sometimes she thinks things in her head that she doesn't say to me. I don't know why mommy doesn't like me and Bobby doesn't know either, but we like it best when mommy lets us go outdoors to play in the barn or down by the creek. If I get my feet wet mommy says I am very bad so I stay on the bank and let Bobby go in, but one day when Bobby went into the water just before we went home for supper mommy scolded me and told me I was bad for letting Bobby go into the water and when I told her she hadn't told me not to let Bobby go in she was angry and I could tell that she didn't like me at all that day.

Almost every day I do something that mommy says is bad even when I try specially to be good. Sometimes right after daddy goes away in the morning I know that mommy is angry and is going to spank me sooner or later that day because she is already thinking how she will spank me, but she never says so out loud. Sometimes she pretends that she's not angry and takes me up on her lap and says I'm her nice little boy but all the time I can hear her thinking that she doesn't really like me even when she tries and she doesn't even want to touch me if she can help it. I can hear her wondering why my hair doesn't grow nice like the Bennet twins that live up the road. I don't see how mommy can be saying one thing out loud and something else inside her head at the same time but when I look at her she puts me down and says she's busy and will I get out from underfoot, and then pretty soon I do something that makes her angry and she makes me go to my room or she spanks me. Bobby doesn't like this. Once when she spanked me he growled at mommy, and mommy chased him outdoors with a broom before she sent me to bed. I cried all day that day because it was cold outdoors and I wanted to have Bobby with me.

I wonder why mommy doesn't like me?

*

One day I was a bad boy and let Bobby come into the house before mommy told me I could. Bobby hadn't done anything bad but mommy hit him on the back with the broom and hurt him and chased him back outdoors and then she told me I was a very bad boy. I could tell that she was going to spank me and I knew she would hurt me because she was so big, and I ran upstairs and hid in my room. Then mommy stamped her foot hard and said Jimmy you come down here this minute. I didn't answer and then she said if I have to come upstairs and get you I'll whip you until you can't sit down, and I still didn't answer because mommy hurts me when she gets angry like that. Then I heard her coming up the stairs and into my room and she opened the closet door and found me. I said please don't hurt me mommy but she reached down and caught my ear and dragged me out of the closet. I was so scared I bit her hand and she screamed and let go and I ran and locked myself in the bathroom because I knew she would hurt me bad if I didn't. I stayed there all day long and I could hear mommy running the sweeper downstairs and I couldn't see why she wanted to hurt me so much just because I let Bobby come in before she told me I could. But somehow it seemed that mommy was afraid of me even though she was so big and strong. I don't see why anybody as big as mommy should be afraid of me but she was.

When daddy came home that night I heard him talking to mommy, and then he came up to the bathroom and said open the door Jimmy I want to talk to you. I said I want Bobby first so he went down and called Bobby and then I opened the door and came out of the bathroom. Daddy reached down and lifted me high up on his shoulder and took me into my bedroom and just sat there for a long time patting Bobby's head and I couldn't hear what he was thinking very well. Finally he said out loud Jimmy you've got to be good to your mommy and do what she says and not lock yourself up in rooms any more. I said but mommy was going to hurt me and daddy said when you're a bad boy your mommy has to punish you so you'll remember to be good, but she doesn't like to spank you. She only does it because she loves you.

I knew that wasn't true because mommy likes to punish me but I didn't dare say that to daddy. Daddy isn't afraid of me the way mommy is and he is nice to me most times, so I said all right if you say so. Daddy said fine, will you promise to be nice to mommy from now on? I said yes if mommy won't hit Bobby any more with the broom. And daddy said well after all Bobby can be a bad dog just the way you can be a bad boy, can't he? I knew Bobby was never a bad dog on purpose but I said yes I guessed so. Then I wanted to ask daddy why mommy was afraid of me but I didn't dare because I knew daddy liked mommy more than anybody and maybe he would be angry at me for saying things like that about her.

That night I heard mommy and daddy talking down in the living room and I sat on the top step so I could hear them. Bobby sat there too, but I knew he didn't know what they were saying because Bobby isn't very smart and can't understand word-talk like I can. He can only understand think-talk, and he doesn't understand that very well. But now even I couldn't understand what mommy was saying. She was crying and saying Ben I tell you there's something wrong with the child, he knows what I'm *thinking*, I can tell it by the way he looks at me. And daddy said darling, that's ridiculous, how could he possibly know what you're thinking? Mommy said I don't know but he does! Ever since he was a little boy he's known—oh, Ben, it's horrible, I can't do anything with him because he *knows* what I'm going to do before I do it. Then daddy said Carol, you're upset about today and you're making things up. The child is just a little smarter than most kids, there's nothing wrong with that. And mommy said no, there's more to it than that and I can't stand it any longer. We've got to take him to a doctor, I don't even like to look at him. Daddy said you're tired, you're just letting little things get on your nerves. So maybe the boy does look a little strange, you know the doctor said it was just that the fontanelles hadn't closed as soon as they should have and lots of children don't have a good growth of hair before they're six or seven. After all he said he isn't a *bad* looking boy.

Then mommy said that isn't true, he's horrible! I can't bear it, Ben, *please* do something, and daddy said what can I do? I talked to the boy and he was sorry and promised he'd behave himself. And mommy said then there's that dog—it follows him around wherever he goes, and he's simply wicked if the dog isn't around, and daddy said isn't it perfectly normal for a boy to love his dog? Mommy said no, not like this, talking to him all the time, and the dog acting exactly as if he understands—there's something wrong with the child, something horribly wrong.

Then daddy was quiet for a while, and then he said all right, if it will make you feel any better we can have Doctor Grant take another look at him. Maybe he can convince you that there's nothing wrong with the boy, and mommy said please, Ben, anything, I can't stand much more of this.

When I went back to bed and Bobby curled up on the floor, I asked him what were fontanelles, and Bobby just yawned and said he didn't know but he thought I was nice, and he would always take care of me, so I didn't worry any more and went to sleep.

*

I have a panda out in the barn and the panda's name is Bobby too and at first Bobby the dog was jealous of Bobby the panda until I told him that the panda was only a make-believe Bobby and he was a real Bobby. Then Bobby liked the panda, and the three of us played out in the barn all day. We decided not to tell mommy and daddy about the panda, and kept it for our own secret. It was a big panda, as big as mommy and daddy, and sometimes I thought maybe I would make the panda hurt mommy but then I knew daddy would be sorry so I didn't.

Bobby and I were playing with Bobby the panda the day the doctor came and mommy called me in and made Bobby stay outside. I didn't like the doctor because he smelled like a dirty old cigar and he had a big red nose with three black hairs coming out of it and he wheezed when he bent down to look at me. Daddy and mommy sat on the couch and the doctor said let me have a look at you young fellow and I said but I'm not sick and the doctor said ha ha, of course you aren't, you're a fine looking boy but just let me listen to your chest for a minute. So he put a cold thing on my chest and stuck some tubes in his ears and listened, and then he looked in my eyes with a bright light and looked into my ears, and then he felt my head all over. He had big hairy hands and I didn't like him touching me but I knew mommy would be angry if I didn't hold still so I let him finish. Then he told daddy some big words that I couldn't understand, but in think-talk he was saying that my head still hadn't closed up right and I didn't have as much hair as you'd expect but otherwise I seemed to be all right. He said I was a good stout looking boy but if they wanted a specialist in to look at me he would arrange it. Daddy asked if that would cost very much and the doctor said yes it probably would and he didn't see any real need for it because my bones were just a little slow in developing, and mommy said have you seen other children like that? The doctor said no but if the boy seems to be normal and intelligent why should she be worrying so? Then mommy told me to go upstairs, and I went but I stopped on the top stair and listened.

When I was gone the doctor said now Carol what is it that's really bothering you? Then mommy told him what she had told daddy, how she thought I knew what she was thinking, and the doctor said to daddy, Ben, have you ever felt any such thing about the boy? Daddy said of course not, sometimes he gives you the feeling that he's smarter than you think he is but all parents have that feeling about their children sometimes. And then mother broke down and her voice got loud and she said he's a monster, I know it, there's something wrong and he's different from us, him and that horrible dog. The doctor said but it's a beautiful collie, and mommy said but he *talks* to it and it *understands* him, and the doctor said now, Carol, let's be reasonable. Mommy said I've been reasonable too long, you men just can't see it at all, don't you think I'd know a normal child if I saw one? And then she cried and cried, and finally she said all right, I know I'm making a fool of myself, maybe I'm just overtired, and the doctor said I'm sure that's the trouble, try to get some rest, and sleep longer at night, and mommy said I can't sleep at night, I just lie there and think.

The doctor said well we'll fix that, enough of this nonsense now, you need your sleep and if you're not sleeping well it's *you* that should be seeing the doctor. He gave her some pills from his bag and then he went away, and pretty soon daddy let Bobby in, and Bobby came upstairs and jumped up and licked my face as if he'd been away for a hundred million years. Later mommy called me down for supper, and she wasn't crying any more, and she and daddy didn't say anything about what they had said to the doctor. Mommy made me a special surprise for dessert, some ice cream with chocolate syrup on top, and after supper we all went for a walk, even though it was cold outside and snowing again. Then daddy said well, I think things will be all right, and mommy said I hope so, but I could tell that she didn't really think so, and she was more afraid of me than ever.

*

For a while I thought mommy was really going to be nice to me and Bobby then. She was especially nice when daddy was home but when daddy was away at work sometimes mommy jumped when she saw me looking at her and then sent me outdoors to play and told me not to come in until lunch. I liked that because I knew if I weren't near mommy everything would be all right. When I was with mommy I tried hard not to look at her and I tried not to hear what she was thinking, but lots of times I would see her looking first at me and then at Bobby, and those times I couldn't help hearing what she was thinking because it seemed so loud inside my head that it made my eyes hurt. But I knew mommy would be angry so I pretended I couldn't hear what she was thinking at all.

One day when we were out in the barn playing with Bobby the panda we saw mommy coming down through the snow from the kitchen and Bobby said look out Jimmy mommy is coming and I quick told Bobby the panda to go hide under the hay so mommy couldn't see him. But the panda was so big his whole top and his little pink nose stuck out of the hay. Mommy came in and looked around the barn and said you've been out here for a long time, what have you been doing? I said nothing, and Bobby said nothing too, only in think-talk. And mommy said you are too, you've been doing something naughty, and I said no mommy we haven't done *anything*, and then the panda sneezed and I looked at him and he looked so funny with his nose sticking out of the hay that I laughed out loud.

Mommy looked angry and said well what's so funny, what are you laughing at? I said nothing, because I knew mommy couldn't see the panda, but I couldn't stop laughing because he looked so funny sticking out of the hay. Then mommy got mad and grabbed my ear and shook me until it hurt and said you naughty boy, *don't you lie to me*, what have you been doing out here? She hurt me so much I started to cry and then Bobby snarled at mommy loud and low and curled his lips back over his teeth and snarled some more. And mommy got real white in the face and let go of me and she said get out of here you nasty dog and Bobby snarled louder and then snapped at her. She screamed and she said Jimmy you come in the house this minute and leave that nasty dog outdoors and I said I won't come, I hate you.

Then mommy said Jimmy! You wicked, ugly little monster, and I said I don't care, when I get big I'm going to hurt you and throw you in the wood shed and lock you in until you die and make you eat coconut pudding and Bobby hates you too. And mommy looked terrible and I could feel how much she was afraid of me and I said you just wait, I'll hurt you bad when I get big, and then she turned and ran back to the house. And Bobby wagged his tail and said don't worry, I won't let her hurt you any more and I said Bobby you shouldn't have snapped at her because daddy won't like me when he comes home but Bobby said *I* like you and I won't let anything ever hurt you. I'll always take care of you no matter what. And I said promise? No matter what? And Bobby said I promise. And then we told Bobby the panda to come out but it wasn't much fun playing any more.

After a little while mommy called me and said lunch was ready. She was still white and I said can Bobby come too and she said of course Bobby can come, Bobby's a nice dog, so we went in to eat lunch. Mommy was talking real fast about what fun it was to play in the barn and was I sure I wasn't too cold because it was below zero outside and the radio said a snowstorm was coming, but she didn't say anything about Bobby and me being out in the barn. She was talking so fast I couldn't hear what she was thinking except for little bits while she set my lunch on the table and then she set a bowl of food on the floor for Bobby even though it wasn't Bobby's time to eat and said nice Bobby here's your dinner. Bobby came over and sniffed the bowl and then he looked up at me and said it smells funny and mommy said nice Bobby, it's good hamburger just the way you like it—

And then for just a second I saw what she was thinking and it was terrible because she was thinking that Bobby would soon be dead, and I remembered daddy saying a long time ago that somebody fed bad things to the Bennet's dog and the dog died and I said don't eat it, Bobby, and Bobby snarled at the dish. And then mommy said you tell the dog to eat it and I said no you're bad and you want to hurt Bobby, and then I picked up the dish and threw it at mommy. It missed and smashed on the wall and she screamed and turned and ran out into the other room. She was screaming for daddy and saying I can't stand it, he's a monster, a murderous little monster and we've got to get out of here before he kills us all, he knows what we're thinking, he's horrible, and then she was on the telephone, and she couldn't make the words come out right when she tried to talk.

I was scared and I said come on Bobby let's lock ourselves up in my room and we ran upstairs and locked the door. Mommy was banging things and laughing and crying downstairs and screaming we've got to get out, he'll kill us if we don't, and a while later I heard the car coming up the road fast, and saw daddy run into the house just as it started to snow. Then mommy was screaming please, Ben, we've got to get out of here, he tried to kill me, and the dog is vicious, he bit me when I tried to make him stop.

The next minute daddy was running up the stairs two at a time and I could feel him inside my head for the first time and I knew he was angry. He'd never been this angry before and he rattled the knob and said open this door Jimmy in a loud voice. I said no I won't and he said open the door or I'll break your neck when I get in there and then he kicked the door and kicked it again. The third time the lock broke and the door flew open and daddy stood there panting. His eyes looked terrible and he had a leather belt doubled up in his hand and he said now come out here and his voice was so loud it hurt my ears.

Down below mommy was crying please Ben, take me away, he'll kill us both, he's a monster! I said don't hurt me daddy it was mommy, she was bad to me, and he said I said *come out here* even louder. I was scared then and I said please daddy I'll be good I promise. Then he started for me with the belt and I screamed out Bobby! Don't let him hurt me, Bobby, and Bobby snarled like a wild animal and jumped at daddy and bit his wrist so bad the blood spurted out. Daddy shouted and dropped the belt and kicked at Bobby but Bobby was too quick. He jumped for daddy again and I saw his white teeth flash and heard him snap close to daddy's throat and then Bobby was snarling and snapping and I was excited and I shouted hurt him, Bobby, he's been bad to me too and he wants to hurt me and you've got to stop him.

Then I saw daddy's eyes open wide, and felt something jump in his mind, something that I'd never felt there before and I knew he was understanding my think-talk. I said I want Bobby to hurt you and mommy because you're not nice to me, only Bobby and my panda are nice to me. Go ahead, Bobby, hurt him, bite him again and make him bleed. And then daddy caught Bobby by the neck and threw him across the room and slammed the door shut and dragged something heavy up to block it. In a minute he was running downstairs shouting Carol, *I heard it!* you were right all along—*I felt him, I felt what he was thinking!* And mommy cried please, Ben, take me away, let's leave them and never come back, never, and daddy said it's horrible, he told that dog to kill me and it went right for my throat, the boy is evil and monstrous. Even from downstairs I could feel daddy's fear pounding into my head and then I heard the door banging and looked out the window and saw daddy carrying suitcases out through the snow to the car and then mommy came out running and the car started down the hill and they were gone. Everything downstairs was very quiet. I looked out the window and I couldn't see anything but the big falling snowflakes and the sun going down over the hill.

Now Bobby and I and the panda are all together and I'm glad mommy and daddy are gone. I went to sleep for a little while because my head hurt so but now I'm awake and Bobby is lying across the room licking his feet and I hope mommy and daddy never come back because Bobby will take care of me. Bobby is my friend and he said he'd always take care of me no matter what and he understands my think-talk even if he isn't very smart.

It's beginning to get cold in the house now because nobody has gone down to fix the fire but I don't care about that. Pretty soon I will tell Bobby to push open the door and go down and fix the fire and then I will tell him to get supper for me and then I will stay up all night because mommy and daddy aren't here to make me go to bed. There's just me and Bobby and the panda, and Bobby promised he'd take care of me because he's my friend.

It's getting very cold now, and I'm getting hungry.

CONSIGNMENT

The three shots ripped through the close night air of the prison, sharply, unbelievably. Three guards crumpled like puppets in the dead silence that followed. The thought flashed through Krenner's mind, incredibly, that possibly no one had heard.

He hurled the rope with all his might up the towering rock wall, waited a long eternity as the slim strong line swished through the darkness, and heard the dull "clank" as the hook took hold at the top. Like a cat he started up, frantically, scrambling, and climbing, the sharp heat of the rope searing his fingers. Suddenly daylight was around him, the bright unearthly glare of arc lights, the siren cutting in with its fierce scream. The shouts of alarm were far below him as he fought up the line, knot after knot, the carefully prepared knots. Twenty seconds to climb, he thought, just twenty seconds—

*

Rifle shots rang out below, the shells smashing into the concrete around him. Krenner almost turned and snarled at the little circle of men in the glaring light below, but turning meant precious seconds. A dull, painful blow struck his foot, as his hands grasped the jagged glass at the top of the wall.

In a moment of triumph he crouched at the top and laughed at the little men and the blazing guns below; on the other side lay the blackness of the river. He turned and plunged into the blackness, his foot throbbing, down swiftly until the cool wetness of the river closed about him, soothing his pain, bathing his mind in the terrible beauty of freedom, and what went with freedom. A few dozen powerful strokes would carry him across and down the river, three miles below the prison fortress from which he had broken. Across the hill from that, somewhere, he'd find Sherman and a wide open road to freedom—

*

Free! Twenty-seven years of walls and work, bitterness and hateful, growing, simmering revenge. Twenty-seven years for a fast-moving world to leave him behind, far behind. He'd have to be careful about that. He wouldn't know about things. Twenty-seven years from his life, to kill his ambition, to take his woman, to disgrace him in the eyes of society. But the candle had burned through. He was free, with time, free, easy, patient time, to find Markson, search him out, kill him at last.

Hours passed it seemed, in the cold, moving water. Krenner struggled to stay alert; loss of control now would be sure death. A few shots had followed him from the wall behind, hopeless shots, hopeless little spears of light cutting across the water, searching for him, a tiny dot in the blackness. Radar could never spot him, for he wore no metal, and the sound of his movements in the water were covered by the sighing wind and the splashing of water against the prison walls.

Finally, after ages of pain and coldness, he dragged himself out onto the muddy shore, close to the calculated spot. He sat on the edge and panted, his foot swollen and throbbing. He wanted to scream in pain, but screams would bring farmers and dogs and questions. That would not do, until he found Sherman, somewhere back in those hills, with a 'copter, and food, and medication, and quiet, peaceful rest.

He tried to struggle to his feet, but the pain was too much now. He half walked, half dragged himself into the woods, and started as best he could the trek across the hills.

*

Jerome Markson absently snapped on the radiovisor on his desk. Sipping his morning coffee thoughtfully as he leafed through the reports on his desk, he listened with half an ear until the announcer's voice seeped through to his consciousness. He tightened suddenly in his seat, and the coffee cooled before him, forgotten.

"—Eastern Pennsylvania is broadcasting a four-state alarm with special radiovisor pictures in an effort to pick up the trail of a convict who escaped the Federal Prison here last night. The escaped man, who shot and killed two guards making good his escape, dived into the river adjoining the prison, and is believed to have headed for an outside rendezvous somewhere in the Blue Mountain region. The prisoner is John Krenner, age 51, gray hair, blue eyes, five-foot-nine. He is armed and dangerous, with four unsuccessful escape attempts, and three known murders on his record. He was serving a life term, without leniency, for the brutal murder in July, 1967, of Florence Markson, wife of the now-famous industrialist, Jerome Markson, president of Markson Foundries. Any person with information of this man's whereabouts should report—"

Markson stared unbelieving at the face which appeared in the visor. Krenner, all right. The same cold eyes, the same cruel mouth, the same sneer. He snapped off the set, his face white and drawn. To face the bitter, unreasoning hate of this man, his former partner—even a prison couldn't hold him.

A telephone buzzed, shattering the silence of the huge office.

"Hello, Jerry? This is Floyd Gunn in Pittsburgh. Krenner's escaped!"

"I know. I just heard. Any word?"

"None yet. We got some inside dope from one of the men in the prison that he has an outside escape route, and that he's been digging up all the information he could find in the past three months or so about the Roads. But I wanted to warn you." The policeman's voice sounded distant and unreal. "He promised to get you, Jerry. I'm ordering you and your home heavily guarded—"

"Guards won't do any good," said Markson, heavily. "Krenner will get me if you don't get him first. Do everything you can."

The policeman's voice sounded more cheerful. "At any rate, he's in the eastern part of the state now. He has four hundred miles to travel before he can get to you. Unless he has a 'copter, or somehow gets on the Roads, he can't get to you for a day or so. We're doing everything we can."

Markson hung up the receiver heavily. Twenty-seven years of peace since that devil had finally murdered his way out of his life. And now he was back again. A terrible mistake for a partner, a man with no reason, a man who could not understand the difference between right and wrong. A man with ruthless ambition, who turned on his partner when honesty got in his way, and murdered his partner's wife in rage when his own way of business was blocked. A man so twisted with rage that he threatened on the brink of capital punishment to tear Markson's heart out, yet Markson had saved him from the chair. An appeal, some money, some influence, had snatched him from death's sure grasp, so he could come back to kill again. And a man with such diabolical good fortune that he could now come safely to Markson, and hunt him out, and carry out the fancied revenge that his twisted mind demanded.

Markson took the visiphone in hand again and dialed a number. The face of a young girl appeared. "Hi, dad. Did you see the news report?"

"Yes, I saw it. I want you to round up Jerry and Mike and take the 'copter out to the summer place on Nantucket. Wait for me there. I don't know how soon I can make it, but I don't want you here now. Leave immediately."

The girl knew better than to argue with her father. "Dad, is there any chance—?"

"There's lots of chance. That's why I want you away from here."

He flipped off the connection, and sighed apprehensively. Now to wait. The furnaces had to keep going, the steel had to be turned out, one way or another. He'd have to stay. And hope. Perhaps the police *would* get him—

*

The elderly lady sat on the edge of the kitchen chair, shivering. "We'll be glad to help you, but you won't hurt us, will you?"

"Shut up," said Krenner. The gray plastic of his pistol gleamed dully in the poor light of the farm kitchen. "Get that foot dressed, with tight pressure and plenty of 'mycin. I don't want it to bleed, and I don't want an infection." The woman hurried her movements, swiftly wrapping the swollen foot.

The man lifted a sizzling frying pan from the range, flipping a hamburger onto a plate. He added potatoes and carrots. "Here's the food," he said sullenly. "And you might put the gun away. We don't have weapons, and we don't have a 'phone."

"You have legs," snapped Krenner. "Now shut up."

The woman finished the dressing. "Try it," she said. The convict stood up by the chair, placing his weight on the foot gingerly. Pain leaped through his leg, but it was a clean pain. He could stand it. He took a small map from his pocket. "Any streams or gorges overland between here and Garret Valley?"

The farmer, shook, his head. "No."

"Give me some clothes, then. No, don't leave. The ones you have on."

The farmer slipped out of his clothes silently, and Krenner dropped the prison grays in the corner.

"You'll keep your mouths shut about this," he stated flatly.

"Oh, yes, you can count on us," exclaimed the woman, eyeing the gun fearfully. "We won't tell a soul."

"I'll say you won't," said Krenner, his fingers tightening on the gun. The shots were muted and flat in the stillness of the kitchen.

An hour later Krenner broke through the underbrush, crossed a rutted road, and pushed on over the ridge. His cruel face was dripping with perspiration. "It should be the last ridge," he thought. "I've gone a good, three miles—" The morning sun was bright, filtering down through the trees, making beautiful wet patterns on the damp ground. The morning heat was just beginning, but the food and medications had made progress easy. He pulled himself up onto a rock ledge, over to the edge, and felt his heart stop cold as he peered down into the valley below.

A dark blue police 'copter nestled on the valley floor next to the sleek gray one. It must have just arrived, for the dark uniforms of the police were swarming around the gray machine He saw the pink face and the sporty clothes of the occupant as he came down the ladder, his hands in the air.

Too late! They'd caught Sherman!

He lay back shaking.

Impossible! He *had* to have Sherman. They couldn't possibly have known, unless somehow they had foreseen, or heard—. His mind seethed with helpless rage. Without Sherman he was stuck. No way to reach Markson, no way to settle that score—unless possibly—.

The Roads.

He'd heard about them. Way back in 1967 when he'd gone up, the roads were underway. A whole system of Rolling Roads was proposed then, and the first had already been built, between Pittsburgh and the Lakes. A crude affair, a conveyor belt system, running at a steady seventy-five miles per hour, carrying only ore and freight.

But in the passing years reports had filtered through the prison walls. New men, coming "up for a visit" had brought tales, gross exaggerations, of the Rolling Roads grown huge, a tremendous system building itself up, crossing hills and valleys in unbroken lines, closed in from weather and hijackers, fast and smooth and endless. Criss-crossing the nation, they had said, in never-slowing belts of passengers and freight livestock. The Great Triangle had been first, from Chicago to St. Louis to Old New York, and back to Chicago. Now every town, every village had its small branch, its entrance to the Rolling Roads, and once a man got on the Roads, they had said, he was safe until he tried to get off.

Clearly the memory of the reports filtered through Krenner's mind. The great Central Roads run from Old New York to Chicago, through New Washington and Pittsburgh—

Markson was in Pittsburgh—

Krenner started down through the underbrush, travelling south by the sun, the urgency of his mission spurring him on against the pain of his foot, the difficulty of the terrain over which he travelled. He was too far north. Somewhere to the south he'd find the Roads. And once on the Roads, he'd find a way to get off—

*

He stopped at the brink of the hill and gasped in amazement.

They ran across the wide valley like silver ribbons. The late afternoon sunlight reflected gold and pink from the plasti-glass encasement, concealing the rushing line of travel within the covering. Like twin serpents, they lay across the hills, about a mile apart, the Road travelling east, and the Road moving west. They stretched as far as he could see. And he could see the white sign which said, "Merryvale Entrance, Westbound, Three miles."

As he tramped, across the field he could hear the hum of the Roads grow loud in his ears. An automatic, machinelike hum, a rhythm of motion. Close to the westbound road he moved back eastward along it, toward the little port which formed the entrance to it. And soon he saw the police 'copter which rested near the entrance, and the uniformed men with their rifles, alert. Three of them.

Krenner fingered his weapon easily. It was almost dark; they would not see him easily. He kept a small hill between himself and the police and moved in within gunshot range. He could see the rocket-like car resting on its single rail, waiting for a passenger to enter, to touch the button which would activate the tiny rocket engines and move it forward, ever and ever more swiftly until it reached the acceleration of the Roads, and slid over, and became a part of the Road. Moving carefully, he slipped from rock to rock, closer to the car and the men who guarded it.

Suddenly the bay of a hound cut through the gloom. Two small brown dogs with the men, straining at their leashes. He hadn't counted on that. Swiftly he took cover and lined his sights with the blue uniforms. Before they knew even his approximate location he had cut them down, and the dogs also, and raced wildly down the remainder of the hill to the car.

"Fare may be calculated from the accompanying charts, and will be collected when your car has taken its place on the Roads," said a little sign near the cockpit. Krenner studied the dashboard for a moment, then jammed in the button marked "Forward," and settled back. The monorail slid forward without a sound, and plunged into a tunnel in the hill. Out the other side, with ever-increasing acceleration it slid in alongside the gleaming silver ribbon, faster and faster. With growing apprehension Krenner watched the speedometer mount, past two hundred, two hundred and twenty, forty, sixty, eighty—at three hundred miles per hour the acceleration force eased, and the car suddenly swerved to the left, into a dark causeway. And then into the brightly lighted plasti-glass tunnel.

He was on the Roads!

Alongside the outside lane the little car sped, moving on an independent rail, sliding gently past other cars resting on the middle lane. An opening appeared, and Krenner's car slid over another notch, disengaged its rail, and settled to a stop on the central lane of the Road. The speedometer fell to nothing, for the car's motion was no longer independent, but an integral part of the speeding Road itself. Three hundred miles per hour on a constant, nonstop flight across the rolling land.

A loudspeaker suddenly piped up in his car. "Welcome to the Roads," it said. "Your fare collector will be with you in a short while. After he has arrived, feel free to leave your car and be at ease on the Road outside. Eating, resting, and sleeping quarters will be found at regular intervals. You are warned, however, not to cross either the barriers to the outside lanes, nor the barriers to the freight-carrying areas front and rear. Pleasant travelling."

Krenner chuckled grimly, and settled down in his car, his automatic in his hand. His fare collector would get a surprise. Down the Road a short distance he saw the man approaching, wearing the green uniform of the Roads. And then he stiffened. Three blue uniforms were accompanying him. Opening the car door swiftly, he slipped out onto the soft carpeting of the Road, and raced swiftly away from the approaching men.

They saw him when he started to run. Ahead he could see a crowd of passengers around a dining area. A shout went up as he knocked a woman down in his pell-mell flight, but he was beyond them in an instant. His foot hindered him, and his pursuers were gaining. Suddenly before him he saw a barrier—a four foot metal wall. No carpet beyond it, no furnishings along the sides. A freight area! He hopped over the barrier and plunged into the blackness of the freight tunnel as he heard the shouts of his pursuers. "Stop! Come back! Stop or we'll shoot!"

They didn't shoot. In a moment Krenner came to the first freight carrier, one of the standard metal containers resting on the steel of the Road. He ran past it, and the next. The third and fourth were open cars, stacked high with machinery. He ran on for several moments before he glanced back.

They weren't following him any more. He could see them, far back, where the light began, a whole crowd of people at the barrier he had crossed. But no one followed him. Odd that they should stop. He centered his mind more closely on his surroundings. Freight might conceal him to get him off the Roads where no passenger station would ever let him through. He climbed to the top of a nearby freight container and slipped down in. Chunks of rock were under his feet, and he fell in a heap on the hard bed. What possible kind of freight—? He slipped a lighter from his pocket and snapped it on.

Coal! A normal freight load. He climbed back up and looked along the road. No pursuit. An uneasy chill went through him—this was too easy. To ride a coal car to safety, without a single man pursuing him—to where? He examined the billing on the side of the car, and he forgot his fears in the rush of excitement. The billing read, "Consignment: Coal, twenty tons, Markson Foundries, via Pittsburgh private cutoff."

His car was carrying him to Markson!

His mind was full of the old, ugly hate, the fearful joy of the impending revenge. Fortune's boy, he thought to himself. Even Sherman could not have done so well, to ride the Rolling Roads, not just to Pittsburgh, not to the mountains, but right to Markson's backyard! He shivered with anticipation. Pittsburgh was only a few hundred miles away, and at three hundred miles an hour—Krenner clenched his fists in cruel pleasure. He hadn't long to wait.

*

An hour passed slowly. Krenner's leg was growing stiff after the exertion of running. Still no sign of life. He eased his position, and stiffened when he heard the little relay box above the consignment sheet give a couple of sharp clicks.

Near the end! He hugged himself in excitement. What a neat trick, to ride a consignment of coal to the very yards where Markson would be! The coal yards which he might have owned, the furnaces, the foundry—. There would be men there to receive the car from the line, well he could remember the men, day and night, working and sweating in those yards and mills! There would be men there to brake the car and empty it. He was in old clothes, farm clothes—he would fit in so well; as soon as the car slowed he could jump off, and simply join the other men. Or he could shoot, if he had to. A little agility in getting out of the car, and a little care in inquiring the way to Markson's office—

The car suddenly shifted to the outer lane. Krenner gripped a handle on the inside and held tight. He felt the swerving motion, and suddenly the car moved out of the tunnel into the open night air. He climbed up the side and peered over the edge. There were five cars in the consignment; he was on the last. Travelling almost at Road speed along the auxiliary cutoff. Swiftly they moved along through the night, through the edge of the Pittsburgh steel yards. Outside he fancied he could hear the rattle of machinery in the yards, the shouts of the men at their work. Making steel was a twenty-four hour proposition.

Then they were clear of the first set of yards. The car made another switch, and Krenner's heart beat faster. A white sign along the side said, "Private Property. Keep off. Markson Foundries Line." Soon now they would come to a crunching halt. Men would be there, but his gun was intact. No matter how many men he met, he had to get to Markson.

The car shuddered a little, but the acceleration continued. They were rising high in the air now, above the foundries. He looked down, and could see the mighty furnaces thrusting their slim necks to the sky.

A bolt of fear went through him. How far did the automatic system go? Automatic loading of coal from the fields, automatic switching onto the Rolling Roads. Automatic transfer of cars onto a private line which led the cars to the foundries. Where did the automatic handling stop? Where did the *men* come into it? Twenty-seven-year-old concepts slid through his mind, of how freight was carried, of how machines were tended, of how steel was made. In a world of rapidly changing technology, twenty-seven years can bring changes, in every walk of life, in every form of production—

Even steel—

A voice from within him screamed, "Get off, Krenner, get off! This is a one way road—" He climbed quickly to the top of the car, to find a place to jump, and turned back, suddenly sick with fear.

The car was going too fast.

The first car had moved with its load to a high point on the elevated road. A thundering crash came to Krenner's ears as its bottom opened to dislodge its contents. Without stopping. Without men. Automatically. From below he could hear a rushing, roaring sound, and the air was suddenly warmer than before—

The next car followed the first. And the next. Krenner scrambled to the top of the car in rising horror as the car ahead moved serenely, jerked suddenly, and jolted loose its load with a crash of coal against steel. Twenty tons of coal hurtled down a chute into roaring redness—

Twenty-seven years had changed things. He hadn't heard men, for there were no men. No men to tend the fires. Glowing, white-hot furnaces, Markson's furnaces, which were fed on a regular, unerring, merciless consignment belt, running directly from the Roads. Efficient, economical, completely automatic.

Krenner's car gave a jolt that threw his head against the side and shook him down onto the coal load like a bag of potatoes. He clawed desperately for a grip on the side, clawed and missed. The bottom of the car opened, and the load fell through with a roar, and the roar drowned his feeble scream as Krenner fell with the coal.

The last thing he saw below, rushing up, was the glowing, blistering, white-hot maw of the blast furnace.

SECOND SIGHT

(Note: The following excerpts from Amy Ballantine's journal have never actually been written down at any time before. Her account of impressions and events has been kept in organized fashion in her mind for at least nine years (even she is not certain when she started), but it must be understood that certain inaccuracies in transcription could not possibly have been avoided in the excerpting attempted here. *The Editor.*)

*

Tuesday, 16 May. Lambertson got back from Boston about two this afternoon. He was tired; I don't think I've ever seen Lambertson so tired. It was more than just exhaustion, too. Maybe anger? Frustration? I couldn't be sure. It seemed more like *defeat* than anything else, and he went straight from the 'copter to his office without even stopping off at the lab at all.

It's good to have him back, though! Not that I haven't had a nice enough rest. With Lambertson gone, Dakin took over the reins for the week, but Dakin doesn't really count, poor man. It's such a temptation to twist him up and get him all confused that I didn't do any real *work* all week. With Lambertson back I'll have to get down to the grind again, but I'm still glad he's here. I never thought I'd miss him so, for such a short time away.

But I wish he'd gotten a rest, if he ever rests! And I wish I knew why he went to Boston in the first place. Certainly he didn't *want* to go. I wanted to read him and find out, but I don't think I'm supposed to know yet. Lambertson didn't want to talk. He didn't even tell me he was back, even though he knew I'd catch him five miles down the road. (I can do that now, with Lambertson. Distance doesn't seem to make so much difference any more if I just ignore it.)

So all I got was bits and snatches on the surface of his mind. Something about me, and Dr. Custer; and a nasty little man called Aarons or Barrons or something. I've heard of him somewhere, but I can't pin it down right now. I'll have to dig that out later, I guess.

But if he saw Dr. Custer, *why doesn't he tell me about it?*

*

Wednesday, 17 May. It was *Aarons* that he saw in Boston, and now I'm sure that something's going wrong. I know that man. I remember him from a long time ago, back when I was still at Bairdsley, long before I came here to the Study Center. He was the consulting psychiatrist, and I don't think I could ever forget him, even if I tried!

That's why I'm sure something very unpleasant is going on.

Lambertson saw Dr. Custer, too, but the directors sent him to Boston because Aarons wanted to talk to him. I wasn't supposed to know anything about it, but Lambertson came down to dinner last night. He wouldn't even look at me, the skunk. I fixed *him*. I told him I was going to peek, and then I read him in a flash, before he could shift his mind to Boston traffic or something. (He knows I can't stand traffic.)

I only picked up a little, but it was enough. There was something very unpleasant that Aarons had said that I couldn't quite get. They were in his office. Lambertson had said, "I don't think she's ready for it, and I'd never try to talk her into it, at this point. Why can't you people get it through your heads that she's a *child*, and a human being, not some kind of laboratory animal? That's been the trouble all along. Everybody has been so eager to *grab*, and nobody has given her a wretched thing in return."

Aarons was smooth. Very sad and reproachful. I got a clear picture of him—short, balding, mean little eyes in a smug, self-righteous little face. "Michael, after all she's twenty-three years old. She's certainly out of diapers by now."

"But she's only had two years of training aimed at teaching *her* anything."

"Well, there's no reason that *that* should stop, is there? Be reasonable, Michael. We certainly agree that you've done a wonderful job with the girl, and naturally you're sensitive about others working with her. But when you consider that public taxes are footing the bill—"

"I'm sensitive about others exploiting her, that's all. I tell you, I won't push her. And I wouldn't let her come up here, even if she agreed to do it. She shouldn't be tampered with for another year or two at least." Lambertson was angry and bitter. Now, three days later, he was still angry.

"And you're certain that your concern is entirely—professional?" (Whatever Aarons meant, it wasn't nice. Lambertson caught it, and oh, my! Chart slapping down on the table, door slamming, swearing—from mild, patient Lambertson, can you imagine? And then later, no more anger, just disgust and defeat. That was what hit me when he came back yesterday. He couldn't hide it, no matter how he tried.)

Well, no wonder he was tired. I remember Aarons all right. He wasn't so interested in me, back in those days. *Wild one*, he called me. *We haven't the time or the people to handle anything like this in a public institution. We have to handle her the way we'd handle any other defective. She may be a* plus-*defective instead of a* minus-*defective, but she's as crippled as if she were deaf and blind.*

Good old Aarons. That was years ago, when I was barely thirteen. Before Dr. Custer got interested and started ophthalmoscoping me and testing me, before I'd ever heard of Lambertson or the Study Center. For that matter, before anybody had done anything but feed me and treat me like some kind of peculiar animal or something.

Well, I'm glad it was Lambertson that went to Boston and not me, for Aarons' sake. And if Aarons tries to come down here to work with me, he's going to be wasting his time, because I'll lead him all around Robin Hood's Barn and get him so confused he'll wish he'd stayed home. But I can't help but wonder, just the same. *Am* I a cripple like Aarons said? Does being psi-high mean that? *I* don't think so, but what does Lambertson think? Sometimes when I try to read Lambertson I'm the one that gets confused. I wish I could tell what he *really* thinks.

*

Wednesday night. I asked Lambertson tonight what Dr. Custer had said. "He wants to see you next week," he told me. "But Amy, he didn't make any promises. He wasn't even hopeful."

"But his letter! He said the studies showed that there wasn't any anatomical defect."

Lambertson leaned back and lit his pipe, shaking his head at me. He's aged ten years this past week. Everybody thinks so. He's lost weight, and he looks as if he hasn't slept at all. "Custer's afraid that it isn't a question of anatomy, Amy."

"But what is it, then, for heaven's sake?"

"He doesn't know. He says it's not very scientific, but it may just be that what you don't use, you lose."

"Oh, but that's silly." I chewed my lip.

"Granted."

"But he thinks that there's a chance?"

"Of course there's a chance. And you know he'll do everything he can. It's just that neither of us wants you to get your hopes up."

It wasn't much, but it was something. Lambertson looked so beat. I didn't have the heart to ask him what Aarons wanted, even though I know he'd like to get it off his chest. Maybe tomorrow will be better.

I spent the day with Charlie Dakin in the lab, and did a little work for a change. I've been disgustingly lazy, and poor Charlie thinks it's all his fault. Charlie reads like twenty-point type ninety per cent of the time, and I'm afraid he knows it. I can tell just exactly when he stops paying attention to business and starts paying attention to *me*, and then all of a sudden he realizes I'm reading him, and it flusters him for the rest of the day. I wonder why? Does he really think I'm shocked? Or surprised? Or *insulted*? Poor Charlie!

I guess I must be good enough looking. I can read it from almost every fellow that comes near me. I wonder why? I mean, why me and not Marjorie over in the Main Office? She's a sweet girl, but she never gets a second look from the guys. There must be some fine differential point I'm missing somewhere, but I don't think I'll ever understand it.

I'm not going to press Lambertson, but I *hope* he opens up tomorrow. He's got me scared silly by now. He has a lot of authority around here, but other people are paying the bills, and when he's frightened about something, it can't help but frighten me.

*

Thursday, 18 May. We went back to reaction testing in the lab with Lambertson today. That study is almost finished, as much as anything I work on is ever finished, which isn't very much. This test had two goals: to clock my stimulus-response pattern in comparison to normals, and to find out just exactly *when* I pick up any given thought-signal from the person I'm reading. It isn't a matter of developing speed. I'm already so fast to respond that it doesn't mean too much from anybody else's standpoint, and I certainly don't need any training there. But where along the line do I pick up a thought impulse? Do I catch it at its inception? Do I pick up the thought formulation, or just the final crystalized pattern? Lambertson thinks I'm with it right from the start, and that some training in those lines would be worth my time.

Of course, we didn't find out, not even with the ingenious little random-firing device that Dakin designed for the study. With this gadget, neither Lambertson nor I know what impulse the box is going to throw at him. He just throws a switch and it starts coming. He catches it, reacts, I catch it from him and react, and we compare reaction times. This afternoon it had us driving up a hill, and sent a ten-ton truck rolling down on us out of control. I had my flasher on two seconds before Lambertson did, of course, but our reaction times are standardized, so when we corrected for my extra speed, we knew that I must have caught the impulse about 0.07 seconds after he did.

Crude, of course, not nearly fast enough, and we can't reproduce on a stable basis. Lambertson says that's as close as we can get without cortical probes. And that's where I put my foot down. I may have a gold mine in this head of mine, but nobody is going to put burr-holes through my skull in order to tap it. Not for a while yet.

That's unfair, of course, because it sounds as if Lambertson were trying to force me into something, and he isn't. I've read him about that, and I know he wouldn't allow it. *Let's learn everything else we can learn without it first*, he says. *Later, if you want to go along with it, maybe. But right now you're not competent to decide for yourself.*

He may be right, but why not? Why does he keep acting as if I'm a child? *Am* I, really? With everything (and I mean *everything*) coming into my mind for the past twenty-three years, haven't I learned enough to make decisions for myself? Lambertson says of course everything has been coming in, it's just that I don't know what to do with it all. But somewhere along the line I have to reach a maturation point of some kind.

It scares me, sometimes, because I can't find an answer to it and the answer might be perfectly horrible. I don't know where it may end. What's worse, I don't know what point it has reached *right now*. How much difference is there between my mind and Lambertson's? I'm psi-high, and he isn't—granted. But is there more to it than that? People like Aarons think so. They think it's a difference between *human* function and something else.

And that scares me because it *just isn't true*. I'm as human as anybody else. But somehow it seems that I'm the one who has to prove it. I wonder if I ever will. That's why Dr. Custer has to help me. Everything hangs on that. I'm to go up to Boston next week, for final studies and testing.

If Dr. Custer can do something, what a difference that will make! Maybe then I could get out of this whole frightening mess, put it behind me and forget about it. With just the psi alone, I don't think I ever can.

*

Friday, 19 May. Today Lambertson broke down and told me what it was that Aarons had been proposing. It was worse than I thought it would be. The man had hit on the one thing I'd been afraid of for so long.

"He wants you to work against normals," Lambertson said. "He's swallowed the latency hypothesis whole. He thinks that everybody must have a latent psi potential, and that all that is needed to drag it into the open is a powerful stimulus from someone with full-blown psi powers."

"Well?" I said. "Do you think so?"

"Who knows?" Lambertson slammed his pencil down on the desk angrily. "No, I don't think so, but what does that mean? Not a thing. It certainly doesn't mean I'm right. Nobody knows the answer, not me, nor Aarons, nor anybody. And Aarons wants to use you to find out."

I nodded slowly. "I see. So I'm to be used as a sort of refined electrical stimulator," I said. "Well, I guess you know what you can tell Aarons."

He was silent, and I couldn't read him. Then he looked up. "Amy, I'm not sure we can tell him that."

I stared at him. "You mean you think he could *force* me?"

"He says you're a public charge, that as long as you have to be supported and cared for, they have the right to use your faculties. He's right on the first point. You *are* a public charge. You have to be sheltered and protected. If you wandered so much as a mile outside these walls you'd never survive, and you know it."

I sat stunned. "But Dr. Custer—"

"Dr. Custer is trying to help. But he hasn't succeeded so far. If he can, then it will be a different story. But I can't stall much longer, Amy. Aarons has a powerful argument. You're psi-high. You're the first full-fledged, wide-open, free-wheeling psi-high that's ever appeared in human history. The *first*. Others in the past have shown potential, maybe, but nothing they could ever learn to control. You've got control, you're fully developed. You're *here*, and you're *the only one there is*."

"So I happened to be unlucky," I snapped. "My genes got mixed up."

"That's not true, and you know it," Lambertson said. "We know your chromosomes better than your face. They're the same as anyone else's. There's no gene difference, none at all. When you're gone, you'll be *gone*, and there's no reason to think that your children will have any more psi potential than Charlie Dakin has."

Something was building up in me then that I couldn't control any longer. "You think I should go along with Aarons," I said dully.

He hesitated. "I'm afraid you're going to have to, sooner or later. Aarons has some latents up in Boston. He's certain that they're latents. He's talked to the directors down here. He's convinced them that you could work with his people, draw them out. You could open the door to a whole new world for human beings."

I lost my temper then. It wasn't just Aarons, or Lambertson, or Dakin, or any of the others. It was *all* of them, dozens of them, compounded year upon year upon year. "Now listen to me for a minute," I said. "Have any of you ever considered what *I* wanted in this thing? *Ever?* Have any of you given that one single thought, just once, one time when you were so sick of thinking great thoughts for humanity that you let another thought leak through? Have you ever thought about what kind of a shuffle I've had since all this started? Well, you'd better think about it. *Right now.*"

"Amy, you know I don't want to push you."

"Listen to me, Lambertson. My folks got rid of me fast when they found out about me. Did you know that? They hated me because I *scared* them! It didn't hurt me too much, because I thought I knew *why* they hated me, I could understand it, and I went off to Bairdsley without even crying. They were going to come see me every week, but do you know how often they managed to make it? *Not once* after I was off their hands. And then at Bairdsley Aarons examined me and decided that I was a cripple. He didn't know anything about me then, but he thought psi was a *defect*. And that was as far as it went. I did what Aarons wanted me to do at Bairdsley. Never what *I* wanted, just what *they* wanted, years and years of what *they* wanted. And then you came along, and I came to the Study Center and did what *you* wanted."

It hurt him, and I knew it. I guess that was what I wanted, to hurt him and to hurt everybody. He was shaking his head, staring at me. "Amy, be fair. I've tried, you know how hard I've tried."

"Tried what? To train me? Yes, but why? To give me better use of my psi faculties? Yes, but why? Did you do it for *me*? Is that really why you did it? Or was that just another phoney front, like all the rest of them, in order to use me, to make me a little more valuable to have around?"

He slapped my face so hard it jolted me. I could feel the awful pain and hurt in his mind as he stared at me, and I sensed the stinging in his palm that matched the burning in my cheek. And then something fell away in his mind, and I saw something I had never seen before.

He loved me, that man. Incredible, isn't it? He *loved* me. Me, who couldn't call him anything but Lambertson, who couldn't imagine calling him Michael, to say nothing of Mike—just Lambertson, who did this, or Lambertson who thought that.

But he could never tell me. He had decided that. I was too helpless. I needed him too much. I needed love, but not the kind of love Lambertson wanted to give, so that kind of love had to be hidden, concealed, *suppressed*. I needed the deepest imaginable understanding, but it had to be utterly unselfish understanding, anything else would be taking advantage of me, so a barrier had to be built—a barrier that I should never penetrate and that he should never be tempted to break down.

Lambertson had done that. For me. It was all there, suddenly, so overwhelming it made me gasp from the impact. I wanted to throw my arms around him; instead I sat down in the chair, shaking my head helplessly. I hated myself then. I had hated myself before, but never like this.

"If I could only go somewhere," I said. "Someplace where nobody knew me, where I could just live by myself for a while, and shut the doors, and shut out the thoughts, and *pretend* for a while, just pretend that I'm perfectly normal."

"I wish you could," Lambertson said. "But you can't. You know that. Not unless Custer can really help."

We sat there for a while. Then I said, "Let Aarons come down. Let him bring anybody he wants with him. I'll do what he wants. Until I see Custer."

That hurt, too, but it was different. It hurt both of us together, not separately any more. And somehow it didn't hurt so much that way.

*

Monday, 22 May. Aarons drove down from Boston this morning with a girl named Mary Bolton, and we went to work.

I think I'm beginning to understand how a dog can tell when someone wants to kick him and doesn't quite dare. I could feel the back of my neck prickle when that man walked into the conference room. I was hoping he might have changed since the last time I saw him. He hadn't, but I had. I wasn't afraid of him any more, just awfully tired of him after he'd been here about ten minutes.

But that girl! I wonder what sort of story he'd told her? She couldn't have been more than sixteen, and she was terrorized. At first I thought it was *Aarons* she was afraid of, but that wasn't so. It was *me*.

It took us all morning just to get around that. The poor girl could hardly make herself talk. She was shaking all over when they arrived. We took a walk around the grounds, alone, and I read her bit by bit—a feeler here, a planted suggestion there, just getting her used to the idea and trying to reassure her. After a while she was smiling. She thought the lagoon was lovely, and by the time we got back to the main building she was laughing, talking about herself, beginning to relax.

Then I gave her a full blast, quickly, only a moment or two. *Don't be afraid—I hate him, yes, but I won't hurt you for anything. Let me come in, don't fight me. We've got to work as a team.*

It shook her. She turned white and almost passed out for a moment. Then she nodded, slowly. "I see," she said. "It feels as if it's way inside, *deep* inside."

"That's right. It won't hurt. I promise."

She nodded again. "Let's go back, now. I think I'm ready to try."

We went to work.

I was as blind as she was, at first. There was nothing there, at first, not even a flicker of brightness. Then, probing deeper, something responded, only a hint, a suggestion of something powerful, deep and hidden—but where? What was her strength? Where was she weak? I couldn't tell.

We started on dice, crude, of course, but as good a tool as any. Dice are no good for measuring anything, but that was why I was there. I was the measuring instrument. The dice were only reactors. Sensitive enough, two balsam cubes, tossed from a box with only gravity to work against. I showed her first, picked up her mind as the dice popped out, led her through it. *Take one at a time, the red one first. Work on it, see? Now we try both. Once more—watch it! All right, now.*

She sat frozen in the chair. She was trying; the sweat stood out on her forehead. Aarons sat tense, smoking, his fingers twitching as he watched the red and green cubes bounce on the white backdrop. Lambertson watched too, but his eyes were on the girl, not on the cubes.

It was hard work. Bit by bit she began to grab; whatever I had felt in her mind seemed to leap up. I probed her, amplifying it, trying to draw it out. It was like wading through knee-deep mud—sticky, sluggish, resisting. I could feel her excitement growing, and bit by bit I released my grip, easing her out, baiting her.

"All right," I said. "That's enough."

She turned to me, wide-eyed. "I—I did it."

Aarons was on his feet, breathing heavily. "It worked?"

"It worked. Not very well, but it's there. All she needs is time, and help, and patience."

"But it worked! Lambertson! Do you know what that means? It means I was right! It means others can have it, just like she has it!" He rubbed his hands together. "We can arrange a full-time lab for it, and work on three or four latents simultaneously. It's a wide-open door, Michael! Can't you see what it means?"

Lambertson nodded, and gave me a long look. "Yes, I think I do."

"I'll start arrangements tomorrow."

"Not tomorrow. You'll have to wait until next week."

"Why?"

"Because Amy would prefer to wait, that's why."

Aarons looked at him, and then at me, peevishly. Finally he shrugged. "If you insist."

"We'll talk about it next week," I said. I was so tired I could hardly look up at him. I stood up, and smiled at my girl. Poor kid, I thought. So excited and eager about it now. And not one idea in the world of what she was walking into.

Certainly Aarons would never be able to tell her.

*

Later, when they were gone, Lambertson and I walked down toward the lagoon. It was a lovely cool evening; the ducks were down at the water's edge. Every year there was a mother duck herding a line of ducklings down the shore and into the water. They never seemed to go where she wanted them to, and she would fuss and chatter, waddling back time and again to prod the reluctant ones out into the pool.

We stood by the water's edge in silence for a long time. Then Lambertson kissed me. It was the first time he had ever done that.

"We could go away," I whispered in his ear. "We could run out on Aarons and the Study Center and everyone, just go away somewhere."

He shook his head slowly. "Amy, don't."

"We could! I'll see Dr. Custer, and he'll tell me he can help, I *know* he will. I won't *need* the Study Center any more, or any other place, or anybody but you."

He didn't answer, and I knew there wasn't anything he could answer. Not then.

*

Friday, 26 May. Yesterday we went to Boston to see Dr. Custer, and now it looks as if it's all over. Now even I can't pretend that there's anything more to be done.

Next week Aarons will come down, and I'll go to work with him just the way he has it planned. He thinks we have three years of work ahead of us before anything can be published, before he can really be sure we have brought a latent into full use of his psi potential. Maybe so, I don't know. Maybe in three years I'll find some way to make myself care one way or the other. But I'll do it, anyway, because there's nothing else to do.

There was no anatomical defect—Dr. Custer was right about that. The eyes are perfect, beautiful gray eyes, he says, and the optic nerves and auditory nerves are perfectly functional. The defect isn't there. It's deeper. Too deep ever to change it.

What you no longer use, you lose, was what he said, apologizing because he couldn't explain it any better. It's like a price tag, perhaps. Long ago, before I knew anything at all, the psi was so strong it started compensating, bringing in more and more from *other* minds—such a wealth of rich, clear, interpreted visual and auditory impressions that there was never any need for my own. And because of that, certain hookups never got hooked up. That's only a theory, of course, but there isn't any other way to explain it.

But am I wrong to hate it? More than anything else in the world I want to *see* Lambertson, *see* him smile and light his pipe, *hear* him laugh. I want to know what color *really* is, what music *really* sounds like unfiltered through somebody else's ears.

I want to see a sunset, just once. Just once I want to see that mother duck take her ducklings down to the water. But I never will. Instead, I see and hear things nobody else can, and the fact that I am stone blind and stone deaf shouldn't make any difference. After all, I've always been that way.

Maybe next week I'll ask Aarons what he thinks about it. It should be interesting to hear what he says.

PRoBLEM

The letter came down the slot too early that morning to be the regular mail run. Pete Greenwood eyed the New Philly photocancel with a dreadful premonition. The letter said:

PETER:
Can you come East chop-chop, urgent?
Grdznth problem getting to be a PRoblem, need expert
icebox salesman to get gators out of hair fast.
Yes? Math boys hot on this, citizens not so hot.
Please come.

TOMMY

Pete tossed the letter down the gulper with a sigh. He had lost a bet to himself because it had come three days later than he expected, but it had come all the same, just as it always did when Tommy Heinz got himself into a hole.

Not that he didn't like Tommy. Tommy was a good PR-man, as PR-men go. He just didn't know his own depth. PRoblem in a beady Grdznth eye! What Tommy needed right now was a Bazooka Battalion, not a PR-man. Pete settled back in the Eastbound Rocketjet with a sigh of resignation.

He was just dozing off when the fat lady up the aisle let out a scream. A huge reptilian head had materialized out of nowhere and was hanging in air, peering about uncertainly. A scaly green body followed, four feet away, complete with long razor talons, heavy hind legs, and a whiplash tail with a needle at the end. For a moment the creature floated upside down, legs thrashing. Then the head and body joined, executed a horizontal pirouette, and settled gently to the floor like an eight-foot circus balloon.

Two rows down a small boy let out a muffled howl and tried to bury himself in his mother's coat collar. An indignant wail arose from the fat lady. Someone behind Pete groaned aloud and quickly retired behind a newspaper.

The creature coughed apologetically. "Terribly sorry," he said in a coarse rumble. "So difficult to control, you know. Terribly sorry...." His voice trailed off as he lumbered down the aisle toward the empty seat next to Pete.

The fat lady gasped, and an angry murmur ran up and down the cabin. "Sit down," Pete said to the creature. "Relax. Cheerful reception these days, eh?"

"You don't mind?" said the creature.

"Not at all." Pete tossed his briefcase on the floor. At a distance the huge beast had looked like a nightmare combination of large alligator and small tyrannosaurus. Now, at close range Pete could see that the "scales" were actually tiny wrinkles of satiny green fur. He knew, of course, that the Grdznth were mammals—"docile, peace-loving mammals," Tommy's PR-blasts had declared emphatically—but with one of them sitting about a foot away Pete had to fight down a wave of horror and revulsion.

The creature was most incredibly ugly. Great yellow pouches hung down below flat reptilian eyes, and a double row of long curved teeth glittered sharply. In spite of himself Pete gripped the seat as the Grdznth breathed at him wetly through damp nostrils.

"Misgauged?" said Pete.

The Grdznth nodded sadly. "It's horrible of me, but I just can't help it. I *always* misgauge. Last time it was the chancel of St. John's Cathedral. I nearly stampeded morning prayer—" He paused to catch his breath. "What an effort. The energy barrier, you know. Frightfully hard to make the jump." He broke off sharply, staring out the window. "Dear me! Are we going *east?*"

"I'm afraid so, friend."

"Oh, dear. I wanted *Florida.*"

"Well, you seem to have drifted through into the wrong airplane," said Pete. "Why Florida?"

The Grdznth looked at him reproachfully. "The Wives, of course. The climate is so much better, and they mustn't be disturbed, you know."

"Of course," said Pete. "In their condition. I'd forgotten."

"And I'm told that things have been somewhat unpleasant in the East just now," said the Grdznth.

Pete thought of Tommy, red-faced and frantic, beating off hordes of indignant citizens. "So I hear," he said. "How many more of you are coming through?"

"Oh, not many, not many at all. Only the Wives—half a million or so—and their spouses, of course." The creature clicked his talons nervously.

"We haven't much more time, you know. Only a few more weeks, a few months at the most. If we couldn't have stopped over here, I just don't know *what* we'd have done."

"Think nothing of it," said Pete indulgently. "It's been great having you."

The passengers within earshot stiffened, glaring at Pete. The fat lady was whispering indignantly to her seat companion. Junior had half emerged from his mother's collar; he was busy sticking out his tongue at the Grdznth.

The creature shifted uneasily. "Really, I think—perhaps Florida would be better."

"Going to try it again right now? Don't rush off," said Pete.

"Oh, I don't mean to rush. It's been lovely, but—" Already the Grdznth was beginning to fade out.

"Try four miles down and a thousand miles southeast," said Pete.

The creature gave him a toothy smile, nodded once, and grew more indistinct. In another five seconds the seat was quite empty. Pete leaned back, grinning to himself as the angry rumble rose around him like a wave. He was a Public Relations man to the core—but right now he was off duty. He chuckled to himself, and the passengers avoided him like the plague all the way to New Philly.

But as he walked down the gangway to hail a cab, he wasn't smiling so much. He was wondering just how high Tommy was hanging him, this time.

*

The lobby of the Public Relations Bureau was swarming like an upturned anthill when Pete disembarked from the taxi. He could almost smell the desperate tension of the place. He fought his way past scurrying clerks and preoccupied poll-takers toward the executive elevators in the rear.

On the newly finished seventeenth floor, he found Tommy Heinz pacing the corridor like an expectant young father. Tommy had lost weight since Pete had last seen him. His ruddy face was paler, his hair thin and ragged as though chunks had been torn out from time to time. He saw Pete step off the elevator, and ran forward with open arms. "I thought you'd never get here!" he groaned. "When you didn't call, I was afraid you'd let me down."

"Me?" said Pete. "I'd never let down a pal."

The sarcasm didn't dent Tommy. He led Pete through the ante-room into the plush director's office, bouncing about excitedly, his words tumbling out like a waterfall. He looked as though one gentle shove might send him yodeling down Market Street in his underdrawers. "Hold it," said Pete. "Relax, I'm not going to leave for a while yet. Your girl screamed something about a senator as we came in. Did you hear her?"

Tommy gave a violent start. "Senator! Oh, dear." He flipped a desk switch. "What senator is that?"

"Senator Stokes," the girl said wearily. "He had an appointment. He's ready to have you fired."

"All I need now is a senator," Tommy said. "What does he want?"

"Guess," said the girl.

"Oh. That's what I was afraid of. Can you keep him there?"

"Don't worry about that," said the girl. "He's growing roots. They swept around him last night, and dusted him off this morning. His appointment was for *yesterday*, remember?"

"Remember! Of course I remember. Senator Stokes—something about a riot in Boston." He started to flip the switch, then added, "See if you can get Charlie down here with his giz."

He turned back to Pete with a frantic light in his eye. "Good old Pete. Just in time. Just. Eleventh-hour reprieve. Have a drink, have a cigar—do you want my job? It's yours. Just speak up."

"I fail to see," said Pete, "just why you had to drag me all the way from L.A. to have a cigar. I've got work to do."

"Selling movies, right?" said Tommy.

"Check."

"To people who don't want to buy them, right?"

"In a manner of speaking," said Pete testily.

"Exactly," said Tommy. "Considering some of the movies you've been selling, you should be able to sell anything to anybody, any time, at any price."

"Please. Movies are getting Better by the Day."

"Yes, I know. And the Grdznth are getting worse by the hour. They're coming through in battalions—a thousand a day! The more Grdznth come through, the more they act as though they own the place. Not nasty or anything—it's that infernal politeness that people hate most, I think. Can't get them mad, can't get them into a fight, but they do anything they please, and go anywhere they please, and if the people don't like it, the Grdznth just go right ahead anyway."

Pete pulled at his lip. "Any violence?"

Tommy gave him a long look. "So far we've kept it out of the papers, but there have been some incidents. Didn't hurt the Grdznth a bit—they have personal protective force fields around them, a little point they didn't bother to tell us about. Anybody who tries anything fancy gets thrown like a bolt of lightning hit him. Rumors are getting wild—people saying they can't be killed, that they're just moving in to stay."

Pete nodded slowly. "Are they?"

"I wish I knew. I mean, for sure. The psych-docs say no. The Grdznth agreed to leave at a specified time, and something in their cultural background makes them stick strictly to their agreements. But that's just what the psych-docs think, and they've been known to be wrong."

"And the appointed time?"

Tommy spread his hands helplessly. "If we knew, you'd still be in L.A. Roughly six months and four days, plus or minus a month for the time differential. That's strictly tentative, according to the math boys. It's a parallel universe, one of several thousand already explored, according to the Grdznth scientists working with Charlie Karns. Most of the parallels are analogous, and we happen to be analogous to the Grdznth, a point we've omitted from our PR-blasts. They have an eight-planet system around a hot sun, and it's going to get lots hotter any day now."

Pete's eyes widened. "Nova?"

"Apparently. Nobody knows how they predicted it, but they did. Spotted it coming several years ago, so they've been romping through parallel after parallel trying to find one they can migrate to. They found one, sort of a desperation choice. It's cold and arid and full of impassable mountain chains. With an uphill fight they can make it support a fraction of their population."

Tommy shook his head helplessly. "They picked a very sensible system for getting a good strong Grdznth population on the new parallel as fast as possible. The males were picked for brains, education, ability and adaptability; the females were chosen largely according to how pregnant they were."

Pete grinned. "Grdznth in utero. There's something poetic about it."

"Just one hitch," said Tommy. "The girls can't gestate in that climate, at least not until they've been there long enough to get their glands adjusted. Seems we have just the right climate here for gestating Grdznth, even better than at home. So they came begging for permission to stop here, on the way through, to rest and parturiate."

"So Earth becomes a glorified incubator." Pete got to his feet thoughtfully. "This is all very touching," he said, "but it just doesn't wash. If the Grdznth are so unpopular with the masses, why did we let them in here in the first place?" He looked narrowly at Tommy. "To be very blunt, what's the parking fee?"

"Plenty," said Tommy heavily. "That's the trouble, you see. The fee is so high, Earth just can't afford to lose it. Charlie Karns'll tell you why."

*

Charlie Karns from Math Section was an intense skeleton of a man with a long jaw and a long white coat drooping over his shoulders like a shroud. In his arms he clutched a small black box.

"It's the parallel universe business, of course," he said to Pete, with Tommy beaming over his shoulder. "The Grdznth can cross through. They've been able to do it for a long time. According to our figuring, this must involve complete control of mass, space and dimension, all three. And time comes into one of the three—we aren't sure which."

The mathematician set the black box on the desk top and released the lid. Like a jack-in-the-box, two small white plastic spheres popped out and began chasing each other about in the air six inches above the box. Presently a third sphere rose up from the box and joined the fun.

Pete watched it with his jaw sagging until his head began to spin. "No wires?"

"*Strictly* no wires," said Charlie glumly. "No nothing." He closed the box with a click. "This is one of their children's toys, and theoretically, it can't work. Among other things, it takes null-gravity to operate."

Pete sat down, rubbing his chin. "Yes," he said. "I'm beginning to see. They're teaching you this?"

Tommy said, "They're trying to. He's been working for weeks with their top mathematicians, him and a dozen others. How many computers have you burned out, Charlie?"

"Four. There's a differential factor, and we can't spot it. They have the equations, all right. It's a matter of translating them into constants that make sense. But we haven't cracked the differential."

"And if you do, then what?"

Charlie took a deep breath. "We'll have inter-dimensional control, a practical, utilizable transmatter. We'll have null-gravity, which means the greatest advance in power utilization since fire was discovered. It might give us the opening to a concept of time travel that makes some kind of sense. And power! If there's an energy differential of any magnitude—" He shook his head sadly.

"We'll also know the time-differential," said Tommy hopefully, "and how long the Grdznth gestation period will be."

"It's a fair exchange," said Charlie. "We keep them until the girls have their babies. They teach us the ABC's of space, mass and dimension."

Pete nodded. "That is, if you can make the people put up with them for another six months or so."

Tommy sighed. "In a word—yes. So far we've gotten nowhere at a thousand miles an hour."

*

"I can't do it!" the cosmetician wailed, hurling himself down on a chair and burying his face in his hands. "I've failed. Failed!"

The Grdznth sitting on the stool looked regretfully from the cosmetician to the Public Relations men. "I say—I *am* sorry...." His coarse voice trailed off as he peeled a long strip of cake makeup off his satiny green face.

Pete Greenwood stared at the cosmetician sobbing in the chair. "What's eating *him*?"

"Professional pride," said Tommy. "He can take twenty years off the face of any woman in Hollywood. But he's not getting to first base with Gorgeous over there. This is only one thing we've tried," he added as they moved on down the corridor. "You should see the field reports. We've tried selling the advances Earth will have, the wealth, the power. No dice. The man on the street reads our PR-blasts, and then looks up to see one of the nasty things staring over his shoulder at the newspaper."

"So you can't make them beautiful," said Pete. "Can't you make them cute?"

"With those teeth? Those eyes? Ugh."

"How about the 'jolly company' approach?"

"Tried it. There's nothing jolly about them. They pop out of nowhere, anywhere. In church, in bedrooms, in rush-hour traffic through Lincoln Tunnel—look!"

Pete peered out the window at the traffic jam below. Cars were snarled up for blocks on either side of the intersection. A squad of traffic cops were converging angrily on the center of the mess, where a stream of green reptilian figures seemed to be popping out of the street and lumbering through the jammed autos like General Sherman tanks.

"Ulcers," said Tommy. "City traffic isn't enough of a mess as it is. And they don't *do* anything about it. They apologize profusely, but they keep coming through." The two started on for the office. "Things are getting to the breaking point. The people are wearing thin from sheer annoyance—to say nothing of the nightmares the kids are having, and the trouble with women fainting."

The signal light on Tommy's desk was flashing scarlet. He dropped into a chair with a sigh and flipped a switch. "Okay, what is it now?"

"Just another senator," said a furious male voice. "Mr. Heinz, my arthritis is beginning to win this fight. Are you going to see me now, or aren't you?"

"Yes, yes, come right in!" Tommy turned white. "Senator Stokes," he muttered. "I'd completely forgotten—"

The senator didn't seem to like being forgotten. He walked into the office, looked disdainfully at the PR-men, and sank to the edge of a chair, leaning on his umbrella.

"You have just lost your job," he said to Tommy, with an icy edge to his voice. "You may not have heard about it yet, but you can take my word for it. I personally will be delighted to make the necessary arrangements, but I doubt if I'll need to. There are at least a hundred senators in Washington who are ready to press for your dismissal, Mr. Heinz—and there's been some off-the-record talk about a lynching. Nothing official, of course."

"Senator—"

"Senator be hanged! We want somebody in this office who can manage to *do* something."

"Do something! You think I'm a magician? I can just make them vanish? What do you want me to do?"

The senator raised his eyebrows. "You needn't shout, Mr. Heinz. I'm not the least interested in *what* you do. My interest is focused completely on a collection of five thousand letters, telegrams, and visiphone calls I've received in the past three days alone. My constituents, Mr. Heinz, are making themselves clear. If the Grdznth do not go, I go."

"That would never do, of course," murmured Pete.

The senator gave Pete a cold, clinical look. "Who is this person?" he asked Tommy.

"An assistant on the job," Tommy said quickly. "A very excellent PR-man."

The senator sniffed audibly. "Full of ideas, no doubt."

"Brimming," said Pete. "Enough ideas to get your constituents off your neck for a while, at least."

"Indeed."

"Indeed," said Pete. "Tommy, how fast can you get a PR-blast to penetrate? How much medium do you control?"

"Plenty," Tommy gulped.

"And how fast can you sample response and analyze it?"

"We can have prelims six hours after the PR-blast. Pete, if you have an idea, tell us!"

Pete stood up, facing the senator. "Everything else has been tried, but it seems to me one important factor has been missed. One that will take your constituents by the ears." He looked at Tommy pityingly. "You've tried to make them lovable, but they aren't lovable. They aren't even passably attractive. There's one thing they *are* though, at least half of them."

Tommy's jaw sagged. "Pregnant," he said.

"Now see here," said the senator. "If you're trying to make a fool out of me to my face—"

"Sit down and shut up," said Pete. "If there's one thing the man in the street reveres, my friend, it's motherhood. We've got several hundred thousand pregnant Grdznth just waiting for all the little Grdznth to arrive, and nobody's given them a side glance." He turned to Tommy. "Get some copywriters down here. Get a Grdznth obstetrician or two. We're going to put together a PR-blast that will twang the people's heart-strings like a billion harps."

The color was back in Tommy's cheeks, and the senator was forgotten as a dozen intercom switches began snapping. "We'll need TV hookups, and plenty of newscast space," he said eagerly. "Maybe a few photographs—do you suppose maybe *baby* Grdznth are lovable?"

"They probably look like salamanders," said Pete. "But tell the people anything you want. If we're going to get across the sanctity of Grdznth motherhood, my friend, anything goes."

"It's genius," chortled Tommy. "Sheer genius."

"If it sells," the senator added, dubiously.

"It'll sell," Pete said. "The question is: for how long?"

*

The planning revealed the mark of genius. Nothing sudden, harsh, or crude—but slowly, in a radio comment here or a newspaper story there, the emphasis began to shift from Grdznth in general to Grdznth as mothers. A Rutgers professor found his TV discussion on "Motherhood as an Experience" suddenly shifted from 6:30 Monday evening to 10:30 Saturday night. Copy rolled by the ream from Tommy's office, refined copy, hypersensitively edited copy, finding its way into the light of day through devious channels.

Three days later a Grdznth miscarriage threatened, and was averted. It was only a page 4 item, but it was a beginning.

Determined movements to expel the Grdznth faltered, trembled with indecision. The Grdznth were ugly, they frightened little children, they *were* a trifle overbearing in their insufferable stubborn politeness—but in a civilized world you just couldn't turn expectant mothers out in the rain.

Not even expectant Grdznth mothers.

By the second week the blast was going at full tilt.

In the Public Relations Bureau building, machines worked on into the night. As questionnaires came back, spot candid films and street-corner interview tapes ran through the projectors on a twenty-four-hour schedule. Tommy Heinz grew thinner and thinner, while Pete nursed sharp post-prandial stomach pains.

"Why don't people *respond?*" Tommy asked plaintively on the morning the third week started. "Haven't they got any feelings? The blast is washing over them like a wave and there they sit!" He punched the private wire to Analysis for the fourth time that morning. He got a man with a hag-ridden look in his eye. "How soon?"

"You want yesterday's rushes?"

"What do you think I want? Any sign of a lag?"

"Not a hint. Last night's panel drew like a magnet. The D-Date tag you suggested has them by the nose."

"How about the President's talk?"

The man from Analysis grinned. "He should be campaigning."

Tommy mopped his forehead with his shirtsleeve. "Okay. Now listen: we need a special run on all response data we have for tolerance levels. Got that? How soon can we have it?"

Analysis shook his head. "We could only make a guess with the data so far."

"Fine," said Tommy. "Make a guess."

"Give us three hours," said Analysis.

"You've got thirty minutes. Get going."

Turning back to Pete, Tommy rubbed his hands eagerly. "It's starting to sell, boy. I don't know how strong or how good, but it's starting to sell! With the tolerance levels to tell us how long we can expect this program to quiet things down, we can give Charlie a deadline to crack his differential factor, or it's the ax for Charlie." He chuckled to himself, and paced the room in an overflow of nervous energy. "I can see it now. Open shafts instead of elevators. A quick hop to Honolulu for an afternoon on the beach, and back in time for supper. A hundred miles to the gallon for the Sunday driver. When people begin *seeing* what the Grdznth are giving us, they'll welcome them with open arms."

"Hmmm," said Pete.

"Well, why won't they? The people just didn't trust us, that was all. What does the man in the street know about transmatters? Nothing. But give him one, and then try to take it away."

"Sure, sure," said Pete. "It sounds great. Just a little bit *too* great."

Tommy blinked at him. "Too great? Are you crazy?"

"Not crazy. Just getting nervous." Pete jammed his hands into his pockets. "Do you realize where *we're* standing in this thing? We're out on a limb—way out. We're fighting for time—time for Charlie and his gang to crack the puzzle, time for the Grdznth girls to gestate. But what are we hearing from Charlie?"

"Pete, Charlie can't just—"

"That's right," said Pete. "*Nothing* is what we're hearing from Charlie. We've got no transmatter, no null-G, no power, nothing except a whole lot of Grdznth and more coming through just as fast as they can. I'm beginning to wonder what the Grdznth *are* giving us."

"Well, they can't gestate forever."

"Maybe not, but I still have a burning desire to talk to Charlie. Something tells me they're going to be gestating a little too long."

They put through the call, but Charlie wasn't answering. "Sorry," the operator said. "Nobody's gotten through there for three days."

"Three days?" cried Tommy. "What's wrong? Is he dead?"

"Couldn't be. They burned out two more machines yesterday," said the operator. "Killed the switchboard for twenty minutes."

"Get him on the wire," Tommy said. "That's orders."

"Yes, sir. But first they want you in Analysis."

Analysis was a shambles. Paper and tape piled knee-deep on the floor. The machines clattered wildly, coughing out reams of paper to be gulped up by other machines. In a corner office they found the Analysis man, pale but jubilant.

"The Program," Tommy said. "How's it going?"

"You can count on the people staying happy for at least another five months." Analysis hesitated an instant. "If they see some baby-Grdznth at the end of it all."

There was dead silence in the room. "Baby Grdznth," Tommy said finally.

"That's what I said. That's what the people are buying. That's what they'd better get."

Tommy swallowed hard. "And if it happens to be six months?"

Analysis drew a finger across his throat.

Tommy and Pete looked at each other, and Tommy's hands were shaking. "I think," he said, "we'd better find Charlie Karns right now."

*

Math Section was like a tomb. The machines were silent. In the office at the end of the room they found an unshaven Charlie gulping a cup of coffee with a very smug-looking Grdznth. The coffee pot was floating gently about six feet above the desk. So were the Grdznth and Charlie.

"Charlie!" Tommy howled. "We've been trying to get you for hours! The operator—"

"I know, I know." Charlie waved a hand disjointedly. "I told her to go away. I told the rest of the crew to go away, too."

"Then you cracked the differential?"

Charlie tipped an imaginary hat toward the Grdznth. "Spike cracked it," he said. "Spike is a sort of Grdznth genius." He tossed the coffee cup over his shoulder and it ricochetted in graceful slow motion against the far wall. "Now why don't you go away, too?"

Tommy turned purple. "We've got five months," he said hoarsely. "Do you hear me? If they aren't going to have their babies in five months, we're dead men."

Charlie chuckled. "Five months, he says. We figured the babies to come in about three months—right, Spike? Not that it'll make much difference to us." Charlie sank slowly down to the desk. He wasn't laughing any more. "We're never going to see any Grdznth babies. It's going to be a little too cold for that. The energy factor," he mumbled. "Nobody thought of that except in passing. Should have, though, long ago. Two completely independent universes, obviously two energy systems. Incompatible. We were dealing with mass, space and dimension—but the energy differential was the important one."

"What about the energy?"

"We're loaded with it. Super-charged. Packed to the breaking point and way beyond." Charlie scribbled frantically on the desk pad. "Look, it took energy for them to come through—immense quantities of energy. Every one that came through upset the balance, distorted our whole energy pattern. And they knew from the start that the differential was all on their side—a million of them unbalances four billion of us. All they needed to overload us completely was time for enough crossings."

"And we gave it to them." Pete sat down slowly, his face green. "Like a rubber ball with a dent in the side. Push in one side, the other side pops out. And we're the other side. When?"

"Any day now. Maybe any minute." Charlie spread his hands helplessly. "Oh, it won't be bad at all. Spike here was telling me. Mean temperature in only 39 below zero, lots of good clean snow, thousands of nice jagged mountain peaks. A lovely place, really. Just a little too cold for Grdznth. They thought Earth was much nicer."

"For them," whispered Tommy.

"For them," Charlie said.

They saw Tam's shabby clothing and the small, weather-beaten bag he carried, and they ordered him aside from the flow of passengers, and checked his packet of passports and visas with extreme care. Then they ordered him to wait. Tam waited, a chilly apprehension rising in his throat. For fifteen minutes he watched them, helplessly.

Finally, the Spaceport was empty, and the huge liner from the outer Asteroid Rings was being lifted and rolled by the giant hooks and cranes back into its berth for drydock and repair, her curved, meteor-dented hull gleaming dully in the harsh arc lights. Tam watched the creaking cranes, and shivered in the cold night air, feeling hunger and dread gnawing at his stomach. There was none of the elation left, none of the great, expansive, soothing joy at returning to Earth after eight long years of hard work and bitterness. Only the cold, corroding uncertainty, the growing apprehension. Times had changed since that night back in '87—just how much he hardly dared to guess. All he knew was the rumors he had heard, the whispered tales, the frightened eyes and the scarred backs and faces. Tam hadn't believed them then, so remote from Earth. He had just laughed and told himself that the stories weren't true. And now they all welled back into his mind, tightening his throat and making him tremble—

"Hey, Sharkie. Come here."

Tam turned and walked slowly over to the customs official who held his papers. "Everything's in order," he said, half defiantly, looking up at the officer's impassive face. "There isn't any mistake."

"What were you doing in the Rings, Sharkie?" The officer's voice was sharp.

"Indenture. Working off my fare back home."

The officer peered into Tam's face, incredulously. "And you come back here?" He shook his head and turned to the other officer. "I knew these Sharkies were dumb, but I didn't think they were that dumb." He turned back to Tam, his eyes suspicious. "What do you think you're going to do now?"

Tam shrugged, uneasily. "Get a job," he said. "A man's got to eat."

The officers exchanged glances. "How long you been on the Rings?"

"Eight years." Tam looked up at him, anxiously. "Can I have my papers now?"

A cruel grin played over the officer's lips. "Sure," he said, handing back the packet of papers. "Happy job-hunting," he added sardonically. "But remember—the ship's going back to the Rings in a week. You can always sign yourself over for fare—"

"I know," said Tam, turning away sharply. "I know all about how that works." He tucked the papers carefully into a tattered breast pocket, hefted the bag wearily, and began trudging slowly across the cold concrete of the Port toward the street and the Underground. A wave of loneliness, almost overpowering in intensity, swept over him, a feeling of emptiness, bleak and hopeless. A chilly night wind swept through his unkempt blond hair as the automatics let him out into the street, and he saw the large dirty "New Denver Underground" sign with the arrow at the far side of the road. Off to the right, several miles across the high mountain plateau, the great capitol city loomed up, shining like a thousand twinkling stars in the clear cold air. Tam jingled his last few coins listlessly, and started for the downward ramp. Somewhere, down there, he could find a darkened corner, maybe even a bench, where the police wouldn't bother him for a couple of hours. Maybe after a little sleep, he'd find some courage, hidden away somewhere. Just enough to walk into an office and ask for a job.

That, he reflected wearily as he shuffled into the tunnel, would take a lot of courage—

* * * * *

The girl at the desk glanced up at him, indifferent, and turned her eyes back to the letter she was typing. Tam Peters continued to stand, awkwardly, his blond hair rumpled, little crow's-feet of weariness creeping from the corners of his eyes. Slowly he looked around the neat office, feeling a pang of shame at his shabby clothes. He should at least have found some way to shave, he thought, some way to take some of the rumple from his trouser legs. He looked back at the receptionist, and coughed, lightly.

She finished her letter at a leisurely pace, and finally looked up at him, her eyes cold. "Well?"

"I read your ad. I'm looking for a job. I'd like to speak to Mr. Randall."

The girl's eyes narrowed, and she took him in in a rapid, sweeping glance, his high, pale forehead, the shock of mud-blond hair, the thin, sensitive face with the exaggerated lines of approaching middle age, the slightly misty blue eyes. It seemed to Tam that she stared for a full minute, and he shifted uneasily, trying to meet the cold inspection, and failing, finally settling his eyes on her prim, neatly manicured fingers. Her lip curled very slightly. "Mr. Randall can't see you today. He's busy. Try again tomorrow." She turned back to typing.

A flat wave of defeat sprang up in his chest. "The ad said to apply today. The earlier the better."

She sniffed indifferently, and pulled a long white sheet from the desk. "Have you filled out an application?"

"No."

"You can't see Mr. Randall without filling out an application." She pointed to a small table across the room, and he felt her eyes on his back as he shuffled over and sat down.

He began filling out the application with great care, making the printing as neat as he could with the old-style vacuum pen provided. Name, age, sex, race, nationality, planet where born, pre-Revolt experience, post-Revolt experience, preference—try as he would, Tam couldn't keep the ancient pen from leaking, making an unsightly blot near the center of the form. Finally he finished, and handed the paper back to the girl at the desk. Then he sat back and waited.

Another man came in, filled out a form, and waited, too, shooting Tam a black look across the room. In a few moments the girl turned to the man. "Robert Stover?"

"Yuh," said the man, lumbering to his feet. "That's me."

"Mr. Randall will see you now."

The man walked heavily across the room, disappeared into the back office. Tam eyed the clock uneasily, still waiting.

A garish picture on the wall caught his eyes, a large, very poor oil portrait of a very stout, graying man dressed in a ridiculous green suit with a little white turban-like affair on the top of his head. Underneath was a little brass plaque with words Tam could barely make out:

Abraham L. Ferrel
(1947-1986)
Founder and First President Marsport Mines, Incorporated
"Unto such men as these, we look to leadership."

Tam stared at the picture, his lip curling slightly. He glanced anxiously at the clock as another man was admitted to the small back office.

Then another man. Anger began creeping into Tam's face, and he fought to keep the scowl away, to keep from showing his concern. The hands of the clock crept around, then around again. It was almost noon. Not a very new dodge, Tam thought coldly. Not very new at all. Finally the small cold flame of anger got the better of him, and he rose and walked over to the desk. "I'm still here," he said patiently. "I'd like to see Mr. Randall."

The girl stared at him indignantly, and flipped an intercom switch. "That Peters application is still out here," she said brittlely. "Do you want to see him, or not?"

There was a moment of silence. Then the voice on the intercom grated, "Yes, I guess so. Send him in."

The office was smaller, immaculately neat. Two visiphone units hung on a switchboard at the man's elbow. Tam's eyes caught the familiar equipment, recognized the interplanetary power coils on one. Then he turned his eyes to the man behind the desk.

"Now, then, what are you after?" asked the man, settling his bulk down behind the desk, his eyes guarded, revealing a trace of boredom.

* * * * *

Tam was suddenly bitterly ashamed of his shabby appearance, the two-day stubble on his chin. He felt a dampness on his forehead, and tried to muster some of the old power and determination into his voice. "I need a job," he said. "I've had plenty of experience with radio-electronics and remote control power operations. I'd make a good mine-operator—"

"I can read," the man cut in sharply, gesturing toward the application form with the ink blot in the middle. "I read all about your experience. But I can't use you. There aren't any more openings."

Tam's ears went red. "But you're always advertising," he countered. "You don't have to worry about me working on Mars, either—I've worked on Mars before, and I can work six, seven hours, even, without a mask or equipment—"

The man's eyebrows raised slightly. "How very interesting," he said flatly. "The fact remains that there aren't any jobs open for you."

The cold, angry flame flared up in Tam's throat suddenly, forcing out the sense of futility and defeat. "Those other men," he said sharply. "I was here before them. That girl wouldn't let me in—"

Randall's eyes narrowed amusedly. "What a pity," he said sadly. "And just think, I hired every one of them—" His face suddenly hardened, and he sat forward, his eyes glinting coldly. "Get smart, Peters. I think Marsport Mines can somehow manage without you. You or any other Sharkie. The men just don't like to work with Sharkies."

Rage swelled up in Tam's chest, bitter futile rage, beating at his temples and driving away all thought of caution. "Look," he grated, bending over the desk threateningly. "I know the law of this system. There's a fair-employment act on the books. It says that men are to be hired by any company in order of application when they qualify equally in experience. I can prove my experience—"

Randall stood up, his face twisted contemptuously. "Get out of here," he snarled. "You've got nerve, you have, come crawling in here with your law! Where do you think you are?" His voice grated in the still air of the office. "We don't hire Sharkies, law or no law, get that? Now get out of here!"

Tam turned, his ears burning, and strode through the office, blindly, kicking open the door and almost running to the quiet air of the street outside. The girl at the desk yawned, and snickered, and went back to her typing with an unpleasant grin.

Tam walked the street, block after block, seething, futile rage swelling up and bubbling over, curses rising to his lips, clipped off with some last vestige of self-control. At last he turned into a small downtown bar and sank wearily onto a stool near the door. The anger was wearing down now to a sort of empty, hopeless weariness, dulling his senses, exaggerating the hunger in his stomach. He had expected it, he told himself, he had known what the answer would be—but he knew that he had hoped, against hope, against what he had known to be the facts; hoped desperately that maybe someone would listen. Oh, he knew the laws, all right, but he'd had plenty of time to see the courts in action. Unfair employment was almost impossible to make stick under any circumstances, but with the courts rigged the way they were these days—he sighed, and drew out one of his last credit-coins. "Beer," he muttered as the barkeep looked up.

The bartender scowled, his heavy-set face a picture of fashionable distaste. Carefully he filled every other order at the bar. Then he grudgingly set up a small beer, mostly foam, and flung some small-coin change down on the bar before Tam. Tam stared at the glass, the little proud flame of anger flaring slowly.

A fat man, sitting nearby, stared at him for a long moment, then took a long swill of beer from his glass. "'Smatter, Sharkie? Whyncha drink y'r beer 'n get t' hell out o' here?"

Tam stared fixedly at his glass, giving no indication of having heard a word.

The fat man stiffened a trifle, swung around to face him. "God-dam Sharkie's too good to talk to a guy," he snarled loudly. "Whassa-matter, Sharkie, ya deaf?"

Tarn's hand trembled as he reached for the beer, took a short swallow. Shrugging, he set the glass on the bar and got up from his stool. He walked out, feeling many eyes on his back.

He walked. Time became a blur to a mind beaten down by constant rebuff. He became conscious of great weariness of both mind and body. Instinct screamed for rest....

* * * * *

Tam sat up, shaking his head to clear it. He shivered from the chill of the park—the cruel pressure of the bench. He pulled up his collar and moved out into the street again.

There was one last chance. Cautiously his mind skirted the idea, picked it up, regarded it warily, then threw it down again. He had promised himself never to consider it, years before, in the hot, angry days of the Revolt. Even then he had had some inkling of the shape of things, and he had promised himself, bitterly, never to consider that last possibility. Still—

Another night in the cold out-of-doors could kill him. Suddenly he didn't care any more, didn't care about promises, or pride, or anything else. He turned into a public telephone booth, checked an address in the thick New Denver book—

He knew he looked frightful as he stepped onto the elevator, felt the cold eyes turn away from him in distaste. Once he might have been mortified, felt the deep shame creeping up his face, but he didn't care any longer. He just stared ahead at the moving panel, avoiding the cold eyes, until the fifth floor was called.

The office was halfway down the dark hallway. He saw the sign on the door, dimly: "United Continents Bureau of Employment", and down in small letters below, "Planetary Division, David G. Hawke."

Tarn felt the sinking feeling in his stomach, and opened the door apprehensively. It had been years since he had seen Dave, long years filled with violence and change. Those years could change men, too. Tam thought, fearfully; they could make even the greatest men change. He remembered, briefly, his promise to himself, made just after the Revolt, never to trade on past friendships, never to ask favors of those men he had known before, and befriended. With a wave of warmth, the memory of those old days broke through, those days when he had roomed with Dave Hawke, the long, probing talks, the confidences, the deep, rich knowledge that they had shared each others dreams and ideals, that they had stood side by side for a common cause, though they were such different men, from such very different worlds. Ideals had been cheap in those days, talk easy, but still, Tam knew that Dave had been sincere, a firm, stout friend. He had known, then, the sincerity in the big lad's quiet voice, felt the rebellious fire in his eyes. They had understood each other, then, deeply, sympathetically, in spite of the powerful barrier they sought to tear down—

The girl at the desk caught his eye, looked up from her work without smiling. "Yes?"

"My name is Tam Peters. I'd like to see Mr. Hawke." His voice was thin, reluctant, reflecting overtones of the icy chill in his chest. So much had happened since those long-dead days, so many things to make men change—

The girl was grinning, her face like a harsh mask. "You're wasting your time," she said, her voice brittle.

Anger flooded Tarn's face. "Listen," he hissed. "I didn't ask for your advice. I asked to see Dave Hawke. If you choose to announce me now, that's fine. If you don't see fit, then I'll go in without it. And you won't stop me—"

The girl stiffened, her eyes angry. "You'd better not get smart," she snapped, watching him warily. "There are police in the building. You'd better not try anything, or I'll call them!"

"That's enough Miss Jackson."

The girl turned to the man in the office door, her eyes disdainful.

The man stood in the doorway, a giant, with curly black hair above a high, intelligent forehead, dark brooding eyes gleaming like live coals in the sensitive face. Tam looked at him, and suddenly his knees would hardly support him, and his voice was a tight whisper—

"Dave!"

And then the huge man was gripping his hand, a strong arm around his thin shoulders, the dark, brooding eyes soft and smiling. "Tam, Tam—It's been so damned long, man—oh, it's good to see you, Tam. Why, the last I heard, you'd taken passage to the Rings—years ago—"

Weakly, Tam stumbled into the inner office, sank into a chair, his eyes overflowing, his mind a turmoil of joy and relief. The huge man slammed the door to the outer office and settled down behind the desk, sticking his feet over the edge, beaming. "Where have you *been*, Tam? You promised you'd look me up any time you came to New Denver, and I haven't seen you in a dozen years—" He fished in a lower drawer. "Drink?"

"No, no—thanks. I don't think I could handle a drink—" Tam sat back, gazing at the huge man, his throat tight. "You look bigger and better than ever, Dave."

* * * * *

Dave Hawke laughed, a deep bass laugh that seemed to start at the soles of his feet. "Couldn't very well look thin and wan," he said. He pushed a cigar box across the desk. "Here, light up. I'm on these exclusively these days—remember how you tried to get me to smoke them, back at the University? How you couldn't stand cigarettes? Said they were for women, a man should smoke a good cigar. You finally converted me."

Tam grinned, suddenly feeling the warmth of the old friendship swelling Back. "Yes, I remember. You were smoking that rotten corncob, then, because old Prof Tenley smoked one that you could smell in the back of the room, and in those days the Prof could do no wrong—"

Dave Hawke grinned broadly, settled back in his chair as he lit the cigar. "Yes, I remember. Still got that corncob around somewhere—" he shook his head, his eyes dreamy. "Good old Prof Tenley! One in a million—there was an honest man, Tam. They don't have them like that in the colleges these days. Wonder what happened to the old goat?"

"He was killed," said Tam, softly. "Just after the war. Got caught in a Revolt riot, and he was shot down."

Dave looked at him, his eyes suddenly sad. "A lot of honest men went down in those riots, didn't they? That was the worst part of the Revolt. There wasn't any provision made for the honest men, the really good men." He stopped, and regarded Tam closely. "What's the trouble, Tam? If you'd been going to make a friendly call, you'd have done it years ago. You know this office has always been open to you—"

Tam stared at his shoe, carefully choosing his words, lining them up in his mind, a frown creasing his forehead. "I'll lay it on the line," he said in a low voice. "I'm in a spot. That passage to the Rings wasn't voluntary. I was shanghaied onto a freighter, and had to work for eight years without pay to get passage back. I'm broke, and I'm hungry, and I need to see a doctor—"

"Well, hell!" the big man exploded. "Why didn't you holler sooner? Look, Tam—we've been friends for a long time. You know better than to hesitate." He fished for his wallet. "Here, I can let you have as much as you need—couple hundred?"

"No, no—That's not what I'm getting at." Tam felt his face flush with embarrassment. "I need a job, Dave. I need one bad."

Dave sat back, and his feet came off the desk abruptly. He didn't look at Tam. "I see," he said softly. "A job—" He stared at the ceiling for a moment. "Tell you what," he said. "The government's opening a new uranium mine in a month or so—going to be a big project, they'll need lots of men—on Mercury—"

Tam's eyes fell, a lump growing in his throat. "Mercury," he repeated dully.

"Why, sure, Tam—good pay, chance for promotion."

"I'd be dead in six months on Mercury." Tam's eyes met Dave's, trying to conceal the pain. "You know that as well as I do, Dave—"

Dave looked away. "Oh, the docs don't know what they're talking about—"

"You know perfectly well that they do. I couldn't even stand Venus very long. I need a job on Mars, Dave—or on Earth."

"Yes," said Dave Hawke sadly, "I guess you're right." He looked straight at Tam, his eyes sorrowful. "The truth is, I can't help you. I'd like to, but I can't. There's nothing I can do."

Tam stared, the pain of disillusionment sweeping through him. "Nothing you can do!" he exploded. "But you're the *director* of this bureau! You know every job open on every one of the planets—"

"I know. And I have to help get them filled. But I can't make anyone hire, Tam. I can send applicants, and recommendations, until I'm blue in the face, but I can't make a company hire—" He paused, staring at Tam. "Oh, hell," he snarled, suddenly, his face darkening. "Let's face it, Tam. They won't hire you. Nobody will hire you. You're a Sharkie, and that's all there is to it, they aren't hiring Sharkies. And there's nothing I can do to make them."

Tam sat as if he had been struck, the color draining from his face. "But the law—Dave, you know there's a law. They *have* to hire us, if we apply first, and have the necessary qualifications."

The big man shrugged, uneasily. "Sure, there's a law, but who's going to enforce it?"

Tam looked at him, a desperate tightness in his throat. "*You* could enforce it. You could if you wanted to."

*   *   *   *   *

The big man stared at him for a moment, then dropped his eyes, looked down at the desk. Somehow this big body seemed smaller, less impressive. "I can't do it, Tam. I just can't."

"They'd have to listen to you!" Tam's face was eager. "You've got enough power to put it across—the court would *have* to stick to the law—"

"I can't do it." Dave drew nervously on his cigar, and the light in his eyes seemed duller, now. "If it were just me, I wouldn't hesitate a minute. But I've got a wife, a family. I can't jeopardize them—"

"Dave, you know it would be the right thing."

"Oh, the right thing be damned! I can't go out on a limb, I tell you. There's nothing I can do. I can let you have money, Tam, as much as you need—I could help you set up in business, maybe, or anything—but I can't stick my neck out like that."

Tam sat stiffly, coldness seeping down into his legs. Deep in his heart he had known that this was what he had dreaded, not the fear of rebuff, not the fear of being snubbed, unrecognized, turned out. That would have been nothing, compared to this change in the honest, forthright, fearless Dave Hawke he had once known. "What's happened, Dave? Back in the old days you would have leaped at such a chance. I would have—the shoe was on the other foot then. We talked, Dave, don't you remember how we talked? We were friends, you can't forget that. I *know* you, I *know* what you believe, what you think. How can you let yourself down?"

Dave Hawke's eyes avoided Tam's. "Times have changed. Those were the good old days, back when everybody was happy, almost. Everybody but me and a few others—at least, it looked that way to you. But those days are gone. They'll never come back. This is a reaction period, and the reaction is bitter. There isn't any place for fighters now, the world is just the way people want it, and nobody can change it. What do you expect me to do?" He stopped, his heavy face contorted, a line of perspiration on his forehead. "I hate it," he said finally, "but my hands are tied. I can't do anything. That's the way things are—"

"But *why?*" Tam Peters was standing, eyes blazing, staring down at the big man behind the desk, the bitterness of long, weary years tearing into his voice, almost blinding him. "*Why is that the way things are?* What have I done? Why do we have this mess, where a man isn't worth any more than the color of his skin—"

Dave Hawke slammed his fist on the desk, and his voice roared out in the close air of the office. "Because it was coming!" he bellowed. "It's been coming and now it's here—and there's nothing on God's earth can be done about it!"

Tam's jaw sagged, and he stared at the man behind the desk. "Dave—think what you're saying, Dave—"

"I know right well what I'm saying," Dave Hawke roared, his eyes burning bitterly. "Oh, you have no idea how long I've thought, the fight I've had with myself, the sacrifices I've had to make. You weren't born like I was, you weren't raised on the wrong side of the fence—well, there was an old, old Christmas story that I used to read. Years ago, before they burned the Sharkie books. It was about an evil man who went through life cheating people, hating and hurting people, and when he died, he found that every evil deed he had ever done had become a link in a heavy iron chain, tied and shackled to his waist. And he wore that chain he had built up, and he had to drag it, and drag it, from one eternity to the next—his name was Marley, remember?"

"Dave, you're not making sense—"

"Oh, yes, all kinds of sense. Because you Sharkies have a chain, too. You started forging it around your ankles back in the classical Middle Ages of Earth. Year by year you built it up, link by link, built it stronger, heavier. You could have stopped it any time you chose, but you didn't ever think of that. You spread over the world, building up your chain, assuming that things would always be just the way they were, just the way you wanted them to be."

The big man stopped, breathing heavily, a sudden sadness creeping into his eyes, his voice taking on a softer tone. "You were such fools," he said softly. "You waxed and grew strong, and clever, and confident, and the more power you had, the more you wanted. You fought wars, and then bigger and better wars, until you couldn't be satisfied with gunpowder and TNT any longer. And finally you divided your world into two armed camps, and brought Fury out of her box, fought with the power of the atoms themselves, you clever Sharkies—and when the dust settled, and cooled off, there weren't very many of you left. Lots of us—it was your war, remember—but not very many of you. Of course there was a Revolt then, and all the boxed up, driven in hatred and bloodshed boiled up and over, and you Sharkies at long last got your chain tied right around your waists. You were a long, long time building it, and now you can wear it—"

* * * * *

Tam's face was chalky. "Dave—there were some of us—you know there were many of us that hated it as much as you did, before the Revolt. Some of us fought, some of us at least tried—"

The big man nodded his head, bitterly. "You thought you tried, sure. It was the noble thing to do, the romantic thing, the *good* thing to do. But you didn't really believe it. I know—I thought there was some hope, back then, some chance to straighten things out without a Revolt. For a long time I thought that you, and those like you, really meant all you were saying, I thought somehow we could find an equal footing, an end to the hatred and bitterness. But there wasn't any end, and you never really thought there ever would be. That made it so safe—it would never succeed, so when things were quiet it was a nice idea to toy around with, this equality for all, a noble project that couldn't possibly succeed. But when things got hot, it was a different matter." He stared at Tam, his dark eyes brooding. "Oh, it wasn't just you, Tam. You were my best friend, even though it was a hopeless, futile friendship. You tried, you did the best you could, I know. But it *just wasn't true*, Tam. When it came to the pinch, to a real jam, you would have been just like the rest, basically. It was built up in you, drummed into you, until no amount of fighting could ever scour it out—"

Dave Hawke stood up, walked over to the window, staring out across the great city. Tam watched him, the blood roaring in his ears, hardly able to believe what he had heard from the big man, fighting to keep his mind from sinking into total confusion. Somewhere a voice deep within him seemed to be struggling through with confirmation, telling him that Dave Hawke was right, that he never really *had* believed. Suddenly Dave turned to him, his dark eyes intense. "Look, Tam," he said, quickly, urgently. "There are jobs you can get. Go to Mercury for a while, work the mines—not long, just for a while, out there in the sun—then you can come back—"

Tam's ears burned, fierce anger suddenly bursting in his mind, a feeling of loathing. "Never," he snapped. "I know what you mean. I don't do things that way. That's a coward's way, and by God, I'm no coward!"

"But it would be so easy, Tam—" Dave's eyes were pleading now. "Please—"

Tam's eyes glinted. "No dice. I've got a better idea. There's one thing I can do. It's not very nice, but at least it's honest, and square. I'm hungry. There's one place where I can get food. Even Sharkies get food there. And a bed to sleep in, and books to read—maybe even some Sharkie books, and maybe some paper to write on—" He stared at the big man, oddly, his pale eyes feverish. "Yes, yes, there's one place I can go, and get plenty to eat, and get away from this eternal rottenness—"

Dave looked up at him, his eyes suspicious. "Where do you mean?"

"Prison," said Tam Peters.

"Oh, now see here—let's not be ridiculous—"

"Not so ridiculous," snapped Tam, his eyes brighter. "I figured it all out, before I came up here. I knew what you were going to say. Sure, go to Mercury, Tam, work in the mines a while—well, I can't do it that way. And there's only one other answer."

"But, Tam—"

"Oh, it wouldn't take much. You know how the courts handle Sharkies. Just a small offense, to get me a few years, then a couple of attempts to break out, and I'd be in for life. I'm a Sharkie, remember. People don't waste time with us."

"Tam, you're talking nonsense. Good Lord, man, you'd have no freedom, no life—"

"What freedom do I have now?" Tam snarled, his voice growing wild. "Freedom to starve? Freedom to crawl on my hands and knees for a little bit of food? I don't want that kind of freedom." His eyes grew shrewd, shifted slyly to Dave Hawke's broad face. "Just a simple charge," he said slowly. "Like assault, for instance. Criminal assault—it has an ugly sound, doesn't it, Dave? That should give me ten years—" his fist clenched at his side. "Yes, criminal assault is just what ought to do the trick—"

The big man tried to dodge, but Tam was too quick. His fist caught Dave in the chest, and Tam was on him like a fury, kicking, scratching, snarling, pounding. Dave choked and cried out, "Tam, for God's sake stop—" A blow caught him in the mouth, choking off his words as Tam fought, all the hate and bitterness of long weary years translated into scratching, swearing desperation. Dave pushed him off, like a bear trying to disentangle a maddened dog from his fur, but Tam was back at him, fighting harder. The door opened, and Miss Jackson's frightened face appeared briefly, then vanished. Finally Dave lifted a heavy fist, drove it hard into Tam's stomach, then sadly lifted the choking, gasping man to the floor.

The police came in, seconds later, clubs drawn, eyes wide. They dragged Tam out, one on each arm. Dave sank back, his eyes filling, a sickness growing in the pit of his stomach. In court, a Sharkie would draw the maximum sentence, without leniency. Ten years in prison—Dave leaned forward, his face in his hands, tears running down his black cheeks, sobs shaking his broad, heavy shoulders. "Why wouldn't he listen? Why couldn't he have gone to Mercury? Only a few months, not long enough to hurt him. Why couldn't he have gone, and worked out in the sun, got that hot sun down on his hands and face—not for long, just for a little while. Two or three months, and he'd have been dark enough to pass—"

THE COFFIN CURE

When the discovery was announced, it was Dr. Chauncey Patrick Coffin who announced it. He had, of course, arranged with uncanny skill to take most of the credit for himself. If it turned out to be greater than he had hoped, so much the better. His presentation was scheduled for the last night of the American College of Clinical Practitioners' annual meeting, and Coffin had fully intended it to be a bombshell.

It was. Its explosion exceeded even Dr. Coffin's wilder expectations, which took quite a bit of doing. In the end he had waded through more newspaper reporters than medical doctors as he left the hall that night. It was a heady evening for Chauncey Patrick Coffin, M.D.

Certain others were not so delighted with Coffin's bombshell.

"It's idiocy!" young Dr. Phillip Dawson wailed in the laboratory conference room the next morning. "Blind, screaming idiocy. You've gone out of your mind—that's all there is to it. Can't you see what you've done? Aside from selling your colleagues down the river, that is?" He clenched the reprint of Coffin's address in his hand and brandished it like a broadsword. "'Report on a Vaccine for the Treatment and Cure of the Common Cold,' by C. P. Coffin, *et al.* That's what it says—*et al.* My idea in the first place. Jake and I both pounding our heads on the wall for eight solid months—and now you sneak it into publication a full year before we have any business publishing a word about it."

"Really, Phillip!" Dr. Chauncey Coffin ran a pudgy hand through his snowy hair. "How ungrateful! I thought for sure you'd be delighted. An excellent presentation, I must say—terse, succinct, unequivocal—" he raised his hand—"but *generously* unequivocal, you understand. You should have heard the ovation—they nearly went wild! And the look on Underwood's face! Worth waiting twenty years for."

"And the reporters," snapped Phillip. "Don't forget the reporters." He whirled on the small dark man sitting quietly in the corner. "How about that, Jake? Did you see the morning papers? This thief not only steals our work, he splashes it all over the countryside in red ink."

Dr. Jacob Miles coughed apologetically. "What Phillip is so stormed up about is the prematurity of it all," he said to Coffin. "After all, we've hardly had an acceptable period of clinical trial."

"Nonsense," said Coffin, glaring at Phillip. "Underwood and his men were ready to publish their discovery within another six weeks. Where would we be then? How much clinical testing do you want? Phillip, you had the worst cold of your life when you took the vaccine. Have you had any since?"

"No, of course not," said Phillip peevishly.

"Jacob, how about you? Any sniffles?"

"Oh, no. No colds."

"Well, what about those six hundred students from the University? Did I misread the reports on them?"

"No—98 per cent cured of active symptoms within twenty-four hours. Not a single recurrence. The results were just short of miraculous." Jake hesitated. "Of course, it's only been a month...."

"Month, year, century! Look at them! Six hundred of the world's most luxuriant colds, and now not even a sniffle." The chubby doctor sank down behind the desk, his ruddy face beaming. "Come, now, gentlemen, be reasonable. Think positively! There's work to be done, a great deal of work. They'll be wanting me in Washington, I imagine. Press conference in twenty minutes. Drug houses to consult with. How dare we stand in the path of Progress? We've won the greatest medical triumph of all times—the conquering of the Common Cold. We'll go down in history!"

And he was perfectly right on one point, at least.

They did go down in history.

* * * * *

The public response to the vaccine was little less than monumental. Of all the ailments that have tormented mankind through history none was ever more universal, more tenacious, more uniformly miserable than the common cold. It was a respecter of no barriers, boundaries, or classes; ambassadors and chambermaids snuffled and sneezed in drippy-nosed unanimity. The powers in the Kremlin sniffed and blew and wept genuine tears on drafty days, while senatorial debates on earth-shaking issues paused reverently upon the unplugging of a nose, the clearing of a rhinorrheic throat. Other illnesses brought disability, even death in their wake; the common cold merely brought torment to the millions as it implacably resisted the most superhuman of efforts to curb it.

Until that chill, rainy November day when the tidings broke to the world in four-inch banner heads:

COFFIN NAILS LID ON COMMON COLD

"No More Coughin'" States Co-Finder of Cure

SNIFFLES SNIPED: SINGLE SHOT TO SAVE SNEEZERS

In medical circles it was called the Coffin Multicentric Upper Respiratory Virus-Inhibiting Vaccine; but the papers could never stand for such high-sounding names, and called it, simply, “The Coffin Cure.”

Below the banner heads, world-renowned feature writers expounded in reverent terms the story of the leviathan struggle of Dr. Chauncey Patrick Coffin (*et al.*) in solving this riddle of the ages: how, after years of failure, they ultimately succeeded in culturing the causative agent of the common cold, identifying it not as a single virus or group of viruses, but as a multicentric virus complex invading the soft mucous linings of the nose, throat and eyes, capable of altering its basic molecular structure at any time to resist efforts of the body from within, or the physician from without, to attack and dispel it; how the hypothesis was set forth by Dr. Phillip Dawson that the virus could be destroyed only by an antibody which could “freeze” the virus-complex in one form long enough for normal body defenses to dispose of the offending invader; the exhausting search for such a “crippling agent,” and the final crowning success after injecting untold gallons of cold-virus material into the hides of a group of co-operative and forbearing dogs (a species which never suffered from colds, and hence endured the whole business with an air of affectionate boredom).

And finally, the testing. First, Coffin himself (who was suffering a particularly horrendous case of the affliction he sought to cure); then his assistants Phillip Dawson and Jacob Miles; then a multitude of students from the University—carefully chosen for the severity of their symptoms, the longevity of their colds, their tendency to acquire them on little or no provocation, and their utter inability to get rid of them with any known medical program.

They were a sorry spectacle, those students filing through the Coffin laboratory for three days in October: wheezing like steam shovels, snorting and sneezing and sniffling and blowing, coughing and squeaking, mute appeals glowing in their blood-shot eyes. The researchers dispensed the materials—a single shot in the right arm, a sensitivity control in the left.

With growing delight they then watched as the results came in. The sneezing stopped; the sniffling ceased. A great silence settled over the campus, in the classrooms, in the library, in classic halls. Dr. Coffin's voice returned (rather to the regret of his fellow workers) and he began bouncing about the laboratory like a small boy at a fair. Students by the dozen trooped in for checkups with noses dry and eyes bright.

In a matter of days there was no doubt left that the goal had been reached.

"But we have to be *sure*," Phillip Dawson had cried cautiously. "This was only a pilot test. We need mass testing now, on an entire community. We should go to the West Coast and run studies there—they have a different breed of cold out there, I hear. We'll have to see how long the immunity lasts, make sure there are no unexpected side effects...." And, muttering to himself, he fell to work with pad and pencil, calculating the program to be undertaken before publication.

But there were rumors. Underwood at Stanford, they said, had already completed his tests and was preparing a paper for publication in a matter of months. Surely with such dramatic results on the pilot tests *something* could be put into print. It would be tragic to lose the race for the sake of a little unnecessary caution....

Peter Dawson was adamant, but he was a voice crying in the wilderness. Chauncey Patrick Coffin was boss.

Within a week even Coffin was wondering if he had bitten off just a trifle too much. They had expected that demand for the vaccine would be great—but even the grisly memory of the early days of the Salk vaccine had not prepared them for the mobs of sneezing, wheezing red-eyed people bombarding them for the first fruits.

Clear-eyed young men from the Government Bureau pushed through crowds of local townspeople, lining the streets outside the Coffin laboratory, standing in pouring rain to raise insistent placards.

Seventeen pharmaceutical houses descended like vultures with production plans, cost-estimates, colorful graphs demonstrating proposed yield and distribution programs. Coffin was flown to Washington, where conferences labored far into the night as demands pounded their doors like a tidal wave.

One laboratory promised the vaccine in ten days; another said a week. The first actually appeared in three weeks and two days, to be soaked up in the space of three hours by the thirsty sponge of cold-weary humanity. Express planes were dispatched to Europe, to Asia, to Africa with the precious cargo, a million needles pierced a million hides, and with a huge, convulsive sneeze mankind stepped forth into a new era.

* * * * *

There were abstainers, of course. There always are.

"It doesn't bake eddy differets how much you talk," Ellie Dawson cried hoarsely, shaking her blonde curls. "I dod't wadt eddy cold shots."

"You're being totally unreasonable," Phillip said, glowering at his wife in annoyance. She wasn't the sweet young thing he had married, not this evening. Her eyes were puffy, her nose red and dripping. "You've had this cold for two solid months now, and there just isn't any sense to it. It's making you miserable. You can't eat, you can't breathe, you can't sleep."

"I dod't wadt eddy cold shots," she repeated stubbornly.

"But why not? Just one little needle, you'd hardly feel it."

"But I dod't like deedles!" she cried, bursting into tears. "Why dod't you leave be alode? Go take your dasty old deedles ad stick theb id people that wadt theb."

"Aw, Ellie—"

"I dod't care, *I dod't like deedles*!" she wailed, burying her face in his shirt.

He held her close, making comforting little noises. It was no use, he reflected sadly. Science just wasn't Ellie's long suit; she didn't know a cold vaccine from a case of smallpox, and no appeal to logic or common sense could surmount her irrational fear of hypodermics. "All right, nobody's going to make you do anything you don't want to," he said.

"Ad eddyway, thik of the poor tissue badufacturers," she sniffled, wiping her nose with a pink facial tissue. "All their little childred starvig to death."

"Say, you *have* got a cold," said Phillip, sniffing. "You've got on enough perfume to fell an ox." He wiped away tears and grinned at her. "Come on now, fix your face. Dinner at the Driftwood? I hear they have marvelous lamb chops."

It was a mellow evening. The lamb chops were delectable—the tastiest lamb chops he had ever eaten, he thought, even being blessed with as good a cook as Ellie for a spouse. Ellie dripped and blew continuously, but refused to go home until they had taken in a movie, and stopped by to dance a while. "I hardly ever gedt to see you eddy bore," she said. "All because of that dasty bedicide you're givig people."

It was true, of course. The work at the lab was endless. They danced, but came home early nevertheless. Phillip needed all the sleep he could get.

He awoke once during the night to a parade of sneezes from his wife, and rolled over, frowning sleepily to himself. It was ignominious, in a way—his own wife refusing the fruit of all those months of work.

And cold or no cold, she surely was using a whale of a lot of perfume.

* * * * *

He awoke, suddenly, began to stretch, and sat bolt upright in bed, staring wildly about the room. Pale morning sunlight drifted in the window. Downstairs he heard Ellie stirring in the kitchen.

For a moment he thought he was suffocating. He leaped out of bed, stared at the vanity table across the room. "*Somebody's spilled the whole damned bottle—*"

The heavy sick-sweet miasma hung like a cloud around him, drenching the room. With every breath it grew thicker. He searched the table top frantically, but there were no empty bottles. His head began to spin from the sickening effluvium.

He blinked in confusion, his hand trembling as he lit a cigarette. No need to panic, he thought. She probably knocked a bottle over when she was dressing. He took a deep puff, and burst into a paroxysm of coughing as acrid fumes burned down his throat to his lungs.

"Ellie!" He rushed into the hall, still coughing. The match smell had given way to the harsh, caustic stench of burning weeds. He stared at his cigarette in horror and threw it into the sink. The smell grew worse. He threw open the hall closet, expecting smoke to come billowing out. "Ellie! Somebody's burning down the house!"

"Whadtever are you talking about?" Ellie's voice came from the stair well. "It's just the toast I burned, silly."

He rushed down the stairs two at a time—and nearly gagged as he reached the bottom. The smell of hot, rancid grease struck him like a solid wall. It was intermingled with an oily smell of boiled and parboiled coffee, overpowering in its intensity. By the time he reached the kitchen he was holding his nose, tears pouring from his eyes. "*Ellie, what are you doing in here?*"

She stared at him. "I'b baking breakfast."

"But don't you *smell* it?"

"Sbell whadt?" said Ellie.

On the stove the automatic percolator was making small, promising noises. In the frying pan four sunnyside eggs were sizzling; half a dozen strips of bacon drained on a paper towel on the sideboard. It couldn't have looked more innocent.

Cautiously, Phillip released his nose, sniffed. The stench nearly choked him. "You mean you don't smell anything *strange*?"

"I did't sbell eddythig, period," said Ellie defensively.

"The coffee, the bacon—*come here a minute*."

She reeked—of bacon, of coffee, of burned toast, but mostly of perfume. "Did you put on any fresh perfume this morning?"

"Before breakfast? Dod't be ridiculous."

"Not even a drop?" Phillip was turning very white.

"Dot a drop."

He shook his head. "Now, wait a minute. This must be all in my mind. I'm—just imagining things, that's all. Working too hard, hysterical reaction. In a minute it'll all go away." He poured a cup of coffee, added cream and sugar.

But he couldn't get it close enough to taste it. It smelled as if it had been boiling three weeks in a rancid pot. It was the smell of coffee, all right, but a smell that was fiendishly distorted, overpoweringly, nauseatingly magnified. It pervaded the room and burned his throat and brought tears gushing to his eyes.

Slowly, realization began to dawn. He spilled the coffee as he set the cup down. The perfume. The coffee. The cigarette....

"My hat," he choked. "Get me my hat. I've got to get to the laboratory."

* * * * *

It got worse all the way downtown. He fought down waves of nausea as the smell of damp, rotting earth rose from his front yard in a gray cloud. The neighbor's dog dashed out to greet him, exuding the great-grandfather of all doggy odors. As Phillip waited for the bus, every passing car fouled the air with noxious fumes, gagging him, doubling him up with coughing as he dabbed at his streaming eyes.

Nobody else seemed to notice anything wrong at all.

The bus ride was a nightmare. It was a damp, rainy day; the inside of the bus smelled like the men's locker room after a big game. A bleary-eyed man with three-days' stubble on his chin flopped down in the seat next to him, and Phillip reeled back with a jolt to the job he had held in his student days, cleaning vats in the brewery.

"It'sh a great morning," Bleary-eyes breathed at him, "huh, Doc?" Phillip blanched. To top it, the man had had a breakfast of salami. In the seat ahead, a fat man held a dead cigar clamped in his mouth like a rank growth. Phillip's stomach began rolling; he sank his face into his hand, trying unobtrusively to clamp his nostrils. With a groan of deliverance he lurched off the bus at the laboratory gate.

He met Jake Miles coming up the steps. Jake looked pale, too pale.

"Morning," Phillip said weakly. "Nice day. Looks like the sun might come through."

"Yeah," said Jake. "Nice day. You—uh—feel all right this morning?"

"Fine, fine." Phillip tossed his hat in the closet, opened the incubator on his culture tubes, trying to look busy. He slammed the door after one whiff and gripped the edge of the work table with whitening knuckles. "Why?"

"Oh, nothing. Thought you looked a little peaked, was all."

They stared at each other in silence. Then, as though by signal, their eyes turned to the office at the end of the lab.

"Coffin come in yet?"

Jake nodded. "He's in there. He's got the door locked."

"I think he's going to have to open it," said Phillip.

A gray-faced Dr. Coffin unlocked the door, backed quickly toward the wall. The room reeked of kitchen deodorant. "Stay right where you are," Coffin squeaked. "Don't come a step closer. I can't see you now. I'm—I'm busy, I've got work that has to be done—"

"You're telling *me*," growled Phillip. He motioned Jake into the office and locked the door carefully. Then he turned to Coffin. "When did it start for you?"

Coffin was trembling. "Right after supper last night. I thought I was going to suffocate. Got up and walked the streets all night. My God, what a stench!"

"Jake?"

Dr. Miles shook his head. "Sometime this morning, I don't know when. I woke up with it."

"That's when it hit me," said Phillip.

"But I don't understand," Coffin howled. "Nobody else seems to notice anything—"

"Yet," said Phillip, "we were the first three to take the Coffin Cure, remember? You, and me and Jake. Two months ago."

Coffin's forehead was beaded with sweat. He stared at the two men in growing horror. "*But what about the others?*" he whispered.

"I think," said Phillip, "that we'd better find something spectacular to do in a mighty big hurry. That's what I think."

* * * * *

Jake Miles said, "The most important thing right now is secrecy. We mustn't let a word get out, not until we're absolutely certain."

"But what's *happened?*" Coffin cried. "These foul smells, everywhere. You, Phillip, you had a cigarette this morning. I can smell it clear over here, and it's bringing tears to my eyes. And if I didn't know better I'd swear neither of you had had a bath in a week. Every odor in town has suddenly turned foul—"

"*Magnified*, you mean," said Jake. "Perfume still smells sweet—there's just too much of it. The same with cinnamon; I tried it. Cried for half an hour, but it still smelled like cinnamon. No, I don't think the *smells* have changed any."

"But what, then?"

"Our noses have changed, obviously." Jake paced the floor in excitement. "Look at our dogs! They've never had colds—and they practically live by their noses. Other animals—all dependent on their senses of smell for survival—and none of them ever have anything even vaguely reminiscent of a common cold. The multicentric virus hits primates only—*and it reaches its fullest parasitic powers in man alone!*"

Coffin shook his head miserably. "But why this horrible stench all of a sudden? I haven't had a cold in weeks—"

"Of course not! That's just what I'm trying to say," Jake cried. "Look, why do we have any sense of smell at all? Because we have tiny olfactory nerve endings buried in the mucous membrane of our noses and throats. But we have always had the virus living there, too, colds or no colds, throughout our entire lifetime. It's *always* been there, anchored in the same cells, parasitizing the same sensitive tissues that carry our olfactory nerve endings, numbing them and crippling them, making them practically useless as sensory organs. No wonder we never smelled anything before! Those poor little nerve endings never had a chance!"

"Until we came along in our shining armor and destroyed the virus," said Phillip.

"Oh, we didn't destroy it. We merely stripped it of a very slippery protective mechanism against normal body defences." Jake perched on the edge of the desk, his dark face intense. "These two months since we had our shots have witnessed a battle to the death between our bodies and the virus. With the help of the vaccine, our bodies have won, that's all—stripped away the last vestiges of an invader that has been almost a part of our normal physiology since the beginning of time. And now for the first time those crippled little nerve endings are just beginning to function."

"God help us," Coffin groaned. "You think it'll get worse?"

"And worse. And still worse," said Jake.

"I wonder," said Phillip slowly, "what the anthropologists will say."

"What do you mean?"

"Maybe it was just a single mutation somewhere back there. Just a tiny change of cell structure or metabolism that left one line of primates vulnerable to an invader no other would harbor. Why else should man have begun to flower and blossom intellectually—grow to depend so much on his brains instead of his brawn that he could rise above all others? What better reason than because somewhere along the line in the world of fang and claw *he suddenly lost his sense of smell?*"

They stared at each other. "Well, he's got it back again now," Coffin wailed, "and he's not going to like it a bit."

"No, he surely isn't," Jake agreed. "He's going to start looking very quickly for someone to blame, I think."

They both looked at Coffin.

"Now don't be ridiculous, boys," said Coffin, turning white. "We're in this together. Phillip, it was your idea in the first place—you said so yourself! You can't leave me now—"

The telephone jangled. They heard the frightened voice of the secretary clear across the room. "Dr. Coffin? There was a student on the line just a moment ago. He—he said he was coming up to see you. Now, he said, not later."

"I'm busy," Coffin sputtered. "I can't see anyone. And I can't take any calls."

"But he's already on his way up," the girl burst out. "He was saying something about tearing you apart with his bare hands."

Coffin slammed down the receiver. His face was the color of lead. "They'll crucify me!" he sobbed. "Jake—Phillip—you've got to help me."

Phillip sighed and unlocked the door. "Send a girl down to the freezer and have her bring up all the live cold virus she can find. Get us some inoculated monkeys and a few dozen dogs." He turned to Coffin. "And stop sniveling. You're the big publicity man around here; you're going to handle the screaming masses, whether you like it or not."

"But what are you going to do?"

"I haven't the faintest idea," said Phillip, "but whatever I do is going to cost you your shirt. We're going to find out how to catch cold again if we have to die."

* * * * *

It was an admirable struggle, and a futile one. They sprayed their noses and throats with enough pure culture of virulent live virus to have condemned an ordinary man to a lifetime of sneezing, watery-eyed misery. They didn't develop a sniffle among them. They mixed six different strains of virus and gargled the extract, spraying themselves and every inoculated monkey they could get their hands on with the vile-smelling stuff. Not a sneeze. They injected it hypodermically, intradermally, subcutaneously, intramuscularly, and intravenously. They drank it. They bathed in the stuff.

But they didn't catch a cold.

"Maybe it's the wrong approach," Jake said one morning. "Our body defenses are keyed up to top performance right now. Maybe if we break them down we can get somewhere."

They plunged down that alley with grim abandon. They starved themselves. They forced themselves to stay awake for days on end, until exhaustion forced their eyes closed in spite of all they could do. They carefully devised vitamin-free, protein-free, mineral-free diets that tasted like library paste and smelled worse. They wore wet clothes and sopping shoes to work, turned off the heat and threw windows open to the raw winter air. Then they resprayed themselves with the live cold virus and waited reverently for the sneezing to begin.

It didn't. They stared at each other in gathering gloom. They'd never felt better in their lives.

Except for the smells, of course. They'd hoped that they might, presently, get used to them. They didn't. Every day it grew a little worse. They began smelling smells they never dreamed existed—noxious smells, cloying smells, smells that drove them gagging to the sinks. Their nose-plugs were rapidly losing their effectiveness. Mealtimes were nightmarish ordeals; they lost weight with alarming speed.

But they didn't catch cold.

"*I* think you should all be locked up," Ellie Dawson said severely as she dragged her husband, blue-faced and shivering, out of an icy shower one bitter morning. "You've lost your wits. You need to be protected against yourselves, that's what you need."

"You don't understand," Phillip moaned. "We've *got* to catch cold."

"Why?" Ellie snapped angrily. "Suppose you don't—what's going to happen?"

"We had three hundred students march on the laboratory today," Phillip said patiently. "The smells were driving them crazy, they said. They couldn't even bear to be close to their best friends. They wanted something done about it, or else they wanted blood. Tomorrow we'll have them back and three hundred more. And they were just the pilot study! What's going to happen when fifteen million people find their noses going bad on them?" He shuddered. "Have you seen the papers? People are already going around sniffing like bloodhounds. And *now* we're finding out what a thorough job we did. We can't crack it, Ellie. We can't even get a toe hold. Those antibodies are just doing too good a job."

"Well, maybe you can find some unclebodies to take care of them," Ellie offered vaguely.

"Look, don't make bad jokes—"

"I'm not making jokes! All I want is a husband back who doesn't complain about how everything smells, and eats the dinners I cook, and doesn't stand around in cold showers at six in the morning."

"I know it's miserable," he said helplessly. "But I don't know how to stop it."

He found Jake and Coffin in tight-lipped conference when he reached the lab. "I can't do it any more," Coffin was saying. "I've begged them for time. I've threatened them. I've promised them everything but my upper plate. I can't face them again, I just can't."

"We only have a few days left," Jake said grimly. "If we don't come up with something, we're goners."

Phillip's jaw suddenly sagged as he stared at them. "You know what I think?" he said suddenly. "I think we've been prize idiots. We've gotten so rattled we haven't used our heads. And all the time it's been sitting there blinking at us!"

"What are you talking about?" snapped Jake.

"Unclebodies," said Phillip.

"Oh, great God!"

"No, I'm serious." Phillip's eyes were very bright. "How many of those students do you think you can corral to help us?"

Coffin gulped. "Six hundred. They're out there in the street right now, howling for a lynching."

"All right, I want them in here. And I want some monkeys. Monkeys with colds, the worse colds the better."

"Do you have any idea what you're doing?" asked Jake.

"None in the least," said Phillip happily, "except that it's never been done before. But maybe it's time we tried following our noses for a while."

* * * * *

The tidal wave began to break two days later ... only a few people here, a dozen there, but enough to confirm the direst newspaper predictions. The boomerang was completing its circle.

At the laboratory the doors were kept barred, the telephones disconnected. Within, there was a bustle of feverish—if odorous—activity. For the three researchers, the olfactory acuity had reached agonizing proportions. Even the small gas masks Phillip had devised could no longer shield them from the constant barrage of violent odors.

But the work went on in spite of the smell. Truckloads of monkeys arrived at the lab—cold-ridden monkeys, sneezing, coughing, weeping, wheezing monkeys by the dozen. Culture trays bulged with tubes, overflowed the incubators and work tables. Each day six hundred angry students paraded through the lab, arms exposed, mouths open, grumbling but co-operating.

At the end of the first week, half the monkeys were cured of their colds and were quite unable to catch them back; the other half had new colds and couldn't get rid of them. Phillip observed this fact with grim satisfaction, and went about the laboratory mumbling to himself.

Two days later he burst forth jubilantly, lugging a sad-looking puppy under his arm. It was like no other puppy in the world. This puppy was sneezing and snuffling with a perfect howler of a cold.

The day came when they injected a tiny droplet of milky fluid beneath the skin of Phillip's arm, and then got the virus spray and gave his nose and throat a liberal application. Then they sat back and waited.

They were still waiting three days later.

"It was a great idea," Jake said gloomily, flipping a bulging notebook closed with finality. "It just didn't work, was all."

Phillip nodded. Both men had grown thin, with pouches under their eyes. Jake's right eye had begun to twitch uncontrollably whenever anyone came within three yards of him. "We can't go on like this, you know. The people are going wild."

"Where's Coffin?"

"He collapsed three days ago. Nervous prostration. He kept having dreams about hangings."

Phillip sighed. "Well, I suppose we'd better just face it. Nice knowing you, Jake. Pity it had to be this way."

"It was a great try, old man. A great try."

"Ah, yes. Nothing like going down in a blaze of—"

Phillip stopped dead, his eyes widening. His nose began to twitch. He took a gasp, a larger gasp, as a long-dead reflex came sleepily to life, shook its head, reared back ...

Phillip sneezed.

He sneezed for ten minutes without a pause, until he lay on the floor blue-faced and gasping for air. He caught hold of Jake, wringing his hand as tears gushed from his eyes. He gave his nose an enormous blow, and headed shakily for the telephone.

* * * * *

"It was a sipple edough pridciple," he said later to Ellie as she spread mustard on his chest and poured more warm water into his foot bath. "The Cure itself depedded upod it—the adtiged-adtibody reactiod. We had the adtibody agaidst the virus, all ridght; what we had to find was sobe kide of adtibody agaidst the *adtibody*." He sneezed violently, and poured in nose drops with a happy grin.

"Will they be able to make it fast enough?"

"Just aboudt fast edough for people to get good ad eager to catch cold agaid," said Phillip. "There's odly wud little hitch...."

Ellie Dawson took the steaks from the grill and set them, still sizzling, on the dinner table. "Hitch?"

Phillip nodded as he chewed the steak with a pretence of enthusiasm. It tasted like slightly damp K-ration.

"This stuff we've bade does a real good job. Just a little too good." He wiped his nose and reached for a fresh tissue.

"I bay be wrog, but I thik I've got this cold for keeps," he said sadly. "Udless I cad fide ad adtibody agaidst the adtibody agaidst the adtibody—"

LETTER OF THE LAW

When the discovery was announced, it was Dr. Chauncey Patrick Coffin who announced it. He had, of course, arranged with uncanny skill to take most of the credit for himself. If it turned out to be greater than he had hoped, so much the better. His presentation was scheduled for the last night of the American College of Clinical Practitioners' annual meeting, and Coffin had fully intended it to be a bombshell.

It was. Its explosion exceeded even Dr. Coffin's wilder expectations, which took quite a bit of doing. In the end he had waded through more newspaper reporters than medical doctors as he left the hall that night. It was a heady evening for Chauncey Patrick Coffin, M.D.

Certain others were not so delighted with Coffin's bombshell.

"It's idiocy!" young Dr. Phillip Dawson wailed in the laboratory conference room the next morning. "Blind, screaming idiocy. You've gone out of your mind—that's all there is to it. Can't you see what you've done? Aside from selling your colleagues down the river, that is?" He clenched the reprint of Coffin's address in his hand and brandished it like a broadsword. "'Report on a Vaccine for the Treatment and Cure of the Common Cold,' by C. P. Coffin, *et al.* That's what it says—*et al.* My idea in the first place. Jake and I both pounding our heads on the wall for eight solid months—and now you sneak it into publication a full year before we have any business publishing a word about it."

"Really, Phillip!" Dr. Chauncey Coffin ran a pudgy hand through his snowy hair. "How ungrateful! I thought for sure you'd be delighted. An excellent presentation, I must say—terse, succinct, unequivocal—" he raised his hand—"but *generously* unequivocal, you understand. You should have heard the ovation—they nearly went wild! And the look on Underwood's face! Worth waiting twenty years for."

"And the reporters," snapped Phillip. "Don't forget the reporters." He whirled on the small dark man sitting quietly in the corner. "How about that, Jake? Did you see the morning papers? This thief not only steals our work, he splashes it all over the countryside in red ink."

Dr. Jacob Miles coughed apologetically. "What Phillip is so stormed up about is the prematurity of it all," he said to Coffin. "After all, we've hardly had an acceptable period of clinical trial."

"Nonsense," said Coffin, glaring at Phillip. "Underwood and his men were ready to publish their discovery within another six weeks. Where would we be then? How much clinical testing do you want? Phillip, you had the worst cold of your life when you took the vaccine. Have you had any since?"

"No, of course not," said Phillip peevishly.

"Jacob, how about you? Any sniffles?"

"Oh, no. No colds."

"Well, what about those six hundred students from the University? Did I misread the reports on them?"

"No—98 per cent cured of active symptoms within twenty-four hours. Not a single recurrence. The results were just short of miraculous." Jake hesitated. "Of course, it's only been a month...."

"Month, year, century! Look at them! Six hundred of the world's most luxuriant colds, and now not even a sniffle." The chubby doctor sank down behind the desk, his ruddy face beaming. "Come, now, gentlemen, be reasonable. Think positively! There's work to be done, a great deal of work. They'll be wanting me in Washington, I imagine. Press conference in twenty minutes. Drug houses to consult with. How dare we stand in the path of Progress? We've won the greatest medical triumph of all times—the conquering of the Common Cold. We'll go down in history!"

And he was perfectly right on one point, at least.

They did go down in history.

* * * * *

The public response to the vaccine was little less than monumental. Of all the ailments that have tormented mankind through history none was ever more universal, more tenacious, more uniformly miserable than the common cold. It was a respecter of no barriers, boundaries, or classes; ambassadors and chambermaids snuffled and sneezed in drippy-nosed unanimity. The powers in the Kremlin sniffed and blew and wept genuine tears on drafty days, while senatorial debates on earth-shaking issues paused reverently upon the unplugging of a nose, the clearing of a rhinorrheic throat. Other illnesses brought disability, even death in their wake; the common cold merely brought torment to the millions as it implacably resisted the most superhuman of efforts to curb it.

Until that chill, rainy November day when the tidings broke to the world in four-inch banner heads:

COFFIN NAILS LID ON COMMON COLD

"No More Coughin'" States Co-Finder of Cure

SNIFFLES SNIPED: SINGLE SHOT TO SAVE SNEEZERS

In medical circles it was called the Coffin Multicentric Upper Respiratory Virus-Inhibiting Vaccine; but the papers could never stand for such high-sounding names, and called it, simply, "The Coffin Cure."

Below the banner heads, world-renowned feature writers expounded in reverent terms the story of the leviathan struggle of Dr. Chauncey Patrick Coffin (*et al.*) in solving this riddle of the ages: how, after years of failure, they ultimately succeeded in culturing the causative agent of the common cold, identifying it not as a single virus or group of viruses, but as a multicentric virus complex invading the soft mucous linings of the nose, throat and eyes, capable of altering its basic molecular structure at any time to resist efforts of the body from within, or the physician from without, to attack and dispel it; how the hypothesis was set forth by Dr. Phillip Dawson that the virus could be destroyed only by an antibody which could "freeze" the virus-complex in one form long enough for normal body defenses to dispose of the offending invader; the exhausting search for such a "crippling agent," and the final crowning success after injecting untold gallons of cold-virus material into the hides of a group of co-operative and forbearing dogs (a species which never suffered from colds, and hence endured the whole business with an air of affectionate boredom).

And finally, the testing. First, Coffin himself (who was suffering a particularly horrendous case of the affliction he sought to cure); then his assistants Phillip Dawson and Jacob Miles; then a multitude of students from the University—carefully chosen for the severity of their symptoms, the longevity of their colds, their tendency to acquire them on little or no provocation, and their utter inability to get rid of them with any known medical program.

They were a sorry spectacle, those students filing through the Coffin laboratory for three days in October: wheezing like steam shovels, snorting and sneezing and sniffling and blowing, coughing and squeaking, mute appeals glowing in their blood-shot eyes. The researchers dispensed the materials—a single shot in the right arm, a sensitivity control in the left.

With growing delight they then watched as the results came in. The sneezing stopped; the sniffling ceased. A great silence settled over the campus, in the classrooms, in the library, in classic halls. Dr. Coffin's voice returned (rather to the regret of his fellow workers) and he began bouncing about the laboratory like a small boy at a fair. Students by the dozen trooped in for checkups with noses dry and eyes bright.

In a matter of days there was no doubt left that the goal had been reached.

"But we have to be *sure*," Phillip Dawson had cried cautiously. "This was only a pilot test. We need mass testing now, on an entire community. We should go to the West Coast and run studies there—they have a different breed of cold out there, I hear. We'll have to see how long the immunity lasts, make sure there are no unexpected side effects...." And, muttering to himself, he fell to work with pad and pencil, calculating the program to be undertaken before publication.

But there were rumors. Underwood at Stanford, they said, had already completed his tests and was preparing a paper for publication in a matter of months. Surely with such dramatic results on the pilot tests *something* could be put into print. It would be tragic to lose the race for the sake of a little unnecessary caution....

Peter Dawson was adamant, but he was a voice crying in the wilderness. Chauncey Patrick Coffin was boss.

Within a week even Coffin was wondering if he had bitten off just a trifle too much. They had expected that demand for the vaccine would be great—but even the grisly memory of the early days of the Salk vaccine had not prepared them for the mobs of sneezing, wheezing red-eyed people bombarding them for the first fruits.

Clear-eyed young men from the Government Bureau pushed through crowds of local townspeople, lining the streets outside the Coffin laboratory, standing in pouring rain to raise insistent placards.

Seventeen pharmaceutical houses descended like vultures with production plans, cost-estimates, colorful graphs demonstrating proposed yield and distribution programs. Coffin was flown to Washington, where conferences labored far into the night as demands pounded their doors like a tidal wave.

One laboratory promised the vaccine in ten days; another said a week. The first actually appeared in three weeks and two days, to be soaked up in the space of three hours by the thirsty sponge of cold-weary humanity. Express planes were dispatched to Europe, to Asia, to Africa with the precious cargo, a million needles pierced a million hides, and with a huge, convulsive sneeze mankind stepped forth into a new era.

* * * * *

There were abstainers, of course. There always are.

"It doesn't bake eddy differets how much you talk," Ellie Dawson cried hoarsely, shaking her blonde curls. "I dod't wadt eddy cold shots."

"You're being totally unreasonable," Phillip said, glowering at his wife in annoyance. She wasn't the sweet young thing he had married, not this evening. Her eyes were puffy, her nose red and dripping. "You've had this cold for two solid months now, and there just isn't any sense to it. It's making you miserable. You can't eat, you can't breathe, you can't sleep."

"I dod't wadt eddy cold shots," she repeated stubbornly.

"But why not? Just one little needle, you'd hardly feel it."

"But I dod't like deedles!" she cried, bursting into tears. "Why dod't you leave be alode? Go take your dasty old deedles ad stick theb id people that wadt theb."

"Aw, Ellie—"

"I dod't care, *I dod't like deedles*!" she wailed, burying her face in his shirt.

He held her close, making comforting little noises. It was no use, he reflected sadly. Science just wasn't Ellie's long suit; she didn't know a cold vaccine from a case of smallpox, and no appeal to logic or common sense could surmount her irrational fear of hypodermics. "All right, nobody's going to make you do anything you don't want to," he said.

"Ad eddyway, thik of the poor tissue badufacturers," she sniffled, wiping her nose with a pink facial tissue. "All their little childred starvig to death."

"Say, you *have* got a cold," said Phillip, sniffing. "You've got on enough perfume to fell an ox." He wiped away tears and grinned at her. "Come on now, fix your face. Dinner at the Driftwood? I hear they have marvelous lamb chops."

It was a mellow evening. The lamb chops were delectable—the tastiest lamb chops he had ever eaten, he thought, even being blessed with as good a cook as Ellie for a spouse. Ellie dripped and blew continuously, but refused to go home until they had taken in a movie, and stopped by to dance a while. "I hardly ever gedt to see you eddy bore," she said. "All because of that dasty bedicide you're givig people."

It was true, of course. The work at the lab was endless. They danced, but came home early nevertheless. Phillip needed all the sleep he could get.

He awoke once during the night to a parade of sneezes from his wife, and rolled over, frowning sleepily to himself. It was ignominious, in a way—his own wife refusing the fruit of all those months of work.

And cold or no cold, she surely was using a whale of a lot of perfume.

* * * * *

He awoke, suddenly, began to stretch, and sat bolt upright in bed, staring wildly about the room. Pale morning sunlight drifted in the window. Downstairs he heard Ellie stirring in the kitchen.

For a moment he thought he was suffocating. He leaped out of bed, stared at the vanity table across the room. "*Somebody's spilled the whole damned bottle—*"

The heavy sick-sweet miasma hung like a cloud around him, drenching the room. With every breath it grew thicker. He searched the table top frantically, but there were no empty bottles. His head began to spin from the sickening effluvium.

He blinked in confusion, his hand trembling as he lit a cigarette. No need to panic, he thought. She probably knocked a bottle over when she was dressing. He took a deep puff, and burst into a paroxysm of coughing as acrid fumes burned down his throat to his lungs.

"Ellie!" He rushed into the hall, still coughing. The match smell had given way to the harsh, caustic stench of burning weeds. He stared at his cigarette in horror and threw it into the sink. The smell grew worse. He threw open the hall closet, expecting smoke to come billowing out. "Ellie! Somebody's burning down the house!"

"Whadtever are you talking about?" Ellie's voice came from the stair well. "It's just the toast I burned, silly."

He rushed down the stairs two at a time—and nearly gagged as he reached the bottom. The smell of hot, rancid grease struck him like a solid wall. It was intermingled with an oily smell of boiled and parboiled coffee, overpowering in its intensity. By the time he reached the kitchen he was holding his nose, tears pouring from his eyes. "*Ellie, what are you doing in here?*"

She stared at him. "I'b baking breakfast."

"But don't you *smell* it?"

"Sbell whadt?" said Ellie.

On the stove the automatic percolator was making small, promising noises. In the frying pan four sunnyside eggs were sizzling; half a dozen strips of bacon drained on a paper towel on the sideboard. It couldn't have looked more innocent.

Cautiously, Phillip released his nose, sniffed. The stench nearly choked him. "You mean you don't smell anything *strange?*"

"I did't sbell eddythig, period," said Ellie defensively.

"The coffee, the bacon—*come here a minute.*"

She reeked—of bacon, of coffee, of burned toast, but mostly of perfume. "Did you put on any fresh perfume this morning?"

"Before breakfast? Dod't be ridiculous."

"Not even a drop?" Phillip was turning very white.

"Dot a drop."

He shook his head. "Now, wait a minute. This must be all in my mind. I'm—just imagining things, that's all. Working too hard, hysterical reaction. In a minute it'll all go away." He poured a cup of coffee, added cream and sugar.

But he couldn't get it close enough to taste it. It smelled as if it had been boiling three weeks in a rancid pot. It was the smell of coffee, all right, but a smell that was fiendishly distorted, overpoweringly, nauseatingly magnified. It pervaded the room and burned his throat and brought tears gushing to his eyes.

Slowly, realization began to dawn. He spilled the coffee as he set the cup down. The perfume. The coffee. The cigarette....

"My hat," he choked. "Get me my hat. I've got to get to the laboratory."

* * * * *

It got worse all the way downtown. He fought down waves of nausea as the smell of damp, rotting earth rose from his front yard in a gray cloud. The neighbor's dog dashed out to greet him, exuding the great-grandfather of all doggy odors. As Phillip waited for the bus, every passing car fouled the air with noxious fumes, gagging him, doubling him up with coughing as he dabbed at his streaming eyes.

Nobody else seemed to notice anything wrong at all.

The bus ride was a nightmare. It was a damp, rainy day; the inside of the bus smelled like the men's locker room after a big game. A bleary-eyed man with three-days' stubble on his chin flopped down in the seat next to him, and Phillip reeled back with a jolt to the job he had held in his student days, cleaning vats in the brewery.

"It'sh a great morning," Bleary-eyes breathed at him, "huh, Doc?" Phillip blanched. To top it, the man had had a breakfast of salami. In the seat ahead, a fat man held a dead cigar clamped in his mouth like a rank growth. Phillip's stomach began rolling; he sank his face into his hand, trying unobtrusively to clamp his nostrils. With a groan of deliverance he lurched off the bus at the laboratory gate.

He met Jake Miles coming up the steps. Jake looked pale, too pale.

"Morning," Phillip said weakly. "Nice day. Looks like the sun might come through."

"Yeah," said Jake. "Nice day. You—uh—feel all right this morning?"

"Fine, fine." Phillip tossed his hat in the closet, opened the incubator on his culture tubes, trying to look busy. He slammed the door after one whiff and gripped the edge of the work table with whitening knuckles. "Why?"

"Oh, nothing. Thought you looked a little peaked, was all."

They stared at each other in silence. Then, as though by signal, their eyes turned to the office at the end of the lab.

"Coffin come in yet?"

Jake nodded. "He's in there. He's got the door locked."

"I think he's going to have to open it," said Phillip.

A gray-faced Dr. Coffin unlocked the door, backed quickly toward the wall. The room reeked of kitchen deodorant. "Stay right where you are," Coffin squeaked. "Don't come a step closer. I can't see you now. I'm—I'm busy, I've got work that has to be done—"

"You're telling *me*," growled Phillip. He motioned Jake into the office and locked the door carefully. Then he turned to Coffin. "When did it start for you?"

Coffin was trembling. "Right after supper last night. I thought I was going to suffocate. Got up and walked the streets all night. My God, what a stench!"

"Jake?"

Dr. Miles shook his head. "Sometime this morning, I don't know when. I woke up with it."

"That's when it hit me," said Phillip.

"But I don't understand," Coffin howled. "Nobody else seems to notice anything—"

"Yet," said Phillip, "we were the first three to take the Coffin Cure, remember? You, and me and Jake. Two months ago."

Coffin's forehead was beaded with sweat. He stared at the two men in growing horror. "*But what about the others?*" he whispered.

"I think," said Phillip, "that we'd better find something spectacular to do in a mighty big hurry. That's what I think."

*   *   *   *   *

Jake Miles said, "The most important thing right now is secrecy. We mustn't let a word get out, not until we're absolutely certain."

"But what's *happened?*" Coffin cried. "These foul smells, everywhere. You, Phillip, you had a cigarette this morning. I can smell it clear over here, and it's bringing tears to my eyes. And if I didn't know better I'd swear neither of you had had a bath in a week. Every odor in town has suddenly turned foul—"

"*Magnified*, you mean," said Jake. "Perfume still smells sweet—there's just too much of it. The same with cinnamon; I tried it. Cried for half an hour, but it still smelled like cinnamon. No, I don't think the *smells* have changed any."

"But what, then?"

"Our noses have changed, obviously." Jake paced the floor in excitement. "Look at our dogs! They've never had colds—and they practically live by their noses. Other animals—all dependent on their senses of smell for survival—and none of them ever have anything even vaguely reminiscent of a common cold. The multicentric virus hits primates only—*and it reaches its fullest parasitic powers in man alone*!"

Coffin shook his head miserably. "But why this horrible stench all of a sudden? I haven't had a cold in weeks—"

"Of course not! That's just what I'm trying to say," Jake cried. "Look, why do we have any sense of smell at all? Because we have tiny olfactory nerve endings buried in the mucous membrane of our noses and throats. But we have always had the virus living there, too, colds or no colds, throughout our entire lifetime. It's *always* been there, anchored in the same cells, parasitizing the same sensitive tissues that carry our olfactory nerve endings, numbing them and crippling them, making them practically useless as sensory organs. No wonder we never smelled anything before! Those poor little nerve endings never had a chance!"

"Until we came along in our shining armor and destroyed the virus," said Phillip.

"Oh, we didn't destroy it. We merely stripped it of a very slippery protective mechanism against normal body defences." Jake perched on the edge of the desk, his dark face intense. "These two months since we had our shots have witnessed a battle to the death between our bodies and the virus. With the help of the vaccine, our bodies have won, that's all—stripped away the last vestiges of an invader that has been almost a part of our normal physiology since the beginning of time. And now for the first time those crippled little nerve endings are just beginning to function."

"God help us," Coffin groaned. "You think it'll get worse?"

"And worse. And still worse," said Jake.

"I wonder," said Phillip slowly, "what the anthropologists will say."

"What do you mean?"

"Maybe it was just a single mutation somewhere back there. Just a tiny change of cell structure or metabolism that left one line of primates vulnerable to an invader no other would harbor. Why else should man have begun to flower and blossom intellectually—grow to depend so much on his brains instead of his brawn that he could rise above all others? What better reason than because somewhere along the line in the world of fang and claw *he suddenly lost his sense of smell?*"

They stared at each other. "Well, he's got it back again now," Coffin wailed, "and he's not going to like it a bit."

"No, he surely isn't," Jake agreed. "He's going to start looking very quickly for someone to blame, I think."

They both looked at Coffin.

"Now don't be ridiculous, boys," said Coffin, turning white. "We're in this together. Phillip, it was your idea in the first place—you said so yourself! You can't leave me now—"

The telephone jangled. They heard the frightened voice of the secretary clear across the room. "Dr. Coffin? There was a student on the line just a moment ago. He—he said he was coming up to see you. Now, he said, not later."

"I'm busy," Coffin sputtered. "I can't see anyone. And I can't take any calls."

"But he's already on his way up," the girl burst out. "He was saying something about tearing you apart with his bare hands."

Coffin slammed down the receiver. His face was the color of lead. "They'll crucify me!" he sobbed. "Jake—Phillip—you've got to help me."

Phillip sighed and unlocked the door. "Send a girl down to the freezer and have her bring up all the live cold virus she can find. Get us some inoculated monkeys and a few dozen dogs." He turned to Coffin. "And stop sniveling. You're the big publicity man around here; you're going to handle the screaming masses, whether you like it or not."

"But what are you going to do?"

"I haven't the faintest idea," said Phillip, "but whatever I do is going to cost you your shirt. We're going to find out how to catch cold again if we have to die."

* * * * *

It was an admirable struggle, and a futile one. They sprayed their noses and throats with enough pure culture of virulent live virus to have condemned an ordinary man to a lifetime of sneezing, watery-eyed misery. They didn't develop a sniffle among them. They mixed six different strains of virus and gargled the extract, spraying themselves and every inoculated monkey they could get their hands on with the vile-smelling stuff. Not a sneeze. They injected it hypodermically, intradermally, subcutaneously, intramuscularly, and intravenously. They drank it. They bathed in the stuff.

But they didn't catch a cold.

"Maybe it's the wrong approach," Jake said one morning. "Our body defenses are keyed up to top performance right now. Maybe if we break them down we can get somewhere."

They plunged down that alley with grim abandon. They starved themselves. They forced themselves to stay awake for days on end, until exhaustion forced their eyes closed in spite of all they could do. They carefully devised vitamin-free, protein-free, mineral-free diets that tasted like library paste and smelled worse. They wore wet clothes and sopping shoes to work, turned off the heat and threw windows open to the raw winter air. Then they resprayed themselves with the live cold virus and waited reverently for the sneezing to begin.

It didn't. They stared at each other in gathering gloom. They'd never felt better in their lives.

Except for the smells, of course. They'd hoped that they might, presently, get used to them. They didn't. Every day it grew a little worse. They began smelling smells they never dreamed existed—noxious smells, cloying smells, smells that drove them gagging to the sinks. Their nose-plugs were rapidly losing their effectiveness. Mealtimes were nightmarish ordeals; they lost weight with alarming speed.

But they didn't catch cold.

"*I* think you should all be locked up," Ellie Dawson said severely as she dragged her husband, blue-faced and shivering, out of an icy shower one bitter morning. "You've lost your wits. You need to be protected against yourselves, that's what you need."

"You don't understand," Phillip moaned. "We've *got* to catch cold."

"Why?" Ellie snapped angrily. "Suppose you don't—what's going to happen?"

"We had three hundred students march on the laboratory today," Phillip said patiently. "The smells were driving them crazy, they said. They couldn't even bear to be close to their best friends. They wanted something done about it, or else they wanted blood. Tomorrow we'll have them back and three hundred more. And they were just the pilot study! What's going to happen when fifteen million people find their noses going bad on them?" He shuddered. "Have you seen the papers? People are already going around sniffing like bloodhounds. And *now* we're finding out what a thorough job we did. We can't crack it, Ellie. We can't even get a toe hold. Those antibodies are just doing too good a job."

"Well, maybe you can find some unclebodies to take care of them," Ellie offered vaguely.

"Look, don't make bad jokes—"

"I'm not making jokes! All I want is a husband back who doesn't complain about how everything smells, and eats the dinners I cook, and doesn't stand around in cold showers at six in the morning."

"I know it's miserable," he said helplessly. "But I don't know how to stop it."

He found Jake and Coffin in tight-lipped conference when he reached the lab. "I can't do it any more," Coffin was saying. "I've begged them for time. I've threatened them. I've promised them everything but my upper plate. I can't face them again, I just can't."

"We only have a few days left," Jake said grimly. "If we don't come up with something, we're goners."

Phillip's jaw suddenly sagged as he stared at them. "You know what I think?" he said suddenly. "I think we've been prize idiots. We've gotten so rattled we haven't used our heads. And all the time it's been sitting there blinking at us!"

"What are you talking about?" snapped Jake.

"Unclebodies," said Phillip.

"Oh, great God!"

"No, I'm serious." Phillip's eyes were very bright. "How many of those students do you think you can corral to help us?"

Coffin gulped. "Six hundred. They're out there in the street right now, howling for a lynching."

"All right, I want them in here. And I want some monkeys. Monkeys with colds, the worse colds the better."

"Do you have any idea what you're doing?" asked Jake.

"None in the least," said Phillip happily, "except that it's never been done before. But maybe it's time we tried following our noses for a while."

* * * * *

The tidal wave began to break two days later ... only a few people here, a dozen there, but enough to confirm the direst newspaper predictions. The boomerang was completing its circle.

At the laboratory the doors were kept barred, the telephones disconnected. Within, there was a bustle of feverish—if odorous—activity. For the three researchers, the olfactory acuity had reached agonizing proportions. Even the small gas masks Phillip had devised could no longer shield them from the constant barrage of violent odors.

But the work went on in spite of the smell. Truckloads of monkeys arrived at the lab—cold-ridden monkeys, sneezing, coughing, weeping, wheezing monkeys by the dozen. Culture trays bulged with tubes, overflowed the incubators and work tables. Each day six hundred angry students paraded through the lab, arms exposed, mouths open, grumbling but co-operating.

At the end of the first week, half the monkeys were cured of their colds and were quite unable to catch them back; the other half had new colds and couldn't get rid of them. Phillip observed this fact with grim satisfaction, and went about the laboratory mumbling to himself.

Two days later he burst forth jubilantly, lugging a sad-looking puppy under his arm. It was like no other puppy in the world. This puppy was sneezing and snuffling with a perfect howler of a cold.

The day came when they injected a tiny droplet of milky fluid beneath the skin of Phillip's arm, and then got the virus spray and gave his nose and throat a liberal application. Then they sat back and waited.

They were still waiting three days later.

"It was a great idea," Jake said gloomily, flipping a bulging notebook closed with finality. "It just didn't work, was all."

Phillip nodded. Both men had grown thin, with pouches under their eyes. Jake's right eye had begun to twitch uncontrollably whenever anyone came within three yards of him. "We can't go on like this, you know. The people are going wild."

"Where's Coffin?"

"He collapsed three days ago. Nervous prostration. He kept having dreams about hangings."

Phillip sighed. "Well, I suppose we'd better just face it. Nice knowing you, Jake. Pity it had to be this way."

"It was a great try, old man. A great try."

"Ah, yes. Nothing like going down in a blaze of—"

Phillip stopped dead, his eyes widening. His nose began to twitch. He took a gasp, a larger gasp, as a long-dead reflex came sleepily to life, shook its head, reared back ...

Phillip sneezed.

He sneezed for ten minutes without a pause, until he lay on the floor blue-faced and gasping for air. He caught hold of Jake, wringing his hand as tears gushed from his eyes. He gave his nose an enormous blow, and headed shakily for the telephone.

* * * * *

"It was a sipple edough pridciple," he said later to Ellie as she spread mustard on his chest and poured more warm water into his foot bath. "The Cure itself depedded upod it—the adtiged-adtibody reactiod. We had the adtibody agaidst the virus, all ridght; what we had to find was sobe kide of adtibody agaidst the *adtibody*." He sneezed violently, and poured in nose drops with a happy grin.

"Will they be able to make it fast enough?"

"Just aboudt fast edough for people to get good ad eager to catch cold agaid," said Phillip. "There's odly wud little hitch...."

Ellie Dawson took the steaks from the grill and set them, still sizzling, on the dinner table. "Hitch?"

Phillip nodded as he chewed the steak with a pretence of enthusiasm. It tasted like slightly damp K-ration.

"This stuff we've bade does a real good job. Just a little too good." He wiped his nose and reached for a fresh tissue.

"I bay be wrog, but I thik I've got this cold for keeps," he said sadly. "Udless I cad fide ad adtibody agaidst the adtibody agaidst the adtibody—"

CONTAMINATION CREW

(The following is taken from the files of the Medical Disciplinary Board, Hospital Earth, from the preliminary hearings in re: The Profession vs. Samuel B. Jenkins, Physician; First Court of Medical Affairs, final action pending.)

COM COD S221VB73 VOROCHISLOV SECTOR; 4th GALACTIC PERIOD 22, 2341 GENERAL SURVEY SHIP *MERCY* TO HOSPITAL EARTH

VIA: FASTEST POSSIBLE ROUTING, PRIORITY UNASSIGNED

TO: Lucius Darby,

Physician Grade I, Black Service Director of Galactic Periphery Services, Hospital Earth

FROM: Samuel B. Jenkins, Physician Grade VI, Red Service General Practice Patrol Ship *Lancet* (Attached GSS *Mercy* pro tem)

SIR: The following communication is directed to your attention in hopes that it may anticipate various charges which are certain to be placed against me as a Physician of the Red Service upon the return of the General Survey Ship *Mercy* to Hospital Earth (expected arrival four months from above date).

These charges will undoubtedly be preferred by one Turvold Neelsen, Physician Grade II of the Black Service, and Commander of the *Mercy* on its current survey mission into the Vorochislov Sector. Exactly what the charges will be I cannot say, since the Black Doctor in question refuses either audience or communication with me at the present time; however, it seems likely that treason, incompetence and mutinous insubordination will be among the milder complaints registered. It is possible that even Malpractice might be added, so you can readily understand the reasons for this statement—

The following will also clarify my attached request that the GSS *Mercy*, upon arrival in orbit around Hospital Earth, be met immediately by a decontamination ship carrying a vat of hydrochloric acid, concentration 3.7%, measuring no less than twenty by thirty by fifty feet, and that Quarantine officials be prepared to place the entire crew of the *Mercy* under physical and psychiatric observation for a period of no less than six weeks upon disembarkation.

The facts, in brief, are as follows:

Three months ago, as crew of the General Practice Patrol Ship *Lancet*, my colleague Green Doctor Wallace Stone and myself began investigating certain peculiar conditions existing on the fourth planet of Mauki, Vorochislov Sector (Class I Medical Service Contract.) The entire population of that planet was found to be suffering from a mass psychotic delusion of rather spectacular proportions: namely, that they and their entire planet were in imminent danger of being devoured, in toto, by an indestructible non-humanoid creature which they called a *hlorg*. The Maukivi were insistent that a *hlorg* had already totally consumed a non-existent outer planet in their system, and was now hard at work on neighboring Mauki V. It was their morbid fear that Mauki IV was next on its list. No amount of reassurance could convince them of the foolishness of these fears, although we exhausted our energy, our patience, and our food and medical supplies in the effort. Ultimately we referred the matter to the Grey Service, feeling confident that it was a psychiatric problem rather than medical or surgical. We applied to the GSS *Mercy* to take us aboard to replenish our ship's supplies, and provide us a much-needed recovery period. The Black Doctor in command approved our request and brought us aboard.

The trouble began two days later....

*

There were three classes of dirty words in use by the men who travelled the spaceways back and forth from Hospital Earth.

There were the words you seldom used in public, but which were colorful and descriptive in private use.

Then there were the words which you seldom used even in private, but which effectively relieved feelings when directed at mirrors, inanimate objects, and people who had just left the room.

Finally, there were the words that you just didn't use, period. You knew they existed; you'd heard them used at one time or another, but to hear them spoken out in plain Earth-English was enough to rock the most space-hardened of the Galactic Pill Peddlers back on his well-worn heels.

Black Doctor Turvold Neelsen's Earth-English was spotty at best, but the word came through without any possibility of misinterpretation. Red Doctor Sam Jenkins stared at the little man and felt his face turning as scarlet as the lining of his uniform cape.

"But that's ridiculous!" he finally stammered. "Quite aside from the language you use to suggest it."

"Ah! So the word still has some punch left, eh? At least you puppies bring something away from your Medical Training, even if it's only taboos." The Black Doctor scowled across the desk at Jenkins' lanky figure. "But sometimes, my good Doctor, it is better to face a fact than to wait for the fact to face you. Sometimes we have to crawl out of our ivory towers for a minute or two—you know?"

Jenkins reddened again. He had never had any great love for physicians of the Black Service—who did?—but he found himself disliking this short, blunt-spoken man even more cordially than most. "Why implicate the *Lancet*?" he burst out. "You've landed the *Mercy* on plenty of planets before we brought the *Lancet* aboard her—"

"But we did not have it with us before the *Lancet* came aboard, and we do have it now. The implication is obvious. You have brought aboard a contaminant."

He'd said it again.

Red Doctor Jenkins' face darkened. "The Green Doctor and I have maintained the *Lancet* in perfect conformity with the Sterility Code. We've taken every precaution on both landing and disembarking procedures. What's more, we've spent the last three months on a planet with *no* mutually compatible flora or fauna. From Hospital Earth viewpoint, Mauki IV is sterile. We made only the briefest check-stop on Mauki V before joining you. It was a barren rock, but we decontaminated again after leaving. If you have a—a *contaminant* on board your ship, sir, it didn't come from the *Lancet*. And I won't be held responsible."

It was strong language to use to a Black Doctor, and Sam Jenkins knew it. There were doctors of the Green and Red Services who had spent their professional lives on some god-forsaken planetoid at the edge of the Galaxy for saying less. Red Doctor Sam Jenkins was too near the end of his Internship, too nearly ready for his first Permanent Planetary Appointment with the rank, honor, and responsibility it carried to lightly risk throwing it to the wind at this stage—

But a Red Doctor does not bring a contaminant aboard a survey ship, he thought doggedly, no matter what the Black Doctor says—

Neelsen looked at the young man slowly. Then he shrugged. "Of course, I'm merely a pathologist. I realize that we know nothing of medicine, nor of disease, nor of the manner in which disease is spread. All this is beyond our scope. But perhaps you'll permit one simple question from a dull old man, just to humor him."

Jenkins looked at the floor. "I'm sorry, sir."

"Just so. You've had a very successful cruise this year with the *Lancet*, I understand."

Jenkins nodded.

"A most successful cruise. Four planets elevated from Class IV to Class II contracts, they tell me. Morua II elevated from Class VI to Class I, with certain special riders. A plague-panic averted on Setman I, and a very complex virus-bacteria symbiosis unravelled on Orb III. An illustrious record. You and your colleague from the Green Service are hoping for a year's exemption from training, I imagine—" The Black Doctor looked up sharply. "You searched your holds after leaving the Mauki planets, I presume?"

Jenkins blinked. "Why—no, sir. That is, we decontaminated according to—"

"I see. You didn't search your holds. I suppose you didn't notice your food supplies dwindling at an alarming rate?"

"No—" The Red Doctor hesitated. "Not really."

"Ah." The Black Doctor closed his eyes wearily and flipped an activator switch. The scanner on the far wall buzzed into activity. It focussed on the rear storage hold of the *Mercy* where the little *Lancet* was resting on its landing rack. "Look closely, Doctor."

At first Jenkins saw nothing. Then his eye caught a long, pink glistening strand lying across the floor of the hold. The scanner picked up the strand, followed it to the place where it emerged from a neat pencil-sized hole in the hull of the *Lancet*. The strand snaked completely across the room and disappeared through another neat hole in the wall into the next storage hold.

Jenkins shook his head as the scanner flipped back to the hole in the *Lancet*'s hull. Even as he watched, the hole enlarged and a pink blob began to emerge. The blob kept coming and coming until it rested soggily on the edge of the hole. Then it teetered and fell *splat* on the floor.

"Friend of yours?" the Black Doctor asked casually.

It was a pink heap of jelly just big enough to fill a scrub bucket. It sat on the floor, quivering noxiously. Then it sent out pseudopods in several directions, probing the metal floor. After a few moments it began oozing along the strand of itself that lay on the floor, and squeezed through the hole into the next hold.

"Ugh," said Sam Jenkins, feeling suddenly sick.

"The hydroponic tanks are in there," the Black Doctor said. "You've seen one of those before?"

"Not in person." Jenkins shook his head weakly. "Only pictures. It's a *hlorg*. We thought it was only a Maukivi persecution fantasy."

"This thing is growing pretty fast for a persecution fantasy. We spotted it eight hours ago, demolishing what was left of your food supply. It's twice as big now as it was then."

"Well, we've got to get rid of it," said Jenkins, suddenly coming to life.

"Amen, Doctor."

"I'll get the survey crew alerted right away. We won't waste a minute. And my apologies." Jenkins was hurrying for the door. "I'll get it cleared out of here fast."

"I do hope so," said the Black Doctor. "The thing makes me ill just to think about."

"I'll give you a clean-ship report in twenty-four hours," the Red Doctor said as confidently as he could and beat a hasty retreat down the corridor. He was wishing fervently that he felt as confident as he sounded.

The Maukivi had described the *hlorg* in excruciating detail. He and Green Doctor Stone had listened, and smiled sadly at each other, day after day, marvelling at the fanciful delusion. *Hlorgs*, indeed! And such creatures to dream up—eating, growing, devouring plant, animal and mineral without discrimination—

And the Maukivi had stoutly maintained that this *hlorg* of theirs was indestructible—

*

Green Doctor Wally Stone, true to his surgical calling, was a man of action.

"You mean there *is* such a thing?" he exploded when his partner confronted him with the news. "For real? Not just somebody's pipe dream?"

"There is," said Jenkins, "and we've got it. Here. On board the *Mercy*. It's eating like hell-and-gone and doubling its size every eight hours."

"Well what are you waiting for? Toss it overboard!"

"Fine! And what happens to the next party it happens to land on? We're supposed to be altruists, remember? We're supposed to worry about the health of the Galaxy." Jenkins shook his head. "Whatever we do with it, we have to find out just what we're tossing before we toss."

The creature had made itself at home aboard the *Mercy*. In the spirit of uninvited guests since time immemorial, it had established a toehold with remarkable asperity, and now was digging in for the long winter. Drawn to the hydroponic tanks like a flea to a dog, the *hlorg* had settled its bulbous pink body down in their murky depths with a contented gurgle. As it grew larger the tank-levels grew lower, the broth clearer.

The fact that the twenty-five crewmen of the *Mercy* depended on those tanks for their food supply on the four-month run back to Hospital Earth didn't seem to bother the *hlorg* a bit. It just sank down wetly and began to eat.

Under Jenkins' whip hand, and with Green Doctor Stone's assistance, the Survey Crew snapped into action. Survey was the soul and lifeblood of the medical services supplied by Hospital Earth to the inhabited planets of the Galaxy. Centuries before, during the era of exploration, every Earth ship had carried a rudimentary Survey Crew—a physiologist, a biochemist, an immunologist, a physician—to determine the safety of landings on unknown planets. Other races were more advanced in technological and physical sciences, in sales or in merchandising—but in the biological sciences men of Earth stood unexcelled in the Galaxy. It was not surprising that their casual offerings of medical services wherever their ships touched had led to a growing demand for those services, until the first Medical Service Contract with Deneb III had formalized the planetary specialty. Earth had become Hospital Earth, physician to a Galaxy, surgeon to a thousand worlds, midwife to those susceptible to midwifery and psychiatrist to those whose inner lives zigged when their outer lives zagged.

In the early days it had been a haphazard arrangement; but gradually distinct Services appeared to handle problems of medicine, surgery, radiology, psychiatry and all the other functions of a well-appointed medical service. Under the direction of the Black Service of Pathology, Hospital ships and Survey ships were dispatched to serve as bases for the tiny General Practice Patrol ships that answered the calls of the planets under Contract.

But it was the Survey ships that did the basic dirty-work on any new planet taken under Contract—outlining the physiological and biochemical aspects of the races involved, studying their disease patterns, their immunological types, their susceptibility to medical, surgical, or psychiatric treatment. It was an exacting service to perform, and Survey did an exacting job.

Now, with their own home base invaded by a hungry pink jelly-blob, the Survey Crew of the *Mercy* dug in with all fours to find a way to exorcise it.

The early returns were not encouraging.

Bowman, the anatomist, spent six hours with the creature. He'd go after the functional anatomy first, he thought, as he approached the task with gusto. Special organs, vital organ systems—after all, every Achilles had his heel. Functional would spot it if anything would—

Six hours later he rendered a preliminary report. It consisted of a blank sheet of paper and an expression of wild frustration.

"What's this supposed to mean?" Jenkins asked.

"Just what it says."

"But it says nothing!"

"That's exactly what it means." Bowman was a thin, wistful-looking man with a hawk nose and a little brown mustache. He subbed as ship's cook when things were slow in his specialty. He wasn't a very good cook, but what could anyone do with the sludge from the harvest shelf of a hydroponic tank? Now, with the *hlorg* incumbent, there wasn't even any sludge.

"I drained off a tank and got a good look at it before it crawled over into the next one," Bowman said. "Ugly bastard. But from a strictly anatomical standpoint I can't help you a bit."

Green Doctor Stone glowered over Jenkins' shoulder at the man. "But surely you can give us *something*."

Bowman shrugged. "You want it technical?"

"Any way you like."

"Your *hlorg* is an ideal anamorph. A nothing. Protoplasm, just protoplasm."

Jenkins looked up sharply. "What about his cellular organization?"

"No cells," said Bowman. "Unless they're sub-microscopic, and I'd need an electron-peeker to tell you that."

"No organ systems?"

"Not even an integument. You saw how slippery he looked? That's why. There's nothing holding him in but energy."

"Now, look," said Stone. "He eats, doesn't he? He must have waste materials of some sort."

Bowman shook his head unhappily. "Sorry. No urates. No nitrates. No CO_2. Anyway, he doesn't eat because he has nothing to eat with. He absorbs. And that includes the lining of the tanks, which he seems to like as much as the contents. He doesn't *bore* those holes he makes—he *dissolves* them."

They sent Bowman back to quarters for a hot bath and a shot of Happy-O and looked up Hrunta, the biochemist.

Hrunta was glaring at paper electrophoretic patterns and pulling out chunks of hair around his bald spot. He gave them a snarl and shoved a sheaf of papers into their hands.

"Metabolic survey?" Jenkins asked.

"Plus," said Hrunta. "You're not going to like it, either."

"Why not? If it grows, it metabolizes. If it metabolizes, we can kill it. Axiom number seventeen, paragraph number four."

"Oh, it metabolizes, all right, but you'd better find yourself another axiom, pretty quick."

"Why?"

"Because it not only metabolizes, it *consumes*. There's no sign of the usual protein-carbohydrate-fat metabolism going on here. This baby has an enzyme system that's straight from hell. It bypasses the usual metabolic activities that produce heat and energy and gets right down to basic-basic."

Jenkins swallowed. "What do you mean?"

"It attacks the nuclear structure of whatever matter the creature comes in contact with. There's a partial mass-energy conversion in its rawest form. The creature goes after carbon-bearing substances first, since the C seems to break down more easily than anything else—hence its preference for plant and animal material over non-C stuff. But it can use anything if it has to—"

Jenkins stared at the little biochemist, an image in his mind of the pink creature in the hold, growing larger by the minute as it ate its way through the hydroponics, through the dry stores, through—

"Is there anything it *can't* use?"

"If there is, I haven't found it," Hrunta said sadly. "In fact, I can't see any reason why it couldn't consume this ship and everything in it, right down to the last rivet—"

*

They walked down to the hold for another look at their uninvited guest, and almost wished they hadn't.

It had reached the size of a small hippopotamus, although the resemblance ended there. Twenty hours had elapsed since the survey had begun. The *hlorg* had used every minute of it, draining the tanks, engulfing dry stores, devouring walls and floors as it spread out in search of food, leaving trails of eroded metal wherever it went.

It was ugly—ugly in its pink shapelessness, ugly in its slimy half-sentient movements, in its very *purposefulness*. But its ugliness went even deeper, stirring primordial feelings of revulsion and loathing in their minds as they watched it oozing implacably across the hold to another dry-storage bin.

Wally Stone shuddered. "It's *grown*."

"Too fast. Bowman charts it as geometric progression."

Stone scratched his jaw as a lone pink pseudopod pushed out on the floor toward him. Then he leaped forward and stamped on it, severing the strand from the body.

The severed member quivered and lay still for a moment. Then it flowed back to rejoin the body with a wet gurgle.

Stone looked at his half-dissolved shoe.

"Egotropism," Jenkins said. "Bowman played around with that, too. A severed piece will rejoin if it can. If it can't it just takes up independent residence and we have two *hlorgs*."

"What happens to it outside the ship?" Stone wanted to know.

"It falls dormant for several hours, and then splits up into a thousand independent chunks. One of the boys spent half of yesterday out there gathering them up. I tell you, this thing is equipped to *survive*."

"So are we," said Green Doctor Stone grimly. "If we can't outwit this free-flowing gob of obscenity, we deserve anything we get. Let's have a conference."

They met in the pilot room. The Black Doctor was there; so were Bowman and Hrunta. Chambers, the physiologist, was glumly clasping and unclasping his hands in a corner. The geneticist, Piccione, drew symbols on a scratch pad and stared blankly at the wall.

Jenkins was saying: "Of course, these are only preliminary reports, but they serve to outline the problem. This is not just an annoyance any longer, it's a crisis. We'd all better understand that."

The Black Doctor cut him off with a wave of his hand, and glowered at the papers as he read them through minutely. As he sat hunched at the desk with the black cowl of his office hanging down from his shoulders he looked like a squat black judge, Jenkins thought, a shadow from the Inquisition, a Passer of Spells. But there was no medievalism in Black Doctor Neelsen. In fact, it was for that reason, and only that reason, that the Black Service had come to be the leaders and the whips, the executors and directors of all the manifold operations of Hospital Earth.

*

The physicians of the General Practice Patrol were fledglings, newly trained in their specialties, inexperienced in the rigorous discipline of medicine that was required of the directors of permanent Planetary Dispensaries in the heavily populated systems of the Galaxy. On outlying worlds where little was known of the ways of medicine, the temptation was great to substitute faith for knowledge, cant for investigation, nonsense rituals for hard work. But the physicians of the Black Service were always waiting to jerk wandering neophytes back to the scientific disciplines that made the service of Hospital Earth so effective. The Black Doctors would not tolerate sloppiness. "Show me the tissue, Doctor," they would say. "Prove to me that what you say is so. Prove that what you did was valid medicine...." Their laboratories were the morgues and autopsy rooms of a thousand planets, the Temples of Truth from which no physician since the days of Pasteur and Lister could escape for long and retain his position.

The Black Doctors were the pragmatists, the gadflies of Hospital Earth. For this reason it was surprising to hear Black Doctor Neelsen saying, "Perhaps we are being too scientific, just now. When the creature has exhausted our food stores, it will look elsewhere for food. Perhaps we must cut at the tree and not at the root."

"A frontal attack?" said Jenkins.

"Just so.. Its enzyme system is its vulnerability. Enzyme systems operate under specific optimum conditions, right? And every known enzyme system can be inactivated by adverse conditions of one sort or another. A physical approach may tell us how in this case. Meanwhile we will be on emergency rations, and hope that we don't starve to death finding out." The Black Doctor paused, looking at the men around him. "And in case you are thinking of enlisting help from outside, forget it. I've sent plague-warnings out for Galactic relay. We have this thing isolated, and we're going to keep it that way as long as I command this ship."

They went gloomily back to their laboratories to plan their frontal attack.

That was the night that Hrunta disappeared.

*

He was gone when they came to wake him from his sleep period. His bunk had been slept in, but he wasn't in it. In fact, he wasn't anywhere on the ship.

"But he couldn't just vanish!" the Black Doctor burst out when they told him the news. "Maybe he's hiding somewhere. Maybe this business was working on his mind."

Green Doctor Stone took a crew of men to search the ship again, even though he considered it a waste of precious time. He had his private convictions about where Hrunta had gone.

So did every other man on the ship, including Jenkins.

The *hlorg* had stopped eating. Huge and round and wet and ugly, it squatted in the after-hold, quivering gently, without any other sign of life.

Surfeited. Like a fat man after a turkey dinner.

Jenkins reviewed progress with the others. No stone had been left unturned. They had sliced the *hlorg*, and squeezed it. They had boiled it and frozen it. They had dropped chunks of it in acid vats and covered other chunks with desiccants and alkalis. Nothing seemed to bother it.

A cold environment slowed down its activity, true, but it also stimulated the process of fission. Warmed up again, the portions sucked back together again and resumed eating.

Heat was a little more effective, but not much. It stunned the creature for a brief period, but it would not burn. It hissed frightfully and gave off an overpowering stench, and curled up at the edges, but as soon as the heat was turned off it began to recover.

In Hrunta's lab chunks of the *hlorg* sat in a dozen vats on tables and in sinks. Some contained antibiotics, some concentrated acids, some desiccants. In each vat a blob of pink protoplasm wiggled happily, showing no sign of discomfiture. On another table were the remains of Hrunta's (unsuccessful) attempt to prepare an anti-*hlorg* serum.

But no Hrunta.

"He was down there with the thing all day," Bowman said sadly. "He felt it was his responsibility, really. Hrunta thought biochemistry was the answer to all things, of course. Very conscientious man."

"But he was in *bed*."

"He claimed he did his best thinking in bed. Maybe he had a brainstorm and went down to try it out, and—"

"Yes." Jenkins nodded sourly. "And." He walked down the row of vats. "You'd think that at least concentrated sulphuric would dessicate it a little. But it's just formed a crust of coagulated protein around itself, and sits there—"

Bowman peered over his shoulder, his mustache twitching. "But it does dessicate."

"If you use enough long enough."

"How about concentrated hydrochloric?"

"Same thing. Maybe a little more effective, but not enough to count."

"Okay. Next we try combinations. There's got to be *something* the wretched beast can't tolerate—"

There was, of course.

*

Green Doctor Stone brought it to Jenkins as he was getting ready to turn in for a sleep period. Jenkins had checked to make sure double guards were posted in the *hlorg's* vicinity, and jolted them with Sleep-Not to keep them on their toes. All the same, he tied a length of stout cord around his ankle just to make sure he didn't do any sleepwalking. He was tying it to the bunk when Stone came in with a pan in his hand and a peculiar look on his face.

"Take a look at this," he said.

Jenkins looked at the sickly brown mass in the tray, and then up at Stone. "Where did you find it?"

"Down in the hold. Our *hlorg* has broken precedent. It's *rejected* something that it ate."

"Yeah. What is it?"

"I don't know. I'm taking it to Neelsen for paraffin sections. But I know what it looks like to me."

"Mm. I know." Jenkins felt sick. Stone headed up to the path lab, leaving the Red Doctor settled in his bunk.

Ten minutes later Jenkins sat bolt upright in the darkness. Frantically he untied himself and slid into his clothes. "Idiot!" he growled to himself. "Seventh son of a seventh son—"

Five minutes later he was staring at the vats in Hrunta's laboratory. He found the one he was looking for. A pink blob of *hlorg* wiggled slowly around the bottom.

Jenkins drew a beaker of distilled water and added it to the fluid in the vat. It hissed and sputtered and sent up quantities of acrid steam. When the steam had cleared away, Jenkins peered in eagerly.

The pink thing in the bottom was turning a sickly violet. It had quit wiggling. As Jenkins watched, the violet color changed to mud grey, then to black. He prodded it with a stirring rod. There was no response.

With a whoop Jenkins buzzed Bowman and Stone. "We've got it!" he shouted to them when they appeared. "Look! Look at it!"

Bowman poked and probed and broke into a wide grin. The piece of *hlorg* was truly and sincerely dead. "It inactivates the enzyme system, and renders the base protoplasm vulnerable to anything that normally attacks it. What are we waiting for?"

They began tearing the laboratory apart, searching for the right bottles. The supply was discouragingly small, but there was some in stock. The three of them raced down the corridor for the hold where the *hlorg* was.

It took them three hours of angry work to exhaust the supply. They whittled chunks off the *hlorg*, tossed them in pans of the deadly fluid. With each slice they stopped momentarily to watch it turn violet, then black, as it died. The *hlorg*, dwindling in size, sensed the attack and slapped frantically at their ankles, sending out angry plumes of wet jelly, but they ducked and dodged and whittled some more. The *hlorg* quivered and gurgled and wept pinkish goo all over the floor, but it grew smaller and weaker with every whack.

"Hrunta must have spotted it and come down here alone," Jenkins panted between slices. "Maybe he slipped, lost his footing, I don't know—"

They continued to work until the supply was exhausted. They had reduced the *hlorg* to a quarter its previous size. "Check the other labs, see if they have some more," said Stone.

"I already have," Bowman said. "They don't. This is it."

"But we haven't got it all killed. There's still—" He pointed to the thing quailing in the corner.

"I know. We're licked, that's all. There isn't any more of the stuff on the ship."

They stopped and looked at each other suddenly. Then Jenkins said: "Oh, yes there is."

There was silence. Bowman looked at Stone, and Stone looked at Bowman. They both looked at Jenkins. "Oh, no. Sorry. I decline." Stone shook his head slowly.

"But we have to! There's no other way. If the enzyme system is inactivated, it's just protoplasm—there's no physiological or biochemical reason—"

"You know what you can do with your physiology and biochemistry," Bowman said succinctly. "You can also count me out." He left them and the hatchway clanged after him.

"Wally?"

"Yeah."

"It'll be months before we get back to Hospital Earth. We know how we can hold it in check until we get there."

"Yeah."

"Well?"

Green Doctor Wally Stone sighed. "Greater love hath no man," he said wearily. "We'd better go tell Neelsen, I guess."

*

Black Doctor Turvold Neelsen's answer was a flat, unequivocal no. "It's monstrous and preposterous. I won't stand for it. Nobody will stand for it."

"But you have the proof in your own hands," Jenkins said. "You saw the specimen that the Green Doctor brought you."

Neelsen hunched back angrily. "I saw it."

"And your impression of it? As a pathologist?"

"I fail to see how my impression applies one way or the other—"

"Doctor, sometimes we have to face facts. Remember?"

"All right." Neelsen seemed to curl up into himself still further. "The specimen was stomach."

"Human stomach?"

"Human stomach."

"But the only human on this ship that doesn't have a stomach is Hrunta," said Jenkins.

"So the *hlorg* ate him."

"*Most* of him. Not quite all. It threw out the one part of him it couldn't eat. The part containing a substance that inactivated its enzyme system. Dilute hydrochloric acid, to be specific. We used the entire ship's supply, and cut the *hlorg* down to three-quarters size, but we need a continuous supply to keep it whittled down until we get home. And there's only one good, permanent, reliable source of dilute hydrochloric acid on board this ship—"

The Black Doctor's face was purple. "I said no," he choked. "My answer stands."

The Red Doctor sighed and turned to Green Doctor Stone. "All right, Wally," he said.

*

(*From the files of the Medical Disciplinary Board, Hospital Earth, op. cit.*)

I am certain that you can see from the foregoing that a reasonable effort was made by Green Doctor Stone and myself to put the plan in effect peaceably and with full approval of our commander. It was our conviction, however, that the emergency nature of the circumstances required that it be done with or without his approval. Our subsequent success in containing the *hlorg* to at least reasonable and manageable proportions should bear out the wisdom of our decision.

Actually, it has not been as bad as one might think. It has been necessary to confine the crew to their quarters, and to restrain the Black

Doctor forcibly, but with liberal use of Happy-O we can occasionally convince ourselves that it is rare beefsteak, and the Green Doctor, our pro-tem cook has concocted several very tasty sauces, such as mushroom, onion, etc. We reduce the *hlorg* to half its size each day, and if thoroughly heated the chunks lie still on the plate for quite some time.

No physical ill effects have been noted, and the period of quarantine is recommended solely to allow the men an adequate period for psychological recovery.

I have only one further recommendation: that the work team from the Grey Service be recalled at once from their assignment on Mauki IV. The problem is decidedly not psychiatric, and it would be one of the tragedies of the ages if our excellent psychiatric service were to succeed in persuading the Maukivi out of their 'delusion'.

After all, Hospital Earth cannot afford to jeopardize a Contract—

(Signed) Samuel B. Jenkins,
Physician Grade VI
Red Service
GPP Ship *Lancet*
(Attached GSS *Mercy* pro tem)

THE LINK

It was nearly sundown when Ravdin eased the ship down into the last slow arc toward the Earth's surface. Stretching his arms and legs, he tried to relax and ease the tension in his tired muscles. Carefully, he tightened the seat belt for landing; below him he could see the vast, tangled expanse of Jungle-land spreading out to the horizon. Miles ahead was the bright circle of the landing field and the sparkling glow of the city beyond. Ravdin peered to the north of the city, hoping to catch a glimpse of the concert before his ship was swallowed by the brilliant landing lights.

A bell chimed softly in his ear. Ravdin forced his attention back to the landing operation. He was still numb and shaken from the Warp-passage, his mind still muddled by the abrupt and incredible change. Moments before, the sky had been a vast, starry blanket of black velvet; then, abruptly, he had been hovering over the city, sliding down toward warm friendly lights and music. He checked the proper switches, and felt the throbbing purr of the anti-grav motors as the ship slid in toward the landing slot. Tall spires of other ships rose to meet him, circle upon circle of silver needles pointing skyward. A little later they were blotted out as the ship was grappled into the berth from which it had risen days before.

With a sigh, Ravdin eased himself out of the seat, his heart pounding with excitement. Perhaps, he thought, he was too excited, too eager to be home, for his mind was still reeling from the fearful discovery of his journey.

The station was completely empty as Ravdin walked down the ramp to the shuttles. At the desk he checked in with the shiny punch-card robot, and walked swiftly across the polished floor. The wall panels pulsed a somber blue-green, broken sharply by brilliant flashes and overtones of scarlet, reflecting with subtle accuracy the tumult in his own mind. Not a sound was in the air, not a whisper nor sign of human habitation. Vaguely, uneasiness grew in his mind as he entered the shuttle station. Suddenly, the music caught him, a long, low chord of indescribable beauty, rising and falling in the wind, a distant whisper of life....

The concert, of course. Everyone would be at the concert tonight, and even from two miles away, the beauty of four hundred perfectly harmonized voices was carried on the breeze. Ravdin's uneasiness disappeared; he was eager to discharge his horrible news, get it off his mind and join the others in the great amphitheater set deep in the hillside outside the city. But he knew instinctively that Lord Nehmon, anticipating his return, would not be at the concert.

Riding the shuttle over the edges of Jungle-land toward the shining bright beauty of the city, Ravdin settled back, trying to clear his mind of the shock and horror he had encountered on his journey. The curves and spires of glowing plastic passed him, lighted with a million hues. He realized that his whole life was entangled in the very beauty of this wonderful city. Everything he had ever hoped or dreamed lay sheltered here in the ever-changing rhythm of colors and shapes and sounds. And now, he knew, he would soon see his beloved city burning once again, turning to flames and ashes in a heart-breaking memorial to the age-old fear of his people.

The little shuttle-car settled down softly on the green terrace near the center of the city. The building was a masterpiece of smoothly curving walls and tasteful lines, opening a full side to the south to catch the soft sunlight and warm breezes. Ravdin strode across the deep carpeting of the terrace. There was other music here, different music, a wilder, more intimate fantasy of whirling sound. An oval door opened for him, and he stopped short, staggered for a moment by the overpowering beauty in the vaulted room.

A girl with red hair the color of new flame was dancing with enthralling beauty and abandon, her body moving like ripples of wind to the music which filled the room with its throbbing cry. Her beauty was exquisite, every motion, every flowing turn a symphony of flawless perfection as she danced to the wild music.

"Lord Nehmon!"

The dancer threw back her head sharply, eyes wide, her body frozen in mid-air, and then, abruptly, she was gone, leaving only the barest flickering image of her fiery hair. The music slowed, singing softly, and Ravdin could see the old man waiting in the room. Nehmon rose, his gaunt face and graying hair belying the youthful movement of his body. Smiling, he came forward, clapped Ravdin on the shoulder, and took his hand warmly. "You're too late for the concert—it's a shame. Mischana is the master tonight, and the whole city is there."

Ravdin's throat tightened as he tried to smile. "I had to let you know," he said. "*They're coming*, Nehmon! I saw them, hours ago."

The last overtones of the music broke abruptly, like a glass shattered on stone. The room was deathly still. Lord Nehmon searched the young man's face. Then he turned away, not quite concealing the sadness and pain in his eyes. "You're certain? You couldn't be mistaken?"

"No chance. I found signs of their passing in a dozen places. Then I saw *them*, their whole fleet. There were hundreds. They're coming, I saw them."

"Did they see you?" Nehmon's voice was sharp.

"No, no. The Warp is a wonderful thing. With it I could come and go in the twinkling of an eye. But I could see them in the twinkling of an eye."

"And it couldn't have been anyone else?"

"Could anyone else build ships like the Hunters?"

Nehmon sighed wearily. "No one that we know." He glanced up at the young man. "Sit down, son, sit down. I—I'll just have to rearrange my thinking a little. Where were they? How far?"

"Seven light years," Ravdin said. "Can you imagine it? Just seven, and moving straight this way. *They know where we are*, and they are coming quickly." His eyes filled with fear. "They *couldn't* have found us so soon, unless they too have discovered the Warp and how to use it to travel."

The older man's breath cut off sharply, and there was real alarm in his eyes. "You're right," he said softly. "Six months ago it was eight hundred light years away, in an area completely remote from us. Now just *seven*. In six months they have come so close."

The scout looked up at Nehmon in desperation. "But what can we do? We have only weeks, maybe days, before they're here. We have no time to plan, no time to prepare for them. What can we do?"

The room was silent. Finally the aged leader stood up, wearily, some fraction of his six hundred years of life showing in his face for the first time in centuries. "We can do once again what we always have done before when the Hunters came," he said sadly. "We can run away."

*

The bright street below the oval window was empty and quiet. Not a breath of air stirred in the city. Ravdin stared out in bitter silence. "Yes, we can run away. Just as we always have before. After we have worked so hard, accomplished so much here, we must burn the city and flee again." His voice trailed off to silence. He stared at Nehmon, seeking in the old man's face some answer, some reassurance. But he found no answer there, only sadness. "Think of the concerts. It's taken so long, but at last we've come so close to the ultimate goal." He gestured toward the thought-sensitive sounding boards lining the walls, the panels which had made the dancer-illusion possible. "Think of the beauty and peace we've found here."

"I know. How well I know."

"Yet now the Hunters come again, and again we must run away." Ravdin stared at the old man, his eyes suddenly bright. "Nehmon, when I saw those ships I began thinking."

"I've spent many years thinking, my son."

"Not what I've been thinking." Ravdin sat down, clasping his hands in excitement. "The Hunters come and we run away, Nehmon. Think about that for a moment. We run, and we run, and we run. From what? We run from the Hunters. They're hunting *us*, these Hunters. They've never quite found us, because we've always already run. We're clever, we're fortunate, and we have a way of life that they do not, so whenever they have come close to finding us, we have run."

Nehmon nodded slowly. "For thousands of years."

Ravdin's eyes were bright. "Yes, we flee, we cringe, we hide under stones, we break up our lives and uproot our families, running like frightened animals in the shadows of night and secrecy." He gulped a breath, and his eyes sought Nehmon's angrily. "*Why do we run, my lord?*"

Nehmon's eyes widened. "Because we have no choice," he said. "We must run or be killed. You know that. You've seen the records, you've been taught."

"Oh, yes, I know what I've been taught. I've been taught that eons ago our remote ancestors fought the Hunters, and lost, and fled, and were pursued. But why do we keep running? Time after time we've been cornered, and we've turned and fled. *Why?* Even animals know that when they're cornered they must turn and fight."

"We are not animals." Nehmon's voice cut the air like a whiplash.

"But we could fight."

"Animals fight. We do not. We fought once, like animals, and now we must run from the Hunters who continue to fight like animals. So be it. Let the Hunters fight."

Ravdin shook his head. "Do you mean that the Hunters are not men like us?" he said. "That's what you're saying, that they are animals. All right. We kill animals for our food, isn't that true? We kill the tiger-beasts in the Jungle to protect ourselves, why not kill the Hunters to protect ourselves?"

Nehmon sighed, and reached out a hand to the young man. "I'm sorry," he said gently. "It seems logical, but it's false logic. The Hunters are men just like you and me. Their lives are different, their culture is different, but they are men. And human life is sacred, to us, above all else. This is the fundamental basis of our very existence. Without it we would be Hunters, too. If we fight, we are dead even if we live. That's why we must run away now, and always. Because we know that we must not kill men."

*

On the street below, the night air was suddenly full of voices, chattering, intermingled with whispers of song and occasional brief harmonic flutterings. The footfalls were muted on the polished pavement as the people passed slowly, their voices carrying a hint of puzzled uneasiness.

"The concert's over!" Ravdin walked to the window, feeling a chill pass through him. "So soon, I wonder why?" Eagerly he searched the faces passing in the street for Dana's face, sensing the lurking discord in the quiet talk of the crowd. Suddenly the sound-boards in the room tinkled a carillon of ruby tones in his ear, and she was in the room, rushing into his arms with a happy cry, pressing her soft cheek to his rough chin. "You're back! Oh, I'm so glad, so very glad!" She turned to the old man. "Nehmon, what has happened? The concert was ruined tonight. There was something in the air, everybody felt it. For some reason the people seemed *afraid.*"

Ravdin turned away from his bride. "Tell her," he said to the old man.

Dana looked at them, her gray eyes widening in horror. "The Hunters! They've found us?"

Ravdin nodded wordlessly.

Her hands trembled as she sat down, and there were tears in her eyes. "We came so close tonight, so very close. I *felt* the music before it was sung, do you realize that? I *felt* the fear around me, even though no one said a word. It wasn't vague or fuzzy, it was *clear*! The transference was perfect." She turned to face the old man. "It's taken so long to come this far, Nehmon. So much work, so much training to reach a perfect communal concert. We've had only two hundred years here, only *two hundred*! I was just a little girl when we came, I can't even remember before that. Before we came here we were undisturbed for a thousand years, and before that, four thousand. But *two hundred*—we *can't* leave now. Not when we've come so far."

Ravdin nodded. "That's the trouble. They come closer every time. This time they will catch us. Or the next time, or the next. And that will be the end of everything for us, unless we fight them." He paused, watching the last groups dispersing on the street below. "If we only knew, for certain, what we were running from."

There was a startled silence. The girl's breath came in a gasp and her eyes widened as his words sank home. "Ravdin," she said softly, "*have you ever seen a Hunter*?"

Ravdin stared at her, and felt a chill of excitement. Music burst from the sounding-board, odd, wild music, suddenly hopeful. "No," he said, "no, of course not. You know that."

The girl rose from her seat. "Nor have I. Never, not once." She turned to Lord Nehmon. "Have *you*?"

"Never." The old man's voice was harsh.

"Has *anyone* ever seen a Hunter?"

Ravdin's hand trembled. "I—I don't know. None of us living now, no. It's been too long since they last actually found us. I've read—oh, I can't remember. I think my grandfather saw them, or my great-grandfather, somewhere back there. It's been thousands of years."

"Yet we've been tearing ourselves up by the roots, fleeing from planet to planet, running and dying and still running. But suppose we don't need to run anymore?"

He stared at her. "They keep coming. They keep searching for us. What more proof do you need?"

Dana's face glowed with excitement, alive with new vitality, new hope. "Ravdin, can't you see? *They might have changed.* They might not be the same. Things can happen. Look at us, how we've grown since the wars with the Hunters. Think how our philosophy and culture have matured! Oh, Ravdin, you were to be master at a concert next month. Think how the concerts have changed! Even my grandmother can remember when the concerts were just a few performers playing, and everyone else just sitting and *listening*! Can you imagine anything more silly? They hadn't even thought of transference then, they never dreamed what a *real* concert could be! Why, those people had never begun to understand music until they themselves became a part of it. Even we can see these changes, why couldn't the Hunters have grown and changed just as we have?"

Nehmon's voice broke in, almost harshly, as he faced the excited pair. "The Hunters don't have concerts," he said grimly. "You're deluding yourself, Dana. They laugh at our music, they scoff at our arts and twist them into obscene mockeries. They have no concept of beauty in their language. The Hunters are incapable of change."

"And you can be certain of that when *nobody has seen them for thousands of years?*"

Nehmon met her steady eyes, read the strength and determination there. He knew, despairingly, what she was thinking—that he was old, that he couldn't understand, that his mind was channeled now beyond the approach of wisdom. "You mustn't think what you're thinking," he said weakly. "You'd be blind. You wouldn't know, you couldn't have any idea what you would find. If you tried to contact them, you could be lost completely, tortured, killed. If they haven't changed, you wouldn't stand a chance. You'd never come back, Dana."

"But she's right all the same," Ravdin said softly. "You're wrong, my lord. We can't continue this way if we're to survive. Sometime our people must contact them, find the link that was once between us, and forge it strong again. We could do it, Dana and I."

"I could forbid you to go."

Dana looked at her husband, and her eyes were proud. "You could forbid us," she said, facing the old man. "But you could never stop us."

*

At the edge of the Jungle-land a great beast stood with green-gleaming eyes, licking his fanged jaws as he watched the glowing city, sensing somehow that the mystifying circle of light and motion was soon to become his Jungle-land again. In the city the turmoil bubbled over, as wave after wave of the people made the short safari across the intervening jungle to the circles of their ships. Husbands, wives, fathers, mothers—all carried their small, frail remembrances out to the ships. There was music among them still, but it was a different sort of music, now, an eerie, hopeless music that drifted out of the city in the wind. It caused all but the bravest of the beasts, their hair prickling on their backs, to run in panic through the jungle darkness. It was a melancholy music, carried from thought to thought, from voice to voice as the people of the city wearily prepared themselves once again for the long journey.

To run away. In the darkness of secrecy, to be gone, without a trace, without symbol or vestige of their presence, leaving only the scorched circle of land for the jungle to reclaim, so that no eyes, not even the sharpest, would ever know how long they had stayed, nor where they might have gone.

In the rounded room of his house, Lord Nehmon dispatched the last of his belongings, a few remembrances, nothing more, because the space on the ships must take people, not remembrances, and he knew that the remembrances would bring only pain. All day Nehmon had supervised the loading, the intricate preparation, following plans laid down millennia before. He saw the libraries and records transported, mile upon endless mile of microfilm, carted to the ships prepared to carry them, stored until a new resting place was found. The history of a people was recorded on that film, a people once proud and strong, now equally proud, but dwindling in numbers as toll for the constant roving. A proud people, yet a people who would turn and run without thought, in a panic of age-old fear. They *had* to run, Nehmon knew, if they were to survive.

And with a blaze of anger in his heart, he almost hated the two young people waiting here with him for the last ship to be filled. For these two would not go.

It had been a long and painful night. He had pleaded and begged, tried to persuade them that there was no hope, that the very idea of remaining behind or trying to contact the Hunters was insane. Yet he knew *they* were sane, perhaps unwise, naive, but their decision had been reached, and they would not be shaken.

The day was almost gone as the last ships began to fill. Nehmon turned to Ravdin and Dana, his face lined and tired. "You'll have to go soon," he said. "The city will be burned, of course, as always. You'll be left with food, and with weapons against the jungle. The Hunters will know that we've been here, but they'll not know when, nor where we have gone." He paused. "It will be up to you to see that they don't learn."

Dana shook her head. "We'll tell them nothing, unless it's safe for them to know."

"They'll question you, even torture you."

She smiled calmly. "Perhaps they won't. But as a last resort, we can blank out."

Nehmon's face went white. "You know there is no coming back, once you do that. You would never regain your memory. You must save it for a last resort."

Down below on the street the last groups of people were passing; the last sweet, eerie tones of the concert were rising in the gathering twilight. Soon the last families would have taken their refuge in the ships, waiting for Nehmon to trigger the fire bombs to ignite the beautiful city after the ships started on their voyage. The concerts were over; there would be long years of aimless wandering before another home could be found, another planet safe from the Hunters and their ships. Even then it would be more years before the concerts could again rise from their hearts and throats and minds, generations before they could begin work again toward the climactic expression of their heritage.

Ravdin felt the desolation in the people's minds, saw the utter hopelessness in the old man's face, and suddenly felt the pressure of despair. It was such a slender hope, so frail and so dangerous. He knew of the terrible fight, the war of his people against the Hunters, so many thousand years before. They had risen together, a common people, their home a single planet. And then, the gradual splitting of the nations, his own people living in peace, seeking the growth and beauty of the arts, despising the bitterness and barrenness of hatred and killing—and the Hunters, under an iron heel of militarism, of government for the perpetuation of government, split farther and farther from them. It was an ever-widening split as the Hunters sneered and ridiculed, and then grew to hate Ravdin's people for all the things the Hunters were losing: peace, love, happiness. Ravdin knew of his people's slowly dawning awareness of the sanctity of life, shattered abruptly by the horrible wars, and then the centuries of fear and flight, hiding from the wrath of the Hunters' vengeance. His people had learned much in those long years. They had conquered disease. They had grown in strength as they dwindled in numbers. But now the end could be seen, crystal clear, the end of his people and a ghastly grave.

Nehmon's voice broke the silence. "If you must stay behind, then go now. The city will burn an hour after the count-down."

"We will be safe, outside the city." Dana gripped her husband's hand, trying to transmit to him some part of her strength and confidence. "Wish us the best, Nehmon. If a link can be forged, we will forge it."

"I wish you the best in everything." There were tears in the old man's eyes as he turned and left the room.

*

They stood in the Jungle-land, listening to the scurry of frightened animals, and shivering in the cool night air as the bright sparks of the ships' exhausts faded into the black starry sky. A man and a woman alone, speechless, watching, staring with awful longing into the skies as the bright rocket jets dwindled to specks and flickered out.

The city burned. Purple spumes of flame shot high into the air, throwing a ghastly light on the frightened Jungle-land. Spires of flame seemed to be seeking the stars with their fingers as the plastic walls and streets of the city hissed and shriveled, blackening, bubbling into a vanishing memory before their eyes. The flames shot high, carrying with them the last remnants of the city which had stood proud and tall an hour before. Then a silence fell, deathly, like the lifeless silence of a grave. Out of the silence, little whispering sounds of the Jungle-land crept to their ears, first frightened, then curious, then bolder and bolder as the wisps of grass and little animals ventured out and out toward the clearing where the city had stood. Bit by bit the Jungle-land gathered courage, and the clearing slowly, silently, began to disappear.

Days later new sparks of light appeared in the black sky. They grew to larger specks, then to flares, and finally settled to the earth as powerful, flaming jets.

They were squat, misshapen vessels, circling down like vultures, hissing, screeching, landing with a grinding crash in the tall thicket near the place where the city had stood. Ravdin's signal had guided them in, and the Hunters had seen them, standing on a hilltop above the demolished amphitheater. Men had come out of the ships, large men with cold faces and dull eyes, weapons strapped to their trim uniforms. The Hunters had blinked at them, unbelieving, with their weapons held at ready. Ravdin and Dana were seized and led to the flagship.

As they approached it, their hearts sank and they clasped hands to bolster their failing hope.

The leader of the Hunters looked up from his desk as they were thrust into his cabin. Frankle's face was a graven mask as he searched their faces dispassionately. The captives were pale and seemed to cringe from the pale interrogation light. "Chickens!" the Hunter snorted. "We have been hunting down chickens." His eyes turned to one of the guards. "They have been searched?"

"Of course, master."

"And questioned?"

The guard frowned. "Yes, sir. But their language is almost unintelligible."

"You've studied the basic tongues, haven't you?" Frankle's voice was as cold as his eyes.

"Of course, sir, but this is so different."

Frankle stared in contempt at the fair-skinned captives, fixing his eyes on them for a long moment. Finally he said, "Well?"

Ravdin glanced briefly at Dana's white face. His voice seemed weak and high-pitched in comparison to the Hunter's baritone. "You are the leader of the Hunters?"

Frankle regarded him sourly, without replying. His thin face was swarthy, his short-cut gray hair matching the cold gray of his eyes. It was an odd face, completely blank of any thought or emotion, yet capable of shifting to a strange biting slyness in the briefest instant. It was a rich face, a face of inscrutable depth. He pushed his chair back, his eyes watchful. "We know your people were here," he said suddenly. "Now they've gone, and yet you remain behind. There must be a reason for such rashness. Are you sick? Crippled?"

Ravdin shook his head. "We are not sick."

"Then criminals, perhaps? Being punished for rebellious plots?"

"We are not criminals."

The Hunter's fist crashed on the desk. "Then why are you here? *Why*? Are you going to tell me now, or do you propose to waste a few hours of my time first?"

"There is no mystery," Ravdin said softly. "We stayed behind to plead for peace."

"For peace?" Frankle stared in disbelief. Then he shrugged, his face tired. "I might have known. Peace! Where have your people gone?"

Ravdin met him eye for eye. "I can't say."

The Hunter laughed. "Let's be precise, you don't *choose* to say, just now. But perhaps very soon you will wish with all your heart to tell me."

Dana's voice was sharp. "We're telling you the truth. We want peace, nothing more. This constant hunting and running is senseless, exhausting to both of us. We want to make peace with you, to bring our people together again."

Frankle snorted. "You came to us in war, once, long ago. Now you want peace. What would you do, clasp us to your bosom, smother us in your idiotic music? Or have you gone on to greater things?"

Ravdin's face flushed hotly. "Much greater things," he snapped.

Frankle sat down slowly. "No doubt," he said. "Now understand me clearly. Very soon you will be killed. How quickly or slowly you die will depend largely upon the civility of your tongues. A civil tongue answers questions with the right answers. That is my definition of a civil tongue." He sat back coldly. "Now, shall we commence asking questions?"

Dana stepped forward suddenly, her cheeks flushed. "We don't have the words to express ourselves," she said softly. "We can't tell you in words what we have to say, but music is a language even you can understand. We can tell you what we want in music."

Frankle scowled. He knew about the magic of this music, he had heard of the witchcraft these weak chicken-people could weave, of their strange, magic power to steal strong men's minds from them and make them like children before wolves. But he had never heard this music with his own ears. He looked at them, his eyes strangely bright. "You know I cannot listen to your music. It is forbidden, even you should know that. How dare you propose—"

"But this is different music." Dana's eyes widened, and she threw an excited glance at her husband. "Our music is beautiful, wonderful to hear. If you could only hear it—"

"Never." The man hesitated. "Your music is forbidden, poisonous."

Her smile was like sweet wine, a smile that worked into the Hunter's mind like a gentle, lazy drug. "But who is to permit or forbid? After all, you are the leader here, and forbidden pleasures are all the sweeter."

Frankle's eyes were on hers, fascinated. Slowly, with a graceful movement, she drew the gleaming thought-sensitive stone from her clothing. It glowed in the room with a pearly luminescence, and she saw the man's eyes turning to it, drawn as if by magic. Then he looked away, and a cruel smile curled his lips. He motioned toward the stone. "All right," he said mockingly. "Do your worst. Show me your precious music."

Like a tinkle of glass breaking in a well, the stone flashed its fiery light in the room. Little swirls of music seemed to swell from it, blossoming in the silence. Frankle tensed, a chill running up his spine, his eyes drawn back to the gleaming jewel. Suddenly, the music filled the room, rising sweetly like an overpowering wave, filling his mind with strange and wonderful images. The stone shimmered and changed, taking the form of dancing clouds of light, swirling with the music as it rose. Frankle felt his mind groping toward the music, trying desperately to reach into the heart of it, to become part of it.

Ravdin and Dana stood there, trancelike, staring transfixed at the gleaming center of light, forcing their joined minds to create the crashing, majestic chords as the song lifted from the depths of oblivion to the heights of glory in the old, old song of their people.

A song of majesty, and strength, and dignity. A song of love, of aspiration, a song of achievement. A song of peoples driven by ancient fears across the eons of space, seeking only peace, even peace with those who drove them.

Frankle heard the music, and could not comprehend, for his mind could not grasp the meaning, the true overtones of those glorious chords, but he felt the strangeness in the pangs of fear which groped through his mind, cringing from the wonderful strains, dazzled by the dancing light. He stared wide-eyed and trembling at the couple across the room, and for an instant it seemed that he was stripped naked. For a fleeting moment the authority was gone from his face; gone too was the cruelty, the avarice, the sardonic mockery. For the briefest moment his cold gray eyes grew incredibly tender with a sudden ancient, long-forgotten longing, crying at last to be heard.

And then, with a scream of rage he was stumbling into the midst of the light, lashing out wildly at the heart of its shimmering brilliance. His huge hand caught the hypnotic stone and swept it into crashing, ear-splitting cacophony against the cold steel bulkhead. He stood rigid, his whole body shaking, eyes blazing with fear and anger and hatred as he turned on Ravdin and Dana. His voice was a raging storm of bitterness drowning out the dying strains of the music.

"Spies! You thought you could steal my mind away, make me forget my duty and listen to your rotten, poisonous noise! Well, you failed, do you hear? I didn't hear it, I didn't listen, *I didn't*! I'll hunt you down as my fathers hunted you down, I'll bring my people their vengeance and glory, and your foul music will be dead!"

He turned to the guards, wildly, his hands still trembling. "Take them out! Whip them, burn them, do anything! But find out where their people have gone. Find out! Music! We'll take the music out of them, once and for all."

*

The inquisition had been horrible. Their minds had had no concept of such horror, such relentless, racking pain. The blazing lights, the questions screaming in their ears, Frankle's vicious eyes burning in frustration, and their own screams, rising with each question they would not answer until their throats were scorched and they could no longer scream. Finally they reached the limit they could endure, and muttered together the hoarse words that could deliver them. Not words that Frankle could hear, but words to bring deliverance, to blank out their minds like a wet sponge over slate. The hypnotic key clicked into the lock of their minds; their screams died in their brains. Frankle stared at them, and knew instantly what they had done, a technique of memory obliteration known and dreaded for so many thousands of years that history could not remember. As his captives stood mindless before him, he let out one hoarse, agonized scream of frustration and defeat.

But strangely enough he did not kill them. He left them on a cold stone ledge, blinking dumbly at each other as the ships of his fleet rose one by one and vanished like fireflies in the dark night sky. Naked, they sat alone on the planet of the Jungle-land. They knew no words, no music, nothing. And they did not even know that in the departing ships a seed had been planted. For Frankle *had* heard the music. He had grasped the beauty of his enemies for that brief instant, and in that instant they had become less his enemies. A tiny seed of doubt had been planted. The seed would grow.

The two sat dumbly, shivering. Far in the distance, a beast roared against the heavy night, and a light rain began to fall. They sat naked, the rain soaking their skin and hair. Then one of them grunted, and moved into the dry darkness of the cave. Deep within him some instinct spoke, warning him to fear the roar of the animal.

Blinking dully, the woman crept into the cave after him. Three thoughts alone filled their empty minds. Not thoughts of Nehmon and his people;

to them, Nehmon had never existed, forgotten as completely as if he had never been. No thoughts of the Hunters, either, nor of their unheard-of mercy in leaving them their lives—lives of memoryless oblivion, like animals in this green Jungle-land, but lives nonetheless.

Only three thoughts filled their minds:

It was raining.

They were hungry.

The Saber-tooth was prowling tonight.

They never knew that the link had been forged.

MEETING OF THE BOARD

It was going to be a bad day. As he pushed his way nervously through the crowds toward the Exit Strip, Walter Towne turned the dismal prospect over and over in his mind. The potential gloominess of this particular day had descended upon him the instant the morning buzzer had gone off, making it even more tempting than usual just to roll over and forget about it all. Twenty minutes later, the water-douse came to drag him, drenched and gurgling, back to the cruel cold world. He had wolfed down his morning Koffee-Kup with one eye on the clock and one eye on his growing sense of impending crisis. And now, to make things just a trifle worse, he was going to be late again.

He struggled doggedly across the rumbling Exit strip toward the plant entrance. After all, he told himself, why should he be so upset? He *was* Vice President-in-Charge-of-Production of the Robling Titanium Corporation. What could they do to him, really? He had rehearsed *his* part many times, squaring his thin shoulders, looking the union boss straight in the eye and saying, "Now, see here, Torkleson—" But he knew, when the showdown came, that he wouldn't say any such thing. And this was the morning that the showdown would come.

Oh, not because of the *lateness*. Of course Bailey, the shop steward, would take his usual delight in bringing that up. But this seemed hardly worthy of concern this morning. The reports waiting on his desk were what worried him. The sales reports. The promotion-draw reports. The royalty reports. The anticipated dividend reports. Walter shook his head wearily. The shop steward was a goad, annoying, perhaps even infuriating, but tolerable. Torkleson was a different matter.

He pulled his worn overcoat down over frayed shirt sleeves, and tried vainly to straighten the celluloid collar that kept scooting his tie up under his ear. Once off the moving strip, he started up the Robling corridor toward the plant gate. Perhaps he would be fortunate. Maybe the reports would be late. Maybe his secretary's two neurones would fail to synapse this morning, and she'd lose them altogether. And, as long as he was dreaming, maybe Bailey would break his neck on the way to work. He walked quickly past the workers' lounge, glancing in at the groups of men, arguing politics and checking the stock market reports before they changed from their neat gray business suits to their welding dungarees. Running up the stairs to the administrative wing, he paused outside the door to punch the time clock. 8:04. Damn. If only Bailey could be sick—

Bailey was not sick. The administrative offices were humming with frantic activity as Walter glanced down the rows of cubbyholes. In the middle of it all sat Bailey, in his black-and-yellow checkered tattersall, smoking a large cigar. His feet were planted on his desk top, but he hadn't started on his morning Western yet. He was busy glaring, first at the clock, then at Walter.

"Late again, I see," the shop steward growled.

Walter gulped. "Yes, sir. Just four minutes, this time, sir. You know those crowded strips—"

"So it's *just* four minutes now, eh?" Bailey's feet came down with a crash. "After last month's fine production record, you think four minutes doesn't matter, eh? Think just because you're a vice president it's all right to mosey in here whenever you feel like it." He glowered. "Well, this is three times this month you've been late, Towne. That's a demerit for each time, and you know what that means."

"You wouldn't count four minutes as a whole demerit!"

Bailey grinned. "Wouldn't I, now! You just add up your pay envelope on Friday. Ten cents an hour off for each demerit."

Walter sighed and shuffled back to his desk. Oh, well. It could have been worse. They might have fired him like poor Cartwright last month. He'd just *have* to listen to that morning buzzer.

The reports were on his desk. He picked them up warily. Maybe they wouldn't be so bad. He'd had more freedom this last month than before, maybe there'd been a policy change. Maybe Torkleson was gaining confidence in him. Maybe—

The reports were worse than he had ever dreamed.

"*Towne!*"

Walter jumped a foot. Bailey was putting down the visiphone receiver. His grin spread unpleasantly from ear to ear. "What have you been doing lately? Sabotaging the production line?"

"What's the trouble now?"

Bailey jerked a thumb significantly at the ceiling. "The boss wants to see you. And you'd better have the right answers, too. The boss seems to have a lot of questions."

Walter rose slowly from his seat. This was it, then. Torkleson had already seen the reports. He started for the door, his knees shaking.

It hadn't always been like this, he reflected miserably. Time was when things had been very different. It had *meant* something to be vice president of a huge industrial firm like Robling Titanium. A man could have had a fine house of his own, and a 'copter-car, and belong to the Country Club; maybe even have a cottage on a lake somewhere.

Walter could almost remember those days with Robling, before the switchover, before that black day when the exchange of ten little shares of stock had thrown the Robling Titanium Corporation into the hands of strange and unnatural owners.

*

The door was of heavy stained oak, with bold letters edged in gold:

TITANIUM WORKERS
OF AMERICA
Amalgamated Locals
Daniel P. Torkleson, Secretary

The secretary flipped down the desk switch and eyed Walter with pity. "Mr. Torkleson will see you."

Walter pushed through the door into the long, handsome office. For an instant he felt a pang of nostalgia—the floor-to-ceiling windows looking out across the long buildings of the Robling plant, the pine paneling, the broad expanse of desk—

"Well? Don't just stand there. Shut the door and come over here." The man behind the desk hoisted his three hundred well-dressed pounds and glared at Walter from under flagrant eyebrows. Torkleson's whole body quivered as he slammed a sheaf of papers down on the desk. "Just what do you think you're doing with this company, Towne?"

Walter swallowed. "I'm production manager of the corporation."

"And just what does the production manager *do* all day?"

Walter reddened. "He organizes the work of the plant, establishes production lines, works with Promotion and Sales, integrates Research and Development, operates the planning machines."

"And you think you do a pretty good job of it, eh? Even asked for a raise last year!" Torkleson's voice was dangerous.

Walter spread his hands. "I do my best. I've been doing it for thirty years. I should know what I'm doing."

"*Then how do you explain these reports?*" Torkleson threw the heap of papers into Walter's arms, and paced up and down behind the desk. "*Look* at them! Sales at rock bottom. Receipts impossible. Big orders canceled. The worst reports in seven years, and you say you know your job!"

"I've been doing everything I could," Walter snapped. "Of course the reports are bad, they couldn't help but be. We haven't met a production schedule in over two years. No plant can keep up production the way the men are working."

Torkleson's face darkened. He leaned forward slowly. "So it's the *men* now, is it? Go ahead. Tell me what's wrong with the men."

"Nothing's wrong with the men—if they'd only work. But they come in when they please, and leave when they please, and spend half their time changing and the other half on Koffee-Kup. No company could survive this. But that's only half of it—" Walter searched through the reports frantically. "This International Jet Transport account—they dropped us because we haven't had a new engine in six years. Why? Because Research and Development hasn't had any money for six years. What can two starved engineers and a second rate chemist drag out of an attic laboratory for competition in the titanium market?" Walter took a deep breath. "I've warned you time and again. Robling had built up accounts over the years with fine products and new models. But since the switchover seven years ago, you and your board have forced me to play the cheap products for the quick profit in order to give your men their dividends. Now the bottom's dropped out. We couldn't turn a quick profit on the big, important accounts, so we had to cancel them. If you had let me manage the company the way it should have been run—"

Torkleson had been slowly turning purple. Now he slammed his fist down on the desk. "We should just turn the company back to Management again, eh? Just let you have a free hand to rob us blind again. Well, it won't work, Towne. Not while I'm secretary of this union. We fought long and hard for control of this corporation, just the way all the other unions did. I know. I was through it all." He sat back smugly, his cheeks quivering with emotion. "You might say that I was a national leader in the movement. But I did it only for the men. The men want their dividends. They own the stock, stock is supposed to pay dividends."

"But they're cutting their own throats," Walter wailed. "You can't build a company and make it grow the way I've been forced to run it."

"Details!" Torkleson snorted. "I don't care *how* the dividends come in. That's your job. My job is to report a dividend every six months to the men who own the stock, the men working on the production lines."

Walter nodded bitterly. "And every year the dividend has to be higher than the last, or you and your fat friends are likely to be thrown out of your jobs—right? No more steaks every night. No more private gold-plated Buicks for you boys. No more twenty-room mansions in Westchester. No more big game hunting in the Rockies. No, you don't have to know anything but how to whip a board meeting into a frenzy so they'll vote you into office again each year."

Torkleson's eyes glittered. His voice was very soft. "I've always liked you, Walter. So I'm going to pretend I didn't hear you." He paused, then continued. "But here on my desk is a small bit of white paper. Unless you have my signature on that paper on the first of next month, you are out of a job, on grounds of incompetence. And I will personally see that you go on every White list in the country."

Walter felt the fight go out of him like a dying wind. He knew what the White list meant. No job, anywhere, ever, in management. No chance, ever, to join a union. No more house, no more weekly pay envelope. He spread his hands weakly. "What do you want?" he asked.

"I want a production plan on my desk within twenty-four hours. A plan that will guarantee me a five per cent increase in dividends in the next six months. And you'd better move fast, because I'm not fooling."

*

Back in his cubbyhole downstairs, Walter stared hopelessly at the reports. He had known it would come to this sooner or later. They all knew it—Hendricks of Promotion, Pendleton of Sales, the whole managerial staff.

It was wrong, all the way down the line. Walter had fought it tooth and nail since the day Torkleson had installed the moose heads in Walter's old office, and moved him down to the cubbyhole, under Bailey's watchful eye. He had argued, and battled, and pleaded, and lost. He had watched the company deteriorate day by day. Now they blamed him, and threatened his job, and he was helpless to do anything about it.

He stared at the machines, clicking busily against the wall. An idea began to form in his head. Helpless?

Not quite. Not if the others could see it, go along with it. It was a repugnant idea. But there was one thing they could do that even Torkleson and his fat-jowled crew would understand.

They could go on strike.

*

"It's ridiculous," the lawyer spluttered, staring at the circle of men in the room. "How can I give you an opinion on the legality of the thing? There isn't any legal precedent that I know of." He mopped his bald head with a large white handkerchief. "There just hasn't *been* a case of a company's management striking against its own labor. It—it isn't done. Oh, there have been lockouts, but this isn't the same thing at all."

Walter nodded. "Well, we couldn't very well lock the men out, they own the plant. We were thinking more of a lock-*in* sort of thing." He turned to Paul Hendricks and the others. "We know how the machines operate. They don't. We also know that the data we keep in the machines is essential to running the business; the machines figure production quotas, organize blueprints, prepare distribution lists, test promotion schemes. It would take an office full of managerial experts to handle even a single phase of the work without the machines."

The man at the window hissed, and Pendleton quickly snapped out the lights. They sat in darkness, hardly daring to breathe. Then: "Okay. Just the man next door coming home."

Pendleton sighed. "You're sure you didn't let them suspect anything, Walter? They wouldn't be watching the house?"

"I don't think so. And you all came alone, at different times." He nodded to the window guard, and turned back to the lawyer. "So we can't be sure of the legal end. You'd have to be on your toes."

"I still don't see how we could work it," Hendricks objected. His heavy face was wrinkled with worry. "Torkleson is no fool, and he has a lot of power in the National Association of Union Stockholders. All he'd need to do is ask for managers, and a dozen companies would throw them to him on loan. They'd be able to figure out the machine system and take over without losing a day."

"Not quite." Walter was grinning. "That's why I spoke of a lock-in. Before we leave, we throw the machines into feedback, every one of them. Lock them into reverberating circuits with a code sequence key. Then all they'll do is buzz and sputter until the feedback is broken with the key.

And the key is our secret. It'll tie the Robling office into granny knots, and scabs won't be able to get any more data out of the machines than Torkleson could. With a lawyer to handle injunctions, we've got them strapped."

"For what?" asked the lawyer.

Walter turned on him sharply. "For new contracts. Contracts to let us manage the company the way it should be managed. If they won't do it, they won't get another Titanium product off their production lines for the rest of the year, and their dividends will *really* take a nosedive."

"That means you'll have to beat Torkleson," said Bates. "He'll never go along."

"Then he'll be left behind."

Hendricks stood up, brushing off his dungarees. "I'm with you, Walter. I've taken all of Torkleson that I want to. And I'm sick of the junk we've been trying to sell people."

The others nodded. Walter rubbed his hands together. "All right. Tomorrow we work as usual, until the noon whistle. When we go off for lunch, we throw the machines into lock-step. Then we just don't come back. But the big thing is to keep it quiet until the noon whistle." He turned to the lawyer. "Are you with us, Jeff?"

Jeff Bates shook his head sadly. "I'm with you. I don't know why, you haven't got a leg to stand on. But if you want to commit suicide, that's all right with me." He picked up his briefcase, and started for the door. "I'll have your contract demands by tomorrow," he grinned. "See you at the lynching."

They got down to the details of planning.

*

The news hit the afternoon telecasts the following day. Headlines screamed:

MANAGEMENT SABOTAGES ROBLING MACHINES OFFICE STRIKERS THREATEN LABOR ECONOMY ROBLING LOCK-IN CREATES PANDEMONIUM

There was a long, indignant statement from Daniel P. Torkleson, condemning Towne and his followers for "flagrant violation of management contracts and illegal fouling of managerial processes." Ben Starkey, President of the Board of American Steel, expressed "shock and regret"; the Amalgamated Buttonhole Makers held a mass meeting in protest, demanding that "the instigators of this unprecedented crime be permanently barred from positions in American Industry."

In Washington, the nation's economists were more cautious in their views. Yes, it *was* an unprecedented action. Yes, there would undoubtedly be repercussions—many industries were having managerial troubles; but as for long term effects, it was difficult to say just at present.

On the Robling production lines the workmen blinked at each other, and at their machines, and wondered vaguely what it was all about.

Yet in all the upheaval, there was very little expression of surprise. Step by step, through the years, economists had been watching with wary eyes the growing movement toward union, control of industry. Even as far back as the '40's and '50's unions, finding themselves oppressed with the administration of growing sums of money—pension funds, welfare funds, medical insurance funds, accruing union dues—had begun investing in corporate stock. It was no news to them that money could make money. And what stock more logical to buy than stock in their own companies?

At first it had been a quiet movement. One by one the smaller firms had tottered, bled drier and drier by increasing production costs, increasing labor demands, and an ever-dwindling margin of profit. One by one they had seen their stocks tottering as they faced bankruptcy, only to be gobbled up by the one ready buyer with plenty of funds to buy with. At first, changes had been small and insignificant: boards of directors shifted; the men were paid higher wages and worked shorter hours; there were tighter management policies; and a little less money was spent on extras like Research and Development.

At first—until that fateful night when Daniel P. Torkleson of TWA and Jake Squill of Amalgamated Buttonhole Makers spent a long evening with beer and cigars in a hotel room, and floated the loan that threw steel to the unions. Oil had followed with hardly a fight, and as the unions began to feel their oats, the changes grew more radical.

Walter Towne remembered those stormy days well. The gradual undercutting of the managerial salaries, the tightening up of inter-union collusion to establish the infamous White list of Recalcitrant Managers. The shift from hourly wage to annual salary for the factory workers, and the change to the other pole for the managerial staff. And then, with creeping malignancy, the hungry howling of the union bosses for more and higher dividends, year after year, moving steadily toward the inevitable crisis.

Until Shop Steward Bailey suddenly found himself in charge of a dozen sputtering machines and an empty office.

*

Torkleson was waiting to see the shop steward when he came in next morning. The union boss's office was crowded with TV cameras, newsmen, and puzzled workmen. The floor was littered with piles of ominous-looking paper. Torkleson was shouting into a telephone, and three lawyers were shouting into Torkleson's ear. He spotted Bailey and waved him through the crowd into an inner office room. "Well? Did they get them fixed?"

Bailey spread his hands nervously. "The electronics boys have been at it since yesterday afternoon. Practically had the machines apart on the floor."

"I know that, stupid," Torkleson roared. "I ordered them there. Did they get the machines *fixed*?"

"Uh—well, no, as a matter of fact—"

"Well, *what's holding them up*?"

Bailey's face was a study in misery. "The machines just go in circles. The circuits are locked. They just reverberate."

"Then call American Electronics. Have them send down an expert crew."

Bailey shook his head. "They won't come."

"They *what*?"

"They said thanks, but no thanks. They don't want their fingers in this pie at all."

"Wait until I get O'Gilvy on the phone."

"It won't do any good, sir. They've got their own management troubles. They're scared silly of a sympathy strike."

The door burst open, and a lawyer stuck his head in. "What about those injunctions, Dan?"

"Get them moving," Torkleson howled. "They'll start those machines again, or I'll have them in jail so fast—" He turned back to Bailey. "What about the production lines?"

The shop steward's face lighted. "They slipped up, there. There was one program that hadn't been coded into the machines yet. Just a minor item, but it's a starter. We found it in Towne's desk, blueprints all ready, promotion all planned."

"Good, good," Torkleson breathed. "I have a directors' meeting right now, have to get the workers quieted down a bit. You put the program through, and give those electronics men three more hours to unsnarl this knot, or we throw them out of the union." He started for the door. "What were the blueprints for?"

"Trash cans," said Bailey. "Pure titanium-steel trash cans."

It took Robling Titanium approximately two days to convert its entire production line to titanium-steel trash cans. With the total resources of the giant plant behind the effort, production was phenomenal. In two more days the available markets were glutted. Within two weeks, at a conservative estimate, there would be a titanium-steel trash can for every man, woman, child, and hound dog on the North American continent. The jet engines, structural steels, tubing, and other pre-strike products piled up in the freight yards, their routing slips and order requisitions tied up in the reverberating machines.

But the machines continued to buzz and sputter.

The workers grew restive. From the first day, Towne and Hendricks and all the others had been picketing the plant, until angry crowds of workers had driven them off with shotguns. Then they came back in an old, weatherbeaten 'copter which hovered over the plant entrance carrying a banner with a plaintive message: ROBLING TITANIUM UNFAIR TO MANAGEMENT. Tomatoes were hurled, fists were shaken, but the 'copter remained.

The third day, Jeff Bates was served with an injunction ordering Towne to return to work. It was duly appealed, legal machinery began tying itself in knots, and the strikers still struck. By the fifth day there was a more serious note.

"You're going to have to appear, Walter. We can't dodge this one."

"When?"

"Tomorrow morning. And before a labor-rigged judge, too." The little lawyer paced his office nervously. "I don't like it. Torkleson's getting desperate. The workers are putting pressure on him."

Walter grinned. "Then Pendleton is doing a good job of selling."

"But you haven't got *time*," the lawyer wailed. "They'll have you in jail if you don't start the machines again. They may have you in jail if you *do* start them, too, but that's another bridge. Right now they want those machines going again."

"We'll see," said Walter. "What time tomorrow?"

"Ten o'clock." Bates looked up. "And don't try to skip. You be there, because *I* don't know what to tell them."

Walter was there a half hour early. Torkleson's legal staff glowered from across the room. The judge glowered from the bench. Walter closed his eyes with a little smile as the charges were read: "—breach of contract, malicious mischief, sabotage of the company's machines, conspiring to destroy the livelihood of ten thousand workers. Your Honor, we are preparing briefs to prove further that these men have formed a conspiracy to undermine the economy of the entire nation. We appeal to the spirit of orderly justice—"

Walter yawned as the words went on.

"Of course, if the defendant will waive his appeals against the previous injunctions, and will release the machines that were sabotaged, we will be happy to formally withdraw these charges."

There was a rustle of sound through the courtroom. His Honor turned to Jeff Bates. "Are you counsel for the defendant?"

"Yes, sir." Bates mopped his bald scalp. "The defendant pleads guilty to all counts."

The union lawyer dropped his glasses on the table with a crash. The judge stared. "Mr. Bates, if you plead guilty, you leave me no alternative—"

"—but to send me to jail," said Walter Towne. "Go ahead. Send me to jail. In fact, I *insist* upon going to jail."

The union lawyer's jaw sagged. There was a hurried conference. A recess was pleaded. Telephones buzzed. Then: "Your Honor, the plaintiff desires to withdraw all charges at this time."

"Objection," Bates exclaimed. "We've already pleaded."

"—feel sure that a settlement can be effected out of court—"

The case was thrown out on its ear.

And still the machines sputtered.

*

Back at the plant rumor had it that the machines were permanently gutted, and that the plant could never go back into production. Conflicting scuttlebutt suggested that persons high in uniondom had perpetrated the crisis deliberately, bullying Management into the strike for the sole purpose of cutting current dividends and selling stock to themselves cheaply. The rumors grew easier and easier to believe. The workers came to the plants in business suits, it was true, and lounged in the finest of lounges, and read the *Wall Street Journal*, and felt like stockholders. But to face facts, their salaries were not the highest. Deduct union dues, pension fees, medical insurance fees, and sundry other little items which had formerly been paid by well-to-do managements, and very little was left but the semi-annual dividend checks. And now the dividends were tottering.

Production lines slowed. There were daily brawls on the plant floor, in the lounge and locker rooms. Workers began joking about the trash cans; then the humor grew more and more remote. Finally, late in the afternoon of the eighth day, Bailey was once again in Torkleson's office.

"Well? Speak up! What's the beef this time?"

"Sir—the men—I mean, there's been some nasty talk. They're tired of making trash cans. No challenge in it. Anyway, the stock room is full, and the freight yard is full, and the last run of orders we sent out came back because nobody wants any more trash cans." Bailey shook his head. "The men won't swallow it any more. There's—well, there's been talk about having a board meeting."

Torkleson's ruddy cheeks paled. "Board meeting, huh?" He licked his heavy lips. "Now look, Bailey, we've always worked well together. I consider you a good friend of mine. You've got to get things under control. Tell the men we're making progress. Tell them Management is beginning to weaken from its original stand. Tell them we expect to have the strike broken in another few hours. Tell them anything."

He waited until Bailey was gone. Then, with a trembling hand he lifted the visiphone receiver. "Get me Walter Towne," he said.

*

"I'm not an unreasonable man," Torkleson was saying miserably, waving his fat paws in the air as he paced back and forth in front of the spokesmen for the striking managers. "Perhaps we were a little demanding, I concede it! Overenthusiastic with our ownership, and all that. But I'm sure we can come to some agreement. A hike in wage scale is certainly within reason. Perhaps we can even arrange for better company houses."

Walter Towne stifled a yawn. "Perhaps you didn't understand us. The men are agitating for a meeting of the board of directors. We want to be at that meeting. That's the only thing we're interested in right now."

"But there wasn't anything about a board meeting in the contract your lawyer presented."

"I know, but you rejected that contract. So we tore it up. Anyway, we've changed our minds."

Torkleson sat down, his heavy cheeks quivering. "Gentlemen, be reasonable! I can guarantee you your jobs, even give you a free hand with the management. So the dividends won't be so large—the men will have to get used to that. That's it, we'll put it through at the next executive conference, give you—"

"The board meeting," Walter said gently. "That'll be enough for us."

The union boss swore and slammed his fist on the desk. "Walk out in front of those men after what you've done? You're fools! Well, I've given you your chance. You'll get your board meeting. But you'd better come armed. Because I know how to handle this kind of board meeting, and if I have anything to say about it, this one will end with a massacre."

*

The meeting was held in a huge auditorium in the Robling administration building. Since every member of the union owned stock in the company, every member had the right to vote for members of the board of directors. But in the early days of the switchover, the idea of a board of directors smacked too strongly of the old system of corporate organization to suit the men. The solution had been simple, if a trifle ungainly. Everyone who owned stock in Robling Titanium was automatically a member of the board of directors, with Torkleson as chairman of the board. The stockholders numbered over ten thousand.

They were all present. They were packed in from the wall to the stage, and hanging from the rafters. They overflowed into the corridors. They jammed the lobby. Ten thousand men rose with a howl of anger when Walter Towne walked out on the stage. But they quieted down again as Dan Torkleson started to speak.

It was a masterful display of rabble-rousing. Torkleson paced the stage, his fat body shaking with agitation, pointing a chubby finger again and again at Walter Towne. He pranced and he ranted. He paused at just the right times for thunderous peals of applause.

"This morning in my office we offered to compromise with these jackals," he cried, "and they rejected compromise. Even at the cost of lowering dividends, of taking food from the mouths of your wives and children, we made our generous offers. They were rejected with scorn. These thieves have one desire in mind, my friends, to starve you all, and to destroy your company and your jobs. To every appeal they heartlessly refused to divulge the key to the lock-in. And now this man—the ringleader who keeps the key word buried in secrecy—has the temerity to ask an audience with you. You're angry men; you want to know the man to blame for our hardship."

He pointed to Towne with a flourish. "I give you your man. Do what you want with him."

The hall exploded in angry thunder. The first wave of men rushed onto the stage as Walter stood up. A tomato whizzed past his ear and splattered against the wall. More men clambered up on the stage, shouting and shaking their fists.

Then somebody appeared with a rope.

Walter gave a sharp nod to the side of the stage. Abruptly the roar of the men was drowned in another sound—a soul-rending, teeth-grating, bone-rattling screech. The men froze, jaws sagging, eyes wide, hardly believing their ears. In the instant of silence as the factory whistle died away, Walter grabbed the microphone. "You want the code word to start the machines again? I'll give it to you before I sit down!"

The men stared at him, shuffling, a murmur rising. Torkleson burst to his feet. "It's a trick!" he howled. "Wait 'til you hear their price."

"We have no price, and no demands," said Walter Towne. "We will *give* you the code word, and we ask nothing in return but that you listen for sixty seconds." He glanced back at Torkleson, and then out to the crowd. "You men here are an electing body—right? You own this great plant and company, top to bottom—right? *You should all be rich*, because Robling could make you rich. But not one of you out there is rich. Only the fat ones on this stage are. But I'll tell you how *you* can be rich."

They listened. Not a peep came from the huge hall. Suddenly, Walter Towne was talking their language.

"You think that since you own the company, times have changed. Well, have they? Are you any better off than you were? Of course not. Because you haven't learned yet that oppression by either side leads to misery for both. You haven't learned moderation. And you never will, until you throw out the ones who have fought moderation right down to the last ditch. You know whom I mean. You know who's grown richer and richer since the switchover. Throw him out, and you too can be rich." He paused for a deep breath. "You want the code word to unlock the machines? All right, I'll give it to you."

He swung around to point a long finger at the fat man sitting there. "The code word is TORKLESON!"

*

Much later, Walter Towne and Jeff Bates pried the trophies off the wall of the big office. The lawyer shook his head sadly. "Pity about Dan Torkleson. Gruesome affair."

Walter nodded as he struggled down with a moose head. "Yes, a pity, but you know the boys when they get upset."

"I suppose so." The lawyer stopped to rest, panting. "Anyway, with the newly elected board of directors, things will be different for everybody. You took a long gamble."

"Not so long. Not when you knew what they wanted to hear. It just took a little timing."

"Still, I didn't think they'd elect you secretary of the union. It just doesn't figure."

Walter Towne chuckled. "Doesn't it? I don't know. Everything's been a little screwy since the switchover. And in a screwy world like this—" He shrugged, and tossed down the moose head. "*Anything* figures."

IMAGE OF THE GODS

It was nearly winter when the ship arrived. Pete Farnam never knew if the timing had been planned that way or not. It might have been coincidence that it came just when the colony was predicting its first real bumper crop of all time. When it was all over, Pete and Mario and the rest tried to figure it out, but none of them ever knew for sure just *what* had happened back on Earth, or *when* it had actually happened. There was too little information to go on, and practically none that they could trust. All Pete Farnam really knew, that day, was that this was the wrong year for a ship from Earth to land on Baron IV.

Pete was out on the plantation when it landed. As usual, his sprayer had gotten clogged; tarring should have been started earlier, before it got so cold that the stuff clung to the nozzle and hardened before the spray could settle into the dusty soil. The summer past had been the colony's finest in the fourteen years he'd been there, a warm, still summer with plenty of rain to keep the dirt down and let the *taaro* get well rooted and grow up tall and gray against the purple sky. But now the *taaro* was harvested. It was waiting, compressed and crated, ready for shipment, and the heavy black clouds were scudding nervously across the sky, faster with every passing day. Two days ago Pete had asked Mario to see about firing up the little furnaces the Dusties had built to help them fight the winter. All that remained now was tarring the fields, and then buckling down beneath the wind shields before the first winter storms struck.

Pete was trying to get the nozzle of the tar sprayer cleaned out when Mario's jeep came roaring down the rutted road from the village in a cloud of dust. In the back seat a couple of Dusties were bouncing up and down like happy five-year-olds. The brakes squealed and Mario bellowed at him from the road. "Pete! The ship's in! Better get hopping!"

Pete nodded and started to close up the sprayer. One of the Dusties tumbled out of the jeep and scampered across the field to give him a hand. It was an inexpert hand to say the least, but the Dusties seemed so proud of the little they were able to learn about mechanized farming that nobody had the heart to shoo them away. Pete watched the fuzzy brown creature get its paws thoroughly gummed up with tar before he pulled him loose and sent him back to the jeep with a whack on the backside. He finished the job himself, grabbed his coat from the back of the sprayer, and pulled himself into the front seat of the jeep.

Mario started the little car back down the road. The young colonist's face was coated with dust, emphasizing the lines of worry around his eyes. "I don't like it, Pete. There isn't any ship due this year."

"When did it land?"

"About twenty minutes ago. Won't be cool for a while yet."

Pete laughed. "Maybe Old Schooner is just getting lonesome to swap tall stories with us. Maybe he's even bringing us a locker of T-bones. Who knows?"

"Maybe," said Mario without conviction.

Pete looked at him, and shrugged. "Why complain if they're early? Maybe they've found some new way to keep our fields from blowing away on us every winter." He stared across at the heavy windbreaks between the fields—long, ragged structures built in hope of outwitting the vicious winds that howled across the land during the long winter. Pete picked bits of tar from his beard, and wiped the dirt from his forehead with the back of his hand. "This tarring is mean," he said wearily. "Glad to take a break."

"Maybe Cap Schooner will know something about the rumors we've been hearing," Mario said gloomily.

Pete looked at him sharply. "About Earth?"

Mario nodded. "Schooner's a pretty good guy, I guess. I mean, he'd tell us if anything was *really* wrong back home, wouldn't he?"

Pete nodded, and snapped his fingers. One of the Dusties hopped over into his lap and began gawking happily at the broad fields as the jeep jogged along. Pete stroked the creature's soft brown fur with his tar-caked fingers. "Maybe someday these little guys will show us where *they* go for the winter," he said. "They must have it down to a science."

Somehow the idea was funny, and both men roared. If the Dusties had *anything* down to a science, nobody knew what. Mario grinned and tweaked the creature's tail. "They sure do beat the winter, though," he said.

"So do we. Only we have to do it the human way. These fellas grew up in the climate." Pete lapsed into silence as the village came into view. The ship had landed quite a way out, resting on its skids on the long shallow groove the colonists had bulldozed out for it years before, the first year they had arrived on Baron IV. Slowly Pete turned Mario's words over in his mind, allowing himself to worry a little. There *had* been rumors of trouble back on Earth, persistent rumors he had taken care to soft-pedal, as mayor of the colony. There were other things, too, like the old newspapers and magazines that had been brought in by the lad from Baron II, and the rare radio message they could pick up through their atmospheric disturbance. Maybe something *was* going wrong back home. But somehow political upheavals on Earth seemed remote to these hardened colonists. Captain Schooner's visits were always welcome, but they were few and far between. The colony was small; one ship every three years could supply it, and even then the *taaro* crates wouldn't half fill up the storage holds. There were other colonies far closer to home that sent back more *taaro* in one year than Baron IV could grow in ten.

But when a ship did come down, it was a time of high excitement. It meant fresh food from Earth, meat from the frozen lockers, maybe even a little candy and salt. And always for Pete a landing meant a long evening of palaver with the captain about things back home and things on Baron IV.

Pete smiled to himself as he thought of it. He could remember Earth, of course, with a kind of vague nostalgia, but Baron IV was home to him now and he knew he would never leave it. He had too many hopes invested there, too many years of heartache and desperate hard work, too much deep satisfaction in having cut a niche for himself on this dusty, hostile world, ever to think much about Earth any more.

Mario stopped in front of the offices, and one of the Dusties hopped out ahead of Pete. The creature strode across the rough gravel to the door, pulling tar off his fingers just as he had seen Pete do. Pete followed him to the door, and then stopped, frowning. There should have been a babble of voices inside, with Captain Schooner's loud laugh roaring above the excitement. But Pete could hear nothing. A chill of uneasiness ran through him; he pushed open the door and walked inside. A dozen of his friends looked up silently, avoiding the eyes of the uniformed stranger in the center of the room. When he saw the man, Pete Farnam knew something was wrong indeed.

It wasn't Captain Schooner. It was a man he'd never seen before.

*

The Dustie ran across the room in front of Pete and hopped up on the desk as though he owned it, throwing his hands on his hips and staring at the stranger curiously. Pete took off his cap and parka and dropped them on a chair. "Well," he said. "This is a surprise. We weren't expecting a ship so soon."

The man inclined his head stiffly and glanced down at the paper he held in his hand. "You're Peter Farnam, I suppose? Mayor of this colony?"

"That's right. And you?"

"Varga is the name," the captain said shortly. "Earth Security and Supply." He nodded toward the small, frail-looking man in civilian clothes, sitting beside him. "This is Rupert Nathan, of the Colonial Service. You'll be seeing a great deal of him." He held out a small wallet of papers. "Our credentials, Farnam. Be so good as to examine them."

Pete glanced around the room. John Tegan and Hank Mario were watching him uneasily. Mary Turner was following the proceedings with her sharp little eyes, missing nothing, and Mel Dorfman stood like a rock, his heavy face curiously expressionless as he watched the visitors. Pete reached out for the papers, flipped through them, and handed them back with a long look at Captain Varga.

He was younger than Captain Schooner, with sandy hair and pale eyes that looked up at Pete from a soft baby face. Clean-shaven, his whole person seemed immaculate as he leaned back calmly in the chair. His civilian companion, however, had indecision written in every line of his pink face. His hands fluttered nervously, and he avoided the colonist's eyes.

Pete turned to the captain. "The papers say you're our official supply ship," he said. "You're early, but an Earth ship is always good news." He clucked at the Dustie, who was about to go after one of the shiny buttons on the captain's blouse. The little brown creature hopped over and settled on Pete's knee. "We've been used to seeing Captain Schooner."

The captain and Nathan exchanged glances. "Captain Schooner has retired from Security Service," the captain said shortly. "You won't be seeing him again. But we have a cargo for your colony. You may send these people over to the ship to start unloading now, if you wish—" his eye swept the circle of windburned faces—"while Nathan and I discuss certain matters with you here."

Nobody moved for a moment. Then Pete nodded to Mario. "Take the boys out to unload, Jack. We'll see you back here in an hour or so."

"Pete, are you sure—"

"Don't worry. Take Mel and Hank along to lend a hand." Pete turned back to Captain Varga. "Suppose we go inside to more comfortable quarters," he said. "We're always glad to have word from Earth."

They passed through a dark, smelly corridor into Pete's personal quarters. For a colony house, if wasn't bad—good plastic chairs, a hand-made rug on the floor, even one of Mary Turner's paintings on the wall, and several of the weird, stylized carvings the Dusties had done for Pete. But the place smelled of tar and sweat, and Captain Varga's nose wrinkled in distaste. Nathan drew out a large silk handkerchief and wiped his pink hands, touching his nose daintily.

The Dustie hopped into the room ahead of them and settled into the biggest, most comfortable chair. Pete snapped his fingers sharply, and the brown creature jumped down again like a naughty child and climbed up on Pete's knee. The captain glanced at the chair with disgust and sat down in another. "Do you actually let those horrid creatures have the run of your house?" he asked.

"Why not?" Pete said. "We have the run of their planet. They're quite harmless, really. And quite clean."

The captain sniffed. "Nasty things. Might find a use for the furs, though. They look quite soft."

"We don't kill Dusties," said Pete coolly. "They're friendly, and intelligent too, in a childish sort of way." He looked at the captain and Nathan, and decided not to put on the coffee pot. "Now what's the trouble?"

"No trouble at all," the captain said, "except the trouble you choose to make. You have your year's *taaro* ready for shipping?"

"Of course."

The captain took out a small pencil on a chain and began to twirl it. "How much, to be exact?"

"Twenty thousand, Earth weight."

"Tons?"

Pete shook his head. "Hundredweight."

The captain raised his eyebrows. "I see. And there are—" he consulted the papers in his hand—"roughly two hundred and twenty colonists here on Baron IV. Is that right?"

"That's right."

"Seventy-four men, eighty-one women, and fifty-nine children, to be exact?"

"I'd have to look it up. Margaret Singman had twins the other night."

"Well, don't be ridiculous," snapped the captain. "On a planet the size of Baron IV, with seventy-four men, you should be producing a dozen times the *taaro* you stated. We'll consider that your quota for a starter, at least. You have ample seed, according to my records. I should think, with the proper equipment—"

"Now wait a minute," Pete said softly. "We're fighting a climate here, captain. You should know that. We have only a two-planting season, and the 'proper equipment,' as you call it, doesn't operate too well out here. It has a way of clogging up with dust in the summer, and rusting in the winter."

"Really," said Captain Varga. "As I was saying, with the proper equipment, you could cultivate a great deal more land than you seem to be using. This would give you the necessary heavier yield. Wouldn't you say so, Nathan?"

The little nervous man nodded. "Certainly, captain. With the proper organization of labor."

"That's nonsense," Pete said, suddenly angry. "Nobody can get that kind of yield from this planet. The ground won't give it, and the men won't grow it."

The captain gave him a long look. "Really?" he said. "I think you're wrong. I think the men will grow it."

Pete stood up slowly. "What are you trying to say? This business about quotas and organization of labor—"

"You didn't read our credentials as we instructed you, Farnam. Mr. Nathan is the official governor of the colony on Baron IV, as of now. You'll find him most co-operative, I'm sure, but he's answerable directly to me in all matters. My job is administration of the entire Baron system. Clear enough?"

Pete's eyes were dark. "I think you'd better draw me a picture," he said tightly. "A very clear picture."

"Very well. Baron IV is not paying for its upkeep. *Taaro*, after all, is not the most necessary of crops in the universe. It has value, but not very much value, all things considered. If the production of *taaro* here is not increased sharply, it may be necessary to close down the colony altogether."

"You're a liar," said Pete shortly. "The Colonization Board makes no production demands on the colonies. Nor does it farm out systems for personal exploitation."

The captain smiled. "The Colonization Board, as you call it, has undergone a slight reorganization," he said.

"*Reorganization!* It's a top-level board in the Earth Government! Nothing could reorganize it but a wholesale—" He broke off, his jaw sagging as the implication sank in.

"You're rather out on a limb, you see," said the captain coolly. "Poor communications and all that. The fact is that the entire Earth Government has undergone a slight reorganization also."

*

The Dustie knew that something had happened.

Pete didn't know how he knew. The Dusties couldn't talk, couldn't make *any* noise, as far as Pete knew. But they always seemed to know when something unusual was happening. It was wrong, really, to consider them unintelligent animals. There are other sorts of intelligence than human, and other sorts of communication, and other sorts of culture. The Baron IV colonists had never understood the queer perceptive sense that the Dusties seemed to possess, any more than they knew how many Dusties there were, or what they ate, or where on the planet they lived. All they knew was that when they landed on Baron IV, the Dusties were there.

At first the creatures had been very timid. For weeks the men and women, busy with their building, had paid little attention to the skittering brown forms that crept down from the rocky hills to watch them with big, curious eyes. They were about half the size of men, and strangely humanoid in appearance, not in the sense that a monkey is humanoid (for they did *not* resemble monkeys) but in some way the colonists could not quite pin down. It may have been the way they walked around on their long, fragile hind legs, the way they stroked their pointed chins as they sat and watched and listened with their pointed ears lifted alertly, watching with soft gray eyes, or the way they handled objects with their little four-fingered hands. They were so remarkably human-like in their elfin way that the colonists couldn't help but be drawn to the creatures.

That whole first summer, when the colonists were building the village and the landing groove for the ships, the Dusties were among them, trying pathetically to help, so eager for friendship that even occasional rebuffs failed to drive them away. They *liked* the colony. They seemed, somehow, to savor the atmosphere, moving about like solemn, fuzzy overseers as the work progressed through the summer. Pete Farnam thought that they had even tried to warn the people about the winter. But the colonists couldn't understand, of course. Not until later. The Dusties became a standing joke, and were tolerated with considerable amusement—until the winter struck.

It had come with almost unbelievable ferocity. The houses had not been completed when the first hurricanes came, and they were smashed into toothpicks. The winds came, vicious winds full of dust and sleet and ice, wild erratic twisting gales that ripped the village to shreds, tearing off the topsoil that had been broken and fertilized—merciless, never-ending winds that wailed and screamed the planet's protest. The winds drove sand and dirt and ice into the heart of the generators, and the heating units corroded and jammed and went dead. The jeeps and tractors and bulldozers were scored and rusted. The people began dying by the dozens as they huddled down in the pitiful little pits they had dug to try to keep the winds away.

Few of them were still conscious when the Dusties had come silently, in the blizzard, eyes closed tight against the blast, to drag the people up into the hills, into caves and hollows that still showed the fresh marks of carving tools. They had brought food—what kind of food nobody knew, for the colony's food had been destroyed by the first blast of the hurricane—but whatever it was it had kept them alive. And somehow, the colonists had survived the winter which seemed never to end. There were frozen legs and ruined eyes; there was pneumonia so swift and virulent that even the antibiotics they managed to salvage could not stop it; there was near-starvation—but they were kept alive, until the winds began to die, and they walked out of their holes in the ground to see the ruins of their first village.

From that winter on, nobody considered the Dusties funny any more. What had motivated them no one knew, but the colony owed them their lives. The Dusties tried to help the people rebuild. They showed them how to build windshields that would keep houses intact and anchored to the ground when the winds came again. They built little furnaces out of dirt and rock which defied the winds and gave great heat. They showed the colonists a dozen things they needed to know for life on the rugged planet. The colonists in turn tried to teach the Dusties something about Earth, and how the colonists had lived, and why they had come. But there was a barrier of intelligence that could not be crossed. The Dusties learned simple things, but only slowly and imperfectly. They seemed content to take on their mock overseer's role, moving in and about the village, approving or disapproving, but always trying to help. Some became personal pets, though "pet" was the wrong word, because it was more of a strange personal friendship limited by utter lack of communication, than any animal-and-master relationship. The colonists made sure that the Dusties were granted the respect due them as rightful masters of Baron IV. And somehow the Dusties perceived this attitude, and were so grateful for the acceptance and friendship that there seemed nothing they wouldn't do for the colonists.

There had been many discussions about them. "You'd think they'd resent our moving in on them," Jack Mario had said one day. "After all, we *are* usurpers. And they treat us like kings. Have you noticed the way they mimic us? I saw one chewing tobacco the other day. He hated the stuff, but he chewed away, and spat like a trooper."

One of the Dusties had been sitting on Pete's knee when Captain Varga had been talking, and he had known that something terrible was wrong. Now he sat on the desk in the office, moving uneasily back and forth as Pete looked up at Mario's dark face, and then across at John Tegan and Mel Dorfman. John's face was dark with anger as he ran his fingers through the heavy gray beard that fell to his chest. Mel sat stunned, shaking his head helplessly. Mario was unable to restrain himself. His face was bitter as he stomped across the room, then returned to shake his fist under Pete's nose. "But did you see him?" he choked. "Governor of the colony! What does he know about growing *taaro* in this kind of soil? Did you see those hands? Soft, dainty, pink! How could a man with hands like that govern a colony?"

Pete looked over at John Tegan. "Well, John?"

The big man looked up, his eyes hollow under craggy brows. "It's below the belt, Pete. But if the government's been overthrown, then the captain is right. It leaves us out on a limb."

Pete shook his head. "*I* can't give him an answer," he said. "The answer has got to come from the colony. All I can do is speak for the colony."

Tegan stared at the floor. "We're an Earth colony," he said softly. "I know that. I was born in New York. I lived there for many years. But Earth isn't my home any more. This is." He looked at Pete. "I built it, and so did you. All of us built it, even when things were getting stormy back home. Maybe that's why we came, maybe somehow we saw the handwriting on the wall."

"But when did it happen?" Mel burst out suddenly. "How could *anything* so big happen so fast?"

"Speed was the secret," Pete said gloomily. "It was quick, it was well organized, and the government was unstable. We're just caught in the edge of it. Pity the ones living there, now. But the new government considers the colonies as areas for exploitation instead of development."

"Well, they can't do it," Mario cried. "This is *our* land, *our* home. Nobody can tell us what to grow in our fields."

Pete's fist slammed down on the desk. "Well, how are you going to stop them? The law of the land is sitting out there in that ship. Tomorrow morning he's coming back here to install his fat little friend as governor. He has guns and soldiers on that ship to back him up. What are you going to do about it?"

"Fight it," Mario said.

"How?"

Jack Mario looked around the room. "There are only a dozen men on that ship," he said softly. "We've got seventy-four. When Varga comes back to the village tomorrow, we tell him to take his friend back to the ship and shove off. We give him five minutes to get turned around, and if he doesn't, we start shooting."

"Just one little thing," said Pete quietly. "What about the supplies? Even if we fought them off and won, what about the food, the clothing, the replacement parts for the machines?"

"We don't need machinery to farm this land," said Mario eagerly. "There's food here, food we can live on; the Dusties showed us that the first winter. And we can farm the land for our own use and let the machinery rust. There's nothing they can bring us from Earth that we can't do without."

"We couldn't get away with it!" Mel Dorfman shook his head bitterly. "You're asking us to cut ourselves off from Earth completely. But they'd never let us. They'd send ships to bomb us out."

"We could hide, and rebuild after they had finished."

Pete Farnam sighed. "They'd never leave us alone, Jack. Didn't you see that captain? His kind of mind can't stand opposition. We'd just be a thorn in the side of the new Earth Government. They don't want *any* free colonies."

"Well, let's give them one." Mario sat down tiredly, snapping his fingers at the Dustie. "Furs!" he snarled. He looked up, his dark eyes burning. "It's no good, Pete. We can't let them get away with it. Produce for them, yes. Try to raise the yield for them, yes. But not a governor. If they insist on that we can throw them out, and keep them out."

"I don't think so. They'd kill every one of us first."

John Tegan sat up, and looked Pete Farnam straight in the eye. "In that case, Peter, it might just be better if they did."

Pete stared at him for a moment and slowly stood up. "All right," he said. "Call a general colony meeting. We'll see what the women think. Then we'll make our plans."

*

The ship's jeep skidded to a halt in a cloud of dust. Captain Varga peered through the windshield. Then he stood up, staring at the three men blocking the road at the edge of the village. The little pink-faced man at his side turned white when he saw their faces, and his fingers began to tremble. Each of the men had a gun.

"You'd better clear the road," the captain snapped. "We're driving through."

Pete Farnam stepped forward. He pointed to Nathan. "Take your friend there back to the ship. Leave him there. We don't want him here."

Nathan turned to Varga. "I told you," he said viciously. "Too big for their boots. Go on through."

The captain laughed and gunned the motor, started straight for the men blocking the road. Then Jack Mario shot a hole in his front tire. The jeep lurched to a stop. Captain Varga stood up, glaring at the men. "Farnam, step out here," he said.

"You heard us," Pete said, without moving. "Crops, yes. We'll try to increase our yield. But no overseer. Leave him here and we'll kill him."

"Once more," said the captain, "clear the way. This man is your new governor. He will be regarded as the official agent of the Earth Government until the final production capacity of this colony is determined. Now clear out."

The men didn't move. Without another word, the captain threw the jeep into reverse, jerked back in a curve, and started the jeep, flat tire and all, back toward the ship in a billow of dust.

Abruptly the village exploded into activity. Four men took up places behind the row of windbreaks beyond the first row of cabins. Pete turned and ran back into the village. He found John Tegan commandeering a squad of ten dirty-faced men. "Are the women and children all out?" he shouted.

"All taken care of." Tegan spat tobacco juice, and wiped his mouth with the back of his hand.

"Where's Mel?"

"Left flank. He'll try to move in behind them. Gonna be tough, Pete, they've got good weapons."

"What about the boys last night?"

John was checking the bolt on his ancient rifle. "Hank and Ringo? Just got back an hour ago. If Varga wants to get his surface planes into action, he's going to have to dismantle them and rebuild them outside. The boys jammed up the launching ports for good." He spat again. "Don't worry, Pete. This is going to be a ground fight."

"Okay." Pete held out his hand to the old man. "This may be it. And if we turn them back, there's bound to be more later."

"There's a lot of planet to hide on," said Tegan. "They may come back, but after a while they'll go again."

Pete nodded. "I just hope we'll still be here when they do."

They waited. It seemed like hours. Pete moved from post to post among the men, heavy-faced men he had known all his life, it seemed. They waited with whatever weapons they had available—pistols, home-made revolvers, ortho-guns, an occasional rifle, even knives and clubs. Pete's heart sank. They were bitter men, but they were a mob with no organization, no training for fighting. They would be facing a dozen of Security's best-disciplined shock troops, armed with the latest weapons from Earth's electronics laboratories. The colonists didn't stand a chance.

Pete got his rifle and made his way up the rise of ground overlooking the right flank of the village. Squinting, he could spot the cloud of dust rising up near the glistening ship, moving toward the village. And then, for the first time, he realized that he hadn't seen any Dusties all day.

It puzzled him. They had been in the village in abundance an hour before dawn, while the plans were being laid out. He glanced around, hoping to see one of the fuzzy brown forms at his elbow, but he saw nothing. And then, as he stared at the cloud of dust coming across the valley, he thought he saw the ground moving.

He blinked, and rubbed his eyes. With a gasp he dragged out his binoculars and peered down at the valley floor. There were thousands of them, hundreds of thousands, their brown bodies moving slowly out from the hills surrounding the village, converging into a broad, liquid column between the village and the ship. Even as he watched, the column grew thicker, like a heavy blanket being drawn across the road, a multitude of Dusties lining up.

Pete's hair prickled on the back of his neck. They knew so little about the creatures, so *very* little. As he watched the brown carpet rolling out, he tried to think. Could there be a weapon in their hands, could they somehow have perceived the evil that came from the ship, somehow sensed the desperation in the men's voices as they had laid their plans? Pete stared, a sinking feeling in the pit of his stomach. They were there in the road, thousands upon thousands of them, standing there, waiting—for what?

Three columns of dust were coming from the road now. Through the glasses Pete could see the jeeps, filled with men in their gleaming gray uniforms, crash helmets tight about their heads, blasters glistening in the pale light. They moved in deadly convoy along the rutted road, closer and closer to the crowd of Dusties overflowing the road.

The Dusties just stood there. They didn't move. They didn't shift, or turn. They just waited.

The captain's car was first in line. He pulled up before the line with a screech of brakes, and stared at the sea of creatures before him. "Get out of there!" he shouted.

The Dusties didn't move.

The captain turned to his men. "Fire into them," he snapped. "Clear a path."

There was a blaze of fire, and a half a dozen Dusties slid to the ground, convulsing. Pete felt a chill pass through him, staring in disbelief. The Dusties had a weapon, he kept telling himself, they *must* have a weapon, something the colonists had never dreamed of. The guns came up again, and another volley echoed across the valley, and a dozen more Dusties fell to the ground. For every one that fell, another moved stolidly into its place.

With a curse the captain sat down in the seat, gunned the motor, and started forward. The jeep struck the fallen bodies, rolled over them, and plunged straight into the wall of Dusties. Still they didn't move. The car slowed and stopped, mired down. The other cars picked up momentum and plunged into the brown river of creatures. They too ground to a stop.

The captain started roaring at his men. "Cut them down! We're going to get through here!" Blasters began roaring into the faces of the Dusties, and as they fell the jeeps moved forward a few feet until more of the creatures blocked their path.

Pete heard a cry below him, and saw Jack Mario standing in the road, gun on the ground, hands out in front of him, staring in horror as the Dusties kept moving into the fire. "Do you see what they're doing!" he screamed. "They'll be slaughtered, every one of them!" And then he was running down the road, shouting at them to stop, and so were Pete and Tegan and the rest of the men.

Something hit Pete in the shoulder as he ran. He spun around and fell into the dusty road. A dozen Dusties closed in around him, lifted him up bodily, and started back through the village with him. He tried to struggle, but vaguely he saw that the other men were being carried back also, while the river of brown creatures held the jeeps at bay. The Dusties were hurrying, half carrying and half dragging him back through the village and up a long ravine into the hills beyond. At last they set Pete on his feet again, plucking urgently at his shirt sleeve as they hurried him along.

He followed them willingly, then, with the rest of the colonists at his heels. He didn't know what the Dusties were doing, but he knew they were trying to save him. Finally they reached a cave, a great cleft in the rock that Pete knew for certain had not been there when he had led exploring parties through these hills years before. It was a huge opening, and already a dozen of the men were there, waiting, dazed by what they had witnessed down in the valley, while more were stumbling up the rocky incline, tugged along by the fuzzy brown creatures.

Inside the cavern, steps led down the side of the rock, deep into the dark coolness of the earth. Down and down they went, until they suddenly found themselves in a mammoth room lit by blazing torches. Pete stopped and stared at his friends who had already arrived. Jack Mario was sitting on the floor, his face in his hands, sobbing. Tegan was sitting, too, blinking at Pete as if he were a stranger, and Dorfman was trembling like a leaf. Pete stared about him through the dim light, and then looked where Tegan was pointing at the end of the room.

He couldn't see it clearly, at first. Finally, he made out a raised platform with four steps leading up. A torch lighted either side of a dais at the top, and between the torches, rising high into the gloom, stood a statue.

It was a beautifully carved thing, hewn from the heavy granite that made up the core of this planet, with the same curious styling as other carving the Dusties had done. The design was intricate, the lines carefully turned and polished. At first Pete thought it was a statue of a Dustie, but when he moved forward and squinted in the dim light, he suddenly realized that it was something else indeed. And in that moment he realized why they were there and why the Dusties had done this incredible thing to protect them.

The statue was weirdly beautiful, the work of a dedicated master sculptor. It was a figure, standing with five-fingered hands on hips, head raised high. Not a portrait, but an image seen through other eyes than human, standing high in the room with the lights burning reverently at its feet.

Unmistakably it was the statue of a man.

*

They heard the bombs, much later. The granite roof and floor of the cavern trembled, and the men and women stared at each other, helpless and sick as they huddled in that great hall. But presently the bombing stopped. Later, when they stumbled out of that grotto into the late afternoon light, the ship was gone.

They knew it would be back. Possibly it would bring back search parties to hunt down the rebels in the hills; perhaps it would just wait and again bomb out the new village when it rose. But searching parties would never find their quarry, and the village would rise again and again, if necessary.

And in the end, somehow, Pete knew that the colonists would find a way to survive here and live free as they had always lived. It might be a bitter struggle, but no matter how hard the fight, there would be one strange and wonderful thing they could count on.

No matter what they had to do, he knew the Dusties would help them.

Flicker's mind fought silently and desperately to maintain its fast-receding control, to master his frantic urge to writhe and scream in agony at the burning light. The fetid animal stench of the aliens filled his nostrils, gagging him; the heat of the place seared his skin like a thousand white-hot needles, and seeped into his throat to blister his lungs. It didn't matter that his arms and legs were bound tightly to the pallet, for he knew he dared not move them. The maddening off-and-on of the scorching light set his mind afire, twisted his stomach into a hard knot of fear and agony, but his body lay still as death, relaxed and motionless. He knew that the instant he betrayed his' tortured alertness by so much as a single tremor, his chance for contact would be totally gone.

"The only sensible thing to do is to kill it!"

It was not repetition but a constant, powerful force, crashing into his mind, hateful, cold. He heard no sound but the muffled throb of spaceship engines far back in the ship, but the *thought* was there, adamant and uncompromising. It burst from the garbled, thought-patterns of the others and struck his mind like an electric shock. One of the aliens wanted to kill him.

Thought contact. It was a paralyzing concept to Flicker. The aliens couldn't possibly realize it themselves; they were using sound communication with one another, on a sonic level beyond the sensitivity of Flicker's ears. He could hear no sound—but the thought patterns that guided the sound-talking of the aliens came through to sledge-hammer his brain, coherent, crystal clear.

*

"But why kill it? We have it sedated almost to death-level now. It's completely unconscious, it's securely bound, and we can keep it that way until we reach home. Then it's no longer our worry."

The first thought broke out again with new overtones of anger and fear. "I say we've got to kill it! We had no right picking it up in the first place. What is it? How did it get there? Where was the ship that brought it?" The alien mind was venomous. "Kill it now, while we can!"

Flicker tried desperately to tear his mind from the agonizing rhythm of the light, to catch and hold the alien thoughts. Confusion rose in his mind, and for the first time he felt a chill of fear. His people knew that these aliens were avaricious and venal—a dozen drained and pillaged star-systems which they had overrun bore witness to that—but he had never even considered, before he started on this mission, that they might kill him without even attempting communication. Why must they kill him? All he wanted was a chance—one brief moment to convey his message to them. Five years of planning, and his own life, had been risked just to get the message to them, to gain their confidence and make them understand, but all he found in these alien minds was fear and suspicion and hate, which had become a single ever-developing crescendo: "Kill it now, while we can!"

There were only three of them with him now, but he knew, from some corner of the alien minds, that five others were sleeping in a forward chamber of the ship. He saw himself clearly, alone on an unknown spacecraft with eight alien creatures, gliding through interstellar space at unthinkable speed, bound for that nebulous and threatening somewhere they called home. Their home. He caught a brief mind-picture from one of them of an enormous city, teeming with these alien creatures, watching him, picking at him, trying to question him, deciding how to kill him

And through everything else came the intermittent burning glare of that terrible white light—

Then suddenly the three aliens were leaving the cabin. Flicker sensed their indecision, felt them balancing the question in their minds. Soundlessly, he lifted one eyelid a trifle. The searing light burst in on his retina, blinding him for a moment; then he caught a distorted glimpse of them opening the hatch and withdrawing in their jerking, uneven gait. And still the alien thought came through with a parting jab to his tortured mind: "The only thing we can do is to kill it. The risk of tampering with it is too great. And we don't dare take it back home alive."

The light was gone now. Flicker took a deep breath of the heavy air, allowing his tensed muscles to relax as the sweet coolness and comfort crept through his body. First he stretched his legs, as far as they would go in the restrainers, then his arms, and coughed a time or two to clear his throat. Almost fearfully he opened his eyes to the cool, soothing darkness. His mind still ached with the afterglow of the furious lights, but gradually the details of the cabin appeared. Far in the background the throbbing drive of the great ship altered subtly, then increased slightly in volume. Bound where? Flicker sighed, trying to turn his mind away from the undermining awareness of failure, of something gone very wrong. Carefully he reviewed his rescue, his actions, the aliens' reactions. They had cut their drive almost immediately when they had spotted him, and sent out a lifeboat for him without previous reconnaissance ; surely he had been helpless enough when they dragged him from his crippled *gig*, half-frozen, to allay any suspicions of his immediate dangerousness. A crippled man is no menace, nor an exhausted man. The whole thing had been carefully planned and skillfully executed. The aliens couldn't have detected his own ship which had dropped him off hours before, in the proper place to intercept their ship. And yet they were suspicious and fearful, as well as curious, and their first thought was to kill him first, and examine him after he was dead.

Flicker's face twisted into a sour grin at the irony. To think that he had come, so quietly and naively, to these aliens as a peacemaker! If he were killed, the loss would be theirs far more than his. Because contact, living contact, and a mutual meeting of minds was desperately necessary. They had to be warned. For three decades they had been observed, without contact, in their slow, consuming march across the galaxy, conquering, enslaving, pillaging. The curiosity of their nature had started them on their way; greed and lust for power had carried them on until now, at last, they were coming too close. They could not be allowed to come closer. They had to be warned away.

Flicker had been present at the meeting where that decision had been reached. There had been voices raised in favor of attacking the encroaching aliens, without warning, to deal them a crippling blow and send them reeling back home. But most of the leaders had opposed this, and Flicker could see their point. He knew that his people's struggle for peace and security and economic balance had been exhausting, the final settlement dearly won. Part of the utter distaste of his people for outside contact lay deep within Flicker's own mind: they asked no homage from anyone, they desired no power, they felt no need for expansion. The years of war had left them exhausted and peace-hungry, and they demanded but one thing from any culture approaching them: they wanted to be left alone. Cultural and economic contacts they would eagerly seek with this alien race, but they would tolerate no upset diplomatic relations, no attempts to infiltrate and conquer, no lies and forgeries and socio-economic upheavals. They were tired of all these. They had found their way as a people, and with characteristic independence they wanted to follow it, without interference or advice.

And then the aliens had come. Closer and closer, to the very fringes of their confederation. Like a cancer the aliens came, stealthily, nibbling at the fringes, never quite contacting them, never really annoying them, but preparing little by little for the first small bite. And Flicker knew that they could not be allowed to take that bite, for his people would fight, if necessary, to total extinction for the right to be left alone.

Flicker shifted his weight, and sighed helplessly. The plan of his leaders had been simple. A few individual contacts, to warn the aliens. A few well-planned demonstrations of the horrors they could expect if they would not desist. There were other parts of the galaxy for these aliens to explore, other stars for them to ravage. If they could be made to realize the carnage they were inevitably approaching, the frightful battle they were precipitating, they might gladly settle for cultural and commercial contacts. But first they must be stopped and warned. They must not go any further.

Flicker's mind raced through the plan, the words, carefully imprinted in his mind, the evidence he could present to them.

If only he could have a chance! He felt the dull pain in his stomach—he hadn't been fed since he was brought aboard, and the drug they gave him had drained and exhausted him. At least he would have no more of *that* for another three hours. He sighed quietly, aching for sleep. From the moment the impact of the first dose of drug hit him, he had realized the terrible depths of strength his deception would require. He had been nearly unconscious from exposure in outer space when they had dragged him from his lifeboat into the blazing light of the ship, but the drug had stimulated him to the point of convulsions. An overwhelming dosage for *their* metabolism, no doubt, but it had fallen far short of his sedation threshold, driving his heart into a frenzy of activity as he tried to control his jerking muscles. Still, there would be no more for three hours or so, so he could lie in reasonable comfort, trying to find a solution to the question at hand.

One of them wanted to kill him immediately. That was the one who had poked and probed that first day, tapping his nerves and bones with a little hammer, taking samples of his blood and exhaled breath, opening his eyelid and using that horrid torch that seared his brain like raw fire. The throbbing, intermittent light had begun to bother him as early as that. Either their visual pickup was of extremely low sensitivity, or his own neurovisio pickup had been stepped up to such a degree that what appeared as steady light to them registered on his mind as a rapid and maddening oscillation. But the brilliance and the heat—

His strength was returning slowly after the ordeal. His muscles ached from inactivity, and he began twisting back and forth, testing the limits of his restraints. Each leg could move about four inches back and forth ; 'his right arm seemed tightly secured, but his left—he twisted his wrist back and forth slowly, and suddenly it was free! Unbelieving, Flicker groped for the restrainer. It hung loosely at the side of the pallet, its buckle broken. He moved the arm tentatively, testing the other restrainer, wiping perspiration from his forehead. Finally he lay back, his heart pounding. With one arm free he could free himself completely in a matter of moments. But the aliens mustn't know it, for anything that would startle them or make them suspicious might turn the tide of their indecision instantly, and bring sudden violent, purposeless death.

The arm could be used to keep himself alive—if he had to. The thought of the one alien crept through his mind: the cold, unyielding hate, and the fear. The others were merely curious, and curiosity could be his weapon, to help him establish the link that was so necessary. Somehow, contact must be established without frightening them, or threatening them in any way. Although their thoughts came to him so clearly, he had tried in vain to establish mental rapport with them. They showed no sign of awareness of anything but their own thoughts, and communicated only by sound, for their thinking processes were as sluggish as their motions. Sluggish thinking, but on a high level: they thought logically, using data in most cases to form logical, sound conclusions. They understood friendliness, and affection, and companionship, among themselves, but toward him—they seemed unable to conceive of him except in terms of alien, to be feared, investigated, attacked.

He sighed again and settled back, trying to ease his aching back and shoulders. His mind was almost giddy from lack of sleep, running off into wild, dreamlike ramblings, but he struggled for control, fighting to keep the fingers of sleep from his mind. He knew that to sleep now would be to place himself at a terrible, possibly fatal, disadvantage. He couldn't afford to sleep now—not until contact had been established.

The light flashed on again, directly above him. Flicker cringed, his muscles twitching, tightening before the torturous heat. Anger and frustration crept through to his consciousness—why so soon? No more drug was due for a long while yet. He heard footsteps in the passageway outside, and the hatch squeaked open admit one of the aliens, alone. And with him came a single paralyzing thought wave which tore into Flicker's brain, driving out the pain and frustration, leaving nothing but cold fear:

"If the others find it dead, they can't do much about it—"

This, then, was the one that had wanted him dead. They called him Klock, and he was the biggest alien on the crew. This one especially was afraid of him, wanted him dead immediately, and had come to see that he was dead! Alone, on his own initiative, against the will of the others. And in a cold wave of fear, Flicker knew that he would do it.

There was no curiosity in the assassin's mind, only fear and hate. Through one not-quite closed eye Flicker watched the alien approach. It held a syringe-like instrument in its claws, and the oily skin was oozing a foul-smelling fluid that stood in droplets all over its face. The fear in the alien's mind intensified, impinging on Flicker's brain with the drive and force of a trip-hammer, clear and cold. "If the others find it dead, there is nothing they can do—"

The alien was beside him, its head near Flicker's face, and he caught the bright glint of glass and steel, too near. Like lightning Flicker swung with his free arm, a sudden, crushing blow. The alien emitted one small, audible squeak, and dropped to the floor, its thin skull squashed like an eggshell right down to its neck.

Frantic with the maddening light and heat, Flicker ripped away the restraints on his other arm and legs. Ripping a magna-boot from the alien's foot, he heaved it with all his might at the source of the light. There was a loud pop, and the cabin sank into darkness again. Flicker wiped the moisture from his forehead, and stood numb and panting at the side of the table as the afterglow faded and the wonderful coolness crept through him again. And then he saw, almost with a start, the body on the metal floor before him.

Gagging from the stench of the thing, he knelt beside it and examined it with trembling fingers. With the light gone, the alien *had* changed color, its leathery skin now a pasty white, its shaggy mane brown. White stuff oozed from its macerated head, mingled with a red fluid which resembled blood. Flicker dabbed his finger in it, sniffed it. A red body fluid should mean an oxygen metabolism, like his own, but he had concluded from the heavy atmosphere that the aliens were nitrogen-metabolistic. That would account, in part, for their sluggishness, their slow thinking.

Realization of the situation began to crowd into his brain. This creature was dead! He had killed it. He sat back on the floor, panting, trying to channel his wheeling thoughts into a coherent pattern. He'd killed one of the aliens ; that meant that his last hope for peaceful contact was gone. The mission was lost, and his danger critical. Even if he could succeed in concealing himself, it was unthinkable to go with them to their home planet. Escape? Equally unthinkable. They were vengeful creatures, as well as 'curious. Their vengeance might be murderous—

Briefly his wife and family flashed through his mind, waiting for him, so proud that he had been chosen for the mission, so eager for his success. And his leaders, watching, waiting daily for his return. There could be no success to report now, nothing but failure.

But he had to survive, he had to get back! There could be other missions, but somehow he. had to get back.

The situation fell sharply into his mind, crystal clear. There was no alternative now. He would have to destroy every creature on the ship.

One against seven. He considered the odds swiftly, the sudden urgency of the situation slamming home. They had weapons, the ship was known to them, they could signal for help. There must be *something* to turn to his advantage—

He kicked the alien's foot, thoughtfully—

The lights!

Flicker jumped to his feet, his heart pounding audibly in his throat. Why such brilliant light, why such a slow-cycle current that he could see the intermittent off-and-on? Obviously, what he saw as an oscillation was a steady light to them. With such low light-sensitivity the aliens it have awakened? to have such brilliant lights. They couldn't see without them! The agonizing brilliance that sent Flicker into convulsions was merely the light necessary for them to see at all.

And comfortable seeing-light for him was to them—total darkness!

Far forward in the ship a metal door clanged. Flicker was instantly alert, nerves alive, every muscle tense. Klock was dead, he would be missed by the others. He took a quick glance around him; and removed the weapon from Klock's side, an ordinary, clumsily designed heat pistol, almost unrecognizable, but similar enough to the type of weapon Flicker knew to be serviceable. He strapped it to his side, and moved silently toward the hatchway.

The lights had to go first. Flicker's body ached. His mind was reeling with fatigue, sliding momentarily into hazy attenuation, snapping back with a start. Unless he slept soon, he knew, his reactions would become dangerously slow, and hunger was now tormenting him also. Food and sleep would have to take priority over the lights, no matter how dangerous.

A thought flashed through his mind, and he glanced back at the alien body on the floor. Some of the blood had oozed out on the aluminum floor, forming a dark pool. The thought slid into focus, and the hunger reintensified, into a gnawing knot in his stomach; then he turned away in disgust. He just wasn't that hungry. Not yet.

Quickly he stepped out into the passageway, moving in the direction of the engine sounds. The ship was silent as a tomb except for the distant throbbing of the motors. Far below him he heard the clang of metal on metal, as if a hatch had been slammed. Then dead silence again. No sign that Klock had been missed, not yet. Flicker breathed the cool darkness of the corridor for a moment, and then moved quickly to the ladder at the end of the passageway. His muscles ached, and his neck was cramped, but he felt some degree of his normal agility returning as he peered into the dark hold below, and eased himself down the ladder.

The grainy odor he had smelled above was stronger down here. Halfway to the ceiling the coarsely woven bags were stacked, filling almost every available inch of the hold except for the walkways. A grain freighter! No wonder it had such a small crew for its size. Not many hands were needed to ferry staple food-grains to the aliens on distant planets. Flicker blinked and searched the walkways, finally finding what he wanted—a cubbyhole, behind the stacks, and up against the outer bulkhead. He slid into the narrow space with a sigh, and curled himself up as comfortably as he could. Clearing his mind of every thought but alertness to sound, he sank into untroubled sleep.

He heard the steps on the deck above him, and sat up in the darkness, instantly alert. There were muffled sounds above, then steps on the metal ladder. Abruptly the hold was thrown into brilliant light. Flicker whimpered and twisted with pain as the light exploded into his eyes, and felt a flash of panic as he saw two of the aliens at the bottom of the ladder.

The waves of thought force struck Flicker, heavy with anger and fear. "It couldn't have come far forward in the ship. If Klock was right, that first day, it has a high-order intelligence. It would seek a good hiding place, and then venture out to explore a little at a time. It could be anywhere." The one called Sha-Lee looked back up the ladder anxiously.

The other's mind was a turmoil of jagged peaks and curves. Then his thought cleared abruptly. "But how could it happen? The creature was sedated, almost dead, as far as we could see. It had a shot just an hour before Klock went up there. How *could* it have awakened? And why did Klock go up there in the first place? I thought you left strict orders—"

The two cautiously moved down the walkway. "Whatever happened, it's loose. And there won't be any sedating when we find it again—"

Trembling with pain, Flicker forced his burning eyes to the source of the light in the overhead. He aimed the heat pistol he had taken from Klock, sending a burst of searing energy at the fixture. The hold fell dark as the light exploded into metallic steam.

"*He's in here!*"

There was a long, pause, in dead silence. Flicker strained to catch the flow of thoughts that streamed from the alien minds.

"I can't see a thing!"

"Neither can I. It got the lights."

They were so near Flicker could almost feel their warmth. Swift and silent as lightning, he sprang up on the grain bags, leaned out just above them. A small bit of wood was near his foot; he grabbed it and threw it with all his might against the far bulkhead. A surge of fear swept from the alien minds at the crash, and they swung and fired wildly. Like a flash Flicker sprang to the deck behind them, pausing the barest instant for breath and balance, then springing quickly forward and striking one of them a crushing blow across the neck. The alien dropped with a small squeak. The other fired wildly, but Flicker was too quick, zig-zagging back to a retreat behind the bags. After a moment he peered over the top of the pile.

Sha-Lee was standing poised, peering into the blackness toward the other alien' who lay quite motionless on the floor, its head twisted at an unnatural angle from its body. Something in Flicker's mind screamed, "Get the other now, while you can!" But he took a deep breath of the sticky air, and then turned and ran silently to the hatch at the back of the hold, and out into the large corridor.

He had to get the lights first. With the lights gone, the others could be taken care of in good time. But he knew that he couldn't stand the torture of the lights much longer; already his eyes felt like sandpaper, and the paralysis which took him for several seconds when the lights first went on could give the aliens a fatal advantage. He, came to a darkened hatchway, half open at the end of the corridor, took a brief inventory, and hurried through. Far below he could hear the generators buzzing, growing stronger and mingling with the sobbing of the motors as he descended ladder after ladder. He hurried down a dimly-lit corridor and tried a hatchway where the noise seemed most intense.

The light from within stabbed at his eyes, blinding him, but he forced himself through the hatch. To the right was the glittering control panel for the atomic pile; to the left were the gauges for the gas storage control. An alien was standing before the main control panel, a larger creature than his brothers, his mind swiftly pulsating, carrying overtones of great physical strength. Flicker slid silently behind one of the generators and studied it and the room, his mind growing progressively, more frantic. His eyes burned furiously, and finally, with a groan, he unstrapped the heat gun and sent a burst toward the ceiling. The light blew with a loud pop, and the alien whirled.

"Who's there?"

Flicker sat tight. The generator he was using for concealment was not functioning probably a standby. Three of them were running in series over to one side, with a fuse-box above them. Flicker's heart pounded. It would have to be quick and sure.

The alien moved swiftly over to the side of the room, and a thin blade of light stabbed out at Flicker. A battle lamp. The suddenness of its appearance startled him, stalled his movement just an instant too long. He saw the burst of red from the alien's weapon, and he screamed out as the scorching energy caught him in the side and doubled him over. In agony he jumped aside and sprang suddenly up onto a catwalk. The alien swung the lamp around below, searching for him, tense, gun poised. In a burst of speed Flicker moved along the catwalk toward the alien, and crouched on the edge directly over him, panting, *gagging* at the smell of the creature mingled with the odor of his own burned flesh. He felt cold rage creep into his mind, recklessness, the age-old instinct of his people to claw and scratch and kill. Suddenly he sprang down past the alien, striking him a light tap on the shoulder as he went by, pinning the creature around like a dervish. The battle lamp went crashing to the deck; the heat gun flew off to one side, struck a bulkhead, and spluttered twice as it shorted out. Flicker spun on the alien, catching him a crippling blow across the chest. Fear broke strong from the alien's mind as he toppled to the floor. Flicker was upon him in an instant, like an animal, ripping, tearing, crushing. The exhilaration roared through his mind like a narcotic, and he lifted the twitching body by the neck, half-dragging it over to the generators. Carefully he placed one of, the alien's paws on one of the generator leads, the other on the other. The terrific voltage sputtered, and the alien gave two jerks and crackled into a steaming, reeking cinder, while the generator turned cherry red, melted, and fused. Flicker blasted the fuse-box with his pistol, fusing it into a glob of molten metal and plastic, then turned the pistol on the auxiliary generators. The smell of ozone rose strongly in the air, and the generators were beyond hope of repair.

Flicker rose and stretched easily, his heart pounding. His side throbbed painfully, but he felt an incongruent flush of satisfaction and well-being. Now there would be no more lights. No more painful, burning agony in his eyes. Now he could take his time—even enjoy himself. He sprang up onto the catwalk again, located a concealed corner, and sank down to sleep.

The five of them were gathered in the control room of the ship. Open paneling of *plastiglass* at the end of the room looked out at the infinity of black starlit space. Far below the engines throbbed, thrusting the ship onward and onward. The aliens moved restlessly, fear and desperation clinging about them like a cloak.

In the darkness of the rear of the control room, high above them on an acceleration cot, crouched Flicker, hunger gnawing at his stomach. He peered down at the flimsy little creatures, studying their features closely for the first time. ShaLee stood with his back to the instrument panel, facing the others, who sat or lounged on the short table-like seats before him. A pair of battle lamps sat on the instrument panel, trained on the two hatchways leading into the control room, and each of the aliens carried a heat pistol in his paw. They looked so weak, so frightened, so utterly helpless, standing there, that it seemed almost impossible for Flicker to believe that these were the creatures who were threatening his people—who were responsible for the draining and pillaging of planets that Flicker had seen. These were the ones, deadly for all their apparent helplessness. Flicker blink ed, leaning closer and closing his eyes, soaking in and separating each thought pattern that reached him from the group.

"So what are we going to do about it?" Sha-Lee's thought came through sharply. "We might be able to manage without the lights, but he got the generators, so that took our radio out too. We got only one message home, and that was brief—not even enough for them to get a fix on us. They know approximately where we are, but they'd never find us in a million years. We can't hope for help from them. We're stuck."

Another one shifted uneasily. "He's out to get us all. And without light we can't find him. We don't even dare go looking for him—it looks as if he can see in the dark."

"Let's consider what we're really up against," said ShaLee. "As you say, he can see in the dark, and we've got darkness here. That's point number one. Number two, he's quiet as a mouse and fast as the -wind. When he got To-may in the grain-storage vault, he came and went so fast I didn't even know what had happened before he was gone. Number three, he's acquainted with spaceships, and with the lights gone he's more at home on this ship than we are. Wherever he came from, he's no primitive. He's got a mind that doesn't miss a trick."

"But what does he want?" Jock toyed with his heat pistol nervously. "What was he doing when we found him out there ? He was nearly frozen to death—"

"—or seemed to be! Motive? It might be anything, or nothing at all. Maybe he's just hateful. The point is, there's one thing he can't do, unless he's *really* got some technology, and that may be our way out."

"Which is?"

"I doubt if he can be in two places at one time. Or three. There are five of us here, and some of us have to get home to tell about this. This could be death to our exploratories. Certainly we don't dare to take him home with us alive, but we'd have to find him to kill him, and he'd get us first. Now here's a plan we might be able to put across. Two of us should stay with the ship, myself and one other. The other three take lifeboats, and get out now. We approach within lifeboat range of Cagli in about an hour. The Caglians won't be happy to see you, but they won't hurt you, and you can bluff your way to a radio. Maybe the two of us here can keep him off until you get help. At any rate, I hope we can."

Flicker lost track of their thoughts as the information integrated in his mind. A chill went through him, driving out even the gnawing hunger for a moment. If they got off in lifeboats, they'd get help, and the mission would really be lost, irreparable damage done. He had to prevent them from making any contact with their home. This ship was a freighter; freighters were slow. Any culture as advanced as theirs would have ships—fast ships—to overtake slow old freighters

Quickly and silently Flicker slipped over toward the hatch. The lamp shown on it full, but the aliens weren't watching. Like a shadow he flashed through the hatch and down the corridor. There he paused, for a fraction of a second, and listened.

No thoughts, no alarm. Flicker felt a wave of contempt. They hadn't even seen him.

At the top of the ladder Flicker crouched and waited. The meeting below was breaking up; he heard a hatchway clang, followed by the muffled pounding of their heavy feet as two of the aliens started down the corridor below. The battle lamp swung back and forth before them, its flash pattern swinging weirdly on the bulkheads and deck. Flicker waited. The aliens started up the ladder before him, their thoughts a muddle, fear oozing from them, but carrying with it a curious overtone of incaution. "We can check the lifeboat for supplies now," came a thought, "and be ready to blast in an hour." At the top of the ladder they passed so close to Flicker that he nearly gagged, yet in his desperate hunger there was something almost tasty—about that smell. They moved on, toward the lifeboat locks, and Flicker followed, trying eagerly to separate their thoughts into a coherent pattern.

"*He's behind us*!" It came suddenly, like a knife through the air.

"Don't turn around." The first alien gripped his companion's sleeve. "Pretend you don't know it." They moved along, with no outward sign of their sudden terrible awareness. Their minds were racing, fearful, but they kept on. Flicker crouched along the bulkhead and followed.

The aliens came to the hatch. Flicker tensed, ready for them. He heard them undog the hatch, heard its squeak as it opened, and he tensed, his muscles quivering eagerly.

Three beams of light stabbed down the passageway at him, brilliant, staggering him LL back against the bulkhead. He grasped frantically at the closing hatch, but it clanged shut, the heavy dogs scraping into place on the opposite side. And at the other end of the corridor

He was trapped! Of course they had been incautious, nonchalant! Of course they had led him on. And now—

"There he is! GET HIM!"

A heat gun whined, its searing energy ricocheting in the closed end of the corridor. With a snarl Flicker sprang, high up on the bulkhead, dragging himself onto a shelf carrying emergency spacesuits. Blast after blast came from the alien guns, rebounding like furies, all missing. "I can't kill it!" a thought pounded through. "It's moving too fast!"

Frantically Flicker trained his own pistol on the hatchway, blasted a steady stream until the metal melted through. With an exultant snarl he dived through the opening, and without pausing sprang up onto the lifeboat locks. He paused, breathing heavily, his burned side throbbing painfully. The two aliens inside were swinging their battle lamp in wild arcs. One spotted him and blasted, but he was gone before the alien triggered. With careful aim he blasted the battle lamp, resting easy for a moment in the ensuing darkness. Then he was across the lock, tearing, ripping, scratching, snarling into the two aliens, roaring in savage glee. One of them fell with a crushed skull, its body horribly mutilated. The other slipped from his grasp and started running through the blackness for the hatch. Flicker was there before it.

He picked up the alien bodily and threw him across the lock. In an instant he was upon him, ripping off an arm at the socket. The alien screamed in pain, and tried to wriggle away. Flicker let him wriggle about three feet. Then he gave him a cuff that sent him sprawling, and ripped off the other arm. The alien twisted and turned like a worm on a stick, but Flicker didn't kill him. Instead, he broke a leg, and twisted off an ear.

The three aliens in the corridor threw open the hatch and flooded the dark lock with the beams of the battle lamps. They saw blood on the deck, and nothing more.

"We know you're in here. Come out now, or we'll come get you." Flicker caught the thought clearly, and snickered comfortably. He was much more comfortable, now that he wasn't so hungry. He picked up a long white bone and threw it against the opposite bulkhead. It clanged, and the three lamps swung instantly in the direction of the sound. "There he is! Blast him!"

Three heat guns spoke sharply, and dead stillness echoed the despairing thought, "That wasn't it—"

They moved across the room, and dragged the charred and mutilated body of their companion away from the bulkhead. "Let's get out of here! We can't fight this thing!" Sha-Lee started for the hatch, followed by the other two.

Only two of the three reached the control room. Flicker played with the third for quite a long while before he killed him.

"We aren't going to get out of this alive," said Sha-Lee. "You know that, as well as I do, I guess."

Jock nodded. "I've been sure of it since he got Klock in the first place. He moves too fast, he thinks too fast, he can see too well. And savage! He has a heat gun, do you realize that? But not One of us was killed with a heat gun. It's butchery, I tell you—no, we won't get out of here, alive."

"And this thing that's stalking us. What will it do? Take the ship back home? Run loose there the way he's run loose here? Killing and maiming? We've got to stop it, Jock. We can't let it get home."

Jock stared at the instrument panel. "I know one way we can stop him," he said slowly. "It's suicide, but it would keep him from going home. And it would mean the end of him, too, finally."

Charlie looked up, tired lines on his face. The fear was gone to resignation now, replaced by another more terrible fear—the fear that they would be killed and leave this thing running loose—on the ship "What is it, Jacques?"

Jacques picked up a space chart, and slowly ripped it in two. "This," he said. "We can cripple the ship, foul up the controls, the gas storage, the charts —cripple it beyond repair. Then he can't do anything! Wreck the engines, destroy the food, smash this ship so no one could ever do anything with it. Completely wreck his chances to get home—"

They moved with sudden desperate swiftness. The heat gun sent up the space charts in wreaths of flame, fused the chart file into a molten heap of aluminum. The engines stopped throbbing, giving way to deathly silence broken only by the heat blasts and the heavy breathing of the two men. The instrument panel melted and exploded, the gas control was smashed. The men worked in a frenzy of fearful destruction, their own last escape going up in searing heat blasts, destruction that no man could even hope to repair, ever

And back in the corner, behind the acceleration cots, Flicker purred and purred. Easy, satisfied contentment filled him for the first time in days; he snickered as the alien creatures went on their path of self-destruction. Everything would be all right now, and his leaders would be pleased at how it turned out. He could bring back first-hand information about these creatures, vital, invaluable information. The contact could be made another time. And then he could go back to his family—they'd really enjoy hearing him tell about that alien, squirming and screeching with both arms ripped off—and have a long, comfortable rest.

The helpless, simple fools! They could kill him so easily, if they only knew. Just a breath of hydrogen, to combine with his high-oxygen metabolism, to explode him like a bomb. But they were destroying everything they could, in a mad, frenzied attempt to stall the spaceship, to keep him out here in space to perish with them! Such a complete job they were doing, and it was so completely and utterly useless.

True, no human being could ever repair those controls to regulate the atomic engines of the ship. No human being could survive the weakening atmosphere long enough to repair the gas units. And even with these repaired and functioning, a human being would be forever stranded in the vast, cold, friendless reaches of space, without a perfect, detailed, visual memory of the space charts easily at his command. For no human being could ever direct a ship blind to a destination, without the charts of the space through which he flew. No human being would ever find his way out of the dead emptiness of such uncharted space.

Flicker curled up and placed his nose gently on his tail, disinterested; unconcerned. A human being would be hopelessly, irreparably doomed out here.

Flicker purred contentedly to himself as he considered the weaknesses of the human race which he had observed. From their view, he was completely stranded.

But a cat can always find its way home.

DERELICT

John Sabo, second in command, sat bolt upright in his bunk, blinking wide-eyed at the darkness. The alarm was screaming through the Satellite Station, its harsh, nerve-jarring clang echoing and re-echoing down the metal corridors, penetrating every nook and crevice and cubicle of the lonely outpost, screaming incredibly through the dark sleeping period. Sabo shook the sleep from his eyes, and then a panic of fear burst into his mind. The alarm! Tumbling out of his bunk in the darkness, he crashed into the far bulkhead, staggering giddily in the impossible gravity as he pawed about for his magnaboots, his heart pounding fiercely in his ears. The *alarm*! Impossible, after so long, after these long months of bitter waiting— In the corridor he collided with Brownie, looking like a frightened gnome, and he growled profanity as he raced down the corridor for the Central Control.

Frightened eyes turned to him as he blinked at the bright lights of the room. The voices rose in a confused, anxious babble, and he shook his head and swore, and ploughed through them toward the screen. "Kill that damned alarm!" he roared, blinking as he counted faces. "Somebody get the Skipper out of his sack, pronto, and stop that clatter! What's the trouble?"

The radioman waved feebly at the view screen, shimmering on the great side panel. "We just picked it up—"

It was a ship, moving in from beyond Saturn's rings, a huge, gray-black blob in the silvery screen, moving in toward the Station with ponderous, clumsy grace, growing larger by the second as it sped toward them. Sabo felt the fear spill over in his mind, driving out all thought, and he sank into the control chair like a well-trained automaton. His gray eyes were wide, trained for long military years to miss nothing; his fingers moved over the panel with deft skill. "Get the men to stations," he growled, "and will somebody kindly get the Skipper down here, if he can manage to take a minute."

"I'm right here." The little graying man was at his elbow, staring at the screen with angry red eyes. "Who told you to shut off the alarm?"

"Nobody told me. Everyone was here, and it was getting on my nerves."

"What a shame." Captain Loomis' voice was icy. "I give orders on this Station," he said smoothly, "and you'll remember it." He scowled at the great gray ship, looming closer and closer. "What's its course?"

"Going to miss us by several thousand kilos at least. Look at that thing! It's *traveling*."

"Contact it! This is what we've been waiting for." The captain's voice was hoarse.

Sabo spun a dial, and cursed. "No luck. Can't get through. It's passing us—"

"Then *grapple* it, stupid! You want me to wipe your nose, too?"

Sabo's face darkened angrily. With slow precision he set the servo fixes on the huge gray hulk looming up in the viewer, and then snapped the switches sharply. Two small servos shoved their blunt noses from the landing port of the Station, and slipped silently into space alongside. Then, like a pair of trained dogs, they sped on their beams straight out from the Station toward the approaching ship. The intruder was dark, moving at tremendous velocity past the Station, as though unaware of its existence. The servos moved out, and suddenly diverged and reversed, twisting in long arcs to come alongside the strange ship, finally moving in at the same velocity on either side. There was a sharp flash of contact power; then, like a mammoth slow-motion monster, the ship jerked in midspace and turned a graceful end-for-end arc as the servo-grapplers gripped it like leeches and whined, glowing ruddy with the jolting power flowing through them. Sabo watched, hardly breathing, until the great ship spun and slowed and stopped. Then it reversed direction, and the servos led it triumphantly back toward the landing port of the Station.

Sabo glanced at the radioman, a frown creasing his forehead. "Still nothing?"

"Not a peep."

He stared out at the great ship, feeling a chill of wonder and fear crawl up his spine. "So this is the mysterious puzzle of Saturn," he muttered. "This is what we've been waiting for."

There was a curious eager light in Captain Loomis' eyes as he looked up. "Oh, no. Not this."

"What?"

"Not this. The ships we've seen before were tiny, flat." His little eyes turned toward the ship, and back to Sabo's heavy face. "This is something else, something quite different." A smile curved his lips, and he rubbed his hands together. "We go out for trout and come back with a whale. This ship's from space, deep space. Not from Saturn. This one's from the stars."

*

The strange ship hung at the side of the Satellite Station, silent as a tomb, still gently rotating as the Station slowly spun in its orbit around Saturn.

In the captain's cabin the men shifted restlessly, uneasily facing the eager eyes of their captain. The old man paced the floor of the cabin, his white hair mussed, his face red with excitement. Even his carefully calm face couldn't conceal the eagerness burning in his eyes as he faced the crew. "Still no contact?" he asked Sparks.

The radioman shook his head anxiously. "Not a sign. I've tried every signal I know at every wave frequency that could possibly reach them. I've even tried a dozen frequencies that couldn't possibly reach them, and I haven't stirred them up a bit. They just aren't answering."

Captain Loomis swung on the group of men. "All right, now, I want you to get this straight. This is our catch. We don't know what's aboard it, and we don't know where it came from, but it's our prize. That means not a word goes back home about it until we've learned all there is to learn. We're going to get the honors on this one, not some eager Admiral back home—"

The men stirred uneasily, worried eyes seeking Sabo's face in alarm. "What about the law?" growled Sabo. "The law says everything must be reported within two hours."

"Then we'll break the law," the captain snapped. "I'm captain of this Station, and those are your orders. You don't need to worry about the law—I'll see that you're protected, but this is too big to fumble. This ship is from the stars. That means it must have an Interstellar drive. You know what that means. The Government will fall all over itself to reward us—"

Sabo scowled, and the worry deepened in the men's faces. It was hard to imagine the Government falling all over itself for anybody. They knew too well how the Government worked. They had heard of the swift trials, the harsh imprisonments that awaited even the petty infringers. The Military Government had no time to waste on those who stepped out of line, they had no mercy to spare. And the men knew that their captain was not in favor in top Government circles. Crack patrol commanders were not shunted into remote, lifeless Satellite Stations if their stand in the Government was high. And deep in their minds, somehow, the men knew they couldn't trust this little, sharp-eyed, white-haired man. The credit for such a discovery as this might go to him, yes—but there would be little left for them.

"The law—" Sabo repeated stubbornly.

"Damn the law! We're stationed out here in this limbo to watch Saturn and report any activity we see coming from there. There's nothing in our orders about anything else. There have been ships from there, they think, but not this ship. The Government has spent billions trying to find an Interstellar, and never gotten to first base." The captain paused, his eyes narrowing. "We'll go aboard this ship," he said softly. "We'll find out what's aboard it, and where it's from, and we'll take its drive. There's been no resistance yet, but it could be dangerous. We can't assume anything. The boarding party will report everything they find to me. One of them will have to be a drive man. That's you, Brownie."

The little man with the sharp black eyes looked up eagerly. "I don't know if I could tell anything—"

"You can tell more than anyone else here. Nobody else knows space drive. I'll count on you. If you bring back a good report, perhaps we can cancel out certain—unfortunate items in your record. But one other should board with you—" His eyes turned toward John Sabo.

"Not me. This is your goat." The mate's eyes were sullen. "This is gross breach, and you know it. They'll have you in irons when we get back. I don't want anything to do with it."

"You're under orders, Sabo. You keep forgetting."

"They're illegal orders, sir!"

"I'll take responsibility for that."

Sabo looked the old man straight in the eye. "You mean you'd sell us down a rat hole to save your skin. That's what you mean."

Captain Loomis' eyes widened incredulously. Then his face darkened, and he stepped very close to the big man. "You'll watch your tongue, I think," he gritted. "Be careful what you say to me, Sabo. Be very careful. Because if you don't, *you'll* be in irons, and we'll see just how long you last when you get back home. Now you've got your orders. You'll board the ship with Brownie."

The big man's fists were clenched until the knuckles were white. "You don't know what's over there!" he burst out. "We could be slaughtered."

The captain's smile was unpleasant. "That would be such a pity," he murmured. "I'd really hate to see it happen—"

*

The ship hung dark and silent, like a shadowy ghost. No flicker of light could be seen aboard it; no sound nor faintest sign of life came from the tall, dark hull plates. It hung there, huge and imponderable, and swung around with the Station in its silent orbit.

The men huddled about Sabo and Brownie, helping them into their pressure suits, checking their equipment. They had watched the little scanning beetles crawl over the surface of the great ship, examining, probing every nook and crevice, reporting crystals, and metals, and irons, while the boarding party prepared. And still the radioman waited alertly for a flicker of life from the solemn giant.

Frightened as they were of their part in the illegal secrecy, the arrival of the ship had brought a change in the crew, lighting fires of excitement in their eyes. They moved faster, their voices were lighter, more cheerful. Long months on the Station had worn on their nerves—out of contact with their homes, on a mission that was secretly jeered as utter Governmental folly. Ships *had* been seen, years before, disappearing into the sullen bright atmospheric crust of Saturn, but there had been no sign of anything since. And out there, on the lonely guard Station, nerves had run ragged, always waiting, always watching, wearing away even the iron discipline of their military background. They grew bitterly weary of the same faces, the same routine, the constant repetition of inactivity. And through the months they had watched with increasing anxiety the conflict growing between the captain and his bitter, sullen-eyed second-in-command, John Sabo.

And then the ship had come, incredibly, from the depths of space, and the tensions of loneliness were forgotten in the flurry of activity. The locks whined and opened as the two men moved out of the Station on the little propulsion sleds, linked to the Station with light silk guy ropes. Sabo settled himself on the sled, cursing himself for falling so foolishly into the captain's scheme, cursing his tongue for wandering. And deep within him he felt a new sensation, a vague uneasiness and insecurity that he had not felt in all his years of military life. The strange ship was a variant, an imponderable factor thrown suddenly into his small world of hatred and bitterness, forcing him into unknown territory, throwing his mind into a welter of doubts and fears. He glanced uneasily across at Brownie, vaguely wishing that someone else were with him. Brownie was a troublemaker, Brownie talked too much, Brownie philosophized in a world that ridiculed philosophy. He'd known men like Brownie before, and he knew that they couldn't be trusted.

The gray hull gleamed at them as they moved toward it, a monstrous wall of polished metal. There were no dents, no surface scars from its passage through space. They found the entrance lock without difficulty, near the top of the ship's great hull, and Brownie probed the rim of the lock with a dozen instruments, his dark eyes burning eagerly. And then, with a squeal that grated in Sabo's ears, the oval port of the ship quivered, and slowly opened.

Silently, the sleds moved into the opening. They were in a small vault, quite dark, and the sleds settled slowly onto a metal deck. Sabo eased himself from the seat, tuning up his audios to their highest sensitivity, moving over to Brownie. Momentarily they touched helmets, and Brownie's excited voice came to him, muted, but breathless. "No trouble getting it open. It worked on the same principle as ours."

"Better get to work on the inner lock."

Brownie shot him a sharp glance. "But what about—inside? I mean, we can't just walk in on them—"

"Why not? We've tried to contact them."

Reluctantly, the little engineer began probing the inner lock with trembling fingers. Minutes later they were easing themselves through, moving slowly down the dark corridor, waiting with pounding hearts for a sound, a sign. The corridor joined another, and then still another, until they reached a great oval door. And then they were inside, in the heart of the ship, and their eyes widened as they stared at the thing in the center of the great vaulted chamber.

"My God!" Brownie's voice was a hoarse whisper in the stillness. "Look at them, Johnny!"

Sabo moved slowly across the room toward the frail, crushed form lying against the great, gleaming panel. Thin, almost boneless arms were pasted against the hard metal; an oval, humanoid skull was crushed like an eggshell into the knobs and levers of the control panel. Sudden horror shot through the big man as he looked around. At the far side of the room was another of the things, and still another, mashed, like lifeless jelly, into the floors and panels. Gently he peeled a bit of jelly away from the metal, then turned with a mixture of wonder and disgust. "All dead," he muttered.

Brownie looked up at him, his hands trembling. "No wonder there was no sign." He looked about helplessly. "It's a derelict, Johnny. A wanderer. How could it have happened? How long ago?"

Sabo shook his head, bewildered. "Then it was just chance that it came to us, that we saw it—"

"No pilot, no charts. It might have wandered for centuries." Brownie stared about the room, a frightened look on his face. And then he was leaning over the control panel, probing at the array of levers, his fingers working eagerly at the wiring. Sabo nodded approvingly. "We'll have to go over it with a comb," he said. "I'll see what I can find in the rest of the ship. You go ahead on the controls and drive." Without waiting for an answer he moved swiftly from the round chamber, out into the corridor again, his stomach almost sick.

It took them many hours. They moved silently, as if even a slight sound might disturb the sleeping alien forms, smashed against the dark metal panels. In another room were the charts, great, beautiful charts, totally unfamiliar, studded with star formations he had never seen, noted with curious, meaningless symbols. As Sabo worked he heard Brownie moving down into the depths of the ship, toward the giant engine rooms. And then, some silent alarm clicked into place in Sabo's mind, tightening his stomach, screaming to be heard. Heart pounding, he dashed down the corridor like a cat, seeing again in his mind the bright, eager eyes of the engineer. Suddenly the meaning of that eagerness dawned on him. He scampered down a ladder, along a corridor, and down another ladder, down to the engine room, almost colliding with Brownie as he crossed from one of the engines to a battery of generators on the far side of the room.

"Brownie!"

"What's the trouble?"

Sabo trembled, then turned away. "Nothing," he muttered. "Just a thought." But he watched as the little man snaked into the labyrinth of dynamos and coils and wires, peering eagerly, probing, searching, making notes in the little pad in his hand.

[Illustration]

Finally, hours later, they moved again toward the lock where they had left their sleds. Not a word passed between them. The uneasiness was strong in Sabo's mind now, growing deeper, mingling with fear and a premonition of impending evil. A dead ship, a derelict, come to them by merest chance from some unthinkably remote star. He cursed, without knowing why, and suddenly he felt he hated Brownie as much as he hated the captain waiting for them in the Station.

But as he stepped into the Station's lock, a new thought crossed his mind, almost dazzling him with its unexpectedness. He looked at the engineer's thin face, and his hands were trembling as he opened the pressure suit.

*

He deliberately took longer than was necessary to give his report to the captain, dwelling on unimportant details, watching with malicious amusement the captain's growing annoyance. Captain Loomis' eyes kept sliding to Brownie, as though trying to read the information he wanted from the engineer's face. Sabo rolled up the charts slowly, stowing them in a pile on the desk. "That's the picture, sir. Perhaps a qualified astronomer could make something of it; I haven't the knowledge or the instruments. The ship came from outside the system, beyond doubt. Probably from a planet with lighter gravity than our own, judging from the frailty of the creatures. Oxygen breathers, from the looks of their gas storage. If you ask me, I'd say—"

"All right, all right," the captain breathed impatiently. "You can write it up and hand it to me. It isn't really important where they came from, or whether they breathe oxygen or fluorine." He turned his eyes to the engineer, and lit a cigar with trembling fingers. "The important thing is *how* they got here. The drive, Brownie. You went over the engines carefully? What did you find?"

Brownie twitched uneasily, and looked at the floor. "Oh, yes, I examined them carefully. Wasn't too hard. I examined every piece of drive machinery on the ship, from stem to stern."

Sabo nodded, slowly, watching the little man with a carefully blank face. "That's right. You gave it a good going over."

Brownie licked his lips. "It's a derelict, like Johnny told you. They were dead. All of them. Probably had been dead for a long time. I couldn't tell, of course. Probably nobody could tell. But they must have been dead for centuries—"

The captain's eyes blinked as the implication sank in. "Wait a minute," he said. "What do you mean, *centuries?*"

Brownie stared at his shoes. "The atomic piles were almost dead," he muttered in an apologetic whine. "The ship wasn't going any place, captain. It was just wandering. Maybe it's wandered for thousands of years." He took a deep breath, and his eyes met the captain's for a brief agonized moment. "They don't have Interstellar, sir. Just plain, simple, slow atomics. Nothing different. They've been traveling for centuries, and it would have taken them just as long to get back."

The captain's voice was thin, choked. "Are you trying to tell me that their drive is no different from our own? That a ship has actually wandered into Interstellar space *without a space drive?*"

Brownie spread his hands helplessly. "Something must have gone wrong. They must have started off for another planet in their own system, and something went wrong. They broke into space, and they all died. And the ship just went on moving. They never intended an Interstellar hop. They couldn't have. They didn't have the drive for it."

The captain sat back numbly, his face pasty gray. The light had faded in his eyes now; he sat as though he'd been struck. "You—you couldn't be wrong? You couldn't have missed anything?"

Brownie's eyes shifted unhappily, and his voice was very faint. "No, sir."

The captain stared at them for a long moment, like a stricken child. Slowly he picked up one of the charts, his mouth working. Then, with a bitter roar, he threw it in Sabo's face. "Get out of here! Take this garbage and get out! And get the men to their stations. We're here to watch Saturn, and by god, we'll watch Saturn!" He turned away, a hand over his eyes, and they heard his choking breath as they left the cabin.

Slowly, Brownie walked out into the corridor, started down toward his cabin, with Sabo silent at his heels. He looked up once at the mate's heavy face, a look of pleading in his dark brown eyes, and then opened the door to his quarters. Like a cat, Sabo was in the room before him, dragging him in, slamming the door. He caught the little man by the neck with one savage hand, and shoved him unceremoniously against the door, his voice a vicious whisper. "*All right, talk! Let's have it now!*"

Brownie choked, his eyes bulging, his face turning gray in the dim light of the cabin. "Johnny! Let me down! What's the matter? You're choking me, Johnny—"

The mate's eyes were red, with heavy lines of disgust and bitterness running from his eyes and the corners of his mouth. "You stinking little liar! *Talk*, damn it! You're not messing with the captain now, you're messing with *me*, and I'll have the truth if I have to cave in your skull—"

"I told you the truth! I don't know what you mean—"

Sabo's palm smashed into his face, jerking his head about like an apple on a string. "That's the wrong answer," he grated. "I warn you, don't lie! The captain is an ambitious ass, he couldn't think his way through a multiplication table. He's a little child. But I'm not quite so dull." He threw the little man down in a heap, his eyes blazing. "You silly fool, your story is so full of holes you could drive a tank through it. They just up and died, did they? I'm supposed to believe that? Smashed up against the panels the way they were? Only one thing could crush them like that. Any fool could see it. Acceleration. And I don't mean atomic acceleration. Something else." He glared down at the man quivering on the floor. "They had Interstellar drive, didn't they, Brownie?"

Brownie nodded his head, weakly, almost sobbing, trying to pull himself erect. "Don't tell the captain," he sobbed. "Oh, Johnny, for god's sake, listen to me, don't let him know I lied. I was going to tell you anyway, Johnny, really I was. I've got a plan, a good plan, can't you see it?" The gleam of excitement came back into the sharp little eyes. "They had it, all right. Their trip probably took just a few months. They had a drive I've never seen before, non-atomic. I couldn't tell the principle, with the look I had, but I think I could work it." He sat up, his whole body trembling. "Don't give me away, Johnny, listen a minute—"

Sabo sat back against the bunk, staring at the little man. "You're out of your mind," he said softly. "You don't know what you're doing. What are you going to do when His Nibs goes over for a look himself? He's stupid, but not that stupid."

Brownie's voice choked, his words tumbling over each other in his eagerness. "He won't get a chance to see it, Johnny. He's got to take our word until he sees it, and we can stall him—"

Sabo blinked. "A day or so—maybe. But what then? Oh, how could you be so stupid? He's on the skids, he's out of favor and fighting for his life. That drive is the break that could put him on top. Can't you see he's selfish? He has to be, in this world, to get anything. Anything or anyone who blocks him, he'll destroy, if he can. Can't you see that? When he spots this, your life won't be worth spitting at."

Brownie was trembling as he sat down opposite the big man. His voice was harsh in the little cubicle, heavy with pain and hopelessness. "That's right," he said. "My life isn't worth a nickle. Neither is yours. Neither is anybody's, here or back home. Nobody's life is worth a nickle. Something's happened to us in the past hundred years, Johnny—something horrible. I've seen it creeping and growing up around us all my life. People don't matter any more, it's the Government, what the Government thinks that matters. It's a web, a cancer that grows in its own pattern, until it goes so far it can't be stopped. Men like Loomis could see the pattern, and adapt to it, throw away all the worthwhile things, the love and beauty and peace that we once had in our lives. Those men can get somewhere, they can turn this life into a climbing game, waiting their chance to get a little farther toward the top, a little closer to some semblance of security—"

"Everybody adapts to it," Sabo snapped. "They have to. You don't see me moving for anyone else, do you? I'm for *me*, and believe me I know it. I don't give a hang for you, or Loomis, or anyone else alive—just me. I want to stay alive, that's all. You're a dreamer, Brownie. But until you pull something like this, you can learn to stop dreaming if you want to—"

"No, no, you're wrong—oh, you're horribly wrong, Johnny. Some of us *can't* adapt, we haven't got what it takes, or else we have something else in us that won't let us go along. And right there we're beat before we start. There's no place for us now, and there never will be." He looked up at the mate's impassive face. "We're in a life where we don't belong, impounded into a senseless, never-ending series of fights and skirmishes and long, lonely waits, feeding this insane urge of the Government to expand, out to the planets, to the stars, farther and farther, bigger and bigger. We've got to go, seeking newer and greater worlds to conquer, with nothing to conquer them with, and nothing to conquer them for. There's life somewhere else in our solar system, so it must be sought out and conquered, no matter what or where it is. We live in a world of iron and fear, and there was no place for me, and others like me, *until this ship came*—"

Sabo looked at him strangely. "So I was right. I read it on your face when we were searching the ship. I knew what you were thinking...." His face darkened angrily. "You couldn't get away with it, Brownie. Where could you go, what could you expect to find? You're talking death, Brownie. Nothing else—"

"No, no. Listen, Johnny." Brownie leaned closer, his eyes bright and intent on the man's heavy face. "The captain has to take our word for it, until he sees the ship. Even then he couldn't tell for sure—I'm the only drive engineer on the Station. We have the charts, we could work with them, try to find out where the ship came from; I already have an idea of how the drive is operated. Another look and I could make it work. Think of it, Johnny! What difference does it make where we went, or what we found? You're a misfit, too, you know that—this coarseness and bitterness is a shell, if you could only see it, a sham. You don't really believe in this world we're in—who cares where, if only we could go, get away? Oh, it's a chance, the wildest, freak chance, but we could take it—"

"If only to get away from *him*," said Sabo in a muted voice. "Lord, how I hate him. I've seen smallness and ambition before—pettiness and treachery, plenty of it. But that man is our whole world knotted up in one little ball. I don't think I'd get home without killing him, just to stop that voice from talking, just to see fear cross his face one time. But if we took the ship, it would break him for good." A new light appeared in the big man's eyes. "He'd be through, Brownie. Washed up."

"And we'd be *free*—"

Sabo's eyes were sharp. "What about the acceleration? It killed those that came in the ship."

"But they were so frail, so weak. Light brittle bones and soft jelly. Our bodies are stronger, we could stand it."

Sabo sat for a long time, staring at Brownie. His mind was suddenly confused by the scope of the idea, racing in myriad twirling fantasies, parading before his eyes the long, bitter, frustrating years, the hopelessness of his own life, the dull aching feeling he felt deep in his stomach and bones each time he set back down on Earth, to join the teeming throngs of hungry people. He thought of the rows of drab apartments, the thin faces, the hollow, hunted eyes of the people he had seen. He knew that that was why he was a soldier—because soldiers ate well, they had time to sleep, they were never allowed long hours to think, and wonder, and grow dull and empty. But he knew his life had been barren. The life of a mindless automaton, moving from place to place, never thinking, never daring to think or speak, hoping only to work without pain each day, and sleep without nightmares.

And then, he thought of the nights in his childhood, when he had lain awake, sweating with fear, as the airships screamed across the dark sky above, bound he never knew where; and then, hearing in the far distance the booming explosion, he had played that horrible little game with himself, seeing how high he could count before he heard the weary, plodding footsteps of the people on the road, moving on to another place. He had known, even as a little boy, that the only safe place was in those bombers, that the place for survival was in the striking armies, and his life had followed the hard-learned pattern, twisting him into the cynical mold of the mercenary soldier, dulling the quick and clever mind, drilling into him the ways and responses of order and obey, stripping him of his heritage of love and humanity. Others less thoughtful had been happier; they had succeeded in forgetting the life they had known before, they had been able to learn easily and well the lessons of the repudiation of the rights of men which had crept like a blight through the world. But Sabo, too, was a misfit, wrenched into a mold he could not fit. He had sensed it vaguely, never really knowing when or how he had built the shell of toughness and cynicism, but also sensing vaguely that it was built, and that in it he could hide, somehow, and laugh at himself, and his leaders, and the whole world through which he plodded. He had laughed, but there had been long nights, in the narrow darkness of spaceship bunks, when his mind pounded at the shell, screaming out in nightmare, and he had wondered if he had really lost his mind.

His gray eyes narrowed as he looked at Brownie, and he felt his heart pounding in his chest, pounding with a fury that he could no longer deny. "It would have to be fast," he said softly. "Like lightning, tonight, tomorrow—very soon."

"Oh, yes, I know that. But we *can* do it—"

"Yes," said Sabo, with a hard, bitter glint in his eyes. "Maybe we can."

*

The preparation was tense. For the first time in his life, Sabo knew the meaning of real fear, felt the clinging aura of sudden death in every glance, every word of the men around him. It seemed incredible that the captain didn't notice the brief exchanges with the little engineer, or his own sudden appearances and disappearances about the Station. But the captain sat in his cabin with angry eyes, snapping answers without even looking up. Still, Sabo knew that the seeds of suspicion lay planted in his mind, ready to burst forth with awful violence at any slight provocation. As he worked, the escape assumed greater and greater proportions in Sabo's mind; he knew with increasing urgency and daring that nothing must stop him. The ship was there, the only bridge away from a life he could no longer endure, and his determination blinded him to caution.

Primarily, he pondered over the charts, while Brownie, growing hourly more nervous, poured his heart into a study of his notes and sketches. A second look at the engines was essential; the excuse he concocted for returning to the ship was recklessly slender, and Sabo spent a grueling five minutes dissuading the captain from accompanying him. But the captain's eyes were dull, and he walked his cabin, sunk in a gloomy, remorseful trance.

The hours passed, and the men saw, in despair, that more precious, dangerous hours would be necessary before the flight could be attempted. And then, abruptly, Sabo got the call to the captain's cabin. He found the old man at his desk, regarding him with cold eyes, and his heart sank. The captain motioned him to a seat, and then sat back, lighting a cigar with painful slowness. "I want you to tell me," he said in a lifeless voice, "exactly what Brownie thinks he's doing."

Sabo went cold. Carefully he kept his eyes on the captain's face. "I guess he's nervous," he said. "He doesn't belong on a Satellite Station. He belongs at home. The place gets on his nerves."

"I didn't like his report."

"I know," said Sabo.

The captain's eyes narrowed. "It was hard to believe. Ships don't just happen out of space. They don't wander out interstellar by accident, either." An unpleasant smile curled his lips. "I'm not telling you anything new. I wouldn't want to accuse Brownie of lying, of course—or you either. But we'll know soon. A patrol craft will be here from the Triton supply base in an hour. I signaled as soon as I had your reports." The smile broadened maliciously. "The patrol craft will have experts aboard. Space drive experts. They'll review your report."

"An hour—"

The captain smiled. "That's what I said. In that hour, you could tell me the truth. I'm not a drive man, I'm an administrator, and organizer and director. You're the technicians. The truth now could save you much unhappiness—in the future."

Sabo stood up heavily. "You've got your information," he said with a bitter laugh. "The patrol craft will confirm it."

The captain's face went a shade grayer. "All right," he said. "Go ahead, laugh. I told you, anyway."

Sabo didn't realize how his hands were trembling until he reached the end of the corridor. In despair he saw the plan crumbling beneath his feet, and with the despair came the cold undercurrent of fear. The patrol would discover them, disclose the hoax. There was no choice left—ready or not, they'd *have* to leave.

Quickly he turned in to the central control room where Brownie was working. He sat down, repeating the captain's news in a soft voice.

"An *hour*! But how can we—"

"We've *got* to. We can't quit now, we're dead if we do."

Brownie's eyes were wide with fear. "But can't we stall them, somehow? Maybe if we turned on the captain—"

"The crew would back him. They wouldn't dare go along with us. We've got to run, nothing else." He took a deep breath. "Can you control the drive?"

Brownie stared at his hands. "I—I think so. I can only try."

"You've got to. It's now or never. Get down to the lock, and I'll get the charts. Get the sleds ready."

He scooped the charts from his bunk, folded them carefully and bound them swiftly with cord. Then he ran silently down the corridor to the landing port lock. Brownie was already there, in the darkness, closing the last clamps on his pressure suit. Sabo handed him the charts, and began the laborious task of climbing into his own suit, panting in the darkness.

And then the alarm was clanging in his ear, and the lock was flooded with brilliant light. Sabo stopped short, a cry on his lips, staring at the entrance to the control room.

The captain was grinning, a nasty, evil grin, his eyes hard and humorless as he stood there flanked by three crewmen. His hand gripped an ugly power gun tightly. He just stood there, grinning, and his voice was like fire in Sabo's ears. "Too bad," he said softly. "You almost made it, too. Trouble is, two can't keep a secret. Shame, Johnny, a smart fellow like you. I might have expected as much from Brownie, but I thought you had more sense—"

Something snapped in Sabo's mind, then. With a roar, he lunged at the captain's feet, screaming his bitterness and rage and frustration, catching the old man's calves with his powerful shoulders. The captain toppled, and Sabo was fighting for the power gun, straining with all his might to twist the gun from the thin hand, and he heard his voice shouting, "Run! *Go, Brownie, make it go!*"

The lock was open, and he saw Brownie's sled nose out into the blackness. The captain choked, his face purple. "Get him! Don't let him get away!"

The lock clanged, and the screens showed the tiny fragile sled jet out from the side of the Station, the small huddled figure clinging to it, heading straight for the open port of the gray ship. "Stop him! The guns, you fools, the guns!"

The alarm still clanged, and the control room was a flurry of activity. Three men snapped down behind the tracer-guns, firing without aiming, in a frenzied attempt to catch the fleeing sled. The sled began zig-zagging, twisting wildly as the shells popped on either side of it. The captain twisted away from Sabo's grip with a roar, and threw one of the crewmen to the deck, wrenching the gun controls from his hands. "Get the big ones on the ship! Blast it! If it gets away you'll all pay."

Suddenly the sled popped into the ship's port, and the hatch slowly closed behind it. Raving, the captain turned the gun on the sleek, polished hull plates, pressed the firing levels on the war-head servos. Three of them shot out from the Satellite, like deadly bugs, careening through the intervening space, until one of them struck the side of the gray ship, and exploded in purple fury against the impervious hull. And the others nosed into the flame, and passed on through, striking nothing.

Like the blinking of a light, the alien ship had throbbed, and jerked, and was gone.

With a roar the captain brought his fist down on the hard plastic and metal of the control panel, kicked at the sheet of knobs and levers with a heavy foot, his face purple with rage. His whole body shook as he turned on Sabo, his eyes wild. "You let him get away! It was your fault, yours! But *you* won't get away! I've got you, and you'll pay, do you hear that?" He pulled himself up until his face was bare inches from Sabo's, his teeth bared in a frenzy of hatred. "Now we'll see who'll laugh, my friend. You'll laugh in the death chamber, if you can still laugh by then!" He turned to the men around him. "Take him," he snarled. "Lock him in his quarters, and guard him well. And while you're doing it, take a good look at him. See how he laughs now."

They marched him down to his cabin, stunned, still wondering what had happened. Something had gone in his mind in that second, something that told him that the choice had to be made, instantly. Because he knew, with dull wonder, that in that instant when the lights went on he could have stopped Brownie, could have saved himself. He could have taken for himself a piece of the glory and promotion due to the discoverers of an Interstellar drive. But he had also known, somehow, in that short instant, that the only hope in the world lay in that one nervous, frightened man, and the ship which could take him away.

And the ship was gone. That meant the captain was through. He'd had his chance, the ship's coming had given him his chance, and he had muffed it. Now he, too, would pay. The Government would not be pleased that such a ship had leaked through his fingers. Captain Loomis was through.

And him? Somehow, it didn't seem to matter any more. He had made a stab at it, he had tried. He just hadn't had the luck. But he knew there was more to that. Something in his mind was singing, some deep feeling of happiness and hope had crept into his mind, and he couldn't worry about himself any more. There was nothing more for him; they had him cold. But deep in his mind he felt a curious satisfaction, transcending any fear and bitterness. Deep in his heart, he knew that *one* man had escaped.

And then he sat back and laughed.

THE NATIVE SOIL

Before the first ship from Earth made a landing on Venus, there was much speculation about what might be found beneath the cloud layers obscuring that planet's surface from the eyes of all observers.

One school of thought maintained that the surface of Venus was a jungle, rank with hot-house moisture, crawling with writhing fauna and man-eating flowers. Another group contended hotly that Venus was an arid desert of wind-carved sandstone, dry and cruel, whipping dust into clouds that sunlight could never penetrate. Others prognosticated an ocean planet with little or no solid ground at all, populated by enormous serpents waiting to greet the first Earthlings with jaws agape.

But nobody knew, of course. Venus was the planet of mystery.

When the first Earth ship finally landed there, all they found was a great quantity of mud.

There was enough mud on Venus to go all the way around twice, with some left over. It was warm, wet, soggy mud—clinging and tenacious. In some places it was gray, and in other places it was black. Elsewhere it was found to be varying shades of brown, yellow, green, blue and purple. But just the same, it was still mud. The sparse Venusian vegetation grew up out of it; the small Venusian natives lived down in it; the steam rose from it and the rain fell on it, and that, it seemed, was that. The planet of mystery was no longer mysterious. It was just messy. People didn't talk about it any more.

But technologists of the Piper Pharmaceuticals, Inc., R&D squad found a certain charm in the Venusian mud.

They began sending cautious and very secret reports back to the Home Office when they discovered just what, exactly was growing in that Venusian mud besides Venusian natives. The Home Office promptly bought up full exploratory and mining rights to the planet for a price that was a brazen steal, and then in high excitement began pouring millions of dollars into ships and machines bound for the muddy planet. The Board of Directors met hoots of derision with secret smiles as they rubbed their hands together softly. Special crews of psychologists were dispatched to Venus to contact the natives; they returned, exuberant, with test-results that proved the natives were friendly, intelligent, co-operative and resourceful, and the Board of Directors rubbed their hands more eagerly together, and poured more money into the Piper Venusian Installation.

It took money to make money, they thought. Let the fools laugh. They wouldn't be laughing long. After all, Piper Pharmaceuticals, Inc., could recognize a gold mine when they saw one.

They thought.

*

Robert Kielland, special investigator and trouble shooter for Piper Pharmaceuticals, Inc., made an abrupt and intimate acquaintance with the fabulous Venusian mud when the landing craft brought him down on that soggy planet. He had transferred from the great bubble-shaped orbital transport ship to the sleek landing craft an hour before, bored and impatient with the whole proposition. He had no desire whatever to go to Venus. He didn't like mud, and he didn't like frontier projects. There had been nothing in his contract with Piper demanding that he travel to other planets in pursuit of his duties, and he had balked at the assignment. He had even balked at the staggering bonus check they offered him to help him get used to the idea.

It was not until they had convinced him that only his own superior judgment, his razor-sharp mind and his extraordinarily shrewd powers of observation and insight could possibly pull Piper Pharmaceuticals, Inc., out of the mudhole they'd gotten themselves into, that he had reluctantly agreed to go. He wouldn't like a moment of it, but he'd go.

Things weren't going right on Venus, it seemed.

The trouble was that millions were going in and nothing was coming out. The early promise of high production figures had faltered, sagged, dwindled and vanished. Venus was getting to be an expensive project to have around, and nobody seemed to know just why.

Now the pilot dipped the landing craft in and out of the cloud blanket, braking the ship, falling closer and closer to the surface as Kielland watched gloomily from the after port. The lurching billows of clouds made him queasy; he opened his Piper samples case and popped a pill into his mouth. Then he gave his nose a squirt or two with his Piper Rhino-Vac nebulizer, just for good measure. Finally, far below them, the featureless gray surface skimmed by. A sparse scraggly forest of twisted gray foliage sprang up at them.

The pilot sighted the landing platform, checked with Control Tower, and eased up for the final descent. He was a skillful pilot, with many landings on Venus to his credit. He brought the ship up on its tail and sat it down on the landing platform for a perfect three-pointer as the jets rumbled to silence.

Then, abruptly, they sank—landing craft, platform and all.

The pilot buzzed Control Tower frantically as Kielland fought down panic. Sorry, said Control Tower. Something must have gone wrong. They'd have them out in a jiffy. Good lord, no, *don't* blast out again, there were a thousand natives in the vicinity. Just be patient, everything would be all right.

They waited. Presently there were thumps and bangs as grapplers clanged on the surface of the craft. Mud gurgled around them as they were hauled up and out with the sound of a giant sipping soup. A mud-encrusted hatchway flew open, and Kielland stepped down on a flimsy-looking platform below. Four small rodent-like creatures were attached to it by ropes; they heaved with a will and began paddling through the soupy mud dragging the platform and Kielland toward a row of low wooden buildings near some stunted trees.

As the creatures paused to puff and pant, the back half of the platform kept sinking into the mud. When they finally reached comparatively solid ground, Kielland was mud up to the hips, and mad enough to blast off without benefit of landing craft.

He surveyed the Piper Venusian Installation, hardly believing what he saw. He had heard the glowing descriptions of the Board of Directors. He had seen the architect's projections of fine modern buildings resting on water-proof buoys, neat boating channels to the mine sites, fine orange-painted dredge equipment (including the new Piper Axis-Traction Dredges that had been developed especially for the operation). It had sounded, in short, just the way a Piper Installation ought to sound.

But there was nothing here that resembled that. Kielland could see a group of little wooden shacks that looked as though they were ready at a moment's notice to sink with a gurgle into the mud. Off to the right across a mud flat one of the dredges apparently had done just that: a swarm of men and natives were hard at work dragging it up again. Control Tower was to the left, balanced precariously at a slight tilt in a sea of mud.

The Piper Venusian Installation didn't look too much like a going concern. It looked far more like a ghost town in the latter stages of decay.

Inside the Administration shack Kielland found a weary-looking man behind a desk, scribbling furiously at a pile of reports. Everything in the shack was splattered with mud. The crude desk and furniture was smeared; the papers had black speckles all over them. Even the man's face was splattered, his clothing encrusted with gobs of still-damp mud. In a corner a young man was industriously scrubbing down the wall with a large brush.

The man wiped mud off Kielland and jumped up with a gleam of hope in his tired eyes. "Ah! Wonderful!" he cried. "Great to see you, old man. You'll find all the papers and reports in order here, everything ready for you—" He brushed the papers away from him with a gesture of finality. "Louie, get the landing craft pilot and don't let him out of your sight. Tell him I'll be ready in twenty minutes—"

"Hold it," said Kielland. "Aren't you Simpson?"

The man wiped mud off his cheeks and spat. He was tall and graying. "That's right."

"Where do you think you're going?"

"Aren't you relieving me?"

"I am not!"

"Oh, my." The man crumbled behind the desk, as though his legs had just given way. "I don't understand it. They told me—"

"I don't care what they told you," said Kielland shortly. "I'm a trouble shooter, not an administrator. When production figures begin to drop, I find out why. The production figures from this place have never gotten high enough to drop."

"This is supposed to be news to me?" said Simpson.

"So you've got troubles."

"Friend, you're right about that."

"Well, we'll straighten them out," Kielland said smoothly. "But first I want to see the foreman who put that wretched landing platform together."

Simpson's eyes became wary. "Uh—you don't really want to see him?"

"Yes, I think I do. When there's such obvious evidence of incompetence, the time to correct it is now."

"Well—maybe we can go outside and see him."

"We'll see him right here." Kielland sank down on the bench near the wall. A tiny headache was developing; he found a capsule in his samples case and popped it in his mouth.

Simpson looked sad and nodded to the orderly who had stopped scrubbing down the wall. "Louie, you heard the man."

"But boss—"

Simpson scowled. Louie went to the door and whistled. Presently there was a splashing sound and a short, gray creature padded in. His hind feet were four-toed webbed paddles; his legs were long and powerful like a kangaroo's. He was covered with thick gray fur which dripped with thick black mud. He squeaked at Simpson, wriggling his nose. Simpson squeaked back sharply.

Suddenly the creature began shaking his head in a slow, rhythmic undulation. With a cry Simpson dropped behind the desk. The orderly fell flat on the floor, covering his face with his arm. Kielland's eyes widened; then he was sitting in a deluge of mud as the little Venusian shook himself until his fur stood straight out in all directions.

Simpson stood up again with a roar. "I've told them a thousand times if I've told them once—" He shook his head helplessly as Kielland wiped mud out of his eyes. "This is the one you wanted to see."

Kielland sputtered. "Can it talk to you?"

"It doesn't talk, it squeaks."

"Then ask it to explain why the platform it built didn't hold the landing craft."

Simpson began whistling and squeaking at length to the little creature. Its shaggy tail crept between its legs and it hung its head like a scolded puppy.

"He says he didn't know a landing craft was supposed to land on the platform," Simpson reported finally. "He's sorry, he says."

"But hasn't he seen a landing craft before?"

Squeak, squeak. "Oh, yes."

"Wasn't he told what the platform was being made for?"

Squeak, squeak. "Of course."

"Then why didn't the platform stand up?"

Simpson sighed. "Maybe he forgot what it was supposed to be used for in the course of building it. Maybe he never really did understand in the first place. I can't get questions like that across to him with this whistling, and I doubt that you'll ever find out which it was."

"Then fire him," said Kielland. "We'll find some other—"

"Oh, no! I mean, let's not be hasty," said Simpson. "I'd hate to have to fire this one—for a while yet, at any rate."

"Why?"

"Because we've finally gotten across to him—at least I *think* we have—just how to take down a dredge tube." Simpson's voice was almost tearful. "It's taken us months to teach him. If we fire him, we'll have to start all over again with another one."

Kielland stared at the Venusian, and then at Simpson. "So," he said finally, "I see."

"No, you don't," Simpson said with conviction. "You don't even begin to see yet. You have to fight it for a few months before you really see." He waved the Venusian out the door and turned to Kielland with burden of ten months' frustration in his voice. "They're *stupid*," he said slowly. "They are so incredibly stupid I could go screaming into the swamp every time I see one of them coming. Their stupidity is positively abysmal."

"Then why use them?" Kielland spluttered.

"Because if we ever hope to mine anything in this miserable mudhole, we've got to use them to do it. There just isn't any other way."

With Simpson leading, they donned waist-high waders with wide, flat silicone-coated pans strapped to the feet and started out to inspect the installation.

A crowd of a dozen or more Venusian natives swarmed happily around them like a pack of hounds. They were in and out of the steaming mud, circling and splashing, squeaking: and shaking. They seemed to be having a real field day.

"Of course," Simpson was saying, "since Number Four dredge sank last week there isn't a whale of a lot of Installation left for you to inspect. But you can see what there is, if you want."

"You mean Number Four dredge is the only one you've got to use?" Kielland asked peevishly. "According to my records you have five Axis-Traction dredges, plus a dozen or more of the old kind."

"Ah!" said Simpson. "Well, Number One had its vacuum chamber corroded out a week after we started using dredging. Ran into a vein of stuff with 15 per cent acid content, and it got chewed up something fierce. Number Two sank without a trace—over there in the swamp someplace." He pointed across the black mud flats to a patch of sickly vegetation. "The Mud-pups know where it is, they think, and I suppose they could go drag it up for us if we dared take the time, but it would lose us a month, and you know the production schedule we've been trying to meet."

"So what about Numbers Three and Five?"

"Oh, we still have them. They won't work without a major overhaul, though."

"Overhaul! They're brand new."

"They *were*. The Mud-pups didn't understand how to sluice them down properly after operations. When this guck gets out into the air it hardens like cement. You ever see a cement mixer that hasn't been cleaned out after use for a few dozen times? That's Numbers Three and Five."

"What about the old style models?"

"Half of them are out of commission, and the other half are holding the islands still."

"Islands?"

"Those chunks of semisolid ground we have Administration built on. The chunk that keeps Control Tower in one place."

"Well, what are they going to do—walk away?"

"That's just about right. The first week we were in operation we kept wondering why we had to travel farther every day to get to the dredges. Then we realized that solid ground on Venus isn't solid ground at all. It's just big chunks of denser stuff that floats on top of the mud like dumplings in a stew. But that was nothing compared to the other things—"

They had reached the vicinity of the salvage operation on Number Five dredge. To Kielland it looked like a huge cylinder-type vacuum cleaner with a number of flexible hoses sprouting from the top. The whole machine was three-quarters submerged in clinging mud. Off to the right a derrick floated hub-deep in slime; grapplers from it were clinging to the dredge and the derrick was heaving and splashing like a trapped hippopotamus. All about the submerged machine were Mud-pups, working like strange little beavers as the man supervising the operation wiped mud from his face and carried on a running line of shouts, curses, whistles and squeaks.

Suddenly one of the Mud-pups saw the newcomers. He let out a squeal, dropped his line in the mud and bounced up to the surface, dancing like a dervish on his broad webbed feet as he stared in unabashed curiosity. A dozen more followed his lead, squirming up and staring, shaking gobs of mud from their fur.

"No, *no*!" the man supervising the operation screamed. "*Pull*, you idiots. Come back here! Watch *out*—"

The derrick wobbled and let out a whine as steel cable sizzled out. Confused, the Mud-pups tore themselves away from the newcomers and turned back to their lines, but it was too late. Number Five dredge trembled, with a wet sucking sound, and settled back into the mud, blub—blub—blub.

The supervisor crawled down from his platform and sloshed across to where Simpson and Kielland were standing. He looked like a man who had suffered the torment of the damned for twenty minutes too long. "No more!" he screamed in Simpson's face. "That's all. I'm through. I'll pick up my pay any time you get it ready, and I'll finish off my contract at home, but I'm through here. One solid week I work to teach these idiots what I want them to do, and you have to come along at the one moment all week when I really need their concentration." He glared, his face purple. "Concentration! I should hope for so much! You got to have a brain to have concentration—"

"Barton, this is Kielland. He's here from the Home Office, to solve all our problems."

"You mean he brought us an evacuation ship?"

"No, he's going to tell us how to make this Installation pay. Right, Kielland?" Simpson's grin was something to see.

Kielland scowled. "What are you going to do with the dredge—just leave it there?" he asked angrily.

"No—I'm going to dig it out, again," said Barton, "after we take another week off to drum into those quarter-brained mud-hens just what it is we want them to do—again—and then persuade them to do it—again—and then hope against hope that nothing happens along to distract them—again. Any suggestions?"

Simpson shook his head. "Take a rest, Barton. Things will look brighter in the morning."

"Nothing ever looks brighter in the morning," said Barton, and he sloshed angrily off toward the Administration island.

"You see?" said Simpson. "Or do you want to look around some more?"

*

Back in Administration shack, Kielland sprayed his throat with Piper Fortified Bio-Static and took two tetracycline capsules from his samples case as he stared gloomily down at the little gob of blue-gray mud on the desk before him.

The Venusian bonanza, the sole object of the multi-million-dollar Piper Venusian Installation, didn't look like much. It ran in veins deep beneath the surface. The R&D men had struck it quite by accident in the first place, sampled it along with a dozen other kinds of Venusian mud—and found they had their hands on the richest 'mycin-bearing bacterial growth since the days of the New Jersey mud flats.

The value of the stuff was incalculable. Twenty-first century Earth had not realized the degree to which it depended upon its effective antibiotic products for maintenance of its health until the mutating immune bacterial strains began to outpace the development of new antibacterials. Early penicillin killed 96 per cent of all organisms in its spectrum—at first—but time and natural selection undid its work in three generations. Even the broad-spectrum drugs were losing their effectiveness to a dangerous degree within decades of their introduction. And the new drugs grown from Earth-born bacteria, or synthesized in the laboratories, were too few and too weak to meet the burgeoning demands of humanity—

Until Venus. The bacteria indigenous to that planet were alien to Earth—every attempt to transplant them had failed—but they grew with abandon in the warm mud currents of Venus. Not all mud was of value: only the singular blue-gray stuff that lay before Kielland on the desk could produce the 'mycin-like tetracycline derivative that was more powerful than the best of Earth-grown wide spectrum antibiotics, with few if any of thc unfortunate side-effects of the Earth products.

The problem seemed simple: find the mud in sufficient quantities for mining, dredge it up, and transport it back to Earth to extract the drug. It was the first two steps of the operation that depended so heavily on the mud-acclimated natives of Venus for success. They were as much at home in the mud as they were in the dank, humid air above. They could distinguish one type of mud from another deep beneath the surface, and could carry a dredge-tube down to a lode of the blue-gray muck with the unfailing accuracy of a homing pigeon.

If they could only be made to understand just what they were expected to do. And that was where production ground down to a slow walk.

The next few days were a nightmare of frustration for Kielland as he observed with mounting horror the standard operating procedure of the Installation.

Men and Mud-pups went to work once again to drag Number Five dredge out of the mud. It took five days of explaining, repeating, coaxing and threatening to do it, but finally up it came—with mud caked and hardened in its insides until it could never be used again.

So they ferried Number Six down piecemeal from the special orbital transport ship that had brought it. Only three landing craft sank during the process, and within two weeks Simpson and Barton set bravely off with their dull-witted cohorts to tackle the swamp with a spanking new piece of equipment. At last the delays were over—

Of course, it took another week to get the actual dredging started. The Mud-pups who had been taught the excavation procedure previously had either disappeared into the swamp or forgotten everything they'd ever been taught. Simpson had expected it, but it was enough to keep Kielland sleepless for three nights and drive his blood pressure to suicidal levels. At length, the blue-gray mud began billowing out of the dredge onto the platforms built to receive it, and the transport ship was notified to stand by for loading. But by the time the ferry had landed, the platform with the load had somehow drifted free of the island and required a week-long expedition into the hinterland to track it down. On the trip back they met a rainstorm that dissolved the blue-gray stuff into soup which ran out between the slats of the platform, and back into the mud again.

They did get the platform back, at any rate.

Meanwhile, the dredge began sucking up green stuff that smelled of sewage instead of the blue-gray clay they sought—so the natives dove mud-ward to explore the direction of the vein. One of them got caught in the suction tube, causing a three-day delay while engineers dismantled the dredge to get him out. In re-assembling, two of the dredge tubes got interlocked somehow, and the dredge burned out three generators trying to suck itself through itself, so to speak. That took another week to fix.

Kielland buried himself in the Administration shack, digging through the records, when the reign of confusion outside became too much to bear. He sent for Tarnier, the Installation physician, biologist, and erstwhile Venusian psychologist. Dr. Tarnier looked like the breathing soul of failure; Kielland had to steel himself to the wave of pity that swept through him at the sight of the man. "You're the one who tested these imbeciles originally?" he demanded.

Dr. Tarnier nodded. His face was seamed, his eyes lustreless. "I tested 'em. God help me, I tested 'em."

"How?"

"Standard procedures. Reaction times. Mazes. Conditioning. Language. Abstractions. Numbers. Associations. The works."

"Standard for Earthmen, I presume you mean."

"So what else? Piper didn't want to know if they were Einsteins or not. All they wanted was a passable level of intelligence. Give them natives with brains and they might have to pay them something. They thought they were getting a bargain."

"Some bargain."

"Yeah."

"Only your tests say they're intelligent. As intelligent, say, as a low-normal human being without benefit of any schooling or education. Right?"

"That's right," the doctor said wearily, as though he had been through this mill again and again. "Schooling and education don't enter into it at all, of course. All we measured was potential. But the results said they had it."

"Then how do you explain the mess we've got out there?"

"The tests were wrong. Or else they weren't applicable even on a basic level. Or something. I don't know. I don't even care much any more."

"Well I care, plenty. Do you realize how much those creatures are costing us? If we ever do get the finished product on the market, it'll cost too much for anybody to buy."

Dr. Tarnier spread his hands. "Don't blame me. Blame them."

"And then this so-called biological survey of yours," Kielland continued, warming to his subject. "From a scientific man, it's a prize. Anatomical description: limited because of absence of autopsy specimens. Apparently have endoskeleton, but organization of the internal organs remains obscure. Thought to be mammalianoid—there's a fence-sitter for you—but can't be certain of this because no young have been observed, nor any females in gestation. Extremely gregarious, curious, playful, irresponsible, etc., etc., etc. Habitat under natural conditions: uncertain. Diet: uncertain. Social organization: uncertain." Kielland threw down the paper with a snort. "In short, the only thing we're certain of is that they're here.

Very helpful. Especially when every dime we have in this project depends on our teaching them how to count to three without help."

Dr. Tarnier spread his hands again. "Mr. Kielland, I'm a mere mortal. In order to measure something, it has to stay the same long enough to get it measured. In order to describe something, it has to hold still long enough to be observed. In order to form a logical opinion of a creature's mental capacity, it has to demonstrate some perceptible mental capacity to start with. You can't get very far studying a creature's habitat and social structure when most of its habitating goes on under twenty feet of mud."

"How about the language?"

"We get by with squeaks and whistles and sign language. A sort of pidgin-Venusian. They use a very complex system among themselves." The doctor paused, uncertainly. "Anyway, it's hard to get too tough with the Pups," he burst out finally. "They really seem to try hard—when they can just manage to keep their minds to it."

"Just stupid, carefree, happy-go-lucky kids, eh?"

Dr. Tarnier shrugged.

"Go away," said Kielland in disgust, and turned back to the reports with a sour taste in his mouth.

Later he called the Installation Comptroller. "What do you pay Mud-pups for their work?" he wanted to know.

"Nothing," said the Comptroller.

"*Nothing!*"

"We have nothing they can use. What would you give them—United Nations coin? They'd just try to eat it."

"How about something they *can* eat, then?"

"Everything we feed them they throw right back up. Planetary incompatibility."

"But there must be *something* you can use for wages," Kielland protested. "Something they want, something they'll work hard for."

"Well, they liked tobacco and pipes all right—but it interfered with their oxygen storage so they couldn't dive. That ruled out tobacco and pipes. They liked Turkish towels, too, but they spent all their time parading up and down in them and slaying the ladies and wouldn't work at all. That ruled out Turkish towels. They don't seem to care too much whether they're paid or not, though—as long as we're decent to them. They seem to like us, in a stupid sort of way."

"Just loving, affectionate, happy-go-lucky kids. I know. Go away." Kielland growled and turned back to the reports ... except that there weren't any more reports that he hadn't read a dozen times or more. Nothing that made sense, nothing that offered a lead. Millions of Piper dollars sunk into this project, and every one of them sitting there blinking at him expectantly.

For the first time he wondered if there really *was* any solution to the problem. Stumbling blocks had been met and removed before—that was Kielland's job, and he knew how to do it. But stupidity could be a stumbling block that was all but insurmountable.

Yet he couldn't throw off the nagging conviction that something more subtle than stupidity was involved....

Then Simpson came in, cursing and sputtering and bellowing for Louie. Louie came, and Simpson started dictating a message for relay to the transport ship. "Special order, rush, repeat, rush," Simpson grated. "For immediate delivery Piper Venusian Installation—one Piper Axis-Traction Dredge, previous specifications applicable—"

Kielland stared at him. "Again?"

Simpson gritted his teeth. "Again."

"Sunk?"

"Blub," said Simpson. "Blub, blub, blub."

Slowly, Kielland stood up, glaring first at Simpson, then at the little muddy creatures that were attempting to hide behind his waders, looking so forlorn and chastised and woebegone. "All right," Kielland said, after a pregnant pause. "That's all. You won't need to relay that order to the ship. Forget about Number Seven dredge. Just get your files in order and get a landing craft down here for me. The sooner the better."

Simpson's face lit up in pathetic eagerness. "You mean we're going to *leave?*"

"That's what I mean."

"The company's not going to like it—"

"The company ought to welcome us home with open arms," Kielland snarled. "They should shower us with kisses. They should do somersaults for joy that I'm not going to let them sink another half billion into the mud out here. They took a gamble and got cleaned, that's all. They'd be as stupid as your pals here if they kept coming back for more." He pulled on his waders, brushing penitent Mud-pups aside as he started for the door.

"Send the natives back to their burrows or whatever they live in and get ready to close down. *I've* got to figure out some way to make a report to the Board that won't get us all fired."

He slammed out the door and started across to his quarters, waders going splat-splat in the mud. Half a dozen Mud-pups were following him. They seemed extraordinarily exuberant as they went diving and splashing in the mud. Kielland turned and roared at them, shaking his fist. They stopped short, then slunk off with their tails between their legs.

But even at that, their squeaking sounded strangely like laughter to Kielland....

In his quarters the light was so dim that he almost had his waders off before he saw the upheaval. The little room was splattered from top to bottom with mud. His bunk was coated with slime; the walls dripped blue-gray goo. Across the room his wardrobe doors hung open as three muddy creatures rooted industriously in the leather case on the floor.

Kielland let out a howl and threw himself across the room. *His samples case!* The Mud-pups scattered, squealing. Their hands were filled with capsules, and their muzzles were dripping with white powder. Two went between Kielland's legs and through the door. The third dove for the window with Kielland after him. The company man's hand closed on a slippery tail, and he fell headlong across the muddy bed as the culprit literally slipped through his fingers.

He sat up, wiping mud from his hair and surveying the damage. Bottles and boxes of medicaments were scattered all over the floor of the wardrobe, covered with mud but unopened. Only one large box had been torn apart, its contents ravaged.

Kielland stared at it as things began clicking into place in his mind. He walked to the door, stared out across the steaming gloomy mud flats toward the lighted windows of the Administration shack. Sometimes, he mused, a man can get so close to something that he can't see the obvious. He stared at the samples case again. Sometimes stupidity works both ways—and sometimes what looks like stupidity may really be something far more deadly.

He licked his lips and flipped the telephone-talker switch. After a misconnection or two he got Control Tower. Control Tower said yes, they had a small exploratory scooter on hand. Yes, it could be controlled on a beam and fitted with cameras. But of course it was special equipment, emergency use only—

He cut them off and buzzed Simpson excitedly. "Cancel all I said—about leaving. I mean. Change of plan. Something's come up. No, don't order anything—but get one of those natives that can understand your whistling and give him the word."

Simpson bellowed over the wire. "What word? What do you think you're doing?"

"I may just be saving our skins—we won't know for a while. But however you manage it, tell them we're definitely *not leaving Venus.* Tell them they're all fired—we don't want them around any more. The Installation is off limits to them from here on in. And tell them we've devised a way to mine the lode without them—got that? Tell them the equipment will be arriving as soon as we can bring it down from the transport."

"Oh, now look—"

"You want me to repeat it?"

Simpson sighed. "All right. Fine. I'll tell them. Then what?"

"Then just don't bother me for a while. I'm going to be busy. Watching TV."

An hour later Kielland was in Control Tower, watching the pale screen as the little remote-controlled explorer circled the installation. Three TV cameras were in operation as he settled down behind the screen. He told Sparks what he wanted to do, and the ship whizzed off in the direction the Mud-pup raiders had taken.

At first, there was nothing but dreary mud flats sliding past the cameras' watchful eyes. Then they picked up a flicker of movement, and the ship circled in lower for a better view. It was a group of natives—a large group. There must have been fifty of them working busily in the mud, five miles away from the Piper Installation. They didn't look so carefree and happy-go-lucky now. They looked very much like desperately busy Mud-pups with a job on their hands, and they were so absorbed they didn't even see the small craft circling above them.

They worked in teams. Some were diving with small containers; some were handling lines attached to the containers; still others were carrying and dumping. They came up full, went down empty, came up full. The produce was heaped in a growing pile on a small semisolid island with a few scraggly trees on it. As they worked the pile grew and grew.

It took only a moment for Kielland to tell what they were doing. The color of the stuff was unmistakable. They were mining piles of blue-gray mud, just as fast as they could mine it.

With a gleam of satisfaction in his eye, Kielland snapped off the screen and nodded at Sparks to bring the cameras back. Then he rang Simpson again.

"Did you tell them?"

Simpson's voice was uneasy. "Yeah—yeah, I told them. They left in a hurry. Quite a hurry."

"Yes, I imagine they did. Where are your men now?"

"Out working on Number Six, trying to get it up."

"Better get them together and pack them over to Control Tower, fast," said Kielland. "I mean everybody. Every man in the Installation. We may have this thing just about tied up, if we can get out of here soon enough—"

Kielland's chair gave a sudden lurch and sailed across the room, smashing into the wall. With a yelp he tried to struggle up the sloping floor; it reared and heaved over the other way, throwing Kielland and Sparks to the other wall amid a heap of instruments. Through the windows they could see the gray mud flats careening wildly below them. It took only an instant to realize what was happening. Kielland shouted, "Let's get out of here!" and headed down the stairs, clinging to the railing for dear life.

Control Tower was sinking in the mud. They had moved faster than he had anticipated, Kielland thought, and snarled at himself all the way down to the landing platform below. He had hoped at least to have time to parley, to stop and discuss the whys and wherefores of the situation with the natives. Now it was abundantly clear that any whys and wherefores that were likely to be discussed would be discussed later.

And very possibly under twenty feet of mud—

A stream of men were floundering out of Administration shack, plowing through the mud with waders only half strapped on as the line of low buildings began shaking and sinking into the morass. From the direction of Number Six dredge another crew was heading for the Tower. But the Tower was rapidly growing shorter as the buoys that sustained it broke loose with ear-shattering crashes.

Kielland caught Sparks by the shoulder, shouting to be heard above the racket. "The transport—did you get it?"

"I—I think so."

"They're sending us a ferry?"

"It should be on its way."

Simpson sloshed up, his face heavy with dismay. "The dredges! They've cut loose the dredges."

"Bother the dredges. Get your men collected and into the shelters. We'll have a ship here any minute."

"But what's happening?"

"We're leaving—if we can make it before these carefree, happy-go-lucky kids here sink us in the mud, dredges, Control Tower and all."

Out of the gloom above there was a roar and a streak of murky yellow as the landing craft eased down through the haze. Only the top of Control Tower was out of the mud now. The Administration shack gave a lurch, sagging, as a dozen indistinct gray forms pulled and tugged at the supporting structure beneath it. Already a circle of natives was converging on the Earthmen as they gathered near the landing platform shelters.

"They're cutting loose the landing platform!" somebody wailed. One of the lines broke with a resounding snap, and the platform lurched. Then a dozen men dived through the mud to pull away the slippery, writhing natives as they worked to cut through the remaining guys. Moments later the landing craft was directly overhead and men and natives alike scattered as she sank down.

The platform splintered and jolted under her weight, began skidding, then held firm to the two guy ropes remaining. A horde of gray creatures hurled themselves on those lines as a hatchway opened above and a ladder dropped down. The men scurried up the ropes just as the plastic dome of the Control Tower sank with a gurgle.

Kielland and Simpson paused at the bottom of the ladder, blinking at the scene of devastation around them.

"Stupid, you say," said Kielland heavily. "Better get up there, or we'll go where Control Tower went."

"But—everything—gone!"

"Wrong again. Everything saved." Kielland urged the administrator up the ladder and sighed with relief as the hatch clanged shut. The jets bloomed and sprayed boiling mud far and wide as the landing craft lifted soggily out of the mire and roared for the clouds above.

Kielland wiped sweat from his forehead and sank back on his cot with a shudder. "*We* should be so stupid," he said.

"I must admit," he said later to a weary and mystified Simpson, "that I didn't expect them to move so fast. But when you've decided in your mind that somebody's really pretty stupid, it's hard to adjust to the idea that maybe he *isn't*, all of a sudden. We should have been much more suspicious of Dr. Tarnier's tests. It's true they weren't designed for Venusians, but they were designed to assess intelligence, and intelligence isn't a quality that's influenced by environment or species. It's either there or it isn't, and the good Doctor told us unequivocally that it was there."

"But their behavior."

"Even that should have tipped us off. There is a very fine line dividing incredible stupidity and incredible *stubbornness*. It's often a tough differential to make. I didn't spot it until I found them wolfing down the tetracycline capsules in my samples case. Then I began to see the implications. Those Mud-pups were stubbornly and tenaciously determined to drive the Piper Venusian Installation off Venus permanently, by fair means or foul. They didn't care how it got off—they just wanted it off."

"But why? We weren't hurting them. There's plenty of mud on Venus."

"Ah—but not so much of the blue-gray stuff we were after, perhaps. Suppose a space ship settled down in a wheatfield in Kansas along about harvest time and started loading wheat into the hold? I suppose the farmer wouldn't mind too much. After all, there's plenty of vegetation on Earth—"

"They're *growing* the stuff?"

"For all they're worth," said Kielland. "Lord knows what sort of metabolism uses tetracycline for food—but they are growing mud that yields an incredibly rich concentration of antibiotic ... their native food. They grow it, harvest it, live on it. Even the way they shake whenever they come out of the mud is a giveaway—what better way to seed their crop far and wide? We were mining away their staff of life, my friend. You really couldn't blame them for objecting."

"Well, if they think they can drive us off that way, they're going to have to get that brilliant intelligence of theirs into action," Simpson said ominously. "We'll bring enough equipment down there to mine them out of house and home."

"Why?" said Kielland. "After all, they're mining it themselves a lot more efficiently than we could ever do it. And with Piper warehouses back on Earth full of old, useless antibiotics that they can't sell for peanuts? No, I don't think we'll mine anything when a simple trade arrangement will do just as well." He sank back in his cot, staring dreamily through the port as the huge orbital transport loomed large ahead of them. He found his throat spray and dosed himself liberally in preparation for his return to civilization. "Of course, the natives are going to be wondering what kind of idiots they're dealing with to sell them pure refined extract of Venusian beefsteak in return for raw chunks of unrefined native soil. But I think we can afford to just let them wonder for a while."

BRIGHTSIDE CROSSING

JAMES BARON was not pleased to hear that he had had a visitor when he reached the Red Lion that evening. He had no stomach for mysteries, vast or trifling, and there were pressing things to think about at this time. Yet the doorman had flagged him as he came in from the street: "A thousand pardons, Mr. Baron. The gentleman—he would leave no name. He said you'd want to see him. He will be back by eight."

Now Baron drummed his fingers on the table top, staring about the quiet lounge. Street trade was discouraged at the Red Lion, gently but persuasively; the patrons were few in number. Across to the right was a group that Baron knew vaguely—Andean climbers, or at least two of them were. Over near the door he recognized old Balmer, who had mapped the first passage to the core of Vulcan Crater on Venus. Baron returned his smile with a nod. Then he settled back and waited impatiently for the intruder who demanded his time without justifying it.

Presently a small, grizzled man crossed the room and sat down at Baron's table. He was short and wiry. His face held no key to his age—he might have been thirty or a thousand—but he looked weary and immensely ugly. His cheeks and forehead were twisted and brown, with scars that were still healing.

The stranger said, "I'm glad you waited. I've heard you're planning to attempt the Brightside."

Baron stared at the man for a moment. "I see you can read telecasts," he said coldly. "The news was correct. We are going to make a Brightside Crossing."

"At perihelion?"

"Of course. When else?"

The grizzled man searched Baron's face for a moment without expression. Then he said slowly, "No, I'm afraid you're not going to make the Crossing."

"Say, who are you, if you don't mind?" Baron demanded.

"The name is Claney," said the stranger.

There was a silence. Then: "Claney? *Peter* Claney?"

"That's right."

Baron's eyes were wide with excitement, all trace of anger gone. "Great balls of fire, man—*where have you been hiding?* We've been trying to contact you for months!"

"I know. I was hoping you'd quit looking and chuck the whole idea."

"Quit looking!" Baron bent forward over the table. "My friend, we'd given up hope, but we've never quit looking. Here, have a drink. There's so much you can tell us." His fingers were trembling.

Peter Claney shook his head. "I can't tell you anything you want to hear."

"But you've *got* to. You're the only man on Earth who's attempted a Brightside Crossing and lived through it! And the story you cleared for the news—it was nothing. We need *details*. Where did your equipment fall down? Where did you miscalculate? What were the trouble spots?" Baron jabbed a finger at Claney's face. "That, for instance—epithelioma? Why? What was wrong with your glass? Your filters? We've got to know those things. If you can tell us, we can make it across where your attempt failed—"

"You want to know why we failed?" asked Claney.

"Of course we want to know. We *have* to know."

"It's simple. We failed because it can't be done. We couldn't do it and neither can you. No human beings will ever cross the Brightside alive, not if they try for centuries."

"Nonsense," Baron declared. "We will."

Claney shrugged. "I was there. I know what I'm saying. You can blame the equipment or the men—there were flaws in both quarters—but we just didn't know what we were fighting. It was the *planet* that whipped us, that and the *Sun*. They'll whip you, too, if you try it."

"Never," said Baron.

"Let me tell you," Peter Claney said.

*

I'd been interested in the Brightside for almost as long as I can remember (Claney said). I guess I was about ten when Wyatt and Carpenter made the last attempt—that was in 2082, I think. I followed the news stories like a tri-V serial and then I was heartbroken when they just disappeared.

I know now that they were a pair of idiots, starting off without proper equipment, with practically no knowledge of surface conditions, without any charts—they couldn't have made a hundred miles—but I didn't know that then and it was a terrible tragedy. After that, I followed Sanderson's work in the Twilight Lab up there and began to get Brightside into my blood, sure as death.

But it was Mikuta's idea to attempt a Crossing. Did you ever know Tom Mikuta? I don't suppose you did. No, not Japanese—Polish-American. He was a major in the Interplanetary Service for some years and hung onto the title after he gave up his commission.

He was with Armstrong on Mars during his Service days, did a good deal of the original mapping and surveying for the Colony there. I first met him on Venus; we spent five years together up there doing some of the nastiest exploring since the Matto Grasso. Then he made the attempt on Vulcan Crater that paved the way for Balmer a few years later.

I'd always liked the Major—he was big and quiet and cool, the sort of guy who always had things figured a little further ahead than anyone else and always knew what to do in a tight place. Too many men in this game are all nerve and luck, with no judgment. The Major had both. He also had the kind of personality that could take a crew of wild men and make them work like a well-oiled machine across a thousand miles of Venus jungle. I liked him and I trusted him.

He contacted me in New York and he was very casual at first. We spent an evening here at the Red Lion, talking about old times; he told me about the Vulcan business, and how he'd been out to see Sanderson and the Twilight Lab on Mercury, and how he preferred a hot trek to a cold one any day of the year—and then he wanted to know what I'd been doing since Venus and what my plans were.

"No particular plans," I told him. "Why?"

He looked me over. "How much do you weigh, Peter?"

I told him one-thirty-five.

"That much!" he said. "Well, there can't be much fat on you, at any rate. How do you take heat?"

"You should know," I said. "Venus was no icebox."

"No, I mean *real* heat."

Then I began to get it. "You're planning a trip."

"That's right. A hot trip." He grinned at me. "Might be dangerous, too."

"What trip?"

"Brightside of Mercury," the Major said.

I whistled cautiously. "At aphelion?"

He threw his head back. "Why try a Crossing at aphelion? What have you done then? Four thousand miles of butcherous heat, just to have some joker come along, use your data and drum you out of the glory by crossing at perihelion forty-four days later? No, thanks. I want the Brightside without any nonsense about it." He leaned across me eagerly. "I want to make a Crossing at perihelion and I want to cross on the surface. If a man can do that, he's got Mercury. Until then, *nobody's* got Mercury. I want Mercury—but I'll need help getting it."

I'd thought of it a thousand times and never dared consider it. Nobody had, since Wyatt and Carpenter disappeared. Mercury turns on its axis in the same time that it wheels around the Sun, which means that the Brightside is always facing in. That makes the Brightside of Mercury at perihelion the hottest place in the Solar System, with one single exception: the surface of the Sun itself.

It would be a hellish trek. Only a few men had ever learned just *how* hellish and they never came back to tell about it. It was a real hell's Crossing, but someday, I thought, somebody would cross it.

I wanted to be along.

*

The Twilight Lab, near the northern pole of Mercury, was the obvious jumping-off place. The setup there wasn't very extensive—a rocket landing, the labs and quarters for Sanderson's crew sunk deep into the crust, and the tower that housed the Solar 'scope that Sanderson had built up there ten years before.

Twilight Lab wasn't particularly interested in the Brightside, of course—the Sun was Sanderson's baby and he'd picked Mercury as the closest chunk of rock to the Sun that could hold his observatory. He'd chosen a good location, too. On Mercury, the Brightside temperature hits 770° F. at perihelion and the Darkside runs pretty constant at -410° F. No permanent installation with a human crew could survive at either extreme. But with Mercury's wobble, the twilight zone between Brightside and Darkside offers something closer to survival temperatures.

Sanderson built the Lab up near the pole, where the zone is about five miles wide, so the temperature only varies 50 to 60 degrees with the libration. The Solar 'scope could take that much change and they'd get good clear observation of the Sun for about seventy out of the eighty-eight days it takes the planet to wheel around.

The Major was counting on Sanderson knowing something about Mercury as well as the Sun when we camped at the Lab to make final preparations.

Sanderson did. He thought we'd lost our minds and he said so, but he gave us all the help he could. He spent a week briefing Jack Stone, the third member of our party, who had arrived with the supplies and equipment a few days earlier. Poor Jack met us at the rocket landing almost bawling, Sanderson had given him such a gloomy picture of what Brightside was like.

Stone was a youngster—hardly twenty-five, I'd say—but he'd been with the Major at Vulcan and had begged to join this trek. I had a funny feeling that Jack really didn't care for exploring too much, but he thought Mikuta was God, followed him around like a puppy.

It didn't matter to me as long as he knew what he was getting in for. You don't go asking people in this game why they do it—they're liable to get awfully uneasy and none of them can ever give you an answer that makes sense. Anyway, Stone had borrowed three men from the Lab, and had the supplies and equipment all lined up when we got there, ready to check and test.

We dug right in. With plenty of funds—tri-V money and some government cash the Major had talked his way around—our equipment was new and good. Mikuta had done the designing and testing himself, with a big assist from Sanderson. We had four Bugs, three of them the light pillow-tire models, with special lead-cooled cut-in engines when the heat set in, and one heavy-duty tractor model for pulling the sledges.

The Major went over them like a kid at the circus. Then he said, "Have you heard anything from McIvers?"

"Who's he?" Stone wanted to know.

"He'll be joining us. He's a good man—got quite a name for climbing, back home." The Major turned to me. "You've probably heard of him."

I'd heard plenty of stories about Ted McIvers and I wasn't too happy to hear that he was joining us. "Kind of a daredevil, isn't he?"

"Maybe. He's lucky and skillful. Where do you draw the line? We'll need plenty of both."

"Have you ever worked with him?" I asked.

"No. Are you worried?"

"Not exactly. But Brightside is no place to count on luck."

The Major laughed. "I don't think we need to worry about McIvers. We understood each other when I talked up the trip to him and we're going to need each other too much to do any fooling around." He turned back to the supply list. "Meanwhile, let's get this stuff listed and packed. We'll need to cut weight sharply and our time is short. Sanderson says we should leave in three days."

Two days later, McIvers hadn't arrived. The Major didn't say much about it. Stone was getting edgy and so was I. We spent the second day studying charts of the Brightside, such as they were. The best available were pretty poor, taken from so far out that the detail dissolved into blurs on blow-up. They showed the biggest ranges of peaks and craters and faults, and that was all. Still, we could use them to plan a broad outline of our course.

"This range here," the Major said as we crowded around the board, "is largely inactive, according to Sanderson. But these to the south and west *could* be active. Seismograph tracings suggest a lot of activity in that region, getting worse down toward the equator—not only volcanic, but sub-surface shifting."

Stone nodded. "Sanderson told me there was probably constant surface activity."

The Major shrugged. "Well, it's treacherous, there's no doubt of it. But the only way to avoid it is to travel over the Pole, which would lose us days and offer us no guarantee of less activity to the west. Now we might avoid some if we could find a pass through this range and cut sharp east—"

It seemed that the more we considered the problem, the further we got from a solution. We knew there were active volcanoes on the Brightside—even on the Darkside, though surface activity there was pretty much slowed down and localized.

But there were problems of atmosphere on Brightside, as well. There was an atmosphere and a constant atmospheric flow from Brightside to Darkside. Not much—the lighter gases had reached escape velocity and disappeared from Brightside millennia ago—but there was CO_2, and nitrogen, and traces of other heavier gases. There was also an abundance of sulfur vapor, as well as carbon disulfide and sulfur dioxide.

The atmospheric tide moved toward the Darkside, where it condensed, carrying enough volcanic ash with it for Sanderson to estimate the depth and nature of the surface upheavals on Brightside from his samplings. The trick was to find a passage that avoided those upheavals as far as possible. But in the final analysis, we were barely scraping the surface. The only way we would find out what was happening where was to be there.

Finally, on the third day, McIvers blew in on a freight rocket from Venus. He'd missed the ship that the Major and I had taken by a few hours, and had conned his way to Venus in hopes of getting a hop from there. He didn't seem too upset about it, as though this were his usual way of doing things and he couldn't see why everyone should get so excited.

He was a tall, rangy man with long, wavy hair prematurely gray, and the sort of eyes that looked like a climber's—half-closed, sleepy, almost indolent, but capable of abrupt alertness. And he never stood still; he was always moving, always doing something with his hands, or talking, or pacing about.

Evidently the Major decided not to press the issue of his arrival. There was still work to do, and an hour later we were running the final tests on the pressure suits. That evening, Stone and McIvers were thick as thieves, and everything was set for an early departure after we got some rest.

*

"And that," said Baron, finishing his drink and signaling the waiter for another pair, "was your first big mistake."

Peter Claney raised his eyebrows. "McIvers?"

"Of course."

Claney shrugged, glanced at the small quiet tables around them. "There are lots of bizarre personalities around a place like this, and some of the best wouldn't seem to be the most reliable at first glance. Anyway, personality problems weren't our big problem right then. *Equipment* worried us first and *route* next."

Baron nodded in agreement. "What kind of suits did you have?"

"The best insulating suits ever made," said Claney. "Each one had an inner lining of a fiberglass modification, to avoid the clumsiness of asbestos, and carried the refrigerating unit and oxygen storage which we recharged from the sledges every eight hours. Outer layer carried a monomolecular chrome reflecting surface that made us glitter like Christmas trees. And we had a half-inch dead-air space under positive pressure between the two layers. Warning thermocouples, of course—at 770 degrees, it wouldn't take much time to fry us to cinders if the suits failed somewhere."

"How about the Bugs?"

"They were insulated, too, but we weren't counting on them too much for protection."

"You weren't!" Baron exclaimed. "Why not?"

"We'd be in and out of them too much. They gave us mobility and storage, but we knew we'd have to do a lot of forward work on foot." Claney smiled bitterly. "Which meant that we had an inch of fiberglass and a half-inch of dead air between us and a surface temperature where lead flowed like water and zinc was almost at melting point and the pools of sulfur in the shadows were boiling like oatmeal over a campfire."

Baron licked his lips. His fingers stroked the cool, wet glass as he set it down on the tablecloth.

"Go on," he said tautly. "You started on schedule?"

"Oh, yes," said Claney, "we started on schedule, all right. We just didn't quite end on schedule, that was all. But I'm getting to that."

He settled back in his chair and continued.

*

We jumped off from Twilight on a course due southeast with thirty days to make it to the Center of Brightside. If we could cross an average of seventy miles a day, we could hit Center exactly at perihelion, the point of Mercury's closest approach to the Sun—which made Center the hottest part of the planet at the hottest it ever gets.

The Sun was already huge and yellow over the horizon when we started, twice the size it appears on Earth. Every day that Sun would grow bigger and whiter, and every day the surface would get hotter. But once we reached Center, the job was only half done—we would still have to travel another two thousand miles to the opposite twilight zone. Sanderson was to meet us on the other side in the Laboratory's scout ship, approximately sixty days from the time we jumped off.

That was the plan, in outline. It was up to us to cross those seventy miles a day, no matter how hot it became, no matter what terrain we had to cross. Detours would be dangerous and time-consuming. Delays could cost us our lives. We all knew that.

The Major briefed us on details an hour before we left. "Peter, you'll take the lead Bug, the small one we stripped down for you. Stone and I will flank you on either side, giving you a hundred-yard lead. McIvers, you'll have the job of dragging the sledges, so we'll have to direct your course pretty closely. Peter's job is to pick the passage at any given point. If there's any doubt of safe passage, we'll all explore ahead on foot before we risk the Bugs. Got that?"

McIvers and Stone exchanged glances. McIvers said: "Jack and I were planning to change around. We figured he could take the sledges. That would give me a little more mobility."

The Major looked up sharply at Stone. "Do you buy that, Jack?"

Stone shrugged. "I don't mind. Mac wanted—"

McIvers made an impatient gesture with his hands. "It doesn't matter. I just feel better when I'm on the move. Does it make any difference?"

"I guess it doesn't," said the Major. "Then you'll flank Peter along with me. Right?"

"Sure, sure." McIvers pulled at his lower lip. "Who's going to do the advance scouting?"

"It sounds like I am," I cut in. "We want to keep the lead Bug light as possible."

Mikuta nodded. "That's right. Peter's Bug is stripped down to the frame and wheels."

McIvers shook his head. "No, I mean the *advance* work. You need somebody out ahead—four or five miles, at least—to pick up the big flaws and active surface changes, don't you?" He stared at the Major. "I mean, how can we tell what sort of a hole we may be moving into, unless we have a scout up ahead?"

"That's what we have the charts for," the Major said sharply.

"Charts! I'm talking about *detail* work. We don't need to worry about the major topography. It's the little faults you can't see on the pictures that can kill us." He tossed the charts down excitedly. "Look, let me take a Bug out ahead and work reconnaissance, keep five, maybe ten miles ahead of the column. I can stay on good solid ground, of course, but scan the area closely and radio back to Peter where to avoid the flaws. Then—"

"No dice," the Major broke in.

"But why not? We could save ourselves days!"

"I don't care what we could save. We stay together. When we get to the Center, I want live men along with me. That means we stay within easy sight of each other at all times. Any climber knows that everybody is safer in a party than one man alone—any time, any place."

McIvers stared at him, his cheeks an angry red. Finally he gave a sullen nod. "Okay. If you say so."

"Well, I say so and I mean it. I don't want any fancy stuff. We're going to hit Center together, and finish the Crossing together. Got that?"

McIvers nodded. Mikuta then looked at Stone and me and we nodded, too.

"All right," he said slowly. "Now that we've got it straight, let's go."

It was hot. If I forget everything else about that trek, I'll never forget that huge yellow Sun glaring down, without a break, hotter and hotter with every mile. We knew that the first few days would be the easiest and we were rested and fresh when we started down the long ragged gorge southeast of the Twilight Lab.

I moved out first; back over my shoulder, I could see the Major and McIvers crawling out behind me, their pillow tires taking the rugged floor of the gorge smoothly. Behind them, Stone dragged the sledges.

Even at only 30 per cent Earth gravity they were a strain on the big tractor, until the ski-blades bit into the fluffy volcanic ash blanketing the valley. We even had a path to follow for the first twenty miles.

I kept my eyes pasted to the big polaroid binocs, picking out the track the early research teams had made out into the edge of Brightside. But in a couple of hours we rumbled past Sanderson's little outpost observatory and the tracks stopped. We were in virgin territory and already the Sun was beginning to bite.

We didn't *feel* the heat so much those first days out. We *saw* it. The refrig units kept our skins at a nice comfortable seventy-five degrees Fahrenheit inside our suits, but our eyes watched that glaring Sun and the baked yellow rocks going past, and some nerve pathways got twisted up, somehow. We poured sweat as if we were in a superheated furnace.

We drove eight hours and slept five. When a sleep period came due, we pulled the Bugs together into a square, threw up a light aluminum sun-shield and lay out in the dust and rocks. The sun-shield cut the temperature down sixty or seventy degrees, for whatever help that was. And then we ate from the forward sledge—sucking through tubes—protein, carbohydrates, bulk gelatin, vitamins.

The Major measured water out with an iron hand, because we'd have drunk ourselves into nephritis in a week otherwise. We were constantly, unceasingly thirsty. Ask the physiologists and psychiatrists why—they can give you have a dozen interesting reasons—but all we knew, or cared about, was that it happened to be so.

We didn't sleep the first few stops, as a consequence. Our eyes burned in spite of the filters and we had roaring headaches, but we couldn't sleep them off. We sat around looking at each other. Then McIvers would say how good a beer would taste, and off we'd go. We'd have murdered our grandmothers for one ice-cold bottle of beer.

After a few driving periods, I began to get my bearings at the wheel. We were moving down into desolation that made Earth's old Death Valley look like a Japanese rose garden. Huge sun-baked cracks opened up in the floor of the gorge, with black cliffs jutting up on either side; the air was filled with a barely visible yellowish mist of sulfur and sulfurous gases.

It was a hot, barren hole, no place for any man to go, but the challenge was so powerful you could almost feel it. No one had ever crossed this land before and escaped. Those who had tried it had been cruelly punished, but the land was still there, so it had to be crossed. Not the easy way. It had to be crossed the hardest way possible: overland, through anything the land could throw up to us, at the most difficult time possible.

Yet we knew that even the land might have been conquered before, except for that Sun. We'd fought absolute cold before and won. We'd never fought heat like this and won. The only worse heat in the Solar System was the surface of the Sun itself.

Brightside was worth trying for. We would get it or it would get us. That was the bargain.

I learned a lot about Mercury those first few driving periods. The gorge petered out after a hundred miles and we moved onto the slope of a range of ragged craters that ran south and east. This range had shown no activity since the first landing on Mercury forty years before, but beyond it there were active cones. Yellow fumes rose from the craters constantly; their sides were shrouded with heavy ash.

We couldn't detect a wind, but we knew there was a hot, sulfurous breeze sweeping in great continental tides across the face of the planet. Not enough for erosion, though. The craters rose up out of jagged gorges, huge towering spears of rock and rubble. Below were the vast yellow flatlands, smoking and hissing from the gases beneath the crust. Over everything was gray dust—silicates and salts, pumice and limestone and granite ash, filling crevices and declivities—offering a soft, treacherous surface for the Bug's pillow tires.

I learned to read the ground, to tell a covered fault by the sag of the dust; I learned to spot a passable crack, and tell it from an impassable cut. Time after time the Bugs ground to a halt while we explored a passage on foot, tied together with light copper cable, digging, advancing, digging some more until we were sure the surface would carry the machines. It was cruel work; we slept in exhaustion. But it went smoothly, at first.

Too smoothly, it seemed to me, and the others seemed to think so, too.

McIvers' restlessness was beginning to grate on our nerves. He talked too much, while we were resting or while we were driving; wisecracks, witticisms, unfunny jokes that wore thin with repetition. He took to making side trips from the route now and then, never far, but a little further each time.

Jack Stone reacted quite the opposite; he grew quieter with each stop, more reserved and apprehensive. I didn't like it, but I figured that it would pass off after a while. I was apprehensive enough myself; I just managed to hide it better.

And every mile the Sun got bigger and whiter and higher in the sky and hotter. Without our ultra-violet screens and glare filters we would have been blinded; as it was our eyes ached constantly and the skin on our faces itched and tingled at the end of an eight-hour trek.

But it took one of those side trips of McIvers' to deliver the penultimate blow to our already fraying nerves. He had driven down a side-branch of a long canyon running off west of our route and was almost out of sight in a cloud of ash when we heard a sharp cry through our earphones.

I wheeled my Bug around with my heart in my throat and spotted him through the binocs, waving frantically from the top of his machine. The Major and I took off, lumbering down the gulch after him as fast as the Bugs could go, with a thousand horrible pictures racing through our minds....

We found him standing stock-still, pointing down the gorge and, for once, he didn't have anything to say. It was the wreck of a Bug; an old-fashioned half-track model of the sort that hadn't been in use for years. It was wedged tight in a cut in the rock, an axle broken, its casing split wide open up the middle, half-buried in a rock slide. A dozen feet away were two insulated suits with white bones gleaming through the fiberglass helmets.

This was as far as Wyatt and Carpenter had gotten on *their* Brightside Crossing.

*

On the fifth driving period out, the terrain began to change. It looked the same, but every now and then it *felt* different. On two occasions I felt my wheels spin, with a howl of protest from my engine. Then, quite suddenly, the Bug gave a lurch; I gunned my motor and nothing happened.

I could see the dull gray stuff seeping up around the hubs, thick and tenacious, splattering around in steaming gobs as the wheels spun. I knew what had happened the moment the wheels gave and, a few minutes later, they chained me to the tractor and dragged me back out of the mire. It looked for all the world like thick gray mud, but it was a pit of molten lead, steaming under a soft layer of concealing ash.

I picked my way more cautiously then. We were getting into an area of recent surface activity; the surface was really treacherous. I caught myself wishing that the Major had okayed McIvers' scheme for an advanced scout; more dangerous for the individual, maybe, but I was driving blind now and I didn't like it.

One error in judgment could sink us all, but I wasn't thinking much about the others. I was worried about *me*, plenty worried. I kept thinking, better McIvers should go than me. It wasn't healthy thinking and I knew it, but I couldn't get the thought out of my mind.

It was a grueling eight hours and we slept poorly. Back in the Bug again, we moved still more slowly—edging out on a broad flat plateau, dodging a network of gaping surface cracks—winding back and forth in an effort to keep the machines on solid rock. I couldn't see far ahead, because of the yellow haze rising from the cracks, so I was almost on top of it when I saw a sharp cut ahead where the surface dropped six feet beyond a deep crack.

I let out a shout to halt the others; then I edged my Bug forward, peering at the cleft. It was deep and wide. I moved fifty yards to the left, then back to the right.

There was only one place that looked like a possible crossing; a long, narrow ledge of gray stuff that lay down across a section of the fault like a ramp. Even as I watched it, I could feel the surface crust under the Bug trembling and saw the ledge shift over a few feet.

The Major's voice sounded in my ears. "How about it, Peter?"

"I don't know. This crust is on roller skates," I called back.

"How about that ledge?"

I hesitated. "I'm scared of it, Major. Let's backtrack and try to find a way around."

There was a roar of disgust in my earphones and McIvers' Bug suddenly lurched forward. It rolled down past me, picked up speed, with McIvers hunched behind the wheel like a race driver. He was heading past me straight for the gray ledge.

My shout caught in my throat; I heard the Major take a huge breath and roar: "Mac! *stop that thing*, you fool!" and then McIvers' Bug was out on the ledge, lumbering across like a juggernaut.

The ledge jolted as the tires struck it; for a horrible moment, it seemed to be sliding out from under the machine. And then the Bug was across in a cloud of dust, and I heard McIvers' voice in my ears, shouting in glee. "Come on, you slowpokes. It'll hold you!"

Something unprintable came through the earphones as the Major drew up alongside me and moved his Bug out on the ledge slowly and over to the other side. Then he said, "Take it slow, Peter. Then give Jack a hand with the sledges." His voice sounded tight as a wire.

Ten minutes later, we were on the other side of the cleft. The Major checked the whole column; then he turned on McIvers angrily. "One more trick like that," he said, "and I'll strap you to a rock and leave you. Do you understand me? *One more time—*"

McIvers' voice was heavy with protest. "Good Lord, if we leave it up to Claney, he'll have us out here forever! Any blind fool could see that that ledge would hold."

"*I* saw it moving," I shot back at him.

"All right, all right, so you've got good eyes. Why all the fuss? We got across, didn't we? But I say we've got to have a little nerve and use it once in a while if we're ever going to get across this lousy hotbox."

"We need to use a little judgment, too," the Major snapped. "All right, let's roll. But if you think I was joking, you just try me out once." He let it soak in for a minute. Then he geared his Bug on around to my flank again.

At the stopover, the incident wasn't mentioned again, but the Major drew me aside just as I was settling down for sleep. "Peter, I'm worried," he said slowly.

"McIvers? Don't worry. He's not as reckless as he seems—just impatient. We are over a hundred miles behind schedule and we're moving awfully slow. We only made forty miles this last drive."

The Major shook his head. "I don't mean McIvers. I mean the kid."

"Jack? What about him?"

"Take a look."

Stone was shaking. He was over near the tractor—away from the rest of us—and he was lying on his back, but he wasn't asleep. His whole body was shaking, convulsively. I saw him grip an outcropping of rock hard.

I walked over and sat down beside him. "Get your water all right?" I said.

He didn't answer. He just kept on shaking.

"Hey, boy," I said. "What's the trouble?"

"It's hot," he said, choking out the words.

"Sure it's hot, but don't let it throw you. We're in really good shape."

"*We're not*," he snapped. "We're in rotten shape, if you ask me. *We're not going to make it*, do you know that? That crazy fool's going to kill us for sure—" All of a sudden, he was bawling like a baby. "I'm scared—I shouldn't be here—I'm *scared*. What am I trying to prove by coming out here, for God's sake? I'm some kind of hero or something? I tell you I'm scared—"

"Look," I said. "Mikuta's scared, *I'm* scared. So what? We'll make it, don't worry. And nobody's trying to be a hero."

"Nobody but Hero Stone," he said bitterly. He shook himself and gave a tight little laugh. "Some hero, eh?"

"We'll make it," I said.

"Sure," he said finally. "Sorry. I'll be okay."

I rolled over, but waited until he was good and quiet. Then I tried to sleep, but I didn't sleep too well. I kept thinking about that ledge. I'd known from the look of it what it was; a zinc slough of the sort Sanderson had warned us about, a wide sheet of almost pure zinc that had been thrown up white-hot from below, quite recently, just waiting for oxygen or sulfur to rot it through.

I knew enough about zinc to know that at these temperatures it gets brittle as glass. Take a chance like McIvers had taken and the whole sheet could snap like a dry pine board. And it wasn't McIvers' fault that it hadn't.

Five hours later, we were back at the wheel. We were hardly moving at all. The ragged surface was almost impassable—great jutting rocks peppered the plateau; ledges crumbled the moment my tires touched them; long, open canyons turned into lead-mires or sulfur pits.

A dozen times I climbed out of the Bug to prod out an uncertain area with my boots and pikestaff. Whenever I did, McIvers piled out behind me, running ahead like a schoolboy at the fair, then climbing back again red-faced and panting, while we moved the machines ahead another mile or two.

Time was pressing us now and McIvers wouldn't let me forget it. We had made only about three hundred twenty miles in six driving periods, so we were about a hundred miles or even more behind schedule.

"We're not going to make it," McIvers would complain angrily. "That Sun's going to be out to aphelion by the time we hit the Center—"

"Sorry, but I can't take it any faster," I told him. I was getting good and mad. I knew what he wanted, but didn't dare let him have it. I was scared enough pushing the Bug out on those ledges, even knowing that at least *I* was making the decisions. Put him in the lead and we wouldn't last for eight hours. Our nerves wouldn't take it, at any rate, even if the machines would.

Jack Stone looked up from the aluminum chart sheets. "Another hundred miles and we should hit a good stretch," he said. "Maybe we can make up distance there for a couple of days."

The Major agreed, but McIvers couldn't hold his impatience. He kept staring up at the Sun as if he had a personal grudge against it and stamped back and forth under the sunshield. "That'll be just fine," he said. "*If* we ever get that far, that is."

We dropped it there, but the Major stopped me as we climbed aboard for the next run. "That guy's going to blow wide open if we don't move faster, Peter. I don't want him in the lead, no matter what happens. He's right though, about the need to make better time. Keep your head, but crowd your luck a little, okay?"

"I'll try," I said. It was asking the impossible and Mikuta knew it. We were on a long downward slope that shifted and buckled all around us, as though there were a molten underlay beneath the crust; the slope was broken by huge crevasses, partly covered with dust and zinc sheeting, like a vast glacier of stone and metal. The outside temperature registered 547° F. and getting hotter. It was no place to start rushing ahead.

I tried it anyway. I took half a dozen shaky passages, edging slowly out on flat zinc ledges, then toppling over and across. It seemed easy for a while and we made progress. We hit an even stretch and raced ahead. And then

I quickly jumped on my brakes and jerked the Bug to a halt in a cloud of dust.

I'd gone too far. We were out on a wide, flat sheet of gray stuff, apparently solid—until I'd suddenly caught sight of the crevasse beneath in the corner of my eye. It was an overhanging shell that trembled under me as I stopped.

McIvers' voice was in my ear. "What's the trouble now, Claney?"

"Move back!" I shouted. "It can't hold us!"

"Looks solid enough from here."

"You want to argue about it? It's too thin, it'll snap. Move back!"

I started edging back down the ledge. I heard McIvers swear; then I saw his Bug start to creep *outward* on the shelf. Not fast or reckless, this time, but slowly, churning up dust in a gentle cloud behind him.

I just stared and felt the blood rush to my head. It seemed so hot I could hardly breathe as he edged out beyond me, further and further—

I think I felt it snap before I saw it. My own machine gave a sickening lurch and a long black crack appeared across the shelf—and widened. Then the ledge began to upend. I heard a scream as McIvers' Bug rose up and up and then crashed down into the crevasse in a thundering slide of rock and shattered metal.

I just stared for a full minute, I think. I couldn't move until I heard Jack Stone groan and the Major shouting, "Claney! I couldn't see—what *happened?*"

"It snapped on him, that's what happened," I roared. I gunned my motor, edged forward toward the fresh broken edge of the shelf. The crevasse gaped; I couldn't see any sign of the machine. Dust was still billowing up blindingly from below.

We stood staring down, the three of us. I caught a glimpse of Jack Stone's face through his helmet. It wasn't pretty.

"Well," said the Major heavily, "that's that."

"I guess so." I felt the way Stone looked.

"Wait," said Stone. "I heard something."

He had. It was a cry in the earphones—faint, but unmistakable.

"Mac!" The Major called. "Mac, can you hear me?"

"Yeah, yeah. I can hear you." The voice was very weak.

"Are you all right?"

"I don't know. Broken leg, I think. It's—hot." There was a long pause. Then: "I think my cooler's gone out."

The Major shot me a glance, then turned to Stone. "Get a cable from the second sledge fast. He'll fry alive if we don't get him out of there. Peter, I need you to lower me. Use the tractor winch."

I lowered him; he stayed down only a few moments. When I hauled him up, his face was drawn. "Still alive," he panted. "He won't be very long, though." He hesitated for just an instant. "We've got to make a try."

"I don't like this ledge," I said. "It's moved twice since I got out. Why not back off and lower him a cable?"

"No good. The Bug is smashed and he's inside it. We'll need torches and I'll need one of you to help." He looked at me and then gave Stone a long look. "Peter, you'd better come."

"Wait," said Stone. His face was very white. "Let me go down with you."

"Peter is lighter."

"I'm not so heavy. Let me go down."

"Okay, if that's the way you want it." The Major tossed him a torch. "Peter, check these hitches and lower us slowly. If you see any kind of trouble, *anything*, cast yourself free and back off this thing, do you understand? This whole ledge may go."

I nodded. "Good luck."

They went over the ledge. I let the cable down bit by bit until it hit two hundred feet and slacked off.

"How does it look?" I shouted.

"Bad," said the Major. "We'll have to work fast. This whole side of the crevasse is ready to crumble. Down a little more."

Minutes passed without a sound. I tried to relax, but I couldn't. Then I felt the ground shift, and the tractor lurched to the side.

The Major shouted, "*It's going, Peter—pull back!*" and I threw the tractor into reverse, jerked the controls as the tractor rumbled off the shelf. The cable snapped, coiled up in front like a broken clockspring. The whole surface under me was shaking wildly now; ash rose in huge gray clouds. Then, with a roar, the whole shelf lurched and slid sideways. It teetered on the edge for seconds before it crashed into the crevasse, tearing the side wall down with it in a mammoth slide. I jerked the tractor to a halt as the dust and flame billowed up.

They were gone—all three of them, McIvers and the Major and Jack Stone—buried under a thousand tons of rock and zinc and molten lead. There wasn't any danger of anybody ever finding their bones.

*

Peter Claney leaned back, finishing his drink, rubbing his scarred face as he looked across at Baron.

Slowly, Baron's grip relaxed on the chair arm. "*You* got back," he said.

Claney nodded. "I got back, sure. I had the tractor and the sledges. I had seven days to drive back under that yellow Sun. I had plenty of time to think."

"You took the wrong man along," Baron said. "That was your mistake. Without him you would have made it."

"Never." Claney shook his head. "That's what I was thinking the first day or so—that it was *McIvers'* fault, that *he* was to blame. But that isn't true. He was wild, reckless and had lots of nerve."

"But his judgment was bad!"

"It couldn't have been sounder. We had to keep to our schedule even if it killed us, because it would positively kill us if we didn't."

"But a man like that—"

"A man like McIvers was necessary. Can't you see that? It was the Sun that beat us, that surface. Perhaps we were licked the very day we started." Claney leaned across the table, his eyes pleading. "We didn't realize that, but it was *true*. There are places that men can't go, conditions men can't tolerate. The others had to die to learn that. I was lucky, I came back. But I'm trying to tell you what I found out—that *nobody* will ever make a Brightside Crossing."

"We will," said Baron. "It won't be a picnic, but we'll make it."

"But suppose you do," said Claney, suddenly. "Suppose I'm all wrong, suppose you *do* make it. Then what? *What comes next?*"

"The Sun," said Baron.

Claney nodded slowly. "Yes. That would be it, wouldn't it?" He laughed. "Good-by, Baron. Jolly talk and all that. Thanks for listening."

Baron caught his wrist as he started to rise. "Just one question more, Claney. Why did you come here?"

"To try to talk you out of killing yourself," said Claney.

"You're a liar," said Baron.

Claney stared down at him for a long moment. Then he crumpled in the chair. There was defeat in his pale blue eyes and something else.

"Well?"

Peter Claney spread his hands, a helpless gesture. "When do you leave, Baron? I want you to take me along."

THE DARK DOOR

1

It was almost dark when he awoke, and lay on the bed, motionless and trembling, his heart sinking in the knowledge that he should never have slept. For almost half a minute, eyes wide with fear, he lay in the silence of the gloomy room, straining to hear some sound, some indication of their presence.

But the only sound was the barely audible hum of his wrist watch and the dismal splatter of raindrops on the cobbled street outside. There was no sound to feed his fear, yet he knew then, without a flicker of doubt, that they were going to kill him.

He shook his head, trying to clear the sleep from his brain as he turned the idea over and over in his mind. He wondered why he hadn't realized it before, long before, back when they had first started this horrible, nerve-wracking cat-and-mouse game. The idea just hadn't occurred to him. But he knew the game-playing was over. They wanted to kill him now. And he knew that ultimately they *would* kill him. There was no way for him to escape.

He sat up on the edge of the bed, painfully, perspiration standing out on his bare back, and he waited, listening. How could he have slept, exposing himself so helplessly? Every ounce of his energy, all the skill and wit and shrewdness at his command were necessary in this cruel hunt; yet he had taken the incredibly terrible chance of sleeping, of losing consciousness, leaving himself wide open and helpless against the attack which he knew was inevitable.

How much had he lost? How close had they come while he slept?

Fearfully, he walked to the window, peered out, and felt his muscles relax a little. The gray, foggy streets were still light. He still had a little time before the terrible night began.

He stumbled across the small, old-fashioned room, sensing that action of some sort was desperately needed. The bathroom was tiny; he stared in the battered, stained reflector unit, shocked at the red-eyed stubble-faced apparition that stared back at him.

This is Harry Scott, he thought, thirty-two years old, and in the prime of life, but not the same Harry Scott who started out on a ridiculous quest so many months ago. This Harry Scott was being hunted like an animal, driven by fear, helpless, and sure to die, unless he could find an escape, somehow. But there were too many of them for him to escape, and they were too clever, and they *knew* he knew too much.

He stepped into the shower-shave unit, trying to relax, to collect his racing thoughts. Above all, he tried to stay the fear that burned through his mind, driving him to panic and desperation. The memory of the last hellish night was too stark to allow relaxation—the growing fear, the silent, desperate hunt through the night; the realization that their numbers were increasing; his frantic search for a hiding place in the New City; and finally his panic-stricken, pell-mell flight down into the alleys and cobbled streets and crumbling frame buildings of the Old City.... Even more horrible, the friends who had turned on him, who turned out to be *like* them.

Back in the bedroom, he lay down again, his body still tense. There were sounds in the building, footsteps moving around on the floor overhead, a door banging somewhere. With every sound, every breath of noise, his muscles tightened still further, freezing him in fear. His own breath was shallow and rapid in his ears as he lay, listening, waiting.

If only something would happen! He wanted to scream, to bang his head against the wall, to run about the room smashing his fist into doors, breaking every piece of furniture. It was the *waiting*, the eternal waiting, and running, waiting some more, feeling the net drawing tighter and tighter as he waited, feeling the measured, unhurried tread behind him, always following, coming closer and closer, as though he were a mouse on a string, twisting and jerking helplessly.

If only they would move, do something he could counter.

But he wasn't even sure any more that he could detect them. And they were so careful never to move into the open.

He jumped up feverishly, moved to the window, and peered between the slats of the dusty, old-fashioned blind at the street below.

An empty street at first, wet, gloomy. He saw no one. Then he caught the flicker of light in an entry several doors down and across the street, as a dark figure sparked a cigarette to life. Harry felt the chill run down his back again. Still there, then, still waiting, a hidden figure, always present, always waiting....

Harry's eyes scanned the rest of the street rapidly. Two three-wheelers rumbled by, their rubber hissing on the wet pavement. One of them carried the blue-and-white of the Old City police, but the car didn't slow up or hesitate as it passed the dark figure in the doorway. They would never help me anyway, Harry thought bitterly. He had tried that before, and met with ridicule and threats. There would be no help from the police in the Old City.

Another figure came around a corner. There was something vaguely familiar about the tall body and broad shoulders as the man walked across the wet street, something Harry faintly recognized from somewhere during the spinning madness of the past few weeks.

The man's eyes turned up toward the window for the briefest instant, then returned steadfastly to the street. Oh, they were sly! You could never spot them looking at you, never for *sure*, but they were always there, always nearby. And there was no one he could trust any longer, no one to whom he could turn.

Not even George Webber.

Swiftly his mind reconsidered that possibility as he watched the figure move down the street. True, Dr. Webber had started him out on this search in the first place. But even Webber would never believe what he had found. Webber was a scientist, a researcher.

What could he do—go to Webber and tell him that there were men alive in the world who were *not* men, who were somehow men and something more?

Could he walk into Dr. Webber's office in the Hoffman Medical Center, walk through the gleaming bright corridors, past the shining metallic doors, and tell Dr. Webber that he had found people alive in the world who could actually see in four dimensions, live in four dimensions, *think* in four dimensions?

Could he explain to Dr. Webber that he knew this simply because in some way he had sensed them, and traced them, and discovered them; that he had not one iota of proof, except that he was being followed by them, hunted by them, even now, in a room in the Old City, waiting for them to strike him down?

He shook his head, almost sobbing. That was what was so horrible. He couldn't tell Webber, because Webber would be certain that he had gone mad, just like the rest. He couldn't tell anyone, he couldn't do anything. He could just wait, and run, and wait—

It was almost dark now and the creaking of the old board house intensified the fear that tore at Harry Scott's mind. Tonight was the night;

he was sure of it. Maybe he had been foolish in coming here to the slum area, where the buildings were relatively unguarded, where anybody could come and go as he pleased. But the New City had hardly been safer, even in the swankiest private chamber in the highest building. They had had agents there, too, hunting him, driving home the bitter lesson of fear they had to teach him. Now he was afraid enough; now they were ready to kill him.

Down below he heard a door bang, and he froze, his back against the wall. There were footsteps, quiet voices, barely audible. His whole body shook and his eyes slid around to the window. The figure in the doorway still waited—but the other figure was not visible. He heard the steps on the stair, ascending slowly, steadily, a tread that paced itself with the powerful throbbing of his own pulse.

Then the telephone screamed out—

Harry gasped. The footsteps were on the floor below, moving steadily upward. The telephone rang again and again; the shrill jangling filled the room insistently. He waited until he couldn't wait any longer. His hand fumbled in a pocket and leveled a tiny, dull-gray metal object at the door. With the other hand, he took the receiver from the hook.

"Harry! Is that you?"

His throat was like sandpaper and the words came out in a rasp. "What is it?"

"Harry, this is George—George Webber."

His eyes were glued to the door. "All right. What do you want?"

"You've got to come talk to us, Harry. We've been waiting for weeks now. You promised us. We've *got* to talk to you."

Harry still watched the door, but his breath came easier. The footsteps moved with ridiculous slowness up the stairs, down the hall toward the room.

"What do you want me to do? They've come to kill me."

There was a long pause. "Harry, are you sure?"

"Dead sure."

"Can you make a break for it?"

Harry blinked. "I could try. But it won't do any good."

"Well, at least try, Harry. Get here to the Hoffman Center. We'll help you all we can."

"I'll try." Harry's words were hardly audible as he set the receiver down with a trembling hand.

The room was silent. The footsteps had stopped. A wave of panic passed up Harry's spine; he crossed the room, threw open the door, stared up and down the hall, unbelieving.

The hall was empty. He started down toward the stairs at a dead run, and then, too late, saw the faint golden glow of a Parkinson Field across the dingy corridor. He gasped in fear, and screamed out once as he struck it.

And then, for seconds stretching into hours, he heard his scream echoing and re-echoing down long, bitter miles of hollow corridor.

2

George Webber leaned back in the soft chair, turning a quizzical glance toward the younger man across the room. He lit a long black cigar.

"Well?" His heavy voice boomed out in the small room. "Now that we've got him here, what do you think?"

The younger man glanced uncomfortably through the glass wall panel into the small dark room beyond. In the dimness, he could barely make out the still form on the bed, grotesque with the electrode-vernier apparatus already in place at its temples. Dr. Manelli looked away sharply, and leafed through the thick sheaf of chart papers in his hand.

"I don't know," he said dully. "I just don't know what to think."

The other man's laugh seemed to rise from the depths of his huge chest. His heavy face creased into a thousand wrinkles. Dr. Webber was a large man, his broad shoulders carrying a suggestion of immense power that matched the intensity of his dark, wide-set eyes. He watched Dr. Manelli's discomfort grow, saw the younger doctor's ears grow red, and the almost cruel lines in his face were masked as he laughed still louder.

"Trouble with you, Frank, you just don't have the courage of your convictions."

"Well, I don't see anything so funny about it!" Manelli's eyes were angry. "The man has a suspicious syndrome—so you've followed him, and spied on him for weeks on end, which isn't exactly highest ethical practice in collecting a history. I still can't see how you're justified."

Dr. Webber snorted, tossing his cigar down on the desk with disgust. "The man is insane. That's my justification. He's out of touch with reality.

He's wandered into a wild, impossible, fantastic dream world. And we've got to get him out of it, because what he knows, what he's trying to hide from us, is so incredibly dangerous that we don't dare let him go."

The big man stared at Manelli, his dark eyes flashing. "Can't you see that? Or would you rather sit back and let Harry Scott go the way that Paulus and Wineberg and the others went?"

"But to use the Parkinson Field on him—" Dr. Manelli shook his head hopelessly. "He'd offered to come over, George. We didn't need to use it."

"Sure, he offered to come—fine, fine. But supposing he changed his mind on the way? For all we know, he had us figured into his paranoia, too, and never would have come near the Hoffman Center."

Dr. Webber shook his head. "We're not playing a game any more, Frank. Get that straight. I thought it was a game a couple of years ago, when we first started. But it ceased to be a game when men like Paulus and Wineberg walked in sane, healthy men, and came out blubbering idiots. That's no game any more. We're onto something big. And, if Harry Scott can lead us to the core of it, then I can't care too much what happens to Harry Scott."

Dr. Manelli stood up sharply, walked to the window, and looked down over the bright, clean buildings of the Hoffman Medical Center. Out across the terraced park that surrounded the glassed towers and shining metal of the Center rose the New City, tier upon tier of smooth, functional architecture, a city of dreams built up painfully out of the rubble of the older, ruined city.

"You could kill him," the young man said finally. "The psycho-integrator isn't any standard interrogative technique; it's dangerous and treacherous. You never know for sure just what you're doing when you dig down into a man's brain tissue with those little electrode probes."

"But we can learn the truth about Harry Scott," Dr. Webber broke in. "Six months ago, Harry Scott was working with us, a quiet, affable, pleasant young fellow, extremely intelligent, intensely co-operative. He was just the man we needed to work with us, an engineer who could take our data and case histories, study them, and subject them to a completely nonmedical analysis. Oh, we had to have it done—the problem's been with us for a hundred years now, growing ever since the 1950s and 60s—insanity in the population, growing, spreading without rhyme or reason, insinuating itself into every nook and cranny of our civilized life."

The big man blinked at Manelli. "Harry Scott was the new approach. We were too close to the problem. We needed a nonmedical outsider to take a look, to tell us what we were missing. So Harry Scott walked into the problem, and then abruptly lost contact with us. We finally track him down and find him gone, out of touch with reality, on the same wretched road that all the others went. With Harry, it's paranoia. He's being persecuted; he has the whole world against him, but most important—the factor we don't dare overlook—*he's no longer working on the problem.*"

Manelli shifted uneasily. "I suppose that's right."

"Of course it's right!" Dr. Webber's eyes flashed. "Harry found something in those statistics. Something about the data, or the case histories; or something Harry Scott himself dug up opened a door for him to go through, a door that none of us ever dreamed existed. We don't know what he found on the other side of that door. Oh, we know what he *thinks* he found, all this garbage about people that look normal but walk through walls when nobody's looking, who think around corners instead of in straight-line logic. But what he *really* found there, we don't have any way of telling. We just know that whatever he *really* found is something new, something unsuspected; something so dangerous it can drive an intelligent man into the wildest delusions of paranoid persecution."

A new light appeared in Dr. Manelli's eyes as he faced the other doctor. "Wait a minute," he said softly. "The integrator is an *experimental* instrument, too."

Dr. Webber smiled slyly. "Now you're beginning to think," he said.

"But you'll see only what Scott himself believes. And *he* thinks his story is true."

"Then we'll have to break his story."

"*Break* it?"

"Certainly. For some reason, this delusion of persecution is far safer for Harry Scott than facing what he really found out. What we've got to do is to make this delusion *less* safe than the truth."

The room was silent for a long moment. Manelli looked up, his fingers trembling. "Let's hear it."

"It's very simple. Up to now, Harry Scott has had *delusions* of persecution. But now we're *really* going to persecute Harry Scott, as he's never been persecuted before."

3

At first he thought he was at the bottom of a deep well and he lay quite still, his eyes clamped shut, wondering where he was and how he could possibly have gotten there. He could feel the dampness and chill of the stone floor under him, and nearby he heard the damp, insistent drip of water splashing against stone. He felt his muscles tighten as the dripping sound forced itself against his senses. Then he opened his eyes.

His first impulse was to scream out wildly in unreasoning, suffocating fear. He fought it down, struggling to sit up in the blackness, his whole mind turned in bitter, hopeless hatred at the ones who had hunted him for so long, and now had trapped him.

Why?

Why did they torture him? Why not kill him outright, have done with it? He shuddered, and struggled to his feet, staring about him in horror.

It was not a well, but a small room, circular, with little rivulets of stale water running down the granite walls. The ceiling closed low over his head, and the only source of light came from the single doorway opening into a long, low stone passageway.

Wave after wave of panic rose in Harry's throat. Each time he fought down the urge to scream, to lie down on the ground and cover his face with his hands and scream in helpless fear. How could they have known the horror that lay in his own mind, the horror of darkness, of damp slimy walls and scurrying rodents, of the clinging, stale humidity of dungeon passageways? He himself had seldom recalled it, except in his most hideous dreams, yet he had known such fear as a boy, so many years ago, and now it was all around him. They had known somehow and *used it against him.*

Why?

He sank down on the floor, his head in his hands, trying to think straight, to find some clue in the turmoil bubbling through his mind that would tell him what had happened.

He had started down the hallway from his room, to find Dr. Webber and tell him about the other people—

He stopped short, looked up wide-eyed. *Had* he been going to Dr. Webber? Had he actually decided to go? Perhaps—yes, perhaps he had, though Webber would only laugh at such a ridiculous story. But the not-men who had hunted him would not laugh; to them, it would not be funny. They knew that it was true. And they knew he knew it was true.

But why not kill him? Why this torture? Why this horrible persecution that dug into the depths of his own nightmares to haunt him?

His breath came fast and a chilly sweat broke out on his forehead. *Where* was he? Was this some long forgotten vault in the depths of the Old City? Or was this another place, another world, perhaps, that the not-men, with their impossible powers, had created to torture him?

His eyes sought the end of the hall, saw the turn at the end, saw the light which seemed to come from the end; and then in an instant he was running down the damp passageway, his pulse pounding at his temples, until he could hardly gasp enough breath as he ran. Finally he reached the turn in the corridor where the light was brighter, and he swung around to stare at the source of the light, a huge, burning, smoky torch which hung from the wall.

Even as he looked at it, the torch went out, shutting him into inky blackness. The only sound at first was the desperation of his own breath; then he heard little scurrying sounds around his feet, and screamed involuntarily as something sleek and four-footed jumped at his chest with snapping jaws.

Shuddering, he fought the thing off, his fingers closing on wiry fur as he caught and squeezed. The thing went limp, and suddenly melted in his hands. He heard it splash as it struck the damp ground at his feet.

What were they doing to his mind?

He screamed out in horror, and followed the echoes of his own scream as he ran down the stone corridor, blindly, slipping on the wet stone floor, falling on his knees into inches of brackish water, scraping back to his feet with an uncontrollable convulsion of fear and loathing, only to run more—

The corridor suddenly broke into two and he stopped short. He didn't know how far, or how long, he had run, but it suddenly occurred to him that he was still alive, still safe. Only his mind was under attack, only his mind was afraid, teetering on the edge of control. And this maze of dungeon tunnels—where could such a thing exist, so perfectly outfitted to horrify him, so neatly fitting into his own pattern of childhood fears and terrors; from where could such a *very individual* attack on his sanity have sprung? From nowhere except....

Except from his own mind!

For an instant, he saw a flicker of light, thought he grasped the edge of a concept previously obscure to him. He stared around him, at the mist swirling down the damp, dark corridor, and thought of the rat that had melted in his hand. Suddenly, his mind was afire, searching through his experience with the strange not-men he had learned to detect, trying to remember everything he had learned and deduced about them before they began their brutal persecution.

They were men, and they looked like men, but they were different. They had other properties of mind, other capabilities that men did not have.

They were not-men. They could exist, and co-exist, two people in one frame, one person known, realized by all who saw, the other one concealed except from those who learned how to look. They could use their minds; they could rationalize correctly; they could use their curious four-dimensional knowledge to bring them to answers no three-dimensional man could reach.

But they couldn't project into men's minds!

Carefully, Harry peered down the misty tunnels. They were clever, these creatures, and powerful. Since they had discovered that he knew them, they had done their work of fear and terror on his mind skillfully. But they were limited, too; they couldn't make things happen that were not true—fantasies, illusions....

Yes, this dungeon was an illusion. It *had* to be.

He cursed and started down the right-hand corridor, his heart sinking. There was no such place and he knew it. He was walking in a dream, a fantasy that had no substance, that could do no more than frighten him, drive him insane; yet he must already have lost his mind to be accepting such an illusion.

Why had he delayed? Why hadn't he gone to the Hoffman Center, laid the whole story before Dr. Webber and Dr. Manelli at the very first, told them what he had found? True, they might have thought him insane, but they wouldn't have put him to torture. They might even have believed him enough to investigate what he told them, and then the cat would have been out of the bag. The tale would have been incredible, but at least his mind would have been safe.

He turned down another corridor and walked suddenly into waist-deep water, so cold it numbed his legs. He stopped again to force back the tendrils of unreasoning horror that brushed his mind. Nothing could really harm him. He would merely wait until his mind finally reached a balance again. There might be no end; it might be a ghastly trap, but he would wait.

Strangely, the mist was becoming greenish in color as it swirled toward him in the damp vaulted passageway. His eyes began watering a little and the lining of his nose started to burn. He stopped short, newly alarmed, and stared at the walls, rubbing the tears away to clear his vision. The greenish-yellow haze grew thicker, catching his eyes and burning like a thousand furies, ripping into his throat until he was choking and coughing, as though great knives sliced through his lungs.

He tried to scream, and started running, blindly. Each gasping breath was an agony as the blistering gas dug deeper and deeper into his lungs. Reason departed from him; he was screaming incoherently as he stumbled up a stony ramp, crashed into a wall, spun around and smashed blindly into another. Then something caught at his shirt.

He felt the heavy planks and pounded iron scrollwork of a huge door, and threw himself upon it, wrenching at the old latch until the door swung open with a screech of rusty hinges. He fell forward on his face, and the door swung shut behind him.

He lay face down, panting and sobbing in the stillness.

Coarse hands grasped his collar, jerking him rudely to his feet, and he opened his eyes. Across the dim, vaulted room he could see the shadowy form of a man, a big man, with a broad chest and powerful shoulders, a man whose rich voice Harry almost recognized, but whose face was deep in shadow. As Harry wiped the tears from his tortured eyes, he heard the man's voice rumble out at him:

"Perhaps you've had enough now to change your mind about telling us the truth."

Harry stared, not quite comprehending. "The—the truth?"

The man's voice was harsh, cutting across the room impatiently. "The truth, I said. The problem, you fool, what you saw, what you learned; you know perfectly well what I'm referring to. But we'll swallow no more of this silly four-dimensional superman tale, so don't bother to start it."

"I—I don't understand you. It's—it's true—" Again he tried to peer across the room. "Why are you hunting me like this? What are you trying to do to me?"

"We want the truth. We want to know what you saw."

"But—but *you're* what I saw. You know what I found out. I mean—" He stopped, his face going white. His hand went to his mouth, and he stared still harder. "Who are you?" he whispered.

"The truth!" the man roared. "You'd better be quick, or you'll be back in the corridor."

"*Webber!*"

"Your last chance, Harry."

Without warning, Harry was across the room, flying across the desk, crashing into the big man's chest. With a scream of fury he fought, driving his fists into the powerful chest, wrenching at the thick, flailing arms of the startled man.

"*It's you!*" he screamed. "It's you that's been torturing me. It's you that's been hunting me down all this time, not the other people, you and your crowd of ghouls have been at my throat!"

He threw the big man off balance, dropped heavily on him as he fell back to the ground, glared down into the other's angry brown eyes.

And then, as though he had never been there at all, the big man vanished, and Harry sat back on the floor, his whole body shaking with frustrated sobs as his mind twisted in anguish.

He had been wrong, completely wrong, ever since he had discovered the not-men. Because he had thought *they* had been the ones who hunted and tortured him for so long. And now he knew how far he had been wrong. For the face of the shadowy man, the man behind the nightmare he was living, was the face of Dr. George Webber.

*

"You're a fool," said Dr. Manelli sharply, as he turned away from the sleeping figure on the bed to face the older man. "Of all the ridiculous things, to let him connect you with this!" The young doctor turned abruptly and sank down in a chair, glowering at Dr. Webber. "You haven't gotten to first base yet, but you've just given Scott enough evidence to free himself from integrator control altogether, if he gives it any thought. But I suppose you realize that."

"Nonsense," Dr. Webber retorted. "He had enough information to do that when we first started. I'm no more worried now than I was then. I'm sure he doesn't know enough about the psycho-integrator to be able voluntarily to control the patient-operator relationship to any degree. Oh, no, he's safe enough. But you've missed the whole point of that little interview." Dr. Webber grinned at Manelli.

"I'm afraid I have. It looked to me like useless bravado."

"The persecution, man, the *persecution*! He's shifted his sights! Before that interview, the *not-men* were torturing him, remember? Because they were afraid he would report his findings to me, of course. But now it's *I* that's against him." The grin widened. "You see where that leads?"

"You're talking almost as though you believed this story about a different sort of people among us."

Dr. Webber shrugged. "Perhaps I do."

"Oh, come now, George."

Dr. Webber's eyebrows went up and the grin disappeared from his face.

"Harry Scott believes it, Frank. We mustn't forget that, or miss its significance. Before Harry started this investigation of his, he wouldn't have paid any attention to such nonsense. But he believes it now."

"But Harry Scott is insane. You said it yourself."

"Ah, yes," said Dr. Webber. "Insane. Just like the others who started to get somewhere along those lines of investigation. Try to analyze the growing incidence of insanity in the population and you yourself go insane. You've got to be crazy to be a psychiatrist. It's an old joke, but it isn't very funny any more. And it's too much for coincidence.

"And then consider the nature of the insanity—a full-blown paranoia—oh, it's amazing. A cunning organization of men who are *not*-men, a regular fairy story, all straight from Harry Scott's agile young mind. But now it's *we* who are persecuting him, *and he still believes his fairy tale*."

"So?"

Dr. Webber's eyes flashed angrily. "It's too neat, Frank. It's clever, and it's powerful, whatever we've run up against. But I think we've got an ace in the hole. We have Harry Scott."

"And you really think he'll lead us somewhere?"

Dr. Webber laughed. "That door I spoke of that Harry peeked through, I think he'll go back to it again. I think he's started to open that door already. And this time I'm going to follow him through."

4

It seemed incredible, yet Harry Scott knew he had not been mistaken. It had been Dr. Webber's face he had seen, a face no one could forget, an unmistakable face. And that meant that it had been Dr. Webber who had been persecuting him.

But why? He had been going to report to Webber when he had run into that golden field in the rooming-house hallway. And suddenly things had changed.

Harry felt a chill reaching to his fingers and toes. Yes, something had changed, all right. The attack on him had suddenly become butcherous, cruel, sneaking into his mind somehow to use his most dreaded nightmares against him. There was no telling what new horrors might be waiting for him. But he knew that he would lose his mind unless he could find an escape.

He was on his feet, his heart pounding. He had to get out of here, wherever he was. He had to get back to town, back to the city, back to where people were. If he could find a place to hide, a place where he could rest, he could try to think his way out of this ridiculous maze, or at least try to understand it.

He wrenched at the door to the passageway, started through, and smashed face-up against a solid brick wall.

He cried out and jumped back from the wall. Blood trickled from his nose. The door was *walled up*, the mortar dry and hard.

Frantically, he glanced around the room. There were no other doors, only the row of tiny windows around the ceiling of the room, pale, ghostly squares of light.

He pulled the chair over to the windows, peered out through the cobwebbed openings to the corridor beyond.

It was not the same hallway as before, but an old, dirty building corridor, incredibly aged, with bricks sagging away from the walls. At the end he could see stairs, and even the faintest hint of sunlight coming from above.

Wildly, he tore at the masonry of the window, chipping away at the soggy mortar with his fingers until he could squeeze through the opening. He fell to the floor of the corridor outside.

It was much colder and the silence was no longer so intense. He seemed to feel, rather than hear, the surging power, the rumble of many machines, the little, almost palpable vibrations from far above him.

He started in a dead run down the musty corridor to the stairs and began to climb them, almost stumbling over himself in his eagerness.

After several flights, the brick walls gave way to cleaner plastic, and suddenly a brightly lighted corridor stretched before him.

Panting from the climb, Harry ran down the corridor to the end, wrenched open a door, and looked out anxiously.

He was almost stunned by the bright light. At first he couldn't orient himself as he stared down at the metal ramp, the moving strips of glowing metal carrying the throngs of people, sliding along the thoroughfare before him, unaware of him watching, unaware of any change from the usual. The towering buildings before him rose to unbelievable heights, bathed in ever-changing rainbow colors, and he felt his pulse thumping in his temples as he gaped.

He was in the New City, of that there was no doubt. This was the part of the great metropolis which had been built again since the devastating war that had nearly wiped the city from the Earth a decade before. These were the moving streets, the beautiful residential apartments, following the modern neo-functional patterns and participational design which had completely altered the pattern of city living. The Old City still remained, of course—the slums, the tenements, the skid-rows of the metropolis—but this was the teeming heart of the city, a new home for men to live in.

And this was the stronghold where the not-men could be found, too. The thought cut through Harry's mind, sending a tremor up his spine. He had found them here; he had uncovered his first clues here, and discovered them; and even now his mind was filled with the horrible, paralyzing fear he had felt that first night when he had made the discovery. Yet he knew now that he dared not go back where he had come from.

At least he could understand why the not-men might have feared and persecuted him, but he could not understand the horrible assault that Dr. Webber had unleashed. And somehow he found Dr. Webber's attack infinitely more frightening.

He seemed to be safe here, though, at least for the moment.

Quickly he moved down onto the nearest moving sidewalk heading toward the living section of the New City. He knew where he could go there, where he could lock himself in, a place where he could think, possibly find a way to fight off Dr. Webber's attack of nightmares.

He settled back on a bench on the moving sidewalk, watching the city slide past him for several minutes before he noticed the curious shadow-form which seemed to whisk out of his field of vision every time he looked.

They were following him again! He looked around wildly as the sidewalk moved swiftly through the cool evening air. Far above, he could see the shimmering, iridescent screen that still stood to protect the New City from the devastating virus attacks which might again strike down from the skies without warning. Far ahead he could see the magnificent "bridge" formed by the sidewalk crossing over to the apartment area, where the thousands who worked in the New City were returning to their homes.

Someone was still following him.

Presently he heard the sound, so close to his ear he jumped, yet so small he could hardly identify it as a human voice. "What was it you found, Harry? What did you discover? Better tell, better tell."

He saw the rift in the moving sidewalk coming, far ahead, a great, gaping rent in the metal fabric of the swiftly moving escalator, as if a huge blade were slicing it down the middle. Harry's hand went to his mouth, choking back a scream as the hole moved with incredible rapidity down the center of the strip, swallowing up whole rows of the seats, moving straight toward his own.

He glanced in fright over the side just as the sidewalk moved out onto the "bridge," and he gasped as he saw the towering canyons of buildings fall far below, saw the seats tumble end over end, heard the sounds of screaming blend into the roar of air by his ears.

Then the rift screamed by him with a demoniac whine and he sank back onto his bench, gasping as the two cloven halves of the strip clanged back together again.

He stared at the people around him on the strip and they stared back at him, mildly, unperturbed, and returned to their evening papers as the strip passed through the first local station on the other side of the "bridge."

Harry Scott sprang to his feet, moving swiftly across the slower strips for the exit channels. He noted the station stop vaguely, but his only thought now was speed, desperate speed, fear-driven speed to put into action the plan that had suddenly burst in his mind.

He knew that he had reached his limit. He had come to a point beyond which he couldn't fight alone.

Somehow, Webber had burrowed into his brain, laid his mind open to attacks of nightmare and madness that he could never hope to fight. Facing this alone, he would lose his mind. His only hope was to go for help to the ones he feared only slightly less, the ones who had minds capable of fighting back for him.

He crossed under the moveable sidewalks and boarded the one going back into the heart of the city. Somewhere there, he hoped, he would find the help he needed. Somewhere back in that city were men he had discovered who were men and something more.

*

Frank Manelli carefully took the blood pressure of the sleeping figure on the bed; then turned to the other man. "He'll be dead soon," he snapped. "Another few minutes now is all it'll take. Just a few more."

"Absurd. There's nothing in these stimuli that can kill him." George Webber sat tense, his eyes fixed on the pale fluctuating screen near the head of the bed.

"His own mind can kill him! He's on the run now; you've broken him loose from his nice safe paranoia. His mind is retreating, running back to some other delusions. It's escaping to the safety his fantasy people can afford him, these not-men he thinks about."

"Yes, yes," agreed Dr. Webber, his eyes eager. "Oh, he's on the run now."

"But what will he do when he finds there aren't any 'not-men' to save him? What will he do then?"

Webber looked up, frowning and grim. "Then we'll know what he found behind the dark door that he opened, that's what."

"No, you're wrong! He'll die. He'll find nothing and the shock will kill him. My God, Webber, you can't tamper with a man's mind like this and hope to save his life! You're obsessed; you've always been obsessed by this impossible search for something in our society, some undiscovered factor to account for the mental illness, the divergent minds, but you can't kill a man to trace it down!"

"It's too neat," said Webber. "He comes back to tell us the truth, and we call him insane. We say he's paranoid, throw him in restraint, place him in an asylum; and we never *know* what he found. The truth is too incredible; when we hear it, it must be insanity we're hearing."

The big doctor laughed, jabbing his thumb at the screen. "This isn't insanity we're seeing. Oh, no, this is the answer we're following. I won't stop now. I've waited too long for this show."

"Well, I say stop it while he's still alive."

Dr. Webber's eyes were deadly. "Get out, Frank," he said softly. "I'm not stopping now."

His eyes returned to the screen, to the bobbing figure that the psycho-integrator traced on the fluorescent background. Twenty years of search had led him here, and now he knew the end was at hand.

5

It was a wild, nightmarish journey. At every step, Harry's senses betrayed him: his wrist watch turned into a brilliant blue-green snake that snapped at his wrist; the air was full of snarling creatures that threatened him at every step. But he fought them off, knowing that they would harm him far less than panic would. He had no idea where to hunt, nor whom to try to reach, but he knew they were there in the New City, and somehow he knew they would help him, if only he could find them.

He got off the moving strip as soon as the lights of the center of the city were clear below, and stepped into the self-operated lift that sped down to ground level. From the elevator, he moved on to one of the long, honeycombed concourses, filled with passing shoppers who stared at the colorful, enticing three-dimensional displays.

At one of the intersections ahead, he spotted a visiphone station, and dropped onto the little seat before the screen. There had been a number, if only he could recall it. But as he started to dial, the silvery screen shattered into a thousand sparkling glass chips, showering the floor with crystal and sparks.

Harry cursed, grabbed the hand instrument, and jangled frantically for the operator. Before she could answer, the instrument grew warm in his hand, then hot and soft, like wax. Slowly, it melted and ran down his arm.

He bolted out into the stream of people, trying desperately to draw some comfort from the crowd around him.

He felt utterly alone; he *had* to contact the not-men who were in the city, warn them, before they spotted him, of the attack he carried with him. If he were leading his pursuer, he could expect no mercy from the ones whose help he sought. He knew the lengths to which they would go to remain undetected in the society around them. Yet he had to find them.

In the distance, he saw a figure waiting, back against one of the show windows. Harry stopped short, ducked into a doorway, and peered out fearfully. Their eyes locked for an instant; then the figure moved on. Harry felt a jolt of horror surge through him. Dr. Webber hunting him in person!

He ducked out of the doorway, turned and ran madly in the opposite direction, searching for an up escalator he could catch. Behind him he heard shots, heard the angry whine of bullets past his ear.

He breathed in great, gasping sobs as he found an almost empty escalator, and bounded up it four steps at a time. Below, he could see Webber coming too, his broad shoulders forcing their way relentlessly through the mill of people.

Panting, Harry reached the top, checked his location against a wall map, and started down the long ramp which led toward the building he had tried to call.

Another shot broke out behind him. The wall alongside powdered away, leaving a gaping hole. On impulse, he leaped into the hole, running through to the rear of the building as the weakened wall swayed and crumbled into a heap of rubble just as Webber reached the place Harry had entered.

Harry breathed a sigh of relief and raced up the stairs of the building to reach a ramp on another level. He turned his eyes toward the tall building at the end of the concourse. There he could hide and relax and try, somehow, to make a contact.

Someone fell into step beside him and took his arm gently but firmly. Harry jerked away, turning terrified eyes to the one who had joined him.

"Quiet," said the man, steering him over toward the edge of the concourse. "Not a sound. You'll be all right."

Harry felt a tremor pass through his mind, the barest touching of mental fingertips, a recognition that sent a surge of eager blood through his heart.

He stopped short, facing the man. "I'm being followed," he gasped. "You can't take me anywhere you don't want Webber to follow, or you'll be in terrible danger."

The stranger shrugged and smiled briefly. "You're not here. You're in a psycho-integrator. It can hurt you, if you let it. But it can't hurt me." He stepped up his pace slightly, and in a moment they turned abruptly into a darkened cul-de-sac.

Suddenly, they were moving *through* the wall of the building into the brilliantly lit lobby of the tall building. Harry gasped, but the stranger led him without a sound toward the elevator, stepped aboard with him, and sped upward, the silence broken only by the whish-whish-whish of the passing floors. Finally they stepped out into a quiet corridor and down through a small office door.

A man sat behind the desk in the office, his face quiet, his eyes very wide and dark. He hardly glanced at Harry, but turned his eyes to the other man.

"Set?" he asked.

"Couldn't miss now."

The man nodded and looked at last at Harry. "You're upset," he murmured. "What's bothering you?"

"Webber," said Harry hoarsely. "He's following me here. He'll spot you. I tried to warn you before I came, but I couldn't."

The man at the desk smiled. "Webber again, eh? Our old friend Webber. That's all right. Webber's at the end of his tether. There's nothing he can do to stop us. He's trying to attack with force, and he fails to realize that time and thought are on our side. The time when force would have succeeded against us is long past. But now there are many of us, almost as many as not."

Harry stared shrewdly at the man behind the desk. "Then why are you so afraid of Webber?" he asked.

"Afraid?"

"You know you are. Long ago you threatened me, if I reported to him. You watched me, played with me. Why are you afraid of him?"

The man sighed. "Webber is premature. We are stalling for time, that's all. We wait. We have grown from so very few, back in the 1940s and 50s, but the time for quiet usurpation of power has not quite arrived. But men like Webber force our hand, discover us, try to expose us."

Harry Scott's face was white, his hands shaking. "And what do you do to them?"

"We—deal with them."

"And those like me?"

The man smiled lopsidedly. "Those like Paulus and Wineberg and the rest—they're happy, really, like little children. But one like you is so much more useful." He pointed almost apologetically to the small screen on his desk.

Harry looked at it, realization dawning. He watched the huge, broad-shouldered figure moving down the hallway toward the door.

"Webber was dangerous to you?"

"Unbelievably dangerous. So dangerous we would use any means to trap him."

Suddenly the door burst open and there stood Webber, a triumphant Webber, face flushed, eyes wide, as he stared at the man behind the desk.

The man smiled back and said, "Come on in, George. We've been waiting for you."

Webber stepped through the door. "Manelli, you fool!"

There was a blinding flash as he crossed the threshold. A faint crackle of sound reached Harry's ears; then the world blacked out....

*

It might have been minutes, or hours, or days. The man who had been behind the desk was leaning over Harry, smiling down at him, gently bandaging the trephine wounds at his temples.

"Gently," he said, as Harry tried to sit up. "Don't try to move. You've been through a rough time."

Harry peered up at him. "You're—not Dr. Webber."

"No. I'm Dr. Manelli. Dr. Webber's been called away—an accident. He'll be some time recovering. I'll be taking care of you."

Vaguely, Harry was aware that something was peculiar, something not quite as it should be. The answer slowly dawned on him.

"The statistical analysis!" he exclaimed. "I was supposed to get some data from Dr. Webber about an analysis, something about rising insanity rates."

Dr. Manelli looked blank. "Insanity rates? You must be mistaken. You were brought here for an immunity examination, nothing more. But you can check with Dr. Webber, when he gets back."

6

George Webber sat in the little room, trembling, listening, his eyes wide in the thick, misty darkness. He knew it would be a matter of time now. He couldn't run much farther. He hadn't seen them, true. Oh, they had been very clever, but they thought they were dealing with a fool, and they weren't. He *knew* they'd been following him; he'd known it for a long time now.

It was just as he had been telling the man downstairs the night before: they were everywhere—your neighbor upstairs, the butcher on the corner, your own son or daughter, maybe even the man you were talking to—*everywhere*!

And of course he had to warn as many people as he possibly could before *they* caught him, throttled him off, as they had threatened to if he talked to anyone.

If only the people would *listen* to him when he told them how cleverly it was all planned, how it would only be a matter of months, maybe only weeks or days before the change would happen, and the world would be quietly, silently taken over by the *other* people, the different people who could walk through walls and think in impossibly complex channels. And no one would know the difference, because business would go on as usual.

He shivered, sinking down lower on the bed. If only people would listen to him—

It wouldn't be long now. He had heard the stealthy footsteps on the landing below his room some time ago. This was the night they had chosen to make good their threats, to choke off his dangerous voice once and for all. There were footsteps on the stairs now, growing louder.

Wildly he glanced around the room as the steps moved down the hall toward his door. He rushed to the window, threw up the sash and screamed hoarsely to the silent street below: "Look out! They're here, all around us! They're planning to take over! Look out! Look out!"

The door burst open and there were two men moving toward him, grim-faced, dressed in white; tall, strong men with sad faces and strong arms.

One was saying, "Better come quietly, mister. No need to wake up the whole town."

INFINITE INTRUDER

It was the second time they tried that Roger Strang realized someone was trying to kill his son.

The first time there had been no particular question. Accidents happen. Even in those days, with all the Base safety regulations and strict speed-way lane laws, young boys would occasionally try to gun their monowheels out of the slow lanes into the terribly swift traffic; when they did, accidents did occur. The first time, when they brought David home in the Base ambulance, shaken but unhurt, with the twisted smashed remains of his monowheel, Roger and Ann Strang had breathed weakly, and decided between themselves that the boy should be scolded within an inch of his young life. And the fact that David maintained tenaciously that he had never swerved from the slow monowheel lane didn't bother his parents a bit. They were acquainted with another small-boy frailty. Small boys, on occasion, are inclined to fib.

But the second time, David was not fibbing. Roger Strang *saw* the *accident* the second time. He saw all the circumstances involved. And he realized, with horrible clarity, that someone, somehow, was trying to kill his son.

It had been late on a Saturday afternoon. The free week-ends that the Barrier Base engineers had once enjoyed to take their families for picnics "outside," or to rest and relax, were things of the past, for the work on the Barrier was reaching a critical stage, demanding more and more of the technicians, scientists and engineers engaged in its development. Already diplomatic relations with the Eurasian Combine were becoming more and more impossible; the Barrier *had* to be built, and quickly, or another more terrible New York City would be the result. Roger had never cleared from his mind the flaming picture of that night of horror, just five years before, when the mighty metropolis had burst into radioactive flame, to announce the beginning of the first Atomic War. The year 2078 was engraved in millions of minds as the year of the most horrible—and the shortest—war in all history, for an armistice had been signed not four days after the first bomb had been dropped. An armistice, but an uneasy peace, for neither of the great nations had really known what atomic war would be like until it had happened. And once upon them, they found that atomic war was not practical, for both mighty opponents would have been gutted in a matter of weeks. The armistice had stopped the bombs, but hostilities continued, until the combined scientific forces of one nation could succeed in preparing a defense.

That particular Saturday afternoon had been busy in the Main Labs on the Barrier Base. The problem of erecting a continent-long electronic Barrier to cover the coast of North America was a staggering proposition. Roger Strang was nearly finished and ready for home as dusk was falling. Leaving his work at the desk, he was slipping on his jacket when David came into the lab. He was small for twelve years, with tousled sand-brown hair standing up at odd angles about a sharp, intelligent face. "I came to get you, Daddy," he said.

Roger smiled. "You rode all the way down here—just to go home with me?"

"Maybe we could get some Icy-pops for supper on the way home," David remarked innocently.

Roger grinned broadly and slapped the boy on the back. "You'd sell your soul for an Icy-pop," he grinned.

The corridor was dark. The man and boy walked down to the elevator, and in a moment were swishing down to the dark and deserted lobby below.

David stepped first from the elevator when the men struck. One stood on either side of the door in the shadow. The boy screamed and reeled from the blow across the neck. Suddenly Roger heard the sharp pistol reports. David dropped with a groan, and Roger staggered against the wall from a powerful blow in the face. He shook his head groggily, catching a glimpse of the two men running through the door into the street below, as three or four people ran into the lobby, flushed out by the shots.

*

Roger shouted, pointing to the door, but the people were looking at the boy. Roger sank down beside his son, deft fingers loosening the blouse. The boy's small face was deathly white, fearful sobs choking his breath as he closed his eyes and shivered. Roger searched under his blouse, trying to find the bullet holes—and found to his chagrin that there weren't any bullet holes.

"Where did you feel the gun?"

David pointed vaguely at his lower ribs. "Right there," he said. "It hurt when they shoved the gun at me."

"But they couldn't have pulled the trigger, if the gun was pointed there—" He examined the unbroken skin on the boy's chest, fear tearing through his mind.

A Security man was there suddenly, asking about the accident, taking Roger's name, checking over the boy. Roger resented the tall man in the gray uniform, felt his temper rise at the slightly sarcastic tone of the questions. Finally the trooper stood up, shaking his head. "The boy must have been mistaken," he said. "Kids always have wild stories to tell. Whoever it was may have been after *somebody*, but they weren't aiming for the boy."

Roger scowled. "This boy is no liar," he snapped. "I saw them shoot—"

The trooper shrugged. "Well, he isn't hurt. Why don't you go on home?"

Roger helped the boy up, angrily. "You're not going to do anything about this?"

"What can I do? Nobody saw who the men were."

Roger grabbed the boy's hand, helped him to his feet, and turned angrily to the door. In the failing light outside the improbability of the attack struck through him strongly. He turned to the boy, his face dark. "David," he said evenly, "you wouldn't be making up stories about feeling that gun in your ribs, would you?"

David shook his head vigorously, eyes still wide with fear. "Honest, dad. I told you the truth."

"But they *couldn't* have shot you in the chest without breaking the skin—" He glanced down at the boy's blouse and jacket, and stopped suddenly, seeing the blackened holes in the ripped cloth. He stooped down and sniffed the holes suspiciously, and shivered suddenly in the cold evening air.

The burned holes smelled like gunpowder.

*

"Strang, you must have been wrong." The large man settled back in his chair, his graying hair smoothed over a bald spot. "Someone trying to kill you I could see—there's plenty of espionage going on, and you're doing important work here. But your boy!" The chief of the Barrier Base Security shook his head. "You must have been mistaken."

"But I *wasn't* mistaken!" Roger Strang sat forward in his chair, his hands gripping the arms until his knuckles were white. "I told you exactly what happened. They got him as he came off the elevator, and shot at him. Not at me, Morrel, at my son. They just clubbed me in the face to get me out of the way—"

"What sort of men?" Morrel's eyes were sharp.

Roger scowled, running his hand through his hair. "It was too dark to see. They wore hats and field jackets. The gun could be identified by ballistics. But they were *fast*, Morrel. They knew who they were looking for."

Morrel rose suddenly, his face impatient. "Strang," he said. "You've been here at the Base for quite awhile. Ever since a month after the war, isn't that right? August, 2078? Somewhere around there, I know. But you've been working hard. I think maybe a rest would do you some good—"

"Rest!" Roger exploded. "Look, man—I'm not joking. This isn't the first time. The boy had a monowheel accident three weeks ago, and he swore he was riding in a safe lane where he belonged. It looked like an accident then—now it looks like a murder attempt. The slugs from the gun *must* be in the building—embedded in the plasterwork somewhere. Surely you could try to trace the gun." He glared at the man's impassive face bitterly, "Or maybe you don't want to trace the gun—"

Morrel scowled. "I've already checked on it. The gun wasn't registered in the Base. Security has a check on every firearm within a fifty-mile range. The attackers must have been outsiders."

Roger's face flushed. "That's not true, Morrel," he said softly, "and you know it's not true."

Morrel shrugged. "Have it your own way," he said, indifferently. "Take a rest, Strang. Go home. Get some rest. And don't bother me with any more of your fairy tales." He turned suddenly on Roger. "And be careful what *you* do with guns, Strang. The only thing about this that I *do* know is that somebody shot a pistol off and scared hell out of your son. You were the only one around, as far as I know. I don't know your game, but you'd better be careful—"

*

Strang left Security Headquarters, and crossed across to the Labs, frustrated and angry. His mind spun over the accident—incredulous, but more incredulous that Morrel would practically laugh at him. He stopped by the Labs building to watch the workmen putting up a large electronic projector in one of the test yards. Work was going ahead. But so slowly.

Roger was aware of the tall thin man who had joined him before he looked around. Martin Drengo put a hand on his shoulder. "Been avoiding me lately?"

"Martin!" Roger Strang turned, his face lighting up. "No, not avoiding you—I've been so busy my own wife hasn't seen me in four days. How are things in Maintenance?"

The thin man smiled sadly. "How are things ever in Maintenance? First a railroad breaks down, then there's a steel strike, then some paymaster doesn't make a payroll—the war knocked things for a loop, Roger. Even now things are still loopy. And how are things in Production?"

Roger scowled. "Let's have some coffee," he said.

They sat in a back corner booth of the Base Dispensary as Roger told about David. Martin Drengo listened without interruption. He was a thin man from top to bottom, a shock of unruly black hair topping an almost cadaverous face, blue eyes large behind thick lenses. His whole body was like a skeleton, his fingers long and bony as he lit a cigarette. But the blue eyes were quick, and the nods warm and understanding. He listened, and then he said, "It couldn't have been an outsider?"

Roger shrugged. "Anything is possible. But why? Why go after a kid?"

Drengo hunched his shoulders forward. "I don't get it," he said. "David has done nothing to give him enemies." He drew on his cigarette. "What did Morrel have to say?"

"He laughed at me! Wouldn't even listen to me. Told me to go home and go to bed, that I was all wet. I tell you, Martin, I *saw* it! You know I wouldn't lie, you know I don't see things that don't happen."

"Yes," said Martin, glumly. "I believe you, all right. But I can't see why your son should be the target. You'd be more likely." He stood up, stretching his long legs. "Look, old boy. Take Morrel's advice, at least temporarily. Go home and get some sleep now; you're all worked up. I'll go in and talk to Morrel. Maybe I can handle that old buzzard better than you can."

Roger watched his friend amble down the aisle and out of the store. He felt better now that he had talked to Drengo. Smiling to himself, he finished off his coffee. Many a scrape he and Martin had seen through together. He remembered that night of horror when the bomb fell on the city, his miraculous rescue, the tall thin figure, reflecting the red glare from his glasses, forcing his way through the burning timbers of the building, tearing Roger's leg loose from the rubble covering it; the frightful struggle through the rubbish, fighting off fear-crazed mobs that sought to stop them, rob them, kill them. They had made the long trek together, Martin and he, the Evacuation Road down to Maryland, the Road of Horrors, lined with the rotting corpses of the dead and the soon-dead, the dreadful refuse of that horrible night. Martin Drengo had been a stout friend to Roger; he'd been with Martin the night he'd met Ann; took the ring from Martin's finger when they stood at the altar on their wedding day; shared with Martin his closest confidence.

Roger sighed and paid for the coffee. What to do? The boy was home now, recovering from the shock of the attack. Roger caught an out-bound tri-wheel, and sped down the busy thoroughfare toward his home. If Martin could talk to Morrel, and get something done, perhaps they could get a line. Somehow, perhaps they could trace the attackers. In the morning he'd see Martin again, and they could figure out a scheme.

But he didn't have a chance to see Martin again. For at 11:30 that night, the marauders struck again. For the third time.

*

Through his sleep he heard a door close down below, and sat bolt upright in bed, his heart pounding wildly. Only a tiny sound, the click of a closing door—

Ann was sitting up beside him, brown hair close around her head, her body tense. "Roger!" she whispered. "Did you hear something?"

Roger was out of bed, bounding across the room, into the hall. Blood pounded in his ears as he rushed to David's room, stopped short before the open door.

The shots rang out like whip cracks, and he saw the yellow flame from the guns. There were two men in the dark room, standing at the bed where the boy lay rolled into a terrified knot. The guns cracked again and again, ripping the bedding, bursting the pillow into a shower of feathers, tearing the boy's pajamas from his thin body, a dozen blazing shots—

Roger let out a strangled cry, grabbed one of the men by the throat, in a savage effort to stop the murderous pistols. The other man caught him a coarse blow behind the ear, and he staggered hard against the wall. Dully he heard the door slam, heavy footsteps down the corridor, running down the stairs.

He struggled feebly to his feet, glancing at the still form on the bed. Choking back a sob he staggered down the hall, shouting to Ann as he went down the stairs, redoubling his speed as he heard the purr of autojets in the driveway. In a·moment he was in his own car, frantically stamping on the starter. It started immediately, the motor booming, and the powerful jet engines forced the heavy car ahead dangerously, taking the corner on two of its three wheels. He knew that Ann would call Security, and he raced to gain on the tail lights that were disappearing down the winding residential road to the main highway. Throwing caution to the winds, Roger swerved the car across a front lawn, down between two houses, into an alley, and through another driveway, gaining three blocks. Ahead, at the junction with the main Base highway he saw the long black autojet turn right.

*

Roger snaked into traffic on the highway and bore down on the black car. Traffic was light because of the late hour, but the patrol was on the road and might stop him instead of the killers. The other car was traveling at top speed, swerving around the slower cars. Roger gained slowly. He fingered the spotlight, preparing to snap it in the driver's eyes. Taking a curve at 90, he crept up alongside the black car as he heard the siren of a patrol car behind him. Cursing, he edged over on the black car, snapped the spotlight full in the face of the driver—

The screaming siren forced him off the road, and he braked hard, his hands trembling. A patrolman came over to the car, gun drawn. He took a quick look at Roger, and his face tightened. "Mr. Strang," he said sharply. "We've been looking for you. You're wanted at Security."

"That car," Roger started weakly. "You've got to stop that car I was chasing—"

"Never mind that car," the patrolman snarled. "It's you they want. Hop out. We'll go in the patrol car."

"You've got to stop them—"

The patrolman fingered his gun. "Security wants to talk to you, Mr. Strang. Hop out."

Roger moved dazedly from his car. He didn't question the patrolman; he hardly even heard him. His mind raced in a welter of confusion, trying desperately to refute the brilliant picture in his mind from that split-second that the spotlight had rested on the driver of the black car, trying to fit the impossible pieces into their places. For the second man in the black autojet had been John Morrel, chief of Barrier Base Security, and the driver had been Martin Drengo—

*

The man at the desk was a stranger to Roger Strang. He was an elderly man, stooped, with graying hair and a small clipped mustache that seemed to stick out like antennae. He watched Roger impassively with steel gray eyes, motioning him to a chair.

"You led us a merry chase," he said flatly, his voice brittle. "A very merry chase. The alarm went out for you almost an hour ago."

Strang's cheeks were red with anger. "My son was shot tonight. I was trying to follow the killers—"

"Killers?" The man raised his eyebrows.

"Yes, killers!" Roger snapped. "Do I have to draw you a picture? They shot my son down in his bed."

The gray-haired man stared at him for a long time. "Well," he said finally in a baffled tone. "Now I've heard everything."

It was Roger's turn to stare. "Can't you understand what I've said? My *son was murdered.*"

The gray-haired man flipped a pencil down on the desk impatiently. "Mr. Strang," he said elaborately. "My name is Whitman. I flew down here from Washington tonight, after being called from my bed by the commanding officer of this base. I am the National Chief of the Federal Bureau of Security, Mr. Strang, and I am not interested in fairy tales. I would like you to come off it now, and answer some questions for me. And I don't want double-talk. I want answers. Do I make myself quite clear?"

Roger stared at him, finally nodded his head. "Quite," he said sourly.

Whitman hunched forward in his chair. "Mr. Strang, how long have you been working in the Barrier Base?"

"Five years. Ever since the bombing of New York."

Whitman nodded. "Oh, yes. The bombing of New York." He looked sharply at Roger. "And how old are you, Mr. Strang?"

Roger looked up, surprised. "Thirty-two, of course. You have my records. Why are you asking?"

The gray-haired man lit a cigarette. "Yes, we have your records," he said offhandedly. "Very interesting records, quite normal, quite in order. Nothing out of the ordinary." He stood up and looked out on the dark street. "Just one thing wrong with your records, Mr. Strang. They aren't true."

Roger stared. "This is ridiculous," he blurted. "What do you mean, they aren't true?"

Whitman took a deep breath, and pulled a sheet of paper out of a sheaf on his desk. "It says here," he said, "that you are Roger Strang, and that you were born in Indianola, Iowa, on the fourteenth of June, 2051. That your father was Jason Strang, born 11 August, 2023, in Chicago, Illinois. That you lived in Indianola until you were twelve, when your father moved to New York City, and was employed with the North American Electronics Laboratories. That you entered International Polytechnic Institute at the age of 21, studying physics and electronics, and graduated in June 2075 with the degree of Bachelor of Electronics. That you did further work, taking a Masters and Doctorate in Electronics at Polytech in 2077."

Whitman took a deep breath. "That's what it says here. A very ordinary record. But there is no record there of your birth in Indianola, Iowa, in 2051 or any other time. There is no record there of your father, the alleged Jason Strang, nor in Chicago. No one by the name of Jason Strang was ever employed by North American Electronics. No one by the name of Roger Strang ever attended Polytech." Whitman watched him with cold eyes. "To the best of our knowledge, and according to all available records, *there never was anyone named Roger Strang until after the bombing of New York.*"

Roger sat stock still, his mind racing. "This is silly," he said finally. "Perfectly idiotic. Those schools *must* have records—"

Whitman's face was tight. "They do have records. Complete records. But the name of Roger Strang is curiously missing from the roster of graduates in 2075. Or any other year." He snubbed his cigarette angrily. "I wish you would tell me, and save us both much unpleasantness. *Just who are you, Mr. Strang, and where do you come from?*"

Strang stared at the man, his pulse pounding in his head. Filtering into his mind was a vast confusion, some phrase, some word, some nebulous doubt that frightened him, made him almost believe that gray-haired man in the chair before him. He took a deep breath, clearing his mind of the nagging doubt. "Look here," he said, exasperated. "When I was drafted for the Barrier Base, they checked for my origin, for my education and credentials. If they had been false, I'd have been snapped up right then.

Probably shot—they were shooting people for chewing their fingernails in those days. I wouldn't have stood a chance."

Whitman nodded his head vigorously. "Exactly!" he snapped. "You *should* have been picked up. But you weren't even suspected until we did a little checking after that accident in the Labs building yesterday. Somehow, false credentials got through for you. Security does not like false credentials. I don't know how you did it, but you did. I want to know how."

"But, I tell you—" Roger stood up, fear suddenly growing in his mind. He lit a cigarette, took two nervous puffs, and set it down, forgotten, on the ash-tray. "I have a wife," he said shakily. "I married her in New York City. We had a son, born in a hospital in New York City. He went to school there. Surely there must be some kind of record—"

Whitman smiled grimly, almost mockingly. "Good old New York City," he snarled. "Married there, you say? Wonderful! Son born there? In the one city in the country where that information *can never be checked*. That's very convenient, Mr. Strang. Or whoever you are. I think you'd better talk."

Roger snubbed out the cigarette viciously. "My son," he said after a long pause. "He was murdered tonight. Shot down in his bed—"

The Security Chief's face went white. "Garbage!" he snapped. "What kind of a fool do you think I am, Strang? Your son murdered—bah! When the alarm went out for you I personally drove to your home. Oddly enough this wife of yours wasn't at home, but your son was. Nice little chap. He made us some coffee, and explained that he didn't know where his parents were, because he'd been asleep all night. Quietly asleep in his bed—"

The words were clipped out, and rang in Roger's ears, incredibly. His hand shook violently as he puffed his cigarette, burning his fingers on the short butt. "I don't believe it," he muttered hollowly. "I saw it happen—"

Whitman sneered. "Are you going to talk or not?"

Roger looked up helplessly. "I don't—know—" he said, weakly. "I don't know."

The Security Chief threw up his hands in disgust. "Then we'll do it the hard way," he grated. Flipping an intercom switch, his voice snapped out cold in the still room. "Send in Psych squad," he growled. "We've got a job to do—"

*

Roger Strang lay back on the small bunk, his nerves yammering from the steady barrage, lights still flickering green and red in his eyes. His body was limp, his mind functioning slowly, sluggishly. His eyelids were still heavy from the drugs, his wrists and forehead burning and sore where the electrodes had been attached. His muscles hardly responded when he tried to move, his strength completely gone—washed out. He simply lay there, his shallow breathing returning to him from the dark stone walls.

The inquisition had been savage. The hot lights, the smooth-faced men firing questions, over and over, the drugs, the curious sensation of mouthing nonsense, of hearing his voice rambling on crazily, yet being unable in any way to control it; the hypnotic effect of Whitman's soft voice, the glitter in his steel-gray eyes, and the questions, questions, questions. The lie detector had been going by his side, jerking insanely at his answers, every time the same answers, every time setting the needle into wild gyrations. And finally the foggy, indistinct memory of Whitman mopping his forehead and stamping savagely on a cigarette, and muttering desperately, "It's no use! Lies! Nothing but lies, lies, lies! He *couldn't* be lying under this treatment, but he is. *And he knows he is!*"

Lies? Roger stretched his heavy limbs, his mind struggling up into a tardy rejection. Not lies! He hadn't lied—he had been answering the truth to the questions. He couldn't have been lying, for the answers were there, clear in his memory. And yet—the same nagging doubt crept through, the same feeling that had plagued him throughout the inquisition, the nagging, haunting, horrible conviction, somewhere in the depths of his numb brain that he *was* lying! Something was missing somewhere, some vast gap in his knowledge, something of which he simply was not aware. The incredible turnabout of Martin Drengo, the attack on David, who was killed, but somehow was not dead. He *had* to be lying—

But how could he lie, and still know that he was not lying? His sluggish mind wrestled, trying to choke back the incredible doubt. Somewhere in the morass, the picture of Martin Drengo came through—Drengo, the traitor, who was trying to kill his son—but the conviction swept through again, overpowering, the certain knowledge that Drengo was *not* a traitor, that he must trust Drengo. Drengo was his friend, his stalwart—

HIS AGENT!

Strang sat bolt upright on the cot, his head spinning. The thought had broken through crystal clear in the darkness, revealed itself for the briefest instant, then swirled down again into the foggy gulf. Agent? Why should he have an agent? What purpose? Frantically he scanned his memory for Drengo, down along the dark channels, searching. Drengo had come through the fire, into the burning building, carried him like a child through the flames into safety. Drengo had been best man at his wedding—but he'd been married before the bombing of the city. *Or had he?* Where did Drengo fit in? Was the fire the first time he had seen Drengo?

Something deep in his mind forced its way through, saying NO! YOU HAVE KNOWN HIM ALL YOUR LIFE! Roger fought it back, frantically. Never! Back in Iowa there had been no Drengo. Nor in Chicago. Nor in New York. He hadn't even known him in—IN NEW ALBANY!

*

Roger Strang was on his feet, shaking, cold fear running through his body, his nerves screaming. Had they ruined his mind? He couldn't think straight any more. Telling him things that weren't true, forcing lies into his mind—frightening him with the horrible conviction that his mind was really helpless, full of false data. What had happened to him? Where had the thought of "New Albany" come from? He shivered, now thoroughly frightened. There wasn't any "New Albany." Nowhere in the world. There just *wasn't* any such place.

Could he have two memories? Conflicting memories?

He walked shakily to the door, peered through the small peephole. In the morning they would try again, they had said. He shuddered, terribly afraid. He had felt his mind cracking under the last questioning; another would drive him completely insane. But Drengo would have the answers. Why had he shot little Davey? How did that fit in? Was this false-credential business part of some stupendous scheme against him? Impossible! But what else? He knew with sudden certain conviction that he must see Martin Drengo, immediately, before they questioned him again, before the fear and uncertainty drove him out of his mind. He called tentatively through the peephole, half-hoping to catch a guard's attention. And the call echoed through silent halls.

And then he heard Ann's voice, clear, cool, sharp in the prison darkness. Roger whirled, fear choking the shouts still ringing in his ears, gaped at the woman who stood in his cell—

She was lovelier than he had ever seen her, her tiny body clothed in a glowing fabric which clung to every curve, accenting her trim figure, her slender hips. Brown hair wreathed her lovely face, and Roger choked as the deep longing for her welled up in his throat. Speechlessly he took her in his arms, holding her close, burying his face in her hair, sobbing in joy and relief. And then he saw the glowing circle behind her, casting its eerie light into the far corners of the dark cell. In fiery greenness the ring shimmered in an aurora of violent power, but Ann paid no attention to it. She stepped back and smiled at him, her eyes bright. "Don't be frightened," she said softly, "and don't make any noise. I'm here to help you."

"But where did you come from?" The question forced itself out in a sort of strangled gasp.

"We have—means of going where we want to. And we want you to come with us." She pointed at the glowing ring. "We want to take you back to the time-area from which you came."

Roger goggled at her, confusion welling strong into his mind again. "Ann," he said weakly. "What kind of trick is this?"

She smiled again. "No trick," she said. "Don't ask questions, darling. I know you're confused, but there isn't much time. You'll just have to do what I say right now." She turned to the glowing ring. "We just step through here. Be careful that you don't touch the substance of the portal going through."

Roger Strang approached the glowing ring curiously, peered through, blinked, peered again. It was like staring at an inscrutable flat-black surface in the shadow. No light reflected through it; nothing could be seen. He heard a faint whining as he stood close to the ring, and he looked up at Ann, his eyes wide. "You can't see through it!" he exclaimed.

Ann was crouching on the floor near a small metallic box, gently turning knobs, checking the dial reading against a small chronometer on her wrist. "Steady, darling," she said. "Just follow me, carefully, and don't be afraid. We're going back home—to the time-area where we belong. You and I. I know—you don't remember. And you'll be puzzled, and confused, because the memory substitution job was very thorough. But you'll remember Martin Drengo, and John Morrel, and me. And I was your wife there, too—Are you ready?"

Roger stared at the ring for a moment. "Where are we going?" he asked. "How far ahead? Or behind—?"

"Ahead," she said. "Eighty years ahead—as far as we can go. That will bring us to the present time, the *real* present time, as far as we, and you, are concerned."

She turned abruptly, and stepped through the ring, and vanished as effectively as if she had disintegrated into vapor. Roger felt fear catch at his throat; then he followed her through.

They were standing in a ruins. The cell was gone, the prison, the Barrier Base. The dark sky above was bespeckled with a myriad of stars, and a cool night breeze swept over Roger's cheek. Far in the distance a low rumble came to his ears. "Sounds like a storm coming," he muttered to Ann, pulling his jacket closer around him.

"No storm," she said grimly. "Look!" She pointed a finger toward the northern horizon. Brazen against the blackness the yellow-orange of fire was rising, great spurts of multi-colored flames licking at the horizon. The rumble became a drone, a roar. Ann grasped Roger's arm and pulled him down to cover in the rubble as the invisible squadron swished across the sky, trailing jet streams of horrid orange behind them. Then to the south, in the direction of the flight, the drone of the engines gave way to the hollow boom-booming of bombing, and the southern horizon flared. Then, as suddenly as it had appeared, the rumble died away, leaving the flames licking the sky to the north and south.

Roger shivered. "War," he said. "Eurasia?"

She shook her head. "If only it were. There is no Eurasia now. The dictator took care of that. Nothing but gutted holes, and rubble." She stood up, helping Roger to his feet. Together they filed through the rubbish down to a roadway. Ann dialed a small wrist radio; in a few moments, out of the dark sky, the dim-out lights of a small 'copter came into view, and the machine settled delicately to the road. Two strange men were inside; they saluted Ann, and helped Roger aboard. Swiftly they clamped down the hatch tight, and the ship rose again silently into the air.

"Where are we going?" asked Roger Strang.

"We have a headquarters. Our data must be checked first. We can't reach a decision without checking. Then we can talk."

The 'copter swung high over the blazing inferno of a city far below. Strang glanced from the window, eyes widening at the holocaust. The crater holes were mammoth, huge spires of living flame rising to the sky, leaving mushroom columns of gray-black smoke that glowed an evil red from the furnace on the ground. "Not Eurasia?" Roger asked suddenly, his mind twisting in amazement. "But who? This is America, isn't it?"

"Yes. This is America. There is no Eurasia now. Soon there may not be an America. Nor even an Earth."

Roger looked up at Ann, eyes wide. "But those jet-planes—the bombing—*who is doing the bombing?*"

Ann Strang stared down at the sullen red fires of the city for a moment, her quiet eyes sad. "Those are Martian planes," she said.

*

The 'copter settled silently down into the heart of the city, glowing red from the flames and bombing. They hovered over the shining Palace, still tall, and superb, and intact, gleaming like a blood-streaked jewel in the glowing night. The 'copter settled on the roof of a low building across a large courtyard from the glittering Palace. Ann Strang stepped out, and motioned Roger to follow down a shaft and stairway into a small room below. She knocked at a door, and a strange man dressed in the curious glowing fabric opened it. His face lit up in a smile.

"Roger!" he cried. "We were afraid we couldn't locate you. We weren't expecting the Security to meddle. Someone got suspicious, somewhere, and began checking your references from their sources—and of course they were false. We were lucky to get you back at all, after Security got you." He clapped Roger on the back, and led him into the room.

John Morrel and Martin Drengo were standing near the rounded window, their faces thrown into grotesque relief against the red-orange glow outside. They turned and saluted, and Roger almost cried out, his mind spinning, a thousand questions cutting into his consciousness, demanding answers. But quite suddenly he was feeling a new power, a new effectiveness in his thinking, in his activity. He turned to Martin Drengo, his eyes questioning but no longer afraid. "What year is this?" he asked.

"This is 2165. March, 2165, and you're in New Albany, in the United States of North America. This is the city where you were born, the city you loved—and look at it!"

Roger walked to the window. The court below was full of people now, ragged people, some of them screaming, a disconsolate muttering rising from a thousand throats—burned people, mangled people. They milled about the mammoth courtyard before the glorious Palace, aimlessly, mindlessly. Far down the avenue leading from the Palace Roger could see the people evacuating the city, a long, desolate line of people, strange autos, carts, even animals, running down the broad avenue to escape from the flaming city.

"We're not in danger here," said Drengo, at his elbow. "No fire nor bomb can reach us here—that is the result of your mighty Atlantic Coast Barrier. Nothing more. It never was perfected in time, before the great Eastern Invasion and the second Atomic War. That was due to occur three years after the time-area where we visited. We were trying to stem it, to turn it aside. We don't know yet whether we succeeded or not."

He turned to the tall man standing at the door. "Markson, all the calculations are prepared. The Calc is evaluating the data against the Equation now, figuring all the variables. If our work did any good, we should know it soon." He sighed and pointed to the Palace. "But our fine Dictator is still alive, and the attack on Mars should be starting any minute—If we didn't succeed, nothing in all Time will stop him."

Roger lit a cigarette, his eyes questioning Drengo. "Dictator?"

Drengo sat down and stretched his legs. "The Dictator appeared four years ago, a nobody, a man from the masses of people on the planet. He rose into public favor like a sky-rocket, a remarkable man, an amazing man—a man who could talk to you, and control your thoughts in a single interview. There has never been a man with such personal magnetism and power, Roger, in all the history of Earth. A man who raised himself from nothing into absolute Dictatorship, and has handled the world according to his whim ever since.

"He is only a young man, Roger, just 32 years of age, but an irresistible man who can win anything from anybody. He writhed into the presidency first, and then deliberately set about rearranging the government to suit himself. And the people let him get away with it, followed him like sheep. And then he was Dictator, and he began turning the social and economic balance of the planet into a whirlwind. And then came Mars."

Martin stretched again, and lit a cigarette, his thin face grave in the darkened room. "The first landing was thirty years ago, and the possibilities for rich and peaceful commerce between Earth and Mars were clear from the first. Mars had what Earth lacked: the true civilization, the polished culture, the lasting socio-economic balance, the permanent peace. Mars could have taught us so much. She could have guided us out of the mire of war and hatred that we have been wallowing in for centuries. But the

Dictator put an end to those possibilities." Drengo shrugged. "He was convinced that the Martians were weak, backward, decadent. He saw their uranium, their gold, their jewelry, their labor—and started on a vast impossible imperialism. If he had had his way, he would have stripped the planet in three years, but the Martians fought against us, turned from peace to suspicion, and finally to open revolt. And the Dictator could not see. He mobilized Earth for total war against Mars, draining our resources, decimating our population, building rockets, bombs, guns—" He stopped for a moment, breathing deeply. "But the Dictator didn't know what he was doing. He had never been on Mars. He has never seen Martians. He had no idea what they think, what they are capable of doing. He doesn't know what we know—that the Martians will win. He doesn't realize that the Martians can carry out a war for years without shaking their economy one iota, while he has drained our planet to such a degree that a war of more than two or three months will break us in half. He doesn't know that Mars can win, and that the Earth can't—"

Roger walked across the room, thoughtfully, his mind fitting pieces into place. "But where do I come in? David—Ann—I don't understand—"

Drengo looked Roger straight in the eye. "The Dictator's name," he said, "is Farrel Strang."

Roger stopped still. "Strang?" he echoed.

"Your son, Roger. Yours and Ann's."

"But—you said the Dictator was only 32—" Roger trailed off, regarding Ann in amazement.

Martin smiled. "People don't grow old so quickly nowadays," he said. "You are 57 years old, Roger. Ann is 53." He leaned back in his chair, his gaunt smile fading. "The Dictator has not been without opposition. You, his parents, opposed him at the very start, and he cast you off. People wiser than the crowds were able to rebuff his powerful personal appeal, to see through the robe of glory he had wrapped around himself. He has opposition, but he has built himself an impregnable fortress, and dealt swift death to any persons suspected of treason. A few have escaped—scientists, technologists, sociologists, physicists. The work of one group of men gave us a weapon which we hoped to use to destroy the Dictator. We found a way to move back in Time. We could leave the normal time-stream and move to any area of past time. So four of us went back, searching for the core of the economic and social upheaval on Earth, and trying to destroy the Dictator before he was born. Given Time travel, it should have been possible. So we went back—myself, John Morrel, Ann Strang, and you."

Roger shook his head, a horrible thought forming in his mind. "You were trying to kill David—my son—" he stopped short. "David *couldn't* have been my son!" He whirled on Martin Drengo. "*Who was that boy?*"

Martin looked away then, his face white. "The boy was your father," he said.

*

The drone of the jet bombers came again, whining into the still room. Roger Strang stood very still, staring at the gaunt man. Slowly the puzzle was beginning to fit together, and horror filtered into his mind. "My father—" he said. "Only twelve years old, but he was to be my father." He stared helplessly at the group in the room. "You were trying—to kill him!"

Martin Drengo stood up, his lean face grave. "We were faced with a terrific problem. Once we returned to a time-area, we had no way of knowing to what extent we could effect people and events that had already happened. We had to go back, to fit in, somehow, in an area where we never had been, to *make* things happen that had never happened before. We knew that if there was any way of doing it, we had to destroy Farrel Strang. But the patterns of history which had allowed him to rise had to be altered, too; destroying the man would not have been enough. So we tried to destroy him in the time-area where the leading time-patterns of *our* time had been formed. We had to kill his grandfather."

Roger shivered. "But if you had killed David—what would have happened *to me?*"

"Presumably the same thing that would have happened to the Dictator. In theory, *if we had succeeded* in killing your father, David, both you and the Dictator would have ceased to exist." Drengo took a deep breath. "The idea was yours, Roger. You knew the terrible damage your son was doing as Dictator. It was a last resort, and Ann and John and I pleaded with you to reconsider. But it was the obvious step."

Ann walked over to Roger, her face pale. "You insisted, Roger. So we did what we could to make it easy. We used the Dictator's favorite trick—a psycho-purge—to clear your mind of all conscious and subconscious memory of your true origin and environment, replacing it with a history and memory of the past-time area where we were going. We chose the contact-time carefully, so that we appeared in New York in the confusion of the bombing of 2078, making sure that your records would stand up under all but the closest examination. From then on, when Martin carried you out from the fire, you stored your own memory of that time-area and became a legitimate member of that society."

"But how could we pose as David's *parents*, if he was my father?"

Ann smiled. "Both David's parents were killed in the New York bombing; we knew that David survived, and we knew where he could be found. There was a close physical resemblance between you and the boy, though actually the resemblance was backwards, and he accepted you as a foster-father without question. With you equipped with a complete memory of your marriage to me in that time, of David's birth, and of your own history before and after the bombing of New York, you fit in well and played the part to perfection. Also, you acted as a control, to guide us, since you had no conscious knowledge beyond that time-area. Martin and Morrel were to be the assassins, the Intruders, and I was to keep tabs on you—"

"And the success of the attempt?"

Ann's face fell. "We don't know yet. We don't know what we accomplished, whether we stemmed the war or not—"

The tall man who had stepped into the room moved forward and threw a sheaf of papers on the floor, his face heavy with anger, his voice hoarse. "Yes, I'm afraid we do know," he said bitterly.

Martin Drengo whirled on him, his face white. "What do you mean, Markson?"

The tall man sank down in a chair tiredly. "We've lost, Martin. We don't need these calculations to tell. The word was just broadcast on the telecast. Farrel Strang's armada has just begun its attack on Mars—"

*

For a moment the distant bombing was the only sound in the room. Then Martin Drengo said, "So he gave the order. And we've lost."

"We only had a theory to work on," said Morrel, staring gloomily at the curved window. "A theory and an equation. The theory said that a man returning through time could alter the social and technological trends of the people and times to which he returned, in order to change history that was already past. The theory said that if we could turn the social patterns and technological trends just slightly away from what they were, we could alter the entire makeup of society in our own time. And the Equation was the tool, the final check on any change. The Equation which evaluates the sum of social, psychological and energy factors in any situation, any city or nation or human society. The Equation has been proven, checked time and time again, but the theory didn't fit it. The theory was wrong."

Roger Strang sat up, suddenly alert. "That boy," he said, his voice sharp. "You nearly made a sieve of him, trying to shoot him. Why didn't he die?"

"Because he was on a high-order variable. Picture it this way: From any point in time, the possible future occurrences could be seen as vectors, an infinite number of possible vectors. Every activity that makes an alteration, or has any broad effect on the future is a high-order variable, but many activities have no grave implications for future time, and could be considered unimportant, or low-order variables. If a man turns a corner and sees something that stimulates him into writing a world-shaking manifesto, the high-order variable would have started when he decided to turn the corner instead of going the other way. But if he took one way home instead of another, and nothing of importance occurred as a result of the decision, a low-order variable would be set up.

"We found that the theory of alterations held quite well, for low-order variables. Wherever we appeared, whatever we did, we set up a definite friction in the normal time-stream, a distortion, like pulling a taut rubber band out. And we could produce changes—on low-order variables. But the elasticity of the distortion was so great as to warp the change back into the time-stream without causing any lasting alteration. When it came to high-order changes, *we simply couldn't make any*. We tried putting wrong data into the machines that were calculating specifications for the Barrier, and the false data went in, but the answers that came out were answers that *should* have appeared with the *right* data. We tried to commit a murder, to kill David Strang, and try as we would we couldn't do it. Because it would have altered a high-order variable, and they simply *wouldn't be altered*!"

"But you, Morrel," Roger exclaimed. "How about you? You were top man in the Barrier Base Security office. You must have made an impression."

Morrel smiled tiredly. "I really thought I had, time after time. I would start off a series of circumstances that should have had a grave alterative effect, and it would look for awhile as if a long-range change was going to be affected—and then it would straighten itself out again, with no important change occurring. It was maddening. We worked for five years trying to make even a small alteration—and brought back our data—" He pointed to the papers on the floor. "There are the calculations, applied on the Equation. Meaningless. We accomplished nothing. And the Dictator is still there."

Drengo slumped in his chair. "And he's started the war. The real attack. This bombardment outside is nothing. There are fifteen squadrons of space-destroyers already unloading atomic bombs on the surface of Mars, and that's the end, for us. Farrel Strang has started a war he can never finish—"

Roger Strang turned sharply to Drengo. "This Dictator," he said. "Where is he? Why can't he be reached now, and destroyed?"

"The Barrier. He can't be touched in the Palace. He has all his offices there, all his controls, and he won't let anyone in since the attempted assassination three months ago. He's safe there, and we can't touch him."

Roger scowled at the control panel on the wall. "How does this time-portal work?" he asked. "You say it can take us back—*why not forward?*"

"No good. The nature of Time itself makes that impossible. At the present instant of Time, everything that has happened has happened. The three-dimensional world in which we live has passed through the fourth temporal dimension, and nothing can alter it. But at this instant there are an infinite number of things that could happen next. The future is an infinite series of variables, and there's no conceivable way to predict which variable will actually be true."

Roger Strang sat up straight, staring at Drengo. "Will that portal work both ways?" he asked tensely.

Drengo stared at him blankly. "You mean, can it be reverse-wired? I suppose so. But—anyone trying to move into the future would necessarily become an *infinity* of people—he couldn't maintain his identity, because he'd have to have a body in every one of an infinite number of places he might be—"

"*—until the normal time stream caught up with him in the future!* And then he'd be in whatever place he fit!" Roger's voice rose excitedly. "Martin, can't you see the implications? Send me ahead—just a little ahead, an hour or so—and let me go into the Palace. If I moved my consciousness to the place where the Palace should be, where the Dictator should be, then when normal time caught up with me, *I could kill him*!"

Drengo was on his feet, staring at Roger with rising excitement. Suddenly he glanced at his watch. "By God!" he muttered. "*Maybe you could—*"

*

Blackness.

He had no body, no form. There was no light, no shape, nothing but eternal, dismal, unbroken blackness. This was the Void, the place where time had not yet come. Roger Strang shuddered, and felt the cold chill of the blackness creep into his marrow. He had to move. He wanted to move, to find the right place, moving with the infinity of possible bodies. A stream of consciousness was all he could grasp, for the blackness enclosed everything. A sort of death, but he knew he was not dead. Blackness was around him, and in him, and through him.

He could feel the timelessness, the total absence of anything. Suddenly he felt the loneliness, for he knew there was no going back. He had to transfer his consciousness, his mind, to the place where the Dictator was, hoping against hope that he could find the place before time caught him wedged in the substance of the stone walls of the Palace. He reached the place that *should* be right, and waited—

And waited. There was no time in this place, and he had to wait for the normal time stream. The blackness worked at his mind, filling him with fear, choking him, making him want to scream in frightened agony—waiting—

And suddenly, abruptly, he was standing in a brightly lighted room. The arched dome over his head sparkled with jewels, and through paneled windows the red glow of the city's fires flickered grimly. *He was in the Palace!*

He looked about swiftly, and crossed the room toward a huge door. In an instant he had thrown it open. The bright lights of the office nearly blinded him, and the man behind the desk rose angrily, caught Roger's eye full—

Roger gasped, his eyes widening. For a moment he thought he was staring into a mirror. For the man behind the desk, clothed in a rich glowing tunic was a living image of—*himself!*

The Dictator's face opened into startled surprise and fear as he recognized Roger, and a frightened cry came from his lips. There was no one else in the room, but his eyes ran swiftly to the visiphone. With careful precision Roger Strang brought the heat-pistol to eye level, and pulled the trigger. Farrel Strang crumpled slowly from the knees, a black hole scorched in his chest.

Roger ran to the fallen man, stared into his face incredulously. His son—and himself, as alike as twin dolls, for all the age difference. Drengo's words rose in Roger's mind: "Medicine is advanced, you know. People don't grow old so soon these days—"

Swiftly Roger slipped from his clothes, an impossibly bold idea translating itself into rapid action. He stripped the glowing tunic from the man's flaccid body, and slipped his arms into the sleeves, pulling the cape in close to cover the burned spot.

He heard a knock on the door. Frantically he forced the body under the heavy desk, and sat down in the chair behind it, eyes wide with fear. "Come in," he croaked.

A young deputy stepped through the door, approached the desk deferentially. "The first reports, sir," he said, looking straight at Roger. Not a flicker of suspicion crossed his face. "The attack is progressing as expected."

"Turn all reports over to my private teletype," Roger snapped. The man saluted. "Immediately, sir!" He turned and left the room, closing the door behind him.

Roger panted, closing his eyes in relief. He could pass! Turning to the file, he examined the detailed plans for the Martian attack; the numbers of ships, the squadron leaders, the zero hours—then he was at the teletype keyboard, passing on the message of peace, the message to stop the War with Mars, to make an armistice; ALL SQUADRONS AND SHIPS ATTENTION: CEASE AND DESIST IN ATTACK PLANS: RETURN TO TERRA IMMEDIATELY: BY ORDER OF FARREL STRANG.

Wildly he tore into the files, ripping out budget reports, stabilization plans, battle plans, evacuation plans. It would be simple to dispose of the Dictator's body as that of an imposter, an assassin—and simply take control himself in Farrel's place. They would carry on with *his* plans, *his* direction. And an era of peace, and stability and rich commerce would commence at long last. The sheaf of papers grew larger and larger as Roger emptied out the files: plans of war, plans of conquest, of slavery—he aimed the heat-pistol at the pile, saw it spring into yellow flame, and circle up to the vaulted ceiling in blue smoke.

*

And then he sat down, panting, and flipped the visiphone switch. "Send one man, unarmed, to the building across the courtyard. Have him bring Martin Drengo to me."

The deputy's eyes widened on the screen. "Unarmed, sir?"

"Unarmed," Roger repeated. "By order of your Dictator."

BEAR TRAP

The man's meteoric rise as a peacemaker in a nation tired by the long years of war made the truth even more shocking.

The huge troop transport plane eased down through the rainy drizzle enshrouding New York International Airport at about five o'clock in the evening. Tom Shandor glanced sourly through the port at the wet landing strip, saw the dim landing lights reflected in the steaming puddles. On an adjacent field he could see the rows and rows of jet fighters, wings up in the foggy rain, poised like ridiculous birds in the darkness. With a sigh he ripped the sheet of paper from the small, battered portable typewriter on his lap, and zipped the machine up in its slicker case.

Across the troop hold the soldiers were beginning to stir, yawning, shifting their packs, collecting their gear. Occasionally they stared at Shandor as if he were totally alien to their midst, and he shivered a little as he collected the sheets of paper scattered on the deck around him, checked the date, 27 September, 1982, and rolled them up to fit in the slim round mailing container. Ten minutes later he was shouldering his way through the crowd of khaki-clad men, scowling up at the sky, his nondescript fedora jammed down over his eyes to keep out the rain, slicker collar pulled up about his ears. At the gangway he stopped before a tired-looking lieutenant and flashed the small fluorescent card in his palm. "Public Information Board."

The officer nodded wearily and gave his coat and typewriter a cursory check, then motioned him on. He strode across the wet field, scowling at the fog, toward the dimmed-out waiting rooms.

He found a mailing chute, and popped the mailing tube down the slot as if he were glad to be rid of it. Into the speaker he said: "Special Delivery. PIB business. It goes to press tonight."

The female voice from the speaker said something, and the red "clear" signal blinked. Shandor slipped off his hat and shook it, then stopped at a coffee machine and extracted a cup of steaming stuff from the bottom after trying the coin three times. Finally he walked across the room to an empty video booth, and sank down into the chair with an exhausted sigh. Flipping a switch, he waited several minutes for an operator to appear. He gave her a number, and then said, "Let's scramble it, please."

"Official?"

He showed her the card, and settled back, his whole body tired. He was a tall man, rather slender, with flat, bland features punctuated only by blond caret-shaped eyebrows. His grey eyes were heavy-lidded now, his mouth an expressionless line as he waited, sunk back into his coat with a long-cultivated air of lifeless boredom. He watched the screen without interest as it bleeped a time or two, then shifted into the familiar scrambled-image pattern. After a moment he muttered the Public Information Board audio-code words, and saw the screen even out into the clear image of a large, heavyset man at a desk.

"Hart," said Shandor. "Story's on its way. I just dropped it from the Airport a minute ago, with a rush tag on it. You should have it for the morning editions."

The big man in the screen blinked, and his heavy face lit up. "The story on the Rocket Project?"

Shandor nodded. "The whole scoop. I'm going home now." He started his hand for the cutoff switch.

"Wait a minute—" Hart picked up a pencil and fiddled with it for a moment. He glanced over his shoulder, and his voice dropped a little. "Is the line scrambled?"

Shandor nodded.

"What's the scoop, boy? How's the Rocket Project coming?"

Shandor grinned wryly. "Read the report, daddy. Everything's just ducky, of course—it's all ready for press. You've got the story, why should I repeat it?"

Hart scowled impatiently. "No, no— I mean the *scoop*. The real stuff. How's the Project going?"

"Not so hot." Shandor's face was weary. "Material cutoff is holding them up something awful. Among other things. The sabotage has really fouled up the west coast trains, and shipments haven't been coming through on schedule. You know—they ask for one thing, and get the wrong weight, or their supplier is out of material, or something goes wrong. And there's personnel trouble, too—too much direction and too little work. It's beginning to look as if they'll never get going. And now it looks like there's going to be another administration shakeup, and you know what that means—"

Hart nodded thoughtfully. "They'd better get hopping," he muttered. "The conference in Berlin is on the skids—it could be hours now." He looked up. "But you got the story rigged all right?"

Shandor's face flattened in distaste. "Sure, sure. You know me, Hart. Anything to keep the people happy. Everything's running as smooth as satin, work going fine, expect a test run in a month, and we should be on the moon in half a year, more or less, maybe, we hope—the usual swill. I'll be in to work out the war stories in the morning. Right now I'm for bed."

He snapped off the video before Hart could interrupt, and started for the door. The rain hit him, as he stepped out, with a wave of cold wet depression, but a cab slid up to the curb before him and he stepped in. Sinking back he tried to relax, to get his stomach to stop complaining, but he couldn't fight the feeling of almost physical illness sweeping over him. He closed his eyes and sank back, trying to drive the ever-plaguing thoughts from his mind, trying to focus on something pleasant, almost hoping that his long-starved conscience might give a final gasp or two and die altogether. But deep in his mind he knew that his screaming conscience was almost the only thing that held him together.

Lies, he thought to himself bitterly. White lies, black lies, whoppers—you could take your choice. There should be a flaming neon sign flashing across the sky, telling all people: "Public Information Board, Fabrication Corporation, fabricating of all lies neatly and expeditiously done." He squirmed, feeling the rebellion grow in his mind. Propaganda, they called it. A nice word, such a very handy word, covering a multitude of seething pots. PIB was the grand clearing house, the last censor of censors, and he, Tom Shandor, was the Chief Fabricator and Purveyor of Lies.

He shook his head, trying to get a breath of clean air in the damp cab. Sometimes he wondered where it was leading, where it would finally end up, what would happen if the people ever really learned, or ever listened to the clever ones who tried to sneak the truth into print somewhere. But people couldn't be told the truth, they had to be coddled, urged, pushed along. They had to be kept somehow happy, somehow hopeful, they had to be kept whipped up to fever pitch, because the long, long years of war and near war had exhausted them, wearied them beyond natural resiliency. No, they had to be spiked, urged and goaded—what would happen if they learned?

He sighed. No one, it seemed, could do it as well as he. No one could take a story of bitter diplomatic fighting in Berlin and simmer it down to a public-palatable "peaceful and progressive meeting;" no one could quite so skillfully reduce the bloody fighting in India to a mild "enemy losses topping American losses twenty to one, and our boys are fighting staunchly, bravely,"— No one could write out the lies quite so neatly, so smoothly as Tom Shandor—

The cab swung in to his house, and he stepped out, tipped the driver, and walked up the walk, eager for the warm dry room. Coffee helped sometimes when he felt this way, but other things helped even more. He didn't even take his coat off before mixing and downing a stiff rye-and-ginger, and he was almost forgetting his unhappy conscience by the time the video began blinking.

He flipped the receiver switch and sat down groggily, blinked at John Hart's heavy face as it materialized on the screen. Hart's eyes were wide, his voice tight and nervous as he leaned forward. "You'd better get into the office pronto," he said, his eyes bright. "You've *really* got a story to work on now—"

Shandor blinked. "The War—"

Hart took a deep breath. "Worse," he said. "David Ingersoll is dead."

*

Tom Shandor shouldered his way through the crowd of men in the anteroom, and went into the inner office. Closing the door behind him coolly, he faced the man at the desk, and threw a thumb over his shoulder. "Who're the goons?" he growled. "You haven't released a story yet—?"

John Hart sighed, his pinkish face drawn. "The press. I don't know how they got the word—there hasn't been a word released, but—" He shrugged and motioned Shandor to a seat. "You know how it goes."

Shandor sat down, his face blank, eyeing the Information chief woodenly. The room was silent for a moment, a tense, anticipatory silence. Then Hart said: "The Rocket story was great, Tommy. A real writing job. You've got the touch, when it comes to a ticklish news release—"

Shandor allowed an expression of distaste to cross his face. He looked at the chubby man across the desk and felt the distaste deepen and crystallize. John Hart's face was round, with little lines going up from the eyes, an almost grotesque, burlesque-comic face that belied the icy practical nature of the man behind it. A thoroughly distasteful face, Shandor thought. Finally he said, "The story, John. On Ingersoll. Let's have it, straight out."

Hart shrugged his stocky shoulders, spreading his hands. "Ingersoll's dead," he said. "That's all there is to it. He's stone-cold dead."

"But he can't be dead!" roared Shandor, his face flushed. "We just can't *afford* to have him dead—"

Hart looked up wearily. "Look, I didn't kill him. He went home from the White House this evening, apparently sound enough, after a long, stiff, nasty conference with the President. Ingersoll wanted to go to Berlin and call a showdown at the International conference there, and he had a policy brawl with the President, and the President wouldn't let him go, sent an undersecretary instead, and threatened to kick Ingersoll out of the cabinet unless he quieted down. Ingersoll got home at 4:30, collapsed at 5:00, and he was dead before the doctor arrived. Cerebral hemorrhage, pretty straightforward. Ingersoll's been killing himself for years—he knew it, and everyone else in Washington knew it. It was bound to happen sooner or later."

"He was trying to prevent a war," said Shandor dully, "and he was all by himself. Nobody else wanted to stop it, nobody that mattered, at any rate. Only the people didn't want war, and who ever listens to them? Ingersoll got the people behind him, so they gave him a couple of Nobel Peace Prizes, and made him Secretary of State, and then cut his throat every time he tried to do anything. No wonder he's dead—"

Hart shrugged again, eloquently indifferent. "So he was a nice guy, he wanted to prevent a war. As far as I'm concerned, he was a pain in the neck, the way he was forever jumping down Information's throat, but he's dead now, he isn't around any more—" His eyes narrowed sharply. "The important thing, Tommy, is that the people won't like it that he's dead. They trusted him. He's been the people's Golden Boy, their last-ditch hope for peace. If they think their last chance is gone with his death, they're going to be mad. They won't like it, and there'll be hell to pay—"

Shandor lit a smoke with trembling fingers, his eyes smouldering. "So the people have to be eased out of the picture," he said flatly. "They've got to get the story so they won't be so angry—"

Hart nodded, grinning. "They've got to have a real story, Tommy. Big, blown up, what a great guy he was, defender of the peace, greatest, most influential man America has turned out since the half-century—you know what they lap up, the usual garbage, only on a slightly higher plane. They've got to think that he's really saved them, that he's turned over the reins to other hands just as trustworthy as his—you can give the president a big hand there—they've got to think his work is the basis of our present foreign policy—can't you see the implications? It's got to be spread on with a trowel, laid on skillfully—"

Shandor's face flushed deep red, and he ground the stub of his smoke out viciously. "I'm sick of this stuff, Hart," he exploded. "I'm sick of you, and I'm sick of this whole rotten setup, this business of writing reams and reams of lies just to keep things under control. Ingersoll was a great man, a *really* great man, and he was *wasted*, thrown away. He worked to make peace, and he got laughed at. He hasn't done a thing—because he couldn't. Everything he has tried has been useless, wasted. *That's* the truth—why not tell that to the people?"

Hart stared. "Get hold of yourself," he snapped. "You know your job. There's a story to write. The life of David Ingersoll. It has to go down smooth." His dark eyes shifted to his hands, and back sharply to Shandor. "A propagandist has to write it, Tommy—an ace propagandist. You're the only one I know that could do the job."

"Not me," said Shandor flatly, standing up. "Count me out. I'm through with this, as of now. Get yourself some other whipping boy. Ingersoll was one man the people could trust. And he was one man I could never face. I'm not good enough for him to spit on, and I'm not going to sell him down the river now that he's dead."

With a little sigh John Hart reached into the desk. "That's very odd," he said softly. "Because Ingersoll left a message for you—"

Shandor snapped about, eyes wide. "Message—?"

The chubby man handed him a small envelope. "Apparently he wrote that a long time ago. Told his daughter to send it to Public Information Board immediately in event of his death. Read it."

Shandor unfolded the thin paper, and blinked unbelieving:

In event of my death during the next few months, a certain amount of biographical writing will be inevitable. It is my express wish that this writing, in whatever form it may take, be done by Mr. Thomas L. Shandor, staff writer of the Federal Public Information Board.

I believe that man alone is qualified to handle this assignment.

(Signed) David P. Ingersoll
Secretary of State,
United States of America.
4 June, 1981

Shandor read the message a second time, then folded it carefully and placed it in his pocket, his forehead creased. "I suppose you want the story to be big," he said dully.

Hart's eyes gleamed a moment of triumph. "As big as you can make it," he said eagerly. "Don't spare time or effort, Tommy. You'll be relieved of all assignments until you have it done—if you'll take it."

"Oh, yes," said Shandor softly. "I'll take it."

*

He landed the small PIB 'copter on an airstrip in the outskirts of Georgetown, haggled with Security officials for a few moments, and grabbed an old weatherbeaten cab, giving the address of the Ingersoll estate as he settled back in the cushions. A small radio was set inside the door; he snapped it on, fiddled with the dial until he found a PIB news report. And as he listened he felt his heart sink lower and lower, and the old familiar feeling of dirtiness swept over him, the feeling of being a part in an enormous, overpowering scheme of corruption and degradation. The Berlin conference was reaching a common meeting ground, the report said, with Russian, Chinese, and American officials making the first real progress in the week of talks. Hope rising for an early armistice on the Indian front. Suddenly he hunched forward, blinking in surprise as the announcer continued the broadcast: "The Secretary of State, David Ingersoll, was stricken with a slight head cold this evening on the eve of his departure for the Berlin Conference, and was advised to postpone the trip temporarily. John Harris Darby, first undersecretary, was dispatched in his place. Mr. Ingersoll expressed confidence that Mr. Darby would be able to handle the talks as well as himself, in view of the optimistic trend in Berlin last night—"

Shandor snapped the radio off viciously, a roar of disgust rising in his throat, cut off just in time. Lies, lies, lies. Some people *knew* they were lies—what could they really think? People like David Ingersoll's wife—

Carefully he reined in his thoughts, channelled them. He had called the Ingersoll home the night before, announcing his arrival this morning—

The taxi ground up a gravelled driveway, stopped before an Army jeep at the iron-grilled gateway. A Security Officer flipped a cigarette onto the ground, shaking his head. "Can't go in, Secretary's orders."

Shandor stepped from the cab, briefcase under his arm. He showed his card, scowled when the officer continued shaking his head. "Orders say *nobody*—"

"Look, blockhead," Shandor grated. "If you want to hang by your toes, I can put through a special check-line to Washington to confirm my appointment here. I'll also recommend you for the salt mines."

The officer growled, "Wise guy," and shuffled into the guard shack. Minutes later he appeared again, jerked his thumb toward the estate. "Take off," he said. "See that you check here at the gate before you leave."

He was admitted to the huge house by a stone-faced butler, who led him through a maze of corridors into a huge dining room. Morning sunlight gleamed through a glassed-in wall, and Shandor stopped at the door, almost speechless.

He knew he'd seen the girl somewhere. At one of the Washington parties, or in the newspapers. Her face was unmistakable; it was the sort of face that a man never forgets once he glimpses it—thin, puckish, with wide-set grey eyes that seemed both somber and secretly amused, a full, sensitive mouth, and blonde hair, exceedingly fine, cropped close about her ears. She was eating her breakfast, a rolled up newspaper by her plate, and as she looked up, her eyes were not warm. She just stared at Shandor angrily for a moment, then set down her coffee cup and threw the paper to the floor with a slam. "You're Shandor, I suppose."

Shandor looked at the paper, then back at her. "Yes, I'm Tom Shandor. But you're not Mrs. Ingersoll—"

"A profound observation. Mother isn't interested in seeing anyone this morning, particularly you." She motioned to a chair. "You can talk to me if you want to."

Shandor sank down in the proffered seat, struggling to readjust his thinking. "Well," he said finally. "I—I wasn't expecting you—" he broke into a grin—"but I should think you could help. You know what I'm trying to do—I mean, about your father. I want to write a story, and the logical place to start would be with his family—"

The girl blinked wide eyes innocently. "Why don't you start with the newspaper files?" she asked, her voice silky. "You'd find all sorts of information about daddy there. Pages and pages—"

"No, no— I don't want that kind of information. You're his daughter, Miss Ingersoll, you could tell me about him as a man. Something about his personal life, what sort of man he was—"

She shrugged indifferently, buttered a piece of toast, as Shandor felt most acutely the pangs of his own missed breakfast. "He got up at seven every morning," she said. "He brushed his teeth and ate breakfast. At nine o'clock the State Department called for him—"

Shandor shook his head unhappily. "No, no, that's not what I mean."

"Then perhaps you'd tell me precisely what you *do* mean?" Her voice was clipped and hard.

Shandor sighed in exasperation. "The personal angle. His likes and dislikes, how he came to formulate his views, his relationship with his wife, with you—"

"He was a kind and loving father," she said, her voice mocking. "He loved to read, he loved music—oh, yes, put that down, he was a *great* lover of music. His wife was the apple of his eye, and he tried, for all the duties of his position, to provide us with a happy home life—"

"Miss Ingersoll."

She stopped in mid-sentence, her grey eyes veiled, and shook her head slightly. "That's not what you want, either?"

Shandor stood up and walked to a window, looking out over the wide veranda. Carefully he snubbed his cigarette in an ashtray, then turned sharply to the girl. "Look. If you want to play games, I can play games too. Either you're going to help me, or you're not—it's up to you. But you forget one thing. I'm a propagandist. I might say I'm a very expert propagandist. I can tell a true story from a false one. You won't get anywhere lying to me, or evading me, and if you choose to try, we can call it off right now. You know exactly the type of information I need from you. Your father was a great man, and he rates a fair shake in the write-ups. I'm asking you to help me."

Her lips formed a sneer. "And *you're* going to give him a fair shake, I'm supposed to believe." She pointed to the newspaper. "With garbage like that? Head cold!" Her face flushed, and she turned her back angrily. "I know your writing, Mr. Shandor. I've been exposed to it for years. You've never written an honest, true story in your life, but you always want the truth to start with, don't you? I'm to give you the truth, and let you do what you want with it, is that the idea? No dice, Mr. Shandor. And you even have the gall to brag about it!"

Shandor flushed angrily. "You're not being fair. This story is going to press straight and true, every word of it. This is one story that won't be altered."

And then she was laughing, choking, holding her sides, as the tears streamed down her cheeks. Shandor watched her, reddening, anger growing up to choke him. "I'm not joking," he snapped. "I'm breaking with the routine, do you understand? I'm through with the lies now, I'm writing this one straight."

She wiped her eyes and looked at him, bitter lines under her smile. "You couldn't do it," she said, still laughing. "You're a fool to think so. You could write it, and you'd be out of a job so fast you wouldn't know what hit you. But you'd never get it into print. And you know it. You'd never even get the story to the inside offices."

Shandor stared at her. "That's what you think," he said slowly. "This story will get to the press if it kills me."

The girl looked up at him, eyes wide, incredulous. "You *mean* that, don't you?"

"I never meant anything more in my life."

She looked at him, wonderingly, motioned him to the table, a faraway look in her eyes. "Have some coffee," she said, and then turned to him, her eyes wide with excitement. The sneer was gone from her face, the coldness and hostility, and her eyes were pleading. "If there were some way to do it, if you really meant what you said, if you'd really *do* it—give people a true story—"

Shandor's voice was low. "I told you, I'm sick of this mill. There's something wrong with this country, something wrong with the world. There's a rottenness in it, and your father was fighting to cut out the rottenness. This story is going to be straight, and it's going to be printed if I get shot for treason. And it could split things wide open at the seams."

She sat down at the table. Her lower lip trembled, and her voice was tense with excitement. "Let's get out of here," she said. "Let's go someplace where we can talk—"

*

They found a quiet place off the business section in Washington, one of the newer places with the small closed booths, catering to people weary of eavesdropping and overheard conversations. Shandor ordered beers, then lit a smoke and leaned back facing Ann Ingersoll. It occurred to him that she was exceptionally lovely, but he was almost frightened by the look on her face, the suppressed excitement, the cold, bitter lines about her mouth. Incongruously, the thought crossed his mind that he'd hate to have this woman against him. She looked as though she would be capable of more than he'd care to tangle with. For all her lovely face there was an edge of thin ice to her smile, a razor-sharp, dangerous quality that made him curiously uncomfortable. But now she was nervous, withdrawing a cigarette from his pack with trembling fingers, fumbling with his lighter until he struck a match for her. "Now," he said. "Why the secrecy?"

She glanced at the closed door to the booth. "Mother would kill me if she knew I was helping you. She hates you, and she hates the Public Information Board. I think dad hated you, too."

Shandor took the folded letter from his pocket. "Then what do you think of this?" he asked softly. "Doesn't this strike you a little odd?"

She read Ingersoll's letter carefully, then looked up at Tom, her eyes wide with surprise. "So this is what that note was. This doesn't wash, Tom."

"You're telling me it doesn't wash. Notice the wording. 'I believe that man alone is qualified to handle this assignment.' Why me? And of all things, why me *alone*? He knew my job, and he fought me and the PIB every step of his career. Why a note like this?"

She looked up at him. "Do you have any idea?"

"Sure, I've got an idea. A crazy one, but an idea. I don't think he wanted me because of the writing. I think he wanted me because I'm a propagandist."

She scowled. "It still doesn't wash. There are lots of propagandists—and why would he want a propagandist?"

Shandor's eyes narrowed. "Let's let it ride for a moment. How about his files?"

"In his office in the State Department."

"He didn't keep anything personal at home?"

Her eyes grew wide. "Oh, no, he wouldn't have dared. Not the sort of work he was doing. With his files under lock and key in the State Department nothing could be touched without his knowledge, but at home anybody might have walked in."

"Of course. How about enemies? Did he have any particular enemies?"

She laughed humorlessly. "Name anybody in the current administration. I think he had more enemies than anybody else in the cabinet." Her mouth turned down bitterly. "He was a stumbling block. He got in people's way, and they hated him for it. They killed him for it."

Shandor's eyes widened. "You mean you think he was murdered?"

"Oh, no, nothing so crude. They didn't have to be crude. They just let him butt his head against a stone wall. Everything he tried was blocked, or else it didn't lead anywhere. Like this Berlin Conference. It's a powder keg. Dad gambled everything on going there, forcing the delegates to face facts, to really put their cards on the table. Ever since the United Nations fell apart in '72 dad had been trying to get America and Russia to sit at the same table. But the President cut him out at the last minute. It was planned that way, to let him get up to the very brink of it, and then slap him down hard. They did it all along. This was just the last he could take."

Shandor was silent for a moment. "Any particular thorns in his side?"

Ann shrugged. "Munitions people, mostly. Dartmouth Bearing had a pressure lobby that was trying to throw him out of the cabinet. The President sided with them, but he didn't dare do it for fear the people would squawk. He was planning to blame the failure of the Berlin Conference on dad and get him ousted that way."

Shandor stared. "But if that conference fails, *we're in full-scale war*!"

"Of course. That's the whole point." She scowled at her glass, blinking back tears. "Dad could have stopped it, but they wouldn't let him. *It killed him*, Tom!"

Shandor watched the smoke curling up from his cigarette. "Look," he said. "I've got an idea, and it's going to take some fast work. That conference could blow up any minute, and then I think we're going to be in real trouble. I want you to go to your father's office and get the contents of his personal file. Not the business files, his personal files. Put them in a briefcase and subway-express them to your home. If you have any trouble, have them check with PIB—we have full authority, and I'm it right now. I'll call them and give them the word. Then meet me here again, with the files, at 7:30 this evening."

She looked up, her eyes wide. "What—what are you going to do?"

Shandor snubbed out his smoke, his eyes bright. "I've got an idea that we may be onto something—just something I want to check. But I think if we work it right, we can lay these boys that fought your father out by the toes—"

*

The Library of Congress had been moved when the threat of bombing in Washington had become acute. Shandor took a cab to the Georgetown airstrip, checked the fuel in the 'copter. Ten minutes later he started the motor, and headed upwind into the haze over the hills. In less than half an hour he settled to the Library landing field in western Maryland, and strode across to the rear entrance.

The electronic cross-index had been the last improvement in the Library since the war with China had started in 1958. Shandor found a reading booth in one of the alcoves on the second floor, and plugged in the index. The cold, metallic voice of the automatic chirped twice and said, "Your reference, pleeyuz."

Shandor thought a moment. "Give me your newspaper files on David Ingersoll, Secretary of State."

"Through which dates, pleeyuz."

"Start with the earliest reference, and carry through to current." The speaker burped, and he sat back, waiting. A small grate in the panel before him popped open, and a small spool plopped out onto a spindle. Another followed, and another. He turned to the reader, and reeled the first spool into the intake slot. The light snapped on, and he began reading.

Spools continued to plop down. He read for several hours, taking a dozen pages of notes. The references commenced in June, 1961, with a small notice that David Ingersoll, Republican from New Jersey, had been nominated to run for state senator. Before that date, nothing. Shandor scowled, searching for some item predating that one. He found nothing.

Scratching his head, he continued reading, outlining chronologically. Ingersoll's election to state senate, then to United States Senate. His rise to national prominence as economist for the post-war Administrator of President Drayton in 1966. His meteoric rise as a peacemaker in a nation tired from endless dreary years of fighting in China and India. His tremendous popularity as he tried to stall the re-intensifying cold-war with Russia. The first Nobel Peace Prize, in 1969, for the ill-fated Ingersoll Plan for World Sovereignty. Pages and pages and pages of newsprint. Shandor growled angrily, surveying the pile of notes with a sinking feeling of incredulity. The articles, the writing, the tone—it was all too familiar.

Carefully he checked the newspaper sources. Some of the dispatches were Associated Press; many came direct desk from Public Information Board in New York; two other networks sponsored some of the wordage. But the tone was all the same.

Finally, disgusted, Tom stuffed the notes into his briefcase, and flipped down the librarian lever. "Sources, please."

A light blinked, and in a moment a buzzer sounded at his elbow. A female voice, quite human, spoke as he lifted the receiver. "Can I help you on sources?"

"Yes. I've been reading the newspaper files on David Ingersoll. I'd like the by-lines on this copy."

There was a moment of silence. "Which dates, please?"

Shandor read off his list, giving dates. The silence continued for several minutes as he waited impatiently. He was about to hang up and leave when the voice spoke up again. "I'm sorry, sir. Most of that material has no by-line. Except for one or two items it's all staff-written."

"By whom?"

"I'm sorry, no source is available. Perhaps the PIB offices could help you—"

"All right, ring them for me, please." He waited another five minutes, saw the PIB cross-index clerk appear on the video screen. "Hello, Mr. Shandor. Can I help you?"

"I'm trying to trace down the names of the Associated Press and PIB writers who covered stories on David Ingersoll over a period from June 1961 to the present date—"

The girl disappeared for several moments. When she reappeared, her face was puzzled. "Why, Mr. Shandor, you've been doing the work on Ingersoll from August, 1978 to Sept. 1982. We haven't closed the files on this last month yet—"

He scowled in annoyance. "Yes, yes, I know that. I want the writers before I came."

The clerk paused. "Until you started your work there was no definite assignment. The information just isn't here. But the man you replaced in PIB was named Frank Mariel."

Shandor turned the name over in his mind, decided that it was familiar, but that he couldn't quite place it. "What's this man doing now?"

The girl shrugged. "I don't know, just now, and have no sources. But according to our files he left Public Information Board to go to work in some capacity for Dartmouth Bearing Corporation."

Shandor flipped the switch, and settled back in the reading chair. Once again he fingered through his notes, frowning, a doubt gnawing through his mind into certainty. He took up a dozen of the stories, analyzed them carefully, word for word, sentence by sentence. Then he sat back, his body tired, eyes closed in concentration, an incredible idea twisting and writhing and solidifying in his mind.

It takes one to catch one. That was his job—telling lies. Writing stories that weren't true, and making them believable. Making people think one thing when the truth was something else. It wasn't so strange that he could detect exactly the same sort of thing when he ran into it. He thought it through again and again, and every time he came up with the same answer. There was no doubt.

Reading the newspaper files had accomplished only one thing. He had spent the afternoon reading a voluminous, neat, smoothly written, extremely convincing batch of bold-faced lies. Lies about David Ingersoll. Somewhere, at the bottom of those lies was a shred or two of truth, a shred hard to analyze, impossible to segregate from the garbage surrounding it. But somebody had written the lies. That meant that somebody knew the truths behind them.

Suddenly he galvanized into action. The video blinked protestingly at his urgent summons, and the Washington visiphone operator answered. "Somewhere in those listings of yours," Shandor said, "you've got a man named Frank Mariel. I want his number."

*

He reached the downtown restaurant half an hour early, and ducked into a nearby visiphone station to ring Hart. The PIB director's chubby face materialized on the screen after a moment's confusion, and Shandor said: "John—what are your plans for releasing the Ingersoll story? The morning papers left him with a slight head cold, if I remember right—" Try as he would, he couldn't conceal the edge of sarcasm in his voice.

Hart scowled. "How's the biography coming?"

"The biography's coming along fine. I want to know what kind of quicksand I'm wading through, that's all."

Hart shrugged and spread his hands. "We can't break the story proper until you're ready with your buffer story. Current plans say that he gets pneumonia tomorrow, and goes to Walter Reed tomorrow night. We're giving it as little emphasis as possible, running the Berlin Conference stories for right-hand column stuff. That'll give you all day tomorrow and half the next day for the preliminary stories on his death. Okay?"

"That's not enough time." Shandor's voice was tight.

"It's enough for a buffer-release." Hart scowled at him, his round face red and annoyed. "Look, Tom, you get that story in, and never mind what you like or don't like. This is dynamite you're playing with—the Conference is going to be on the rocks in a matter of hours—that's straight from the Undersecretary—and on top of it all, there's trouble down in Arizona—"

Shandor's eyes widened. "The Rocket Project—?"

Hart's mouth twisted. "Sabotage. They picked up a whole ring that's been operating for over a year. Caught them red-handed, but not before they burnt out half a calculator wing. They'll have to move in new machines now before they can go on—set the Project back another week, and that could lose the war for us right there. Now *get that story in.*" He snapped the switch down, leaving Shandor blinking at the darkened screen.

Ten minutes later Ann Ingersoll joined him in the restaurant booth. She was wearing a chic white linen outfit, with her hair fresh, like a blonde halo around her head in the fading evening light. Her freshness contrasted painfully with Tom's curling collar and dirty tie, and he suddenly wished he'd picked up a shave. He looked up and grunted when he saw the fat briefcase under the girl's arm, and she dropped it on the table between them and sank down opposite him, studying his face. "The reading didn't go so well," she said.

"The reading went lousy," he admitted sheepishly. "This the personal file?"

She nodded shortly and lit a cigarette. "The works. They didn't even bother me. But I can't see why all the precaution— I mean, the express and all that—"

Shandor looked at her sharply. "If what you said this morning was true, that file is a gold mine, for us, but more particularly, for your father's enemies. I'll go over it closely when I get out of here. Meantime, there are one or two other things I want to talk over with you."

She settled herself, and grinned. "Okay, boss. Fire away."

He took a deep breath, and tiredness lined his face. "First off: what did your father do before he went into politics?"

Her eyes widened, and she arrested the cigarette halfway to her mouth, put it back on the ashtray, with a puzzled frown on her face. "That's funny," she said softly. "I thought I knew, but I guess I don't. He was an industrialist—way, far back, years and years ago, when I was just a little brat—and then we got into the war with China, and I don't know what he did. He was always making business trips; I can remember going to the airport with mother to meet him, but I don't know what he did. Mother always avoided talking about him, and I never got to see him enough to talk—"

Shandor sat forward, his eyes bright. "Did he ever entertain any business friends during that time—any that you can remember?"

She shook her head. "I can't remember. Seems to me a man or two came home with him on a couple of occasions, but I don't know who. I don't remember much before the night he came home and said he was going to run for Congress. Then there were people galore—have been ever since."

"And what about his work at the end of the China war? After he was elected, while he was doing all that work to try to smooth things out with Russia—can you remember him saying anything, to you, or to your mother, about *what* he was doing, and how?"

She shook her head again. "Oh, yes, he'd talk—he and mother would talk—sometimes argue. I had the feeling that things weren't too well with mother and dad many times. But I can't remember anything specific, except that he used to say over and over how he hated the thought of another war. He was afraid it was going to come—"

Shandor looked up sharply. "But he hated it—"

"Yes." Her eyes widened. "Oh, yes, he hated it. Dad was a good man, Tom. He believed with all his heart that the people of the world wanted peace, and that they were being dragged to war because they couldn't find any purpose to keep them from it. He believed that if the people of the world had a cause, a purpose, a driving force, that there wouldn't be any more wars. Some men fought him for preaching peace, but he wouldn't be swayed. Especially he hated the pure-profit lobbies, the patriotic drum-beaters who stood to get rich in a war. But dad had to die, and there aren't many men like him left now, I guess."

"I know." Shandor fell silent, stirring his coffee glumly. "Tell me," he said, "did your father have anything to do with a man named Mariel?"

Ann's eyes narrowed. "Frank Mariel? He was the newspaper man. Yes, dad had plenty to do with him. He hated dad's guts, because dad fought his writing so much. Mariel was one of the 'fight now and get rich' school that were continually plaguing dad."

"Would you say that they were enemies?"

She bit her lip, wrinkling her brow in thought. "Not at first. More like a big dog with a little flea, at first. Mariel pestered dad, and dad tried to scratch him away. But Mariel got into PIB, and then I suppose you could call them enemies—"

Shandor sat back, frowning, his face dark with fatigue. He stared at the table top for a long moment, and when he looked up at the girl his eyes were troubled. "There's something wrong with this," he said softly. "I can't quite make it out, but it just doesn't look right. Those newspaper stories I read—pure bushwa, from beginning to end. I'm dead certain of it. And yet—" he paused, searching for words. "Look. It's like I'm looking at a jigsaw puzzle that *looks* like it's all completed and lying out on the table. But there's something that tells me I'm being foxed, that it isn't a complete puzzle at all, just an illusion, yet somehow I can't even tell for sure where pieces are missing—"

The girl leaned over the table, her grey eyes deep with concern. "Tom," she said, almost in a whisper. "Suppose there *is* something, Tom. Something big, what's it going to do to *you*, Tom? You can't fight anything as powerful as PIB, and these men that hated dad could break you."

Tom grinned tiredly, his eyes far away. "I know," he said softly. "But a man can only swallow so much. Somewhere, I guess, I've still got a conscience—it's a nuisance, but it's still there." He looked closely at the lovely girl across from him. "Maybe it's just that I'm tired of being sick of myself. I'd like to *like* myself for a change. I haven't liked myself for years." He looked straight at her, his voice very small in the still booth. "I'd like some other people to like me, too. So I've got to keep going—"

Her hand was in his, then, grasping his fingers tightly, and her voice was trembling. "I didn't think there was anybody left like that," she said. "Tom, you aren't by yourself—remember that. No matter what happens, I'm with you all the way. I'm—I'm afraid, but I'm with you."

He looked up at her then, and his voice was tight. "Listen, Ann. Your father planned to go to Berlin before he died. What was he going to *do* if he went to the Berlin Conference?"

She shrugged helplessly. "The usual diplomatic fol-de-rol, I suppose. He always—"

"No, no—that's not right. He wanted to go so badly that he died when he wasn't allowed to, Ann. He must have had something in mind, something concrete, something tremendous. Something that would have changed the picture a great deal."

And then she was staring at Shandor, her face white, grey eyes wide. "Of course he had something," she exclaimed. "He *must* have—oh, I don't know what, he wouldn't say what was in his mind, but when he came home after that meeting with the President he was furious— I've never seen him so furious, Tom, he was almost out of his mind with anger, and he paced the floor, and, swore and nearly tore the room apart. He wouldn't speak to anyone, just stamped around and threw things. And then we heard him cry out, and when we got to him he was unconscious on the floor, and he was dead when the doctor came—" She set her glass down with trembling fingers. "He had something big, Tom, I'm sure of it. He had some information that he planned to drop on the conference table with such a bang it would stop the whole world cold. *He knew something* that the conference doesn't know—"

Tom Shandor stood up, trembling, and took the briefcase. "It should be here," he said. "If not the whole story, at least the missing pieces." He started for the booth door. "Go home," he said. "I'm going where I can examine these files without any interference. Then I'll call you." And then he was out the door, shouldering his way through the crowded restaurant, frantically weaving his way to the street. He didn't hear Ann's voice as she called after him to stop, didn't see her stop at the booth door, watch in a confusion of fear and tenderness, and collapse into the booth, sobbing as if her heart would break. Because a crazy, twisted, impossible idea was in his mind, an idea that had plagued him since he had started reading that morning, an idea with an answer, an acid test, folded in the briefcase under his arm. He bumped into a fat man at the bar, grunted angrily, and finally reached the street, whistled at the cab that lingered nearby.

The car swung up before him, the door springing open automatically. He had one foot on the running board before he saw the trap, saw the tight yellowish face and the glittering eyes inside the cab. Suddenly there was an explosion of bright purple brilliance, and he was screaming, twisting and screaming and reeling backward onto the sidewalk, doubled over with the agonizing fire that burned through his side and down one leg, forcing scream after scream from his throat as he blindly staggered to the wall of the building, pounded it with his fists for relief from the searing pain. And then he was on his side on the sidewalk, sobbing, blubbering incoherently to the uniformed policeman who was dragging him gently to his feet, seeing through burning eyes the group of curious people gathering around. Suddenly realization dawned through the pain, and he let out a cry of anger and bolted for the curb, knocking the policeman aside, his eyes wild, searching the receding stream of traffic for the cab, a picture of the occupant burned indelibly into his mind, a face he had seen, recognized. The cab was gone, he knew, gone like a breath of wind. The briefcase was also gone—

*

He gave the address of the Essex University Hospital to the cabby, and settled back in the seat, gripping the hand-guard tightly to fight down the returning pain in his side and leg. His mind was whirling, fighting in a welter of confusion, trying to find some avenue of approach, some way to make sense of the mess. The face in the cab recurred again and again before his eyes, the gaunt, putty-colored cheeks, the sharp glittering eyes. His acquaintance with Frank Mariel had been brief and unpleasant, in the past, but that was a face he would never forget. But how could Mariel have known where he would be, and when? There was precision in that attack, far too smooth precision ever to have been left to chance, or even to independent planning. His mind skirted the obvious a dozen times, and each time rejected it angrily. Finally he knew he could no longer reject the thought, the only possible answer. Mariel had known where he would be, and at what time. Therefore, someone must have told him.

He stiffened in the seat, the pain momentarily forgotten. Only one person could have told Mariel. Only one person knew where the file was, and where it would be after he left the restaurant—he felt cold bitterness creep down his spine. She had known, and sat there making eyes at him, and telling him how wonderful he was, how she was with him no matter what happened—and she'd already sold him down the river. He shook his head angrily, trying to keep his thoughts on a rational plane. *Why?* Why had she strung him along, why had she even started to help him? And why, above all, turn against her own father?

The Hospital driveway crunched under the cab, and he hopped out, wincing with every step, and walked into a phone booth off the lobby. He gave a name, and in a moment heard the P.A. system echoing it: "Dr. Prex; calling Dr. Prex." In a moment he heard a receiver click off, and a familiar voice said, "Prex speaking."

"Prex, this is Shandor. Got a minute?"

The voice was cordial. "Dozens of them. Where are you?"

"I'll be up in your quarters." Shandor slammed down the receiver and started for the elevator to the Resident Physicians' wing.

He let himself in by a key, and settled down in the darkened room to wait an eternity before a tall, gaunt man walked in, snapped on a light, and loosened the white jacket at his neck. He was a young man, no more than thirty, with a tired, sober face and jet black hair falling over his forehead. His eyes lighted as he saw Shandor, and he grinned. "You look like you've been through the mill. What happened?"

Shandor stripped off his clothes, exposing the angry red of the seared skin. The tall man whistled softly, the smile fading. Carefully he examined the burned area, his fingers gentle on the tender surface, then he turned troubled eyes to Shandor. "You've been messing around with dirty guys, Tom. Nobody but a real dog would turn a scalder on a man." He went to a cupboard, returned with a jar of salve and bandages.

"Is it serious?" Shandor's face was deathly white. "I've been fighting shock with thiamin for the last hour, but I don't think I can hold out much longer."

Prex shrugged. "You didn't get enough to do any permanent damage, if that's what you mean. Just fried the pain-receptors in your skin to a crisp, is all. A little dose is so painful you can't do anything but holler for a while, but it won't hurt you permanently unless you get it all over you. Enough can kill you." He dressed the burned areas carefully, then bared Shandor's arm and used a pressure syringe for a moment. "Who's using one of those things?"

Shandor was silent for a moment. Then he said, "Look, Prex. I need some help, badly." His eyes looked up in dull anger. "I'm going to see a man tonight, and I want him to talk, hard and fast. I don't care right now if he nearly dies from pain, but I want him to talk. I need somebody along who knows how to make things painful."

Prex scowled, and pointed to the burn. "This the man?"

"That's the man."

Prex put away the salve. "I suppose I'll help you, then. Is this official, or grudge?"

"A little of both. Look, Prex, I know this is a big favor to ask, but it's on the level. Believe me, it's square, nothing shady about it. The method may not be legal, but the means are justified. I can't tell you what's up, but I'm asking you to trust me."

Prex grinned. "You say it's all right, it's all right. When?"

Shandor glanced at his watch. "About 3:00 this morning, I think. We can take your car."

They talked for a while, and a call took the doctor away. Shandor slept a little, then made some black coffee. Shortly before three the two men left the Hospital by the Physicians' entrance, and Prex's little beat-up Dartmouth slid smoothly into the desultory traffic for the suburbs.

*

The apartment was small and neatly furnished. Shandor and the Doctor had been admitted by a sleepy doorman who had been jolted to sudden attention by Tom's PIB card, and after five minutes pounding on the apartment door, a sleepy-eyed man opened the door a crack. "Say, what's the idea pounding on a man's door at this time of night? Haven't you—"

Shandor gave the door a shove with his shoulder, driving it open into the room. "Shut up," he said bluntly. He turned so the light struck his face, and the little man's jaw dropped in astonishment. "Shandor!" he whispered.

Frank Mariel looked like a weasel—sallow, sunken-cheeked, with a yellowish cast to his skin that contrasted unpleasantly with the coal black hair. "That's right," said Shandor. "We've come for a little talk. Meet the doctor."

Mariel's eyes shifted momentarily to Prex's stoney face, then back to Shandor, ghosts of fear creeping across his face. "What do you want?"

"I've come for the files."

The little man scowled. "You've come to the wrong man. I don't have any files."

Prex carefully took a small black case from his pocket, unsnapped a hinge, and a small, shiny instrument fell out in his hand. "The files," said Shandor. "Who has them?"

"I—I don't know—"

Shandor smashed a fist into the man's face, viciously, knocking him reeling to the floor. "You tried to kill me tonight," he snarled. "You should have done it up right. You should stick to magazine editing and keep your nose out of dirty games, Mariel. Who has the files?"

Mariel picked himself up, trembling, met Shandor's fist, and sprawled again, a trickle of blood appearing at his mouth. "Harry Dartmouth has the files," he groaned. "They're probably in Chicago now."

"What do you know about Harry Dartmouth?"

Mariel gained a chair this time before Shandor hit him. "I've only met him a couple of times. He's the president of Dartmouth Bearing Corporation and he's my boss—Dartmouth Bearing publishes '*Fighting World*.' I do what he tells me."

Shandor's eyes flared. "Including murder, is that right?" Mariel's eyes were sullen. "Come on, talk! Why did Dartmouth want Ingersoll's personal files?"

The man just stared sullenly at the floor. Prex pressed a stud on the side of the shiny instrument, and a purple flash caught Mariel's little finger. Mariel jerked and squealed with pain. "Speak up," said Shandor. "I didn't hear you."

"Probably about the bonds," Mariel whimpered. His face was ashen, and he eyed Prex with undisguised pleading. "Look, tell him to put that thing away—"

Shandor grinned without humor. "You don't like scalders, eh? Get a big enough dose, and you're dead, Mariel—but I guess you know that, don't you? Think about it. But don't think too long. What about the bonds?"

"Ingersoll has been trying to get Dartmouth Bearing Corporation on legal grounds for years. Something about the government bonds they held, bought during the China wars. You know, surplus profits—Dartmouth Bearing could beat the taxes by buying bonds. Harry Dartmouth thought Ingersoll's files had some legal dope against them—he was afraid you'd try to make trouble for the company—"

"So he hired his little pixie, eh? Seems to me you'd have enough on your hands editing that rag—"

Mariel shot him an injured look. "'*Fighting World*' has the second largest magazine circulation in the country. It's a good magazine."

"It's a warmonger propaganda rag," snapped Shandor. He glared at the little man. "What's your relation to Ingersoll?"

"I hated his guts. He was carrying his lily-livered pacifism right to the White House, and I couldn't see it. So I fought him every inch of the way. I'll fight what he stands for now he's dead—"

Shandor's eyes narrowed. "That was a mistake, Mariel. You weren't supposed to know he is dead." He walked over to the little man, whose face was a shade whiter yet. "Funny," said Shandor quietly. "You say you hated him, but I didn't get that impression at all."

Mariel's eyes opened wide. "What do you mean?"

"Everything you wrote for PIB seems to have treated him kindly."

A shadow of deep concern crossed Mariel's face, as though for the first time he found himself in deep water. "PIB told me what to write, and I wrote it. You know how they work."

"Yes, I know how they work. I also know that most of your writing, while you were doing Public Information Board work, was never ordered by PIB. Ever hear of Ben Chamberlain, Mariel? Or Frank Eberhardt? Or Jon Harding? Ever hear of them, Mariel?" Shandor's voice cut sharply through the room. "Ben Chamberlain wrote for every large circulation magazine in the country, after the Chinese war. Frank Eberhardt was the man behind Associated Press during those years. Jon Harding was the silent publisher of three newspapers in Washington, two in New York, and one in Chicago. Ever hear of those men, Mariel?"

"No, no—"

"You know damned well you've heard of them. Because *those men were all you*. Every single one of them—" Shandor was standing close to him, now, and Mariel sat like he had seen a ghost, his lower lip quivering, forehead wet. "No, no, you're wrong—"

"No, no, I'm right," mocked Shandor. "I've been in the newspaper racket for a long time, Mariel. I've got friends in PIB—real friends, not the shamus crowd you're acquainted with that'll take you for your last nickel and then leave you to starve. Never mind how I found out. You hated Ingersoll so much you handed him bouquets all the time. How about it, Mariel? All that writing—you couldn't praise him enough. Boosting him, beating the drum for him and his policies—every trick and gimmick known in the propaganda game to give him a boost, make him the people's darling—how about it?"

Mariel was shaking his head, his little eyes nearly popping with fright. "It wasn't him," he choked. "Ingersoll had nothing to do with it. It was Dartmouth Bearing. They bought me into the spots. Got me the newspapers, supported me. Dartmouth Bearing ran the whole works, and they told me what to write—"

"Garbage! Dartmouth Bearing—the biggest munitions people in America, and I'm supposed to believe that they told you to go to bat for the country's strongest pacifist! What kind of sap do you take me for?"

"It's true! Ingersoll had nothing to do with it, nothing at all." Mariel's voice was almost pleading. "Look, I don't know what Dartmouth Bearing had in mind. Who was I to ask questions? You don't realize their power, Shandor. Those bonds I spoke of—they hold millions of dollars worth of bonds! They hold enough bonds to topple the economy of the nation, they've got bonds in the names of ten thousand subsidiary companies. They've been telling Federal Economics Commission what to do for the past ten years! And they're getting us into this war, Shandor—lock, stock and barrel. They pushed for everything they could get, and they had the money, the power, the men to do whatever they wanted. You couldn't fight them, because they had everything sewed up so tight nobody could approach them—"

Shandor's mind was racing, the missing pieces beginning, suddenly, to come out of the haze. The incredible, twisted idea broke through again, staggering him, driving through his mind like icy steel. "Listen, Mariel. I swear I'll kill you if you lie to me, so you'd better tell the truth. Who put you on my trail? Who told you Ingersoll was dead, and that I was scraping up Ingersoll's past?"

The little man twisted his hands, almost in tears. "Harry Dartmouth told me—"

"And who told Harry Dartmouth?"

Mariel's voice was so weak it could hardly be heard. "The girl," he said.

Shandor felt the chill deepen. "And where are the files now?"

"Dartmouth has them. Probably in Chicago—I expressed them. The girl didn't dare send them direct, for fear you would check, or that she was being watched. I was supposed to pick them up from you, and see to it that you didn't remember—"

Shandor clenched his fist. "Where are Dartmouth's plants located?"

"The main plants are in Chicago and Newark. They've got a smaller one in Nevada."

"And what do they make?"

"In peacetime—cars. In wartime they make tanks and shells."

"And their records? Inventories? Shipping orders, and files? Where do they keep them?"

"I—I don't know. You aren't thinking of—"

"Never mind what I'm thinking of, just answer up. Where are they?"

"All the administration offices are in Chicago. But they'd kill you, Shandor—you wouldn't stand a chance. They can't be fought, I tell you."

Shandor nodded to Prex, and started for the door. "Keep him here until dawn, then go on home, and forget what you heard. If anything happens, give me a ring at my home." He glared at Mariel. "Don't worry about me, bud—they won't be doing anything to me when I get through with them. They just won't be doing anything at all."

*

The idea had crystallized as he talked to Mariel. Shandor's mind was whirling as he walked down toward the thoroughfare. Incredulously, he tried to piece the picture together. He had known Dartmouth Bearing was big—but that big? Mariel might have been talking nonsense, or he might have been reading the Gospel. Shandor hailed a cab, sat back in the seat scratching his head. How big could Dartmouth Bearing be? Could *any* corporation be that big? He thought back, remembering the rash of post-war scandals and profit-gouging trials, the anti-trust trials. In wartime, bars are let down, *no one* can look with disfavor on the factories making the weapons. And if one corporation could buy, and expand, and buy some more—it might be too powerful to be prosecuted after the war—

Shandor shook his head, realizing that he was skirting the big issue. Dartmouth Bearing connected up, in some absurd fashion, but there was a missing link. Mariel fit into one side of the puzzle, interlocking with Dartmouth. The stolen files might even fit, for that matter. But the idea grew stronger. A great, jagged piece in the middle of the puzzle was missing—the key piece which would tie everything together. He felt his skin prickle as he thought. An impossible idea—and yet, he realized, if it were true, everything else would fall clearly into place—

He sat bolt upright. It *had* to be true—

He leaned forward and gave the cabby the landing field address, then sat back, feeling his pulse pounding through his arms and legs. Nervously he switched on the radio. The dial fell to some jazz music, which he tolerated for a moment or two, then flipped to a news broadcast. Not that news broadcasts really meant much, but he wanted to hear the Ingersoll story release for the day. He listened impatiently to a roundup of local news: David Ingersoll stricken with pneumonia, three Senators protesting the current tax bill—he brought his attention around sharply at the sound of a familiar name—

"—disappeared from his Chicago home early this morning. Mr. Dartmouth is president of Dartmouth Bearing Corporation, currently engaged in the manufacture of munitions for Defense, and producing much of the machinery being used in the Moon-rocket in Arizona. Police are following all possible leads, and are confident that there has been no foul play.

"On the international scene, the Kremlin is still blocking—" Shandor snapped off the radio abruptly, his forehead damp. Dartmouth disappeared, and with him the files—why? And where to go now to find them? If the idea that was plaguing him was true, sound, valid—he'd *have* to have the files. His whole body was wet with perspiration as he reached the landing field.

The trip to the Library of Congress seemed endless, yet he knew that the Library wouldn't be open until 8:00 anyway. Suddenly he felt a wave of extreme weariness sweep over him—when had he last slept? Bored, he snapped the telephone switch and rang PIB offices for his mail. To his surprise, John Hart took the wire, and exploded in his ear, "Where in hell have you been? I've been trying to get you all night. Listen, Tom, drop the Ingersoll story cold, and get in here. The faster the better."

Shandor blinked. "Drop the story? You're crazy!"

"*Get in here*!" roared Hart. "From now on you've *really* got a job. The Berlin Conference blew up tonight, Tom—high as a kite. *We're at war with Russia—*"

Carefully, Shandor plopped the receiver down on its hook, his hands like ice. Just one item first, he thought, just one thing I've got to know. *Then* back to PIB, maybe.

He found a booth in the Library, and began hunting, time pressing him into frantic speed. The idea was incredible, but it *had* to be true. He searched the micro-film files for three hours before he found it, in a "Who's Who" dating back to 1958, three years before the war with China. A simple, innocuous listing, which froze him to his seat. He read it, unbelievingly, yet knowing that it was the only possible link. Finally he read it again.

David P. Ingersoll. Born 1922, married 1947. Educated at Rutgers University and MIT. Worked as administrator for International Harvester until 1955. Taught Harvard University from 1955 to 1957.

David P. Ingersoll, becoming, in 1958, the executive president of Dartmouth Bearing Corporation....

*

He found a small, wooded glade not far from the Library, and set the 'copter down skillfully, his mind numbed, fighting to see through the haze to the core of incredible truth he had uncovered. The great, jagged piece, so long missing, was suddenly plopped right down into the middle of the puzzle, and now it didn't fit. There were still holes, holes that obscured the picture and twisted it into a nightmarish impossibility. He snapped the telephone switch, tried three numbers without any success, and finally reached the fourth. He heard Dr. Prex's sharp voice on the wire.

"Anything happen since I left, Prex?"

"Nothing remarkable." The doctor's voice sounded tired. "Somebody tried to call Mariel on the visiphone about an hour after you had gone, and then signed off in a hurry when he saw somebody else around. Don't know who it was, but he sounded mighty agitated." The doctor's voice paused. "Anything new, Tom?"

"Plenty," growled Shandor bitterly. "But you'll have to read it in the newspapers." He flipped off the connection before Prex could reply.

Then Shandor sank back and slept, the sleep of total exhaustion, hoping that a rest would make the shimmering, indefinite picture hold still long enough for him to study it. And as he drifted into troubled sleep a greater and more pressing question wormed upward into his mind.

He woke with a jolt, just as the sun was going down, and he knew then with perfect clarity what he had to do. He checked quickly to see that he had been undisturbed, and then manipulated the controls of the 'copter. Easing the ship into the sky toward Washington, he searched out a news report on the radio, listened with a dull feeling in the pit of his stomach as the story came through about the breakdown of the Berlin Conference, the declaration of war, the President's meeting with Congress that morning, his formal request for full wartime power, the granting of permission by a wide-eyed, frightened legislature. Shandor settled back, staring dully at the ground moving below him, the whisps of evening haze rising over the darkening land. There was only one thing to do. He had to have Ingersoll's files. He knew only one way to get them.

Half an hour later he was settling the ship down, under cover of darkness, on the vast grounds behind the Ingersoll estate, cutting the motors to effect a quiet landing. Tramping down the ravine toward the huge house, he saw it was dark; down by the gate he could see the Security Guard, standing in a haze of blue cigarette smoke under the dim-out lights. Cautiously he slipped across the back terrace, crossing behind the house, and jangled a bell on a side porch.

Ann Ingersoll opened the door, and gasped as Shandor forced his way in. "Keep quiet," he hissed, slipping the door shut behind him. Then he sighed, and walked through the entrance into the large front room.

"Tom! Oh, Tom, I was afraid— Oh, *Tom*!" Suddenly she was in his arms sobbing, pressing her face against his shirt front. "Oh, I'm so glad to see you, Tom—"

He disengaged her, turning from her and walking across the room. "Let's turn it off, Ann," he said disgustedly. "It's not very impressive."

"Tom—I—I *wanted* to tell you. I just didn't know what to do. I didn't believe them when they said you wouldn't be harmed, I was afraid. Oh, Tom, I wanted to tell you, believe me—"

"You didn't tell me," he snapped. "They were nervous, they slipped up. That's the only reason I'm alive. They planned to kill me."

She stared at him tearfully, shaking her head from side to side, searching for words. "I—I didn't want that—"

He whirled, his eyes blazing. "You silly fool, what do you think you're doing when you play games with a mob like this? Do you think they're going to play fair? You're no clod, you know better than that—" He leaned over her, trembling with anger. "You set me up for a sucker, but the plan fell through. And now I'm running around loose, and if you thought I was dangerous before, you haven't seen anything like how dangerous I am now. You're going to tell me some things, now, and you're going to tell them straight. You're going to tell me where Harry Dartmouth went with those files, where they are right now. Understand that? *I want those files.* Because when I have them I'm going to do exactly what I started out to do. I'm going to write a story, the whole rotten story about your precious father and his two-faced life. I'm going to write about Dartmouth Bearing Corporation and all its flunky outfits, and tell what they've done to this country and the people of this country." He paused, breathing heavily, and sank down on a chair, staring at her. "I've learned things in the past twenty-four hours I never dreamed could be true. I should be able to believe anything, I suppose, but these things knocked my stilts out from under me. This country has been had—right straight down the line, for a dozen years. We've been sold down the river like a pack of slaves, and now we're going to get a look at the cold ugly truth, for once."

She stared at him. "What do you mean—about my preçious father—?"

"Your precious father was at the bottom of the whole slimy mess."

"No, no—not dad." She shook her head, her face chalky. "Harry Dartmouth, maybe, but not dad. Listen a minute. I didn't set you up for anything. I didn't know what Dartmouth and Mariel were up to. Dad left instructions for me to contact Harry Dartmouth immediately, in case he died. He told me that—oh, a year ago. Told me that before I did anything else, I should contact Dartmouth, and do as he said. So when he died, I contacted Harry, and kept in contact with him. He told me you were out to burn my father, to heap garbage on him after he was dead before the people who loved him, and he said the first thing you would want would be his personal files. Tom, I didn't know you, then—I knew Harry, and knew that dad trusted him, for some reason, so I believed him. But I began to realize that what he said wasn't true. I got the files, and he said to give them to you, to string you along, and he'd pick them up from you before you had a chance to do any harm with them. He said he wouldn't hurt you, but I—I didn't believe him, Tom. I believed you, that you wanted to give dad a fair shake—"

Shandor was on his feet, his eyes blazing. "So you turned them over to Dartmouth anyway? And what do you think he's done with them? Can you tell me that? Where has he gone? Has he burnt them? If not, what's he going to do with them?"

Her voice was weak, and she looked as if she were about to faint. "That's what I'm trying to tell you," she said, shakily. "He doesn't have them. I have them."

Shandor's jaw dropped. "Now, wait a minute," he said softly. "You gave me the briefcase, Mariel snatched it and nearly killed me—"

"A dummy, Tom. I didn't know who to trust, but I knew I believed you more than I believed Harry. Things happened so fast, and I was so confused—" She looked straight at him. "I gave you a dummy, Tom."

His knees walked out from under him, then, and he sank into a chair. "You've got them here, then," he said weakly.

"Yes. I have them here."

*

The room was in the back of the house, a small, crowded study, with a green-shaded desk lamp. Shandor dumped the contents of the briefcase onto the desk, and settled down, his heart pounding in his throat. He started at the top of the pile, sifting, ripping out huge sheafs of papers, receipts, notes, journals, clippings. He hardly noticed when the girl slipped out of the room, and he was deep in study when she returned half an hour later with steaming black coffee. With a grunt of thanks he drank it, never shifting his attention from the scatter of papers, papers from the personal file of a dead man. And slowly, the picture unfolded.

An ugly picture. A picture of deceit, a picture full of lies, full of secret promises, a picture of scheming, of plotting, planning, influencing, coercing, cheating, propagandizing—all with one single-minded aim, with a single terrible goal.

Shandor read, numbly, his mind twisting in protest as the picture unfolded. David Ingersoll's control of Dartmouth Bearing Corporation and its growing horde of subsidiaries under the figurehead of his protege, Harry Dartmouth. The huge profits from the Chinese war, the relaxation of control laws, the millions of war-won dollars ploughed back into government bonds, in a thousand different names, all controlled by Dartmouth Bearing Corporation—

And Ingersoll's own work in the diplomatic field—an incredibly skillful, incredibly evil channeling of power and pressure toward the inevitable goal, hidden under the cloak of peaceful respectability and popular support. The careful treaties, quietly disorganizing a dozen national economics, antagonizing the great nation to the East under the all too acceptable guise of "peace through strength." Reciprocal trade agreements bitterly antagonistic to Russian economic development. The continual bickering, the skillful manipulation hidden under the powerful propaganda cloak of a hundred publications, all coursing to one ultimate, terrible goal, all with one purpose, one aim—

War. War with anybody, war in the field and war on the diplomatic front. Traces even remained of the work done within the enemy nations, bitter anti-Ingersoll propaganda from within the ranks of Russia herself, manipulated to strengthen Ingersoll in America, to build him up, to drive the nations farther apart, while presenting Ingersoll as the pathetic prince of world peace, fighting desperately to stop the ponderous wheels of the irresistible juggernaut—

And in America, the constant, unremitting literary and editorial drumbeating, pressuring greater war preparation, distilling hatreds in a thousand circles, focussing them into a single channel. Tremendous propaganda pressure to build armies, to build weapons, to get the Moon-rocket project underway—

Shandor sat back, eyes drooping, fighting to keep his eyes open. His mind was numb, his body trembling. A sheaf of papers in a separate folder caught his eye, production records of the Dartmouth Bearing Corporation, almost up to the date of Ingersoll's death. Shandor frowned, a snag in the chain drawing his attention. He peered at the papers, vaguely puzzled. Invoices from the Chicago plant, materials for tanks, and guns, and shells. Steel, chemicals. The same for the New Jersey plant, the same with a dozen subsidiary plants. Shipments of magnesium and silver wire to the Rocket Project in Arizona, carried through several subsidiary offices. The construction of a huge calculator for the Project in Arizona. Motors and materials, all for Arizona—something caught his mind, brought a frown to his large bland face, some off-key note in the monstrous symphony of production and intrigue that threw up a red flag in his mind, screamed for attention—

And then he sipped the fresh coffee at his elbow and sighed, and looked up at the girl standing there, saw her hand tremble as she steadied herself against the desk, and sat down beside him. He felt a great confusion, suddenly, a vast sympathy for this girl, and he wanted to take her in his arms, hold her close, *protect* her, somehow. She didn't know, she *couldn't* know about this horrible thing. She couldn't have been a party to it, a part of it. He knew the evidence said yes, she knows the whole story, she *helped* them, but he also knew that the evidence, somehow, was wrong, that somehow, he still didn't have the whole picture—

She looked at him, her voice trembling. "You're wrong, Tom," she said.

He shook his head, helplessly. "I'm sorry. It's horrible, I know. But I'm not wrong. This war was planned. We've been puppets on strings, and one man engineered it, from the very start. Your father."

Her eyes were filled with tears, and she shook her head, running a tired hand across her forehead. "You didn't know him, Tom. If you did, you'd know how wrong you are. He was a great man, fine man, but above all he was a *good* man. Only a monster could have done what you're thinking. Dad hated war, he fought it all his life. He couldn't be the monster you think."

Tom's voice was soft in the darkened room, his eyes catching the downcast face of the trembling girl, fighting to believe in a phantom, and his hatred for the power that could trample a faith like that suddenly swelled up in bitter hopeless rage. "It's here, on paper, it can't be denied. It's hateful, but it's here, it's what I set out to learn. It's not a lie this time, Ann, it's the truth, and this time it's *got to be told*. I've written my last false story. This one is going to the people the way it is. This one is going to be the truth."

He stopped, staring at her. The puzzling, twisted hole in the puzzle was suddenly there, staring him in the face, falling down into place in his mind with blazing clarity. Staring, he dived into the pile of papers again, searching, frantically searching for the missing piece, something he had seen, and passed over, the one single piece in the story that didn't make sense. And he found it, on the lists of materials shipped to the Nevada plant. Pig Iron. Raw magnesium. Raw copper. Steel, electron tubes, plastics, from all parts of the country, all being shipped to the Dartmouth Plant in Nevada—

Where they made only shells—

At first he thought it was only a rumble in his mind, the shocking realization storming through. Then he saw Ann jump up suddenly, white-faced and race to the window, and he heard the small scream in her throat. And then the rumbling grew louder, stronger, and the house trembled. He heard the whine of jet planes scream over the house as he joined her at the window, heard the screaming whines mingled with the rumbling thunder. And far away, on the horizon, the red glare was glowing, rising, burning up to a roaring conflagration in the black night sky—

"Washington!" Her voice was small, infinitely frightened.

"Yes. That's Washington."

"Then it really *has* started." She turned to him with eyes wide with horror, and snuggled up to his chest like a frightened child. "Oh, Tom—"

"It's here. What we've been waiting for. What your father started could never be stopped any other way than this—"

The roar was louder now, rising to a whining scream as another squad of dark ships roared overhead, moving East and South, jets whistling in the night. "This is what your father wanted."

She was crying, great sobs shaking her shoulders. "You're wrong, you're wrong—oh, Tom, you must be wrong—"

His voice was low, almost inaudible in the thundering roar of the bombardment. "Ann, I've got to go ahead. I've got to go tonight. To Nevada, to the Dartmouth plant there. I know I'm right, but I have to go, to check something—to make sure of something." He paused, looking down at her. "I'll be back, Ann. But I'm afraid of what I'll find out there. I need you behind me. Especially with what I have to do, I need you. You've got to decide. Are you for me? Or against me?"

She shook her head sadly, and sank into a chair, gently removing his hands from her waist. "I loved my father, Tom," she said in a beaten voice. "I can't help what he's done—I loved him. I—I can't be with you, Tom."

*

Far below him he could see the cars jamming the roads leaving Washington. He could almost hear the noise, the screeching of brakes, the fistfights, the shouts, the blatting of horns. He moved south over open country, hoping to avoid the places where the 'copter might be spotted and stopped for questioning. He knew that Hart would have an alarm out for him by now, and he didn't dare risk being stopped until he reached his destination, the place where the last piece to the puzzle could be found, the answer to the question that was burning through his mind. Shells were made of steel and chemicals. The tools that made them were also made of steel. Not manganese. Not copper. Not electron relays, nor plastic, nor liquid oxygen. Just steel.

The 'copter relayed south and then turned west over Kentucky. Shandor checked the auxiliary tanks which he had filled at the Library landing field that morning; then he turned the ship to robot controls and sank back in the seat to rest. His whole body clamored for sleep, but he knew he dare not sleep. Any slip, any contact with Army aircraft or Security patrol could throw everything into the fire— For hours he sat, gazing hypnotically at the black expanse of land below, flying high over the pitch-black countryside. Not a light showed, not a sign of life.

Bored, he flipped the radio button, located a news broadcast. "—the bombed area did not extend west of the Appalachians. Washington DC was badly hit, as were New York and Philadelphia, and further raids are expected to originate from Siberia, coming across the great circle to the West coast or the Middle west. So far the Enemy appears to have lived up to its agreement in the Ingersoll pact to outlaw use of atomic bombs, for no atomic weapons have been used so far, but the damage with block-busters has been heavy. All citizens are urged to maintain strictest blackout regulations, and to report as called upon in local work and civil defense pools as they are set up. The attack began—"

Shandor sighed, checked his instrument readings. Far in the East the horizon was beginning to lighten, a healthy, white-grey light. His calculations placed him over Eastern Nebraska, and a few moments later he nosed down cautiously and verified his location. Lincoln Airbase was in a flurry of activity; the field was alive with men, like little black ants, preparing the reserve fighters and pursuits for use in a fever of urgent speed. Suddenly the 'copter radio bleeped, and Tom threw the switch. "Over."

An angry voice snarled, "You up there, whoever you are, where'd you leave your brains? No civilian craft are allowed in the air, and that's orders straight from Washington. Don't you know there's a war on? Now get down here, before you're shot down—"

Shandor thought quickly. "This is a Federal Security ship," he snapped. "I'm just on a reconnaissance—"

The voice was cautious. "Security? What's your corroboration number?"

Shandor cursed. "JF223R-864. Name is Jerry Chandler. Give it a check if you want to." He flipped the switch, and accelerated for the ridge of hills that marked the Colorado border as the radio signal continued to bleep angrily, and a trio of pursuit planes on the ground began warming up. Shandor sighed, hoping they would check before they sent ships after him. It might at least delay them until he reached his destination.

Another hour carried him to the heart of the Rockies, and across the great salt fields of Utah. His fuel tanks were low, being emptied one by one as the tiny ship sped through the bright morning sky, and Tom was growing uneasy, until suddenly, far to the west and slightly to the north he spotted the plant, nestling in the mountain foothills. It lay far below, sprawling like some sort of giant spider across the rugged terrain. Several hundred cars spread out to the south of the plant, and he could see others speeding in from the temporary village across the ridge. Everything was quiet, orderly. He could see the shipments, crated, sitting in freight cars to the north. And then he saw the drill line running over to the right of the plant. He followed it, quickly checking a topographical map in the cockpit, and his heart started pounding. The railroad branch ran between two low peaks and curved out toward the desert. Moving over it, he saw the curve, saw it as it cut off to the left—and seemed to stop dead in the middle of the desert sand—

Shandor circled even lower, keeping one ear cocked on the radio, and settled the ship on the railroad line. And just as he cut the motors, he heard the shrill whine of three pursuit ships screaming in from the Eastern horizon—

He was out of the 'copter almost as soon as it had touched, throwing a jacket over his arm, and racing for the place where the drill line ended. Because he had seen as he slid in for a landing, just what he had suspected from the topographical map. The drill didn't end in the middle of a desert at all. It went right on into the mountainside.

The excavation was quite large, the entrance covered and camouflaged neatly to give the very impression that he had gotten from the air. Under the camouflage the space was crowded, stacked with crates, boxes, materials, stacked all along the walls of the tunnel. He followed the rails in, lighting his way with a small pocket flashlight when the tunnel turned a corner, cutting off the daylight. Suddenly the tunnel widened, opening out into a much wider room. He sensed, rather than saw, the immense size of the vault, smelt the odd, bitter odor in the air. With the flashlight he probed the darkness, spotting the high, vaulted ceiling above him. And below him—

At first he couldn't see, probing the vast excavation before him, and then, strangely, he saw but couldn't realize what he saw. He stared for a solid minute, uncomprehending, then, stifling a gasp, he *knew what he was looking at*—

Lights. He had to have lights, to see clearly what he couldn't believe. Frantically, he spun the flashlight, seeking a light panel, and then, fascinated, he turned the little oval of light back to the pit. And then he heard the barest whisper of sound, the faintest intake of breath, and he ducked, frozen, as a blow whistled past his ear. A second blow from the side caught him solidly in the blackness, grunting, flailing out into a tangle of legs and arms, cursing, catching a foot in his face, striking up into soft, yielding flesh—

And his head suddenly exploded into a million dazzling lights as he sank unconscious to the ground—

*

It was a tiny room, completely without windows, the artificial light filtering through from ventilation slits near the top. Shandor sat up, shaking as the chill in the room became painfully evident. A small electric heater sat in the corner beaming valiantly, but the heat hardly reached his numbed toes. He stood up, shaking himself, slapping his arms against his sides to drive off the coldness—and he heard a noise through the door as soon as he had made a sound.

Muted footsteps stopped outside the door, and a huge man stepped inside. He looked at Shandor carefully, then closed the door behind him, without locking it. "I'm Baker," he rasped cheerfully. "How are you feeling?"

Shandor rubbed his head, suddenly and acutely aware of a very sore nose and a bruised rib cage. "Not so hot," he muttered. "How long have I been out?"

"Long enough." The man pulled out a plug of tobacco, ripped off a chunk with his teeth. "Chew?"

"I smoke." Shandor fished for cigarettes in an empty pocket.

"Not in here you don't," said Baker. He shrugged his huge shoulders and settled affably down on a bench near the wall. "You feel like talking?"

Shandor eyed the unlocked door, and turned his eyes to the huge man. "Sure," he said. "What do you want to talk about?"

"I don't want to talk about nothin'," the big man replied, indifferently. "Thought you might, though."

"Are you the one that roughed me up?"

"Yuh." Baker grinned. "Hope I didn't hurt you much. Boss said to keep you in one piece, but we had to hurry up, and take care of those Army guys you brought in on your tail. That was dumb. You almost upset everything."

Memory flooded back, and Shandor's eyes widened. "Yes—they followed me all the way from Lincoln—what happened to them?"

Baker grinned and chomped his tobacco. "They're a long way away now. Don't worry about them."

Shandor eyed the door uneasily. The latch hadn't caught, and the door had swung open an inch or two. "Where am I?" he asked, inching toward the door. "What—what are you planning to do to me?"

Baker watched him edging away. "You're safe," he said. "The boss'll talk to you pretty soon if you feel like it—" He squinted at Tom in surprise, pointing an indolent thumb toward the door. "You planning to go out or something?"

Tom stopped short, his face red. The big man shrugged. "Go ahead. I ain't going to stop you." He grinned. "Go as far as you can."

Without a word Shandor threw open the door, looked out into the concrete corridor. At the end was a large, bright room. Cautiously he started down, then suddenly let out a cry and broke into a run, his eyes wide—

He reached the room, a large room, with heavy plastic windows. He ran to one of the windows, pulse pounding, and stared, a cry choking in his throat. The blackness of the crags contrasted dimly with the inky blackness of the sky beyond. Mile upon mile of jagged, rocky crags, black rock, ageless, unaged rock. And it struck him with a jolt how easily he had been able to run, how lightning-swift his movements. He stared again, and then he saw what he had seen in the pit, standing high outside the building on a rocky flat, standing bright and silvery, like a phantom finger pointing to the inky heavens, sleek, smooth, resting on polished tailfins, like an other-worldly bird poised for flight—

A voice behind him said, "You aren't really going anyplace, you know. Why run?" It was a soft voice, a kindly voice, cultured, not rough and biting like Baker's voice. It came from directly behind Shandor, and he felt his skin crawl. He had heard that voice before—many times before. Even in his dreams he had heard that voice. "You see, it's pretty cold out there. And there isn't any air. You're on the Moon, Mr. Shandor—"

He whirled, his face twisted and white. And he stared at the small figure standing at the door, a stoop-shouldered man, white hair slightly untidy, crow's-feet about his tired eyes. An old man, with eyes that carried a sparkle of youth and kindliness. The eyes of David P. Ingersoll.

*

Shandor stared for a long moment, shaking his head like a man seeing a phantom. When he found words, his voice was choked, the words wrenched out as if by force. "You're—you're alive."

"Yes. I'm alive."

"Then—" Shandor shook his head violently, turning to the window, and back to the small, white-haired man. "Then your death was just a fake."

The old man nodded tiredly. "That's right. Just a fake."

Shandor stumbled to a chair, sat down woodenly. "I don't get it," he said dully. "I just don't get it. The war—that—that I can see. I can see how you worked it, how you engineered it, but this—" he gestured feebly at the window, at the black, impossible landscape outside. "This I can't see. They're bombing us to pieces, they're bombing out Washington, probably your own home, your own family—last night—" he stopped, frowning in confusion—"no, it couldn't have been last night—two days ago?—well, whatever day it was, they were bombing us to pieces, and you're up here—*why*? What's it going to get you? This war, this whole rotten intrigue mess, and then *this*?"

The old man walked across the room and stared for a moment at the silent ship outside. "I hope I can make you understand. We had to come here. We had no choice. We couldn't do what we wanted any other way than to come here—*first*. Before anybody else."

"But why *here*? They're building a rocket there in Arizona. They'll be up here in a few days, maybe a few weeks—"

"Approximately forty-eight hours," corrected Ingersoll quietly. "Within forty-eight hours the Arizona rocket will be here. If the Russian rocket doesn't get here first."

"It doesn't make sense. It won't do you any good to be here if the Earth is blasted to bits. Why come here? And why bring *me* here, of all people? What do you want with me?"

Ingersoll smiled and sat down opposite Shandor. "Take it easy," he said gently. "You're here, you're safe, and you're going to get the whole story. I realize that this is a bit of a jolt—but you had to be jolted. With you I think the jolt will be very beneficial, since we want you with us. That's why we brought you here. We need your help, and we need it very badly. It's as simple as that."

Shandor was on his feet, his eyes blazing. "No dice. This is your game, not mine. I don't want anything to do with it—"

"But you don't know the game—"

"I know plenty of the game. I followed the trail, right from the start. I know the whole rotten mess. The trail led me all the way around Robin Hood's barn, but it told me things—oh, it told me plenty! It told me about you, and this war. And now you want me to help you! What do you want me to do? Go down and tell the people it isn't really so bad being pounded to shreds? Should I tell them they aren't really being bombed, it's all in their minds? Shall I tell them this is a war to defend their freedoms, that it's a great crusade against the evil forces of the world? What kind of a sap do you think I am?" He walked to the window, his whole body trembling with anger. "I followed this trail down to the end, I scraped my way down into the dirtiest, slimiest depths of the barrel, and I've found you down there, and your rotten corporations, and your crowd of heelers. And on the other side are three hundred million people taking the lash end of the whip on Earth, helping to feed you. And you ask me to help you!"

"Once upon a time," Ingersoll interrupted quietly, "there was a fox."

Shandor stopped and stared at him.

"—and the fox got caught in a trap. A big bear trap, with steel jaws, that clamped down on him and held him fast by the leg. He wrenched and he pulled, but he couldn't break that trap open, no matter what he did. And the fox knew that the farmer would come along almost any time to open that bear trap, and the fox knew the farmer would kill him. He knew that if he didn't get out of that trap, he'd be finished, sure as sin. But he was a clever fox, and he found a way to get out of the bear trap." Ingersoll's voice was low, tense in the still room. "Do you know what he did?"

Shandor shook his head silently.

"It was a very simple solution," said Ingersoll. "Drastic, but simple. *He gnawed off his leg.*"

Another man had entered the room, a small, weasel-faced man with sallow cheeks and slick black hair. Ingersoll looked up with a smile, but Mariel waved him on, and took a seat nearby.

"So he chewed off his leg," Shandor repeated dully. "I don't get it."

"The world is in a trap," said Ingersoll, watching Shandor with quiet eyes. "A great big bear trap. It's been in that trap for decades—ever since the first World War. The world has come to a wall it can't climb, a trap it can't get out of, a vicious, painful, torturous trap, and the world has been struggling for seven decades to get out. It hasn't succeeded. And the time is drawing rapidly nigh for the farmer to come. Something had to be done, and done fast, before it was too late. The fox had to chew off its leg. And I had to bring the world to the brink of a major war."

Shandor shook his head, his mind buzzing. "I don't see what you mean. We never had a chance for peace, we never had a chance to get our feet on the ground from one round to the next. No time to do anything worthwhile in the past seventy years—I don't see what you mean about a trap."

Ingersoll settled back in his chair, the light catching his face in sharp profile. "It's been a century of almost continuous war," he said. "You've pointed out the whole trouble. We haven't had time to catch our breath, to make a real peace. The first World War was a sorry affair, by our standards—almost a relic of earlier European wars. Trench fighting, poor rifles, soap-box aircraft—nothing to distinguish it from earlier wars but its scope. But twenty uneasy years went by, and another war began, a very different sort of war. This one had fast aircraft, fast mechanized forces, heavy bombing, and finally, to cap the climax, atomics. That second World War could hold up its head as a real, strapping, fighting war in any society of wars. It was a stiff war, and a terrible one. Quite a bit of progress, for twenty years. But essentially, it was a war of ideologies, just as the previous one had been. A war of intolerance, of unmixable ideas—"

The old man paused, and drew a sip of water from the canister in the corner. "Somewhere, somehow, the world had missed the boat. Those wars didn't solve anything, they didn't even make a very strong pretense. They just made things worse. Somewhere, human society had gotten into a trap, a vicious circle. It had reached the end of its progressive tether, it had no place to go, no place to expand, to great common goal. So ideologies arose to try to solve the dilemma of a basically static society, and they fought wars. And they reached a point, finally, where they could destroy themselves unless they broke the vicious circle, somehow."

Shandor looked up, a deep frown on his face. "You're trying to say that they needed a new frontier."

"Exactly! They desperately needed it. There was only one more frontier they could reach for. A frontier which, once attained, has no real end." He gestured toward the black landscape outside. "There's the frontier. Space. The one thing that could bring human wars to an end. A vast, limitless frontier which could drive men's spirits upward and outward for the rest of time. And that frontier seemed unattainable. It was blocked off by a wall, by the jaws of a trap. Oh, they tried. After the first war the work began. The second war contributed unimaginably to the technical knowledge. But after the second war, they could go no further. Because it cost money, it required a tremendous effort on the part of the people of a great nation to do it, and they couldn't see why they should spend the money to get to space. After all, they had to work up the atomics and new weapons for the next war—it was a trap, as strong and treacherous as any the people of the world had ever encountered.

"The answer, of course, was obvious. Each war brought a great surge of technological development, to build better weapons, to fight bigger wars. Some developments led to extremely beneficial ends, too—if it hadn't been for the second war, a certain British biologist might still be piddling around his understaffed, underpaid laboratory, wishing he had more money, and wondering why it was that that dirty patch of mold on his petri dish seemed to keep bacteria from growing—but the second war created a sudden, frantic, urgent demand for something, anything, that would *stop infection—fast.* And in no time, penicillin was in mass production, saving untold thousands of lives. There was no question of money. Look at the Manhattan project. How many millions went into that? It gave us atomic power, for war, and for peace. For peaceful purposes, the money would never have been spent. But if it was for the sake of war—"

Ingersoll smiled tiredly. "Sounds insane, doesn't it? But look at the record. I looked at the record, way back at the end of the war with China. Other men looked at the record, too. We got together, and talked. We knew that the military advantage of a rocket base on the moon could be a deciding factor in another major war. Military experts had recognized that fact back in the 1950's. Another war could give men the technological kick they needed to get them to space—possibly *in time.* If men got to space before they destroyed themselves, the trap would be broken, the frontier would be opened, and men could turn their energies away from destruction toward something infinitely greater and more important. With space on his hands men could get along without wars. But if we waited for peacetime to go to space, we might never make it. It might be too late.

"It was a dreadful undertaking. I saw the wealth in the company I directed and controlled at the end of the Chinese war, and the idea grew strong. I saw that a huge industrial amalgamation could be undertaken, and succeed. We had a weapon in our favor, the most dangerous weapon ever devised, a thousand times more potent than atomics. Hitler used it, with terrible success. Stalin used it. Haro-Tsing used it. Why couldn't Ingersoll use it? Propaganda—a terrible weapon. It could make people think the right way—it could make them think almost *any* way. It made them think war. From the end of the last war we started, with propaganda, with politics, with money. The group grew stronger as our power became more clearly understood. Mariel handled propaganda through the newspapers, and PIB, and magazines—a clever man—and Harry Dartmouth handled production. I handled the politics and diplomacy. We had but one aim in mind—to bring about a threat of major war that would drive men to space. To the moon, to a man-made satellite, *somewhere or anywhere* to break through the Earth's gravity and get to space. And we aimed at a controlled war. We had the power to do it, we had the money and the plants. We just had to be certain it wasn't the *ultimate* war. It wasn't easy to make sure that atomic weapons wouldn't be used this time—but they will not. Both nations are too much afraid, thanks to our propaganda program. They both leaped at a chance to make a face-saving agreement. And we hoped that the war could be held off until we got to the moon, and until the Arizona rocket project could get a ship launched for the moon. The wheels we had started just moved too fast. I saw at the beginning of the Berlin Conference that it would explode into war, so I decided the time for my 'death' had arrived. I had to come here, to make sure the war doesn't go on any longer than necessary."

Shandor looked up at the old man, his eyes tired. "I still don't see where I'm supposed to fit in. I don't see why you came here at all. Was that a wild-goose chase I ran down there, learning about this?"

"Not a wild goose chase. The important work can't start, you see, until the rocket gets here. It wouldn't do much good if the Arizona rocket got here, to fight the war. It may come for war, but it must go back for peace. We built this rocket to get us here first—built it from government specifications, though they didn't know it. We had the plant to build it in, and we were able to hire technologists *not* to find the right answers in Arizona until we were finished. Because the whole value of the war-threat depended solely and completely upon our getting here *first*. When the Arizona rocket gets to the moon, the war must be stopped. Only then can we start the real 'operation Bear Trap.' That ship, whether American or Russian, will meet with a great surprise when it reaches the Moon. We haven't been spotted here. We left in darkness and solitude, and if we were seen, it was chalked off as a guided missile. We're well camouflaged, and although we don't have any sort of elaborate base—just a couple of sealed rooms—we have a ship and we have weapons. When the first ship comes up here, the control of the situation will be in our hands. Because when it comes, it will be sent back with an ultimatum to *all* nations—to cease warfare, or suffer the most terrible, nonpartisan bombardment the world has ever seen. A pinpoint bombardment, from our ship, here on the Moon. There won't be too much bickering I think. The war will stop. All eyes will turn to us. And then the big work begins."

He smiled, his thin face showing tired lines in the bright light. "I may die before the work is done. I don't know, nor care. I have no successor, nor have we any plans to perpetuate our power once the work is done. As soon as the people themselves will take over the work, the job is theirs, because no group can hope to ultimately control space. But first people must be sold on space, from the bottom up. They must be forced to realize the implications of a ship on the moon. They must realize that the first ship was the hardest, that the trap is sprung. The amputation is a painful one, there wasn't any known anaesthetic, but it will heal, and from here there is no further need for war. But the people must see that, understand its importance. They've got to have the whole story, in terms that they can't mistake. And that means a propagandist—"

"You have Mariel," said Shandor. "He's had the work, the experience—"

"He's getting tired. He'll tell you himself his ideas are slow, he isn't on his toes any longer. He needs a new man, a helper, to take his place. When the first ship comes, his job is done." The old man smiled. "I've watched you, of course, for years. Mariel saw that you were given his job when he left PIB to edit '*Fighting World*.' He didn't think you were the man, he didn't trust you—thought you had been raised too strongly on the sort of gibberish you were writing. I thought you were the only man we could use. So we let you follow the trail, and watched to see how you'd handle it. And when you came to the Nevada plant, we *knew* you were the man we had to have—"

Shandor scowled, looking first at Ingersoll, then at Mariel's impassive face. "What about Ann?" he asked, and his voice was unsteady. "She knew about it all the time?"

"No. She didn't know anything about it. We were afraid she had upset things when she didn't turn my files over to Dartmouth as he'd told her. We were afraid you'd go ahead and write the story as you saw it then, which would have wrecked our plan completely. As it was, she helped us sidestep the danger in the long run, but she didn't know what she was really doing." He grinned. "The error was ours, of course. We simply underestimated our man. We didn't know you were that tenacious."

Shandor's face was haggard. "Look. I—I don't know what to think. This ship in Arizona—how long? When will it come? How do you know it'll ever come?"

"We waited until our agents there gave us a final report. The ship may be leaving at any time. But there's no doubt that it'll come. If it doesn't, one from Russia will. It won't be long." He looked at Shandor closely. "You'll have to decide by then, Tom."

"And if I don't go along with you?"

"We could lose. It's as simple as that. Without a spokesman, the plan could fall through completely. There's only one thing you need to make your decision, Tom—faith in men, and a sure conviction that man was made for the stars, and not for an endless circle of useless wars. Think of it, Tom. That's what your decision means."

Shandor walked to the window, stared out at the bleak landscape, watched the great bluish globe of earth, hanging like a huge balloon in the black sky. He saw the myriad pinpoints of light in the blackness on all sides of it, and shook his head, trying to think. So many things to think of, so very many things—

"I don't know," he muttered. "I just don't know—"

*

It was a long night. Ideas are cruel, they become a part of a man's brain, an inner part of his chemistry, they carve grooves deep in his mind which aren't easily wiped away. He knew he'd been living a lie, a bitter, hopeless, endless lie, all his life, but a liar grows to believe his own lies. Even to the point of destruction, he believes them. It was so hard to see the picture, now that he had the last piece in place.

A fox, and a bear trap. Such a simple analogy. War was a hellish proposition, it was cruel, it was evil. It could be lost, so very easily. And it seemed so completely, utterly senseless to cut off one's own leg—

And then he thought, somewhere, sometime, he'd see her again. Perhaps they'd be old by then, but perhaps not—perhaps they'd still be young, and perhaps she wouldn't know the true story yet. Perhaps he could be the first to tell her, to let her know that he had been wrong— Maybe there could be a chance to be happy, on Earth, sometime. They might marry, even, there might be children. To be raised for what? Wars and wars and more wars? Or was there another alternative? Perhaps the stars were winking brighter—

*

A hoarse shout rang through the quiet rooms. Ingersoll sat bolt upright, turned his bright eyes to Mariel, and looked down the passageway. And then they were crowding to the window as one of the men snapped off the lights in the room, and they were staring up at the pale bluish globe that hung in the sky, squinting, breathless—

And they saw the tiny, tiny burst of brightness on one side of that globe, saw a tiny whisp of yellow, cutting an arc from the edge, moving farther and farther into the black circle of space around the Earth, slicing like a thin scimitar, moving higher and higher, and then, magically, winking out, leaving a tiny, evaporating trail behind it.

"You saw it?" whispered Mariel in the darkness. "You saw it, David?"

"Yes. I saw it." Ingersoll breathed deeply, staring into the blackness, searching for a glimmer, a glint, some faint reassurance that it had not been a mirage they had seen. And then Ingersoll felt a hand in his, Tom Shandor's hand, gripping his tightly, wringing it, and when the lights snapped on again, he was staring at Shandor, tears of happiness streaming from his pale, tired eyes. "You saw it?" he whispered.

Shandor nodded, his heart suddenly too large for his chest, a peace settling down on him greater than any he had ever known in his life.

"They're coming," he said.

MARTYR

"I can break him, split his Criterion Committee wide open *now* while there's still a chance, and open rejuvenation up to everybody...."

*

Four and one half hours after Martian sunset, the last light in the Headquarters Building finally blinked out.

Carl Golden stamped his feet nervously against the cold, cupping his cigarette in his hand to suck up the tiny spark of warmth. The night air bit his nostrils and made the smoke tasteless in the darkness. Atmosphere screens kept the oxygen in, all right—but they never kept the biting cold out. As the light disappeared he dropped the cigarette, stamping it sharply into darkness. Boredom vanished, and warm blood prickled through his shivering legs.

He slid back tight against the coarse black building front, peering across the road in the gloom.

It was the girl. He had thought so, but hadn't been sure. She swung the heavy stone door shut after her, glanced both left and right, and started down the frosty road toward the lights of the colony.

Carl Golden waited until she was gone. He glanced at his wrist-chrono, and waited ten minutes more. He didn't realize that he was trembling until he ducked swiftly across the road. Through the window of the low, one-story building he could see the lobby call-board, with the little colored studs all dark. He smiled in unpleasant satisfaction—no one was left in the building. It was routine, just like everything else in this god-forsaken hole. Utter, abysmal, trancelike routine. The girl was a little later than usual, probably because of the ship coming in tomorrow. Reports to get ready, supply requisitions, personnel recommendations—

—and the final reports on Armstrong's death. Mustn't forget that. The *real* story, the absolute, factual truth, without any nonsense. The reports that would go, ultimately, to Rinehart and only Rinehart, as all other important reports from the Mars Colony had been doing for so many years.

Carl skirted the long, low building, falling into the black shadows of the side wall. Halfway around he came to the supply chute, covered with a heavy moulded-stone cover.

Now?

It had taken four months here to know that he would have to do it this way. Four months of ridiculous masquerade—made idiotic by the incredible fact that everyone took him for exactly what he pretended to be, and never challenged him—not even Terry Fisher, who drunk or sober always challenged everything and everybody! But the four months had told on his nerves, in his reactions, in the hollows under his quick brown eyes. There was always the spectre of a slip-up, an aroused suspicion. And until he had the reports before his eyes, he couldn't fall back on Dan Fowler's name to save him. He had shook Dan's hand the night he had left, and Dan had said, "Remember, son—I don't know you. Hate to do it this way, but we can't risk it now—" And they couldn't, of course. Not until they knew, for certain, who had murdered Kenneth Armstrong.

They already knew why.

*

The utter stillness of the place reassured him; he hoisted up the chute cover, threw it high, and shinned his long body into the chute. It was a steep slide; he held on for an instant, then let go. Blackness gulped him down as the cover snapped closed behind him.

He struck hard and rolled. The chute opened into the commissary in the third deep-level of the building, and the place was black as the inside of a pocket. He tested unbroken legs with a sigh of relief, and limped across to where the door should be.

In the corridor there was some light—dim phosphorescence from the Martian night-rock lining the walls and tiling the floor. He walked swiftly, cursing the clack-clack his heels made on the ringing stone. When he reached the end of the corridor he tried the heavy door.

It gave, complaining. Good, good! It had been a quick, imperfect job of jimmying the lock, so obviously poor that it had worried him a lot—but why should they test it? There was still another door.

He stepped into the blackness again, started across the room as the door swung shut behind him.

A shoe scraped, the faintest rustle of sound. Carl froze. His own trouser leg? A trick of acoustics? He didn't move a muscle.

Then: "Carl?"

His pocket light flickered around the room, a small secretary's ante-room. It stopped on a pair of legs, a body, slouched down in the soft plastifoam chair—a face, ruddy and bland, with a shock of sandy hair, with quixotic eyebrows. "Terry! For Christ sake, what—"

The man leaned forward, grinning up at him. "You're late, Carl." His voice was a muddy drawl. "Should have made it sooner than this, sheems—seems to me."

Carl's light moved past the man in the chair to the floor. The bottle was standing there, still half full. "My god, you're *drunk*!"

"Course I'm drunk. Whadj-ya think, I'd sober up after you left me tonight? No thanks, I'd rather be drunk." Terry Fisher hiccupped loudly. "I'd always rather be drunk, around this place."

"All right, you've got to get out of here—" Carl's voice rose with bitter anger. Of all times, of *all* times—he wanted to scream. "How did you get in here? You've *got* to get out—"

"So do you. They're on to you, Carl. I don't think you know that, but they are." He leaned forward precariously. "I had a talk with Barness this morning, one of his nice 'spontaneous' chats, and he pumped the hell out of me and thought I was too drunk to know it. They're expecting you to come here tonight—"

Carl heaved at the drunken man's arm, frantically in the darkness. "Get *out* of here, Terry, or so help me—"

Terry clutched at him. "Didn't you hear me? They *know* about you. Personell supervisor! They think you're spying for the Eastern boys—they're starting a Mars colony too, you know. Barness is sure you're selling them info—" The man hiccupped again. "Barness is an ass, just like all the other Retreads running this place, but I'm not an ass, and you didn't fool me for two days—"

Carl gritted his teeth. How could Terry Fisher know? "For the last time—"

Fisher lurched to his feet. "They'll get you, Carl. They can try you and shoot you right on the spot, and Barness will do it. I had to tell you, you've walked right into it, but you might still get away if—"

It was cruel. The drunken man's head jerked up at the blow, and he gave a little grunt, then slid back down on the chair. Carl stepped over his legs, worked swiftly at the door beyond. If they caught him now, Terry Fisher was right. But in five more minutes—

The lock squeaked, and the door fell open. Inside he tore through the file cases, wrenched at the locked drawers in frantic haste, ripping the weak aluminum sheeting like thick tinfoil. Then he found the folder marked KENNETH ARMSTRONG on the tab.

Somewhere above him an alarm went off, screaming a mournful note through the building. He threw on the light switch, flooding the room with whiteness, and started through the papers, one by one, in the folder. No time to read. Flash retinal photos were hard to superimpose and keep straight, but that was one reason why Carl Golden was on Mars instead of sitting in an office back on Earth—

He flipped the last page, and threw the folder onto the floor. As he went through the door, he flipped out the light, raced with clattering footsteps down the corridor.

Lights caught him from both sides, slicing the blackness like hot knives. "*All right, Golden. Stop right there.*"

Dark figures came out of the lights, ripped his clothing off without a word. Somebody wrenched open his mouth, shined a light in, rammed coarse cold fingers down into his throat. Then: "All right, you bastard, up stairs. Barness wants to see you."

They packed him naked into the street, hurried him into a three-wheeled ground car. Five minutes later he was wading through frosty dust into another building, and Barness was glaring at him across the room.

*

Odd things flashed through Carl's mind. You seldom saw a Repeater get really angry—but Barness was angry. The man's young-old face (the strange, utterly ageless amalgamation of sixty years of wisdom, superimposed by the youth of a twenty-year-old) had unaccustomed lines of wrath about the eyes and mouth. Barness didn't waste words. "What did you want down there?"

"Armstrong." Carl cut the word out almost gleefully. "And I got it, and there's nothing you or Rinehart or anybody else in between can do about it. I don't know *what* I saw yet, but I've got it in my eyes and in my cortex, and you can't touch it."

"You stupid fool, we can *peel* your cortex," Barness snarled.

"Well, you won't. You won't dare."

Barness glanced across at the officer who had brought him in. "Tommy—"

"Dan Fowler won't like it," said Carl.

Barness stopped short, blinking. He took a slow breath. Then he sank down into his chair. "Fowler" he said, as though dawn were just breaking.

"That's right. He sent me up here. I've found what he wants. Shoot me now, and when they probe you Dan will know I found it, and you won't be around for another rejuvenation."

Barness looked suddenly old. "What did he want?"

"The truth about Armstrong. Not the 'accident' story you fed to the teevies.... "*Tragic End for World Hero, Died With His Boots On*". Dan wanted the truth. Who killed him. Why this colony is grinding down from compound low to stop, and turning men like Terry Fisher into alcoholic bums. Why this colony is turning into a glorified, super-refined Birdie's Rest for old men. But mostly who killed Armstrong, how he was murdered, who gave the orders. And if you don't mind, I'm beginning to get cold."

"And you got all that," said Barness.

"That's right."

"You haven't read it, though."

"Not yet. Plenty of time for that on the way back."

Barness nodded wearily, and motioned the guard to give Carl his clothes. "I think you'd better read it tonight. Maybe it'll surprise you."

Golden's eyes widened. Something in the man's voice, some curious note of defeat and hopelessness, told him that Barness was not lying. "Oh?"

"Armstrong didn't have an accident, that's true. But nobody murdered him, either. Nobody gave any orders, to anybody, from anybody. Armstrong put a bullet through his head—quite of his own volition."

II

"All right, Senator," the young red-headed doctor said. "You say you want it straight—that's how you're going to get it." Moments before, Dr. Moss had been laughing. Now he wasn't laughing. "Six months, at the outside. Nine, if you went to bed tomorrow, retired from the Senate, and lived on tea and crackers. But where I'm sitting I wouldn't bet a plugged nickel that you'll be alive a month from now. If you think I'm joking, you just try to squeeze a bet out of me."

Senator Dan Fowler took the black cigar from his mouth, stared at the chewed-up end for a moment, and put it back in again. He had had something exceedingly witty all ready to say at this point in the examination; now it didn't seem to be too funny. If Moss had been a mealy-mouthed quack like the last Doc he had seen, okay. But Moss wasn't. Moss was obviously not impressed by the old man sitting across the desk from him, a fact which made Dan Fowler just a trifle uneasy. And Moss knew his turnips.

Dan Fowler looked at the doctor and said, "Garbage."

The red-headed doctor shrugged. "Look, Senator—sometimes a banana is a banana. I know heart disease, and I know how it acts. I know that it kills people if they wait too long. And when you're dead, no rejuvenation lab is going to bring you back to life again."

"Oh, hell! Who's dying?" Fowler's grey eyebrows knit in the old familiar scowl, and he bit down hard on the cigar. "Heart disease! So I get a little pain now and then—sure it won't last forever, and when it gets bad I'll come in and take the full treatment. But I can't do it now!" He spread his hands in a violent gesture. "I only came in here because my daughter dragged me. My heart's doing fine—I've been working an eighteen hour day for forty years now, and I can do it for another year or two—"

"But you have pain," said Dr. Moss.

"So? A little twinge, now and then."

"Whenever you lose your temper. Whenever anything upsets you."

"All right—a twinge."

"Which makes you sit down for ten or fifteen minutes. Which doesn't go away with one nitro-tablet any more, so you have to take two, and sometimes three—right?"

*

Dan Fowler blinked. "All right, sometimes it gets a little bad—"

"And it used to be only once or twice a month, but now it's almost every day. And once or twice you've blacked clean out for a while, and made your staff work like demons to cover for you and keep it off the teevies, right?"

"Say, who's been talking to you?"

"Jean has been talking to me."

"Can't even trust your own daughter to keep her trap shut." The Senator tossed the cigar butt down in disgust. "It happened once, yes. That god damned Rinehart is enough to make anybody black out." He thrust out his jaw and glowered at Dr. Moss as though it were all *his* fault. Then he grinned. "Oh, I know you're right, Doc. It's just that this is the wrong *time*. I can't take two months out now—there's too much to be done between now and the middle of next month."

"Oh, yes. The Hearings. Why not turn it over to your staff? They know what's going on."

"Nonsense. They know, but not like I know. After the Hearings, fine—I'll come along like a lamb. But now—"

Dr. Moss reddened, slammed his fist down on the desk. "Dammit, man, are you blind and deaf? Or just plain stupid? Didn't you hear me a moment ago? *You may not live through the Hearings.* You could *go*, just like that, any minute. But this is 2134 A.D., not the middle ages. It would be so utterly, hopelessly pointless to let that happen—"

Fowler champed his cigar and scowled. "After it was done I'd have to Free-Agent for a year, wouldn't I?" It was an accusation.

"You *should*. But that's a formality. If you want to go back to what you were doing the day you came from the Center—"

"Yes, *if*! But supposing I didn't? Supposing I was all changed?"

The young doctor looked at the old man shrewdly. Dan Fowler was 56 years old—and he looked forty. It seemed incredible even to Moss that the man could have done what he had done, and look almost as young and fighting-mad now as he had when he started. Clever old goat, too—but Dan Fowler's last remark opened the hidden door wide. Moss smiled to himself. "You're afraid of it, aren't you, Senator?"

"Of rejuvenation? Nonsense."

"But you are. You aren't the only one—it's a pretty frightening thing. Cash in the old model, take out a new one, just like a jet racer or a worn out talk-writer. Only it isn't machinery, it's your body, and your life." Dr. Moss grinned. "It scares a man. *Rejuvenation* isn't the right word, of course. Aside from the neurones, they take away every cell in your body, one way or another, and give you new ones. A hundred and fifty years ago Cancelmo and Klein did it on a dog, and called it *sub-total prosthesis*. A crude job—I've seen their papers and films. Vat-grown hearts and kidneys, revitalized vascular material, building up new organ systems like a patchwork quilt, coaxing new tissues to grow to replace old ones—but they got a living dog out of it, and that dog lived to the ripe old age of 37 years before he died."

*

Moss pushed back from his desk, watching Dan Fowler's face. "Then in 1992 Nimrock tried it on a man, and almost got himself hanged because the man died. That was a hundred and forty-two years ago. And then while he was still on trial, his workers completed the second job, and the man *lived*, and oh, how the jig changed for Nimrock!"

The doctor shrugged. As he talked, Dan Fowler sat silent, chewing his cigar furiously. But listening—he was listening, all right. "Well, it was crude, then," Moss said. "It's not so crude any more." He pointed to a large bronze plaque hanging on the office wall. "You've seen that before. Read it."

Dan Fowler's eyes went up to the plaque. A list of names. At the top words said, "*These ten gave life to Mankind.*"

Below it were the names:

Martin Aronson, Ph. D. Education

Thomas Bevalaqua Literature and Art

Chauncy Devlin Music

Frederick A. Kehler, M. S. Engineering

William B. Morse, L. L. D. Law

Rev. Hugh H. F. Norton Philosophy and Theology

Jacob Prowsnitz, Ph. D. History

Arthur L. Rodgers, M. D. Medicine

Carlotta Sokol, Ph. D. Sociopsychology

Harvey Tatum Business

"I know," said Dan Fowler. "June 1st, 2005. They were volunteers."

"Ten out of several dozen volunteers," Moss amended. "Those ten were chosen by lot. Already people were dreaming of what sub-total prosthesis could do. It could preserve the great minds, it could compound the accumulated wisdom of one lifetime with another lifetime—and maybe more. Those ten people—representing ten great fields of study—risked their lives. Not to live forever—just to see if rejuvenation could really preserve their minds in newly built bodies. All of them were old, older than you are, Senator, some were sicker than you, and all of them were afraid. But seven of the ten are *still alive today*, a hundred and thirty years later. Rodgers died in a jet crash. Tatum died of neuro-toxic virus, because we couldn't do anything to rebuild neurones in those days. Bevalaqua suicided. The rest are still alive, after two more rejuvenations."

"Fine," said Dan Fowler. "I still can't do it now."

"That was just ten people," Moss cut in. "It took five years to get ready for them. But now we can do five hundred a year—only five hundred select individuals, to live on instead of dying. And you've got the gall to sit there and tell me you don't have the time for it!"

*

The old man rose slowly, lighting another cigar. "It could be five thousand a year. That's why I don't have the time. Fifteen thousand, fifty thousand. We could do it—but we're not doing it. Walter Rinehart's been rejuvenated—twice already! *I'm* on the list because I shouted so loud they didn't dare leave me off. But *you're* not on it. Why not? You could be. Everybody could be."

Dr. Moss spread his hands. "The Criterion Committee does the choosing."

"*Rinehart's* criteria! Only five hundred a year. Use it for a weapon. Build power with it. Get a strangle-hold on it, and never, never let it go." The Senator leaned across the desk, his eyes bright with anger. "I haven't got time to stop what I'm doing now—because I can *stop* Rinehart, if I only live that long, I can break him, split his Criterion Committee wide open *now* while there's still a chance, and open rejuvenation up to everybody instead of five hundred lucky ones a year. I can stop him because I've dug at him and dug at him for twenty-nine years, and shouted and screamed and fought and made people listen. And if I fumble now, it'll all be down the drain, finished, washed up.

"If that happens, *nobody* will ever stop him."

There was silence in the room for a moment. Then Moss spread his hands. "The hearings are that critical, eh?"

"I'm afraid so."

"Why has it got to be *your* personal fight? Other people could do it."

"They'd fumble it. They'd foul it up. Senator Libby fouled it up once already, a long time ago. Rinehart's lived for a hundred and nineteen years, and he's learning new tricks every year. I've only lived fifty-six of them, but I know his tricks. I can beat him."

"But why *you?*"

"Somebody's got to do it. My card is on top."

A 'phone buzzer chirped. "Yes, he's here." Dr. Moss handed Dan the receiver. A moment later the Senator was grinning like a cat struggling into his overcoat and scarf. "Sorry, Doc—I know what you tell me is true, and I'm no fool. If I have to stop, I'll stop."

"Tomorrow, then."

"Not tomorrow. One of my lads is back from the Mars Colony. Tomorrow we pow-wow—but hard. After the hearings, Doc. And meanwhile, keep your eye on the teevies. I'll be seeing you."

The door clicked shut with a note of finality, and Dr. David Moss stared at it gloomily. "I hope so," he said. But nobody in particular heard him.

III

A Volta two-wheeler was waiting for him outside. Jean drove off down the drive with characteristic contempt for the laws of gravity when Dan had piled in, and Carl Golden was there, looking thinner, more gaunt and hawk-like than ever before, his brown eyes sharp under his shock of black hair, his long, thin aquiline nose ("If you weren't a Jew you'd be a discredit to the Gentiles," Dan Fowler had twitted him once, years before, and Carl had looked down his long, thin, aquiline nose, and sniffed, and let the matter drop, because until then he had never been sure whether his being a Jew had mattered to Dan Fowler or not, and now he knew, and was quite satisfied with the knowledge) and the ever-present cigarette between thin, sensitive fingers. Dan clapped him on the shoulder, and shot a black look at his daughter, relegating her to an indescribable Fowler limbo, which was where she belonged, and would reside until Dan got excited and forgot how she'd betrayed him to Dr. Moss, which would take about ten or fifteen minutes all told. Jean Fowler knew her father far too well to worry about it, and squinted out the window at the afternoon traffic as the car skidded the corner into the Boulevard Throughway, across the river toward home. "God damn it, boy, you could have *wired* me at least. One of Jean's crew spotted the passage list, so I knew you'd left, and got the hearing moved up to next month—"

Carl scowled. "I thought it was all set for February 15th."

Dan chuckled. "It was. But I was only waiting for you, and got the ball rolling as soon as I knew you were on your way. Dwight McKenzie is still writing the Committee's business calendar, of course, and he didn't like it a bit, but he couldn't find any solid reason why it *shouldn't* be set ahead. And I think our good friend Senator Rinehart is probably wriggling on the stick about now, just on the shock value of the switch. Always figure in the shock value of everything you do, my boy—it pays off more than you'd ever dream—"

Carl Golden shook his head. "I don't like it, Dan."

"What, the switch in dates?"

"The switch. I wish you hadn't done that."

"But why? Look, son, I know that with Ken Armstrong dead our whole approach has to be changed—it's going to be trickier, but it might even work out better. The Senate knows what's been going on between Rinehart and me, and so does the President. They know elections are due next June. They know I want a seat on his Criterion Committee before elections, and they know that to get on it I'll do my damnedest to unseat him. They know I've shaken him up, that he's scared of me. Okay, fine. With Armstrong there to tell how he was chosen for Retread back in '87, we'd have had Rinehart running for his life...."

"But you don't," Carl cut in flatly, "and that's that."

"What, are you crazy, son? *I needed Armstrong, bad.* Rinehart knew it, and had him taken care of. It was fishy—it stunk from here to Mars, but Rinehart covered it up fast and clean. But with the stuff you got up in the Colony, we can charge Rinehart with murder, and the whole Senate knows his motive already. He didn't *dare* to let Armstrong testify."

*

Carl was shaking his head sadly.

"Well, what's wrong?"

"You aren't going to like this, Dan. Rinehart's clean. Armstrong comitted suicide."

Fowler's mouth fell open, and he sat back hard. "Oh, no."

"Sorry."

"Ken Armstrong? Suicided?" He shook his head helplessly, groping for words. "I—I—oh, Jesus. I don't believe it. If Ken Armstrong suicided, I'm the Scarlet Whore of Babylon."

"Well, we'll try to keep *that* off the teevies."

"There's no chance that you're wrong," said the old man.

Carl shook his head. "There's plenty that's funny about that Mars Colony, but Armstrong's death was suicide. Period. Even Barness didn't understand it."

Sharp eyes went to Carl's face. "What's funny about the Colony?"

Carl shrugged, and lit a cigarette. "Hard to say. This was my first look, I had nothing to compare it with. But there's *something* wrong. I always thought the Mars Colony was a frontier, a real challenge—you know, Man against the Wilderness, and all that. Saloons jammed on Saturday nights with rough boys out to get some and babes that had it to give. A place that could take Earthbound softies and toughen them up in a week, working to tame down the desert—"

His voice trailed off. "They've got a saloon, all right—but everybody just comes in quietly and gets slobbery drunk. Met a guy named Fisher, thought the same thing I did when he came up five years ago. A real go-getter, leader type, lots of ideas and the guts to put them across. Now he's got a hob-nail liver and he came back here on the ship with me, hating Mars and everything up there, most of all himself. Something's wrong up there, Dan. Maybe that's why Armstrong bowed out."

The Senator took a deep breath. "Not a man like Ken Armstrong. Why, I used to worship him when I was a kid. I was ten when he came back to Earth for his second Retread." The old man shook his head. "I wanted to go back to Mars with him—I actually packed up to run away, until dear brother Paul caught me and squealed to Dad. Imagine."

"I'm sorry, Dan."

The car whizzed off the Throughway, and began weaving through the residential areas of Arlington. Jean swung under an arched gate, stopped in front of a large greystone house of the sort they hadn't built for a hundred years. Dan Fowler stared out at the grey November afternoon. "Well, then we're really on thin ice at the Hearings. We can still do it. It'll take some steam-rollering, but we can manage it." He turned to the girl. "Get Schirmer on the wire as soon as we get inside. I'll go over Carl's report for whatever I can find. Tell Schirmer if he wants to keep his job as Coordinator of the Medical Center next year, he'd better have all the statistics available on all rejuvenated persons past and present, in my office tomorrow morning."

Jean gave her father a queer look. "Schirmer's waiting for you inside right now."

"Oh? Why?"

"He wouldn't say. Nothing to do with politics, he said. Something about Paul."

*

Nathan Shirmer was waiting in the library, sipping a brandy and pretending to scan a Congressional Record in the viewer-box. He looked up, bird-like, as Dan Fowler strode in. "Well, Nate. Sit down, sit down. I see you're into my private stock already, so I won't offer you any. What's this about my brother?"

Schirmer coughed into his hand. "Why—Dan, I don't quite know how to tell you this. He was in Washington this afternoon—"

"Of course he was. He was supposed to go to the Center—" Dan broke off short, whirling on Schirmer. "Wait a minute! There wasn't a slip-up on this permit?"

"Permit?"

"For rejuvention, you ass! He's on the Starship Project, coordinating engineer of the whole works out there. He's got a fair place on the list coming to him three ways from Sunday. Follmer put the permit through months ago, and Paul has just been diddling around getting himself clear so he could come in—"

The little Coordinator's eyes widened. "Oh, there wasn't anything wrong on *our* side, if that's what you mean. The permit was perfectly clear, the doctors were waiting for him. It was nothing like that."

"Then what was it like?"

Nathan Schirmer wriggled, and tried to avoid Dan's eyes. "Your brother refused it. He laughed in our faces, and told us to go to hell, and took the next jet back to Nevada. All in one afternoon."

The vibration of the jet engines hung just at perception level, nagging and nagging at Dan Fowler, until he threw his papers aside with a snarl of disgust, and peered angrily out the window.

They were high, and moving fast. Far below was a tiny spot of light in the blackness. Pittsburgh. Maybe Cleveland. It didn't matter which. Jets traveled at such-and-such a rate of speed; they left at such-and-such a time and arrived elsewhere at such-and-such a time later. He could worry, or he could not-worry. The jet would bring him down in Las Vegas in exactly the same time, to the second, either way. Another half-hour taxi ride over dusty desert roads would bring him to the glorified quonset hut his brother called home. Nothing Dan Fowler could do would hurry the process of getting there.

Dan had called, and received no answer.

He had talked to the Las Vegas authorities, and even gotten Lijinsky at the Starship, and neither of them knew anything. The police said yes, they would check at Dr. Fowler's residence, if he wasn't out at the Ship, and check back. But they hadn't checked back, and that was two hours ago. Meanwhile, Carl had chartered him a plane.

God damn Paul to three kinds of hell. Of all miserable times to start playing games, acting like an imbecile child! And the work and sweat Dan had gone through to get that permit, to buy it beg it, steal it, gold-plate it. Of course the odds were good that Paul would have gotten it without a whisper from Dan—he was high on the list, he was critical to Starship, and certainly Starship was critical enough to rate. But Dan had gone out on a limb, way out—The Senator's fist clenched, and he drummed it helplessly on the empty seat, and felt a twinge of pain spread up his chest, down his arm. He cursed, fumbled for the bottle in his vest pocket. God damned heart and god damned brother and god damned Rinehart—did *everything* have to split the wrong way? Now? Of all times of all days of all his fifty-six years of life, *now?*

All right, Dan. Cool, boy. Relax. Shame on you. Can't you quit being selfish just for a little while? Dan didn't like the idea as it flickered through his mind, but then he didn't like anything too much right then, so he forced the thought back for a rerun.

Big Dan Fowler, *Senator* Dan Fowler, Selfish Dan Fowler loves Dan Fowler mostly.

Poor Paul.

*

The words had been going through his mind like a silly chant since the first moment he had seen Nate Schirmer in the library. Poor Paul. Dan did all right for himself, he did—made quite a name down in Washington, you know, a fighter, a real fighter. The Boy with the Golden Touch (joke, son, laugh now). Everything he ever did worked out with him on top, somehow. Paul was different. Smart enough, plenty of the old gazoo, but he never had Dan's drive. Bad breaks, right down the line. Kinda tough on a guy, with a comet like Dan in the family. Poor Paul.

He let his mind drift back slowly, remembering little things, trying to spot the time, the single instant in time, when he stopped fighting Paul and started feeling sorry for him. It had been different, years ago. Paul was the smart one, all right. Never had Dan's build but he could think rings around him. Dan was always a little slow—never forgot anything he learned, but he learned slow. Still, there were ways to get around that—

Dad and Mom always liked Paul the best (their first boy, you know) and babied him more, and that was decidedly tougher to get around—Still there were ways.

Like the night the prize money came from the lottery, when he and Paul had split a ticket down the middle. How old was he then—ten? Eleven? And Paul was fifteen. He'd grubbed up the dollar polishing cars, and met Paul's dollar halfway, never dreaming the thing would pay off. And when it did! Oh, he'd never forget that night. He wanted the jet-racer. The ticket paid two thousand, a hell of a lot of cash for a pair of boys—and the two thousand would buy the racer. He'd been so excited tears had poured down his face.... But Paul had said no. Split it even, just like the ticket, Paul had said. There were hot words, and pleading, and threats, and Paul had just laughed at him until he got so mad he wanted to kill him with only his fists. Bad mistake, that. Paul was skinny, not much muscle, read books all the time it looked like a cinch. But Paul had five years on him that he hadn't counted on. Important five years. Paul connected with just one—enough to lay Dan flat on his back with a concussion and a broken jaw, and that, my boy, was that.

Almost.

Dan had won the fight, of course. It was the broken jaw that did it, that night, later the fight Mom and Dad had, worse than usual, a cruel one, low blows, mean—But Dan got his racer, on the strength of the broken jaw. That jaw had done him a lot of good. Never grew quite right after that, got one of the centers of ossification, the doc had said, and Dan had been god's gift to the pen-and-brush men with that heavy, angular jaw—a fighter's jaw, they called it.

*

That started it, of course. He knew then that he could beat Paul. Good to know. But never *sure* of it, always having to prove it. The successes came, and always he let Paul know about them, watched Paul's face like a cat. And Paul would squirm, and sneer, and tell Dan that in the end it was brains that would pay off. Sour grapes, of course. If Paul had ever squared off to him again, man to man, they might have had it over with. But Paul just seemed content to sit and quietly hate him.

Like the night he broke the Universalists in New Chicago, at the hundred-dollar-a-plate dinner. He'd told them, that night. That was the night they'd cold-shouldered him, and put Libby up to run for Mayor. Oh, he'd raised a glorious stink that night—he'd never enjoyed himself so much in his life, turning their whole twisted machine right over to the public on a silver platter. Cutting loose from the old crowd, appointing himself a committee of one to nominate himself on an Independent Reform ticket, campaign himself, and elect himself. A whippersnapper of thirty-two. Paul had been amused by it all, almost indulgent. "You *do* get melodramatic, don't you, Dan? Well, if you want to cut your own throat, that's your affair." And Dan had burned, and told Paul to watch the teevies, he'd see a thing or two, and he did, all right. He remembered Paul's face a few months later, when Libby conceded at 11:45 PM on election night, and Dan rode into office with a new crowd of livewires who were ready to help him plow into New Chicago and clean up that burg like it'd never been cleaned up. And the sweetest part of the victory pie had been the look on Paul's face that night—

So they'd fought, and he'd won and rubbed it in, and Paul had lost, and hated him for it, until that mysterious day—when had it really happened?—when "that big-brained brother of mine" changed subtly into "Christ, man, quit floundering! Who wants engineers? They're all over the place, you'll starve to death" and then finally, to "poor Paul."

When had it happened? Why?

Dan wondered, suddenly, if he had ever really forgiven Paul that blow to the jaw—

Perhaps.

He shook himself, scowling into the plastiglass window blackness. Okay, they'd fought it out. Always jolly, always making it out to be a big friendly game, only it never was a game. He knew how much he owed to Paul. He'd known it with growing concern for a lot of years. And now if he had to drag him back to Washington by the hair, he'd drag the silly fool—

IV

They didn't look very much alike. There was a spareness about Paul—a tall, lean, hungry-looking man, with large soft eyes that hid their anger and a face that was lined with tiredness and resignation. A year ago, when Dan had seen him last, he had looked a young 60, closer to 45; now he looked an old, old 61. How much of this was the cancer Dan didn't know. The pathologist had said: "Not a very malignant tumor right now, but you can never tell when it'll blow up. He'd better be scheduled at the Center, if he's got a permit—"

But some of it was Paul, just Paul. The house was exactly as Dan had expected it would be (though he had never been inside this house since Paul had come to Starship Project fifteen years ago)—stuffy, severe, rather gloomy, rooms packed with bookshelves, drawing boards, odds and ends of papers and blueprints and inks, thick, ugly furniture from the early 2000's, a cluttered, improvised, helter-skelter barn of a testing-lab, with modern equipment that looked lost and alien scattered among the mouldering junk of two centuries.

"Get your coat," said Dan. "It's cold outside. We're going back to Washington."

"Have a drink." Paul waved him toward the sideboard. "Relax. Your pilot needs a rest."

"Paul, I didn't come here to play games. The games are over now."

Paul poured a brandy with deliberation. Handed Dan one, sipped his own. "Good brandy," he murmured. "Wish I could afford more of it."

"*Paul.* You're going with me."

The old man shrugged with a little tired smile. "I'll go with you if you insist, of course. But I'm not going."

"Do you know what you're saying?"

"Perfectly."

"Paul, you don't just say 'Thanks, but I don't believe I'll have any' when they give you a rejuvenation permit. *Nobody* refuses rejuvenation. Why, there are a million people out there begging for a place on the list. It's *life*, Paul. You can't just turn it down—"

"This *is* good brandy," said Paul. "Would you care to take a look at my lab, by the way? Not too well equipped, but sometimes I can work here better than—"

Dan swung on his brother viciously. "I will tell you what I'm going to do," he grated, hitting each word hard, like knuckles rapping the table. "I'm going to take you to the plane. If you won't come, my pilot and I will drag you. When we get to Washington, we'll take you to the Center. If you won't sign the necessary releases, I'll forge them. I'll bribe two witnesses who will swear in the face of death by torture that they saw you signing. I'll buy out the doctors that can do the job, and if they won't do it, I'll sweat them down until they *will*."

*

He slammed the glass down on the table, feeling his heart pounding in his throat, feeling the pain creep up. "I've got lots of things on lots of people, and I can get things done when I want them done. People don't fool with me in Washington any more, because when they do they get their fingers burned off at the knuckles. For Christ sake, Paul, I knew you were stubborn but I didn't think you were block-headed stupid!"

Paul shrugged, apologetically. "I'm impressed, Dan. Really."

"You don't think I can do it?" Dan roared.

"Oh, no doubt you *could.* But such a lot of trouble for an unwilling victim. And I'm your brother, Dan. Remember?"

Dan Fowler spread his hands in defeat, then sank down in the chair. "Paul, tell me *why.*"

"I don't want to be rejuvenated." As though he were saying, "I don't want any sugar in my coffee."

"Why not? If I could only see why, if I knew what was going through your mind, maybe I could understand. But I can't."

Dan looked up at Paul, practically pleading. "You're *needed.* I had a tape from Lijinsky last month—do you know what he said? He said why couldn't you have come to Starship ten years earlier? Nobody knows that ship like you do, you're making it go. That ship can take men to the stars, now, with rejuvenation, and the same men can come back again to find the same people waiting for them when they get here. They can *live* that long, now. We've been tied down to seventy years of life, to a tight little universe of one sun and nine planets for thousands of years. Well, we can change that now. We can go out. That's what your work can do for us." He stared helplessly at his brother. "You could go out on that ship you're building, Paul. You've always wanted to. *Why not?*"

Paul looked across at him for a long moment. There was pity in his eyes. There was also hatred there, and victory, long awaited, bitterly won. "Do you really want me to tell you?"

"I want you to tell me."

Then Paul told him. It took about ten minutes. It was not tempered with mercy.

It split Dan Fowler's world wide open at the seams.

*

"You've been talking about the Starship," said Paul Fowler. "All right, that's as good a starting place as any. I came to Starship Project—what was it, fifteen years ago? Almost sixteen, I guess. This was my meat. I couldn't work well with people, I worked with *things*, processes, ideas. I dug in hard on Starship. I loved it, dreamed it, lived with it. I had dreams in those days. Work hard, make myself valuable here, maybe I'd *get* rejuvenation, so I could work more on Starship. I believed everything you just said. Alpha Centauri, Arcturus, Vega, anywhere we wanted to go—and I could go along! It wouldn't be long, either. We had Lijinsky back with us after his rejuvenation, directing the Project, we had Keller and Stark and Eddie Cochran—great men, the men who had pounded Starship Project into reality, took it out of the story books and made the people of this country want it bad enough to pay for it. Those men were back now—new men, rebuilt bodies, with all their knowledge and experience preserved. Only now they had something even more precious than life: *time*. And I was part of it, and I too could have time."

Paul shook his head, slowly, and sank back into the chair. His eyes were very tired. "A dream, nothing more. A fantasy. It took me fifteen years to learn what a dream it was. Not even a suspicion at first—only a vague puzzlement, things happening that I couldn't quite grasp. Easy to shrug off, until it got too obvious. Not a matter of wrong decisions, really. The decisions were right, but they were in the wrong places. Something about Starship Project shifting, changing somehow. Something being lost. Slowly. Nothing you could nail down, at first, but growing month by month.

"Then one night I saw what it was. That was when I equipped the lab here, and proved to myself that Starship Project was a dream."

*

He spread his hands and smiled at Dan like a benign old Chips to a third-form schoolboy. "The Starship isn't going to Alpha Centauri or anywhere else. It's not going to leave the ground. I thought I'd live long enough to launch that ship and be one of its crew. Well, I won't. That ship wouldn't leave the ground if I lived a million years."

"Garbage," said Dan Fowler succinctly.

"No, Dan. Not garbage. Unfortunately, we sometimes have to recognize our dreams as dreams, and look reality right square in the face. Starship Project is dying. Our whole civilization is dying. Nimrock drove the first nail into the coffin a hundred and thirty years ago—lord, if they'd only hanged him when his first rejuvenation failed! But that would only have delayed it. Now we're dying, slowly right now, but soon it will be fast, very fast. And do you know who's getting set to land the death-blow?" He smiled sadly across at his brother. "You are, Dan."

Dan Fowler sprang from his chair with a roar. "My god, Paul, you're *sick*! Of all the idiot's delights I ever heard, I—I—oh, Jesus." He stood shaking, groping for words, staring at his brother.

"You said you wanted me to tell you."

"Tell me! Tell me what?" Dan took a trembling breath, and sat down, visibly, gripping himself. "All right, all right, I heard what you said—you must mean something, but I don't know what. Let's be reasonable. Let's forget philosophy and semantics and concepts and all the frills for just a minute and talk about facts, huh? *Just facts.*"

"All right, facts," said Paul. "Kenneth Armstrong wrote MAN ON MARS in 2028—he was fifty-seven years old then, and he hadn't been rejuvenated yet. Fundamentally a good book, analyzing his first Mars Colony, taking it apart right down to the silk undies, to show why it had failed so miserably, and why the next one could succeed if he could ever get up there again. He had foresight; with rejuvenation just getting started, he had a whole flock of ideas about overpopulation and the need for a Mars Colony—he was all wet on the population angle, of course, but nobody knew that then. He kicked Keller and Lijinsky off on the Starship idea. They admit it—it was MAN ON MARS that first started them thinking. They were both young, with lots of fight in them. Okay?"

"Just stick to facts," said Dan coldly.

*

"Okay. Starship Project got started, and blossomed into the people's Baby. They started work on the basic blueprints about 60 years ago. Everybody knew it would be a long job—cost money, plenty of it, and there was so much to do before the building ever began. That was where I came in, fifteen years ago. Building. They were looking for engineers who weren't eager to get rich. It went fine. We started to build. Then Keller and Stark came back from rejuvenation. Lijinsky had been rejuvenated five years before."

"Look, I don't need a course in history," Dan exploded.

"Yes, you do," Paul snapped. "You need to sit down and listen for once, instead of shooting your big mouth off all the time. That's what you need real bad, Dan." Paul Fowler rubbed his chin. There were red spots in his cheeks. "Okay, there were some changes made. I didn't like the engine housing—I never had, so I went along with them a hundred percent on that. Even though I designed it—I'd learned a few things since. And there were bugs. It made perfectly good sense, talking to Lijinsky. Starship Project was pretty important to all of us. Dangerous to risk a fumble on the first play, even a tiny risk. We might never get another chance. Lijinsky knew we youngsters were driving along on adrenalin and nerves, and couldn't wait to get out there, but when you thought about it, what was the rush? Was it worth a chance of a fumble to get out there *this* year instead of *next*? Couldn't we take time to find a valid test for that engine at ultra-high acceleration before we put it back in? After all, we *had* time now—Keller and Stark just back with sixty more years to live—why the rush?

"Okay. I bought it. We worked out a valid test on paper. Took us four years of work on it to find out you couldn't build such a device on Earth, but never mind that. Other things were stalling all the while. The colony-plan for the ship. Choosing the crew—what criteria, what qualifications? There was plenty of time—why not make *sure* it's right? Don't leave anything crude, if we can refine it a little first—"

Paul sighed wearily. "It snowballed. Keller and Stark backed Lijinsky to the hilt. There was some trouble about money—I think you had your thumb in the pie there, getting it fixed for us, didn't you? More refining. Work it out. Detail. Get sidetracked on some aspect for a few years—so what? Lots of time. Rejuvenation, and all that, talk about the Universalists beating Rinehart out and throwing the Center open to everybody. Et cetera, et cetera. But somewhere along the line I began to see that it just wasn't true. The holdups, the changes, the digressions and snags and refinements were all excuses, all part of a big, beautiful, exquisitely reasonable facade built up to obscure the real truth. *Lijinsky and Keller and Stark had changed.*"

Dan Fowler snorted. "I know a very smart young doctor who told me that there *weren't* any changes."

"I don't mean anything physical—their bodies were fine. Nothing mental, either—they had the same sharp minds they always had. It was a change in values. They'd lost something that they'd had before. The *drive* that made them start Starship Project, the *urgency*, the vital importance of the thing—it was all gone. They just didn't have the push any more. They began to look for the easy way, and it was far easier to build and rebuild, and refine, and improve the Starship here on the ground than to throw that Starship out into space—"

*

There was a long, long silence. Dan Fowler sat grey-faced, staring at Paul, just shaking his head and staring. "I don't believe it," he said finally. "You do maybe, because you want to, but you're mixed up, Paul. I've seen Lijinsky's reports. There's been progress, regular progress, month by month. You've been too close to it, maybe. Of course there have been delays, but only when they were necessary. The progress has gone on—"

Paul stood up suddenly. "Come in here, Dan. Look." He threw open a door, strode rapidly down a corridor and a flight of stairs into the long, low barn of a laboratory. "Here, here, let me show you something." He pulled out drawers, dragged out rolls of blueprints. "These are my own. They're based on the working prints from Starship that we drew up ten years ago, scaled down to model size. I've tested them, I've run tolerances, I've checked the math five ways and back again. I've tested the parts, the engine—model size. The blueprints haven't got a flaw in them. They're perfect as they'll ever get. No, wait a minute, look—"

He strode fiercely across to slide back a floor panel, drew up the long, glittering thing from a well in the floor—sleek, beautiful, three feet long. Paul maneuvered a midget loading crane, guided the thing into launching position on the floor, then turned back to Dan. "There it is. Just a model, but it's perfect. Every detail is perfect. There's even fuel in it. No men, but there could be if there were any men small enough."

Anger was blazing in Paul's voice now, bitterness and frustration. "I built it, because I had to be sure. I've tested its thrust. I could launch this model for Alpha Centauri tonight—and *it would get there*. If there were little men who could get into it, *they'd* get there, too—alive. Starship Project is completed, it's been completed for ten years now, but do you know what happened to these blueprints, the originals? They were studied. They were improvements. They almost had the ship built, and then they took it apart again."

"But I've read the reports," Dan cried.

"Have you *seen* the Starship? Have you *talked* to them over there? It isn't just there, it's *everywhere*, Dan. There are only about 70,000 rejuvenated men alive in this hemisphere so far, but already the change is beginning to show. Go talk to the Advertising people—*there's* a delicate indicator of social change if there ever was one. See what they say. Who are they backing in the Government? You? Like hell. Rinehart? No, they're backing up 'Moses' Tyndall and his Abolitionist goon-squad who preach that rejuvenation is the work of Satan, and they're giving him enough strength that he's even getting *you* worried. How about Roderigo Aviado and his Solar Energy Project down in Antarctica? Do you know what he's been doing down there lately? You'd better find out, Dan. What's happening to the Mars Colony? Do you have any idea? You'd better find out. Have you gone to see any of the Noble Ten that are still rattling around? Oh, you ought to. How about all the suicides we've been having in the last ten years? What do the insurance people say about that?"

*

He stopped, from lack of breath. Dan just stared at him, shaking his head like Silly Willy on the teevies. "Find out what you're doing, Dan—before you push this universal rejuvenation idea of yours through. Find out—if you've got the guts to find out, that is. We've got a monster on our hands, and now you've got to be Big Dan Fowler playing God and turning him loose on the world. Well, be careful. Find out first, while you can. It's all here to see, if you'll open your eyes, but you're all so dead sure that you want life everlasting that nobody's even bothered to *look*. And now it's become such a political bludgeon that nobody *dares* to look."

The model ship seemed to gleam in the dim laboratory light. Dan Fowler walked over to it, ran a finger up the shiny side to the pinpoint tip. His face was old, and something was gone from his eyes when he turned back to Paul. "You've known this for so long, and you never told me. You never said a word." He shook his head slowly. "I didn't know you hated me so much. But I'm not going to let you win this one, either, Paul. You're wrong. I'm going to prove it if it kills me."

V

"Well, try his home number, then," Dan Fowler snarled into the speaker. He gnawed his cigar and fumed as long minutes spun off the wall clock. His fingers drummed the wall. "How's that? Dammit, I want to speak to

Dwight McKenzie, his aide will *not* do—well, of course he's in town. I just saw him yesterday—"

He waited another five minutes, and then his half dollar clanked back in the return, with apologies. "All right, get his office when it opens, and call me back." He reeled off the number of the private booth.

Carl Golden looked up as he came back to the table and stirred sugar-cream into half-cold coffee. "No luck?"

"Son of a bitch has vanished." Dan leaned back against the wall, glowering at Carl and Jean. Through the transparent walls of the glassed-in booth, they could see the morning breakfast-seekers drifting into the place. "We should have him pretty soon." He bit off the end of a fresh cigar, and assaulted it with a match.

"Dad, you know what Dr. Moss said—"

"Look, little girl—if I'm going to die in ten minutes, I'm going to smoke for those ten minutes and enjoy them," Dan snapped. The coffee was like lukewarm dishwater. Both the young people sipped theirs with bleary early-morning resignation. Carl Golden needed a shave badly. He opened his second pack of cigarettes. "Did you sleep on the way back?"

Dan snorted. "What do you think?"

"I think Paul might be lying to you."

Dan shot him a sharp glance. "Maybe—but I don't think so. Paul has always been fussy about telling the truth. He's all wrong, of course—" (fresh coffee, sugar-cream)—"but I think *he* believes his tale. Does it sound like he's lying to you?"

Carl sighed and shook his head. "No. I don't like it. It sounds to me as though he's pretty sure he's right."

Dan clanked the cup down and swore. "He's demented, that's what he is! He's waited too long, his brain's starting to go. If that story of his were true, why has he waited so long to tell somebody about it?"

"Maybe he wanted to see you hang yourself."

"But I can only hang myself on facts, not on the paranoid ramblings of a sick old man. The horrible thing is that he probably believes it—he almost had me believing it, for a while. But it isn't true. He's wrong—good lord, he's *got* to be wrong." Dan broke off, staring across at Carl. He gulped the last of the coffee. "If he *isn't* wrong, then that's all, kiddies. The mountain sinks into the sea, with us just ten feet from the top of it."

"Well, would *you* walk into the Center for a Retread now without being sure he's wrong?"

"Of course I wouldn't," said Dan peevishly. "Paul has taken the game right out from under our noses. We've got to stop everything and find out *now*, before we do another damned thing." The Senator dragged a sheaf of yellow paper out of his breast pocket and spread it out on the table. "I worked it out on the way back. We've got a nasty job on our hands. More than we can possibly squeeze in before the Hearing come up on December 15th. So number one job is to shift the Hearings back again. I'll take care of that as soon as I can get McKenzie on the wire."

"What's your excuse going to be?" Jean wanted to know.

"Anything but the truth. McKenzie thinks I'm going to win the fight at the Hearings, and he wants to be on the right side of the toast when it's buttered. He'll shift the date back to February 15th. Okay, next step: we need a crew. A crowd that can do fast, accurate, hard work and not squeal if they don't sleep for a month or so. Tommy Sandborn should be in Washington—he can handle statistics for us. In addition, we need a couple of good sharp detectives. Jean?"

*

The girl nodded. "I can handle that end. It'll take some time getting them together, though."

"How much time?"

"Couple of days."

"Fine, we can have lots of work for them in a couple of days." The Senator turned back to Carl. "I want you to hit Starship Project first thing."

Carl shook his head. "I've got a better man for that job. Saw him last night, and he's dying for something to do. You don't know him—Terry Fisher. He'll know how to dig out what we want. He was doing it for five years on Mars."

"The alky?" Dan didn't like it. "We can't risk a slip to the teevies. We just don't dare."

"There won't be any slip. Terry jumped in the bottle to get away from Mars, that's all. He'll stay cold when it counts."

"Okay, if you say so. I want to see the setup there, too, but I want it ready for a quick scan. Get him down there this morning to soften things up and get it all out on the table for me. You'd better tackle the ad-men, then. Let's see—Tenner's Agency in Philly is a good place to start. Then hit Metro Insurance. Don't waste time with underlings, go to the top and wave my name around like an orange flag. They won't like it a damned bit, but they know I have the finger on Kornwall in Communications. We'll take his scalp if they don't play ball. All you'll have to do is convince them of that."

"What's on Kornwall?"

"Kornwall has been fronting for 'Moses' Tyndall for years. That's why Tyndall never bothered me too much, because we could get him through Kornwall any time we wanted to. And the ad-men and Metro have everything they own sunk into Tyndall's plans." Carl's frown still lingered. "Don't worry about it, son. It's okay."

"I think maybe you're underestimating John Tyndall."

"Why?"

"I worked for him once, remember? He doesn't like you. He knows it's going to be you or him, in the long haul, with nobody else involved. And you realize what happens if 'Moses' gets wind of this mess? Finds out what your brother told you, or even finds out that you're worried about something?"

Dan chewed his lip. "He *could* be a pain, couldn't he?"

"He sure could. More than a pain, and Kornwall wouldn't be much help after the news got out."

"Well, we'll have to take the risk, that's all. We'll have to be fast and quiet." He pushed aside his coffee cup as the phone blinker started in. "I think that gets us started. Jean, you'll keep somebody on the switchboard, and keep track of us all. When I get through with McKenzie, I may be leaving the country for a while. You'll have to be my ears, and cover for me. *Yes*, yes. I was calling Dwight McKenzie—"

The phonebox squawked for a moment or two.

"Hello, Dwight?—What? Oh, thunder! Well, where is he? Timagami—Ontario? An island!" He covered the speaker and growled, "He's gone moose-hunting." Then: "Okay, get me Eastern Sea-Jet Charter Service."

Five minutes later they walked out onto the street and split up in three different directions.

*

A long series of grey, flickering pictures, then, for Dan Fowler. A fast meal in the car to the Charter Service landing field. Morning sun swallowed up, sky gray, then almost black, temperature dropping, a grey drizzling rain. Cold. Wind carrying it across the open field in waves, slashing his cheeks with icy blades of water. Grey shape of the ski-plane ("Eight feet of snow up there, according to the IWB reports. Lake's frozen three feet thick. Going to be a rough ride, Senator"). Jean's quick kiss before he climbed up, the sharp worry in her eyes ("Got your pills, Dad? Try to sleep. Take it easy. Give me a call about anything—") (But there aren't any phones, the operator said. Better not tell her that. Why scare her any more? Damned heart, anyway). A wobbly takeoff that almost dumped his stomach in his lap, sent the briefcase flying across the cabin. Then rain, and grey-black nothing out through the mid-day view ports, heading north. Faster, faster, why can't you get this crate to move? Sorry, Senator. Nasty currents up here. Maybe we can try going higher—

Time! Paul had called it more precious than life, and now time flew screaming by in great deadly sweeps, like a black-winged buzzard. And through it all, weariness, tiredness that he had never felt before. Not years, not work. Weary body, yes—and time was running out, he should have rejuvenated years ago. But now—*what if Paul were right?*

Can't do it now. Not until Paul is wrong, a thousand times wrong. That was it, of course, that was the weariness that wasn't time-weariness or body-weariness. Just mind-weariness. Weariness at the thought of wasted work, the wasted years—a wasted life. Unless Paul is very wrong.

A snarl of disgust, a toggle switch snapped, a flickering teevie screen. Wonderful pickup these days. News of the World brought to you by Atomics International, the fuel to power the Starship—the President returned to Washington today after three-week vacation conference in Calcutta with Chinese and Indian dignitaries—full accord and a cordial ending to the meeting—American medical supplies to be made available—and on the home front, appropriations renewed for Antarctica Project, to bring solar energy into every home, Aviado was quoted as saying—huge Abolitionist rally last night in New Chicago as John 'Moses' Tyndall returned to that city to celebrate the fifteenth birthday of the movement that started there back in 2119—no violence reported as Tyndall lashed out at Senator Daniel Fowler's universal rejuvenation program—twenty-five hour work week hailed by Senator Rinehart of

Alaska as a great progressive step for the American people—Senator Rinehart, chairman of the policy-making Criterion Committee held forth hope last night that rejuvenation techniques may increase the number of candidates to six hundred a year within five years—and now, news from the entertainment world—

Going down, then, into flurries of Northern snow, peering out at the whiter gloom below, a long stretch of white with blobs of black on either side, resolving into snow-laden black pines, a long flat lake-top of ice and snow. Taxi-ing down, engines roaring, sucking up snow into steam in the orange afterblast. And ahead, up from the lake, a black blot of a house, with orange window lights reflecting warmth and cheer against the wilderness outside—

Then Dwight McKenzie, peering out into the gloom, eyes widening in recognition, little mean eyes with streaks of fear through them, widening and then smiling, pumping his hand. "Dan! My god, I couldn't *imagine*—hardly ever see anybody up here, you know. Come in, come in, you must be half frozen. What's happened? Something torn loose down in Washington?" And more questions, fast, tumbling over each other, no answers wanted, talky-talk questions to cover surprise and fear and the one large question of why Dan Fowler should be dropping down out of the sky on *him*, which question he didn't think he wanted answered just yet—

*

A huge, rugged room, blazing fire in a mammoth fireplace at the end, moose heads, a rug of thick black bear hide. "Like to come up here a day or two ahead of the party, you know," McKenzie was saying. "Does a man good to commune with his soul once in a while. Do you like to hunt? You should join us, Dan. Libby and Donaldson will be up tomorrow with a couple of guides. We could find you an extra gun. They say hunting should be good this year—"

One chair against the fireplace, a book hastily thrown down beside it, SEXTRA SPECIAL, Cartoons by Kulp. Great book for soul-searching Senators. Things were all out of focus after the sudden change from the cold, but now Dan was beginning to see. One book, one chair, but two half-filled sherry glasses at the sideboard—

"Can't wait, Dwight, I have to get back to the city, but I couldn't find you down there, and they didn't know when you were coming back. I just wanted to let you know that I put you to all that trouble for nothing—we don't need the Hearing date in December, after all."

Wariness suddenly in McKenzie's eyes. "Well! Nice of you to think of it, Dan—but it wasn't really any trouble. No trouble at all. December 15th is fine, as a matter of fact, better than the February date would have been. Give the Committee a chance to collect itself during the Holidays, ha, ha."

"Well, it now seems that it *wouldn't* be so good for me, Dwight. I'd much prefer it to be changed back to the February date."

"Well, now." Pause. "Dan, we *have* to settle these things sooner or later, you know. I don't know whether we can do that now—"

"Don't know! Why not?"

The moose-hunter licked both lips, couldn't keep his eyes on Dan's eyes, focused on his nose instead,—as if the nose were *really* the important part of the conversation. "It isn't just me that makes these decisions, Dan. Other people have to be consulted. It's pretty late to catch them now, you know. It might be pretty hard to do that—"

No more smiles from Dan. "Now look—you make the calendar, and you can change it." Face getting red, getting angry—careful, Dan, those two sherry glasses, watch what you say—"I want it changed back. And I've got to know right now."

"But you told me you'd be all ready to roll by December 15th—"

To hell with caution—he *had* to have time. "Look, there's no reason you can't do it if you want to, Dwight. I'd consider it a personal favor—I repeat, a very large personal favor—if you'd make the arrangements. I won't forget it—" What did the swine want, an arm off at the roots?

"Sorry," said a voice from the rear door of the room. Walter Rinehart walked across to the sideboard. "You don't mind if I finish this, Dwight?"

A deep breath from McKenzie, like a sigh of relief. "Go right ahead, Walt. Sherry, Dan?"

"No, I don't think so." It was Walter, all right. Tall, upright, dignified Walter, fine shock of wavy hair that was white as the snow outside. Young-old lines on his face. Some men looked finer after rejuvenation, much finer than before. There had been a chilly look about Walter Rinehart's eyes before his first Retread. Not now. A fine man, like somebody's dear old grandfather. Just give him a chunk of wood to whittle and a jack-blade to whittle it with—

But inside, the mind was the same. Inside, no changes. Author of the Rinehart Criteria, the royal road to a self-perpetuating "immortal elite."

*

Dan turned his back on Rinehart and said to McKenzie: "I want the date changed."

"I—I can't do it, Dan." An inquiring glance at Rinehart, a faint smiling nod in return.

He knew he'd blundered then, blundered badly. McKenzie was afraid. McKenzie wanted another lifetime, one of these days. He'd decided that Rinehart would be the one who could give it to him. But worse, far worse: Rinehart knew now that something had happened, something was wrong.

"What's the matter, Dan?" he said smoothly. "You need more time? Why? You had it before, and you were pretty eager to toss it up. Well, what's happened, Dan?"

That was all. Back against the wall. The thought of bluffing it through, swallowing the December 15th date and telling them to shove it flashed through his mind. He threw it out violently, his heart sinking. That was only a few more days. They had weeks of work ahead of them. They needed more time, they *had* to have it—

Rinehart was grinning confidently. "Of course I'd like to cooperate, Dan. Only I have some plans for the Hearings, too. You've been getting on people's nerves, down in the city. There's even been talk of reconsidering your rejuvenation permit—"

Your move, Dan. God, what a blunder! Why did you ever come up here? And every minute you stand there with your jaw sagging just tells Rinehart how tight he's got you—*do* something, *anything*—

There was a way. Would Carl understand it? Carl had begged him never to use it, ever, under any circumstances. And Carl had trusted him when he had said he wouldn't—but if Carl were standing here now, he'd say yes, go ahead, use it, wouldn't he? He'd have to—

"I want the Hearings on February 15th," Dan said to Rinehart.

"Sorry, Dan. We can't be tossing dates around like that. Unless you'd care to tell me why."

"Okay." Dan grabbed his hat angrily. "I'll make a formal request for the change tomorrow morning, and read it on the teevies. Then I'll also announce a feature attraction that the people can look forward to when the Hearing date comes. We weren't planning to use it, but I guess you'd like to have both barrels right in the face, so that's what we'll give you."

Walter Rinehart roared with laughter. "*Another* feature attraction? You do dig them up, don't you? Ken Armstrong's dead, you know."

"Peter Golden's widow isn't."

*

The smile faded on Rinehart's face. He looked suddenly like a man carved out of grey stone. Dan trembled, let the words sink in. "You didn't think *anybody* knew about that, did you, Walt? Sorry. We've got the story on Peter Golden. Took us quite a while to piece it together, but we did with the help of his son. Carl remembers his father before the accident, you see, quite well. His widow remembers him even before that. And we have some fascinating recordings that Peter Golden made when he applied for rejuvenation, and when he appealed the Committee's decisions. Some of the private interviews, too, Walter."

"I gave Peter Golden forty more years of life," Rinehart said.

"You crucified him," said Dan, bluntly.

There was silence, long silence. Then: "Are you selling?"

"I'm selling." Cut out my tongue, Carl, but I'm selling.

"How do I know you won't break it anyway?"

"You don't know. Except that I'm telling you I won't."

Rinehart soaked that in with the last gulp of sherry. Then he smashed the glass on the stone floor. "Change the date," he said to McKenzie. "Then throw this vermin out of here."

Back in the snow and darkness Dan tried to breathe again, and couldn't quite make it. He had to stop and rest twice going down to the plane. Then he was sick all the way back.

VI

Early evening, as the plane dropped him off in New York Crater, and picked up another charter. Two cold eggs and some scalding coffee, eaten standing up at the airport counter. Great for the stomach, but there wasn't time to stop. Anyway, Dan's stomach wasn't in the mood for dim lights and pale wine, not just this minute. Questions howling through his mind. The knowledge that he had made the one Class A colossal blunder of his thirty years in politics, this last half-day. A miscalculation of a man! He should have known about McKenzie—at least suspected. McKenzie was getting old, he wanted a Retread, and wanted it badly. Before, he had planned to get it through Dan. Then something changed his mind, and he decided Rinehart would end up on top.

Why?

Armstrong's suicide, of course. Pretty good proof that even Rinehart hadn't known it was a suicide. If Carl had brought back evidence of murder, Dan would win, McKenzie thought. But evidence of suicide—it was shaky. Walt Rinehart has his hooks in too deep.

They piped down the fifteen minute warning for the Washington Jet. Dan gulped the last of his coffee, and found a visi-phone booth with a scrambler in working order. Two calls. The first one to Jean, to line up round-the-clock guards for Peter Golden's widow on Long Island. Jean couldn't keep surprise out of her voice. Dan grunted and didn't elaborate—just get them out there.

Then a call to locate Carl. He chewed his cigar nervously.

Two minutes of waiting while they called Carl from wherever he was. Then: "I just saw McKenzie. I found him hiding in Rhinehart's hip pocket."

"Jesus, Dan. We've got to have time."

"We've got it—but the price was very steep, son."

Silence then as Carl peered at him. Finally: "I see."

"If I hadn't been in such a hurry, if I'd only thought it out," Dan said miserably. "It was an awful error—and all mine, too."

"Well, don't go out and shoot yourself. I suppose it had to happen sooner or later. What about Mother?"

"She'll be perfectly safe. They won't get within a mile of her. Look, son—is Fisher doing all right?"

Carl nodded. "I talked to him an hour ago. He'll be ready for you by tomorrow night, he thinks."

"Sober?"

"Sober. And mad. He's the right guy for the job." Worried lines deepened on Golden's forehead. "Everything's O.K.? Rinehart won't dare—"

"I scared him. He'd almost forgotten. Everything's fine." Dan rang off, scowling. He wished he was as sure as he sounded. Rinehart's back was to the wall, now. Dan wasn't too sure he liked it that way.

An hour later he was in Washington, and Jean was dragging him into the Volta. "If you don't sleep now, I'll have you put to sleep. Now shut up while I drive you home."

A soft bed, darkness, escape. When had he slept last? It was heaven.

*

He slept the clock around, which he had not intended, and caught the next night-jet to Las Vegas, which he had intended. There was some delay with the passenger list after he had gone aboard, a fight of some sort, and the jet took off four minutes late. Dan slept again, fitfully.

Somebody slid into the adjoining seat. "Well! Good old Dan Fowler!"

A gaunt, frantic-looking man, with skin like cracked parchment across his high cheekbones, and a pair of Carradine eyes looking down at Dan. If Death should walk in human flesh, Dan thought, it would look like John Tyndall.

"What do you want, 'Moses'?"

"Just dropped by to chat," said Tyndall. "You're heading for Las Vegas, eh? Why?"

Dan jerked, fumbled for the upright-button. "I like the climate out there. If you want to talk, talk and get it over with."

Tyndall lifted a narrow foot and gave the recline-button a sharp jab, dumping the Senator back against the seat. "You're onto something. I can smell it cooking, and I want my share, right now."

Dan stared into the gaunt face, and burst out laughing. He had never actually been so close to John Tyndall before, and he did *not* like the smell, which had brought on the laugh, but he knew all about Tyndall. More than Tyndall himself knew, probably. He could even remember the early rallies Tyndall had led, feeding on the fears and suspicions and nasty rumors grown up in the early days. It was evil, they had said. This was not God's way, this was Man's way, as evil as Man was evil. If God had wanted Man to live a thousand years, he would have given him such a body—

Or:

They'll use it for a tool! Political football. They'll buy and sell with it. They'll make a cult of it, they're doing it right now! Look at Walter Rinehart. Did you hear about his scheme? To keep it down to five hundred a year? They'll make themselves a ruling class, an immortal elite, with Rinehart for their Black Pope. Better that *nobody* should have it—

Or:

Immortality, huh? But what kind? You hear what happened to Harvey Tatum? That's right, the jet-car man, big business. He was one of their 'Noble Ten' they're always bragging about. But they say he had to have special drugs every night, that he had *changed*. That's right, if he didn't get these drugs, see, he'd go mad and try to suck blood and butcher up children—oh, they didn't dare publish it, had to put him out of the way quietly, but my brother-in-law was down in Lancaster one night when—

*

All it really needed was the man, and one day there was 'Moses' Tyndall. Leader of the New Crusade for God. Small, at first. But the ad-men began supporting him, broadcasting his rallies, playing him up big. Abolish rejuvenation, it's a blot against Man's immortal soul. Amen. Then the insurance people came along, with money. (The ad-men and the insurance people weren't too concerned about Man's immortal soul—they'd take their share now, thanks—but this didn't bother Tyndall too much. Misguided, but they were on God's side. He prayed for them.) So they gave Tyndall the first Abolitionist seat in the Senate, in 2124, just nine years ago, and the fight between Rinehart and Dan Fowler that was brewing even then had turned into a three-cornered fight—

*

Dan grinned up at Tyndall and said, "Go away, John. Don't bother me."

"You've got something," Tyndall snarled. "What is that damn shadow of yours nosing around Tenner's for? Why the sudden leaping interest in Nevada? Two trips in three days—what are you trying to track down?"

"Why on Earth should I tell you anything, Holy Man?"

The parchment face wrinkled unpleasantly. "Because it would be very smart, that's why. Rinehart's out of it, now. Washed up, finished, thanks to you. Now it's just you or me, one or the other. You're in the way, and you're going to be gotten out of the way when you've finished up Rinehart, because I'm going to start rolling them. Go along with me now and you won't get smashed, Dan."

"Get out of here," Dan snarled, sitting bolt upright. "You gave it to Carl Golden, a long time ago when he was with you, remember? Carl's my boy now—do you think I'll swallow the same bait?"

"You'd be smart if you did." The man leaned forward. "I'll let you in on a secret. I've just recently had a—*vision*, you might say. There are going to be riots and fires and shouting, around the time of the Hearings. People will be killed. Lots of people—spontaneous outbursts of passion, of course, the great voice of the people rising against the Abomination. And against *you*, Dan. A few Repeaters may be taken out and hanged, and then when you have won against Rinehart, you'll find people thinking that you're really a traitor—"

"Nobody will swallow that," Dan snapped.

"Just watch and see. I can still call it off, if you say so." He stood up quickly as Dan's face went purple. "New Chicago," he said smoothly. "Have to see a man here, and then get back to the Capitol. Happy hunting, Dan. You know where to reach me."

He strode down the aisle of the ship, leaving Dan staring bleakly at an empty seat.

Paul, Paul—

*

He met Terry Fisher at the landing field in Las Vegas. A firm handshake, clear brown eyes looking at him the way a four-year-old looks at Santa Claus. "Glad you could come tonight, Senator. I've had a busy couple of days. I think you'll be interested." Remarkable restraint in the man's voice. His face was full of things unsaid. Dan caught it; he knew faces, read them like typescript. "What is it, son?"

"Wait until you see." Fisher laughed nervously. "I thought for a while that I was back on Mars."

"Cigar?"

"No thanks. I never use them."

The car broke through darkness across bumpy pavement. The men sat silently. Then a barbed-wire enclosure loomed up, and a guard walked over, peered at their credentials, and waved them through. Ahead lay a long, low row of buildings, and a tall something spearing up into the clear desert night. They stopped at the first building, and hurried up the steps.

Small, red-faced Lijinsky greeted them, all warm handshake and enthusiasm and unmistakable happiness and surprise. "A real pleasure, Senator! We haven't had a direct governmental look-see in quite a while. I'm glad I'm here to show you around."

"Everything is going right along, eh?"

"Oh, yes! She'll be a ship to be proud of. Now, I think we can arrange some quarters for you for the night, and in the morning we can sit down and have a nice, long talk."

Terry Fisher was shaking his head. "I think the Senator would like to see the ship now—isn't that right, Senator?"

Lijinsky's eyes opened wide, his head bobbed in surprise. Young-old creases on his face flickered. "Tonight? Oh, you can't really be serious. Why, it's almost two in the morning! We only have a skeleton crew working at night. Tomorrow you can see—"

"Tonight, if you don't mind." Dan tried to keep the sharp edge out of his voice. "Unless you have some specific objection, of course."

"Objection? None whatsoever." Lijinsky seemed puzzled, and a little hurt. But he bounced back: "Tonight it is, then. Let's go." There was no doubting the little man's honesty. He wasn't hiding anything, just surprised. But a moment later there was concern on his face as he led them out toward the factory compounds. "There's no question of appropriations, I hope, Senator?"

"No, no. Nothing of the sort."

"Well, I'm certainly glad to hear that. Sometimes our contacts from Washington are a little disappointed in the Ship, of course."

Dan's throat tightened. "Why?"

"No reason, really. We're making fine progress, it isn't that. Yes, things really buzz around here; just ask Mr. Fisher about *that*—he was here all day watching the workers. But there are always minor changes in plans, of course, as we recognize more of the problems."

Terry Fisher grimaced silently, and followed them into a small Whirlwind groundcar. The little gyro-car bumped down the road on its single wheel, down into a gorge, then out onto the flats. Dan strained his eyes, peering ahead at the spear of Starship gleaming in the distant night-lights. Pictures from the last Starship Progress Report flickered through his mind, and a frown gathered as they came closer to the ship. Then the car halted on the edge of the building-pit and they blinked down and up at the scaffolded monster.

Dan didn't even move from the car. He just stared. The report had featured photos, projected testing dates—even ventured a possible date for launching, with the building of the Starship so near to completion. That had been a month ago. Now Dan stared at the ship and shook his head, uncomprehending.

The hull-plates were off again, lying in heaps on the ground in a mammoth circle. The ship was a skeleton, a long, gawky structure of naked metal beams. Even now a dozen men were scampering around the scaffolding, before Dan's incredulous eyes, and he saw some of the beaming coming *off* the body of the ship, being dropped onto the crane, moving slowly to the ground.

Ten years ago the ship had looked the same. As he watched, he felt a wave of hopelessness sweep through him, a sense of desolate, empty bitterness. Ten years—

His eyes met Terry Fisher's in the gloom of the car, begging to be told it wasn't so. Fisher shook his head.

Then Dan said: "I think I've seen enough. Take me back to the air field."

*

"It was the same thing on Mars," Fisher was telling him as the return jet speared East into the dawn. "The refining and super-refining, the slowing down, the changes in viewpoint and planning. I went up there ready to beat the world barehanded, to work on the frontier, to build that colony, and maybe lead another one. I even worked out the plans for a break-away colony—we would need colony-builders when we went to the stars, I thought." He shrugged sadly. "Carl told you, I guess. They considered the break-away colony, carefully, and then Barness decided it was really too early. Too much work already, with just one colony. And there was, in a sense: frantic activity, noise, hubbub, hard work, fancy plans—all going nowhere. No drive, no real direction." He shrugged again. "I did a lot of drinking before they threw me off Mars."

"Nobody saw it happening?"

"It wasn't the sort of thing you see. You could only *feel* it. It started when Armstrong came to the colony, rejuvenated, to take over its development. And eventually, I think Armstrong did see it. That's why he suicided."

"But the Starship," Dan cried. "It was almost built, and they were *tearing it down*. I saw it with my own eyes."

"Ah, yes. For the twenty-seventh time, I think. A change in the engineering thinking, that's all. Keller and Lijinsky suddenly came to the conclusion that the whole thing might fall apart in midair at the launching. Can you imagine it? When rockets have been built for years, running to Mars every two months? But they could prove it on paper, and by the time they got through explaining it every damned soul on the project was saying yes, it might fall apart at the launching. Why, it's a standing joke with the workers. They call Keller "Old Jet Propulsion" and always have a good laugh. But then, Keller and Stark and Lijinsky should know what's what. They've all been rejuvenated, and working on the ship for years." Fisher's voice was heavy with anger.

Dan didn't answer. There didn't seem to be much *to* answer, and he just couldn't tell Fisher how it felt to have a cold blanket of fear wrapping around his heart, so dreadful and cold that he hardly dared look five minutes ahead right now. *We have a Monster on our hands—*

VII

He was sick when they reached Washington. The pain in his chest became acute as he walked down the gangway, and by the time he found a seat in the terminal and popped a nitro-tablet under his tongue he was breathing in deep, ragged gasps. He sat very still, trying to lean back against the seat, and quite suddenly he realized that he was very, very ill. The good red-headed Dr. Moss would smile in satisfaction, he thought bitterly. There was sweat on his forehead; it had never seemed very probable to him that he might one day die—he didn't *have* to die in this great, wonderful world of new bodies for old, he could live on, and on, and on. He could live to see the Golden Centuries of Man. A solar system teeming with life. Ships to challenge the stars, the barriers breaking, crumbling before their very eyes. Other changes, as short-lived Man became long-lived Man. Changes in teaching, in thinking, in feeling. Disease, the Enemy, was crushed. Famine, the Enemy, slinking back into the dim memory of history. War, the Enemy, pointless to extinction.

All based on one principle: Man must live. He need not die. If a man could live forty years instead of twenty, had it been wrong to fight the plagues that struck him down in his youth? If he could live sixty years instead of forty, had the great researchers of the 1940's and '50's and '60's been wrong? Was it any more wrong to want to live a thousand years? Who could say that it was?

He took a shuddering breath, and then nodded to Terry Fisher, and walked unsteadily to the cab stand. He would not believe what he had seen at Starship Project. It was not enough. Collect the evidence, *then* conclude. He gave Fisher an ashen smile. "It's nothing. The ticker kicks up once in a while, that's all. Let's go see what Carl and Jean and the boys have dug up." Fisher smiled grimly, an eager gleam in his eye.

Carl and Jean and the boys had dug up plenty. The floor of offices Dan rented for the work of his organization was going like Washington Terminal at rush hour. A dozen people were here and there, working with tapes, papers, program cards. Jean met them at the door, hustled them into the private offices in the back. "Carl just got here, too. He's down eating. The boys outside are trying to make sense out of his insurance and advertising figures."

"He got next to them okay?"

"Sure—but you were right, they didn't like it."

"What sort of reports?"

*

The girl sighed. "Only prelims. Almost all of the stuff is up in the air, which makes it hard to evaluate. The ad-men have to be figuring what they're going to do next half-century, so that they'll be there with the right thing when the time comes. But it seems they don't like what they see. People have to buy what the ad-men are selling, or the ad-men shrivel up, and already the trend seems to be showing up. People aren't in such a rush to buy. Don't have the same sense of urgency that they used to—" Her hands fluttered. "Well, as I say, it's all up in the air. Let the boys analyze for a while. The suicide business is a little more tangible. The rates are up, all over. But break it into first-generation and Repeaters, and it's pretty clear who's pushing it up."

"Like Armstrong," said Dan slowly.

Jean nodded. "Oh, here's Carl now."

He came in, rubbing his hands, and gave Dan a queer look. "Everything under control, Dan?"

Dan nodded. He told Carl about Tyndall's proposition. Carl gave a wry grin. "He hasn't changed a bit, has he?"

"Yes, he has. He's gotten lots stronger."

Carl scowled, and slapped the desk with his palm. "You should have stopped him, Dan. I told you that a long time ago—back when I first came in with you. He was aiming for your throat even then, trying to use me and what I knew about Dad to sell the country a pack of lies about you. He almost did, too. I hated your guts back then. I thought you were the rottenest man that ever came up in politics, until you got hold of me and pounded sense into my head. And Tyndall's never forgiven you that, either."

"All right—we're still ahead of him. Have you just finished with the ad-men?"

"Oh, no. I just got back from a trip south. My nose is still cold."

Dan's eyebrows went up. "And how was Dr. Aviado? I haven't seen a report from Antarctica Project for five years."

"Yes you have. You just couldn't read them. Aviado is quite a theoretician. That's how he got his money and his Project, down there, with plenty of room to build his reflectors and nobody around to get hurt if something goes wrong. Except a few penguins. And he's done a real job of development down there since his rejuvenation."

"Ah." Dan glanced up hopefully.

"Now there," said Carl, "is a real lively project. Solar energy into power on a utilitarian level. The man is fanatic, of course, but with his plans he could actually be producing in another five years." He lit a cigarette, drew on it as though it were bitter.

"Could?"

"Seems he's gotten sidetracked a bit," said Carl.

Dan glanced at Terry Fisher. "How?"

"Well, his equipment is working fine, and he can concentrate solar heat from ten square miles onto a spot the size of a manhole cover. But he hasn't gone too far converting it to useful power yet." Carl suddenly burst out laughing. "Dan, this'll kill you. Billions and billions of calories of solar heat concentrated down there, and what do you think he's doing with it? He's digging a hole in the ice two thousand feet deep and a mile wide. That's what."

"A hole in the ice!"

"Exactly. Conversion? Certainly—but first we want to be sure we're right. So right now his whole crew is very busy *trying to melt down Antarctica.* And if you give him another ten years, he'll have it done, by god."

*

This was the last, most painful trip of all.

Dan didn't even know why he was going, except that Paul had told him he should go, and no stone could be left unturned.

The landing in New York Crater had been rough, and Dan had cracked his elbow on the bulkhead; he nursed it now as he left the Volta on the deserted street of the crater city, and entered the low one-story lobby of the groundscraper. The clerk took his name impassively, and he sat down to wait.

An hour passed, then another.

Then: "Mr. Devlin will see you now, Senator."

Down in the elevator, four—five—six stories. Above him was the world; here, deep below, with subtly efficient ventilators and shafts and exotic cubby-holes for retreat, a man could forget that a world above existed.

Soft lighting in the corridor, a golden plastic door. The door swung open, and a tiny old man blinked out.

"Mr. Chauncey Devlin?"

"Senator Fowler!" The little old man beamed. "Come in, come in—my dear fellow, if I'd realized it was you, I'd never have dreamed of keeping you so long—" He smiled, obviously distressed. "Retreat has its disadvantages, too, you see. Nothing is perfect but life, as they say. When *you've* lived for a hundred and ninety years, you'll be glad to get away from people, and to be able to keep them out, from time to time."

In better light Dan stared openly at the man. A hundred and ninety years. It was incredible. He told the man so.

"Isn't it, though?" Chauncey Devlin chirped. "Well, I was a was-baby! Can you imagine? Born in London in 1945. But I don't even think about those horrid years any more. Imagine—people dropping bombs on each other!"

A tiny bird of a man—three times rejuvenated, and still the mind was sharp, the eyes were sharp. The face was a strange mixture of recent youth and very great age. It stirred something deep inside Dan—almost a feeling of loathing. An uncanny feeling.

"We've always known your music," he said. "We've always loved it. Just a week ago we heard the Washington Philharmonic doing—"

"The eighth." Chauncey Devlin cut him off disdainfully. "They always do the eighth."

"It's a great symphony," Dan protested.

Devlin chuckled, and bounced about the room like a little boy. "It was only half finished when they chose me for the big plunge," he said. "Of course I was doing a lot of conducting then, too. Now I'd much rather just write." He hurried across the long, softly-lit room to the piano, came back with a sheaf of papers. "Do you read music? This is just what I've been doing recently. Can't get it quite right, but it'll come, it'll come."

"Which will this be?" asked Dan.

"The tenth. The ninth was under contract, of course—strictly a pot-boiler, I'm afraid. Thought it was pretty good at the time, but *this* one—ah!" He fondled the smooth sheets of paper. "In this one I could *say* something. Always before it was hit and run, make a stab at it, then rush on to stab at something else. Not *this* one." He patted the manuscript happily. "With this one there will be _nothing_ wrong."

"It's almost finished?"

"Oh, no. Oh, my goodness no! A fairly acceptable first movement, but not what I *will* do on it—as I go along."

"I see. I—understand. How long have you worked on it now?"

"Oh, I don't know—I must have it down here somewhere. Oh, yes. Started it in April of 2057. Seventy-seven years."

They talked on, until it became too painful. Then Dan rose, and thanked his host, and started back for the corridor and life again. He had never even mentioned his excuse for coming, and nobody had missed it.

Chauncey Devlin, a tiny, perfect wax-image of a man, so old, so wise, so excited and full of enthusiasm and energy and carefulness, working eagerly, happily—

Accomplishing nothing. Seventy-seven years. The picture of a man who had been great, and who had slowly ground to a standstill.

And now Dan knew that he hadn't really been looking at Chauncey Devlin at all. He had been looking at the whole human race.

VIII

February 15th, 2135.

The day of the Hearings, to consider the charges and petition formally placed by The Honorable Daniel Fowler, Independent Senator from the Great State of Illinois. The long oval hearing-room was filling early; the gallery above was packed by 9:05 in the morning. Teevie-boys all over the place. The Criterion Committee members, taking their places in twos and threes—some old, some young, some rejuvenated, some not, taking their places in the oval. Then the other Senators—not the President, of course, but he'll be well represented by Senator Rinehart himself, ah yes. Don't worry about the President.

*

Bad news in the papers. Trouble in New Chicago, where so much trouble seems to start these days. Bomb thrown in the Medical Center out there, a *bomb* of all things! Shades of Lenin. Couple of people killed, and one of the doctors nearly beaten to death on the street before the police arrived to clear the mob away. Dan Fowler's name popping up here and there, not pleasantly. Whispers and accusations, *sotto voce*. And 'Moses' Tyndall's network hookup last night—of course nobody with any sense listens to *him*, but did you hear that hall go wild?

Rinehart—yes, that's him. Well, he's got a right to look worried. If Dan can unseat him here and now, he's washed up. According to the rules of the Government, you know, Fowler can legally petition for Rinehart's chairmanship without risking it as a platform plank in the next election, and get a hearing here, and then if the Senate votes him in, he's got the election made. Dan's smart. They're scared to throw old Rinehart out, of course—after all, he's let them keep their thumbs on rejuvination all these years with his Criteria, and if they supported him they got named, and if they didn't, they didn't get named. Not quite as crude as that, of course, but that's what it boiled down to, let me tell you! But now, if they reject Dan's petition and the people give him the election over their heads, they're *really* in a spot. Out on the ice on their rosy red—

How's that? Can't be too long now. I see Tyndall has just come in, Bible and all. See if he's got any tomatoes in his pockets. Ol' Moses really gets you going—ever listen to him talk? Well, it's just as well. Damn, but it's hot in here—

In the rear chamber, Dan mopped his brow, popped a pill under his tongue, dragged savagely on the long black cigar. "You with me, son?"

Carl nodded.

"You know what it means."

"Of course. There's your buzzer. Better get in there." Carl went back to Jean and the others around the 80-inch screen, set deep in the wall. Dan put his cigar down, gently, as though he planned to be back to smoke it again before it went out, and walked through the tall oak doors.

*

The hubbub caught, rose up for a few moments, then dropped away. Dan took his seat, grinned across at Libby, leaned his head over to drop an aside into Parker's ear. Rinehart staring at the ceiling as the charges are read off in a droning voice—

—Whereas the criteria for selection of candidates for sub-total prosthesis, first written by the Honorable Walter Rinehart of the Great State of Alaska, have been found to be inadequate, outdated, and utterly inappropriate to the use of sub-total prosthesis that is now possible—

—And whereas that same Honorable Walter Rinehart has repeatedly used the criteria, not in the just, honorable, and humble way in which such criteria must be regarded, but rather as a tool and weapon for his own furtherance and for that of his friends and associates—

Dan waited, patiently. Was Rinehart's face whiter than it had been? Was the Hall quieter now? Maybe not—but wait for the petition—

—The Senate of the United States of North America is formally petitioned that the Honorable Walter Rinehart should be displaced from his seat as Chairman in the Criterion Committee, and that his seat as Chairman of that committee should be resumed by the Honorable Daniel Fowler, author of this petition, who has hereby pledged himself before God to seek through this Committee in any and every way possible, the extention of the benefits of sub-total prosthesis techniques to all the people of this land and not to a chosen few—

Screams, hoots, cat-calls, applause, all from the gallery. None below—Senatorial dignity forbade, and the anti-sound glass kept the noise out of the chamber below. Then Dan Fowler stood up, an older Dan Fowler than most of them seemed to remember. "You have heard the charges which have been read. I stand before you now, formally, to withdraw them—"

What, what? Jaws sagging, eyes wide; teevie camera frozen on the Senator's face, then jerking wildly around the room to catch the reaction—

"You have also heard the petition which has been read. I stand before you now, formally, to withdraw it—"

Slowly, measuring each word, he told them. He knew that words were not enough, but he told them. "Only 75,000 men and women have undergone the process, at this date, out of almost two hundred million people on this continent, yet it has already begun to sap our strength. We were told that no change was involved, and indeed we saw no change, but it was there, my friends. The suicides of men like Kenneth Armstrong did not just *occur*. There are many reasons that might lead a man to take his life in this world of ours—selfishness, self-pity, hatred of the world or of himself, bitterness, resentment—but it was none of these that motivated Kenneth Armstrong. *His death was the act of a bewildered, defeated mind*—for he saw what I am telling you now and knew that it was true. He saw Starships built and rebuilt, and never launched—colonies dying of lethargy, because there was no longer any drive behind them—brilliant minds losing sight of goals, and drifting into endless inconsequential digressions—lifetimes wasted in repetition, in re-doing and re-writing and re-living. He saw it: the downward spiral which could only lead to death for all of us in the last days.

"This is why I withdraw the charges and petition of this Hearing. This is why I reject rejuvenation, and declare that it is a monstrous thing *which we must not allow to continue*. This is why I now announce that I personally will nominate the Honorable John Tyndall for President in the elections next spring, and will promise him my pledged support, my political organization and experience, and my every personal effort to see that he is elected."

*

It seemed that there would be no end to it, when Dan Fowler had finished. 'Moses' Tyndall had sat staring as the blood drained out of his sallow face; his jaw gaped, and he half-rose from his chair, then sank back with a ragged cough, staring at the Senator as if he had been transformed into a snake. Carl and Terry were beside Dan in a moment, clearing a way back to the rear chambers, then down the steps of the building to a cab. Senator Libby intercepted them there, his face purple with rage, and McKenzie, bristling and indignant. "You've lost your mind, Dan."

"I have not. I am perfectly sane."

"But *Tyndall*! He'll turn Washington into a grand revival meeting, he'll—"

"Then we'll cut him down to size. He's *my* candidate, remember, not his own. He'll play my game if it pays him well enough. But I want an Abolitionist administration, and I'm going to get one."

In the cab he stared glumly out the window, his heart racing, his whole body shaking in reaction now. "You know what it means," he said to Carl for the tenth time.

"Yes, Dan, I know."

"It means no rejuvenation, for you or for any of us. It means proving something; to people that they just don't want to believe, and cramming it down their throats if we have to. It means taking away their right to keep on living."

"I know all that."

"Carl, if you want out—"

"Yesterday was the time."

"Okay then. We've got work to do."

IX

Up in the offices again, Dan was on the phone immediately. He knew politics, and people—like the jungle cat knows the whimpering creatures he stalks. He knew that it was the first impact, the first jolting blow that would win for them, or lose for them. Everything had to hit right. He had spent his life working with people, building friends, building power, banking his resources, investing himself. Now the time had come to cash in.

Carl and Jean and the others worked with him—a dreadful afternoon and evening, fighting off newsmen, blocking phone calls, trying to concentrate in the midst of bedlam. The campaign to elect Tyndall had to start *now*. They labored to record a work-schedule, listing names, outlining telegrams, drinking coffee, as Dan swore at his dead cigar like old times once again, and grinned like a madman as the plans slowly developed and blossomed out.

Then the phone jangled, and Dan reached out for it. It was that last small effort that did it. A sledge-hammer blow, from deep within him, sharp agonizing pain, a driving hunger for the air that he just couldn't drag into his lungs. He let out a small, sharp cry, and doubled over with pain. They found him seconds later, still clinging to the phone, his breath so faint as to be no breath at all.

*

He regained consciousness hours later. He stared about him at the straight lines of the ceiling, at the hospital bed and the hospital window. Dimly he saw Carl Golden, head dropping on his chest, dozing at the side of the bed.

There was a hissing sound, and he raised a hand, felt the tiny oxygen mask over his mouth and nose. But even with that help, every breath was an agony of pain and weariness.

He was so very tired. But slowly, through the fog, he remembered. Cold sweat broke out on his forehead, drenched his body. *He was alive.* Yet he remembered crystal clear the thought that had exploded in his mind in the instant the blow had come. *I'm dying. This is the end—it's too late now.* And then, cruelly, *why did I wait so long?*

He struggled against the mask, sat bolt upright in bed. "I'm going to die," he whispered, then caught his breath. Carl sat up, smiled at him.

"Lie back, Dan. Get some rest."

Had he heard? Had Carl heard the fear he had whispered? Perhaps not. He lay back, panting, as Carl watched. Do you know what I'm thinking, Carl? I'm thinking how much I want to live. People don't *need* to die—wasn't that what Dr. Moss had said? It's such a terrible waste, he had said.

Too late, now. Dan's hands trembled. He remembered the Senators in the oval hall, hearing him speak his brave words; he remembered Rinehart's face, and Tyndall's, and Libby's. He was committed now. Yesterday, no. Now, yes.

Paul had been right, and Dan had proved it.

His eyes moved across to the bedside table. A telephone. He was still alive, Moss had said that sometimes it was possible *even when you were dying*. That was what they did with your father, wasn't it, Carl? Brave Peter Golden, who had fought Rinehart so hard, who had begged and pleaded for universal rejuvenation, waited and watched and finally caught Rinehart red-handed, to prove that he was corrupting the law and expose him. Simple, honest Peter Golden, applying so naively for his rightful place on the list, when his cancer was diagnosed. Peter Golden had been all but dead when he had finally whispered defeat, and given Rinehart his perpetual silence in return for life. They had snatched him from death, indeed. But he had been crucified all the same. They had torn away everything, and found a coward underneath.

Coward? Why? Was it wrong to want to live? Dan Fowler was dying. Why must it be him? He had committed himself to a fight, yes, but there were others, young men, who could fight. Men like Peter Golden's son.

But you are their leader, Dan. If you fail them, they will never win.

Carl was watching him silently, his lean dark face expressionless. Could the boy read his mind? Was it possible that he knew what Dan Fowler was thinking? Carl had always understood before. It had seemed that sometimes Carl had understood Dan far better than Dan did. He wanted to cry out to Carl now, spill over his dreadful thoughts.

There was no one to run to. He was facing himself now. No more cover-up, no deceit. Life or death, that was the choice. No compromise. Life or death, but decide *now*. Not tomorrow, not next week, not in five minutes—

He knew the answer then, the flaw, the one thing that even Paul hadn't known. That life is too dear, that a man loves life—not what he can *do* with life, but very life itself for its own sake—too much to die. It was no choice, not really. A man will *always* choose life, as long as the choice is really his. Dan Fowler knew that now.

It would be selling himself—like Peter Golden did. It would betray Carl, and Jean, and all the rest. It would mean derision, and scorn, and oblivion for Dan Fowler.

Carl Golden was standing by the bed when he reached out his arm for the telephone. The squeaking of a valve—what? Carl's hand, infinitely gentle, on his chest, bringing up the soft blankets, and his good clean oxygen dwindling, dwindling—

Carl!

How did you know?

*

She came in the room as he was reopening the valve on the oxygen tank. She stared at Dan, grey on the bed, and then at Carl. One look at Carl's face and she knew too.

Carl nodded, slowly. "I'm sorry, Jean."

She shook her head, tears welling up. "But you loved him so."

"More than my own father."

"Then *why*?"

"He wanted to be immortal. Always, that drove him. Greatness, power—all the same. Now he will be immortal, because we needed a martyr in order to win. Now we will win. The other way we would surely lose, and he would live on and on, and die every day." He turned slowly to the bed and brought the sheet up gently. "This is better. This way he will never die."

They left the quiet room.

A Man Obsessed

Table of Contents

CHAPTER ONE

Jeffrey Meyer sat back in his chair and waited. He could hardly breathe in the stifling air of the place. His hand clenched his glass until the knuckles were white, and his lip curled slightly as he watched the crowd around him. His whole body was tense. His legs, knotted tightly under the seat, were ready to move in an instant, and his eyes roved from the front to the back of the place. They were pale gray eyes that were never still—moving, watching, waiting. He had waited for so long, waited and hunted with bitter patience. But now he knew the long wait was drawing to a close. He knew that Conroe was coming and the trap was set.

For the thousandth time that evening, a shiver of chilly pleasure passed through him at the thought. He squirmed in eagerness, hardly daring to breathe. With his free hand he caressed the cool plastic handle of the gun that was close to his side, and a tight smile appeared on his thin lips. Conroe was coming ... at last ... at last.... And tonight he would kill Conroe.

The place was a madhouse around him. In the front of the room, by the street door, was a long horseshoe bar. It was already crowded by the early revelers. A screechie in the corner blatted out the tinny, nervous music that had recently become so popular, and a loud, hysterical burst of feminine laughter echoed to the back of the room.

Jeff Meyer rubbed his eyes, smarting from the bluish haze filling the long, low-ceilinged room. The unhealthy laughter broke out again, and someone burst into a bellow of song, half giggle, half noise.

At the adjoining table an alky-siky stirred, muttered something unintelligible and returned his nose sadly to his glass. Jeff's eyes flicked over the man with distaste. The scrawny neck, the sagging jaw, the idiotic, almost unearthly expression of intent listening on the vapid face: a typical picture of the type. Jeff watched him for a moment in disgust, then moved his eyes on, still watching as a flicker of apprehension passed through his mind.

A girl, quite naked except for the tray slung at her waist, strolled by his table, wagging her hips and turning on her heaviest personality smile.

"Drive a nail, mister?"

"Beat it."

The smile cooled slightly on the girl's lips. "Just askin'," she whined. "You don't have to get—"

"Beat it!" Jeff shot her a venomous look, trying frantically to keep his attention from straying from the front of the room. It would be too much to slip up now, more than he could stand to make a mistake like the last time.

The trap was perfect. It *couldn't* fail this time. Each step of the way had been carefully sketched, plotted through long sleepless nights of conference and planning. They couldn't have hunted a man like Conroe all these years without learning something about him—about his personality, about the things he liked and disliked, the things he did, the places he frequented, the friends he made.

Last time, after Jeff's own blundering error had allowed him to slip through the net at the last frantic minute, there seemed to be no hope. Everything seemed all the more hopeless when the man had disappeared as completely as if he were dead. But then they had found the girl—the key to his hiding place. She had formed the top link in the long, meticulous chain which had been drawn tighter each day, drawing Paul Conroe at last closer and closer to the hands of the man who was going to kill him. And now the trap was set; there could be no slip this time. There might never be another chance.

The street door opened sharply, and a short, bull-necked man with sandy hair walked in. He was followed by two other men in neat business suits. The first man stepped quickly to the bar, shouldering his way through the crowd, and stood sipping beer for several minutes. He glanced closely at the people around the bar and the surrounding tables before he walked toward the back and seated himself next to Meyer. Looking at Jeff with an indefinable expression, he finished his beer at a gulp and set the glass down on the table top with a snap.

"What's up?" Jeff said hoarsely.

"Something's funny." The sandy-haired man's voice was a smooth bass, and a frown appeared on his pink forehead. "He should have been here by now. He left the hotel over in Camden-town an hour ago, private three-wheeler, and he headed for here."

Jeff leaned forward, his face going white. "You've got somebody on him?"

"Yes, yes, of course." The man's voice was sharp, and there were tired lines around his eyes. "Take it easy, Jeff. You wouldn't be able to get him if he did come in—the way you are. He'd spot you in two seconds."

Jeff's hand trembled as he gripped his glass, and he settled tensely back in his chair. "It can't go wrong, Ted. It's got to come off."

"It should. The girl is here and she got word from him last night."

"Can she be trusted?"

The sandy-haired man shrugged. "Don't be silly. In this game, nobody can be trusted. If she's scared enough, she'll play along—okay? We've done our best to scare her. We've scared the hell out of her. Maybe she's more scared of Conroe—I don't know. But it looks cold to me. On a platter. So get a grip on yourself."

"It's got to come off." Jeff growled the words savagely, and drained his glass at a gulp. The sandy-haired man blinked, his pale little eyes curious. He leaned back thoughtfully. "Suppose it doesn't, Jeff? Suppose something goes wrong? Then what?"

Jeff's heavy hand caught the man's wrist in a grip that was like a vise. "You don't talk like that," he grated. "Your men I don't mind, but not you—understand? It can't go wrong. That's all there is to it. No if's, no maybe's. You got that now?"

Ted rubbed his wrist, his face red. "All right," he muttered. "So it can't go wrong. So I shouldn't talk, I shouldn't ask questions. But if it does go wrong, you're going to be dead. Do you know that? Because you're killing yourself with this—" He sighed, staring at Meyer. "What's it worth, Jeff? This constant tearing yourself apart? You've been obsessed with it for years. I know, I've been working with you and watching you for the last five of them—five long years of hunting. And for what? To get a man and kill him. That's all. What's it worth?"

Jeff took a deep breath and took a pack of cigarettes from his jacket. "Drive a nail," he said, offering the pack. "And don't worry about me. Worry about Conroe. He's the one who'll be dead."

Ted shrugged and took the smoke. "Okay. But if this blows up, I'm through. Because this is all I can take."

"Nothing will blow up. I'll get him. If I don't get him now, I'll get him the next time, or the next, or the next. With or without you, I'll get him."

Jeff took a trembling breath, his gray eyes cold under heavy black brows. "But there hadn't better be any next time."

He sat back in his chair, his face falling into the lines so familiar to Ted Bahr. Jeff Meyer had been a handsome man, before the long years of hate had done their work on his face. He was a huge, powerfully built man, heavy-shouldered, with a strong neck and straight nose, and a shock of jet black hair, neatly clipped. Only his face showed the bitterness of the past five years—years filled with anger and hatred, and a growing savagery which had driven the man almost to the breaking point.

The lines about his eyes and mouth were cruel—heavy lines that had been carved deeply and indelibly into the strong face, giving it a harsh, almost brutal cast in the dim light of the bistro. He breathed regularly and slowly as he sat, but his pale eyes were ice-hard as they moved slowly across the little show floor. They took in every face, every movement in the growing throng.

He was out of place and he knew it. He had no use for the giddy, half-hysterical people who crowded these smoke-filled holes night after night. They came in droves from the heart of the city to drink the watery gin and puff frantically on the contraband cigarettes as they tried desperately to drive off the steam and pressure of their daily lives.

Meyer hated the smell and stuffiness of the place; he hated the loud screams of laughter, the idiotic giggles; he hated the blubbering alky-sikys who crowded the bars with their whisky and their strange, unearthly dream-worlds. Above all, he hated the horrible, resounding artificiality, the brassiness and clanging noise of the crowd. His skin crawled. He knew that he couldn't possibly disappear into such a crowd, that he was as obvious, sitting there, as if he had been painted with red polka dots. And he knew that if Conroe spotted him a second before he spotted Conroe—He eased back in the chair and fought for control of his trembling hands.

The lights dimmed suddenly and a huge red spotlight caught the curtain at the back of the show floor. Jeff heard Bahr catch his breath for a moment, then let out a small, uneasy sigh. The crowd hushed as the girl parted the curtains and stepped out onto the middle of the floor, to a fanfare of tinny music. Jeff's eyes widened as they followed her to the center of the red light.

"That's her."

Jeff glanced sharply at Bahr. "The girl? She's the one?"

Bahr nodded. "Conroe knows how to pick them. He's supposed to meet her later. This is her first show for the evening. Then she has another at ten and another at two. He's supposed to take her home." He glanced around the room carefully. "Watch yourself," he muttered, and silently slipped away from the table.

The girl was nervous. Jeff sat close enough to see the fear in her face as she whirled around the floor. The music had shifted into a slow throbbing undertone, as she started to dance. She moved slowly, circling the floor. Her hair was long and black, flowing around her shoulders, and her body moved with carefully calculated grace to the music. But there was fear in her face as she whirled, and her eyes sought the faces on the fringe of the circle.

The music quickened imperceptibly and Jeff felt a chill run up his spine. The upper part of the shimmering gown slipped from the girl's shoulders, and slowly the tempo of the dance began to change from the stately rhythm it had a moment before. The throb of the music became hypnotic, moving faster and faster. Jeff's hands trembled as he tried to draw his eyes away from the undulating figure. There had been nothing to mark the change, but suddenly the dance had become obscene as the music rose—so viciously obscene that Jeff nearly gagged.

He felt the tension in the crowd around him. He heard their breathing rise, felt the desperate eagerness in their hard, bright eyes as they watched. The nervousness had left the girl's face. She had forgotten her fear, and a little smile appeared on her face as her body moved in abandon to the quickening beat.

Slowly she moved toward the tables, and the spotlight followed her, playing tricks with her hair and gown, concealing and revealing, twisting and swaying.... Jeff felt his body freeze. He fought to move, fought to take his eyes from the writhing figure as she drew closer and closer—

And then she was among the people, moving from table to table, never slowing her motion, graceful as a cat, twisting and twirling in the flickering red light. In and out she moved until she reached Jeff's table, her face inscrutable—a peacefully smiling mask. With amazing grace she leaped up on the table top and gave Jeff's glass a kick that sent it spinning onto the floor with a crash. And then the red light hit him full in the face—

"Get out of the light!"

Like a cat he threw his chair back and struck the girl, knocking her from the table. Someone screamed and the light swung to the girl, then back to him. The table went over. He rolled out of the light, twisting and fighting through the stunned and screaming crowd. His gun was in his hand, and he frantically searched the shouting room with his eyes.

"Get him! There he goes!"

He heard Bahr's voice roar from the side of the room. Jeff swung sharply to the sound of the voice. He saw the tall, slender figure crouched with his back to the bar, eyes wide with fear and desperation. There was no mistaking the face, the hollow cheeks and the high forehead, the graying hair. It was the face he had seen in his dreams, the twisted lips, the evil, ghoulish face of the man he had hunted to the ends of the earth. For a fraction of a second he saw Paul Conroe, crouched at bay, and then the figure was gone, twisting through the crowd toward the door—

"Stop him!" Jeff swung savagely into the crowd, screaming at Bahr across the room. "He's heading for the street! Get him!" The gun kicked sharply against his hand as he fired at the moving head. Rising for an instant, it disappeared again into the sea of heads. A scream rose at the shot. Women dropped to the floor, glasses crashed, tables went over. Someone clawed ineffectually for Jeff's leg. Then, abruptly, the lights went out and there was another scream.

"The door, the door—Don't let him get out—"

Jeff plunged to the side of the room, wrenched open the emergency exit and plunged down the dark, narrow walkway to the street. He heard shots as he ran. Turning the corner of the building, he saw the tall figure running pell-mell down the wet street.

"There he goes! Get him!"

Ted Bahr hung from the door. He gasped as he held his side, his face twisted in pain. "He hit me," he panted. "He's broken away—" A jet car slid from the curb and whined down the street toward the fleeing figure. "He can't make it—I've got men on every corner in cars. They'll get him, drive him back—"

"But where's he going?" A sob of rage choked Jeff's voice. "She sold us out, the bitch. She fingered me when she saw him come in—" His whole body trembled and the words tumbled out, almost incoherent. "But he must know the streets are blocked. Where's he running?"

"You think I'm a mind reader? I don't know. There are no open buildings in the whole block but this place and the Hoffman Center. He can't go anywhere else and he can't get out of the block. We've got every escapeway sewed up tight. He'll have to come back here or be shot down out there."

They watched the gloomy street, tears of rage in Jeff's eyes. His hands shook uncontrollably and his shoulders sagged in exhaustion and defeat. The tavern door had burst open and people were crowding out. Jeff and Ted Bahr moved back into the shadows of the alleyway and waited and listened.

"There's got to be a shot!" Jeff burst out. "He couldn't have slipped through." He turned to Bahr frantically. "Could he have gone into the Center?"

"On what pretense? They'd throw him to the Mercy Men—or the booby hatch, one or the other. He'd know better than to try." The sandy-haired man sank down on his haunches and gripped his side tightly. "He'll be back or we'll hear the shooting. He couldn't have slipped through."

A three-wheeled jet car slid in to the curb, and a man came up to them, eyes wide. "Get him?"

Bahr scowled. "No sign. How about the other boys?"

The man blinked. "Not a whisper. He never reached the end of the block."

"Did you check with Klett and Barker?"

"They haven't seen a soul down here."

Bahr glanced at Jeff sharply. "How about the streets behind? Any chance of a breakthrough there?"

The man's voice was matter-of-fact. "It's airtight. He couldn't get through without somebody seeing him." He stepped back to the car and spoke rapidly into the talker for a moment or two. "Nothing yet."

"Damn. How about Howie and the boys inside the place?"

"Nothing from them either."

Jeff's face darkened. "The Hoffman Center," he said slowly. "He got into the Center, somehow. He must have."

"He'd have to have gilt-edged medical credentials to get in after hours. They don't mess around over there. And what would it gain him?"

Jeff peered at Bahr in the darkness. "Maybe he wanted to be thrown to the Mercy Men. Maybe he's figured that as a last resort, he'll go in and volunteer, make a stab at the Big Cash."

Bahr stared at the big man in horror. "Look—Conroe may be desperate, but he hasn't lost his mind. My God, man! He isn't crazy."

"But he's scared."

"Of course he's scared, but—"

"How scared?"

Bahr shrugged angrily. "He'd have to be on his last legs to take a gamble like that."

"But they'd take him. They wouldn't ask any questions. They'd swallow him up; *they'd hide him*, whether they knew it or not." Jeff's voice rose in excitement. "Look. We've hunted him down for years. We've never rested; we've never quit. He knows that and he knows why. He knows me. He knows I'm not going to quit until I get him. And he knows I will get him, sooner or later. I'm cutting too close; I'm undermining his friends; I'm always moving closer. Everywhere he goes, everything he does, I'm onto him. And he knows when I do get him, he's going to die. What does that add up to?"

Bahr blinked in silence. Jeff's face hardened. "Well, I'll tell you what it adds up to. A man can take just so much. He can slide and twist and hide and keep moving just so long. Then he finds there aren't any more hiding places. But there's one last place a man can go to hide—if he's really at the end of his tether—and that's the Mercy Men. Because there he could vanish as though he'd never existed."

Ted Bahr carefully lit a smoke. "If that's where he went, we're through, Jeff. We'll never get him. We don't even need to worry about trying. Because if he's gone there, he'll never come out again."

"Some of them do."

Bahr grunted. "One in a million, maybe. The odds are so heavy that there's no sense thinking about it. If Paul Conroe has gone to the Mercy Men, then he's dead. And that is that."

Jeff returned his weapon to his pocket sharply and walked out to the car at the curb. "Keep your men where they are," he said to Bahr. "Keep them there for the rest of the night. If he's found a loophole, I want to know it. If he's hidden in the buildings, he'll have to come out sometime. Get some men to search the roofs, and you and I can start on the alleyways. If he's out there, we'll get him." He straightened his shoulders and the sullen fire was back in his eyes—an angry, bitter fire. "And if he's gone into the Center, we'll still get him."

Bahr's eyes were wide. "He'll never come out if he's gone where you think, Jeff. We could wait weeks or months, even years, and we still wouldn't know. Even if he did come out, we might never recognize him."

"I'll recognize him," Jeff snarled, looking down into Bahr's face. "I'm going to kill him. I'm going to know that he's dead, because I'll see him die. And I'll kill him if I have to follow him into the Center to do it."

CHAPTER TWO

The news report blatted in Jeff Meyer's ear from the little car radio. The words came through, but he hardly heard them as his eyes watched the huge glass doors of the administration building of the Hoffman Medical Center.

... no word has yet been received, but it is believed that the Eurasian governments may be in session several hours more in an attempt to stem the inflation. On the home front, the stock-market nosedive, which resulted from the new Senate taxation bill yesterday, leveled off when the Secretary of Corporative Business announced this morning that the government would abandon attempts to enforce the new law, at least for the time being. Secretary Barnes stated that further study of the bill would be undertaken when more pressing governmental problems had been cleared—

Jeff snapped off the switch with a snarl. The street passing the Center was crowded. Lines of cars moved into and out of the traffic stream from the huge Center parking tiers. The building rose high, tier upon tier. Its walls gleamed white in the bright morning sunlight, reflecting brilliant facets of golden light from thousands of polished windows.

It was an immense building, sprawling across six perfectly landscaped city blocks, tall trees and cool green terraces setting off the glistening beauty of the architecture. The structure sent tower after tower up from the dingy street below, and at the foot of the towers was a buzz of furious activity. Supply trucks, carrying food and supplies for the twenty-two thousand beds and the people in them, and for the additional thirteen thousand people who worked day and night to keep the huge hospital running, moved toward the unloading platforms.

The Hoffman Medical Center was an age-old dream which had finally come true. Even those who had conceived it had not realized the tremendous need it would fulfill. From its very inception, no expense had been spared. The finest architects had thrown up the shimmering ward-towers, turned toward the sun, to bring light to the sick and injured who rested and healed within. Equipment unequaled anywhere in the world had filled the Center's dressing and surgical rooms. The doctors, nurses, researchers and technicians who staffed the institution had been gathered from the world over. And all the world had conceded the Hoffman Center its place as leader in the realm of medicine, ever since the cornerstone had been laid that rainy morning in the spring of the year 2085. Twenty-four years had passed since that day, and in those years the Hoffman Center had never once faltered in its leadership.

The men in the car sat in stony silence. Finally, Jeff Meyer stirred, extended his hand briefly to Ted Bahr. "You'll cover things out here?"

"Don't worry about it." Bahr shook the hand. "Well wait to hear from you." He watched, almost wistfully, as the huge man cut through the traffic and headed for the large glass doors. Then, with a sigh, he stepped on the starter button and snaked the little jet car into the stream of traffic moving toward the city.

*

Jeff Meyer stopped in the great, bustling lobby and stared about him almost in awe. He had never been inside the Hoffman Center before, though he had heard of it many times and in many places. Since it had taken over service of the huge metropolis of Boston-New Haven-New York-Philadelphia, the newspapers and TV had been full of stories of the lifesaving and healing that had gone on within its walls. The disease research, conducted by specialists in all phases of medicine who were for the first time gathered together under one agency, had startled the world again and again.

But there had been other stories, too—not from the papers and TV, not these stories. These tales had come by word of mouth: a short sentence or two, a nervous laugh, a sneering joke, a rumor, a whispered story from a wide-eyed alky hanging over a bar. Not the sort of stories one really believed, but the sort that made one wonder.

Several dozen white-garbed women moved across the floor of the huge lobby and talked quietly among themselves. Jeff sniffed uneasily. There was a curiously distasteful odor in the air, an odor of almost unhealthy cleanliness and spotless preservation. The lobby was a mill of activity: the elevators and interbuilding jitneys terminated here; people moved briskly, carrying with them the familiar air of hurry and vast pressure that infected the whole world outside.

Jeff watched, spotting the corridor leading to the main administrative offices. He saw the elevators constantly rising to and returning from the huge admission offices. He noted the corridor twisting off to the staff living quarters. He stood silent, his quick gray eyes cautiously probing and watching. He tried to print an indelible picture in his mind of the layout of the building and was almost floored by the hive-like bustle of the place. There was a complexity in the curved doorways and the brightly lighted corridors.

Somewhere here he could find Paul Conroe. Somewhere in this maze of buildings and passageways was the man he had hunted for. Logic told him that. They had spent the night searching every possible alternative. His muscles ached and his eyes were red from sleeplessness, but there was a hot, angry glow in his heart. He knew that this was the only place that Conroe could have gone. Yet the place where he must be hiding was a place Jeff had heard of only in rumor, a place whose mention carried with it a half-knowledge of staggering wealth and almost indescribable horror.

Someone tapped him on the shoulder. He turned, startled, to face a huge, burly man with a suspicious face and a gray uniform. "You got business here, mister, or are we just sight-seeing?"

Jeff forced a grin. "I don't know where to go," he said truthfully.

"Maybe you should go back out then. No visitors until this afternoon."

"No, I'm not a visitor. I'm looking for the Volunteer's Bank. The ads said to come to the administration offices—"

The guard's face softened a little. He pointed a finger toward a corridor marked RESEARCH ADMINISTRATION. "Right over there," he said. "Office is the first door to your right. The nurse will take care of you."

Meyer strolled toward the corridor, his mind fumbling with the rumors and bits of half-knowledge that were all that he had to work on: stories of drunks stumbling into the Emergency Rooms and never coming out; tales of quiet, swift raids on narcotics houses, of people who never reached the police stations.

But how could he make the right contact here? "Research Administration" covered a multitude of meanings. He had read the advertisements for Hoffman volunteers in all the buses, in the 'copters, on the roads. Newspapers and TV had carried them for years. Meyer glanced down at his unpolished shoes, rubbed a finger over his purposely unshaven chin. What would they expect a volunteer to look like? How could they detect a fraud, an interloper? He shivered as he faced the office door. It would be a gamble, a terrible chance. Because with all the other publicity, no mention had ever been made of the Mercy Men. He glanced back, found the guard still staring at him, and walked into the office.

Several people sat along the wall. A small, mousy-looking man with a bald head and close-set eyes had just sat down in the chair before the desk. He waited for the prim-looking woman wearing a ridiculous little white hat to put down her pen. She didn't even glance up as Jeff took a seat, and she kept writing for several minutes before turning her attention to the little bald man. Then she looked up and gave a frosty smile at him. "Yes, sir?"

"Dr. Bennet asked me to come back today," the little man said. "Follow-up on last week's work."

"Name please?" The woman took his name and punched the button on a panel before her; an instant later a card flipped down in a slot. She checked it, made an entry and nodded to the man. "Dr. Bennet will be ready for you at eleven. You'll find magazines in the lounge." She indicated another door, and the little man disappeared through it.

Another person, a middle-aged woman, moved to take the little man's place before the desk. Jeff felt restless and glanced at his watch. It was almost eleven. Must she move so slowly? Nothing seemed to hurry her. She worked from person to person, smiling, impersonal, just a trifle chilly. Finally she nodded to Jeff, and he moved to the chair.

"Name, please?"

"You don't have a card on me."

She looked up briefly. "A new volunteer? We're happy to have you, sir. Now if you'll give me your name, I can start the papers through."

Jeff cleared his throat, felt his pulse pounding in his forehead. "I'm not sure just what I want to volunteer for," he said cautiously.

The woman smiled. "We have a rather large selection to choose from. There are the regular 'mycin drug runs every week on Tuesdays and Thursdays. You take the drug by mouth in the morning and give blood samples at ten, two and four. Many of our new Volunteers start on that. It pays six dollars and your lunch while you're here. Or you could give blood, but the law restricts you to once every three months on that, and it only pays thirty-five dollars. Or—"

Jeff shook his head and leaned forward. He looked directly into her eyes. "I don't think you understand," he said softly. "I want money. Lots of it.

Not five or ten dollars." He looked down at the desk. "I've heard you have other kinds of work."

The woman's eyes narrowed. "There are higher-paying categories of Volunteer work, of course. But you must understand that they are higher paying because they involve a greater risk to the health of the Volunteer. For instance, we've been running circulation studies with heart catheterizations. We pay a hundred dollars for these, but there is an appreciable risk involved. Or sternal marrow punctures for blood studies. Usually we start—"

"I said money," said Jeff implacably. "Not peanuts."

Her eyes widened and she stared at him for a long moment. It was a strange, penetrating stare that took him in from his face to his feet. Her smile faded and her fingers were suddenly nervous. "Have you any idea what you're talking about?"

"I have. I'm talking about the Mercy Men."

She stood up abruptly and disappeared into an inner office. Jeff waited, his whole body trembling. Beads of sweat broke out on his forehead, and he gave a visible start when the woman opened the door again.

"Come in here, please."

Then he was on the right track. He tried to conceal the excitement in his eyes as he took a seat in the small room. He waited, fidgeting. The woman packed up a small telephone on the desk and punched several buttons in rapid succession. The silence was almost intolerable as he waited, a silence that was alive and vibrant. Finally a signal light flickered and she took up the receiver.

"Dr. Schiml? This is the Volunteer office, Doctor." She shot Jeff a swift glance. "There's another man here to see you."

Meyer felt his heart pound. He shifted in his chair and started to take out a cigarette. Then he checked himself.

"That's right," the woman was saying, eyeing him as if he were a biological specimen. "I'm sorry, he hasn't given a name.... Ten minutes? All right, Doctor, I'll have him wait." With that, she replaced the receiver and left the room without a word.

Jeff stood up, stretched his legs and looked about the room. It was small, with just a desk and two or three chairs. Obviously it served as a conference room of some sort. One wall held the panel of file buttons;

another held the telephone and visiphone viewer. Over the visiphone screen, a large lighted panel announced the date in sharp black letters: 32 April, 2109. Below it, the little transistor clock had just changed to read 11:23 A.M. Almost noon. And every passing minute his quarry drew farther and farther away.

He glanced out the window at the rising tiers of buildings. Across the courtyard the first of the ward-towers rose. To one side of it were a series of long, low structures with skylights. These were the kitchens, perhaps, or maintenance buildings. There were dozens of them—any one of which could be hiding Paul Conroe. Jeff clenched his hands until the nails bit his palms. He stared down at the buildings. Conroe could be anywhere down there. *Another man had already seen Dr. Schiml....*

A door clicked behind him and he turned sharply. A man entered the room and closed the door behind him. Smiling, he walked over to the desk. Meyer nodded and watched the man. He felt a sinking feeling in the pit of his stomach. For the briefest instant the doctor had caught his eye, and Jeff felt everything that he had planned to say crumble like dust around him.

The man hardly looked like a doctor, although his white jacket was immaculate and a stethoscope peeped from his side pocket. He was tall and slender, almost fifty years old, with round, cheerful pink cheeks and a little pug nose that seemed completely out of place on his face.

A harmless-looking man, Jeff thought, except for his eyes. But his eyes—they were the sharpest, most penetrating eyes Jeff had ever seen. And they were watching him. Quite independent of the smiling face, they watched his every move, studying him. The eyes were full of wisdom, but they were also tinged with caution.

The doctor sat down and motioned Jeff to the seat facing the desk. He pushed a cigar case across the desk to him.

Jeff hesitated, then took one. "I thought these were slightly illegal," he said.

The doctor grinned. "Slightly. Thanks to us, as you probably know. We did most of the work here on tobacco smoke and cancer—actually got legislation pushed through on it." He leaned back easily in his chair as he lit his own cigar. "Still, one once in a while won't do too much harm. And there's nothing like a good smoke to get things talked out. I'm Roger Schiml, by the way. I didn't get your name."

"Meyer," said Jeff. "Jeffrey Meyer."

The doctor's eyes narrowed quizzically. "I hope my girl didn't bother you too much. She channels most of the volunteer work here, as you see. Then, occasionally, cases come in which she'd rather turn over to me." He paused for a moment. "Cases like yours, for instance."

Jeff blinked, his mind racing. It would take acting, he thought, real acting to fool this man. The face was deceptively young and benign, almost complacent. But the eyes were far from young. They were old, old eyes. They had seen more than eyes should see. They missed nothing. To fool a man with eyes like that—Jeff took a deep breath and said, "I want to join the Mercy Men."

Dr. Schiml's eyes widened very slightly. For a long moment he said nothing, just stared at the huge man before him. Then he said, "That's interesting. It's also very curious. The name, I mean—oh, I can understand the attraction such an idea might have for people, but the name that's become so popular—it baffles me. 'Mercy Men.' It gives you a curious feeling, don't you think? Brings up mental pictures of handsome young interns fighting the forces of evil and death, the brave heroes giving their all for the upward flight of humanity—all that garbage, you know." The eyes hardened quite suddenly. "Where did you hear of the Mercy Men, I wonder?"

Jeff shrugged. "The word's been around for quite a while. A snatch here, a story there—even though it isn't advertised too openly."

Dr. Schiml looked him straight in the eye. "And suppose I told you that there is no such organization, either here or anywhere else on Earth that I know of?"

A tight smile appeared on Jeff's face. "I'd call you a class-A liar."

Schiml's eyebrows went up. "I see. That's a big word. Maybe you can support it."

"I can. There are Mercy Men here. There have been for several years."

"You're sure of that."

"Quite. I know one. He was a skid-rower with a taste for morphine when I first ran into him—a champagne appetite to go with a beer income. Then he went out of circulation for about six months. Now he has a place up in the Catskills, with many, many thousands of dollars in the bank. Of course, he uses the money to feed several hundred cats in his basement." Jeff's eyes narrowed. "He never liked cats very much before he left here. There are other funny things he does—nothing serious, of course, but peculiar. Still, he doesn't need the dope any more."

Schiml smiled and put his fingers together. "That would be Luke Tandy. Yes, Luke was a little different when he left, but the work was satisfactory and we paid off."

"Yes," said Jeff softly. "One hundred and fifty thousand dollars. Cash on the line. To him or his heirs. He was lucky."

"So what are you doing here?"

"I want a hundred and fifty thousand dollars too."

The doctor's eyes met Jeff's squarely. "And you are a liar too."

Jeff reddened. "What do you mean—"

"Look, let's get this straight right now. Don't lie to me. I'll catch you every time." The doctor's eyes were hard. "I see a man who's eaten well for a long time, wearing dirty but expensive clothes, who doesn't drink, who doesn't use drugs, who is young and strong and capable. He tells me he wants to join the Mercy Men for money. He tells me a lie. Now I'll ask you again: why are you here?"

"For money. For one hundred and fifty thousand dollars."

The doctor sighed and leaned back. "All right, no matter. We'll go into it later, I suppose. But I think you'd better understand certain things. It's no accident that your information on the Mercy Men is so vague. We've been careful to keep it that way, of course. The more vague the stories, the fewer curiosity-seekers and busybodies we have to contend with. Also, the more distasteful the stories, the more desperate people will become before they come to us. This we particularly desire. Because the work we do here requires a very desperate man to volunteer."

As he talked, the doctor brought out a pack of cards from the desk and began riffling them nervously in his fingers. Jeff's eyes caught them and a chill went down his back. They were curious cards, not the regular playing variety. These were smaller, with a peculiar marking system in bright red on the white faces. Jeff shivered and he was puzzled at the chill that gripped his body. He shifted in his chair in growing tension and tried to take his eyes from the cards.

The doctor snubbed out his cigar, leaned back in the chair and gave the cards a riffle and regarded Jeff closely. "We've done a lot here since the Center opened—work based on years of background research. A century or more ago there were terrible medical problems to be faced: polio was a killer then; they had no idea of cancer control; they were faced with a terrific death rate from heart disease. All those things are beaten now, a thing of the past. But as the old killers moved out, new ones took their place. Look at the half-dozen NVI plagues we've had in the past few years—neurotoxic virus infections that started to appear out of nowhere twenty years ago. Look at the alky-sikys you see in every bar today, a completely new type of alcoholism-psychosis that we haven't even been able to describe, much less cure. Look at the statistics on mental disease, rising in geometric progression almost every year."

The tall doctor stood up and walked to the window. "We don't know why it's happening, but it is. Something's on the march, something ghastly and evil among the people. Something that has to be stopped." He gave the cards a sharp riffle and tossed them onto the desk with a sigh. "We can't stop it until we know something about the human brain and how it works, and why it does what it does, and how. We don't even understand fully the structure of the nervous system, much less understand its function. And we've learned all we can from cats and dogs and monkeys. Any further study of a monkey's brain will give us great insight into the neuroses and complexes of monkeys, no doubt. But it won't teach us anything more about *men*." His voice was very soft. "You can see where this leads, I think."

Jeff Meyer nodded slowly. "You need men," he said.

"We need men. Men to study. Cruel as it may sound, men to experiment upon. We can't learn any more from any other variety of ... experimental animal. But there are problems. Toy around with a man's brain and he is likely to die, quite abruptly. Or he may be deranged, or he may go violently insane. Most of the work, however well planned, however certain we were of results, however safe it appeared, proved to be completely unpredictable. Much of the work and many of the results were quite horrible. But we're making progress, slow—but progress nonetheless. So the work continues.

"It hasn't been very popular. No man in his right mind would volunteer for such a job. So we hired men. For the most truly altruistic work in the world, our workers come with the most mercenary of motives: we pay for their services and we pay well. A hundred thousand dollars is a small fee, on our scale. We have the government behind us. The sky is the limit, if we need a man for a job. The money is paid, when the work is completed, either to the man himself or to his heirs. You see why the name they've given themselves is so curious—Medical Mercenaries, the 'Mercy Men.' That's why a man must be desperate to come to us. That's why we must be so very careful who joins us, for what motives."

Jeff Meyer stared at his hands and waited in the silence of the room. His eyes strayed once again to the curious cards, and the chill of fear went through him like a ghastly breeze. This was a port of last resort, a road that could end in horror and death. Ted Bahr had said it wasn't worth it—that Conroe would never escape alive—but he knew that Conroe could. And he knew Conroe well enough to know that he would.

Jeff felt the old bitterness and hatred swell up in his mind, and his hands trembled as he sat. He had long since thrown aside his life as he had known it, cast off the veneer of civilized life that he had acquired, to hunt Paul Conroe down and kill him. There was nothing else in his life that mattered. It had been a long, grueling hunt, tracking him, following him, studying him, tracing his movements and habits, plotting trap after trap, driving the man to desperation. But there had been no indication, anywhere along the line, that Conroe would turn to such a desperate gamble as this.

But he must have known that death otherwise was inevitable. Here he could be changed. He might disappear from the face of the Earth in the oblivion of quiet death, to be sure, but he also might emerge, unscathed, to live in wealth the rest of his life, unrecognizable and safe.

Jeff Meyer looked up at the doctor and his eyes were hard. "I haven't changed my mind," he said. "What has to be done to join?"

Dr. Schiml sighed, and turned resignedly to the file panel. "There are tests that are necessary and rules to be obeyed. You'll be confined and regimented. And once you're assigned to a job and sign a release, you're in." He leaned forward and punched the visiphone button. Tapping his fingers idly on the desk, he waited until an image blinked and cleared on the screen. “Blackie,” he said tiredly. “Better send the Nasty Frenchman up here. We’ve got a new recruit.”

The visiphone snapped off and Jeff sat frozen to his seat, his pulse throbbing in his neck, every nerve in his body screaming in excitement. The face on the screen had been clearly visible for a moment: a pale face with large gray eyes—a woman’s face, surrounded by flowing black hair. It was a face that was impressed indelibly on his memory. It belonged to the girl who had danced the night before in the red light.

CHAPTER THREE

There was no doubt of it. She was the girl in the night club, the dancing girl with the flowing black hair and the mask-like smile, who had led him to Conroe and then brought the spotlight to his face to spring the trap too soon. Frantically Jeff fought to control his excitement. He knew his face was white and he avoided the doctor's puzzled glance. But he couldn't control the angry fire burning in his mind, the little voice screaming out: "*He's here; he's here, somewhere!*"

But why was she here? The doctor had called her "Blackie." He had spoken to her with familiarity. Jeff's mind whirled. He had the strangest feeling that he had missed something somewhere along the line, that he knew the answer but couldn't quite grasp it. What could the girl's sudden appearance in the Center involve?

Or had her appearance at the night club been the unusual one?

A buzzer rang and the office door opened to admit a small, weasel-faced man. The doctor looked up and smiled. "Hello, Jacques. This is Jeff Meyer, the new recruit. Take him down and get him quartered in, all right? And you might brief him a little. He's awfully green."

The little man scratched his long nose and regarded Jeff with a nasty smile. "A new one, huh? Where are you going to line him up?"

"No telling. We'll see where the tests put him, first. Then we'll talk about jobs."

The smile widened on the little man's face, turning down the end of his long pointed nose and revealing a dirty yellow row of teeth. His eyes ran over Jeff from head to toe. "Big one too. But then, they fall just as hard as the rest. Want me to take him right down?"

Schiml nodded. "Maybe he can still get lunch." His eyes shifted to Jeff. "This is the Nasty Frenchman," he said, motioning toward the little man with his thumb. "He's been around for a long time; he can show you the ropes. And don't let him bother you too much—his sense of humor, I mean. Like I say, he's been around here a long time. You'll get quarters and you'll be expected to stay with your group for meals and everything else. That means no contacts outside the hospital as long as you're here. You'll get the daily news reports, and there are magazines and books in the library. If you've got other business outside, you haven't any business in here. Any time you leave the Center it's considered an automatic breach of contract."

He paused for a long moment and gave Jeff a strange look, almost a half smile. "And you'll find that questions aren't appreciated around here, Jeff. Any kind of questions. The men don't like people too much when they ask questions."

The Nasty Frenchman shuffled his feet nervously, and Jeff started out the door. Then the little man turned back to Dr. Schiml. "They brought Tinker back from the table about ten minutes ago. He's in pretty bad shape. Maybe you should look at him?"

"This was the big job today, wasn't it?" Schiml's eyes were sharp. "What did Dr. Bartel say?"

"He said no dice. It was a bust."

"I see. Well, it may be just the diodrax wearing off now, but I'll be down to see."

The Nasty Frenchman grunted and turned back to Jeff. His face still wore the nasty little grin. "Let's go, big boy," he said, and started down the hall.

*

Jeff watched the corridors as they passed, counting them one by one, trying desperately to keep himself oriented. He glanced at his watch and angrily sucked in his breath. Minutes were slipping by, precious minutes, minutes that could mean success or failure. A thousand questions crowded his mind, and behind them all was the girl. She was the key, he was sure of it. She would know where Conroe was, where he could be found....

They reached an elevator, stepped aboard and shot down at such dizzying speed that Jeff nearly choked. Then, suddenly, they came to a jolting stop and stepped into a dingy, gray corridor that was dimly lit by bare bulbs in the ceiling.

The Nasty Frenchman punched a button in the wall and turned to regard Jeff. The sneering little smile was still on his lips as the far-off rumble of a jitney grew to a sharp clatter. A little car dropped down from its ceiling track. The little man hopped in nimbly and motioned Jeff in beside him. Then the car took off for the ceiling again, swinging crazily and speeding down the maze of corridors and curves.

Jeff stirred uneasily, growing more and more confused with every turn. "Look," he broke out finally, "where's this thing taking us?"

The Nasty Frenchman turned pale eyes toward him. "You worried or something?"

"Well, it looks like we're headed for the center of the Earth. I'd like to be able to find my way out sometime—"

"Why?"

The question was so blunt that it left Jeff's jaw sagging for a moment. "Well, I'm not planning to spend the rest of my life in here."

The Nasty Frenchman guffawed. It was not a pleasant laugh. "Here for a nice restful vacation, huh? You wise guys are all the same. Go ahead, dream—I won't bother you."

The little man turned his attention to the controls and the car swung sharply to the right and headed down another corridor. Jeff scowled as he watched the lighted corridors flash by. Were they speeding so far, so deep in the depths of the building? Or was this part of a definite plan to confuse, to lose recruits in the mammoth place so completely that they could never find their way out? Jeff shrugged, finally. It really didn't matter too much. He had one job and only one. He could worry about escape when it had been accomplished.

"That girl," he said finally. "The doctor called her 'Blackie.' Is she down here where we're going?"

"How should I know? I don't keep her on a leash." The little man's face darkened and his eyes turned suspiciously to Jeff.

"I mean, is she one of the group—one of the Mercy Men?"

The Nasty Frenchman threw a switch sharply, swerving the speeding car through a long, dim passage. He ignored the question, as if he hadn't heard it. In the dim light his skin was pasty yellow and wrinkled like a mummy. The cruelty and avarice on his face was frightening.

Jeff watched him for a moment or two, then said, "What brought you here? To the Mercy Men, I mean?"

The Nasty Frenchman's eyes flashed poisonously, his face a horrid mask. "Did I ask you your racket before you came in?"

"No."

"Then don't ask me mine. And you won't forget that, if you're smart." He turned his attention sharply to the controls, ignoring Jeff for several moments. Finally he said, "You'll share a room and you'll eat at eight, noon and six. Tests should start tomorrow morning at eight-thirty. You'll be in your room when the doctors come for you. You won't have any status here until you're tested. Then you'll sign a release and wait for a job assignment. You won't have any choice of work; that's just for the older ones. Some of the work is with central nervous system, some is with sympathetic; some work concentrates on spinal cord and peripherals, but most of the interest these days is in cortical lesions and repair. That pays the best, too—couple hundred thousand at a crack, with a fairly good risk."

"And what's a fairly good risk in here?"

The grin reappeared on the little man's face again. It was almost savage in its cruelty. "Ten per cent full recovery is a good risk. That means complete recovery from the work, no secondary infection, complete recovery of faculties—in other words complete success in the work. Then a *fairly* good risk runs slightly lower—more casualty, maybe five per cent recovery. And a high-risk job averages two per cent—"

The grin broadened. "You've got a better chance of living sitting under an atom bomb, my friend. And once you sign a release, relieving the hospital and the doctors of all responsibility, you're in, and held to your contract by law. This is no vacation, but if you're lucky enough to come through—" The little man's eyes were bright with eagerness. "They pay off—oh, how they pay off. If you're lucky, you'll get a good starter, maybe a hundred thousand, with good risk." He scratched his nose and regarded Jeff closely. "Of course, there are incomplete recoveries, too. They have trouble keeping them out of the news, if they ever leave. Pretty messy, sometimes, too."

Jeff felt his face paling at the cruel eagerness in the little man's voice. What could bring a man to a place like this—especially this kind of a man? Or had he been a different kind of a man before he came in? How long had he been here, waiting from experiment to experiment, waiting to live or to die, waiting for the payoff, the Big Cash that waited at the end of a job? What could such an existence do to a man? What could there be to drive him on? Jeff shuddered, then gasped as the car gave a sudden lurch around a corner and settled to the floor.

The Nasty Frenchman hopped out, motioned to Jeff to follow. They started walking toward the escalator at the end of the passageway. Jeff searched each doorway they passed, keeping alert for a sign of the black-haired woman. "Look," he said finally. "This girl—Blackie, I mean—who is she?"

The Nasty Frenchman stopped in his tracks, glared at Jeff. "What is she, an old family friend or something? You keep asking about her."

"I know her from somewhere."

"So why bother me with your questions?"

Jeff's face darkened angrily. "I want to see her, all right? Don't get so jumpy—"

The little man whirled on him like a cat. Jeff's arm was wrenched behind his back until he felt the tendons rip. With unbelievable strength the Nasty Frenchman twisted the huge man back against the wall and glared up at him with blazing eyes. "You're a smart guy, coming around here, asking questions," he snarled, giving Jeff's arm a vicious wrench. "You think you can fool me? You ask about this, you ask about that—why so nosey? Blackie ... me ... everything. What are you doing here? Going after the Big Cash or asking questions?"

"The Cash!" Jeff gasped. He twisted to wriggle free of the iron-like grip.

"Then don't ask questions! We don't like nosey people here; we like people that roll dice square and mind their own business." The little man gave the arm a final agonizing wrench and released it. He jumped back, poised, eyes savagely eager.

Every instinct screamed at Jeff to rush him, but he slumped against the wall. Rubbing his aching arm, he fought for control. He knew a fight now could ruin things completely. Already he had blundered terribly. He cursed under his breath. How stupid he'd been not to have realized how unpopular questions would be to people in a place like this. And surely the word would get to the girl now that he was asking about her. Unless he could get to her first—

Still rubbing his elbows painfully, he turned to the Nasty Frenchman. "Okay, let it go," he growled. "Where do we go from here?"

The room was small and barren. Dingy and gray, it matched Jeff's spirit perfectly. He entered it with the Nasty Frenchman at his heels and stared at the two stark hospital beds against the far wall, the two foot lockers, the two small desk-and-chair combinations. There was no window in the room. Indeed, there was nothing about the room or corridor to prove that they were not twenty miles underground. Certainly the jitney ride had been no reassurance to the contrary.

The dim wall lights glowed on scrubbed, peeling paint, and the floor was covered with clean but well-worn plastic matting. Against one wall was a TV set. Between the beds a door led into a compact lavatory and shower. Glancing in, Jeff saw the lavatory was also connected with the adjoining room.

"It's no Grand Hotel," the Nasty Frenchman said sourly. "But it's clean and it's a bed. This corridor quarters your whole unit—the C unit. Other units are on other floors, up and down."

Jeff looked around the room gloomily. "Where can I eat?"

"The mess hall's four flights down. Take the escalator at the end of the hall. It closes in half an hour, so you'd better step on it. And if you're smart, you won't go wandering around. These boys in gray you see here and there don't like us very much." His face creased into a sardonic grin as he started for the door. "And you'd be smart to change before you come down. The faster people stop thinking you're new here, the happier you'll be." With that, he turned and disappeared down the hall.

Jeff gave a sigh, and prowled the room. One of the foot lockers held an amazing assortment of clean and dirty clothes. On the floor of it lay a large heap of dirty shirts and trousers, and nested squarely in the center of the pile was a heap of gold rings and wrist watches. Jeff blinked, not quite believing his eyes. He hadn't thought to ask about his room-mate, but apparently he had one who had not yet made his appearance.

Apparently everyone wore similar clothing. He found the other locker filled with clean shirts and dungarees. Swiftly he started to change, his mind racing. His body was sore all over and he felt a dry, hot feeling around his ears from lack of sleep. His arm ached miserably every time he moved it. If only he could sleep for a little while. But he knew there was no time to be wasted. In the mess hall there would still be people. Somewhere among them he would find the girl....

Carefully he considered the problem. The girl was the key. He had to find her, to make certain that Conroe was here. And he had to find her quickly, catch her unawares, before she had a chance to alibi or hide. Conroe would be hidden; he would never come into the open until he was sure that he had not been followed. He too must be taken unawares. Jeff had seen Conroe slip out of too many traps in the past. A blunder now could be the last. And if Conroe had time to plan, there would be many, many blunders.

A car buzzed down the hall as he stood in the room and stopped a little way from the door. There were voices, subdued, yet carrying a sharp note of frantic excitement. Jeff paused, listening to the combination of unfamiliar sounds: a grunt, a low curse, a rustle of whispered conversation, a low whistle. Then the door to the next room banged open and a rumble and squeak of wheels came to his ears.

"Jeez, what a job!"

"Yeah, looks bad. Did the doc see him?"

"He said he'd be down—"

"—gotta let it wear off before you can tell. This was the works, this time."

Jeff walked quietly to the door of the connecting lavatory, his nerves tingling. A new sound was apparent, an unearthly sound of labored, gurgling breathing. Jeff shivered. He had heard a sound like that only once before in his life: in a rocket during the Asian war, when a man had been struck in the throat with a chunk of shrapnel. Carefully, he pushed the door open an inch, peered through....

There were three men standing in the room, maneuvering a man—if it was a man—from the four-wheeled cart onto the bed. The man's head was covered to the shoulders with bandage. A patch of fresh blood showed near the temple, and a rubber tube emerged where the mouth should have been.

"Got him down? Better cover him closer. Restrainers—he may jump around. Doc said three weeks for shock to wear off, if he makes it through the night."

"Yeah—and this is the Big Cash for Tinker too. Harpo nearly beat him to the job, but Schiml had promised him—"

Jeff shuddered. This, then, was one of the Mercy Men, finished with a "job." The gurgling sound grew louder, measuring itself with the man's breathing—short, shallow, a measure of death. An experiment had been completed.

Jeff closed the door silently. His face in the mirror was pasty white and his hands were shaking. Here was the factor that had been plaguing him from the start, finally breaking through to the surface. The road he was traveling was a one-way road. He had to find Conroe and get off the road quickly, while he could. *Because he dared not travel the road too far....*

*

The air in the corridor seemed fresher as Jeff started for the escalator. It was almost two o'clock and he hurried, anxious to reach the mess hall before it closed. He consciously fought the picture of the man on the bed out of his mind. With effort he focused his attention once again on the girl. At the end of the corridor he stepped onto the creaky, down-going escalator.

If only he could check with Ted Bahr, make certain that the trail had really ended at the Hoffman Center, make sure that Conroe was not really somewhere outside, still hiding, still running. One thing seemed certain: if Conroe were really here, he too would be faced with the testing and classification; he too would be traveling the same grim road as Jeff himself. And as a newcomer, he too would be under suspicion and scrutiny.

Jeff stopped short on a landing. He was suddenly aware that he had lost count of the flights he had gone down. He looked back to check his bearings, then moved around to the stairs moving up. The escalator creaked and groaned, as if every turn would be its last, and Jeff stared dreamily at the moving wall, waiting—until he passed the open well to the opposite stairs.

He froze, his mind screaming. Unable to move, he stared at the pale, frightened face of the man on the down-going stairway. In the brief seconds while they passed, he stood rooted, paralyzed, unable to cry out. Then with a hoarse yell he turned. Half-stumbling, half-falling, he ran down the up-going stairs until he reached the opening.

Then he vaulted across the barrier, crashing his shoulder against the wall as he went through. He caught a glimpse of the tall, slender figure running from the bottom of the stairs into the corridor at the bottom, and he shouted again in a burst of blinding rage. He took the steps three at a time, his mind numb to the pain as his foot struck the solid floor and twisted, sending him sprawling on his face. In an instant he was on his feet again, running, frantically, blindly, to the end of the corridor.

It broke into two hallways, going off in a Y. Both were dark and both were empty. Jeff stood panting, almost screaming out in rage, his whole body trembling. He started blindly down one corridor, jerked open a door and stared in at the small, empty office. He tried another door and another. Then he turned and ran back to the Y, spun around the corner and ran pell-mell down the second corridor. Only his own desperate footfalls echoed back to him in the darkness.

Back at the Y, he sank to the floor. Still panting, he sobbed aloud in his rage, clenching his fists as he tried to regain control of his spinning mind. Rage there was—yes, and hatred and bitter frustration. But also, tumbling through his mind in a wild, elated cadence, was a cry of sheer, incoherent savage joy. Because he knew now, beyond any shadow of doubt, that Paul Conroe was among the Mercy Men.

He looked up suddenly at the two figures approaching him from the lighted corridor. One of them held a tiny, deadly scorcher pistol trained on his chest. The other, a huge, burly man, reached down and jerked Jeff's face up into the light. "What's your unit?" the harsh voice grated.

Jeff glimpsed the gray cloth of the man's jacket, the official-looking black belt over his shoulder. "C unit," he panted.

The blow caught him full on the chin, twisting his head around with a jolt. "Wise guy, wandering around without a pass," the voice growled. "You goddam scabs think you run the place, don't you?" Another blow struck him behind the ear, and a fist caught him hard in the pit of the stomach. As he doubled over retching, a smashing blow caught his chin, and he tasted blood in his mouth as his knees buckled under him.

*

He felt them, vaguely, half-carrying, half-dragging him down the corridor. He heard a door open and fell face down on the floor. A harsh voice said, "Here's your room-mate, scut. Keep him home from now on." And the door slammed behind him.

Painfully, he raised himself on his hands, shook his head dazedly.

"You look like you're sick or something." The voice from the bed was hard and insolent.

Painfully, Jeff jerked his head up and stared. The girl blinked coldly and pulled a frazzled cigarette from her blue cotton shirt. She flicked a match with her thumb and touched off the smoke. Then she stared down at Jeff mockingly. "Sorry, Jack," said the girl called Blackie. "But it looks like we're roomies. So you might as well get used to the idea."

CHAPTER FOUR

Something exploded in Jeff's brain then, something he could no more control than the creeping, vicious hatred of Paul Conroe that had driven him for so long. The jangling, tinny music of the tavern was screaming through his mind; the indelible picture of the swerving, gyrating figure: the long raven hair, the impassive face, the full lips. His knees buckled and his head was reeling, but he lurched across the room at the girl. Catching her by the collar, he drew her face up to his with a wrench that knocked the cigarette from her hand and brought her breath out in a gasp.

"All right," he grated. "Where is he? Come on, come on, talk! Where is he? And don't tell me he's not here, because I know he is, understand? I just saw him. I just chased him, down below. I know he's here! I want to know where."

Her foot came up sharply and caught him in the leg, sending an agony of pain into his thigh. Suddenly she began to fight like a cat, clawing, biting—blue fire in her eyes. Jeff brought his hand up and slapped her face twice, hard. With a snarl she caught him in the stomach with her foot and tore herself free, sending him reeling back against the wall.

He bounded off, then stopped dead in his tracks. A horrible realization exploded in his mind. She was standing poised, her face twisted, her eyes burning, a stream of poisonous language pouring at him. In her hand was a knife, blade up, balanced in her hand with deadly intent. But Jeff hardly noticed the knife; he didn't hear the words as he stared unbelievingly at her face, his heart sinking. Because the face was wrong, somehow.

The lips were not right, the nose was shaped differently, the glow in the eyes was not right. His panting turned into a bitter sob of disbelief, of incredible disappointment. There couldn't be any doubt—it simply was not the right girl.

"Where—where is he?" he asked weakly, his heart pounding helplessly in his throat.

"Not another step," the girl snarled. "Another inch and I'll slice you up like putty."

"No, no—" Jeff shook his head, trying desperately to clear his mind, to understand. This was the girl he had seen in the visiphone screen. Yes, the same clothes, the same face. But she wasn't the girl in the tavern. "Conroe," he blurted out, plaintively. "You—you must know Conroe—"

"I've never heard of Conroe."

"But you must have—last night, in that dive—dancing—"

Her jaw dropped as she stared at him in disgust. Then she gave the knife a flip into the desk top and sank down on her bed, her face relaxing. "Go away," she said tiredly. "That goddam Frenchman's sense of humor. Go on, beat it. I'm not rooming with any hoppy—at least until he's off the stuff."

"You don't know Conroe?"

The girl looked at him closely. "Look, Jack," she said with patient bitterness, "I don't know who you are and I don't know your pal Comstock or whatever it is. And I sure as hell wasn't dancing anywhere last night. I was working in the tank last night getting some looped-up hophead cooled off for the axe this morning. And it wasn't fun for either of us, and you'll be down there yourself if you don't cool off. And you won't like it, either. So go away, don't bother me."

Jeff sank down on the opposite bed, his head in his hands. "You—you looked so much like her—"

"So I looked so much like her!" She spat out a filthy word and drew her legs up, glaring at him.

Jeff reddened, his whole body aching. "All right, I'm sorry. I got excited. I couldn't help it. And I can't leave here—I tried it a little while ago and ran into a couple of fists."

Blackie's lip curled. "The guards don't like us down here. They don't like anything about us. They'll kill you if you give them half an excuse."

Jeff looked up at her. "But why? I didn't do anything."

The girl laughed harshly. "Do you think that makes any difference to them? Look, Jack, let's face it: you're in a prison, understand? They don't call it that, and there aren't any bars. But you're not going anywhere, and the boys in gray are here to see that you don't. And they hate us because we're not good enough for them, and we're in line for the kind of money they don't dare go after. You're here for one thing: to make money, big money, or to get your brains jolted loose, and nothing else—" She looked up at him, her eyes narrowing. "Or are you?"

Jeff shook his head miserably. "No, nothing else. I'm waiting for testing. This other thing is an old fight, that's all. You wouldn't understand. You just looked so much like the girl—" He looked up at her, studying her face more closely. She wasn't as young as he had thought at first. There were little wrinkles around her eyes, a shade too much make-up showing where her mouth crinkled when she talked. Her lips were painted too full, and there was a tiredness in her eyes, a beaten, hunted look that she couldn't quite hide.

She leaned back on the bed, and even relaxation didn't erase the hardness. Only the jet black hair and the smooth black eyebrows looked young and fresh.

Jeff shook his head and kept staring at her. "I don't get it," he said helplessly. "I was assigned to this room—"

"So was I." The girl's eyes hardened.

"Are you one of the ... workers?"

She sneered bitterly. "You mean one of the experimental animals? That's right. The Mercy Men. Full of mercy, that's me." She spat on the floor.

"But the mixed company—"

There was no humor in her laugh. "What did you think, they'd have a separate boudoir for the ladies? How do they treat any kind of experimental animal? Get off it, Jack. They don't care what we do or how we live. All they want is good healthy human livestock when they're ready for it. Nothing more. That means they have to feed us and bunk us down. Period. And if you've got any wise ideas"—her eyes widened with a look of open viciousness, shocking in its intensity—"just try something. Just once. You'll find out a lot about Blackie in a hell of a rush." She rolled over contemptuously, turning her back to him. "You'll find out I don't like loonies for roommates, for instance."

Jeff lit a cigarette, his hands trembling. The room seemed to be spinning, and he felt his muscles sagging in pain and fatigue. He had counted so much on information from the girl. But incredible as the resemblance was, Blackie couldn't have been the girl he had seen in the tavern. If she had recognized him, he would have spotted it. She couldn't have hidden it completely.

Suddenly he felt terribly alone, almost beaten, helpless to go on. Where could he go? What could he do? How could he follow a trail that led straight into stone walls? He leaned back on the bed and yielded to the fatigue that plagued him. His mind sank into a confusion of hopelessness. Maybe, he thought wearily, maybe that plaguing doubt that lay in the fringes of his mind was right. Maybe he'd never find Conroe. He sighed as the darkness of utter exhaustion closed in on him, and his head sank back to the pillow—

*

He knew he was dreaming. Some tiny corner of his mind stood aside, prodding him, telling him he dare not sleep, that he must be up, moving, hunting, that the danger was too grave for sleep. But he slept, and the little corner of his mind prodded and cried out and watched....

He was walking along a brook, a walk he had taken once before, so very many years ago. A cool breeze struck down from the meadow, rumpling his hair. He heard the tinkle of the water as it sparkled across the rock. And he was afraid, so desperately afraid. The voice in his mind screamed out to him at every footstep, until he faltered and slowed and stopped.

Not here, Jeff, not here. Stop, stop now! If you go farther, you'll be dead—

Sweat broke out on his forehead. He tried to move forward, felt an iron grip on his legs. *Stop, Jeff, stop, you'll die, Jeff*—An overpowering wave of fear swept over him, and he turned. He ran like the wind, with the voice following him, crying out in his ear, following him on ghostly wings. In the dream he became a little boy again, running, screaming in fear. A man stood in his pathway, arms outstretched, and Jeff threw himself into his father's arms, sobbing as though his heart would break, clutching at him with incredible relief, burying his face in the strong, comforting chest. *Oh, daddy, daddy, you're safe. You're here, daddy.*

He looked up at his father's smiling face and he saw the strong, sensitive lines around the big man's mouth, the power and wisdom in the eyes. Nowhere else was there this sense of strength, of unlimited power, of complete comfort. He buried his face again in old Jacob Meyer's chest. A flood of deep peacefulness passed through his mind—

Jeff, Jeff, watch out!

He stiffened, his whole body going cold. The strong arms were no longer around him, and he was suddenly afraid again—afraid with a terror that bit deep into his mind. He looked up and screamed, a scream that echoed and re-echoed. It came again and again—a scream of pure terror. Because his father's face was no longer next to him. There was another face, hanging bodiless and luminous above him. It was chalk white—a face of pure ghoulish evil, staring at him.

It was Conroe's face. He screamed again, tried to cover his eyes, tried to shrink down into nothing. But the hideous, twisted face followed him. The horrible fear intensified, sweeping through him like a flame, twisting into fiery hate in his heart, as he watched the evil, glowing face.

He killed your father, Jeff. He butchered your father, shot him down like an animal, in cold blood—

Jeff screamed and the evil face grinned and moved closer, until the rank breath was hot on Jeff's neck.

You must kill him, Jeff. He killed your father—

But why? Why did he do it, why ... why ... *why*? There was no answer. The voice trailed off into horrible laughter. Quite suddenly the face was gone. In its place was a tiny, distant figure—running, running like the wind, down the narrow, darkened hospital corridor. And Jeff was running too, burning with hatred, fighting desperately to catch up with the fleeing figure, to close the gap between them.

The walls were of gray stone. Conroe was running swiftly, unhindered. But horrid objects swept out of the walls at Jeff. He tripped on a wet, slimy thing on the floor and fell on his face. He scrambled up again as the figure disappeared around a far corner. The walls were gray and wet around him. He reached the Y, waiting, panting, screaming out his hatred down the empty, re-echoing hallways.

Then suddenly he glimpsed the figure and started running again, but they were no longer in the Hoffman Center. They were running down a hillside, a horrible, barren hillside, studded with long knives and spears and swords—shiny blades standing straight up from the ground, gleaming in the bluish light.

Conroe was far ahead, moving nimbly through the gauntlet of swords. But Jeff couldn't follow his path, for new knives sprang up before him, cutting his ankles, ripping his clothes. He panted, near exhaustion, as the figure vanished in the distance. Sinking down to the ground, Jeff sobbed, his whole body shaking. And the voice screamed mockingly in his ear: *You'll never get him, Jeff. No matter how hard you try, you'll never get him ... never ... never ... never....*

But I've got to, I've got to. I've got to find him and kill him. Daddy told me to—

He woke with a jolt, his screams still echoing in the still room, sweat pouring from his forehead and body, soaking his clothes. He sat bolt upright. He searched for his watch, but couldn't find it. *How long had he slept?*

His eyes shot to the opposite bed, standing empty, and he rolled out onto his feet. He had the horrible feeling that the world had passed him by, that he had missed something critical while he slept.

He stared at his wrist. The watch was definitely gone. Then, with a curse, he crossed the room and ripped open Blackie's foot locker. Sure enough, the watch lay with the heap of gold jewelry on the dirty clothes pile. He stared at it as he re-strapped it on his wrist. Then he walked into the lavatory, splashed cold water into his face and tried to quell the fierce painful throbbing in his head. The watch said eight-thirty. He had slept for five hours—five precious hours for Conroe to hide, cover his tracks, disappear deeper into this mire of human trash.

Jeff stumbled to the door, glanced out to see two gray-clothed guards passing in the corridor. Quietly he pulled the door shut. His stomach was screaming from hunger and he searched the room restlessly. Finally, he unearthed a box of crackers and a quarter pound of cheese in the bottom of Blackie's locker. He ate ravenously and drank some water from the lavatory tap. Then he sank down on the edge of the bed.

The dream again, the same horrible, frightening, desperate dream—the dream that recurred and recurred; always different, yet always the same. The same face that had haunted him all his life, the face that had almost driven him insane that day, five years before, when he met it face to face for the first time; the face of the man he had hunted to the ends of the earth. But never had he caught the man, never had he seen him but for brief glimpses. Conroe had slipped from every trap before it was sprung. Yet finally he had become so desperate that he was forced to retreat down a one-way road that led to hellish death.

Jeff shook his head hopelessly as he tried to piece together the situation. He was in a half-world of avaricious men and women out to sell themselves for incredible fees. It was a half-world that seemed to Jeff only slightly more insane than the warped, intense world of pressure and fear and insecurity that lay outside the Hoffman Center. And in this half-world were a doctor who knew Jeff was a fraud, a kleptomaniac girl who thought he was an addict, and somewhere—the slender figure of the man he hunted.

Again he walked to the door. After peering out cautiously, he started down the corridor. From the far end he heard a burst of laughter, the sound of many voices. The smell of coffee floated down the corridor to tantalize him. He followed the sounds and reached the large, long room that served as a lounge and library for the Mercy Men in his unit.

The room was crowded. A dozen groups were huddled on the floor in a buzz of frantic excitement. The room was blue with cigarette smoke, and the lights glowed harshly from the walls. He saw the dice rolling in the centers of the groups and he also saw half a dozen tables, crowded with bright-eyed people. He heard the riffle of playing cards and the harsh, tense laugh of a winner drawing in a pot. And then he spied the Nasty Frenchman, his eyes bright with excitement, a cup of exceedingly black coffee in one hand and a pile of white paper tags in the other.

He grinned at Jeff with undisguised malice and said, "Come on in, wise guy. Things are just beginning to get hot."

Blinking, Jeff walked into the room.

CHAPTER FIVE

His first impulse was to turn and run. There was no explaining it, no rationalizing the feeling of dread and danger that struck him as he walked into the room. The feeling swept over him with almost overpowering intensity; something was unbearably wrong here.

Jeff walked in slowly, closing the door behind him. The door seemed to be pulled tight shut, sucked out of his hand. That was when the tension in the air struck Jeff like an almost physical force, and his mind filled with dread.

No one noticed him. He stared around himself curiously. He watched the Nasty Frenchman shoulder his way through the crowd. One of Silly Giggin's particularly maddening nervous-jazz arrangements was squawking from a player somewhere in the room, and the air itself was filled with a jagged rattle of conversation that rose above the music.

Most of the faces were new to Jeff. There were tired, old ones, marked indelibly with lines of fear, lines of hunted hopelessness. There were faces with tight, compressed, bloodless lips; faces with eyes full of coldness and cynicism, and faces radiating sharp, perverted intelligence.

Crowds leaned tensely around the tables and watched the cards with eager, calculating eyes. Side bets were made as the hands were opened. Other groups huddled on the floor and watched the dice with beady, avaricious eyes.

The music jangled and scraped, and little bursts of harsh laughter broke out to compete with it. And through it all ran the chilling inescapable feeling of error, of something missed, something gone horribly wrong.

He moved slowly through the room and searched the faces milling around him. His eyes caught Blackie's, far across the room, for the barest instant, and the chill of something gone wrong intensified and sent a quiver up his spine. He stopped a passerby and motioned at the nearest dice huddle. "How do you get in?" he asked.

The man shrugged, looking at him strangely. "You lay down your money and you play," he snapped. "If you got no money, then you've got the next job's payoff to bet with. 'Smatter, Jack, you new around here?" And the man moved on, shaking his head.

Jeff nodded, realization striking. What would be more natural to a group of people teetering from day to day on the brink of death? The need for excitement, for activity, would be overpowering in a dismal prison-place like this. And with the huge sums of money yet unearned to bet with—Jeff shuddered. Cut-throat games, yes, but could they really explain this strange tension he sensed? Or had something happened, something to change the atmosphere, to pervade every nook and cranny of the room with an air of explosive tension?

Jeff started moving toward the Nasty Frenchman. The little man was gulping coffee in the corner. He sucked on a long, black cigar and appeared to be in deep conversation with a bald-headed giant who leaned against the wall. Jeff spotted Blackie again. She was across the room on her knees. She faced a little buck-toothed man, as she swiftly rolled the three colored dice. Her eyes followed them, quick and unnaturally bright.

Jeff shook his head. Panmumjon was a high-speed, high-tension game—a game for the steel-nerved. Its famous dead-locks had often led to murder, as the pots rose higher and higher. The girl seemed to be winning. She rolled the dice with trance-like regularity, and the little buck-toothed man's face darkened as his money pile dwindled.

Across the room a corner crap game was moving swiftly, with staggering sums of money passing from hand to hand; the card games, though slower, left the mark of their tension on the players' faces. Jeff still stared, until he had seen every face in the room. Paul Conroe's face was not one of them.

No, he had not expected that. But what had happened? It was maddening to stand there, to feel the tension in the room, sense that it was growing until it seemed to pound at his temples. No one else seemed to notice it. Was he the only one aware of the change in the air, in the sounds, even in the color of the light against the walls? Something was impelling him, urging him to run, to get away, to leave the room now while he could. Yet when he tried to analyze the creeping, poisonous fear, tried to pin it down, it wriggled away into the fringes of his mind, and mocked him.

Finally, he reached the corner of the room. His ear caught the Nasty Frenchman's nasal voice, and he froze as he stared at the little man.

"I tell you, Harpo, I heard it with my own ears. You never saw Schiml so excited. And then Shaggy Parsons was saying that the whole unit was being split up—that's the A unit. I saw him when I was going through this afternoon. He was all excited, too."

"But why split it up?" The huge bald-headed man called Harpo growled, his heavy lips twisting in disgust. "I don't trust Shaggy Parsons for nothin', and I think you hear what you want to hear. What's the point to it? Schiml's coming along fine in the work he's using us in—"

The Nasty Frenchman turned red. "That's just it: we've been in and we're going to be out, right out in the cold. Can't you get that straight? Something's going to break. They're onto something—Schiml and his boys—something big. And they've got a new man, somebody they're excited about, somebody that's been knocking walls down just by looking at them, or something—"

Harpo made a disgusted noise. "You mean, the old ESP story again. So maybe they go off on another spook hunt. They'll get over it, same as they did the last time or the time before."

The Nasty Frenchman's voice was tense. "But they're *changing things.* And changes mean trouble." He glanced at Jeff and his eyebrows went up. "Look, they get on a line of work, they assign men to different parts of a job, they get work lined up months in advance. Then all of a sudden something new comes along. They get excited about something and they toss out a couple dozen workers, add on a couple dozen new ones, change the fees, change the work. And they end up handing the best pay to somebody who's just come in. I don't like it. I've been in this place too long. I've had too many tough, lousy jobs here to just get pushed aside because they don't happen to be interested any more in what they were doing to me before. And they never tell us! We never know for sure. We just have to wait and guess and hope."

The little man's eyes blazed. "But we can pick up some things, a little here, a little there—you learn how, after a while. And I can tell you, something's wrong, something's going to happen. You can even feel it in here."

Jeff's skin crawled. That was it, of course. There was something wrong. But it hadn't happened yet. It was going to happen. He stared at a huddled group around a panmumjon game, watched the bright-colored dice cubes roll across and back, across and back. A newcomer, the Nasty Frenchman had said, someone who had come in and disrupted the smooth work schedule of the Center, someone who had the doctors suddenly excited. Someone whom they were planning to use—on a spook hunt.

What kind of a spook hunt? Why that choice of words? Could Conroe conceivably be the newcomer they had been talking about? It didn't seem possible that it could have happened so suddenly if Conroe were the one—but who? And what did this have to do with the ever-growing sense of impending danger that pervaded the room, right now?

Jeff's eyes wandered to the dice game, and the fear in his mind suddenly grew to a screaming torrent. *Go away, Jeff. Don't watch, don't look*—He scowled, suddenly angry. Why not look? What was there so dangerous in a dice game? He moved over to the nearby huddle and watched the moving cubes in fascination. No, Jeff, no, don't do it, Jeff—With a curse, he dropped to his knees and reached out for the dice.

"You in?" somebody asked. Jeff nodded, his face like a rock. The voice had stopped screaming in his ear, and now something else grew in his mind: a wild exhilaration that caught his breath and swept through his brain like a whirl-wind. His eyes sparkled and he pulled money from his pocket. He laid the bills on the floor and his hands closed on the dice.

He faced a little, pimple-faced man with beady black eyes and he raised the three brightly colored dice, rolling into the familiar pattern. The dice deadlocked in four throws. He sweated out seven more with new dice. Then Jeff saw a break in the odds, boosted the ante on his next throw and caught his breath as the man facing him matched it.

The dice rolled, fell into deadlock again, and the crowd around them gasped, moved in closer around them. The third set of dice was brought out, for the attempts at dead-lock-breaking. Then a fourth set followed, as the complex structure of the game built up like a house of cards. Then Jeff's dice at last rolled the critical number, and the structure began to break apart—throw after throw falling faster and faster into his hands.

Four or five people moved in at his side with side bets and began to collect along with him, as he moved into another game, built it up. This one he lost cold, but still he played on, his excitement growing.

And then, suddenly, pandemonium broke loose in the room. Eyes glanced up, startled, at the two men, far across the room, who stood facing each other, eyes blazing.

"Throw them down! Go on! Throw them, see how they land!"

Somebody shouted, "What happened, Archie?"

"He's got loaded dice in here, somehow." Archie pointed an accusing finger at the other man. "They don't fall right. There's something wrong with them—"

The other man snarled. "So you aren't winning any more—so what? You brought the dice in yourself."

"But the odds aren't right. There's something funny going on."

Jeff turned back to the dice, his mind still screaming, sensing that disaster hung in the air like a heavy sword. His own game moved on, faster and faster. Somewhere across the room another fight broke out, and another. Several men dropped out of games and stood up against the walls. Their eyes were wide with anger as they watched the other players. And then Jeff rolled three sixes, fourteen times in a row. He tossed the dice down in front of his gaping opponents with a curse and walked shakily back to the corner. The whole room spun around his head.

Suddenly, in this room, probabilities had gone mad. He could feel the shifting instability of the atmosphere, as real and oppressive to him as if it were solid and he were attempting to wade through it. This was what had been bothering him, plaguing him. Quite suddenly and without explanation, something impossible had begun to happen. Cards had begun to fall in unbelievable sequences, repeating themselves with idiotic regularity; dice had defied the laws of gravity as they spun on the tables and floor.

A hubbub filled the room as the players stopped and stared at each other, unable to comprehend the impossible that was happening before their eyes. And then Blackie was passing Jeff, her face flushed, a curious light of desperation in her eyes.

An impulse passed through Jeff's mind. He reached out an arm, stopped the girl. "Game," he said sharply.

Her eyes flashed at him. "What game?"

"Anything." He held up his wrist before her eyes and showed her the gold watch. "We can play for this."

Something flared in her eyes for a moment before she gained control. Then she was down on her knees, pushing her sleeves up, a tight look of fear and dread haunting her eyes as she looked up at Jeff. "Something's happening," she said softly. "The dice—they're not right."

"I know it. Why not?" His voice was hoarse, his eyes hard on her face.

She threw him a baffled look. "There isn't any reason. Nothing is different, but the dice don't fall right. That's all, they just don't."

Jeff grinned tightly. "Go on, throw them."

She threw the dice, saw them dance on the floor, caught her number. Jeff rolled them, beat her on it, picked up the money. He rolled again, then again. The tightness grew around the girl's eyes; little tense lines hardened near her mouth. Nervously, she fumbled a cigarette into her mouth, lit it, puffed as the dice rolled.

She lost. She lost again. Side bets picked up around them, the people as they watched catching the tension that was building up.

"What's happening?"

"The dice—my God! They've gone crazy!"

"Blackie's losing. What do you think—"

"—losing? She never loses on dice. Who's the guy?"

"Never saw him before. Look, he took another one! Those dice are hexed."

"My cards were crazy too: king high full every time, a dozen hands in a row. How can you bet on something like that, I ask you."

The Silly Giggins record screeched louder, then gave a squawk as the record suddenly shattered in a thousand pieces. Somebody cursed and threw a pack of cards on the floor, and a scream broke out across the room. One group came suddenly to blows; several dice games tightened down to bloody conflict between individuals. A man burst into tears, suddenly, and sat back on his haunches, his face stricken. "They can't act this way," he wailed. "They just *can't*—"

Jeff's eyes watched the spinning dice, and again something was screaming in his ear. He felt as though his head were going to burst, but he continued to roll and he saw the girl's face darken with each throw. He saw the fear shine out from her blue eyes. Suddenly she let out a curse, snatched the dice from Jeff's hand and threw them sharply across the room. She stared at Jeff venomously, then glared at the people around her as if she were a cornered animal.

"It's all of you," she snarled. "You're turning them against me. You're making them fall wrong." She spat on the floor and started for the door. Jeff moved after her but felt a restraining hand on his arm.

"Leave her alone," said the Nasty Frenchman. "You'll have trouble on your hands if you don't. You see what I meant about something being wrong? The whole crowd here is on edge, as if somebody were picking them up and throwing them down. Who ever saw dice fall that way, or cards fall that way"—the little man's eyes flashed slyly—" *unless somebody was controlling them.*"

Jeff's breath was faster as he stared at the Nasty Frenchman, and his voice was hoarse. "What are you talking about?"

The little man's lips twisted angrily. "You saw what happened in here, didn't you?"

Jeff turned away in anger. He wove through the crowd, his jaw tight as he moved toward the door. The Nasty Frenchman could only glimpse the truth, but someone else saw more, much more. Somehow, Jeff knew that this past hour held the key to the whole problem, if he could only see it. Here was the answer to the whole tangled puzzle of the girl and Paul Conroe, of Dr. Schiml and the Mercy Men.

And he knew that when he reached the room, the girl would be waiting. She would be waiting with cold fire in her eyes, as she sat at the table, a small pair of colored dice lying before her in the dim light.

Jeff hurried down the darkened corridor, fear exploding in his brain. She would be there and he knew why she would be smoldering when he walked into the room. He had seen her eyes, seen her face as they had thrown the dice. He knew beyond any shadow of doubt who had been controlling the dice.

The girl was waiting, just as he had known she would. He stepped into the room and closed the door gently behind him, facing her desperate eyes as she rolled the colored dice back and forth in front of her. "Game," she challenged, her voice harsh and metallic.

The room was tense with silent fear as he sank down opposite her at the table.

CHAPTER SIX

Jeff reached out and took the dice from the girl's hand. "Put them away, Blackie," he said softly, "You don't have to prove anything. I know—"

"Game," she repeated harshly, shaking her head.

"Look. Think a minute. Back there, do you know what happened in that room?"

Her eyes caught his and were wide with fear. "Game," she whispered, her hands trembling. "You've got to play me!"

He shrugged, his eyes tired as he watched her face. He took the dice and rolled them out on the table. A three, a four and a five fell; he saw her eyes flash across the table, taking in the sequence. Then her hand reached out, grasped the dice, gave them a throw. The hostility in her mind struck out at him, reinforcing the terrible dread that he already felt. He fought the hostility, staring at the dice, his hands gripping the edge of the table. And the dice danced and settled down: a three, a four and a five....

The girl's eyes widened, staring first at him, then back at the dice. Slowly she reached out, took the cube with the five showing, sent it bouncing across the table. It spun and bounced—and settled down once again with the five exposed.

Jeff felt the blast of bitter fear strike out from the girl's eyes. The room seemed to scream with the tension he felt. She took the dice with trembling hands, threw them out hard and clenched her fists as they fell. The three and four settled out immediately. Jeff watched the third cube, spinning on one corner, spinning ... spinning.... He felt his muscles grow tense, his mind screaming, tightening down as he stared at the little cube. It was as though an iron fist held his brain in its palm and was slowly, slowly squeezing. And the little cube continued, ridiculously, to spin and spin, until it quite suddenly flipped over onto its side and lay still with the five exposed.

Blackie gave a choked scream, her face pasty white. "Then it was you." She choked, staring at him as if he were a ghost. "You were doing it deliberately in there, throwing off the odds, twisting things around, turning the dice against me."

Jeff shook his head violently. "No, no, not me—us—both of us. We were fighting each other, without knowing it—"

Her hand went up to her mouth, choking off the words as she stared at him. Jeff stared at the dice, his whole body trembling, huge drops of sweat running down his forehead. And as he watched, the dice hopped about on the table, like jumping beans, turning over and over, jerkily, spinning on their edges in a horrible, incredible little dance. Jeff shook his head, his eyes wide with horror as he watched the dice.

"You knew it all along," the girl choked. "You came in there just to torment me, to show me up—"

"No, no." Jeff turned wide eyes on her. "I didn't know it, until I picked up the dice in that room. Something drove me to do it. I didn't know what I was doing until all of a sudden the dice were doing what I wanted them to do—" He broke off, panting. "I never knew it, I never dreamed it." His eyes sought the girl's, pleading. "I didn't understand it; I couldn't help it. I just knew that something wrong was going on. And then I knew that somebody was fighting me. There was a tension in it. I felt it. I knew somebody was tampering with the dice. Then when I got near you, I knew it was you."

The girl's face was working, tears welling up in her eyes. "I had to—I had to win with them."

"Then you knew you were doing it!" Jeff stared at her. "And when both of us started tampering, opposing each other, the probabilities governing the games went wild, completely wild."

The girl was sobbing, her face in her hands. "I could always control it. It always worked. It was the only thing I could do that came out right. Everything else has always gone wrong." She sobbed like a baby, her shoulders shaking as she choked out great, racking sobs.

Jeff leaned forward, almost cruelly, his eyes burning at her. "When did you find out you could ... make dice fall the way you wanted them to?"

The girl shook her head helplessly. "I didn't know it. I didn't have any idea, until I came here. It was the only thing I could win at. Everything else I lost at. All my life I've been losing."

"What have you been losing?"

"Everything, everything—everything I touch turns black, goes sour, somehow."

"But what, *what?*" Jeff leaned toward the girl, his voice hoarse. "Why did you come here? How did you get here?"

The girl's sobs broke out again, her shoulders shaking in anguish. "I don't know, I don't know. Oh, I could take it, up to a limit, but then I couldn't stand it any more. Everything I tried went wrong; everyone that was near me went wrong too. Even the rackets wouldn't work with me around."

"What rackets?"

Her voice was weak and cracking. "Any of the rackets. I've been in a dozen, two dozen, ever since the war. Dad was killed in the first bombing of the Fourth War, when I was just a kid—twelve, thirteen, I can't remember now. He died trying to get us out of the city and through to the Defense area north of the Trenton section. Radiation burns got him, maybe pneumonia, I don't know. But it got Dad first and Mom later."

She straightened up and wiped her eyes with her sleeve. "We never did get out of the devastated area. We were killing dogs and cats for food for a while. Then when things did get straightened out, we ran into the inflation, the burned-out crops, the whole rat-race. The dirty breaks were coming in hard then. First we were guerrillas, then we were bushwhackers. Then we came into the city again and started shaking down the rich ones that came back from the mountains where they hid."

"But you came in here," Jeff grated. "Why here, if you were doing so well in rackets?"

"I wasn't. Can't you understand? The luck—it was running wrong, worse and worse all the time. And then I got hooked on dope. Narcotics control was all shot to pieces during the war; heroin was all over the place. But they knew I had this hard-luck jinx. They caught me on it, until I was hooked bad."

She shrugged, her face a study in pathetic hopelessness. "They hauled me in here. Schiml sold me his bill of goods. What could I lose? I was so tired, I didn't care. I didn't care if they jolted my brains loose, or what they did to me. All I wanted was to eat and get off the dope and get enough cash so I could try for something decent, where hard luck couldn't touch me. And I didn't really care if I never got out."

"But with the dice you made out."

"Oh, yes, with the dice—" The girl's eyes flickered for a moment. "I found out I could make them sit up and talk for me. I played it cozy, didn't let anybody catch on. But they always worked for me, until tonight—"

Jeff nodded, his face white. "Until tonight, when you found out you were fighting for control. Because tonight I found out they'd talk for me too. And you couldn't beat me with them."

Her voice was weak. "I—I couldn't budge them. They fell the way you called them."

"It isn't possible, you know," Jeff said softly. "Every time they've tried to prove it was, they've found some loophole in the study of it, something wrong somewhere. Nobody's ever proved a thing about psychokinesis."

The girl grinned mirthlessly. "They've been trying to prove it here since the year one. Every now and again they get hot on it. They've just tested somebody that's got them excited and they'll be starting the whole works over again."

Jeff leaned over, his eyes blazing. "Yes, yes, who's that person?"

"I don't know. I just heard it. A new recruit, I guess."

"A recruit named Conroe?"

Her eyes widened at the virulence in his voice. "I—I don't know, I don't know. I've only heard. I don't even know if there *is* such a person."

"Where can I find out?"

Again the fear was in her eyes. "I—I don't know."

Jeff's voice was tense, his eyes fixed on the girl's face in desperate eagerness. "Look, you've got to help me. I know he's here. I must find him. I saw him this afternoon. Remember when the guards brought me in here? I saw him on the stairs. I chased him and lost him, but he's here. He's hiding, running away from me. I've got to find him, somehow. Please, Blackie, you can help me."

Her eyes were wide on his face. "What do you want with him? Why are you after him? I don't want to get mixed up in anything—"

"No, no, it won't mix you up. Look, I want to kill him. Short and sweet, nothing more—just kill him. I want to send one bullet into his brain, watch his face splatter out, watch his skull break open. That's all I want, just one bullet—"

Jeff's voice was low, the words wrenched from his throat, and the hatred in his eyes was poisonous as it washed over the girl's face. "He haunts me, for years he's haunted me." Jeff's voice dropped, the words breaking the stillness of the room in a hoarse, terrible cadence. "He killed my father. This Conroe—he butchered my father like an animal, shot him down in cold blood. It was horrible, ruthless. Conroe was the assassin. He killed my father without a thought of mercy in his mind. And I loved my father, I loved him with all the love I had." He stared at the girl. "I'll kill the man that killed my father if I have to die myself in the killing."

"And that man is here?"

"That man is here. I've hunted him for years. This was his last resort, his final desperate gamble for escape. He had nowhere else to turn. I've got the outside tied up so that he doesn't dare to leave. Now I've got to track him down in here. I've got to find him and kill him, before I'm caught, before I'm tested and classified. I've got to move fast and I need help. I need help so much."

The girl leaned toward him, her eyes dark as she stared at him. "The dice," she said softly. "I've been playing it cozy. I still could—if you'll let me."

His eyes widened. "Anything you say," he said. "We'll play it cozy together. But I've got to have floor plans of the place, information on how to avoid the guards. I've got to know where their records are kept, their lists and rosters and working plans."

"Then it's a deal?"

His eyes caught hers, and for an instant he saw something behind the mask she wore, something of the fear that lay back there, something of a little child who fought against impossible odds to find a toehold in the world. Then the barrier was back up, and her eyes were blank and revealed nothing.

Jeff held out his hand, touched her palm lightly and clenched her fingers. "It's a deal," he said.

*

The trip down the corridor was a nightmare. Jeff's mind was still reeling from the incredible discovery of the dice, the sudden, unbelievable awareness that he and Blackie had been silently and fiercely battling each other for control, fighting with a fury that had somehow shattered the very warp of probability in the room where they had been. How could he have had a part in something like this? He had never had reason to suspect he might carry such a power, yet here was evidence he could not disregard. And how could it fit into the question of Paul Conroe, and the mysterious recruit to the Mercy Men who had just been tested?

A thought struck Jeff, quite suddenly. It came with such impact that he stopped cold in his tracks. It was so simple, so impossible, yet no more impossible than the things he had already seen with his own eyes. Because the incredible record of escapes that Conroe carried, the impossible regularity with which Conroe had managed to avoid capture, time after time, seemed too much to accept as coincidence. And if Conroe were indeed carrying latent extra-sensory powers, he could continue to slip from trap after trap—*unless Jeff could oppose those powers with powers of his own.*

Jeff cursed in his teeth. How could he tell? He had no evidence that Conroe carried any extra-sensory power whatsoever, and surely there was little enough to indicate that he had any more than most latent powers. There were so many, many possibilities, and so little concrete evidence to go on.

And if Conroe had such powers, why had he been so startled to meet Jeff on the stairs? Why the look of fear and disbelief that had streaked across his face? Jeff glanced at his watch, saw the minute hand move to eleven-thirty. He would have to hurry, for the guards would be down the escalator in a few moments. And these thoughts of his could lead to nowhere. Conroe had been jolted to see Jeff. It must have been a horrible shock for him to realize that the Hunter had followed him, even into this death trap, to know that the Hunter would have the outside so well guarded that he, the Hunted, could never get out. Now Conroe would be forced to gamble against being caught and assigned to work as a Mercy Man. Yes, it must have been a horrible jolt for Conroe, driving one last, searing bolt of fear into his already desperate mind. And what would he have tried to do?

A thousand ideas flooded Jeff's mind. He was waiting for testing. Perhaps Conroe, somehow, had been tested already? Could Jeff succeed in stalling Schiml, especially if the rumors spinning down the dark corridors were true? There was no sure way of telling. All Jeff could do was to search the file rooms Blackie had directed him to.

He stopped at the entrance to the escalator, pored over the floor plan Blackie had sketched for him. He spotted the escalator, oriented himself on the plan. The filing rooms were two flights below. If he could reach them without being stopped.... He moved silently onto the down shaft, his eyes moving constantly for a sight of a gray-garbed prowler.

At the foot of the escalator he stopped short. Three men in white were pushing a gurney along the corridor. Jeff glanced quickly at the twitching form under the blankets. Then he looked away hurriedly. One of the men dropped behind and waved at him sharply as he stepped off the stairs. The man still wore the operating mask hanging from his neck, and his hair was tightly enclosed in the green-knit operating cap.

The doctor tipped a thumb over his shoulder and pointed down the corridor. "You coming to fix the pump?"

Jeff blinked rapidly. "That's right," he croaked. "Did—did Jerry come with the tools yet?"

"Nobody came in yet. We just finished. Been in there since three this afternoon, and the damned pump went kerflooey right in the middle. Had to aspirate the poor joe by hand, and if you think *that's* not a job—" The doctor wiped sweat from his forehead. "Better get it fixed tonight. We've got another one going in at eight in the morning and we've got to have the pump."

Jeff nodded, and started down the hall, his heart thudding madly against his ribs. He reached the open door to one of the operating rooms. Slipping quickly into the small dressing-room annex, he snatched one of the gowns and caps from the wall.

If they were still operating this late, it was a heaven-sent chance. No guard would bother him if he were wearing the white of a doctor or the green of a surgeon. He struggled into the clumsy gowning, tying it quickly behind his back, and slipped the cap over his head. Finally he found a mask, snapped it up under his ears as he had seen it worn by the doctors in the corridors.

In a moment he was back on the escalator, descending to the next floor. At the foot of the stairs, he started quickly down the corridor Blackie had indicated, glancing at each door as he passed. The first two had lights under them, indicating that these apparently were operating rooms still in use. Finally he stopped before a large, heavy door, with a simple sign painted on the wooden panel: COMPUTOR TECHNICIANS ONLY. He tried the door, found it locked. Quickly he glanced up and down the corridor, doubled a hard fist and drove it through the panel with a crunch. Then he fumbled inside for the lock.

In an instant he was inside. The torn hole in the panel glared at him. He threw the door wide open and snapped on the overhead lights, throwing the room into bright fluorescent light. Then he drew the pale-green gown closer about him and moved across the room to the huge file panel that faced him.

It was not his first experience with the huge punched-card files which had become so necessary in organizations where the numbers and volumes of records made human operatives too slow or clumsy. Quickly Jeff moved to the master-control panel, searched for the section and coding system for Research: Subject Personnel.

First he would try the simple coding for Conroe's name, on the chance that Conroe had come in using his own name. Jeff rechecked the coding, punched the buttons which would relay through the cards alphabetically; then he waited as the machinery whirred briefly. A panel lighted near the bottom of the control board, spelling the two words: NO INFORMATION.

Jeff's fingers sped over the coding board again, as he started coding in a description. He coded in height, weight, eye color, hair color, bone contour, lip formation—every other descriptive category he could think of. Then again he punched the "Search" button.

This time several dozen cards fell down. He picked them up from the yield-slot and slowly leafed through them, glancing both at the small photograph attached to each card and at the small "date of admission" code symbol at the top of each card. Again he found nothing. Disgusted, he tried the same system again, this time adding two limiting coding symbols: Subject Personnel and Recent Admission. And again the cards were negative. Not a single one could possibly have been connected with Paul Conroe.

Jeff sat down at the desk facing the panel and he searched his mind for another pathway of identification. Suddenly a thought occurred to him. He searched through his pocket for a picture wallet, drew out the small, ID-size photo of Conroe that he carried for identification purposes.

Searching the panel, he finally found the slot he was looking for: the small, photoelectronic chamber for recording picture identification. He slipped the photo into the slot, punched the "Search" button, and waited again, his whole body tense.

The machine buzzed for a long moment. Then a single card dropped into the slot. Eagerly Jeff snatched it up, stared down at the attached photograph which almost perfectly matched the photo from his pocket. Near the top of the card was a small typewritten notation: *Conroe, Paul* A., INFORMATION RESTRICTED. ALL FILE NOTATIONS RECORDED IN HOFFMAN CENTER CENTRAL ARCHIVES.

Below this notation was a list of dates. Jeff read them, staring in disbelief, then read them again. Incredible, those dates—dates of admission to the Hoffman Center and dates of release. It was impossible that Conroe could have been here at the times the dates indicated: ten years ago, when the Hoffman Center was hardly opened; five years ago, during the very time when Jeff had been tracking him down. Yet the dates were there, in black and white, cold, impersonal, indisputable. And below the dates was a final notation, inked in by hand: CENTRAL ARCHIVES CLASSIFICATION: ESP RESEARCH.

Swiftly Jeff stuffed the card into his shirt. He refiled the other cards with trembling fingers, his heart pounding a frightful tattoo in his forehead. Incredible, yet he knew, somehow, that it fit into the picture, that it was a key to the picture. He turned, started for the door, and stopped dead.

"Schiml!" he breathed.

The figure lounged against the door, green cap askew on his head, mask still dangling about his neck. There was a smile on his face as he leaned back, regarding Jeff in amusement. Nonchalantly, he tossed a pair of dice into the air, and caught them, still smiling. "Let's go, Jeff," said Dr. Schiml. "We've got some tests to run."

"You—you mean, in the morning," Jeff stammered, hardly believing his ears.

The smile broadened on the doctor's lips, and he gave the dice another toss and dropped them in his pocket. "Not in the morning, Jeff," he said softly. "Now."

CHAPTER SEVEN

Jeff sank down in the chair, his forehead streaming sweat. He clenched his fists as he tried to regain control of his trembling muscles. *How long had Schiml been standing there*? Just a second or two? Or had he been watching Jeff for ten minutes, watching him punch down the filing codes, watching him stuff the filing card into his shirt? There was nothing to be told from the doctor's face, as the man smiled down at his trembling quarry. There was nothing in the eyes of the guards who stood behind him in the hallway, their hands poised on their heavy sidearms.

Schiml turned to one of them, nodded slightly, and they disappeared, their boots clanging in the still corridor behind them. Then he turned his eyes back to Jeff, the ghost of a knowing smile still flickering about his eyes. "Find anything interesting?" he asked, his eyes narrowing slightly.

Jeff fumbled a cigarette to his lips, gripped the lighter to steady it. "Nothing to speak of," he said hoarsely. "Been a long time since I worked one of these files." His eyes caught Schiml's defiantly, held them in desperation. Finally Schiml blinked and looked away.

"Looking for anything special?" he asked smoothly.

"Nothing special." Jeff blew smoke out into the room, his trembling nerves quieting slightly.

"I see. Just sight-seeing, I suppose."

Jeff shrugged. "More or less. I wanted to see the setup."

A dry smile crossed Schiml's face. "Particularly the setup in the filing room," he said softly. "I thought I'd find you here. Blackie said you'd just stepped out for a short walk, so we just took a guess." The doctor's eyes hardened sharply on Jeff's face. "And all dressed up like a doctor, too."

He stepped across the room, jerked the cap from Jeff's head, snapped the string to the gown with a sharp swipe of his hand. "We don't do this around here," he said, his voice cutting like a razor. "Doctors wear these, nobody else. Got that straight? We also do not wander around breaking into filing rooms, just looking at the setup. If the guards had caught you at it, you wouldn't be alive right now—which would have been a dirty shame, since we have plans for you." He jerked his thumb toward the door. "After you, Jeff. We've got some work to do tonight."

Jeff moved out into the hall, took up beside the tall doctor as he started back for the escalator. "You weren't serious about testing me tonight, surely."

Dr. Schiml stared at him. "And why not?"

"Look, it's late. I'll be here in the morning."

The doctor walked on in silence for a long moment. Jeff followed, his mind racing, a thousand questions tumbling through in rapid succession: questions he dared not ask, questions he couldn't answer. How much did Schiml know? And how much did he suspect? A chill ran down Jeff's back. What had he been doing with the dice? Could Blackie possibly have told him? Or could he have heard about the freakish occurrence in the game room through other channels? And what could he learn in the course of the testing that he didn't know already?

Jeff puzzled as he matched the doctor's rapid pace. They went up the escalator, down the twisting corridor toward an area beyond the living quarters that Jeff hadn't seen before. Above all, he must keep his nerve, keep a tight control on his tongue, on his reactions, make sure that there were no tricks to tear information from him that he didn't dare divulge.

He looked at Schiml, sharply, a frown on his face. "I still don't see why this can't wait till morning. Why the big hurry?"

Schiml stopped, turned to Jeff in exasperation. "You still think we're running a picnic grounds here, don't you?" he snapped. "Well, we're not. We're doing a job, a job that can't wait for morning or anything else. We work a twenty-four-hour schedule here. All you do is provide the where-withal to work with—nothing more."

"But I'll be tired, nervous. I don't see how I could pass any kind of test."

Schiml laughed shortly. "These aren't the kind of tests you pass or fail. Actually, the more tired and nervous you are, the better the results will be for you. They'll give you an extra edge of safety when you're assigned to a job. What the tests tell us is what we can expect from you, the very minimum. Basically, we're working to save your life for you."

Jeff blinked at him, followed him through swinging doors into a long, brightly lighted corridor, with green walls and a gleaming tile floor. "What do you mean, save my life? You seem to delight in just the opposite here, from what I've heard."

The doctor made an impatient noise. "You got the wrong information," he said angrily. "That's the trouble. You people insist upon listening to and believing the morbid stories, all the unpleasantness you hear about the work here. And it's all either completely false or only half-truth. This business of bloodthirstiness, for instance. It's just plain not true.

"One of the biggest factors in our work here is making arrangements for optimum conditions for the success of our experiments. By 'optimum' we mean the best conditions from several standpoints: from the standpoint of what we're trying to learn—the experiment itself, that is—and from the standpoint of the researcher, too. But most particularly, we're working for optimum recovery odds for the experimental animals—you, in this case."

Jeff snorted. "But still, we're just experimental animals, from your viewpoint," he said sharply.

"Not *just* experimental animals," Schiml snapped angrily. "You're *the* experimental animals. Working with human beings isn't the same as working with cats and dogs and monkeys—far from it. Dogs and cats are stronger and tougher, more durable than humans, which is why they're used for preliminary work of great success. But basically, they're expendable. If something goes wrong, that's too bad. But we've learned something, and the dog or cat can be sacrificed without too many tears. But we don't feel quite the same about human beings."

"I'm glad to hear that," said Jeff sourly. "It makes me feel better."

"I'm not trying to be facetious. I mean it. We're not ghouls. We don't have any less regard for human life than anyone else, just because we're responsible for some human death in the work we're doing. For one thing, we study every human being we use, try to dig out his strengths and weaknesses, physical and mental. We want to know how he reacts to what, how fast he recuperates, how much physical punishment his body can take, how far his mental resiliency will extend. Then when we know these things, we can fit him into the program of research which will give him the very best chance of coming out in one piece. At the same time, he will fill a spot that we need filled. No, there's no delight here in taking human life or jeopardizing human safety."

They turned abruptly off the corridor and entered a small office. Schiml motioned Jeff to a chair, sat himself down behind a small desk and began sorting through several stacks of forms. The room was silent for a moment. Then the doctor punched a button on the telephone panel.

When the light blinked an answer to him, he said: "Gabe? He's here. Better come on up."

Then he flipped down the switch and leaned back, lighting a long, slender cigar and undoing the green robe around his neck.

Jeff watched him, still puzzling over what he had just said. The doctor seemed so matter-of-fact. What he had said made sense, but somewhere in the picture there seemed to be a gaping hole. "This sounds like it's a great setup—for you doctors and researchers," he said finally. "But what's it leading to? What good is it doing? Oh, I know, it increases your knowledge of men's minds, but how does it help the man in the street? How does it actually help *anyone*, in the long run? How do you ever get the government to back it with the financial mess they're facing in Washington?"

Schiml threw back his head and laughed aloud. "You've got the cart before the horse," he said, when he got control of his voice. "Support? Listen, my lad, the government is running itself bankrupt just to keep our research going. Did you realize that? *Bankrupting itself*! And why? Because unless our work pays off—and soon—there isn't going to be any government left. That's why. Because we're fighting something that's eating away at the very roots of our civilization, something that's creeping and growing and destroying."

He stared at Jeff, his eyes wide. "Oh, the government knows that the situation is grave. We had to prove it to them, show it to them time and again, until they couldn't miss it any longer. But they saw it finally. They've seen it growing for a century or more, ever since the end of the Second War. They've seen the business instability, the bank runs and the stock market dives. They've seen the mental and moral decay in the cities. They could see it, but it took statistics to prove that there was a pattern to it, a pattern of decay and rot and putrefaction that's been crumbling away the clay feet of this colossal civilization of ours."

The doctor stood up, paced back and forth across the room and sent blue smoke into the air from the cigar as he walked. "Oh, they support us all right. We don't know for sure what we're fighting, but we do know the answer is in the functioning of the minds and brains of man. We're working against a disease—a creeping disease of men's minds—and we are forced to use men to search those minds, to study them, to try to weed out the poison of the disease. And so we have the Mercy Men to help us fight."

The doctor's lips twisted in a bitter sneer as he sat heavily down on the chair again, crunched the cigar out viciously in the tray. "Mercy Men who have no mercy in their souls, who have no interest nor concern with what they're doing, or what it may be accomplishing. They are interested in one thing only: the amount of money they'll be paid for having their brains jogged loose."

The scorn was heavy in Dr. Schiml's eyes. "Well, we don't care who we have: addicts, condemned murderers, prostitutes, the trash from the skid-row gutters. They're all drawn here, like flies to a dung hill. But they're here on errands of mercy, whether they like it or not, or know it or not. And we take them because they're the only ones who can be bought, and we guard them for all we're worth, so that the goal will be accomplished." He took a deep breath and stared scornfully at Jeff. "That's you I'm talking about, you know."

Jeff's hands trembled as he snuffed out his smoke. He stood up as the corridor door opened, admitting a small, dark-haired man with thick glasses. He was dressed in doctor's whites. Jeff rubbed his chest nervously and took a deep breath, still acutely aware of the stiff card in his shirt front.

"All right," he said hoarsely, "so you're talking about me. When do we get started with this?"

*

The little dressing room was cramped; it reeked of anesthetic. Jeff walked in, followed by Dr. Schiml and the other doctor, and started removing his shoes. "This is Doctor Gabriel," Schiml said, indicating his myopic colleague. "He'll start you off with a complete physical. Then you'll have a neurological. Come on into the next room as soon as you're undressed." And with that the two doctors disappeared through swinging doors into an inner room.

Jeff removed his shirt and trousers swiftly, carefully folding the file card and stuffing it under the inner sole of his right shoe. It wasn't exactly the perfect hiding place, if anyone were looking for the card. But not once during the conversation had Schiml's eyes strayed curiously to Jeff's shirt front. Either Schiml had not seen him take the card, or else the doctor's self-control was superhuman. And no mention of the dice had been made, either. Jeff gave his shoes a final pat, tossed his clothes on one of the gurneys lining the walls and pushed through the doors into the next room.

It was huge, dome-ceilinged, with a dozen partitions dividing different sections from one another. One end looked like a classroom, with blackboards occupying a whole wall. Another section carried the paraphernalia of a complete gymnasium. The doctors were sitting in a corner that was obviously outfitted as an examination room: the tables were covered with crisp green sheeting, and the walls had gleaming cabinets full of green-wrapped bundles and instruments.

Schiml sat on the edge of a desk. His eyes watched Jeff closely as he lit a cigarette, leaned back and blew rings into the air. Dr. Gabriel motioned Jeff to the table and started the physical without further delay.

It was the most rigorous, painstaking physical examination Jeff had ever had. The little, squinting doctor poked and probed him from head to toe. He snapped retinal-pattern photos, examined pore-patterns, listened, prodded, thumped, auscultated. He motioned Jeff back onto the chair and started going over him with a rubber hammer, tapping him sharply in dozens of areas, eliciting a most disconcerting variety of muscular jerks and twitches. Then the hammer was replaced by a small electrode, with which the doctor probed and tested, bringing spasmodic jerks to the muscles of Jeff's back and arms and thighs. Finally, Dr. Gabriel relaxed, sat Jeff down in a soft chair and retired to a small portable instrument cabinet nearby.

Dr. Schiml put out his smoke and stood up. "Any questions before we begin?"

Jeff almost sighed aloud. Any questions? His nerves tingled all over and his mind was full of conjecture—wild, ridiculous guesses of what they would discover in the testing, of what the results would bring. Suppose they learned about the dice? Suppose they found out that he was a fraud, that he was in the Center on a private mission, a mission of death all his own, and no party to their own missions of death? And yet, if he had to follow through, the kind of work he would be assigned to would depend upon the results of the tests—that seemed sure. But what if they rendered him unconscious, knocked him out, used drugs?

His mind raced frantically, searching for some way of stalling things, some way of slowing down the red tape of testing and assignment, to give him time to complete his own mission and get out. But he knew that already he must have aroused suspicions. Schiml must have suspected that all the cards were not on the table, yet Schiml seemed willing to overlook his suspicions. And the wheels had begun to move more and more swiftly, carrying him to the critical point where he would have to sign a release and take an assignment, or reveal his real purpose for being in the Center. If he were to find Conroe, he must find him before the chips were down.

He stared at Schiml, his mind still groping for something to hang onto. He found nothing. "No. No questions, I guess," he said.

The doctor looked at him closely, then shrugged in resignation. "All right," he said, tiredly. "You'll have a whole series of tests of all kinds: physical stamina, mental alertness, reaction time, intelligence, sanity—everything we could possibly need to know. But I should warn you of one thing." He looked at Jeff, his eyes deadly serious. "All of these future tests are subjective. All of them will tell us about you as a person: how you think, how you behave. Desperately essential stuff, if you're to survive the sort of work we do here. What we find is the whole basis of our assignments."

He paused for a long moment. "You'd be wise to stick to the truth. No embellishments, no fancy stuff. We can't do anything about it if you don't choose to take the advice. But if you falsify, you're tampering with your own life expectancy here."

Jeff blinked, shifting in his seat uneasily. *Don't worry about that, Jack,* he thought. *I won't be around long enough for it to make any difference.* Nevertheless the doctor's words were far from soothing. If only Jeff could maintain the fraud throughout the testing, keep his wits about him as the tests progressed. Then he could get back to the hunt as soon as they were through.

He watched the doctor prepare a long paper on the desk. Then the rapid-fire series of questions began: family history, personal history, history of family disease and personal illness. The questions were swift and businesslike, and Jeff felt his muscles relaxing as he sat back. He answered almost automatically. Then: "Ever been hypnotized before?"

Something in Jeff's mind froze, screaming a warning. "No," he snapped.

Schiml's eyes widened imperceptibly. "Part of the testing should be done under hypnosis, for your sake, and for the sake of speed." His eyes caught Jeff's hard. "Unless you have some reason for objecting—"

"It won't work," Jeff lied swiftly, his mind racing. "Psychic block of some kind—induced in childhood, probably. My father had a block against it too." Every muscle in his body was tense, and he sat forward in his seat, his eyes wide.

Schiml shrugged. "It would make the testing a hundred per cent easier on you if you'd allow it. Some of these tests are pretty exhausting and some take a powerful long time without hypnotic-recovery aid. And of course we keep all information strictly confidential—"

"No dice," said Jeff hoarsely.

The doctor shrugged again, glancing over at Dr. Gabriel. "Hear that, Gabe?"

The little doctor shrugged. "His funeral," he growled. He rolled a small, shiny-paneled instrument with earphones to Jeff's side. "We'll start on the less strenuous ones, then. This is a hearing test. Very simple. You just listen, mark down the signals you hear. Keep your eyes on the eyepiece; it records visio-audio correlation times, tells us how soon after you hear a word you form a visual image of it." He snapped the earphones over Jeff's head and moved a printed answer sheet in front of him on the desk. And then the earphones started talking.

There was a long series of words, gradually becoming softer and softer. Jeff marked them down, swiftly, gradually forgetting his surroundings, throwing his attention toward the test. The doctors retired to the other side of the room. They talked to each other in low whispers, until he no longer heard them. There was only the low, insistent whispering in the earphones.

And then the words seemed to grow louder again, but somehow he had lost track of what they meant. He listened, his eyes watching the cool gray pearly screen in the eyepieces. His fingers were poised to write down the words, but he couldn't quite understand the syllables.

They were *nonsense syllables*, syllables with no meaning. His eyes opened wide, a bolt of suspicion shooting through him, and his hands gripped the arms of the chair as he began to rise.

And then the light exploded in his eyes with such agonizing brilliance that it sent shooting pain searing through his brain. He let out a stifled cry. He struggled and tried to rise from the chair. But he was blinded by the piercing beam. And then he felt the needle bite his arm, and the nonsense words in his ears straightened out into meaningful phrases. A soft, soothing voice was saying: "Relax ... relax ... sit back and relax ... relax and rest...."

Slowly the warmth crept over his body, and he felt his muscles relax, even as the voice instructed. He eased gently back into the chair, and soon his mind was clear of fear and worry and suspicion. He was still, sleeping with the peaceful ease of a newborn child.

CHAPTER EIGHT

It could never have been done without hypnosis. Within broad limits, the human body is capable of doing just exactly whatever it *thinks* it is capable of. But the human body could hardly be blamed if convention had long since decided that exertion was bad, that straining to the limit of endurance was unhealthy, that approaching—even obliquely—the margin of safety of human resiliency was equivalent to approaching death with arms extended. That convention had so declared was well known to the researchers at the Hoffman Center.

But it was also known that the human body under the soothing suggestion of hypnosis could be carried up to that margin of safety and beyond. Indeed, it could be carried almost to the actual breaking point without stir, without a flicker of protest, without a sign of fear.

And these were the conditions that were critically needed in testing for the Mercy Men. Yet, though hypnosis was necessary, the men who came to the Mercy Men without fail rejected hypnosis. Always they held the fear of divulging some secret of their past. Whether because of distrust of the doctors and the testing in the Center, or plain, ordinary malignance of character—no one knew all the motives. But those who needed hypnosis the most rejected it the most vehemently. This forced the development of techniques of hypnosis-by-force.

It would have annoyed Jeff, if he had known. Indeed, it would have driven him to the heights of anger, for Jeff, among other things, was afraid. But he need not have been, and it made little difference that he was. Now Jeff was not suffering from his fear. His mind was in a quiet, happy haze, and he felt his body half-lifted, half-led across the room to the first section of the testing room.

Even now there was a tiny, sharp-voiced sentinel hiding away in a corner of his mind, screaming out its message of alertness and fear to Jeff. But he laughed to himself, sinking deeper into the peacefulness of his walking slumber. Dr. Gabriel's voice was in his ear, his voice smooth and soothing, talking to him quietly, giving simple instructions. Quickly, he took him through the paces of a testing series that would have taken long, hard days to complete. It would have left him in psychotic break at the end, if he had not had the recuperative buffer of hypnosis to help him.

First, he was dressed in soft flannel clothing and moved into the gymnasium. Recorders were attached to his legs and arms and throat. Then he was formally introduced to the treadmill and quietly asked to run it until he collapsed. He smiled and obliged, running as though the furies were at his heels. He ran until his face went purple and his muscles knotted. At last he fell down, unable to continue.

This happened after ten minutes of top-limit running. Then came five minutes of recuperation under suggestion: "Your heart is beating slower. You're breathing slowly and deeply ... relaxing ... relaxing." Someone took his arm and he was off again, this time on the old, reliable Harvard Step-Test, jumping up on the chair and back down. He did this until once again he lay panting on the floor, hardly able to move as his pulse and respiration changes were carefully recorded.

Next in line came a lively handball game. He was handed a small, hard-rubber ball, and asked to engage in a game of catch with a machine that was stationed at the end of a cubby. The machine played hard, spinning the ball around and hurling it at Jeff with such incredible rapidity that he was forced to abandon all thinking. Instinctively, he reached out to catch the ball. His fingers burned with pain as he caught it and passed it in, only to have it hurled back out again, twice as fast. Soon he moved as automatically as a machine, catching, hurling, his mind refusing to accept the aching and swelling in his fingers, as the ball struck and struck and struck....

Then a small ladder was rolled in. He listened carefully to instructions and then ran up and down the ladder until he collapsed off the top. He was rested gently on the floor while blood samples were taken from his arm. Then he sat, staring dully at the floor. A voice said, "Relax, Jeff, take a rest. Sleep quietly, Jeff. You'll be ready to dig in and fight in a minute. Now just relax."

Several people were about; one brought him a heavy, sugary drink, lukewarm and revolting. He drank it, gagging, spilling it all down his shirt front. Then he grinned and licked his lips while further blood samples were drawn. And then, he was allowed to take a drink of cool water. He was left staring at his feet for five whole minutes of recuperation before the next stage of the testing commenced.

*

The lights were in three long columns. They extended as far as Jeff could see to the horizon. Some were blinking; some shone with steady intensity, while others were dark.

"Call the columns one, two and three," said Dr. Gabriel, close by, his voice soft with patience. "Record the position of the lights as you see them now. Then when the signal sounds, start recording every light change you see in all three columns. Do it fast, Jeff, as fast as you can."

The eye is a wonderful instrument of precision, capable of detecting an infinitude of movement and change. It is delicate enough to distinguish, if necessary, each and every still frame composing the motion picture that flickers so swiftly before it on the white screen. Jeff's fingers moved, his pencil recorded, quickly moving from column one to column two, and on to column three. The pencil moved swiftly until the test was over.

Then on to the next test....

Electrode leads were fastened to each of his ten toes and each of his ten fingers.

"Listen once, Jeff. Right first toe corresponds to left thumb; right second toe to right index finger. (Wonderful stuff, hypno-palamine, only one repetition to learn) When you feel a shock in a toe, press the button for the corresponding finger. Ready now, Jeff, as fast as you can."

Shock, press, shock, press. Jeff's mind was still, silent, a blank, an open circuit for reactions to speed through without hindrance, without modulation. Another round done and on to the next....

Doctor Schiml's pale face loomed up from some distant place. "Everything all right?"

"Going fine, fine. Smooth as can be."

"No snags anywhere?"

"No, no snags. None that I can see—yet."

*

"I want a smoke."

Dr. Gabriel relaxed, offered Jeff a smoke from a crumpled pack, extended his lighter and smiled. He noticed that Jeff's wide eyes missed their focus, could not see the extended flame. "How do you feel, Jeff?"

"Fine, fine—"

"Still got a lot to do."

A flicker of fear crossed the dull eyes. "Fine. Only I hope...."

"Yes?"

"... hope we finish. I'm tired."

"Sleepy?"

"Yeah, sleepy."

"Well, we'll have everything on punched cards for Tilly in a couple of hours or so. All the factors about you that this testing will unearth would take a research staff five hundred years to integrate down to the point where it would mean anything. With Tilly it takes five minutes. She doesn't make mistakes, either."

"Nice Tilly."

"And after the results come through, you're assigned and you sign your release and you're on your way to money."

Again the flicker of fear came, deeper this time. "Money...."

*

More tests, more tests. Hear a sound, punch a button. See a picture, record it. Test after endless test, dozens of records, his brain growing tired, tired. Then into the bright, gleaming room, up onto the green-draped table.

"No pain, Jeff, nothing to worry about. Be over in just a minute."

His eyes caught the slender, wicked-looking trefine; he heard the buzz of the motor, felt the grinding shock. But there was no reaction, no pain. And then he felt a curious tingling in his arms and legs, as the small electro-encephalograph end-plates entered his skull through the tiny drilled holes.

He watched with dull eyes as the little lights on the control board nearby began blinking on and off, on and off. The flashes followed a hectic, nervous pattern, registering individual brain-cell activity onto supersensitive stroboscopic film. This, in turn, was fed down automatically to Tilly for analysis. And then the trefine holes were plugged up again and his head was tightly taped, and he was moved back into another room for another five-minute recovery.

"Hit the ink blots yet?"

"Not yet, Rog. Take it easy, we're coming along. Ink blots and intelligence runs next, and so on."

Something stirred deep in Jeff's mind, even through the soothing delusions of hypnosis. It stirred and cried out at the first sign of the strange, colored forms on the cards. Something deep in Jeff's mind forced its way out to his lips as Dr. Gabriel said softly, "Just look at them, Jeff, and tell me what you see."

"No! Take them away."

"What's that? Gently, Jeff. Relax and take a look."

Jeff was on his feet, backing away, a wild, helpless, cornered fire in his eyes. "Take them away. Get me out of here. Go away—"

"Jeff!" The voice was sharp, commanding. "Sit down, Jeff."

Jeff sank down in the seat, gingerly, eyes wary. The doctor moved his hand and Jeff jumped a foot, his teeth chattering.

"What's the matter, Jeff?"

"I—I don't like ... those ... cards."

"But they're only ink blots, Jeff."

Jeff frowned and squinted at the cards. He scratched his head in perplexity. Slowly he sank back down in the chair, didn't even notice as the web-belt restrainers closed over his arms and legs, tightened down.

"Now look at the pictures, Jeff. Tell me what you see."

The perplexity grew on his heavy face, but he looked and talked, slowly, hoarsely. A dog's head, a little gnome, a big red bat.

"Gently, Jeff. Nothing to be afraid of. Relax, man, relax...."

Then came the word-association tests: half an hour of words and answers, while fear curled up through Jeff's brain, gathering, crouching, ready to spring, waiting in horrible anticipation for something, something that was coming as sure as hour followed hour. Jeff felt the web restrainers cutting his wrists, as the words were read. He trembled in growing foreboding.

Dr. Schiml's face was back, still concerned, his eyes bright. "Going all right, Gabe?"

"Dunno, Rog. Something funny with the ink blots. You can glance at the report. Word association all screwed up too. Can't spot it, but there's something funny."

"Give him a minute's rest and reinforce the palamine. Probably got a powerful vitality opposing it."

Dr. Gabriel was back in a moment, and another needle nibbled Jeff's arm briefly. Then the doctor walked to the desk, took out the small, square plastic box. He dropped the cards out into his hand. They were plain-backed little cards with bright red symbols on their faces.

Dr. Gabriel held them under Jeff's nose. "Rhine cards," he said softly. "Four different symbols, Jeff. Look close. A square, a circle...."

It was like a gouge, jammed down through Jeff's mind, ripping it without mercy. A red-hot, steaming poker was being rammed into the soft, waxy tissue of his brain.

"My God, hold him!"

Jeff screamed, wide awake, his eyes bulging with terror. With an animal-like roar he wrenched at his restrainers, ripped them out of the raw wood and plunged across the room in blind, terrified flight. He ran across the room and struck the solid brick wall full face. He hit with a sickening thud, pounded at the wall with his fists, screaming out again and again. And then he collapsed to the floor, his nose broken, his face bleeding, his fingers raw with the nails broken.

And as he slid into merciful unconsciousness, they heard him blubbering: "He killed my father ... killed him ... killed him ... killed him ... killed him...."

*

Hours later he stirred. He almost screamed out in pain as he tried to move his arm. His chest burned as he breathed. When he opened his eyes, an almost unbearable, pounding ache struck down through his skull. He recognized his room, saw the empty bed across from him. Then he raised an arm, felt the bandaging around his face, his neck.

He listened fearfully and his ears caught only the harsh, gurgling breathing of the man in the next room: the man called Tinker, whose doom as a Mercy Man had not been quite sealed, who breathed on, shallowly, breaking the deadly silence.

What had happened?

Jeff sat bolt upright in the darkness, ignoring the stabbing pain that shot through his chest and neck. What had happened? Why was he bandaged? What was the meaning of the pure, naked, paralyzing fear that was gripping him like a vise? He stared through the darkness at the opposite bed, and blinked. What had happened ... what ... what?

Of course. He had been in the file room. He'd been caught. Schiml had caught him and he had been taken down for testing. And then: *a bright light, nonsense words in his ear, a needle....*

Gasping with pain, Jeff rolled out of bed, searched underneath for his shoes. With an audible sob, he retrieved the crumpled card from under the inner sole. Then they hadn't gotten the card. They didn't know. But what could have happened? Slowly, other things came back: there had been a scream; he had felt a shock, as though molten lead had been sent streaming through his veins, and then he had struck the wall like a ten-ton truck.

He groped for his watch, stared at it, hardly believing his eyes. It read seven P.M. It had been almost one A.M. when they had taken him down to Dr. Gabriel. It couldn't be seven in the evening again. Unless he had slept around the clock. He listened to the watch; it was still running. Whatever had happened had thrown him, thrown him so hard that he had slept for almost twenty-four hours. And in the course of that time....

The horrible loss struck him suddenly, worming its way through to open realization. Twenty-four hours later—a day gone, a whole day for Conroe to use to move deeper into hiding. He sank back on the bed and groaned, despair heavy in his mind. A day gone, a precious day. Somewhere the man was in the Center. But to locate him now, after he had had such time—how could Jeff do it?

He felt a greater urgency now. No matter what they had found in the testing, he had no time left to hunt. The next step on this one-way road was assignment and the signing of a release—the point of no return.

And through it all, something ate at his mind: some curious question, some phantom he could not pin down, a shadow figure which loomed up again and again in his mind, haunting him—the shadow of fearful doubt. Why the shock? Why had he broken loose? What had driven him to punish his arms and legs so mercilessly on the restrainers? What monstrous demon had torn loose in his mind? What gaping sore had the doctors scraped over to drive him to such extremes of fear and horror? *And why was the same feeling there in his mind whenever he thought of Paul Conroe?*

He sighed. He needed help and he knew it. He needed help desperately. Here, in a whirlpool of hatred and selfishness, he needed help more than he had ever needed it, help to track down this phantom shadow, help to corner it, to kill it. And the only ones he could ask for help were those around him, the Mercy Men themselves. He needed their help, if only to escape becoming one of them.

*

He dozed, then woke a little later and listened. There was an air of tension in the room, a whisper of something gone sharply wrong. Jeff forced himself up on his elbow, tried to peer through the darkness. Something had happened just before he awoke. He listened to the deathly stillness in the room.

And then he knew what it was. The breathing in the next room had stopped.

He lay back, his heart pounding, listening to the rasping of his own breath, fear and despair rising up to new heights in his mind. Death had come, then. One man who would never see the payoff he so eagerly awaited. Jeff had felt death pass over the room, and he knew, instinctively, that the entire unit would know it too without a single word passing from a single mouth. For the sense of death was a tangible thing here, moving with silent, imponderable footfalls from room to room.

For the first time, Jeff felt a kinship, a depth of understanding to share with the Mercy Men. And there was a depth of fear, deep down, which he knew now that he must share with them too. Painfully, he rolled over on his side and stared into the darkness for long minutes before he fell into fitful sleep.

CHAPTER NINE

A voice was talking across the room, a muffled, mysterious rumble of up-and-down sounds. Slowly Jeff dragged his mind out of the clinging depths of nightmare, back to the stuffy, dimly lit room. How long had he slept? And how late was it now? The soft voices across the room gave no clue, and his aching mind was too tired to care any more. He just lay in the dim light, every muscle aching, his mind returning again and again to the nightmare he had been reliving for the thousandth time.

It had been horribly sharp this time, clear as noonday: the same subject as always, the same face, the same horrible knowledge, and the same soul-wrenching hatred welling up and bubbling over in his mind. Always it was hatred without plan or form, pure, disorganized animal fury. But this time the dream had been more coherent, clearer, more unmistakable and vicious.

He had been walking down the street in the heart of the city. Yes, it was mid-morning. The sun's heat was unbearable already, and his jacket and shirt were damp. What was he doing that morning? Was he on his way to the survey depot with some information on the next Mars run? It didn't really matter. But he turned into the building and then it hit him.

It was like the shock that had struck him in the testing room, he thought. He had run into the man bodily. Stepping back to beg his pardon, he saw the man's face. That's where the dream went wild, just as his mind had gone wild on that sunny morning so long ago. He saw the man turn and run like the wind, snaking into the flowing stream of people on the street. Jeff followed, shouting, his fists and legs churning through the masses of people. He screamed in hoarse, maddened despair as he saw the figure vanish before his eyes.

And then he was leaning against the wall, panting, tears streaming down his face. Unable to understand, knowing only that this was the man whose face had haunted his dreams all his life, he acknowledged this was the man he would have to kill.

His eyes snapped open. The voices across the room were louder. Jeff listened. One voice was a woman's—Blackie's, of course. There was no mistaking the Nasty Frenchman's nasal twang. But the third voice—Jeff blinked his eyes. He moved his head to see the little group across the room.

They were huddled around a small infra-red coffee maker: Blackie, the Nasty Frenchman, and the huge, bald-headed man called Harpo. Blackie's voice was sharp and pleading as she echoed the Nasty Frenchman in angry protest. Harpo's heavy bass rumbled an undertone to the whispered discussion. Painfully, Jeff drew himself up on an elbow and turned his ear in the direction of the huddle, as the words drifted to him, unclearly:

"I say find out who and do something about it," the Nasty Frenchman was insisting angrily. His face was red and spiteful, and his eyes flashed as he glared up at Harpo. "We're out of it completely. Don't you see that? Because of this switch, we're off the payroll—ditched like common scum! Well, the job I've been on was to pay two hundred thousand dollars, with practically no risk involved. And I'll kill the man that's cutting me out of it."

Harpo's voice was soothing. "So maybe you're daydreaming. Maybe there won't be any switch of jobs at all."

"I saw the report, I tell you. It was signed by Schiml himself."

Harpo looked up sharply. "You actually saw Schiml's signature on it?"

"I saw it. I'm taken off assignment and so are you. We're both shoved out. Can't you get that straight? After all this time—and just because they get somebody in here that gets them excited."

Harpo snorted. "So they've gone off on these spook hunts before. Where do you think it'll take them this time? Extra-sensory powers!" The huge man spat in disdain. "Have you ever seen anybody with extra-sensory powers? Well, neither have I. Look, Jacques, let's face it: Schiml would give his left arm at the shoulder to have proof of extra-sensory powers in any form." Harpo grinned unpleasantly. "You've seen proof of that before. He believes in it, he wants to prove it. And every now and then he's going to have a try at it just to keep himself happy, just to keep in form. There's no call to get excited."

"But he's got a solid prospect this time," Blackie snapped. "From the stories I've heard the guy is a phenomenon. Hit top scores on the cards—highest they've ever recorded here. Other things too, like peeling the paper off the walls just by looking at them, or closing up opened wounds in ten minutes."

"So you hear stories! Around here I don't believe anything I hear." Harpo shifted uneasily. "If there was anything tangible, anything we could put our hands on, I'd listen. But there's not—no proof, no nothing but a lot of wild stories. And I've even heard better stories in my time. You can't go around fighting stories—"

Jeff sat bolt upright, something shouting out in his brain. He grabbed for his shoes, oblivious to the agonizing pain in his muscles, fumbled eagerly, his mind screaming in excitement. "What kind of proof do you want?" he growled.

Harpo stared up at him, as though seeing a ghost. "You awake!" he gasped. And then: "Any kind of proof!"

"Then take a look at this." And Jeff tossed the crumpled card down in the middle of the huddle.

Blackie was on her feet, her eyes eager. "Didn't know you were anywhere near ready to wake up," she said. "You look like they really gave you the works."

"Well, something happened, all right. I don't know whether I'm coming or going."

Blackie nodded. "You never do, after testing. They came here for you, and I told them you'd gone out for a stroll. But I guess they found you." She put a cup of coffee in Jeff's hand and motioned toward the card. "You got that out of the file without being spotted?"

Jeff's eyes met hers for the briefest instant. "That's right. And I heard what you were talking about." He caught the little note of warning in her eyes: the silent, helpless appeal. He shook his head imperceptibly. He knew then that she hadn't told the others about their battle over the dice. He pointed to the card. "I think that answers a lot of things."

Harpo's eyes were suspicious. "How do you know that's the man?"

"Because I drove him in here, that's why." Jeff's voice was a snarl; it sounded sharp in the quiet room. "I knew he was here because he came here to escape me. But I didn't know he had any connection with ESP until I saw the card."

Harpo stared at the card, then at Jeff. "You mean you drove him in here?"

"That's right. Because I'd have killed him if he didn't come." Jeff's face was dark as he turned to the girl. "Tell him, Blackie. Tell him why I'm here."

Blackie told them. They listened with widening eyes, and the room was still as a tomb.

"And you came in here to kill this man—nothing more?" Harpo's voice was incredulous. "But man, you're on thin ice, very thin ice. If they tested you last night, you'll be assigned. Why, you could be forced to sign a release any time."

"I know it, I know it. Can't you see why there isn't time to bicker now?" Jeff's voice cracked in the still room, sharp and urgent. "This is the man, the one I'm looking for and the one you're looking for, the one with ESP that's got Schiml and his men so excited! It's here on the card!"

Harpo's eyes were narrow. "Any other proof besides the card that Conroe is the man?"

Jeff's voice was low with hate. "Look. I've been hunting the man down for five years. A long time. I've hunted him wherever he's gone. I've had the best detective agency in North America working with me hand and foot, tracking him down. But they haven't caught him. We've almost caught him, we've haunted him, we've run him back and forth across the country and world until he's ragged. But we've never caught him. Isn't there some significance to that? Time and again we've come so close that we couldn't miss—and then we missed. We've come too close too many times for coincidence. There's another factor, a factor that's giving Conroe warning, time after time. It's allowed him to slip out of perfectly sealed traps—*a factor like precognition, for instance.*"

There was a long silence. Then the Nasty Frenchman was on his feet, his lips stretched in a malicious grin. "If we move fast enough, we can stop it—cut it off at the bud. We're off the payroll now. But we can get back on it again, if their boy wonder dies."

Harpo's eyes flashed. "And how do you plan to do it?"

"Nothing simpler in the world. We just find the guy." The Nasty Frenchman's grin widened. "Then after we find him, we tell our friend Jeff about it. Nothing more. Jeff'll take it from there. Right, Jeff?"

Jeff's heart pounded against his ribs. "That's right," he said, his voice hoarse with eagerness. "Just find him for me."

Harpo bent over slowly, poured another cup of coffee. "Then let's talk plans," he said softly.

*

The planning went smoothly. Jeff sat forward eagerly. The despair and hopelessness of an hour before evaporated, leaving fingers of wild excitement creeping through his muscles, up and down his spine. These people knew where they were; they knew how to hunt in this evil place, where to go, what to do. This was the help he needed to complete his mission, the help he'd needed from the start. And now, at last, nothing would go wrong. Carefully, the last trap was laid—the final drive in this manhunt that had lasted so long and been so fruitless. This time there would be no slip.

Harpo fingered the card thoughtfully. "These dates must have some significance. Were there any signs of Conroe's visits here at those times?"

Jeff shook his head. "No sign. He couldn't have been here for more than three days at a time, or I'd have known about it."

Harpo grunted, his eyes sharp on Jeff's face. "And you had no definite, direct evidence that he was somehow using an extra-sensory talent in eluding you?"

Jeff scowled. "No direct evidence. I'm afraid not. There was no reason to suspect it, until I found the card. Then hindsight started filling in funny things that had gone unnoticed before."

Harpo nodded. "Yes. That's the way it would be. But Schiml must have had direct enough evidence. This ESP study is just like space travel was. They've been after it for years; they start after it time after time, every time a new angle comes up. Because if they succeed it could mean so much to so many people."

The Nasty Frenchman snorted. "Sure. Like running us out of paying jobs for good and all, after all the risks we've taken. Open the door to ESP for them, and there wouldn't be any other work in the Center for twenty years. And if we don't happen to be what they're looking for—" He ran his finger across his throat and scowled. "The man is here. We've got to have information on him, past and present. That means we'll have to search the Archives. There's no better approach." He turned his sharp little eyes on Jeff. "You know how the electronic files work. You're the one that can dig out what we need to know in the Archives."

Jeff nodded. "But I'll need time to work without interruption. Can you get me into the Archive files without being caught?"

The Nasty Frenchman nodded eagerly. "Nothing to it. Give us half an hour to clear the way and get the guards taken care of." He glanced up at Harpo. "The old fire-alarm gag should do it, all right. Then you can walk right down."

"And can you keep it clear for me, say, for an hour or so?"

"For five hours, if necessary." Harpo stood up sharply. "We'll start now to get things lined up. When it's clear, I'll give you a flicker on the phone. Don't answer it. Just come along. Blackie can draw you a map while you wait." The bald-headed giant started to leave, then turned back. "And don't let any alarm bells disturb you. We've found ways of occupying guards before." He touched his forehead briefly, and he and the Nasty Frenchman disappeared into the corridor.

*

"I think it'll work," Jeff breathed, tucking Blackie's crude penciled map into his pocket. "I think we've got him. Once we know where he is and what they're going to do with him—" He grinned up at her, his eyes shining. "His time's running out, Blackie. He's as good as dead."

The girl leaned forward, pouring coffee, sitting silently. Jeff watched her face, as if seeing it for the first time. Indeed, for the first time, the girl's face seemed softer. In the dim light of the room, the hard lines melted away, magically. Her face appeared younger and fresher, as though some curious mask had dropped away in the course of the evening.

But her eyes were troubled as she watched Jeff and lifted her coffee cup in mock salute. "To the Hunter," she said softly.

Jeff raised his own cup. "Yes. But not for long now."

"It can't go on much longer, Jeff. Your number's up next."

"For assignment?" Jeff's eyes flashed. "Do you think that makes any difference to me? I'm following through to the end on this, no matter what happens."

"But, Jeff, you can't sign a release."

Jeff stared at her in the silent room. "Why not? If it's the only thing I can do—"

Her eyes were wide and very dark. "Oh, Jeff, you're in terrible danger here."

"I know that."

"You don't, you don't." The girl was shaking her head, tears rising to her eyes. "You don't know anything, Jeff, about the Mercy Men or the kind of work they do. Oh, I know, you think you do. But you don't, really. Look, Jeff—look at it straight—you're young, you're smart. There are other ways to spend your life, more important things for you to do. Can't you see that? No man is worth throwing your life away for, no matter what he's done to you. That's what you're doing. You're walking down a blind alley, into a death trap! Get out, while you can."

Jeff's head was shaking, his lips tight, until the color fled them, leaving pale gray lines. "I can't get out. I just can't. Nothing anyone could say could drive me out now."

"But you've got to run while you can! Oh, yes, go down there tonight if you must, try to find him. But if you don't find him, cut and run. Jeff, get out, tonight. They can't stop you; they have no legal hold on you, yet. But once they bring in a release, you're hooked. It'll be too late then."

Jeff's eyes narrowed, and he sat down on the bed and faced the girl. There was an elfin expression on her face, a curious intensity in her large gray eyes that he had never seen before. "What do you care?" he asked suddenly. "What do you care what I do?"

The girl's voice was low, and the words tumbled out so rapidly that he could hardly follow them. "Look, Jeff, you and me—we could work as a team. Don't you see what we could do? We could get out of here, together. We could get out of the city, go to the West Coast. The dice, think of the dice, man—we could clean up! You don't belong in here on the rack for slaughter. And I wouldn't belong here, either, if we could work together—"

Somewhere in the distance an alarm bell began ringing, insistently, clang-clanging down the corridors. Then there was a rush of feet, shouted orders and calls up and down the hallway, and the squeak of three jitneys passing by in rapid succession. Then, abruptly, the corridor fell silent again.

Jeff hardly noticed the clamor. He stared at the girl, his hands trembling. "Blackie, Blackie, think what you're saying. The tough-luck jinx. Have you forgotten? You're safe from it here. But outside, what would happen? We might make a go of it, yes, but what if the jinx followed us?"

"Oh, but Jeff, that's silly." She swallowed, her eyes almost overflowing as she tried to blink back the tears. "It isn't just selfishness, Jeff. I could stay here. I talked to Schiml this afternoon, before Harpo and Jacques started talking. They're out—yes. But I'm not. He wants me to stay, says there's a place for me in the work. But I don't want to stay."

Jeff was shaking his head slowly, his eyes tired. "It's no dice, Blackie. Not now. After I get Conroe, after I get out of here, then maybe I could think about it. But I haven't given this dice business any thought at all. Can't you see? I'd have to think it out, carefully, all its ramifications. And I haven't been able to do that. It hasn't mattered enough. I've got a man to kill, first, before anything else. And I'm going to kill him. I'm going to kill him tonight."

"Then do it for sure. Get him tonight! And then get out, before something happens—"

In the corner the phone gave two sharp rings, then lapsed into silence. Their eyes met, sharply, desperately. "Nothing's going to happen," Jeff said softly. "Don't worry about it. I've been at this too long for anything to happen."

There was a frantic light in the girl's gray eyes as she looked up at him, a depth and sincerity he had never seen before. Her eyes pleaded with him. "You don't know, you don't know...."

And then they were in each other's arms, drawing each other close, desperately. His hard lips met her soft ones, met and held. Then when they parted there was another look in her eyes, and he heard her breath cut sharply by his ear. "Jeff—"

Gently he put a finger to his lips, loosened her arms from around him. "Don't say it," he whispered. "Not now, Blackie. Not now—"

And then he was outside, in the corridor. The cool air caught him and he ran down the corridor toward the stairs. He hurried against the time the men had prepared for his safety. And as he ran, he felt his heart pounding in his ears, and he knew the hour was drawing close.

CHAPTER TEN

Jacques and Harpo were waiting for him at the head of the escalator. He nodded and followed them down the corridor to the small jitney car that was waiting.

"All set?"

"All set. The guards are all busy up in N unit putting out a fire. They won't be down to bother us for a couple of hours." The Nasty Frenchman scowled disdainfully. "But you'll have to hurry. When they come back, we'll have a time stalling them again."

Jeff nodded. "That should be enough. Then maybe we'll have other things to occupy the guards tonight."

The jitney started with a lurch and a squawk. Harpo handled the controls, running the little car swiftly down the corridor. It swung suddenly into a pitch-black tunnel, took an abrupt dip and began to spiral downward at a wild rate. Jeff grabbed the hand rail and gasped.

"It's a long way down," Harpo chuckled, sitting back in the darkness. "The Archives hold the permanent records of the entire Hoffman Center since it was first opened. That's why it's a vault, so that bombing won't destroy it. It's one of the most valuable tombs in history."

The jitney shot out into a lighted corridor. Jeff swallowed and felt his ears pop. The little car whizzed through a maze of tunnels and corridors. Finally it settled down to the floor before the heavy steel doors at the end of a large corridor.

Without a word, Harpo moved down to the end of the corridor, and drew the jitney car with him. He opened the motor hood, started pawing around busily inside.

The Nasty Frenchman chuckled. "If anyone wanders by, that jitney alarm siren goes off, and Harpo's just a poor technician trying to make it stop." The little man walked quickly to the steel doors. "It's not the first time I've had to work on these," he said slyly. "We wanted in here a few months ago, when they were trying to pull a shakedown deal on some of us. I worked out the combination pattern then; it took me three days. They change the combination periodically, of course, but the pattern is built into the lock."

He opened a small leather case and placed an instrument up against the lock. A long, thin wire was poised and ready in his other hand. Jeff heard several muffled clicks; then Jacques inserted the wire sharply into something. An alarm bell above the door gave one dull, half-hearted clunk and relapsed into silence, as though changing its mind at the last moment. A moment later the little Frenchman looked up and winked, and the steel vault door rolled slowly back.

The place smelled damp and empty. Three walls and half of the fourth were occupied with electronic file controls. The bulk of the room was taken up with tables, microviewers, readers, recorders, and other study-apparatus. There was nothing small in the room; the whole place breathed of bigness, of complexity, of many years of work and wisdom, of many lives and many, many deaths. It was a record-room that many lives had built.

Jeff moved in toward the control panel. He located the master coder and sat down in a chair before it, his eyes running over it carefully, sizing up the mammoth filing machine. And then, quite suddenly, he felt terribly afraid. A knot grew in his stomach and a cold sweat broke out on his forehead. A face was again looming up sharply in his mind. It was the huge, ghoulish face that had come to him again and again in his dreams; the face full of hatred and viciousness—pale and inhuman.

It was the face of a heartless, pointless, bloody assassin. But was that all? Or was there more to that face, more to that dream than Jeff had ever suspected? Something deep in his mind stirred, sending a chill down his spine. His hand trembled as he ran a hand over the control panel. A ghost was there at his elbow, a ghost that had followed him on this nebulous trail of bitterness and hatred for so long—a trail which would end in this very room.

He shook his head angrily. There was no time for panic, no time for ruminating. He picked the panel-code combination for the Mercy Men and the research unit. Then he computed the coding for Conroe's name. With trembling fingers, he typed out the coding, punched the tracer button and sat back, his heart thumping wildly. He watched the receiver slot for the telltale file cards and folio.

The file squeaked and chattered and whirred and moaned, and finally the pale instruction panel lighted up: No Information.

Jeff blinked, a chill running up his back. These files were the final appeal; the information had to be here. Quickly, he computed a description coding, fed it in and waited again in mounting tension. Still no information. He picked the code card from his pocket, the card from the Mercy Men's file up above, the card with the Hoffman Center's own picture of Conroe on it. He fed it into the photoelectric tracer, marked in the necessary coding for an unlimited file search: "Any person resembling this description in any way: any information on—" Again he sat back, breathing heavily.

The whirring went on and on. Then, inexorably, the little panel flickered and spelled out a single word:

"Unknown."

Jeff choked. He stared at the panel, his whole body shaking, and went through the coding again, step by step, searching for an error, finding none. It was impossible, it couldn't be so—and yet, the files were empty of information. As though there had never been a Paul Conroe. There was not even a reference card to the card in the Mercy Men's files.

He stared at the panel, his mind rebelling in protest. Nothing, not even a trace in the one place where there had to be complete information. He had come to a dead end—the last dead end there could be in the Hoffman Center.

The Nasty Frenchman lit a cigarette and watched Jeff from bright eyes. "No luck?"

"No luck," said Jeff, brokenly. "We're beaten. That's all."

"But there must be—"

"Well, there's not!" Jeff slammed his fist down on the table with a crash, his eyes blazing. "There's not a trace, not a whisper of the man in here. There has to be—and there's not. It's the same as every other time: a blank wall. Blank wall after blank wall. I'm getting tired of them, so miserably tired of running into blind alley after blind alley." He stood up, his shoulders sagging. "I'm too tired of it to keep it up. There's no point to gambling any longer. I'm getting out of here while I've got a whole skin."

"Maybe you've got more time than you think." The Nasty Frenchman eyed him in alarm. "This is no time to run out. It may be weeks before you're assigned."

Jeff stared at him. "Well, I know one way to find out." He walked over to the control panel, stabbed an angry finger at the master coder, picked out the coding for "J. Meyer." "They'll have me here too," he snapped. "The whole works about me: what the testing said, what they're going to do to me. That's one way to find out." Quickly, he typed out the coding, punched the tracer button....

The machinery whirred again, briefly. Then there was a click in the receiver slot and another and another. Jeff blinked at it as the microfilm rolls continued to fall down. Then he reached out to the single white card which fell on top of the rolls. His fingers were damp as he took the card. His own death warrant, perhaps? He glanced at the card and froze. His head began pounding as if it would burst.

"J. Meyer" he had punched in, and that was what the card said—*but not Jeffrey Meyer*. The card held a photo of a middle-aged, gray-haired man, and the typewritten name at the top said: JACOB MEYER.

And the picture was a photograph of his father's face.

*

It was impossible, incredible, but he stared at the card in his hand. It did not disappear; it stayed there. It still said: "Jacob Meyer"; it still showed the beloved features of his father, staring up at him blankly from the card. *His father*!

His heart pounded as he stared at the brief typewritten notation below the picture: "Born 11 August, 2050, Des Moines, Iowa; married 3 Dec. 2077, wife died childbirth 27 November 2078; one son Jeffrey born 27 November 2078." Then below were a series of dates: date of bachelor's degree, date of Master's and Doctorate; Associate Professor of Statistics at Rutgers University, 2079-2084; joined Government Bureau of Statistics in 2085. Finally, at the bottom of the card were a long series of reference numbers to microfilm files.

Jeff sank down in the chair, his mind spinning helplessly. He turned dazed eyes to the Nasty Frenchman. "You might as well go," he said. "I've got to do some reading."

Feverishly, he scooped up the microfilm rolls, carried them to the nearest reader, twisted the spool into the machine and bent his eyes to the viewing slot, his heart pounding in his throat....

The first roll was a long, detailed series of abstracts of statistical papers, all written by Jacob A. Meyer, Ph.D., all covered with marginal notes in a scrawling, spidery hand and initialed "R.D.S." The papers covered a multitude of studies; some dealt with the very techniques of statistical analyses themselves, others were concerned with specific studies that had been done.

The papers were written in scholarly manner, perfectly well documented, but the marginal notes found fault continually, both with the samplings noted and the conclusions drawn. Jeff read through some of the papers and he scowled. They dated over a period of the four years when his father had been teaching statistics. There were several dozen papers, all with marginal notes, none of which made much sense to Jeff. With a sigh, he pulled out the roll, fed in another.

This one seemed a little more rewarding. It was a letter, signed by Roger D. Schiml, M.D., dated almost twenty years before, addressed to the Government Bureau of Statistics. Jeff's eyes skimmed the letter briefly, catching words here, phrases there:

... as director of research at the Hoffman Center, considered it my duty to bring this unbelievable condition to the attention of higher authorities.... Naturally, a statistical analysis must be made of the matter before it can be concluded that there has been a marked increase in mental illness of any kind in the general populace ... have followed Dr. Meyer's analyses in the past with much interest, and would be pleased if he could come to the Hoffman Center within the next month to commence such a study....

There was nothing tangible, nothing that made sense. Jeff shuffled through the rolls, popped another into place in the reader. This time he read much more closely a letter from an unknown person to Dr. Schiml. It was dated almost a year later than the former letter. This note referred in several places to the "Almost unbelievable results of the statistical study done several months ago." It also referred to the investigation just concluded of possible disturbing elements in the analysis. The final paragraph Jeff read through three times, his eyes nearly popping.

There was no doubt that the data was sound, and properly collected; naturally, the results of the analysis followed mathematically from the data. It seemed, therefore, that we were dealing with a disturbing factor heretofore quite unsuspected. Our investigation leads us to the inavoidable, though hardly credible, conclusion that Dr. Jacob A. Meyer *was himself* the sole disturbing factor in the analysis. No other possibility fits the facts of the picture. We recommend therefore that an intensive study of Dr. Meyer's previous work be undertaken, with a view to answering the obvious questions aroused by such a report. We also recommend that this be undertaken without delay.

At the top of the letter, in red letters, was the government's careful restriction: TOP SECRET.

Another roll went into the reader. This held the letter-head of a New York psychiatrist. Jeff's eyes caught the name and he read eagerly:

Dear Dr. Schiml:

We have studied the microfilm records you posted to us with extreme care, and undertaken the study of Jacob Meyer, as instructed. Although it is impossible to make a positive diagnosis without interviewing and examining the patient in person, we are inclined to support your views as stated in your letter. As to the possibility of other more remarkable phenomena occurring, we are not prepared to comment. But we must point out that this man almost certainly undergoes a regular manic-depressive cycle, may be dangerously depressed, even suicidal, in a depressive low, and may endanger himself and others in a manic period of elation. Such a person is extremely dangerous and should not be allowed freedom to go as he chooses.

Jeff looked up, tears streaming from his eyes. His whole body was wet with perspiration. He could hardly keep his balance as he stood up. What lies! The idea that his father could have been insane, that he could have falsified any sort of statistical report that he had done—it was impossible, a pack of incredible lies. But they were here, on the files of the greatest medical center on the face of the earth—lies about his father, lies that Jeff couldn't even attack because he could not understand them.

The door swung open sharply, and the Nasty Frenchman stuck his head in, panting. "Better get going," he snarled. "There are guards coming." His head disappeared abruptly, and Jeff heard Harpo's voice bellow at him: "Come on, we've got to run!"

Jeff's legs would hardly move. He felt numb as though a thousand nerve centers had been suddenly struck all at once. He fumbled, pouring the microfilm rolls into his pockets, his mind whirling. There was no sense to it: no understanding, no explanation. Somehow, he knew, there was a tie-in between these records of his father, taken so long ago, and the absence of any information on Paul Conroe in the files. But he couldn't find the link.

He ran out into the hall, leaped into the jitney car. He hung on for dear life as it sped up through the tunnel, into the blackness of the spiral once again. Suddenly, in his ears, another sound exploded, the loud, insistent clang of an alarm bell.

Harpo looked at the Nasty Frenchman and then at Jeff. "Oh, oh," he said softly. "They're onto something; that's a general muster. We'd better get back to quarters—and fast!"

He shoved the controls ahead a bit further, and Jeff felt the car leap ahead. Finally it settled down in the quarters corridor. They leaped out, Harpo set the dials for the car to return, and the three men ran for their quarters, the bell still clanging in their ears.

In Jeff's mind thoughts were tumbling as he ran—hopeless thoughts, uneasy thoughts. As he had ridden up, little chinks had fallen into place in his mind. Little spaces that he had never understood suddenly began to make sense, adding up to questions, big questions. It was too pat, too easy that Conroe should come in here and vanish as if he had never been alive. Things didn't happen that way, not even for Conroe.

Other things came into focus, slowly, flickering briefly through his mind—things that had happened years before, things that seemed, suddenly, to mean something. Then, just as they came into focus, they flickered back out of reach again. They were incidents like the night in the gambling room; like the night in the nightclub with the dancer swaying before him; like the sudden, shocking jolt that had awakened him from the depths of hypnosis and driven him face-first into a stone wall; things like the curious viciousness of his hatred for Paul Conroe—a hate that had carried him to the ends of the earth. But now that hate lay stalemated, and new and more frightening information threatened to descend on him.

What did it mean?

Jeff felt the uneasiness crystallize into real fear. He broke into a run down the corridor toward his room. Fear pounded through his mind, suddenly, unreasonably. He tore open the door, fell inside, closed it tight behind him before snapping on the lights.

The room was empty. The coffee pot still stood on the little table. It was still hot, still steaming. Blackie was gone and a cigarette still burned on the edge of the tray.

He had to get out! He knew it then, knew that was at the bottom of the unreasonable fear. The bell was still clanging in the hallway, loudly piercing the still air of the room. He had to flee while he could. Instinctively now he knew that he'd never find Paul Conroe in the Center, never in a thousand years of searching. The fear grew stronger, a little voice screaming in his ear, "*Don't wait. Run, run now, or it's too late.*"

He tore open his foot locker, stared at the empty hooks. The locker was cleaned out, empty of every stitch of clothing. His bag was gone, his shoes, his coat.

It's too late. Don't wait.

His pulse pounded in his temples and a sweat broke out on his forehead. The escalator! If he could get to it, then make the turn into the next corridor, and get a jitney car.... It was the only way to get out and he had no choice. Panting, he broke out into the hall once again, ran pell-mell down the corridor toward the escalator. Then, when he was almost there, a wire cage slammed down across the corridor and blocked his path completely.

Jeff stopped short, his shoes scraping against the concrete floor. His heart pounded a deafening tattoo in his ears as he stared at the wire grill. Then he whirled and ran back down the corridor as fast as his legs would move. If he could get back to the offices, back to the main corridor before they stopped him, he could get a car there. Far ahead he saw the bright light of the main corridor. His breath came in a hoarse whine as he tried to run faster. And then, ten yards ahead, he saw another grill clank down, cutting him off, falling directly in his path.

He cried out, a helpless, desperate cry. He was trapped, caught in the one length of corridor. His mind spun dizzily to Blackie. She had been gone. Where to? Where had everybody gone? He started back, frantically jerking open doors on either side of the corridor, staring into room after room, his breath catching in his throat as he ran. All the rooms were empty. Jeff felt his mind spinning. He felt a curious inevitability, a fantastic pattern falling into shape as he stared into the empty rooms. Finally he reached his own again. Wide-eyed and panting, he threw the door open, strode in and threw himself down in the chair and waited.

He did not wait long. For a few moments there was no sound. Then he heard the sounds of feet coming down the corridor. He tightened his grip on the chair arm. He wasn't thinking any longer. Cold beads of sweat stood out on his forehead as he waited, hearing the steps draw nearer. For the first time that he could remember, sheer terror crept through his mind, paralyzing him. He knew he had waited too long. His chance to jump the road was gone; there was no longer any escape.

Then the door was filled by some figures. One of them was the tall, white figure of Dr. Schiml. He walked into the room and smiled like the cat that ate the canary. Sinking down on the bed with a sigh, he was still smiling at Jeff. The girl followed him into the room. Her eyes were downcast. She tossed a little pair of ivory dice into the air and caught them as they fell.

The doctor smiled, and drew a crisp white paper from his pocket, began unfolding it slowly. "A matter of business," he said, almost apologetically. "It's time we got down to business, I think."

CHAPTER ELEVEN

Jeff raised his eyes to the doctor's face. His throat felt like sandpaper. He tried to swallow and couldn't. "Sorry," he grated. "I've changed my mind. I'm not talking business."

Dr. Schiml smiled, his head slowly moving back and forth. "I hear you're quite handy at the dice, Jeff."

Jeff jumped out of the chair, fists clenched, eyes blazing at the girl. "You bitch," he snarled. "You two-bit tramp stoolie. You'd sell your grandmother short for a bag of salt, wouldn't you? Come to me with your sob stories, beg me to move out of here with you." His voice was biting. "How much did they pay you to sell out? A hundred thousand, maybe? Or was this just a little routine affair? Maybe a thousand or two?"

The girl's face darkened, her eyes bewildered as she stared at him. "No, that's not true. I didn't—"

"Well, it won't do them any good, no matter how much they paid you. Because I'm not signing a release, now or ever."

A guard grabbed Jeff's arm, forcing him back into the chair.

Dr. Schiml still smiled, clasping his knee with his hands. "I guess you didn't quite understand me," he said pleasantly. "You mustn't blame Blackie. She didn't sell you short. She just couldn't help answering a few perfectly innocent questions." His eyes returned to Jeff, coldly. "We're not asking you to sign a release, Jeff. We're telling you."

Jeff stared at him in amazement. "Don't be silly," he blurted. "I'm not signing a release to you people. Do you think I'm out of my mind? Take it away, burn it and get yourself another guinea pig."

Dr. Schiml smiled quietly and shook his head. "We don't want another guinea pig, Jeff. That's just it. We want you."

A little line of sweat broke out on Jeff's forehead. "Look," he said hoarsely. "I'm not signing anything, do you understand? I've changed my mind. I don't care for the work here. I don't like the company."

Schiml's smile faded. He shrugged and tucked the white paper back into his white coat. "Just as you wish," he said. "The release is just a formality. Bring him along, boys."

"Wait!" Jeff was on his feet again, facing the guards, his eyes wide with fright. His eyes caught Schiml's. "Look, you've got things wrong. I'm a fake in here, a fraud. Can't you understand that? I didn't come in here to volunteer. I never intended to volunteer, never planned to go even as far as I did. I came here—"

Schiml made an impatient face and held up a hand. "Oh, yes, yes, I know all that. You came into this place because you'd followed a man in here and you wanted to kill him. You'd been hunting him for years, because you thought he murdered your father in cold blood and nothing would do but you kill him. Right?" Schiml blinked at Jeff, his voice heavy with boredom. "So you came in here and went through testing, hunting down your man, trying to find him. But you *didn't* find him. Now things have suddenly become too hot for your liking, so you figure that it's time to pull out. Right? Or are some of the details wrong?"

Jeff's jaw sagged, his face going pasty. "That slut girl—"

Schiml grimaced. "No, not Blackie. Blackie is discreet, in her own quiet way. She hasn't had anything to do with it. We've known about you all along, Jeff. And through a much more reliable source than Blackie." He glanced over his shoulder at one of the guards. "Bring him in," he said abruptly.

The door to the adjoining room opened and a man walked into the room. He was a tall, lean man; a gaunt-faced man with sallow cheeks and large, sad eyes; a weary-looking man whose hair was graying about the temples—a man whose whole body looked desperately tired.

And Schiml looked at the man and then he looked at the ceiling. "Hello, Paul," he said softly. "There's someone here who's been looking for you—"

A scream broke from Jeff's lips as he stared across the room. A raw animal scream ripped from his mouth like a knife. His lips twisted and he wrenched at the guards who were holding his arms, his face going purple, his eyes bulging.

With a roar he lunged at Conroe, bellowing, a torrent of hatred and abuse pouring from his lips. Again and again he screamed, his eyes blazing with an unholy fire of hatred. Conroe jerked back with a cry, and then Schiml was on his feet as Jeff lunged again, his muscles tightening like bands of steel under the flimsy shirt.

The guards fought to restrain him, and then the doctor was holding him too, crying: "Get out, Paul, quick!"

But Paul Conroe stood stock still, writhing from his hands to his head, his eyes filling with horrible pain. Suddenly the coffee cup jerked from the table, spun in the air and hurled straight for Conroe's head. It missed, smashing against the wall.

Jeff screamed again and the walls and ceiling began powdering off, plaster peeling down in great chunks, smashing off the walls onto the floor. A huge chunk fell from the ceiling, and then the curtains suddenly started to blaze, as if ignited by some magic fire. Finally, Conroe's clothing began smoking and smoldering.

Blackie screamed, staring at Jeff in open horror. Schiml's voice roared through the bedlam: "Get him! Sedate him, for God's sake, before he tears the place down on our ears!" Again Jeff roared his virulent hatred, and this time Conroe was the one who shouted:

"Stop him! He's tearing me apart inside. My God, stop him!"

Someone stepped between Jeff and Conroe. There was a flicker of glass and silver as a plunger was pressed home. Then suddenly Jeff's muscles gave out. His legs walked out from under him, and he felt himself sliding to the floor. But still he screamed, the face of the man who had tormented him all his life growing closer and closer, more and more vicious. Then suddenly everything around him went black. His last conscious impression was that of Blackie. She had her face in her hands and she was sobbing like a child in the corner.

*

He lay on the long table, wrapped in cool green surgical linens, motionless, barely breathing. His eyes were wide open, but sightless. They seemed to be staring straight up at the pale, glowing skylight in the ceiling. It was as if they were staring beyond, eons beyond, into some strange world that no human foot had ever trod.

His breath came slowly, a harsh sound in the still room. Sometimes it slowed almost to a stop, sometimes it accelerated. Dr. Schiml paused motionless by his side, waiting, watching breathlessly until the ragged wheeze slowed once again to normal.

Jeff lay like a corpse, but he was not dead. Near his head the panel of tiny lights flickered on and off, brighter and dimmer, carrying their simple on-or-off messages from the myriad microscopic endings on the tiny electrode that probed through the soft brain tissue.

No human being could ever analyze the waxing and waning of patterns on that panel, not even in five lifetimes. But a camera could film the changes, instant upon instant, flickering and flashing and glowing dully on and off, in a thousand thousand different figures and movements. And the computor could take these patterns from the film and analyze them and compare them. It would integrate them into the constantly changing picture that appeared on the small screen by the bedside.

It was a crude instrument, indeed, for the study of so exquisitely delicate and variable an instrument as a human brain, and no one knew this more painfully than Roger Schiml. But even such a crude instrument could probe into that strange half-world that they had sought so long to enter.

Near the bedside Paul Conroe sat motionless, his face drawn, his gaunt cheeks sunken. His eyes were wide and fearful as he watched the picture panel and his fingers trembled as he lit his pipe. He kept watching.

"It could be so dangerous," he murmured finally, turning to look at Schiml. "So terribly dangerous."

Schiml nodded gravely, adjusting the microvernier that controlled the probing instrument. "Of course it could be dangerous, but not too much so. Twenty years ago he'd have been dead already, but we haven't been wasting time all these years we've been waiting for him. Particularly in this cell-probing technique, we've ironed out the bugs. He'll survive, all right, unless we run into something mighty—"

Conroe shook his head. "Oh, no, no. I don't mean dangerous for him. I mean dangerous for us. Even he doesn't realize his power. How can we predict what sort of power it might be?" He looked up at Schiml, his eyes wide. "That room—it would have been gone in another five minutes, simply torn apart into molecular dust. He did it—and yet, I'd swear he didn't know what he was doing. I doubt if he even realized what was happening. And the fire—that was real fire, Roger. I know, I felt it burn me."

Schiml nodded eagerly. "Of course it was real fire! Set molecules to spinning at terrifically accelerated rates and you have fire. But those are the things we have to learn, Paul."

Conroe shook his head, fearfully. "We could both see the fire, but there was something else. You couldn't feel the hatred that was in that room. I could." He looked up, his eyes haunted. "God, Roger, how could a man hate that way? It was thick; it ran out into the room like syrup. Oh, I've felt hatred before in the minds I've contacted, many times. I've felt vile hatred before, but this was alive, crawling hate—" He sighed, his hands trembling. "It's in his mind, Roger. We don't know what else he might do, even under anesthetic, if we hit the right places. But it's in his mind. That we know. But why?"

Schiml nodded again. "That's the key question, of course. Why does he hate you so much? When we know that"—the doctor spread his hands—"we'll have the answer to twenty years' work, perhaps. And dangerous as it is, we've got to find out, while we have a chance, Paul. You know that. We can't stop now, not with what we know. We know that Jeff's insanity is far less active right now than his father's was. But unless we can locate the areas, find the location of both factors, the psychosis and the extra-sensory powers, we're lost. We'd have no recourse but to turn our findings over to the authorities. And you know what that would mean."

Conroe nodded wearily. "Yes, I know. Mass slaughter, sterilization, fear, panic—all the wrong answers. And even the panic alone would be fatal in our psychotic world."

Dr. Schiml shrugged and went back to the bedside. "We'll know soon, one way or the other," he said softly. "We're coming through right now."

CHAPTER TWELVE

The needle moved, probed ever so slightly, stimulating deep, deep in the soft, fragile tissue ... seeking, probing, recording. A twinge, the barest trace of shock, a sharp series of firing nerve cells, a flicker of light, a picture—Jeff Meyer *shifted, his eyelids lowering very slightly, and a muscle in his jaw began twitching involuntarily....*

*

He was floating gently on his back, resting on huge, fluffy, billowing clouds. He didn't know where he was, nor did he care. He just lay still, spinning gently, like a man in free fall, feeling the gentle clouds around him pressing him downward and downward. His eyes were closed tightly—so tightly that no ray of light might leak in. He knew as he floated that whatever happened, he dare not open them.

But then there were sounds around him. He felt his muscles tighten and he clasped his chest with his arms. There were *things* floating through the air around him, and they were making little sounds: tiny squeaks and groans. He shuddered, suddenly horribly afraid. The noises grew louder and louder, whispering into his ear, laughing at him.

He opened his eyes with a jolt, staring at the long, black, hollow tunnel he was falling through. He was spinning, end over end, faster and faster down the tunnel. He strained to see through the darkness to the bottom, but he couldn't. Then the laughter started. First little, quiet giggles, quite near his ear, but growing louder and louder—unpleasant laughs, chuckles, guffaws. They followed each other, peal upon peal of insane laughter, reverberating from the curved tunnel walls, growing louder and louder, more and more derisive. They were laughing at him—whoever they were—and their laughs rose into screams in his ears. Then to gain silence he was forced to scream out himself. And he clasped his hands to his ears and shut his eyes tight—and abruptly the laughter stopped. *Everything* stopped.

He lay tense, listening. No, not everything. There were some sounds. Somewhere in the distance he could hear the bzz-bzz-bzz of a cicada. It sounded sharp in the summer night air. He rolled over, felt the crisp sheets under him, the soft pillow, the rustling of the light blanket. Where?...

And then it came to him, clearly. He was in his room, waiting, waiting and expecting.

Daddy! Quite suddenly, he knew that Daddy had come home. There had been no sound in the dark house; he hadn't even heard the jet-car go into the garage, nor the front door squeak. But he had known, just the same, that Daddy was here. He blinked at the darkness, and little chills of fright ran up his spine. It was so dark, and he didn't like the dark, and he wished Daddy would come up and turn on the light. But Daddy had said ever since Mommy died that he must be a brave little man, even if he was only four....

He lay and shivered. There were other noises: outside the window, in the room—frightening noises. It was all very well to be a brave little man, but Daddy just didn't understand about the dark and the noises. And Daddy didn't understand about how he wanted somebody to hold him close and cuddle him and whisper to him.

And then he heard Daddy's step on the stair and felt him coming nearer. He rolled over and giggled, pretending to be asleep. Not that he'd fool Daddy for a minute. Daddy would already know he was awake. They played the same game night after night. But it was fun to play little games like that with Daddy. He waited, listening until he heard the door open, and the footsteps reach his bed. He heard Daddy's breathing. And then he rolled over and threw the covers off and jumped up like a little white ghost, shouting, "Boo! Did I scare you, Daddy?"

And then Daddy took him up on his shoulders and laughed, and said he was a big white horse come to carry little Jeff on a long journey. So they took the long journey down to the study for milk and cookies, just as they always did when Daddy came home. He knew Daddy didn't want any milk, of course. Daddy never drank milk at night with him. Daddy was much more interested in the funny cards, the cards he had watched Daddy make that day a year ago. Daddy had him run through them over and over and over ... circle, spiral, figure eight, letter B, letter R.... *It was a letter R, Daddy? But it couldn't have been, I know—oh, you're trying to catch me! Can we play with the marbles now, Daddy? Or the dice tonight? The round-cornered ones—they're much easier, you know.*

But Daddy would watch him as he read the cards, wrinkling up his nose and calling out the figure. And he would see Daddy mark down each right one and each wrong one. And then he would feel Daddy almost beaming happiness and satisfaction. And he would wait eagerly for Daddy to get out the dice, because they were so much more fun than the cards. *The square-cornered dice, Daddy? Oh, Daddy, they're so much harder. Oh, another game, a new one? Oh, good, Daddy. Teach me a new game with them, please. I'll try very hard to make them come out right.*

And then after the new game, Daddy told him a story before bed. It was one of his funny stories, where he *talked* the story, but put in all the fun and jokes and private things without any words.

It was funny. None of the others, like Mary Ann down the block, could feel their daddies like he could. Sometimes he wondered about it. He would tell Mary Ann about it as a special secret, but she wouldn't believe him. Nobody can hear their daddies without their daddies talking, she said. But he knew better.

And then there were thoughts creeping through his mind, feelings coming from Daddy that were uncomfortable feelings. He sat up suddenly in Daddy's arms and felt the chill pass through him.

"Daddy...."

"Yes, son."

"Why—why are you afraid, Daddy? What are you afraid of?"

And Daddy laughed and looked at him in a strange way and said, "Afraid? What do you mean, afraid?" But the afraidness was still there. Even when he went to bed and Daddy left him again, he could still feel the afraidness....

And then, abruptly, he was swinging into a vast, roaring whirlpool that swung around his head. He felt his body twisting in the blackness, swirling about, carried along without effort. He knew, somehow, that he was Jeff Meyer. And he knew that the needle was there, probing in his mind; he could feel it approach and withdraw. He could feel the twinge of recognition, the almost intangible sudden awareness and realization of a truth.

Then the seeker was gone: the probe finished in that area and moved on to the next. The whirlpool was a tunnel of rushing water, swinging about him, whirling him with lightning speed up ... up ... up; around, then down with a sickening rush. Then up again, as though he were riding the Wall of Death in a circus, around and around ... yet always drawing him in closer ... closer ... closer....

To what?

He knew he was fighting it, twisting with all his strength to fight against the impossible whirlpool which choked and carried him like a feather. He clenched his fists and fought, gritting his teeth, desperate, suddenly horribly afraid, more horribly afraid than he had ever been in his life. Down at the end of the tumultuous whirlpool, something lay—something horrid and ugly, something that had been wiped out of his mind, scoured out and disposed of long, long ago. *It was something he dared not face, never again.* Suddenly Jeff screamed and tried to force his mind back to that place. He tried desperately to remember, tried to see where the whirlpool was leading him before it was too late—*before it killed him*!

Something lay down there, waiting for him. It was more hideous than his mind could imagine—*something which could kill him.* Closer and closer he swept, helpless, his body growing rigid with fear, fighting, blood rushing through his veins. But he couldn't escape that closed, frantic alleyway to death.

Daddy was afraid. The thought screamed through Jeff's mind with the impact of a lightning bolt. It paralyzed his thoughts, tightened his muscles into rigid knots. Daddy was afraid ... afraid ... *afraid*—so horribly afraid.

The thought swept through him, congealing his blood. He cried out, shaking his head, trying to fight away the seeping stench of deadly fear, trying to clear it out of his mind. His face twisted in agony and his whole body wrenched. Suddenly, he was screaming and pounding his face against the ground. He was alone and his mind was wracked and obsessed by that horrible fear.

He opened his eyes and saw the turf under his head. Dimly, through the pain sweeping through his mind, he saw the grassy meadow on which he lay, completely by himself. The little singing brook was a few feet away. The afternoon sun was high, but the willow tree hung over him, covering him with cool shade. From somewhere a bird was singing.

"Daddy!" The word broke from his lips in a small scream, and he sat bolt upright, his hair tousled, his small, keen-featured eight-year-old face twisted with the pain and fear that tore through his mind. Some corner of his brain, so very remote, told him that he was not eight, that he was a grown man. But he saw his tiny hands, grubby with the dirt of the barnyard and lane through which he had walked in coming here. He had been driven here by the pain and fear and hatred that had been streaming into his mind.

It was Daddy. He knew it was Daddy, and Daddy was afraid. Daddy was running, with the desperation of a hunted animal, running down a corridor, his mind in a frenzy of fear. He was peering back over his shoulder, his breath coming in great gasps as he reached the end of the hall, wrenched vainly at the door and then collapsed against it. And while he sobbed in great gasps, tears of fear and desperation ran down his cheeks.

Jeff saw the door; he felt Daddy's body heaving, heard the furious pulse pounding in his own head. He saw the cold, darkened corridor, and his mind was picked up in the frenzied sweep of his father's thoughts, carried in a rush he could neither understand nor oppose. Stronger than ever before, his thoughts were Daddy's thoughts. He saw through Daddy's eyes; he felt through Daddy's body. In the closest rapport they had ever known, though Jeff lay here on the grassy plot, his body writhed with the pain and fear that Daddy was suffering miles distant.

They're coming, his mind screamed. *Trapped, trapped—what can I do?* Daddy was racing back up the corridor now, his eye catching an elevator standing open. He ran inside, groped frantically for the switch. He had to get away, had to get down below, somehow get to the street! Oh, God, what a mistake to walk into this place—an office building, of all places, where they could so easily follow him in, cut him off, trap him!

Why had he come? Why? He'd known they were hunting for him, knew they'd been getting closer and closer. But how could he have sensed that this day would bring a panic, that the stock market would take its nosedive this one particular day, putting the finger on him without any question, spotting him, pointing out his exact location to his hunters, beyond shadow of doubt?

How could he have known? This was to have been the final test, the test to prove the force he had in his mind—the force which had been destroying and destroying and destroying. And it had emanated from his own mind in some unspeakable way, uncontrolled, unbelieved and misunderstood. It was the force which had brought the hunters to him.

But not now! Oh, please, please, not now—not when he was so close to the answer. Not when he was so close. Slowly, helpless anger seethed through his mind. They had no right to stop him now. In another day, another week, he could have the answer. In another few days he would have corralled this frightening power, controlled it. He knew he could find the answer. He stood on the very brink. But now the hunters had trapped him—

Why, Daddy? Why are they hunting you? Oh, Daddy, Daddy, please, I'm so scared! Please, Daddy, come home. Please don't be so much afraid, Daddy. I'm so frightened....

The elevator gave a lurch. He fell against the door as the car ground to a halt between floors. Frantically, he pounded the button, waited through long eternities as the car sat, silent, motionless. Then his fingers ran hastily along the cracks in the car door, seeking a hold, trying desperately to wrench open the locked door.

He felt them coming, somewhere above him, somewhere below him. Then something tore loose in his mind; some last dam of control broke, and he was screaming his defiance at them, screaming his hatred, his bitterness. They had him, they were going to kill him without trial, shoot him down like a mad dog. He felt them flinch and cower back at the stream of hatred roaring out of his mind, felt them move back. They were afraid of him, but they were determined to kill him.

A sound above! He flattened back against the elevator wall, wrenching at the metal grating with superhuman strength, trying to twist open the metal, to find some way into the shaft below. Someone was coming down from above, down onto the top of the elevator; someone whose mind was filled with fear, but who moved with determination. There was a scraping sound from above, a dull twang of cable striking against cable.

They could be cutting the car loose.

He leaped for the ceiling of the car, stabbing up with his fingers for the little escape doorway. Sheer hatred drove his legs as he jumped and jumped again, until the door flew up. His hand caught the rim, and he dragged his body up. He jerked his shoulders through the small opening, heaving and lunging through to the top of the car.

He looked up. He saw a face, a single face, hanging mistily above him. Dimly he made out the form of a man hanging on the cable twenty feet above. His legs were wrapped around the cables and one hand carried the small, dully gleaming weapon. His mind screamed hatred at the man, and he grabbed at the cables, wrenching them, shaking them like a huge tree.

He saw the man slowly moving down, spinning back and forth helplessly as the cables vibrated. But he held on tenaciously, moving closer.

Daddy! Stop him! Daddy, don't let him kill you.

The face came into clearer view: a thin face, an evil one, twisted with fear and pain. The figure moved slowly down the cables, slowly turning, lifting the arm with the weapon, patiently trying to take aim. It was a gaunt face, with high cheekbones, slightly bulging eyes, high flat forehead, graying hair. *Remember that face, Jeff. Never forget that face, that face is the face of the man who is butchering your father.* Hatred streamed out at the face; he crouched back against the wall of the shaft, wrenching at the cables, trying vainly to shake the killer loose. He had to get him first; he had to stop him. *He's so close; he's turning; the gun is raising. I'll never get him—*

The face, hovering close, eyes wide—the face of a ghoul—and below the face was the dull, round hole of the gun muzzle, just inches away. A finger tightened. A horrible flash came, straight in the eyes—

Daddy!

The thoughts screamed through his mind: the bitter, naked hatred, the hatred of madness, streaming out in one last searing inferno. Then came a sickening lurch, a lurch of maddened fear and hate. And there was the snuffing out of a light, leaving darkness....

Daddy! No, Daddy. No, I can't feel you any more, Daddy. What have they done to you? Oh, please, Daddy, talk to me. Talk to me. No, no, no. Oh, Daddy, Daddy, Daddy....

Dr. Schiml looked up from the pale, prostrate form after a long time; his forehead was beaded with sweat. The color had drained almost completely from Jeff's face, and his skin had taken a waxy cast. His breathing was so shallow it was hardly audible in the still room, and the panel of flickering lights had become almost completely still.

"We can't go on yet," said Dr. Schiml, his voice hoarse. "We'll have to wait." He turned and walked across the room, trying to keep his eyes away from the prostrate form on the bed; yet everywhere he went, it seemed his eyes caught the idiotic stare in the man's blank eyes. "Well have to wait," he repeated, and his voice was almost a sob.

CHAPTER THIRTEEN

Paul Conroe moved for the first time, running a hand through his thick gray hair as he glanced up at Schiml. "Some of that came through to me, even now," he said weakly. His face, also, was ashen and his eyes were haunted. "To think that he hated me that much, and to think *why* he hated me—" He shook his head and buried his face in his hands. "I never knew about the old man and the son. I just never knew. If I'd known, I'd never have done it."

The room was still for a long moment. Then Schiml blinked at Conroe, his hands trembling. "So this is the tremendous power, the mutant strain we've been trying to trace for so long."

"This is one of the tremendous powers," Conroe replied wearily. "Jeff probably has all the power that his father had, though it hasn't all matured yet. It's just latent, waiting for the time that the genes demand of his body for fulfillment. Nothing more. And other people have the same powers. Hundreds, thousands of other people. Somewhere, a hundred and fifty years ago, there was a change—a little change in one man or one woman."

He looked up at Schiml, the haunted look still in his large eyes. "Extra-sensory powers—no doubt of it, a true mutant strain, but tied in to a sleeper—a black gene that spells insanity. One became two and two spread to four—extra-sensory power and gene-linked insanity. Always together, growing, insidiously growing like a cancer. And it's eating out the roots of our civilization."

He stood up, walked across the room and stared down at the pallid-faced man in the bed. "This answers so many things, Roger," he said finally. "We knew old Jacob Meyer had a son, of course. We even suspected then that the son might share some of his powers. But this! We never dreamed it. The father and son were practically two people with one mind, in almost perfect mutual rapport. Only the son was so young he couldn't understand what was wrong. All he knew was that he 'felt' Daddy and could tell what Daddy was thinking. Actually, everything that went on in his father's mind—*everything*—was in his mind too. At least, in the peak of the old man's cycle of insanity—"

Schiml looked up sharply. "Then there's no doubt in your mind that the old man was insane?"

Conroe shook his head. "Oh, no. There was no doubt. He was insane, all right. A psychiatric analysis of his behavior was enough to convince me of that, even if following him and watching him wasn't. He had a regular cycle of elation and depression, so regular it could almost be clocked. He'd even spotted the symptoms of the psychosis himself, back in his college days. But of course he hadn't realized what it was. All he knew was that at certain times he seemed to be surrounded by these peculiar phenomena, which happened rapidly and regularly at those times when he was feeling elated, on top of the world. And at other times he seemed to carry with him an aura of depression. Actually, when he hit the blackest depths of his depressions, he would be bringing about whole waves of suicides and depression—errors and everything else."

Conroe took a deep breath. "We knew all this at the time, of course. What we didn't know was that the old man had been seeking the answer himself, actively seeking it. All we knew was that he was actively the most dangerous man alive on Earth, and that until he was killed he would become more and more dangerous—dangerous enough to shake the very roots of our civilization."

Schiml nodded slowly. "And you're sure that his destructive use of his power was a result directly of the insanity?"

Conroe frowned. "Not quite," he said after a moment. "Actually, you couldn't say that Jacob Meyer 'used' his extra-sensory powers. They weren't, for the most part, the kind of powers he could either control or 'use.' They were the sort of powers that just happened. He had a power, and when he was running high—in a period of elation, when everything was on top of the world—the power functioned. He fairly exuded this power that he carried, and the higher he rose in his elation, the more viciously dangerous the power became."

Conroe stopped, staring at the bed for a long moment. "The hellish thing was that it couldn't possibly be connected up with a human power at all. After all, how can one human being have an overwhelming effect on the progress of a business cycle? He can't, of course, unless he's a dictator, or a tremendously powerful person in some other field. And Jacob Meyer was neither. He was a simple, half-starved statistician with a bunch of ideas that he couldn't even understand himself, much less sell to anyone who could do anything with them. Or how can a man, *just by being in the vicinity*, tip the balance that topples the stock market into an almost irreparable sag?"

Conroe leaned forward, groping for words. "Jacob Meyer's psychokinesis was not the sort of telekinesis that we saw Jeff turning against me in that room a couple of hours ago. He could probably have managed that, too, if he had hated me enough. But if Jacob Meyer's mind had merely affected physical things—the turn of a card, the fall of the dice, the movement of molecules from one place to another—he would have been a simple problem. We could have isolated him, studied him. But it wasn't that simple."

Paul Conroe sat back, regarding Schiml with large, sad eyes. "It would have been impossible to prove in a court of law. We knew it and the government knew it. That was why they appointed us assassins to deal with him. *Because Jacob Meyer's mind affected probabilities*. By his very presence, in a period of elation, he upset the normal probabilities of occurrences going on around him. We watched him, Roger. It was incredible. We watched him in the stock market, and we saw the panic start almost the moment he walked in. We saw the buyers suddenly and inexplicably change their minds and start selling instead of buying. We saw what happened in the Bank of the Metropolis that first day we tried for him. He was scared, his mind was driven into a peak of fear and anger; it started a bank run that morning that nearly bankrupted the most powerful financial house on the East Coast! We saw this one little man's personal, individual influence on international diplomacy, on finances, on gambling in Reno, on the thinking and acting of the man on the street. It was incredible, Roger."

"But surely Jacob Meyer wasn't the only one—"

"Oh, there were others, certainly. We've a better idea of that, now, after all these years of study. There were and are thousands and thousands—some like me, some much worse—all carrying some degree of extra-sensory power from that original mutant strain, all with the gene-linked psychosis paired up with it every time. And we've seen our civilization struggling against these thousands just to keep its feet. But Jacob Meyer was the first case of the whole, full-blown change in one man that we'd ever found. He was running wild, his mind was completely insane. And the extra-sensory powers he carried were so firmly enmeshed in the insanity that there was no separating the two. Meyer tipped us off. He set us on the trail, and the trail led to his son after he was dead—"

"Yes, the son. We have the son." Schiml scowled at the shallow-breathing form on the bed. "We should have had him before—years before."

"Of course we should. But the son vanished after his father's death. We never knew why he vanished—until now. But now we know that when we killed his father, we did more than just that. We almost killed our last chance to catch this thing and study it before it was too late. Because when we killed Jeff's father, *we killed Jeff Meyer too.*"

Schiml scowled. "I don't follow. He's still alive."

"Oh, of course he's still alive. But can't you see what happened to him? He was living in his father's mind; he knew everything his father knew—but he didn't understand it. He thought with his father's thoughts, he saw through his father's eyes, because they were mutually and completely telepathic. He felt his father's fear and frustration and bitterness when we trapped him in that office building finally. He lay screaming on the ground on a farm somewhere, but actually he was in his father's mind.

"It was a mad mind, a mind rising to the highest screaming heights of mania, as he waited for me to come down and kill him. And Jeff was surrounded with his father's hatred. He saw my face through his father's eyes, and all he could understand was that his daddy was being butchered and that I was butchering him. When the bullet went into his father's brain and split his skull open, Jeff Meyer felt that too. When his father died, Jeff died too—a part of him, that is. They were one mind and part of that one mind was destroyed."

Conroe paused, his forehead covered with perspiration. The room was silent except for the hoarse breathing of the man on the table. Conroe's face, as he looked down, was that of a ghost.

"No wonder the boy disappeared," he whispered. "He'd been shot through the head. He was almost virtually dead. He must have gone into shock for years after such a trauma, Roger. He must have spent years roaming that farm, cared for by an aunt or uncle or cousin, while he slowly recovered. No wonder we could find no trace. And then, when he did get well, all he knew was that his father had been murdered. He didn't know how; he didn't know why, and he dared never remember the truth. Because, the truth was that *he* had been killed. All he dared recognize was my face—a recurrent, nightmarish hallucination, rising out of his dreams, plaguing him on the streets, tormenting him day and night."

"But you were hunting him."

"Oh, yes, we were hunting him. It was inevitable that sooner or later we would come up face to face. But when we did, I received such a horrible mental blow that I couldn't even look to see what he looked like. I could do nothing but scream and run. When he saw me that day in the night club, he took complete leave of his senses. He exploded into hatred and bitterness. And then he resolved to hunt me down and kill me for killing his father."

Conroe spread his hands apologetically. "It seemed good sense to use that hatred and singleness of purpose to draw him here. But it was torture. He followed me with his mind, without even knowing it. It was old Jacob Meyer's face that haunted me everywhere I went. I didn't know why, then, because I didn't know Jeff had been part of that mind. And Jeff didn't know that he carried and broadcast that horror wherever he went."

Conroe leaned back, his body limp in exhaustion. "We needed Jeff so desperately. Yes, we needed him in here, for testing, for this study. It's been a long, tedious job, studying him, observing him, photographing him, learning how much of his father's power he had. And we dared not bring him in here until we were sure it was safe. And now, with what he knows, he is more vitally dangerous than his father ever was. There are hundreds that carry the change, in larger or smaller part, all gene-linked with insanity. And Jeff Meyer is insane as any of the rest of them. But at least there's hope, because we can study him now. Because unless we can somehow separate the function of the insanity from the function of the psychokinesis, we have no choice left, no hope."

Schiml looked up, his eyes wide. "No choice—"

"—but to kill them, every one. To hunt out the strain and wipe it from the face of the Earth so ruthlessly and completely that it can never rise again. And to wipe out with it the first new link in the evolution of Man since the dawn of history."

Slowly Roger Schiml's eyes traveled from Jeff Meyers' form on the bed to Paul Conroe's grave face. "There's no other way?"

"None," said Paul Conroe.

*

"Jeff," said Dr. Schiml. "Jeff Meyer."

The figure on the cot stirred ever so slightly. The eyes slowly closed, then reopened, looking slightly less blank. Jeff's lips parted in an almost inaudible groan, hardly more than a breath.

"Jeff. You've got to hear me a minute. Listen, Jeff, we're trying to help you. Can you hear that? We're trying to help you, Jeff, and we need your help."

The eyes shifted, turned to Schiml's face. They were haunted eyes—eyes that had seen the grave and beyond it.

"Please, Jeff. Listen. We're hunting. We're trying to find a way to help you. You know about your father now, the truth about your father, don't you?"

The eyes wavered, came back, and the head nodded ever so slightly. "I know," came the sighing reply.

"You've got to tell us what to do, Jeff. There are good powers here in your mind, and there are terrible powers, ruinous powers. We've got to find them both, find where they lie, how they work. You must tell us, as we probe—tell us when we strike the good, when we strike the bad. Do you understand, Jeff?"

Again the head nodded. Jeff's jaw tightened a trifle and an expression of infinite fatigue crossed his face. "Go on, Doc."

Dr. Schiml leaned over the proper controls and moved the dial on the microvernier. He moved it again, watching, moving it still again. A fine sweat broke out on his forehead as he worked, and he felt Conroe's soft eyes on him, waiting, hoping....

And then a whimper broke from Jeff's lips, an indefinable sound, helpless and childlike, a little cry of terror. Dr. Schiml looked up, his heart thumping in his throat. Jeff's eyes were wide again, staring lifelessly, and his breath was shallow and thready. Schiml glanced quickly at Conroe, then back, his eyes reflecting the fear and tension in his mind. And as he worked his shoulders slumped forward, prepared for defeat. Because what he was doing was impossible, and he knew it was impossible. But he knew, above all, that it had to succeed.

CHAPTER FOURTEEN

He was spinning like a top, end over end, as though he had sprung off a huge, powerful diving board. He rose higher and higher into the air. Lying tense, Jeff knew that his body was still on the soft bed, yet he felt his feet rising, his head sinking, as he spun head over heels through the blackness. And he could feel the tiny probing needle, seeking, hunting, stimulating....

A siren noise burst in his ears: a shimmering blast of screeching musical sound that sent cold shivers down his back. Then it leveled off to an up-and-down whine that gradually became a blat of static in his ear. Somewhere, out of the uneven grating of the noise, he heard a voice whispering in his ear, hoarsely. He paused, straining to hear, trying to catch an occasional word.

He knew that there were no voices outside of his body. He was sure of that. Yet he heard the sound, deeper in his ear, louder and softer, then louder again. It whispered to him, carrying a note of deepest urgency in the soft sibilants. Quite suddenly, it seemed vitally important to hear what the voice was saying, for the words were clearly directed at him. He shifted slightly and listened harder, until the words came through clearly.

And then he gasped, a feeling of panic sweeping through him. He heard the words and they were nonsense words, sounds without meanings. Something stirred in his mind, some vague memory of nonsense words, of a horrible shock. Had there been a shock? But the strange sounds frightened him, driving fear down through the marrow of his bones. The whispering sounds were sinister: babbling sounds, sounds of words that *needed* meaning and had none—half-words, garbled, twisted, meaningless.

Cautiously he opened his eyes, peered through the murky blackness to see the whisperers. His eyes fastened on two shapeless forms, tall, ghostly, in black robes with hoods drawn up over their faces. The figures leaned on their sticks and held their heads together. They babbled nonsense to each other with such fierce earnestness that they seemed somehow horridly ridiculous. Taking a deep breath, Jeff started toward the two figures, then stopped short, his heart pounding wildly in his throat.

Because the moment he had made a move toward them, the figures turned sharply toward him, and their nonsense voices had suddenly become clear for the briefest moment. They became clear and unmistakable and heavy with horrible meaning: "Stay away, Jeff Meyer. Stay away."

He stared about, trembling, trying to place himself, trying to find some landmark. The hooded figures turned back to each other and began babbling once again. But now they seemed to be standing before an archway—a gloomy, gray archway which they seemed to be guarding. Slowly, slyly, Jeff started to move away from them. But he watched them from stealthy eyes, and as he moved away the gloom about him cleared, and things were suddenly brighter. And then there was singing in his ears, joyous choruses bursting forth in happy song. A great feeling of relief and complacency settled down upon him like a mantle. He smiled and breathed deeper and started to roll over.

"*What was that, Jeff? What did we strike?*"

He shook his head violently, a frown creasing his face. "Stay away," he muttered. "The old men, they were there." Suddenly he felt himself twist around until he was facing the hooded figures again, and his feet were moving him toward them again, involuntarily, inexorably. And then the nonsense words settled out again, more menacingly, louder this time than before: "No closer, Jeff Meyer. Stay away—away—away."

"Can't go there," he muttered aloud.

"*Why not, Jeff?*"

"They won't let me. I've got to stay away."

"*What are they guarding, Jeff?*"

"I don't know. I don't know, I tell you. I've got to stay away!"

And then suddenly the singing dissolved into a hideous cacophony of clashing sounds, a din that nearly deafened him. A huge wave suddenly swept up around him. It was like a breaker at the ocean's edge, swirling up, surrounding him, catching him up and hurling him head over heels down a long, whirling tunnel. Desperately he fought for balance and finally found his feet under him once again. But then the ground was moving under him. He ran frantically, until his breath came in short gasps and his blood pounded in his ears. Then he caught a branch that swept by near him, and raised himself up as the flooding water roared underneath him.

The sky around him was clouding over blackly. Far in the distance he saw a blinding flash of lightning, ripping through the sky, bringing the bleak, wind-torn landscape into sharp relief in his mind as he clung to the branch. He heard a flapping of wings as a huge, black vulture skimmed by. And then the rain began to fall, a cold, soaking rain that ate through his clothes and soaked his skin. It ran in torrents into his eyes and ears and mouth.

And then he heard voices all around him. How could there be voices here? For there were no people, no sign of warm-blooded life. But there were voices, pleasant ones. They came from all sides. He could see no one, but he could *feel* them.

Feel them! He gasped in pure joy, shooting out his mind eagerly, unbelievingly, searching out the sudden feeling of perfect, warm *contact* he had just felt. And then his mind was running from person to person, dozens of persons, and he could feel them all, as clearly, as wondrously as he had ever felt his father—sharply, beautifully.

He cried out, he cried out for joy. Tears of unrelieved happiness rolled down his cheeks as he stretched out his mind and embraced the thoughts of the people he could feel but not see. And he felt his own thoughts being met, being caught and embraced and understood.

"Right here!" he shouted. "Schiml, this is it, don't lose it, man. This is the center. I'm controlling it. You've got it now. *Work it, Schiml. Work it for all you've got.* "

And then he looked at the black, menacing sky around him, and his mind laughed and cried out for the clouds to go away. And there was a wild whirling of clouds and they broke, and the sun was streaming down upon him suddenly. He threw himself from the tree, ran down the hillside. He felt a wonderful, overpowering freedom he had never felt before, his mind free to soar and soar without hindrance. There was nothing now to stand between it and complete understanding of all men. It was a mind which could go wherever he wanted it to go, do whatever he wished.

He ran down toward the bottom of the hill and felt his control growing with every step he took. He knew when he reached the bottom of the hill that the battle would be won, so he ran all the faster.

And then, like some horrible nightmare, the hooded figures loomed up directly in his path, long bony fingers stabbing out at him accusingly. He fell flat on his face at the overpowering warning in the voices that struck him. And he lay at the feet of the figures and sobbed, his whole body shaking with bitter, hopeless sobs. And the dark clouds gathered again. He was too late, too late.

"What are they guarding, Jeff? "

"I don't know. I don't know. I can't break through."

"You've got to, Jeff. You've got to! We've got the extra-sensory center. We've found it, but something is blocking it. Jeff, something is keeping you away. You've got to see what— "

"I can't. Oh, I can't. Please, don't make me!"

"You must, Jeff! "

"No!"

"Go on, Jeff. "

He stood up, facing the hood figures, cowering, his whole body trembling. Deep in his mind he could feel the probing needle, moving, slowly moving, forcing him nearer and nearer to the grim figures. Slowly his feet moved, dragging in fear, a paralyzing fear that demanded every ounce of strength he possessed to make his legs function. And the voices, laden with menace, were grating in his ear, "Stay out, stay away. If you want to live, stay away ... away ... away...."

He moved closer and closer to the hooded figures, leaned forward to peer around them toward the gray, ghastly gate they guarded—a gate heavy with mold and rusty iron braces.

And then he reached up and threw back the hood of the first figure, stared at the face it had covered, and burst into a scream.

It was his own face!

He turned and threw back the other hood and peered intently, fighting to see the face before the features blurred out beyond recognition. It was his face, too, unmistakable. With a roar of anger and frustration he reached out, tore away the hoods, ripped them off, one with each hand, and wrenched away the enclosing shrouds.

The figures were skeletons with his face! He struck them and they shattered like thin glass, falling down in pieces at his feet. And he brushed his feet through the debris and turned to press his shoulder against the gate, heaving against it until it swung open, creaking on rusty hinges. It swung open—*on the face of madness* .

He screamed twice, short, frantic screams, as he tried to hide his eyes from the rotten, writhing horror behind the gate.

"Here!" he screamed. "It's here. You're at the right place. This is what you're looking for. Cut it out. Slice it away. Please, I can't stand it any longer."

His feet moved through the horrible gate, into the swarming, loathsome, horror-ridden madness that lay beyond. And he screamed again as he saw the bright flash. He felt the wrenching, sickening lurch that took him and threw him to the ground, down the long, twisting channels of darkness, as the pain struck through his head.

Suddenly there was another blinding flash, and he felt his muscles and his mind crumble into dust. He fell and quivered and lay helplessly, as his mind sifted and drained away into the porous earth beneath him.

*

When he opened his eyes, he saw Conroe's face. He was tense for a moment, every muscle going into spasm. Then suddenly he relaxed and blinked and stared up at Conroe's face, his eyes filled with wonder.

"I'm sorry, Jeff. I don't know the words to tell you how sorry." There were tears in Conroe's eyes, and Jeff watched them and felt a chill of wonder run down his spine. For Conroe was not using words at all and yet he *knew* what Conroe wanted to say.

Wordlessly he reached up, took the man's hand, pressed it briefly and let it fall on the blanket again. "There aren't those kinds of words," he murmured.

"And you feel all right?"

Jeff blinked, sudden wonder dawning in his eyes. "I—I—I'm alive!" He struggled to sit up, felt the twinge of pain shoot down his spine.

Schiml moved up to the bedside and gently eased him back into the softness of the bed. "Yes," he said happily, "you're alive. And you're well. And there's no irony in calling you a Mercy Man." His eyes gleamed in happy triumph. "You're a whole man, Jeff—the way you were intended to be—for the first time in your life."

The words came to him clearly, yet Jeff knew that not a single word had been audible in the room. "Just like my father," he murmured. "I just felt him, just knew what he was thinking."

Tears were running down Schiml's cheeks, and his face was so infinitely happy that he hardly seemed the same man. He raised a finger, silently pointed to the water glass on the table and looked at Jeff. Jeff turned his eyes to the glass, and it rose half an inch from the table and hung there, glowing slightly in the dim light of the room. Then it gently set back on the stand.

"Control," Jeff said softly. "I have control."

"The power was chained down to something else," Schiml said softly. "You had the extra-sensory power, yes, but it was linked to something that would have prevented you from ever gaining control. A degenerative insanity, part and parcel of the extra-sensory power. You're not alone, Jeff. There are many hundreds like you, in greater or lesser degrees. Conroe is like you, to a very limited extent. And he's been seeking a way to separate the two, for years. That's why you're really a Mercy Man. We knew there were two centers, but we knew no way to separate them. We had to have you to guide us, Jeff. We had to find the center of insanity in your brain to cut it out and deliver you. That's what we've waited twenty years for. And you're free, now. It's gone. And now we have a technique we can use to free a thousand others like you."

Jeff stared at them wonderingly. Sunlight streamed in the window. Across the way, he could see the ward-towers of the Hoffman Medical Center, white and gleaming. He took a deep breath of the fresh air and turned again to the two men standing by the bedside.

"Then it was you who were hunting me," he murmured. "Strange, isn't it. It wasn't me hunting Conroe. It was my father, the ghost of my father still in my mind. The ghost of a madman—" His eyes narrowed and he stared at Schiml closely. "Then there were others who knew too. Blackie knew. She must have been the girl in the night club."

"She was. A little heavy make-up, a little light plastic, those made enough change to deceive you. But she never knew why. Hypnotics can be powerful and they can erase all memory." He paused, smiling at Jeff. "Blackie will be next. We need her so much in the work we have to do, almost as much as we need you. But you've freed Blackie too. She'll be happier than she's ever been since the cloak of bad luck began broadcasting from her mind ten years ago. She'll be happier by far."

*

Hours later, Jeff woke again in the still room. The men were gone and the shadows were lengthening in the room, and his mind was filled with many thoughts.

"You can go if you want," Paul Conroe had said before they left. "Or you can stay, as you see fit. If you go, we can't stop you. But we beg you to stay. We need you so very much."

There would be others staying, Jeff thought. The Nasty Frenchman would stay—sneering, laughing, hating—aiming at the big money that always lurked in the future, unaware completely of the errand of mercy he was running with his life. And Harpo would stay, and all the others....

And Blackie would stay too. Poor, helpless Blackie—beautiful Blackie, desperate Blackie. For her there was a new lease. And there was no way of telling the person she would be after the new lease was signed for her.

And Conroe would stay, delivered after all these years of the burden he carried.

Wearily, yet happily, Jeff stared at the ceiling. He breathed deeply of the quiet air, his mind filled with a maze of wondering thoughts. He knew that thinking now was useless, that there really wasn't any issue any more.

He knew, as he closed his eyes again, that Jeff Meyer would stay too.

GOLD IN THE SKY

TABLE OF CONTENTS

TROUBLE TIMES TWO

The sun was glowing dull red as it slipped down· behind the curving horizon of Mars, but Gregory Hunter was not able to see it.

There was no viewscreen in the ship's cabin; it was too tiny for that. Greg twisted around in the cockpit that had been built just big enough to hold him, and shifted his long legs against the brace-webbing, trying to get them comfortable.

He knew he was afraid ... but nobody else knew that, not even the captain waiting at the control board on the satellite, and in spite of the fear Greg Hunter would not have traded places at this moment with anyone else in the universe.

He had worked too hard and waited too long for this moment.

He heard the count-down monitor clicking in his ears, and his hands clenched into fists. How far from Mars would he be ten minutes from now? He didn't know. Farther than any man had ever traveled before in the space of ten minutes, he knew, and faster. How far and how fast would depend on him alone.

"All set, Greg?" It was the captain's voice in the earphones.

"All set, Captain."

"You understand the program?"

Greg nodded. "Twenty-four hours out, twenty-four hours back, ninety degrees to the ecliptic, and all the accelleration I can stand both ways."

Greg grinned to himself. He thought of the months of conditioning he had gone through to prepare for this run ... the hours in the centrifuge to build up his tolerance to accelleration, the careful diet, the rigorous hours of physical conditioning. It was only one experiment, one tiny step in the work that could someday give men the stars, but to Gregory Hunter at this moment it was everything.

"Good luck, then." The captain cut off, and the blastoff buzzer sounded.

He was off. His heart hammered in his throat, and his eyes ached fiercely, but he paid no attention. His finger crept to the air-speed indicator, then to the cut-off switch. When the pressure became too great, when he began to black out, he would press it.

But not yet. It was speed they wanted; they had to know how much accelleration a man could take for how long and still survive, and now it was up to him to show them.

Fleetingly, he thought of Tom ... poor old stick-in-the-mud Tom, working away in his grubby little Mars-bound laboratory, watching bacteria grow. Tom could never have qualified for a job like this. Tom couldn't even go into free-fall for ten minutes without getting sick all over the place. Greg felt a surge of pity for his brother, and then a twinge of malicious anticipation. Wait until Tom heard the reports on *this* run! It was all right to spend your time poking around with bottles and test tubes if you couldn't do anything else, but it took something special to pilot an XP ship for Project Star-Jump. And after this run was over, even Tom would have to admit it....

There was a lurch, and quite suddenly the enormous pressure was gone.

Something was wrong. He hadn't pushed the cut-off button, yet the ship's engines were suddenly silent. He jabbed at the power switch. Nothing happened. Then the side-jets sputted, and he was slammed sideways into the cot.

He snapped on the radio speaker. "Control ... can you hear me? Something's gone wrong out here...."

"Nothing's wrong," the captain's voice said in his earphones. "Just sit tight. I'm bringing you back in. There's a call here from Sun Lake City. They want you down there in a hurry. We'll have to scratch you on this run."

"*Who* wants me down there?"

"The U.N. Council office. Signed by Major Briarton himself and I can't argue with the Major. We're bringing you in."

Greg Hunter sank back, disappointment so thick he could taste it in his mouth. Sun Lake City! That meant two days at least, one down, one back, maybe more if connections weren't right. It meant that the captain would send Morton or one of the others out in his place. It meant....

Suddenly he thought of what else it meant, and a chill ran up his back.

There was only one reason Major Briarton would call him in like this. Something had happened to Dad.

Greg leaned back in the cot, suddenly tense, as a thousand frightful possibilities flooded his mind. It could only mean that Dad was in some kind of trouble.

And if anything had happened to Dad....

*

The sun was sinking rapidly toward the horizon when the city finally came into sight in the distance, but try as he would, Tom Hunter could not urge more than thirty-five miles an hour from the huge lurching vehicle he was driving.

On an open paved highway the big pillow-wheeled Sloppy Joe would do sixty in a breeze, but this desert route was far from a paved road. Inside the pressurized passenger cab, Tom gripped the shock-bars with one arm and the other leg, and jammed the accelerator to the floor. The engine coughed, but thirty-five was all it would do.

Through the windshield Tom could see the endless rolling dunes of the Martian desert stretching to the horizon on every side. They called Mars the Red Planet, but it was not red when you were close to it. There were multitudes of colors here ... yellow, orange, brown, gray, occasional patches of gray-green ... all shifting and changing in the fading sunlight. Off to the right were the worn-down peaks of the Mesabi II, one of the long, low mountain ranges of almost pure iron ore that helped give the planet its dull red appearance from outer space. And behind him, near the horizon, the tiny sun glowed orange out of a blue-black sky.

Tom fought the wheel as the Sloppy Joe jounced across a dry creek bed, and swore softly to himself. Why hadn't he kept his head and waited for the mail ship that had been due at the Lab to give him a lift back? He'd have been in Sun Lake City an hour ago ... but the urgency of the message had driven caution from his mind.

A summons from the Mars Coordinator of the U.N. Interplanetary Council was the same as an order ... but there was more to Tom's haste than that. There was only one reason that Major Briarton would be calling him in to Sun Lake City, and that reason meant trouble.

Something was wrong. Something had happened to Dad.

Now Tom peered up at the dark sky, squinting into the sun. Somewhere out there between Mars and Jupiter was a no-man's-land of danger, a great circling ring of space dirt and debris, the Asteroid belt. And somewhere out there, Dad was working.

Tom thought for a moment of the pitiful little mining rig that Roger Hunter had taken out to the Belt ... the tiny orbit-ship to be used for headquarters and storage of the ore; the even tinier scout ship, Pete Racely's old *Scavenger* that he had sold to Roger Hunter for back taxes and repairs when he went broke in the Belt looking for his Big Strike. It wasn't much of a mining rig for anybody to use, and the dangers of a small mining operation in the Asteroid Belt were frightening. It took skill to bring a little scout-ship in for a landing on an asteroid rock hardly bigger than the ship itself; it took even more skill to rig the controlled-Murexide charges to blast the rock into tiny fragments, and then run out the shiny magnetic net to catch the explosion debris and bring it in to the hold of the orbit-ship....

Tom Hunter scowled, trying to shake off the feeling of uneasiness that was nibbling at his mind. Asteroid mining was dangerous ... but Dad was no novice. Nobody on Mars knew how to handle a mining rig better than Roger Hunter did. He knew what he was doing out there, there was no real danger for him or was there....

Roger Hunter, a good man, a gentle and peaceful man, had finally seen all he could stomach of Jupiter Equilateral and its company mining policies six months before. He had told them so in plain, simple language when he turned in his resignation. They didn't try to stop him ... a man was still free to quit a job on Mars if he wanted to, even a job with Jupiter Equilateral. But it was an open secret that the big mining outfit had not liked Roger Hunter's way of resigning, taking half a dozen of their first-rate mining engineers with him. There had been veiled threats, rumors of attempts to close the markets to Roger Hunter's ore, in open violation of U.N. Council policies on Mars....

Tom fought the wheel as the big tractor lumbered up another rise, and the huge plastic bubble of Sun Lake City came into view far down the valley below.

He thought of Greg. Had Greg been summoned too? He closed his lips tightly as a wave of anger passed through his mind. If anything had happened, no matter what, he thought, Greg would be there. Taking over and running things, as usual. He thought of the last time he had seen his brother, and then deliberately blocked out the engulfing bitterness.

That had been more than a year ago. Maybe Greg had changed since then.

But somehow, Tom didn't think so.

The Sloppy Joe was on the valley floor now, and ahead the bubble covering the city was drawing closer. The sun was almost gone; lights were appearing inside the plastic shielding. Born and raised on Mars, Tom had seen the teeming cities of Earth only once in his life ... but to him none of the splendors of the Earth cities could match the simple, quiet beauty of this Martian outpost settlement. There had been a time when people had said that Sun Lake City could never be built, that it could never survive if it were, but with each successive year it grew larger and stronger, the headquarters city for the planet that had become the new frontier of Earth.

The radiophone buzzed, and the airlock guard hailed him when he returned the signal. Tom gave his routine ID. He guided the tractor into the lock, waited until pressure and atmosphere rose to normal, and then leaped out of the cab.

Five minutes later he was walking across the lobby of the Interplanetary Council building, stepping into the down elevator. Three flights below he stepped out into the office corridor of the U.N. Interplanetary Council on Mars.

If there was trouble, this was where he would find it.

He paused for a minute before the gray plastic door marked MAJOR FRANK BRIARTON in raised stainless steel letters. Then he pushed open the door and walked into the ante-room.

It was empty. Suddenly he felt a touch on his shoulder. Behind him, a familiar voice said, "Hello, Twin."

*

At first glance they looked like carbon copies of each other, although they were no more identical than identical twins ever are. Greg stood a good two inches taller than Tom. His shoulders were broad, and there was a small gray scar over one eye that stood out in contrast to the healthy tanned color of his face. Tom was of slighter build, and wirier, his skin much more pale.

But they had the same dark hair, the same gray eyes, the same square, stubborn line to the jaw. They looked at each other for a moment without speaking. Then Greg grinned and clapped his brother on the shoulder.

"So you got here, finally," he said. "I was beginning to think I'd have to go out on the desert and find you."

"Oh, I got here, all right," Tom said. "I see you did too."

"Yes," Greg said heavily. "Can't argue with the major, you know."

"But what does he want?"

"How should I know? All he said was to get down here fast. And now he isn't even here himself."

"Is Dad on Mars?" Tom asked.

Greg looked at him. "I don't know."

"We could check the register."

"I already checked it. He has not logged in, but that doesn't mean anything."

"I suppose not," Tom said glumly.

They were silent for a moment. Then Greg said, "Look, what are you worried about? Nothing could have happened to Dad. He's been mining the Belt for years."

"I know. I just wish he were here, that's all. If he's in some kind of trouble...."

"What kind of trouble? You're looking for spooks."

"Spooks like Jupiter Equilateral, maybe," Tom said. "They could make plenty of trouble for Dad."

"With the U.N. in the driver's seat here? They wouldn't dare. Why do you think the major rides them so hard with all the claim-filing regulations? He'd give his right arm for a chance to break that outfit into pieces."

"I still wish somebody had gone out to the Belt with Dad," Tom said.

Just then the door opened. The newcomer was a tall, gray-haired man with U.N. Council stripes on his lapel, and major's rockets on his shoulders. "Sorry I'm late, boys," Major Briarton said. "I'd hoped to be here when you arrived. I'm sorry to pull you in here like this, but I'm afraid I had no choice. When did you boys hear from your father last?"

They looked at each other. "I saw him six weeks ago," Tom said. "Just before he left to go out to the Belt again."

"Nothing since then?"

"Not a word."

The major chewed his lip. "Greg?"

"I had a note at Christmas, I think. But what...."

"What did he say in the note?"

"He said Merry Christmas and Happy New Year. Dad isn't much of a letter writer."

"Nothing at all about what he was doing?"

Greg shook his head. "Look, Major, if there's some sort of trouble...."

"Yes, I'm afraid there's trouble," the major said. He looked up at them, and spread his hands helplessly. "There isn't any easy way to tell you, but you've got to know. There's been an accident, out in the Belt."

"Accident?" Greg said.

"A very serious accident. A fuel tank exploded in the scooter your father was riding back to the *Scavenger*. It must have been very sudden, and by the time help arrived...." The major broke off, unable to find words.

For a long moment there was utter silence in the room. Outside, an elevator was buzzing, and a typewriter clicked monotonously somewhere in the building.

Then Tom Hunter broke the silence. "Who was it, Major?" he said. "Who killed Dad? Tell us, or we'll find out!"

For a moment, Major Briarton just stared at him. Then he was on his feet, shaking his head as he came around the desk. "Tom, use your head," he said. "It's as much of a shock to me as it is to you, but you can't afford to jump to false conclusions...."

Tom Hunter looked up bitterly. "He's dead, isn't he?"

"Yes, he's dead. He must have died the instant of the explosion...."

"You mean you don't know?"

"I wasn't there at the time it happened, no."

"Then who was?"

*

Major Briarton spread his hands helplessly. "Nobody was. Your father was alone. From what we could tell later, he'd left the *Scavenger* to land on one of his claims, using the ship's scooter for the landing. He was on the way back to the *Scavenger* when the rear tank exploded. There wasn't enough left of it to tell what went wrong ... but it was an accident, there was no evidence to suggest anything else."

Tom looked at him. "You really believe that?"

"I can only tell you what we found."

"Well, I don't believe it for a minute," Tom said angrily. "How long have you and Dad been friends? Twenty years? Twenty-five? Do you really think Dad would have an accident with a mining rig?"

"I know he was an expert engineer," the major said. "But things can happen that even an expert can't foresee, mining in the Belt."

"Things like a fuel tank exploding? Not to Dad, they would never happen. I don't care what anybody says...."

"Easy, Tom," Greg said.

"Well, I won't take it easy. Dad was too careful for something like that to happen. If he had an accident, somebody *made* it happen."

Greg turned to the major. "What was Dad doing out there?"

"Mining."

"By himself? No crew at all?"

"No, he was alone."

"I thought the regulations said there always had to be at least two men working an asteroid claim."

"That's right. Your father had Johnny Coombs with him when he left Sun Lake City. They signed out as a team ... and then Johnny came back to Mars on the first shuttle ship."

"How come?"

"Not even Johnny knows. Your father just sent him back, and there was nothing we could do about it then. The U.N. has no jurisdiction in the belt, unless a major crime has been committed." Major Briarton shook his head helplessly. "If a man is determined to mine a claim all by himself out there, he can find a dozen different ways to wiggle out of the regulations."

"But Dad would never be that stupid," Greg said. "If he was alone when it happened, who found him?"

"A routine U.N. Patrol ship. When Roger failed to check in at the regular eight-hour signal, they went out to see what was wrong. But by the time they reached him, it was too late to help."

"I just don't get it," Greg said. "Dad had more sense than to try to mine out there all by himself."

"I know," the major said. "I don't know the answer. I had the Patrol ship go over the scene of the accident with a comb after they found what had happened, but there was nothing there to find. It was an accident, and that's that."

"What about Jupiter Equilateral?" Tom said hotly. "Everybody knows they were out to get Dad ... why don't you find out what *they* were doing when it happened, bring them in for questioning...."

"I can't do that, I haven't a scrap of evidence," the major said wearily.

"Why can't you? You're the Mars Coordinator, aren't you? You act like you're scared of them."

Major Briarton's lips tightened angrily. "All right, since you put it that way ... I *am* scared of them. They're big, and they're powerful. If they had their way, there wouldn't be any United Nations control on Mars, there wouldn't be *anybody* to fight them and keep them in check. There wouldn't be any independent miners out in the Belt, either, because they'd all be bought out or dead, and Earth would pay through the nose for every ounce of metal that they got from the Asteroid Belt. That company has been trying to drive the U.N. off Mars for thirty years, and they've come so close to it that it scares me plenty." He pushed his chair back sharply and rose to his feet. "And that is exactly why I refuse to stir up a mess over this thing, unhappy as it is, without something more than suspicions and rumors to back me up ... because all Jupiter Equilateral needs is one big issue to make us look like fools out here, and we're through."

He crossed the room to a wall cabinet, opened it, and pulled out a scarred aluminum box. "We found this in the cabin of the *Scavenger*. I thought you boys might want it."

They both recognized it instantly ... the battered old spacer's pack that Roger Hunter had used for as long as they could remember. It seemed to them, suddenly, as if a part of him had appeared here in the room with them. Greg looked at the box and turned away. "You open it," he said to Tom in a sick voice.

There was nothing much inside ... some clothing, a pipe and tobacco pouch, a jack knife, half a dozen other items so familiar that Tom could hardly bear to touch them. At the bottom of the pack was the heavy leather gun case which had always held Roger Hunter's ancient .44 revolver. Tom dropped it back without even opening the flap. He closed the box and took a deep breath. "Then you really believe that it was an accident and nothing more?" he said to the major.

Major Briarton shook his head. "What I think or don't think doesn't make any difference. It just doesn't matter. In order to do anything, I've got to have evidence, and there just isn't any evidence. I can't even take a ship out there for a second look, with the evidence I have, and that's all there is to it."

"But you think that maybe it wasn't an accident, just the same," Tom pursued.

The major hesitated. Then he shook his head again. "I'm sorry, but I've got to stand on what I've said. And I think you'd better stand on it, too. There's nothing else to be done."

*

It should have been enough, but it wasn't. As Tom Hunter walked with his brother down the broad Upper Ramp to the business section of Sun Lake City, he could not shake off the feeling of helpless anger, the growing conviction that Roger Hunter's death involved something more than the tragic accident in space that Major Briarton had insisted it was.

"He didn't tell us everything he knew," Tom said fiercely. "He didn't say everything he wanted to say, either. He doesn't think it was an accident any more than I do."

"How do you know, are you a mind reader?"

"No."

"Well, Dad wasn't a superman, either. He was taking an awful risk, trying to work a mining rig by himself, and he had a bad break. Why do you have to have somebody to blame for it?"

"Keep talking," Tom said. "You'll convince yourself yet."

Greg just jammed his hands in his pockets, and they walked in silence for a moment.

For Tom and Greg Hunter, Sun Lake City had always been home. Now they walked along the Main Concourse, Tom with the aluminum box under his arm, Greg with his own spacer's pack thrown over his shoulder. They didn't talk; rather than being drawn closer by the news of the tragedy, it seemed that they had drawn farther apart, as though the one common link that had held them together had suddenly been broken.

Finally Tom broke the silence. "At least there's one thing we can do," he said. "I'm going to call Johnny Coombs."

He shortly found a phone booth and dialed a number. Johnny had been a friend of the family for years; he and Roger Hunter had been partners in many mining ventures in the Asteroid Belt before Roger had taken his position with Jupiter Equilateral. If Johnny had any suspicions that Roger Hunter's accident had been more than an accident, he certainly would not hesitate to voice them....

After a dozen rings, Tom hung up, tried another number. There was no answer there, either. Frowning, Tom rang the city's central paging system. "Put in a personal call for Johnny Coombs," he said when the "record" signal flashed on. "Tell him to contact the Hunters when he comes in. We'll be at home...."

They resumed their silent walk. When they reached H wing on the fourth level, they turned right down an apartment corridor, and stopped in front of a familiar doorway. Tom pressed his palm against the lock-plate, and the door swung open.

It was home to them, the only home they had ever known. Soft lights sprang up on the walls of the apartment as the door opened. Tom saw the old bookcases lining the walls, the drafting-board and light at the far end of the room, the simple chairs and dining table, the door which led into the bedroom and kitchen beyond. The room had the slightly disheveled look that it had had ever since Mom had died ... a slipper on the floor here, a book face down on the couch there....

It looked as though Dad had just stepped out for an hour or so.

Tom was three steps into the room before he saw the visitor.

The man was sitting comfortably in Roger Hunter's easy chair, a short, fat man with round pink cheeks that sagged a little and a double chin that rested on his neck scarf. There were two other men in the room, both large and broad-shouldered; one of them nodded to the fat man, and moved to stand between the boys and the door.

The fat man was out of his seat before the boys could speak, smiling at them and holding out his hand. "I wanted to be sure to see you before you left the city," he was saying, "so we just came on in to wait. I hope you don't mind our ... butting in, so to speak." He chuckled, looking from one twin to the other. "You don't know me, I suppose. I'm Merrill Tawney. Representing Jupiter Equilateral, you know."

Tom took the card he was holding out, looked at the name and the tiny gold symbol in the corner, a letter "J" in the center of a triangle. He handed the card to Greg. "I've seen you before," he told the fat man. "What do you want with us?"

Tawney smiled again, spreading his hands. "We've heard about the tragedy, of course. A shocking thing ... Roger was one of our group so recently. We wanted you to know that if there is anything at all we can do to help, we'd be only too glad...."

"Thanks," Greg said. "But we're doing just fine."

Tawney's smile tightened a little, but he hung onto it. "I always felt close to your father," he said. "All of us at Jupiter Equilateral did. We were all sorry to see him leave."

"I bet you were," Greg said, "he was the best mining engineer you ever had. But Dad could never stand liars, or crooked ways of doing business."

One of the men started for Greg, but the fat man stopped him with a wave of his hand. "We had our differences of opinion," he said. "We saw things one way, your father saw them another way. But he was a fine man, one of the finest...."

"Look, Mr. Tawney, you'd better say what you came to say and get out of here," Greg said dangerously, "before we give your friends here something to do."

"I merely came to offer you some help," Tawney said. He was no longer smiling. "Since your father's death, you two have acquired certain responsibilities. I thought we might relieve you of some of them."

"What sort of responsibilities?"

"You have an unmanned orbit-ship which is now a derelict in the Asteroid Belt. You have a scout-ship out there also. You can't just leave them there as a navigation hazard to every ship traveling in the sector. There are also a few mining claims which aren't going to be of much value to you now."

"I see," Greg said. "Are you offering to buy Dad's mining rig?"

"Well, I doubt very much that we'd have any use for it, as such. But we could save you the trouble of going out there to haul it in."

"That's very thoughtful," Greg said. "How much are you offering?"

Tom looked up in alarm. "Wait a minute," he said. "That rig's not for sale...."

"How much?" Greg repeated.

"Forty thousand dollars," Merrill Tawney said. "Ship, rig and claims. We'll even pay the transfer tax."

Tom stared at the man, wondering if he had heard right. He knew what Roger Hunter had paid for the rig; he had been with Dad when the papers were signed. Tawney's offer was three times as much as the rig was worth.

But Greg was shaking his head. "I don't think we could sell at that price."

The fat man's hands fluttered. "You understand that those ships are hardly suited to a major mining operation like ours," he said, "and the claims...." He dismissed them with a wave of his hand. "Still, we'd want you to be happy with the price. Say, forty-five thousand?"

Greg hesitated, shook his head again. "I guess we'd better think it over, Mr. Tawney."

"Fifty thousand is absolutely the top," Tawney said sharply. "I have the papers right here, drawn up for your signatures, but I'm afraid we can't hold the offer open."

"I don't know, we might want to do some mining ourselves," Greg said. "For all we know, Dad might have struck some rich ore on one of those claims."

Tawney laughed. "I hardly think so. Those claims were all Jupiter Equilateral rejects. Our own engineers found nothing but low grade ore on any of them."

"Still, it might be fun to look."

"It could be very expensive fun. Asteroid mining is a dangerous business, even for experts. For amateurs...." Tawney spread his hands. "Accidents occur...."

"Yes, we've heard about those accidents," Greg said coldly. "I don't think we're quite ready to sell, Mr. Tawney. We may never be ready to sell to you, so don't stop breathing until we call you. Now if there's nothing else, why don't you take your friends and go somewhere else?"

The fat man scowled; he started to say something more, then saw the look on Greg's face, and shrugged. "I'd advise you to give it some careful thought," he said as he started for the door. "It might be very foolish for you to try to use that rig."

Smiling, Greg closed the door in his face. Then he turned and winked at Tom. "Great fellow, Mr. Tawney. He almost had me sold."

"So I noticed," Tom said. "For a while I thought you were serious."

"Well, we found out how high they'd go. That's a very generous outfit Mr. Tawney works for."

"Or else a very crooked one," Tom said. "Are you wondering the same thing I'm wondering?"

"Yes," Greg said slowly. "I think I am."

"Then that makes three of us," a heavy voice rumbled from the bedroom door.

*

Johnny Coombs was a tall man, so thin he was almost gangling, with a long nose and shaggy eyebrows jutting out over his eyes. With his rudely cropped hair and his huge hands, he looked like a caricature of a frontier Mars-farmer, but the blue eyes under the eyebrows were not dull.

"Johnny!" Tom cried. "We were trying to find you."

"I know," Johnny said. "So have a lot of other people, includin' your friends there."

"Well, did you hear what Tawney wanted?"

"I'm not so quick on my feet any more," Johnny Coombs said, "but I got nothin' wrong with my ears." He scratched his jaw and looked up sharply at Greg. "Not many people nowadays get a chance to bargain with Merrill Tawney."

Greg shrugged. "He named a price and I didn't like it."

"Three times what the rig is worth," Coombs said.

"That's what I didn't like," Greg said. "That outfit wouldn't give us a break like that just for old times' sake. Do you think they would?"

"Well, I don't know," Johnny said slowly. "Back before they built the city here, they used to have rats getting into the grub. Came right down off the ships. Got rid of most of them, finally, but it seems to me we've still got some around, even if they've got different shapes now." He jerked his thumb toward the bedroom door. "In case you're wondering, that's why I was standin' back there all this time ... just to make sure you didn't sell out to Tawney no matter what price he offered."

Tom jumped up excitedly. "Then you know something about Dad's accident!"

"No, I can't say I do. I wasn't there."

"Do you really think it was an accident?"

"Can't prove it wasn't."

"But at least you've got some ideas," Tom said.

"Takes more than ideas to make a case," he said at length. "But there's one thing I do know. I've got no proof, not a shred of it, but I'm sure of one thing just as sure as I'm on Mars." He looked at the twins thoughtfully. "Your dad wasn't just prospecting, out in the Belt. He'd run onto something out there, something big."

The twins looked at him. "Run onto something?" Greg said. "You mean...."

"I mean I think your dad hit a Big Strike out there, rich metal, a real bonanza lode. Maybe the biggest strike that's ever been made," the miner said slowly. "And then somebody got to him before he could bring it in."

TOO MANY WARNINGS

For a moment, neither of the boys could say anything at all.

From the time they had learned to talk, they had heard stories and tales that the miners and prospectors told about the Big Strike, the pot of gold at the end of the rainbow, the wonderful, elusive goal of every man who had ever taken a ship into the Asteroid Belt.

For almost a hundred and fifty years ... since the earliest days of space exploration ... there had been miners prospecting in the Asteroids. Out there, beyond the orbit of Mars and inside the orbit of Jupiter, were a hundred thousand ... maybe a hundred million, for all anybody knew ... chunks of rock, metal and debris, spinning in silent orbit around the sun. Some few of the Asteroids were big enough to be called planets ... Ceres, five hundred miles in diameter; Juno, Vesta, Pallas, half a dozen more. A few hundred others, ranging in size from ten to a hundred miles in diameter, had been charted and followed in their orbits by the observatories, first from Earth's airless Moon, then from Mars. There were tens of thousands more that had never been charted. Together they made up the Asteroid Belt, spread out in space like a broad road around the sun, echoing the age-old call of the bonanza.

For there was wealth in the Asteroids ... wealth beyond a man's wildest dreams ... if only he could find it.

Earth, with its depleted iron ranges, its exhausted tin and copper mines, and its burgeoning population, was hungry for metal. Earth needed steel, tin, nickel, and zinc; more than anything, Earth needed ruthenium, the rare-earth catalyst that made the huge solar energy converters possible.

Mars was rich in the ores of these metals ... but the ores were buried deep in the ground. The cost of mining them, and of lifting the heavy ore from Mars' gravitational field and carrying it to Earth was prohibitive. Only the finest carbon steel, and the radioactive metals, smelted and purified on Mars and transported to Earth, could be made profitable.

But from the Asteroid Belt, it was a different story. There was no gravity to fight on the tiny asteroids. On these chunks of debris, the metals lay close to the surface, easy to mine. Ships orbiting in the Belt could fill their holds with their precious metal cargoes and transfer them in space to the interplanetary orbit-ships spinning back toward Earth. It was hard work, and dangerous work; most of the ore was low-grade, and brought little return. But always there was the lure of the Big Strike, the lode of almost-pure metal that could bring a fortune back to the man who found it.

*

A few such strikes had been made. Forty years before a single claim had brought its owner seventeen million dollars in two years. A dozen other men had stumbled onto fortunes in the Belt ... but such metal-rich fragments were grains of sand in a mighty river. For every man who found one, a thousand others spent years looking and then perished in the fruitless search.

And now Johnny Coombs was telling them that their father had been one of that incredible few.

"You really think Dad hit a bonanza lode out there?"

"That's what I said."

"Did you see it with your own eyes?"

"No."

"You weren't even out there with him!"

"No."

"Then why are you so sure he found something?"

"Because he told me so," Johnny Coombs said quietly.

The boys looked at each other. "He actually *said* he'd found a rich lode?" Tom asked eagerly.

"Not exactly," Johnny said. "Matter of fact, he never actually told me *what* he'd found. He needed somebody to sign aboard the *Scavenger* with him in order to get a clearance to blast off, but he never did plan to take me out there with him. 'I can't take you now, Johnny,' he told me. 'I've found something out there, but I've got to work it alone for a while.' I asked him what he'd found, and he just gave me that funny little grin of his and said, 'Never mind what it is, it's big enough for both of us. You just keep your mouth shut, and you'll find out soon enough.' And then he wouldn't say another word until we were homing in on the shuttle ship to drop me off."

Johnny finished his coffee and pushed the cup aside. "I knew he wasn't joking. He was excited, and I think he was scared, too. Just before I left him, he said, 'There's one other thing, Johnny. Things might not work out quite the way I figure them, and if they don't ... make sure the twins know what I've told you.' I told him I would, and headed back. That was the last I heard from him until the Patrol ship found him floating in space with a torn-open suit and a ruined scooter floating a few miles away."

"Do you think that Jupiter Equilateral knew Dad had found something?" Tom asked.

"Who knows? I'm sure that *he* never told them, but it's awful hard to keep a secret like that, and they sound awful eager to buy that rig," Johnny Coombs said.

"Yes, and it doesn't make sense. I mean, if they were responsible for Dad's accident, why didn't they just check in for him on schedule and then quietly bring in their rig to jump the claim?"

"Maybe they couldn't find it," Johnny said. "If they'd killed your dad, they wouldn't have dared hang around very long right then. Even if they'd kept the signal going, a Patrol ship might have come into the region any time. And if a U.N. Patrol ship ever caught them working a dead man's claim without reporting the dead man, the suit would really start to leak." Johnny shook his head. "Remember, your Dad had a dozen claims out there. They might have had to scout the whole works to find the right one. Much easier to do it out in the open, with your signatures on a claim transfer. But one thing is sure ... if they *knew* what Roger found out there, and where it was, Tawney would never be offering you triple price for the rig."

"Then whatever Dad found is still out there," Tom said.

"I'd bet my last dime on it."

"There might even be something to show that the accident wasn't an accident," Tom went on. "Something even the Major would have to admit was evidence."

Johnny Coombs pursed his lips, looking up at Tom. "Might be," he conceded.

"Well, what are we waiting for? We turned Tawney's offer down ... he might be sending a crew out to jump the claim right now."

"If he hasn't already," Johnny said.

"Then we've got to get out there."

Johnny turned to Greg. "You could pilot us out and handle the navigation, and as for Tom...."

"As for Tom, he could get sick all over the place and keep us busy just taking care of him," Greg said sourly. "You and me, yes. Not Tom. You don't know that boy in a spaceship."

Tom started to his feet, glaring at his brother. "That's got nothing to do with it...."

"It's true, isn't it? You'd be a big help out there."

Johnny looked at Tom. "You always get sick in free fall?"

"Look, let's be reasonable," Greg said. "You'd just be in the way. There are plenty of things you could do right here, and Johnny and I could handle the rig alone...."

Tom faced his brother angrily. "If you think I'm going to stay here and keep myself company, you're crazy," he said. "This is one show you're not going to run, so just quit trying. If you go out there, I go."

Greg shrugged. "Okay, Twin. It's your stomach, not mine."

"Then let me worry about it."

"I hope," Johnny said, "that that's the worst we have to worry about. Let's get started planning."

*

Time was the factor uppermost in their minds. They knew that even under the best of conditions, it could take weeks to outfit and prepare for a run out to the Belt. A ship had to be leased and fueled; there were supplies to lay in. There was the problem of clearance to take care of, claims to be verified and spotted, orbit coordinates to be computed and checked ... a thousand details to be dealt with, anyone of which might delay embarkation from an hour to a day or more.

It was not surprising that Tom and Greg were dubious when Johnny told them they could be ready to clear ground in less than twenty-four hours. Even knowing that Merrill Tawney might already have a mining crew at work on Roger Hunter's claims, they could not believe that the red tape of preparation and clearance could be cut away so swiftly.

They underestimated Johnny Coombs.

Six hours after he left them, he was back with a signed lease giving them the use of a scout-ship and fuel to take them out to the Belt and back again; the ship was in the Sun Lake City racks waiting for them whenever they were ready.

"What kind of a ship?" Greg wanted to know.

"A Class III Flying Dutchman with overhauled atomics and hydrazine side-jets," Johnny said, waving the transfer order. "Think you can fly it?"

Greg whistled. "Can I? I trained in a Dutchman ... just about the fastest scouter there is. What condition?"

"Lousy ... but it's fueled, with six weeks' supplies in the hold, and it doesn't cost us a cent. Courtesy of a friend. You'll have to check it over, but it'll do."

They inspected the ship, a weatherbeaten scouter that looked like a relic of the '90's. Inside there were signs of many refittings and overhauls, but the atomics were well shielded, and it carried a surprising chemical fuel auxiliary for the cabin size. Greg disappeared into the engine room, and Tom and Johnny left him testing valves and circuits while they headed down to the U.N. Registry office in the control tower.

On the way Johnny outlined the remaining outfitting steps. Tom would be responsible for getting the clearance permit through Registry; Johnny would check out all supplies, and then contact the observatory for the orbit coordinates of Roger Hunter's claims.

"I thought the orbits were mapped on the claim papers," Tom said. "I mean, every time an asteroid is claimed, the orbit has to be charted...."

"That's right, but the orbit goes all the way around the sun. We know where the *Scavenger* was when the Patrol ship found her ... but she's been travelling in orbit ever since. The observatory computer will pinpoint her for us and chart a collision course so we can cut out and meet her instead of trailing her for a week. Do you have the crew-papers Greg and I signed?"

"Right here."

They were stepping off the ramp below the ship when a man loomed up out of the shadows. It was a miner Tom had never seen before. Johnny nodded as he approached. "Any news, Jack?"

"Quiet as a church," the man said.

"We'll be held up another eight hours at least," Johnny said. "Don't go to sleep on us, Jack."

"Don't worry about us sleepin'," the man said grimly. "There's been nobody around but yourselves, so far ... except the clearance inspector."

Johnny looked up sharply. "You check his papers?"

"*And* his prints. He was all right."

Johnny took Tom's arm, and they headed through the gate toward the control tower. "I guess I'm just naturally suspicious," he grinned, "but I'd sure hate to have a broken cut-off switch, or a fuel valve go out of whack at just the wrong moment."

"You think Tawney would dare to try something here?" Tom said.

"Never hurts to check. We've got our hands full for a few hours getting set, so I just asked my friends to keep an eye on things. Always did say that a man who's going to gamble is smart to cover his bets."

At the control tower they parted, and Tom walked into the clearance office. Johnny's watch-man had startled him, and for the first time he felt a chill of apprehension. If they were right ... if this trip to the Belt were not a wild goose chase from the very start ... then Roger Hunter's accident had been no accident at all.

Quite suddenly, Tom felt very thankful that Johnny Coombs had friends....

*

"I don't like it," the Major said, facing Tom and Greg across the desk in the U.N. Registry office below the control tower. "You've gotten an idea in your heads, and you just won't listen to reason."

Somewhere above them, Tom could hear the low-pitched rumble of a scout-ship blasting from its launching rack. "All we want to do is go out and work Dad's claim," he said for the second time.

"I know perfectly well what you want to do, that's why I told the people here to alert me if you tried to clear a ship. You don't know what you're doing ... and I'm not going to sign those clearance papers."

"Why not?" Greg said.

"Because you're going out there asking for trouble, that's why not."

"But you told us before that there wasn't any trouble. Dad had an accident, that was all. So how could we get in trouble?"

The Major's face was an angry red. He started to say something, then stopped, and scowled at them instead. They met his stare. Finally he threw up his hands. "All right, so I can't legally stop you," he said. "But at least I can beg you to use your heads. You're wasting time and money on a foolish idea. You're walking into dangers and risks that you can't handle, and I hate to see it happen.

"Mining in the Belt is a job for experienced men, not rank novices."

"Johnny Coombs is no novice."

"No, but he's lost his wits, taking you two out there."

"Well, are there any other dangers you have in mind?"

Once more the Major searched for words, and failed to find them. "No," he sighed, "and you wouldn't listen if I did."

"It seems everybody is warning us about how dangerous this trip is likely to be," Greg said quietly. "Last night it was Merrill Tawney. He offered to buy us out, he was so eager for a deal that he offered us a fantastic price. Then Johnny tells us that Dad mined some rich ore when he was out there on his last trip, but never got a chance to bring it in because of his ... accident. Up until now I haven't been so sure Dad *didn't* just have an accident, but now I'm beginning to wonder. Too many people have been warning us...."

"You're determined to go out there, then?"

"That's about right."

The Major picked up the clearance papers, glanced at them quickly, and signed them. "All right, you're cleared. I hate to do it, but I suppose I'd go with you if the law would let me. And I'll tell you one thing ... if you can find a single particle of evidence that will link Jupiter Equilateral or anybody else to your father's death, I'll use all the power I have to break them." He handed the papers back to Tom. "But be careful, because if Jupiter Equilateral is involved in it, they're going to play dirty."

At the door he turned. "Good trip, and good luck."

Tom folded the papers and stuck them thoughtfully into his pocket.

They met Johnny Coombs in the Registry offices upstairs; Tom patted his pocket happily. "We're cleared in forty-five minutes," he said.

Johnny grinned. "Then we're all set." They headed up the ramp, reached ground level, and started out toward the launching racks.

At the far end of the field a powerful Class I Ranger, one of the Jupiter Equilateral scout fleet, was settling down into its slot in a perfect landing maneuver. The triangle-and-J-insignia gleamed brightly on her dark hull. She was a rich, luxurious-looking ship. Many miners on Mars could remember when Jupiter Equilateral had been nothing more than a tiny mining company working claims in the remote "equilateral" cluster of asteroids far out in Jupiter's orbit. Gradually the company had grown and flourished, accumulating wealth and power as it grew, leaving behind it a thousand half-confirmed stories of cheating, piracy, murder and theft. Other small mining outfits had fallen by the wayside until now over two-thirds of all asteroid mining claims were held by Jupiter Equilateral, and the small independent miners were forced more and more to take what was left.

They reached the gate to the Dutchman's launching slot and entered.

Inside the ship Tom and Johnny strapped down while Greg made his final check-down on the engines, gyros and wiring. The cabin was a tiny vault, with none of the spacious "living room" of the orbit-ships. Tom leaned back in the accelleration cot, and listened to the count-down signals that came at one minute intervals now. In the earphones he could hear the sporadic chatter between Greg and the control tower. No hint that this was anything but a routine blastoff....

But there was trouble ahead, Tom was certain of that. Everybody on Mars was aware that Roger Hunter's sons were heading out to the Belt to pick up where he had left off. Greg had secured a leave of absence from Project Star-Jump ... unhappily granted, even though his part in their program had already been disrupted. Even they had heard the rumors that were adrift....

And if there was trouble now, they were on their own. The Asteroid Belt was a wilderness, untracked and unexplored, and except for an almost insignificant fraction, completely unknown. If there was trouble out there, there would be no one to help.

Somewhere below the engines roared, and Tom felt the weight on his chest, sudden and breath-taking.

They were on their way.

BETWEEN MARS AND JUPITER....

After all the tension of preparing for it, the trip out seemed interminable.

They were all impatient to reach their destination. During blastoff and accelleration they had watched Mars dwindle to a tiny red dot; then time seemed to stop altogether, and there was nothing to do but wait.

For the first eight hours of free fall, after the engines had cut out, Tom was violently ill. He fought it desperately, gulping the pills Johnny offered and trying to keep them down. Gradually the waves of nausea subsided, but it was a full twenty-four hours before Tom felt like stirring from his cot to take up the shipboard routine.

And then there was nothing for him to do. Greg handled the navigation skilfully, while Johnny kept radio contact and busied himself in the storeroom, so Tom spent hours at the viewscreen. On the second day he spotted a tiny chunk of rock that was unquestionably an asteroid moving swiftly toward them. It passed at a tangent ten thousand miles ahead of them, and Greg started work at the computer, feeding in the data tapes that would ultimately guide the ship to its goal.

*

Pinpointing a given spot in the Asteroid Belt was a gargantuan task, virtually impossible without the aid of the ship's computer to compute orbits, speeds, and distances. Tom spent more and more time at the viewscreen, searching the blackness of space for more asteroid sightings. But except for an occasional tiny bit of debris hurtling by, he saw nothing but the changeless panorama of stars.

Johnny Coombs found him there on the third day, and laughed at his sour expression. "Gettin' impatient?"

"Just wondering when we'll reach the Belt, is all," Tom said.

Johnny chuckled. "Hope you're not holdin' your breath. We've already been *in* the Belt for the last forty-eight hours."

"Then where are all the asteroids?" Tom said.

"Oh, they're here. You just won't see many of them. People always think there ought to be dozens of them around, like sheep on a hillside, but it just doesn't work that way." Johnny peered at the screen. "Of course, to an astronomer the Belt is just loaded ... hundreds of thousands of chunks, all sizes from five hundred miles in diameter on down. But actually, those chunks are all tens of thousands of miles apart, and the Belt *looks* just as empty as the space between Mars and Earth."

"Well, I don't see how we're ever going to find one particular rock," Tom said, watching the screen gloomily.

"It's not too hard. Every asteroid has its own orbit around the sun, and everyone that's been registered as a claim has the orbit charted. The one we want isn't where it was when your Dad's body was found ... it's been travelling in its orbit ever since. But by figuring in the fourth dimension, we can locate it."

Tom blinked. "Fourth dimension?"

"Time," Johnny Coombs said. "If we just used the three linear dimensions ... length, width and depth ... we'd end up at the place where the asteroid *was*, but that wouldn't help us much because it's been moving in orbit ever since the Patrol Ship last pinpointed it. So we figure in a fourth dimension ... the time that's passed since it was last spotted ... and we can chart a collision course with it, figure out just where *we'll* have to be to meet it."

It was the first time that the idea of time as a "dimension" had ever made sense to Tom. They talked some more, until Johnny started bringing in fifth and sixth dimensions, and problems of irrational space and hyperspace, and got even himself confused.

"Anyway," Tom said, "I'm glad we've got a computer aboard."

"And a navigator," Johnny added. "Don't sell your brother short."

"Fat chance of that. Greg would never stand for it."

Johnny frowned. "You lads don't like each other very much, do you?" he said.

Tom was silent for a moment. Then he looked away. "We get along, I guess."

"Maybe. But sometimes just gettin' along isn't enough. Especially when there's trouble. Give it a thought, when you've got a minute or two...."

Later, the three of them went over the computer results together. Johnny and Greg fed the navigation data into the ship's drive mechanism, checking and rechecking speeds and inclination angles. Already the Dutchman's orbital speed was matching the speed of Roger Hunter's asteroid ... but the orbit had to be tracked so that they would arrive at the exact point in space to make contact. Tom was assigned to the viewscreen, and the long wait began.

He spotted their destination point an hour before the computer had predicted contact ... at first a tiny pinpoint of reflected light in the scope, gradually resolving into two pinpoints, then three in a tiny cluster. Greg cut in the rear and lateral jets momentarily, stabilizing their contact course; the dots grew larger.

Ten minutes later, Tom could see their goal clearly in the viewscreen ... the place where Roger Hunter had died.

*

It was neither large nor small for an asteroid, an irregular chunk of rock and metal, perhaps five miles in diameter, lighted only by the dull reddish glow from the dime-sized sun. Like many such jagged chunks of debris that sprinkled the Belt, this asteroid did not spin on any axis, but constantly presented the same face to the sun.

Just off the bright side the orbit-ship floated, stable in its orbit next to the big rock, but so small in comparison that it looked like a tiny glittering toy balloon. And clamped on its rack on the orbit-ship's side, airlock to airlock, was the *Scavenger*, the little scout ship that Roger Hunter had brought out from Mars on his last journey.

While Greg maneuvered the Dutchman into the empty landing rack below the *Scavenger* on the hull of the orbit-ship, Johnny scanned the blackness around them through the viewscope, a frown wrinkling his forehead.

"Do you see anybody?" Tom asked.

"Not a sign ... but I'm really looking for other rocks. I can see three that aren't too far away, but none of them have claim marks. This one must have been the only one Roger was working."

They stared at the ragged surface of the planetoid. Raw veins of metallic ore cut through it with streaks of color, but most of the sun-side showed only the dull gray of iron and granite. There was nothing unusual about the surface that Tom could see. "Could there be anything on the dark side?"

"Could be," Johnny said. "We'll have to go over it foot by foot ... but first, we should go through the orbit-ship and the *Scavenger*. If the Patrol ship missed anything, we want to know it."

The interior of the orbit-ship was dark. It spun slowly on its axis, giving them just enough weight so they would not float free whenever they moved. Their boots clanged on the metal decks as they climbed up the curving corridor toward the control cabin.

Then Johnny threw a light switch, and they stared around them in amazement.

The cabin was a shambles. Everything that was not bolted down had been ripped open and thrown aside.

Greg whistled through his teeth. "The Major said the Patrol crew had gone through the ship ... but he didn't say they'd wrecked it."

"They didn't," Johnny said grimly. "No Patrol ship would ever do this. Somebody else has been here since." He turned to the control panel, flipped switches, checked gauges. "Hydroponics are all right. Atmosphere is still good; we can take off these helmets. Fuel looks all right, storage holds ..." He shook his head. "They weren't looting, but they were looking for something, all right. Let's look around and see if they missed anything."

It took them an hour to survey the wreckage. Not a compartment had been missed. Even the mattresses on the accelleration cots had been torn open, the spring-stuffing tossed about helter-skelter. Tom went through the lock into the *Scavenger*; the scout ship too had been searched, rapidly but thoroughly.

But there was no sign of anything that Roger Hunter might have found.

Back in the control cabin Johnny was checking the ship's log. The old entries were on microfilm, stored on their spools near the reader. More recent entries were still recorded on tape. From the jumbled order, there was no doubt that marauders had examined them. Johnny ran through them nevertheless, but there was nothing of interest. Routine navigational data; a record of the time of contact with the asteroid; a log of preliminary observations on the rock; nothing more. The last tape recorded the call-schedule Roger Hunter had set up with the Patrol, a routine precaution used by all miners, to bring help if for some reason they should fail to check in on schedule.

There was no hint in the log of any extraordinary discovery.

"Are any tapes missing?" Greg wanted to know.

"Doesn't look like it. There's one here for each day-period."

"I wonder," Tom said. "Dad always kept a personal log. You know, a sort of a diary, on microfilm." He peered into the film storage bin, checked through the spools. Then, from down beneath the last row of spools he pulled out a slightly smaller spool. "Here's something our friends missed, I bet."

It was not really a diary, just a sequence of notes, calculations and ideas that Roger Hunter had jotted down and microfilmed from time to time. The entries on the one spool went back for several years. Tom fed the spool into the reader, and they stared eagerly at the last few entries.

A series of calculations, covering several pages, but with no notes to indicate what, exactly, Roger Hunter had been calculating. "Looks like he was plotting an orbit," Greg said. "But what orbit? And why? Nothing here to tell."

"It must have been important, though, or Dad wouldn't have filmed the pages," Tom said. "Anything else?"

Another sheet with more calculations. Then a short paragraph written in Roger Hunter's hurried scrawl. "No doubt now what it is," the words said. "Wish Johnny were here, show him a *real* bonanza, but he'll know soon enough if...."

They stared at the scribbled, uncompleted sentence. Then Johnny Coombs let out a whoop. "I told you he found something! And he found it *here*, not somewhere else."

"Hold it," Greg said, peering at the film reader. "There's something more on the last page, but I can't read it."

Tom blinked at the entry. "'Inter Jovem et Martem planetam interposui,'" he read. He scratched his head. "That's Latin, and it's famous, too. Kepler wrote it, back before the asteroids were discovered. 'Between Jupiter and Mars I will put a planet.'"

Greg and Johnny looked at each other. "I don't get it," Greg said.

"Dad told me about that once," Tom said. "Kepler couldn't understand the long jump between Mars and Jupiter, when Venus and Earth and Mars were so close together. He figured there ought to be a planet out here ... and he was right, in a way. There wasn't any one planet, unless you'd call Ceres a planet, but it wasn't just empty space between Mars and Jupiter either. The asteroids were here."

"But why would Dad be writing that down?" Greg asked. "And what has it got to do with what he found out here?" He snapped off the reader switch angrily. "I don't understand any of this, and I don't like it. If Dad found something out here, where is it? And who tore this ship apart after the Patrol ship left?"

"Probably the same ones that caused the 'accident' in the first place," Johnny said.

"But why did they come back?" Greg protested. "If they killed Dad, they must have known what he'd found before they killed him."

"You'd think so," Johnny conceded.

"Then why take the risk of coming back here again?"

"Maybe they *didn't* know," Tom said thoughtfully.

"What do you mean?"

"I mean maybe they killed him too soon. Maybe they thought they knew what he'd found and where it was ... and then found out that they didn't, after all. Maybe Dad hid it...."

Johnny Coombs shook his head. "No way a man can hide an ore strike."

"But suppose Dad did, somehow, and whoever killed him couldn't find it? It would be too late to make him tell them. They'd *have* to come back and look again, wouldn't they? And from the way they went about it, it looks as though they weren't having much luck."

"Then whatever Dad found would still be here, somewhere," Greg said.

"That's right."

"But where? There's nothing on this ship."

"Maybe not," Tom said, "but I'd like to take a look at that asteroid before we give up."

*

They paused in the big ore-loading lock to reclamp their pressure suit helmets, and looked down at the jagged chunk of rock a hundred yards below them. In the lock they had found scooters ... the little one-man propulsion units so commonly used for short distance work in space ... but decided not to use them. "They're clumsy," Johnny said, "and the bumper units in your suits will do just as well for this distance." He looked down at the rock. "I'll take the center section. You each take an edge and work in. Look for any signs of work on the surface ... chisel marks, Murexide charges, anything."

"What about the dark side?" Greg asked.

"If we want to see anything there, we'll either have to rig up lights or turn the rock around," Johnny said. "Let's cover this side first and see what we come up with."

He turned and leaped from the airlock, moving gracefully down toward the surface, using the bumper unit to guide himself with short bursts of compressed CO_2, from the nozzle. Greg followed, pushing off harder and passing Johnny halfway down. Tom hesitated. It looked easy enough ... but he remembered the violent nausea of his first few hours of free fall.

Finally he gritted his teeth and jumped off after Greg. Instantly he knew that he had jumped too hard. He shot away from the orbit-ship like a bullet; the jagged asteroid surface leaped up at him. Frantically he grabbed for the bumper nozzle and pulled the trigger, trying to break his fall.

He felt the nozzle jerk in his hand, and then, abruptly, he was spinning off at a wild tangent from the asteroid, head over heels. For a moment it seemed that asteroid, orbit-ship and stars were all wheeling crazily around him. Then he realized what had happened. He fired the bumper again, and went spinning twice as fast. The third time he timed the blast, aiming the nozzle carefully, and the spinning almost stopped.

He fought down nausea, trying to get his bearings. He was three hundred yards out from the asteroid, almost twice as far from the orbit-ship. He stared down at the rock as he moved slowly away from it. Before, from the orbit-ship, he had been able to see only the bright side of the huge rock; now he could see the sharp line of darkness across one side.

But there was something else....

He fired the bumper again to steady himself, peering into the blackness beyond the light-line on the rock. He snapped on his helmet lamp, aimed the spotlight beam down to the dark rock surface. Greg and Johnny were landing now on the bright side, with Greg almost out of sight over the "horizon" ... but Tom's attention was focussed on something he could see only now as he moved away from the asteroid surface.

His spotlight caught it ... something bright and metallic, completely hidden on the dark side, lying in close to the surface but not quite on the surface. Then suddenly Tom knew what it was ... the braking jets of a Class I Ranger, crouching beyond the reach of sunlight in the shadow of the asteroid....

Swiftly he fired the bumper again, turning back toward the orbit-ship. His hand went to the speaker-switch, but he caught himself in time. Any warning shouted to Greg and Johnny would certainly be picked up by the ship. But he had to give warning somehow.

He tumbled into the airlock, searching for a flare in his web belt. It was a risk ... the Ranger ship might pick up the flash ... but he had to take it. He was unscrewing the fuse cap from the flare when he saw Greg and Johnny leap up from the asteroid surface.

Then he saw what had alarmed them. Slowly, the Ranger was moving out from its hiding place behind the rock. Tom reached out to catch Greg as he came plummeting into the lock. There was a flash from the Ranger's side, and Johnny Coombs' voice boomed in his earphones: "Get inside! Get the lock closed, fast ... hurry up, can't waste a second."

Johnny caught the lip of the lock, dragged himself inside frantically. They were spinning the airlock door closed when they heard the thundering explosion, felt the ship lurch under their feet, and all three of them went crashing to the deck.

For a stunned moment they were helpless as they struggled to pick themselves up. The stable airlock deck was suddenly no longer stable ... it was lurching back and forth like a rowboat on a heavy sea, and they grabbed the shock-bars along the bulkheads to steady themselves. "What happened?" Greg yelped. "I saw a ship...."

As if in answer there was another crash belowdecks, and the lurching became worse. "They're firing on us, that's what happened," Johnny Coombs growled.

"Well, they're shaking us loose at the seams," Greg said. "We've got to get this crate out of here." He reached for his helmet, began unsnapping his pressure suit.

"Leave it on," Johnny snapped.

"But we can't move fast enough in these things...."

"Leave it on all the same. If they split the hull open, you'll be dead in ten seconds without a suit."

Somewhere below they heard the steady *clang-clang-clang* of the emergency-station's bell ... already one of the compartments somewhere had been breached, and was pouring its air out into the vacuum of space. "But what can we do?" Greg said. "They could tear us apart!"

"First, we see what they've already done," Johnny said, spinning the wheel on the inner lock. "If they plan to tear us apart, we're done for, but they may want to try to board us.... We'll wait and see."

An orbit-ship under fire was completely vulnerable. One well-placed shell could rip it open like a balloon.

Tom and Greg followed Johnny to where the control cabin was located. In control they found alarm lights flashing in three places on the instrument panel. Another muffled crash roared through the ship, and a new row of lights sprang on along the panel.

"How are the engines?" Greg said, staring at the flickering lights.

"Can't tell. Looks like they're firing at the main jets, but they've ripped open three storage holds, too. They're trying to disable us...."

"What about the *Scavenger*?"

Johnny checked a gauge. "The airlock compartment is all right, so the scout ships haven't been touched. They couldn't fire on them without splitting the whole ship down the middle." Johnny leaned forward, flipped on the viewscreen, and an image came into focus.

*

It was a Class I Ranger, and there was no doubt of its origin. Like the one they had seen berthing at the Sun Lake City racks, this ship had a glossy black hull, with the golden triangle-and-J insignia standing out in sharp relief in the dim sunlight.

"It's our friends, all right," Johnny said.

"But what are they trying to do?" Tom said.

Even as they watched, a pair of scooters broke from the side of the Ranger and slid down toward the sun side of the asteroid. "I don't know," Johnny said. "I think they intended to stay hidden, until Tom lost control of his bumper, and got far enough around there to spot them." He frowned as the first scooter touched down on the asteroid surface.

"Can't we fire on them?" Greg said angrily.

"Not the way this tub is lurching around. They've got our main gyros, and the auxilliaries aren't powerful enough to steady us. Another blast or two could send us spinning like a top, and we'd have nothing to stabilize us...."

There was another flash from the Ranger's hull, and the ship jerked under their feet. "Well, we're a sitting duck here," Greg said. "Maybe those engines will still work." He slid into the control seat, flipped the drive switches to fire the side jets in opposite pairs. They fired, steadying the lurching of the ship somewhat, but there was no response from the main engines. "No good. We couldn't begin to run from them. We're stuck here."

"They could outrun us anyway," Tom said, watching the viewscreen. "And they're moving in closer now."

"They're going to board us," Tom said.

Johnny nodded, his eyes suddenly bright. "I think you're right. And if they do, we may have a chance. But we've got to split up.... Greg, you take the control cabin here, try to keep them out if you can. Tom can cover the main corridor to the storage holds, and I'll take the engine room section.

That will sew up the entrances to control, here, and give us a chance to stop them."

"They may have a dozen men," Tom said. "They could just shoot us down."

"I don't think so," Johnny said. "They want *us*, not the ship, or they wouldn't bother to board us. We may not be able to hold them off, but we can try."

"What about making a run for it in the *Scavenger?*" Greg said.

Johnny chuckled grimly. "It'd be a mighty short run. That Ranger's got homing shells that could blow the *Scavenger* to splinters if we tried it. Our best bet is to put up such a brawl that they think twice about taking us."

They parted in the corridor outside control, Johnny heading down for the engine room corridors, while Tom ran up toward the main outer-shell corridor, a Markheim stunner in his hand. The entire outer shell of the ship was storage space, each compartment separately sealed and connected with the two main corridors that circled the ship. On each side these corridors came together to join the short entry corridors from the scout-ship airlocks.

Tom knew that the only way the ship could be boarded was through those locks; a man stationed at the place where the main corridors joined could block any entry from the locks ... as long as he could hold his position. Tom reached the junction of the corridors, and crouched close to the wall. By peering around the corner, he had a good view of the airlock corridor.

Tom gripped the Markheim tightly, and he dialed it down to a narrow beam. Nobody had ever been killed by a stunner ... but a direct hit with a narrow beam could paralyze a man for three days.

There was movement at the far end of the airlock corridor. A helmeted head peered around the turn in the corridor; then two men in pressure suits moved into view, walking cautiously, weapons in hand. Tom shrank back against the wall, certain they had not seen him. He waited until they were almost to the junction with the main corridor; then he took aim and pressed the trigger stud on his Markheim. There was an ugly ripping sound as the gun jerked in his hand. The two men dropped as though they had been pole-axed.

A shout, a scrape of metal against metal, and a shot ripped back at him from the end of the corridor. Tom jerked back fast, but not quite fast enough. He felt a sledge-hammer blow on his shoulder, felt his arm jerk in a cramping spasm while the corridor echoed the low rumble of sub-sonics. He flexed his arm to work out the spasm ... they were using a wide beam, hardly strong enough to stun a man. His heart pounded. They were being careful, very careful....

Two more men rounded the bend in the corridor. Tom fired, but they hit the deck fast, and the beam missed. The first one jerked to his feet, charged up the corridor toward him, dodging and sliding. Tom followed him in his sights, fired three times as the Markheim heated up in his hand. The beam hit the man's leg, dumping him to the deck, and bounced off to catch the second one.

But now there was another sound, coming from the corridor behind him. Voices, shouts, clanging of boots. He pressed against the wall, listening. The sounds were from below. They must have gotten past Johnny ... probably the men on the scooters. Tom looked around helplessly. If they came up behind him, he was trapped in a crossfire. But if he left his position, more men could come in through the airlock. Even now two more came around the bend, starting up the corridor for him....

Quite suddenly, the lights went out.

The men stopped. Sound stopped. The corridor was pitch black. Tom fired wildly down the corridor, heard shouts and oaths from the men, but he could see nothing. Then, ahead, a flicker of light as a headlamp went on. The men from the airlock were close, moving in on him, and from behind he saw light bouncing off the corridor walls....

He jerked open the hatch to a storage hold, ducked inside, and slammed the hatch behind him. He pressed against the wall, panting.

He waited.

Suddenly an idea flickered in Tom's mind.

It was a chance ... a long chance ... but it was something. If they were going to be captured in spite of anything they could do, even a long chance would be worth trying....

He waited in the darkness, tried to think it through. It was a wild idea, an utterly impossible idea, he had never heard of it being tried before ... but *any* chance was better than none. He remembered what Johnny had said in the control cabin. The Ranger ship would have homing shells. An attempt to make a run with the *Scavenger* might be disastrous.

He thought about it, trying to reason it out. The Jupiter Equilateral men obviously wanted them alive. They did not dare to kill Roger Hunter's sons, because Roger Hunter might have told them where the bonanza was. And Jupiter Equilateral would not dare let anyone of them break away. If one of them got back to Mars, the whole U.N. Patrol would be out in the Belt....

The plan became clear in his mind, but he had to let Greg know. He fingered the control of his helmet radio. The boarding party would have a snooper, but if he was quick, they wouldn't have time to nail him. He buzzed an attention code. "Greg? Can you hear me?"

Silence. He buzzed again, and waited. What was wrong? Had they already broken through to the control cabin and taken Greg? He buzzed again. "Greg! Sound off if you can hear me."

More silence. Then a click. "Tom?"

"Here. Are you all right?"

"So far. You?"

"They got past me, but they didn't hit me. How's Johnny?"

"I don't know," Greg said. "I think he's been hurt. Tom, you'd better get off, they'll have snoopers...."

"All right, listen," Tom said. "How does it look to you?"

"Bad. We're outnumbered, they'll be through to here any minute."

"All right, I've got an idea. It's risky, but it might let us pull something out of this mess. I'll need some time, though."

"How much?"

"Ten, fifteen minutes."

There was an edge to Greg's voice. "What are you planning?"

"I can't tell you, they're listening in. But if it works...."

"Look, don't do anything stupid."

"I can't hear you," Tom said. "You try to hold them for fifteen minutes ... and don't worry. Take care of yourself."

Tom snapped off the speaker and moved to the hatchway. The corridor was empty, and pitch black. He started down toward the airlock, then stopped short at the sound of voices and the flicker of headlamps up ahead.

He crouched back, but the lights were not moving. Guards at the lock, making certain that nobody tried to board their own ship. Tom grinned to himself. They weren't missing any bets, he thought.

Except one. There was one bet they wouldn't even think of.

He backtracked to the storage hold, crossed through it, and out into the far corridor. He followed the gentle curve of the deck a quarter of the way around the ship. Twice along the way he stumbled in the darkness, but saw no sign of the raiders. At last he reached the far side, and the corridor leading to No. 2 airlock. Again he could see the lamps of the guards around the bend; they were stationed directly inside their own lock.

Inching forward, he peered into blackness. Each step made a muffled clang on the deck plates. He edged his boots along as quietly as possible, reaching along the wall with his hand until he felt the lip of a hatchway.

The lights and voices seemed nearer now. In the dim reflected light he saw the sign on the door of the hatchway:

No. 2 Airlock BE SURE PRESSURE GAUGE IS AT ZERO BEFORE OPENING HATCH

He checked the gauge, silently spun the wheel. There was a *ping* as the seals broke. He pulled the hatch open just enough to squeeze into the lock, then closed it behind him. Then he switched on the pumps, waiting impatiently until the red "all clear" signal flashed on. Then he opened the outside lock.

Just beyond, he could see the sleek silvery lines of the *Scavenger*.

It was their only chance.

He took a deep breath, and jumped across the gap to the open lock of the *Scavenger*.

THE LAST RUN OF THE SCAVENGER

To Greg Hunter the siege of the orbit-ship had been a nerve-wracking game of listening and waiting for something to happen.

In the darkness of the control cabin he stretched his fingers, cramped from gripping the heavy Markheim stunner, and checked the corridor outside again. There was no sound in the darkness there, no sign of movement. Somewhere far below he heard metal banging on metal; minutes before he thought he had heard the sharp ripping sound of a stunner blast overhead, but he wasn't sure. Wherever the fighting was going on, it was not here.

He shook his head as his uneasiness mounted. Why hadn't Johnny come back? He'd gone off to try and disable the Ranger ship leaving Greg to guard the control cabin. Why no sign of the marauders in the control cabin corridor? This should have been the first place they would head for, if they planned to take the ship, but there had been nothing but silence and darkness. Johnny had been gone near 15 minutes already. Greg became more uneasy.

He waited. Suddenly, bitterly, he realized the hopelessness of it. Even if Johnny did manage to damage the Ranger ship, what difference would it make? They had been fools to come out here, idiots to ignore Tawney's warning, the three of them. Tawney had told them in so many words that there would be trouble, and they had come out anyway, just begging for it.

Well, now they had what they'd begged for. Greg slammed his fist into his palm angrily. What had they expected? That the big company would step humbly aside for them, with a fortune hanging in the balance? If they had even begun to think it through before they started....

But they hadn't, and now it was too late. They were under attack; Johnny was off on a fool's errand, gone too long for comfort, and Tom ... Greg glanced at his watch. It had been ten minutes since Tom's call. What had he meant by it? A plan, he said. A long chance.

He couldn't shake off the cold feeling in his chest when he thought about Tom. What if something happened to him....

Greg remembered how he had grown to resent his brother. The time when they were very young and Tom had been struck by the sickness, a native Martian virus they called it. He remembered the endless nights of attention given to Tom alone. From then on somehow they weren't friends any more. But now all that seemed to disappear and Greg only wished that Tom would appear down the corridor....

A sound startled him. He tensed, gripping the stunner, peering into the darkness. Had he heard something? Or was it his own foot scraping on the deck plate? He held his breath, listening, and the sound came again, louder.

Someone was moving stealthily up the corridor.

Greg waited, covered by the edge of the hatchway. It might be Johnny returning, or maybe even Tom ... but there was no sign of recognition. Whoever it was was coming silently....

Then a beam of light flared from a headlamp, and he saw the blue crackle of a stunner. He jerked back as the beam bounced off the metal walls. Then he was firing point blank down the corridor, his stunner on a tight beam, a deadly pencil of violent energy. He heard a muffled scream and a bulk loomed up in front of him, crashed to the deck at his feet.

He fired again. Another crash, a shout, and then the sound of footsteps retreating. He waited, his heart pounding, but there was nothing more.

The first attempt on the control cabin had failed.

*

Five minutes later the second attempt began. This time there was no warning sound. A sudden, ear-splitting crash, a groan of tortured metal, and the barricaded hatchway glowed dull red. Another crash followed. The edge of the hatch split open, pouring acrid Murexide fumes into the cabin. A third explosion breached the door six inches; Greg could see headlamps in the corridor beyond.

He fired through the crack, pressing down the stud until the stunner scorched his hand. Then he heard boots clanging up the other corridor. He pressed back against the wall, waited until the sounds were near, then threw open the hatch. For an instant he made a perfect target, but the raiders did not fire. The stunner buzzed in his hand, and once again the footfalls retreated.

They *were* being careful!

Silence then, and blackness. Minutes passed ... five, ten.... Greg checked the time again. It was over twenty minutes since Tom had talked to him. What had happened? Whatever Tom had planned must have misfired, or something would have happened by now. For a moment he considered leaving his post and starting down the dark corridor to search ... but where to search? There was nothing to do but wait and hope for a miracle.

Then suddenly the lights blazed on in the control cabin and the corridor outside. An attention signal buzzed in Greg's earphones. "All right, Hunter, it's all over," a voice grated. "You've got five minutes to get down to No. 3 lock. If you make us come get you, you'll get hurt."

"I'll chance it," Greg snapped back. "Come on up."

"We're through fooling," the voice said. "You'd better get down here. And bring your brother with you."

"Sure," Greg said. "Start holding your breath."

The contact broke for a moment, then clicked on again. This time it was another voice. "We've got Johnny Coombs down here," it said. "You want him to stay alive, you start moving. Without your stunner."

Greg chewed his lip. They could be bluffing ... but they might not be. "I want to see Johnny," he said.

On the control panel a viewscreen flickered to life. "Take a look, then," the voice said in his earphones.

They had Johnny, all right. A burly guard was holding his good arm behind his back. Greg could see the speaker wires jerked loose from his helmet.

"It's up to you," the voice said. "You've got three minutes. If you're not down here by then, this helmet comes off and your friend goes out the lock. It's quick that way, but it's not very pleasant."

Johnny was shaking his head violently; the guard wrenched at his arm, and the miner's face twisted in pain. "Two minutes," the voice said.

"Okay," Greg said. "I'm coming down."

"Drop the stunner right there."

He dropped the weapon onto the deck. Three steps out into the corridor, and two guards were there to meet him, stunners raised. They marched him up the ramp to the outer level corridor and around to No. 3 lock.

They were waiting there with Johnny. A moment later the guards herded them through the lock and into the hold of the Ranger ship, stripped off their suits, and searched them.

A big man with a heavy face and coarse black hair came into the cabin. He looked at Johnny and Greg and grunted. "You must be Hunter," he said to Greg. "Where's the other one?"

"What other one?" Greg said.

"Your brother. Where is he?"

"How would I know?" Greg said.

The man's face darkened. "You'd be smart to watch your tongue," he said. "We know there were three of you, we want the other one."

The man turned to a guard. "What about it?"

"Don't know, Doc. Nobody's reported him."

"Then take a crew and search the ship. We were due back hours ago. He's in there somewhere."

"Sure, Doc." The guard disappeared through the lock. The man called Doc motioned Greg and Johnny through into the main cabin.

"What are you planning to do with us?" Greg demanded.

"You'll find out soon enough." Doc's mouth twisted angrily.

A guard burst into the cabin. "Doc, there's just nobody there! We've scoured the ship."

"You think he just floated away in his space suit?" Doc growled. "*Find him.* Tawney only needs one of them, but we can't take a chance on the other one getting back...." He broke off, his eyes on the viewscreen. "Did you check those scout ships?"

"No, I thought...."

"Get down there and check them." Doc turned back to the viewscreen impatiently.

Greg caught Johnny's eye, saw the big miner's worried frown. "Where is he?" he whispered.

"I don't know. Thought you did...."

"All I know is that he had some kind of scheme in mind."

"Shut up," Doc said to them. "If you're smart, you'll be strapping down before we...." He broke off in mid sentence, listening.

Quite suddenly, the Ranger ship had begun to vibrate. Somewhere, far away, there was the muffled rumble of engines.

Doc whirled to the viewscreen. Greg and Johnny looked at the same instant, and Johnny groaned.

Below them, the *Scavenger*'s jets were flaring. First the pale starter flame, then a long stream of fire, growing longer as the engines developed thrust.

Doc slammed down a switch, roared into a speaker. "That scout ship ... stop it! He's trying to make a break!"

Two guards appeared at the lock almost instantly, but it was too late. Already she was straining at her magnetic cable moorings; then the exhaust flared, and the little scout ship leaped away from the orbit-ship, moving out at a tangent to the asteroid's orbit, picking up speed, moving faster and faster....

In toward the orbit of Mars.

The man called Doc had gone pale. Now he snapped on the speaker again. "Frank? Stand by on missile control. He's asking for it."

"Right," the voice came back. "I'm sighting in."

The *Scavenger* was moving fast now, dwindling in the viewscreen. One panel of the screen went telescopic to track her. "All right," Doc said. "Fire one and two."

From both sides of the Ranger, tiny rockets flared. Like twin bullets the homing shells moved out, side by side, in the track of the escaping *Scavenger*. With a strangled cry, Greg leaped forward, but Johnny caught his arm.

"Johnny, *Tom's on ... that thing....*"

"I know. But he's got a chance."

Already the homing shells were out of sight; only the twin flares were visible. Greg stared helplessly at the tiny light-spot of the *Scavenger*. At first she had been moving straight, but now she was dodging and twisting, her side-jets flaring at irregular intervals. The twin pursuit shells mimicked each change in course, drawing closer to her every second.

And then there was a flash, so brilliant it nearly blinded them, and the *Scavenger* burst apart in space. The second shell struck a fragment; there was another flash. Then there was nothing but a nebulous powdering of tiny metal fragments.

The last run of the *Scavenger* had ended.

Dazed, Greg turned away from the screen, and somewhere, as if in a dream, he heard Doc saying, "All right, boys, strap this pair down. We've got a lot of work to do before we can get out of here."

PRISONERS

Wherever they were planning to take them, the captors took great pains to make sure that their two prisoners did not escape before they were underway. Greg and Johnny were strapped down securely into accelleration cots. Two burly guards were assigned to them, and the guards were taking their job seriously. One of the two was watching them at all times, and both men held their stunners on ready.

Meanwhile, under Doc's orders, the crew of the Jupiter Equilateral ship began a systematic looting of the orbit-ship they had disabled. Earlier they had merely searched the cabins and compartments. Now a steady stream of pressure-suited men crossed through the airlocks into the crippled vessel, marched back with packing cases full of tape records, microfilm spools, stored computer data ... anything that might conceivably contain information. The control cabin was literally torn apart. Every storage hold was ransacked.

A team of six men was dispatched to the asteroid surface, searching for any sign of mining or prospecting activity. They came back an hour later, long-faced and empty handed. Doc took their reports, his scowl growing deeper and deeper.

Finally the last of the searchers reported in. "Doc, we'd scraped it clean, and there's nothing there. Not one thing that we didn't check before."

"There's *got* to be something there," Doc said.

"You tell me where else to look, and I'll do it."

Doc shook his head ominously. "Tawney's not going to like it," he said. "There's no other place it could be...."

"Well, at least we have this pair," the other said, jerking a thumb at Greg and Johnny. "They'll know."

Doc looked at them darkly. "Yes, and they'll tell, too, or I don't know Tawney."

Greg watched it all happening, heard the noises, saw the packing-cases come through the cabin, and still he could not quite believe it. He caught Johnny's eye, then turned away, suddenly sick. Johnny shook his head. "Take it easy, boy."

"He didn't even have a chance," Greg said.

"I know that. He must have known it too."

"But why? What was he thinking of?"

"Maybe he thought he could make it. Maybe he thought it was the only chance...."

There was no other answer that Greg could see, and the ache in his chest was deeper.

There was no way to bring Tom back now. However things had been between them, they could never be changed now. But he knew that as long as he was still breathing, somebody somehow was going to answer for that last desperate run of the *Scavenger*....

*

It had been an excellent idea, Tom Hunter thought to himself, and it had worked perfectly, exactly as he had planned it ... so far. But now, as he clung to his precarious perch, he wondered if it had not worked out a little too well. The first flush of excitement that he had felt when he saw the *Scavenger* blow apart in space had begun to die down now; on its heels came the unpleasant truth, the realization that only the easy part lay behind him so far. The hard part was yet to come, and if that were to fail....

He realized, suddenly, that he was afraid. He was well enough concealed at the moment, clinging tightly against the outside hull of the Ranger ship, hidden behind the open airlock door. But soon the airlock would be pulled closed, and then the real test would come.

Carefully, he ran through the plan again in his mind. He was certain now that his reasoning was right. There had been two dozen men on the raider ship; there had been no question, even from the start, that they would succeed in boarding the orbit-ship and taking its occupants prisoners. The Jupiter Equilateral ship had not appeared there by coincidence. They had come looking for something that they had not found.

And the only source of information left was Roger Hunter's sons. The three of them together might have held the ship for hours, or even days ... but with engines and radios smashed, there had been no hope of contacting Mars for help. Ultimately, they would have been taken.

As he had crouched in the dark storage hold in the orbit-ship, Tom had realized this. He had also realized that, once captured, they would never have been freed and allowed to return to Mars.

If the three of them were taken, they were finished. But what if only two were taken? He had pushed it aside as a foolish idea, at first. The boarding party would never rest until they had accounted for all three. They wouldn't dare go back to their headquarters leaving one live man behind to tell the story....

Unless they thought the third man was dead. If they were sure of that ... *certain* of it ... they would not hesitate to take the remaining two away. And if, by chance, the third man wasn't as dead as they thought he was, and could find a way to follow them home, there might still be a chance to free the other two.

It was then that he thought of the *Scavenger*, and knew that he had found a way.

In the cabin of the little scout ship he had worked swiftly, fearful that at any minute one of the marauders might come aboard to search it. Tom was no rocket pilot, but he did know that the count-down was automatic, and that every ship could run on an autopilot, as a drone, following a prescribed course until it ran out of fuel. Even the shell-evasion mechanism could be set on automatic....

Quickly he set the autopilot, plotted a simple high school math course for the ship, a course the Ranger ship would be certain to see, and to fire upon. He set the count-down clock to give himself plenty of time for the next step.

Both the airlock to the *Scavenger* and to the orbit-ship worked on electric motors. The *Scavenger* was grappled to the orbit-ship's hull by magnetic cables. Tom dug into the ship's repair locker, found the wires and fuses that he needed, and swiftly started to work.

It was an ingenious device. The inner airlock door in the orbit-ship was triggered to a fuse. He had left it ajar; the moment it was closed, by anyone intending to board the *Scavenger*, the fuse would burn, a circuit would open, and the little ship's autopilot would go on active. The ship would blast away from its moorings, head out toward Mars....

And the fireworks would begin. All that he would have to worry about then would be getting himself aboard the Ranger ship without being detected.

Which was almost impossible. But he knew there was a way. There was one place no one would think to look for him, if he could manage to keep out of range of the viewscreen lenses ... the outer hull of the ship. If he could clamp himself to the hull, somehow, and manage to cling there during blastoff, he could follow Greg and Johnny right home.

He checked the fuse on the airlock once again to make certain it would work. Then he waited, hidden behind the little scout ship's hull, until the orbit-ship swung around into shadow. He checked his suit dials ... oxygen for twenty-two hours, heater pack fully charged, soda-ash only half saturated ... it would do. Above him he could see the rear jets of the Ranger. He swung out onto the orbit-ship's hull, and began crawling up toward the enemy ship.

It was slow going. Every pressure suit had magnetic boots and hand-pads to enable crewmen to go outside and make repairs on the hull of a ship in transit. Tom clung, and moved, and clung again, trying to reach the protecting hull of the Ranger before the orbit-ship swung him around to the sun-side again....

He couldn't move fast enough. He saw the line of sunlight coming around the ship as it swung full into the sun. He froze, crouching motionless. If somebody on the Ranger spotted him now, it was all over. He was exposed like a lizard on a rock. He waited, hardly daring to breathe, as the ship spun ponderously around, carrying him into shadow again.

And nothing happened. He started crawling upward again, reached up to grab the mooring cable, and swung himself across to the hull of the Ranger. The airlock hung open; he scuttled behind it, clinging to the hull in its shadow just as Greg and Johnny were herded across by the Jupiter Equilateral guards.

Then he waited. There was no sound, no sign of life. After a while the Ranger's inner lock opened, and a group of men hurried across to the orbit-ship. Probably a searching party, Tom thought. Soon the men came back, then returned to the orbit-ship. After another minute, he felt the vibration of the *Scavenger*'s motors, and he knew that his snare had been triggered.

He saw the little ship break free and streak out in its curving trajectory. He saw the homing shells burst from the Ranger's tubes. The *Scavenger* vanished from his range of vision, but moments later he saw the sudden flare of light reflected against the hull of the orbit-ship, and he knew his plan had worked, but the ordeal lay ahead.

And at the end of it, he might really be a dead man.

*

Hours later, the last group of looters left the orbit-ship, and the airlock to the Ranger clanged shut. Tom heard the sucking sound of the air-tight seals, then silence. The orbit-ship was empty, its insides gutted, its engines no longer operable. The Ranger hung like a long splinter of silver alongside her hull, poised and ready to move on.

He knew that the time had come. Very soon the blastoff and the accelleration would begin. He had a few moments to find a position of safety, no more.

Quickly, he began scrambling toward the rear of the Ranger's hull, hugging the metal sides, moving sideways like a crab. Ahead, he knew, the viewscreen lenses would be active; if one of them picked him up, it would be quite a jolt to the men inside the ship ... but it would be the end of his free ride.

But the major peril was the blastoff. Once the engines cut off, the ship would be in free fall. Then he could cling easily to the hull, walk all over it if he chose to, with the aid of his boots and hand-pads. But unless he found a way to anchor himself firmly to the hull during blastoff, he could be flung off like a pebble.

He heard a whirring sound, and saw the magnetic mooring cables jerk. The ship was preparing for blastoff. Automatic motors were drawing the cables and grappling plates into the hull. Moving quickly, Tom reached the rear cable. Here was his anchor, something to hold him tight to the hull! With one hand he loosened the web belt of his suit, looped it over a corner of the grappling plate as it pulled in to the hull.

The plate pulled tight against the belt. Each plate fit into a shallow excavation in the hull, fitting so tightly that the plates were all but invisible when they were in place. Tom felt himself pulled in tightly as the plate gripped the belt against the metal, and the whirring of the motor stopped.

For an instant it looked like the answer. The belt was wedged tight ... he couldn't possibly pull loose without ripping the nylon webbing of the belt. But a moment later the motor started whirring again. The plate pushed out from the hull a few inches, then started back, again pulling in the belt....

A good idea that just wouldn't work. The automatic machinery on a spaceship was built to perfection; nothing could be permitted to half-work. Tom realized what was happening. Unless the plate fit perfectly in its place, the cable motor could not shut off, and presently an alarm signal would start flashing on the control panel.

He pulled the belt loose, reluctantly. He would have to count on his boots and his hand-pads alone.

He searched the rear hull, looking for some break in the polished metal that might serve as a toehold. To the rear the fins flared out, supported by heavy struts. He made his way back, crouching close to the hull, and straddled one of the struts. He jammed his magnetic boots down against the hull, and wrapped his arms around the strut with all his strength.

Clinging there, he waited.

It wasn't a good position. The metal of the strut was polished and slick, but it was better than trying to cling to the open hull. He tensed now, not daring to relax for fear that the blastoff accelleration would slam him when he was unprepared.

Deep in the ship, the engines began to rumble. He felt it rather than heard it, a low-pitched vibration that grew stronger and stronger. The Ranger would not need a great thrust to move away from the orbit-ship ... but if they were in a hurry, they might start out at nearly Mars-escape....

The jets flared, and something slammed him down against the fin strut. The Ranger moved out, its engines roaring, accellerating hard. Tom felt as though he had been hit by a ton of rock. The strut seemed to press in against his chest; he could not breathe. His hands were sliding, and he felt the pull on his boots. He tightened his grip desperately. This was it. He had to hang on, *had* to hang on....

He saw his boot on the hull surface, sliding slowly, creeping back and stretching his leg, suddenly it broke loose; he lurched to one side, and the other boot began sliding. There was a terrible ache in his arms, as though some malignant giant were tearing at him, trying to wrench him loose as he fought for his hold.

There was one black instant when he knew he could not hold on another second. He could see the blue flame of the jet streaming behind him, the cold blackness of space beyond that. It had been a fool's idea, he thought in despair, a million-to-one shot that he had taken, and lost....

And then the pressure stopped. His boots clanged down on the hull, and he almost lost his hand-grip. He stretched an arm, shook himself, took a great painful breath, and then clung to the strut, almost sobbing, hardly daring to move.

The ordeal was over. Somewhere, far ahead, an orbit-ship was waiting for the Ranger to return. He would have to be ready for the braking thrust and the side-maneuvering thrusts, but he would manage to hold on. Crouching against the fin, he would be invisible to viewers on the orbit-ship ... and who would be looking for a man clinging to the outside of a scout-ship?

Tom sighed, and waited. Jupiter Equilateral would have its prisoners, all right. He wished now that he had not discarded the stunner, but those extra pounds might have made the difference between life and death during the blastoff. And at least he was not completely unarmed. He still had Dad's revolver at his side.

He smiled to himself. The pirates would have their prisoners, indeed ... but they would have one factor to deal with that they had not counted on.

*

For Greg it was a bitter, lonely trip.

After ten hours they saw the huge Jupiter Equilateral orbit-ship looming up in the viewscreen like a minor planet. Skilfully Doc maneuvered the ship into the launching rack. The guards unstrapped the prisoners, and handed them pressure suits.

Moments later they were in a section in crews' quarters where they stripped off their suits. This orbit-ship was much larger than Roger Hunter's; the gravity was almost Mars-normal, and it was comforting just to stretch and relax their cramped muscles.

As long as they didn't think of what was ahead.

Finally Johnny grinned and slapped Greg's shoulder. "Cheer up," he said. "We'll be honored guests for a while, you can bet on that."

"For a while," Greg said bitterly.

Just then the hatchway opened. "Well, who do we have here?" a familiar voice said. "Returning a call, you might say. And maybe this time you'll be ready for a bit of bargaining."

They turned to see the heavy face and angry eyes of Merrill Tawney.

THE SCAVENGERS OF SPACE

The casual observer might have been fooled. Tawney's guard was down only for an instant; then the expression of cold fury and determination on his face dropped away as though the shutter of a camera had clicked, and he was all smiles and affability. They were honored guests here, one would have thought, and this pudgy agent of the Jupiter Equilateral combine was their genial host, anxious for their welfare, eager to do anything he could for their comfort....

They were amazed by the luxuriousness of the ship. For the next few hours they received the best treatment, sumptuous accommodations, excellent food.

They were finishing their second cup of coffee when Tawney asked, "Feeling better, gentlemen?"

"You do things in a big way," Johnny said. "This is real coffee, made from grounds. Must have cost a fortune to ship it out here."

Tawney spread his hands. "We keep it for special occasions. Like when we have special visitors."

"Even when the visits aren't voluntary," Greg added sourly.

"We have to be realistic," Tawney said. "Would you have come if we invited you? Of course not. You gentlemen chose to come out to the Belt in spite of my warnings. You thus made things very awkward for us, upset certain of our plans." He looked at Greg. "We don't ordinarily allow people to upset our plans, but now we find that we're forced to include you in our plans, whether you happen to like the idea or not."

"You're doing a lot of talking," Greg said. "Why don't you come to the point?"

Tawney was no longer smiling. "We happen to know that your father struck a rich lode on one of his claims."

"That's interesting," Greg said. "Did Dad tell you that?"

"He didn't have to. A man can't keep a secret like that, not for very long. Ask your friend here, if you don't believe me. And we make it our business to know what's going on out here. We have to, in order to survive."

"Well, suppose you heard right. The law says that what a man finds on his own claim is his."

"Certainly," Tawney said. "Nobody would think of claim-jumping, these days. But when a man happens to die before he can bring in his bonanza, then it's a question of who gets there first, wouldn't you think?"

"Not when the man is murdered," Greg said hotly, "not by a long shot."

"But you can't prove that your father was murdered."

"If I could, I wouldn't be here."

"Then I think we'll stick to the law," Tawney said, "and call it an accident."

"And what about my brother? Was that an accident?"

"Ah, yes, your brother." Tawney's eyes hardened. "Quite a different matter, that. Sometimes Doc tends to be over-zealous in carrying out his assigned duties. I can assure you that he has been ... disciplined."

"That's not going to help Tom very much."

"Unfortunately not," Tawney said. "Your brother made a very foolish move, under the circumstances. But from a practical point of view, perhaps it's not entirely a tragedy."

"What do you mean by that?"

"From what I've heard," Tawney said, "you didn't have much use for your twin brother. And now you certainly won't have to share your father's legacy...."

It was too much. With a roar Greg swung at the little fat man. The blow caught Tawney full in the jaw, jerked his head back. Greg threw his shoulder into a hard left, slamming Tawney back against the wall. The guard charged across the room, dragging them apart as Tawney blubbered and tried to cover his face. Greg dug his elbow into the guard's stomach, twisted away and started for Tawney again. Then Johnny caught his arm and spun him around. "Stop it," he snapped. "Use your head, boy...."

Greg stopped, glaring at Tawney and gasping for breath. The company man picked himself up, rubbing his hand across his mouth. For a moment he trembled with rage. Then he gripped the table with one hand, forcibly regaining his control. He even managed a sickly smile. "Just like your father," he said, "too hot-headed for your own good. But we'll let it pass. I brought you here to make you an offer, a very generous offer, and I'll still make it. I'm a businessman, when I want something I want I bargain for it.

If I have to share a profit to get it, I share the profit. All right ... you know where your father's strike is. We want it. We can't find it, so you've got us over a barrel. We're ready to bargain."

Greg started forward. "I wouldn't bargain with you for...."

"Shut up, Greg," Johnny said.

Greg stared at him. The big miner's voice had cracked like a whip; now he was drawing Merrill Tawney aside, speaking rapidly into his ear. Tawney listened, shot a venomous glance across at Greg, and finally nodded. "All right," he said, "but I can't wait forever...."

"You won't have to."

Tawney turned to the guard. "You have your orders," he said. "They're to have these quarters, and the freedom of the ship, except for the outer level. They're not to be harmed, and they're not to be out of your sight except when they're locked in here. Is that clear?"

The guard nodded. Tawney looked at Johnny, and started for the door, still rubbing his jaw. "We'll talk again later," he said, and then he was gone.

When the guard had left, and the lock buzzed in the door, Johnny looked at Greg and shook his head sadly. "You just about fixed things, boy, you really did. You've got to use your head if you want to stay alive a while, that's all. Look, there isn't going to be any bargaining with Tawney, he just doesn't work that way. It's heads he wins, tails we lose. Once he has what he wants we won't last six minutes. All right, then there's just one thing that can keep us alive ... stalling him. We've got to make him think you'll give in if he plays his cards right."

Greg was silent for a minute. "I hadn't thought of it that way."

"And we've got to use the time we have to find some way to break for it." Johnny stood up, staring around the luxurious lounge. "If you want my opinion, it's going to take some pretty fancy footwork to get out of here with our skins."

*

True to his word, Tawney had given them the freedom of the ship. Greg and Johnny discovered that their guard was also an excellent guide. All day he had been leading them through the ship, chatting and answering their questions about asteroid mining, until they almost forgot that they were really prisoners here. And the guard's obvious pride in the scope and skill of his company's mining operations was strangely infectious.

Watching the Jupiter Equilateral ship in operation, Greg felt his heart sink. Here was a huge, powerful organization, with all the equipment and men and know-how they could ever need. How could one man, or two or three in a team, hope to compete with them? For the independent miner, the only hope was the Big Strike, the single lode that could make him rich. He might work all his life without finding it, and then stumble upon it by sheer chance....

But if he couldn't keep it when he found it, then what? What if the great mining company became so strong that they could be their own law in the Belt? What if they grew strong enough and powerful enough to challenge the United Nations on Mars itself, and gain control of the entire mining industry? What chance would the independent miner have then?

It was a frightening picture. Suddenly something began to make sense to Greg; he realized something about his father that he had never known before.

Roger Hunter had been a miner, yes. But he had been something else too, something far more important than just a miner.

Roger Hunter had been a fighter, fighting to the end for something he believed in....

Tawney interrupted Greg's thought.

"Quite an operation," he said.

Greg looked at him. "So I see."

"And very efficient, too. Our men have everything they need to work with. We can mine at far less cost than anyone else."

"But you still can't stand the idea of independent miners working the Belt," Greg said.

Tawney's eyebrows went up. "But why not? There's lots of room out here. Our operation with Jupiter Equilateral is no different from an independent miner's operation. We aren't different kinds of people." Tawney smiled. "When you get right down to it, we're both exactly the same thing ... scavengers in space, vultures picking over the dead remains to see what we can find. We come out to the asteroids, and we bring back what we want and leave the rest behind. And it doesn't matter whether we've got one ship working or four hundred ... we're still just scavengers."

"With just one difference," Greg said, turning away from the viewscreen.

"Difference?"

Greg nodded. "Even vultures don't kill their own," he said.

*

Later, when they were alone in their quarters again, Greg and Johnny stared at each other gloomily.

"Didn't you see *anything* that might help us?" Greg said.

"Not much. For an orbit-ship, this place is a fortress. I got a good look at that scout ship coming in ... it was armed to the teeth. Probably they all are. And they're keeping a guard now at every airlock."

"So we're sewed up tight," Greg said.

"Looks that way. They've got us, boy, and I think Tawney's patience is wearing thin, too. We're either going to have to produce or else."

"But what can we do?"

"Start bluffing."

"It seems to me we're just about bluffed out."

"I mean talk business," Johnny said. "Tell Tawney what he wants to know."

"When we don't know any more than he does? How?"

Johnny Coombs scratched his jaw. "I've been thinking about that," he said slowly, "and I wonder if we don't know a whole lot more than we think we do."

"Like what?" Greg said.

"We've all been looking for the same thing ... a Big Strike, a bonanza lode. Tawney's men have raked over every one of your Dad's claims, and they haven't turned up a thing." Johnny looked at Greg. "Makes you wonder a little, doesn't it? Your Dad was smart, but he was no magician. And how does a man go about hiding something like a vein of ore?"

"I don't know," Greg said. "It doesn't seem possible."

"It isn't possible," Johnny said flatly. "There's only one possible explanation, and we've been missing it all along. Whatever he found, *it wasn't an ore strike*. It was something else, something far different from anything we've been thinking of."

Greg stared at him. "But if it wasn't an ore strike, what was it?"

"I don't know," Johnny said. "But I'm sure of one thing ... it was something important enough that he was ready to die before he'd reveal it.

And that means it was important enough that Tawney won't dare kill us until he finds out what it was."

THE INVISIBLE MAN

Crouching back into the shadow, Tom Hunter waited as the heavy footsteps moved up the corridor, then back down, then up and down again. He peered around the corner for a moment, looking quickly up and down the curving corridor. The guard was twenty yards away, moving toward him in a slow measured pace. Tom jerked his head back, then peered out again as the footsteps receded.

The guard was a big man, with a heavy-duty stunner resting in the crook of his elbow. He paused; scratched himself, and resumed his pacing. Tom waited, hoping that something might distract the big man, but he moved stolidly back and forth, not too alert, but far too alert to risk breaking out into the main corridor.

Tom moved back into the darkened corridor where he was standing, trying to decide what to do. It was a side corridor, and a blind alley; it ended in a large hatchway marked HYDROPONICS, and there were no branching corridors. If he were discovered here, there would be no place to hide.

But he knew that he could never hope to accomplish his purpose here....

A hatch clanged open, and there were more footsteps down the main corridor as a change of guards hurried by. There was a rumble of voices, and Tom listened to catch the words.

"... don't care what you think, the boss says tighten it up...."

"But they got them locked in...."

"So tell it to the boss. We're supposed to check every compartment in the section every hour. Now get moving...."

The footsteps moved up and down the corridor then, and Tom heard hatches clanging open. If they sent a light down this spur ... he turned to the hatch, spun the big wheel on the door, and slipped inside just as the footsteps came closer.

The stench inside was almost overpowering. The big, darkened room was extremely warm, the air damp with vapor. The plastic-coated walls streamed with moisture. Against the walls Tom could see the great hydroponic vats that held the yeast and algae cultures that fed the crew of the ship. Water was splashing in one of the vats, and there was a gurgling sound as nutrient broth drained out, to be replaced with fresh.

He moved swiftly across the compartment, into a darkened area behind the rows of vats, and crouched down. He heard footsteps, and the ring of metal as the hatchway came open. One of the guards walked in, peered into the gloom, wrinkled his nose, and walked out again, closing the hatchway behind him.

It would do for a while ... if he didn't suffocate ... but if this ship was organized like smaller ones, it would be a blind alley. Modern hydroponic tanks did not require much servicing, once the cultures were growing; the broth was drained automatically and sluiced through a series of pipes to the rendering plant where the yeasts could be flavored and pressed into surrogate steaks and other items for spaceship cuisine. There would be no other entrances, no way to leave except the way he had come in.

And with the guards on duty, that was out of the question. He waited, listening, as the check-down continued in nearby compartments. Then silence fell again. The heavy yeast aroma had grown more and more oppressive; now suddenly a fan went on with a whir, and a cool draft of freshened reprocessed air poured down from the ventilator shaft above his head.

Getting into the orbit-ship had been easier than he had hoped. In the excitement as the new prisoners were brought aboard, security measures had been lax. No one had expected a third visitor; in consequence, no one looked for one. Huge as it was, the Jupiter Equilateral ship had never been planned as a prison, and it had taken time to stake out the guards in a security system that was at all effective. In addition, every man who served as a guard had been taken from duty somewhere else on the ship.

So there had been no guard at the airlock in the first few moments after the prisoners were taken off the Ranger ship. Tom had waited until the ship was moored, clinging to the fin strut. He watched Greg and Johnny taken through the lock, and soon the last of the crew had crossed over after securing the ship. Presently the orbit-ship airlock had gone dark, and only then had he ventured from his place of concealment, creeping along the dark hull of the Ranger ship and leaping across to the airlock.

A momentary risk, then, as he opened the lock. In the control room, he knew, a signal light would blink on a panel as the lock was opened. Tom moved as quickly as he could, hoping that in the excitement of the new visitors, the signal would go unnoticed ... or if spotted, that the spotter would assume it was only a crewman making a final trip across to the Ranger ship.

But once inside, he began to realize the magnitude of his problem. This was not a tiny independent orbit-ship with a few corridors and compartments. This was a huge ship, a vast complex of corridors and compartments and holds. There was probably a crew of a thousand men on this ship ... and there was no sign where Greg and Johnny might have been taken.

He moved forward, trying to keep to side corridors and darkened areas. In the airlock he had wrapped up his pressure suit and stored it on a rack; no one would notice it there, and it might be handy later. He had strapped his father's gun case to his side, some comfort, but a small one.

Now, crouching behind the yeast vat, he lifted out the gun, hefted it idly in his hand. It was a weapon, at least. He was not well acquainted with guns, and in the shadowy light it seemed to him that this one looked odd for a revolver; it even felt wrong, out of balance in his hand. He slipped it back in the case. After all, it had been fitted to Dad's hand, not his. And Johnny or Greg would know how to use it better than he would.

If he could find them. But to do that, he would have to search the ship. He would have to move about, he couldn't just wait in a storage hold. And with all the guards that were posted, he would certainly stumble into one of them sooner or later if he tried leaving this spot....

He shook his head, and started for the hatch. He would have to chance it. There was no way to tell how much time he had, but it was a sure bet that he didn't have very long.

In the spur corridor again, he waited until the guard's footsteps were muffled and distant. Then he darted out into the main corridor, moving swiftly and silently away from the guard. At the first hatchway he ducked inside, waited in the darkness, panting....

The guard had stopped walking. Then his footsteps resumed, but more quickly, coming down the corridor. He stopped, almost outside the hatchway door. "Funny," Tom heard him mutter. "I'd have sworn...."

Tom held his breath, waiting. This was a storage hold, but he didn't dare to move, even to take cover. The guard stood motionless for a moment, then grunted, and resumed his slow pacing.

When he had moved away Tom caught his breath in huge gasps, his heart beating in his throat. It was no use, he thought in despair. Once or twice he might get away with it, but sooner or later a guard would be alert enough to investigate an obscure noise, a flicker of movement in the corner of his eye....

There had to be another way. His eye probed the storage hold, hopelessly, and then stopped on a metal grill in the wall.

For a moment, he didn't recognize what it was. Then there was a *whoosh-whoosh-whoosh* as a fan went on, and he felt cool air against his cheek. He held out his hand to the grill, found the air coming from there.

A ventilation shaft. Every space craft had to have reconditioning units for the air inside the ship; the men inside needed a constant supply of fresh oxygen, but even more, without pumps to move the air in each compartment they would soon suffocate from the accumulation of carbon dioxide in the air they breathed out, or bake from the heat their bodies radiated. On the other hand, the yeasts and algae required carbon dioxide and yielded copious amounts of oxygen as they grew.

In Roger Hunter's little orbit-ship the ventilation shafts were small, a loose network of foot-square ducts leading from the central pumps and air-reconditioning units to every compartment in the ship. But in a ship of this size....

The grill was over a yard wide, four feet tall. It started about shoulder height and ran up to the overhead. The ducts would network the ship, opening into every compartment, and no one would ever open them unless something went wrong.

And then he was laughing out loud, working the grill out of the slots that held it to the wall, trying to make his hands work in his excitement.

He knew he had found his answer.

The grill came loose, lifted down in a piece. He stopped short as footsteps approached in the corridor, paused, and went on. Then he peered into the black gaping hole behind the grill. It was big enough for a man to crawl in. He shinned up into the hole, and pulled the grill back into its slot behind him.

Somewhere far away he heard a throbbing of giant pumps. There was a rush of cool fresh air past his cheek, cold when it contacted the sweat pouring down his forehead. He could not quite stand up, but there was plenty of room for him to crouch and move.

Ahead of him was a black tunnel, broken only by a patch of light coming through the grill that opened into the next compartment. He started into the blackness, his heart racing.

Somewhere in the ship Johnny Coombs and Greg Hunter were prisoners ... but now, Tom knew, there was a way to escape.

*

It was a completely different world, a world within a world, a world of darkness and silence, of a thousand curving and intersecting tunnels, some large, some small. For hours it seemed to him that he had been wandering through a tomb, moving through the corridors of a dead ship, the lone surviving crewman. There was some contact with the other world, of course, the world of the spaceship outside ... each compartment had its metal grill, and he passed many of them. But there were like doors that only he knew existed. He met no one in *these* corridors, there was no danger of sudden discovery and arrest in these dark alleys....

His boots had made too much noise as he started out, so he had slipped them off, hanging them from his belt and moving on in his stocking feet. As he went from duct to duct, he had an almost ridiculous feeling of freedom and power. In every sense, he was an invisible man. Not one soul on this great ship knew he was here, or even suspected. He had the run of the ship, complete freedom to go wherever he chose. He could move from compartment to compartment as silently and invisibly as if he had no substance at all.

*

He knew the first job was to learn the pattern of the ducts, and orientation was a problem. He had heard stories of men getting lost in the deep underground mining tunnels on Mars, wandering in circles for days until their food gave out and they starved. And there was that hazard here, for every duct looked like every other one.

But there was a difference here, because the ducts curved just as the main ship's corridors did. He could always identify the center of the ship by the force of false gravity pulling the other way. Furthermore, as the ducts drew closer to the pumps and reconditioning units, they opened into larger vents, and the noise of the pumps thundered in his ears. After an hour of exploration, Tom was certain that from any place in the ship he could at least find his way to the outer layer, and from there to one of the scout-ship airlocks.

Finding Greg and Johnny was quite a different matter.

He could not see enough through the compartment grills to identify just what the compartments were; he was forced to rely on what he could hear. The engine rooms were easily identified. In one area he heard the banging of pots and pans, the steaming of kettles ... obviously the galley. He found the control area. He could hear the clatter of typing instruments, the *click-click-click* of the computers working out the orbits and trajectories for the scout-ships as they moved out from the orbit-ship or came back in. In another compartment he heard a dispatcher chattering his own special code-language into a microphone in a low-pitched voice. He passed another grill, and then stopped short as a familiar voice drifted through.

Merrill Tawney's voice.

Tom hugged the grill, straining to catch the words. The company man sounded angry; the man he was talking to sounded even angrier. "I can't help what you want or don't want, Merrill, I can only report what we've found, and that's nothing at all. Every one of those claims has been searched twice over. Doc and his boys went over them, and we didn't find anything they missed. I think you're barking up the wrong tree."

"There's *got* to be something," Tawney said, his voice tight with anger. "Hunter couldn't have taken anything away from there, he didn't have a chance to. You read the reports..."

"I know," the other said wearily, "I know what the reports said."

"Then what he found is still there. There's no other possibility," Tawney said.

"We went over that rock with a microscope. We blew it to shreds. Assay has gone through the fragments literally piece by piece. They found low grade iron, a trace of nickel, a little tin, and lots of granite. If we never found anything richer than that, we'd have been out of business ten years ago."

There was a long silence. Tom pressed closer to the grill. Then he heard Tawney slam his fist into his palm. "You know what Roger Hunter's doing, don't you?" he said. "He's making fools of us, that's what! The man's dead, and he's making us look like idiots. If we hadn't been so sure we had the lode spotted ..." He broke off. "Well, that's done, we can't undo it. But this brat of his...."

"Any luck there?"

"Not a word. He's playing coy."

"Maybe he doesn't know anything. Doc made a bad mistake when he blasted the other one ... suppose *he* was the only one that knew."

"All right, it was a mistake," Tawney snapped. "What was he supposed to do, let him get back to Mars? We've got a good front there, but it's not that good. If the United Nations gets a toehold out here, the whole Belt will go into their pocket, you realize that. They're waiting for us to make one slip." He paused, and Tom heard him pacing the compartment. "But I think we've got our boy. This one knows. We've been spoiling him so far, that's all. Well, now we start digging. When I get through with him, he'll be begging us to let him tell. You just watch me, as soon as the okay comes through...."

Tom drew back from the grill, moving on in the darkness. So far he had not rushed his exploration ... there was a chance to use the ducts for escape, he wanted to know them well. But now he knew the hour was getting late. So far Greg and Johnny had been stalling Tawney ... but Tawney was getting impatient.

He moved quickly and he thought again of what Tawney had said. Tawney was right about one thing ... there was no way that Dad could have hidden a Big Strike so nobody could find it. It had to be there....

And yet it wasn't. He and Greg hadn't found it. Tawney's men hadn't found it, either. Why not? There must be a reason.

But he could not put his finger on it.

Half an hour later he was seriously worried. Half the compartments in the area were deserted, the men leaving for the cafeteria. The thought reminded Tom how hungry he was, and thirsty. His small emergency ration kit was empty. He toyed with the thought of sneaking into a food storage compartment, then thrust it out of his mind as too risky. He had to find Greg and Johnny before anything.

He passed a grill, and heard a murmur of voices; something in the deep bass rumble caught his ear, and he stopped, listened.

The voices stopped also.

He waited for them to begin, pressing against the grill. Johnny Coombs was not the only man with a deep bass voice, he might have been mistaken. He listened, but there was no sound. He heard the whir of a fan begin, still no sound, not even footsteps.

And then it happened, so fast he was taken completely off guard. The grill suddenly gave way, pitching him forward into the compartment. Something struck him behind the ear as he fell; there was a grunt, a sharp command, and he was pinned to the floor in the semi-darkness of the compartment.

Then he heard a gasp, and he opened his eyes. He was staring into his brother's startled face. Greg was pinning his shoulders to the carpeted deck, and behind him Johnny Coombs had a fist raised....

But they had stopped in mid-air, like a tableau of puppets. Greg gaped, his jaw falling open, and Tom heard himself saying, "What are you trying to do, kill a guy? Seems to me one time is enough."

He had found them.

THE TRIGGER

In the first instance of astonishment they were speechless. Later, Tom said it was the first time in his life that he had ever seen Greg totally without words; his brother jumped back, as if he had seen a ghost, and his mouth worked, but no sounds came out.

"Don't worry, it's me all right," Tom said, "and I'm mighty hungry."

Greg and Johnny stared at the black hole behind the grill ... and then Greg was pumelling him, pounding him on the back, so excited he couldn't get a sentence out, and Johnny was hovering over them, incredulous but forced to believe his eyes, like a father overwhelmed by the impossible behavior of a pair of unpredictable children. It was a jubilant reunion. They broke open the cabinets and refrigerator in the back of the lounge and pulled out surro-ham and rolls, while Johnny got some coffee going. Tom was so famished he could hardly wait to make sandwiches of the ham. He ate it as fast as he got it.

But finally he slowed up, got his mouth empty enough to talk. "All right, let's have the story," Greg said, still looking as though he couldn't believe his eyes. "The last we saw, you were blown into atoms out there in that *Scavenger* ... you've got some nerve turning up now and scaring us half out of our skins...."

"You want me to go back in my hole?"

"Just sit still and talk!"

Tom told them, then, starting from the beginning.

Through it all Greg stared in admiration. "We've got a genius among us, that's all," he said finally. "And I always thought you were the timid one...."

"But what else could I do?" Tom said. "You know what they say about grabbing a tiger by the tail ... once you get hold, you've got to hold on."

"Okay," Greg said, "but the next time I make a crack about your retiring nature, remind me to stick my foot in my mouth."

"I'll do it for him," Johnny Coombs rumbled.

Tom nodded toward the open grill. "The only thing I don't see is how you knew I was back there."

Johnny grinned. "We were busy taking down the grill when you came along. We'd found three microphones in this place, and figured they might have one behind the grill. And then we heard somebody breathing back there ... we thought they'd posted a guard back there, just to snoop us."

"Well, I'm glad you didn't hit him any harder...."

Johnny started to say something, then stopped, cocked his head toward the door. There were footsteps in the corridor outside; they came closer, stopped by the door. "Quick," Johnny hissed, "back inside!"

There was no time to look for other concealment. Tom leaped across the room, jumped up into the shaft again, and Greg slammed the grate up into place just as the hatchway door swung open.

Merrill Tawney walked into the room, with two burly guards behind him.

*

For the first few seconds, Greg was certain that they were lost. He stood with his back to the ventilator grill, frozen in his tracks as the fat little company man came in the room. He tried to keep his face blank, but he knew he wasn't succeeding. He saw the puzzled frown form on Tawney's face.

The company man motioned the guards into the room, peered suspiciously at Greg and Johnny. "Am I interrupting something, by any chance?"

"Nothing at all," Johnny blurted. "We were just talking."

"Talking." Tawney repeated the word as if it were some strange language he didn't quite understand. He looked at the guard. "Let's just check them."

While one guard patted down their clothes, the other withdrew a stunner, held it on ready. Tawney prowled the lounge. He glanced at the food on the table, then reached under the chair cushion and withdrew the disconnected microphone, looked at the loose wires, and tossed it aside.

"They're clean," the guard said.

Tawney's face was a study of uneasiness, but he clearly could not pinpoint what the trouble was. Finally he shrugged, turned on the smile again, although his eyes remained watchful. "Well, maybe you won't mind if I join in the talking for a while," he said. "You've been comfortable? No complaints?"

"No complaints," Greg said.

"Then I presume we're ready to talk business." He looked at Greg.

"You said you were ready to bargain," Greg said, "but I haven't heard any terms yet."

"Terms? Very simple. You direct us to the lode, we give you half of everything we realize from it," Tawney said, smiling.

"You mean you'll write us a contract? With a U.N. witness to it?"

"Well, hardly ... under the circumstances. I'm afraid you'll have to take our word."

Greg looked at the company man, and shook his head. "Not that I don't trust you," he said, "but I'm afraid I can't give you what you want," Greg said.

"Why not?"

"Because I don't know where Dad made his strike."

The company man's face darkened. "Somebody knows where it is. Your father would never have found something like that without telling his own sons...."

"Sorry," Greg said. "Of course, I can tell you where you can find out, if you want to go look."

"We've already searched his records...."

"*Some* of his records," Greg said. "Not all of them. There was a compartment behind the main control panel in Dad's orbit-ship. Dad used it to store deeds, claims, other important papers. There was a packet of notes in there before your men fired on the ship. But of course, maybe you searched more thoroughly, the second time."

Tawney stared at him for a moment, then at Johnny. Johnny Coombs shrugged his shoulders solemnly, and shook his head. Without a word, the little company man walked to the intercom speaker on the wall. He spoke sharply into it, waited, then had a brief, pungent conversation with someone. Then he turned back to Greg, his face heavy with suspicion. "You saw these papers?"

"Certainly I saw them. I didn't have time to read them through, but what else could they be?"

"Let me warn you," Tawney said coldly, "if I send a crew out there on a wild goose chase, the party will be over when they get back, do you understand? You've been given every consideration. If this is a fool's errand, you'll pay for it very dearly." He turned on his heel, snarled at one of the guards. "I want them watched every minute," he said. "One of you stay with them constantly. It won't take long to find out if this is a stall...."

He stalked out, and the hatchway clanged behind him. One guard went along; the big one with the stunner stayed behind, eyeing his prisoners unpleasantly. The stunner was in his hand, the safety off.

Johnny Coombs started across the room toward the kitchennette, passing close to the guard. Suddenly he turned, swung his fist heavily down on the guard's neck. The stunner crackled, but Greg had jumped aside. Another blow from Johnny's fist sent the gun flying. Another blow, and the guard's legs slid out from under him. He fell unconscious to the floor.

In an instant they were across the room, lifting down the grill, helping Tom out of his hiding place. "Okay, boy," Johnny said to Greg, "I guess you pulled the trigger with that story of yours."

"Not me," Greg said. "Tom did. He's the one that showed us the way out ... the same way he came in."

*

The guard was out for a while, they made sure of that first. Then there was a hasty consultation. "The airlocks are guarded," Johnny said, "and if they tumble to the ventilator shafts, they can smoke us out in no time. How are we going to get a scout-ship without showing ourselves? For that matter, how are we going to get a scout-ship away from here without being blown up the way the *Scavenger* was blown up?"

"I think I know a way," Tom said. "We have to have something to keep a lot of the crew busy. If we could get to the ship's generators and put them out of commission somehow, it might do it."

"Why?" Greg wanted to know.

"Because of the air supply," Tom said. "Without the generators, the fans won't run. They'll have to get a crew to fix them or they'll suffocate."

"But that would only take a few men," Johnny said. "As soon as the generators went out, they'd look for us, and if we were missing ... well, they'd have the whole crew beating the bushes for us. It wouldn't be long before somebody thought of the ventilators."

"But we've got to do something, and do it fast," Tom said.

"I know." Johnny chewed his lip. "It's a good idea, but we need more than just the generators. We've got to disable the ship ... throw so many things at them so fast from so many different directions that they don't know which way to turn. That means we'd need to split up, and we'd need weapons." He hefted the guard's Markheim. "One stunner between three of us isn't enough."

"Well, we have this." Tom unbuckled Roger Hunter's gun case from his belt. "Dad's revolver. It's not a stunner, but it might help." He tossed the case to Johnny. "I can give you both a rundown on how the shafts go. We could plan to meet at a certain spot in a certain length of time...."

He broke off, looking at Johnny. The big miner had taken Roger Hunter's gun from the case, and hefted it in his hand, started to check it automatically as Tom talked. But now his hand froze as he stared at the weapon.

"What's wrong?" Tom asked.

"This gun is wrong," Johnny said. "All wrong. Where did you get this thing?"

"From Dad's spacer pack, the one the Patrol brought back. The Major gave it to us in Sun Lake City." Tom peered at the gun. "Is it broken or something? It's just Dad's revolver...."

"It is, eh?" Johnny turned the gun over in his hand. "Whoever told you about guns?"

"What's wrong with it?"

There was an odd expression on Johnny's face as he handed the weapon back to Tom. "Take a look at it," he said. "Tell me whether it's loaded or not."

Tom looked at it. Except for a few hours on the firing range, he had had no experience with guns; he couldn't have taken down a Markheim and reassembled it if his life depended on it. But he had seen his father take the old revolver out of the leather case many times before.

Now Tom could see that this was not the same gun.

The thing in his hand was large and awkward. The hand-grips didn't fit; there was no trigger guard, and no trigger. Several inches along the gleaming metal barrel was a shiny stud, and below it a dial with notches on it.

"That's funny," Tom said. "I've never seen this thing before."

Greg took it from him, balanced it in his hand. "Doesn't feel right," he said. "All out of balance."

"Look at the barrel," Johnny said quietly.

Greg looked. There was no hole in the end of the barrel. "This thing's crazy," he said.

"And then some," Johnny said. "You haven't had this out of the case since you took it from the pack?"

"Just once," said Tom. "And I put it right back. I hardly looked at it. Look, maybe it's just a new model Dad got."

"It's no new model. I'm not even sure it's a gun," Johnny said. "Doesn't *feel* like a gun."

"What happens when you push the stud here?" Greg asked.

Johnny licked his lips nervously. "Try it," he said.

Greg leveled the thing at the rear wall of the lounge and pressed the stud. There was a sharp buzzing sound, and a blinding flash of blue light against the wall. It looked for all the world like the flash of a live power line shorting out. They squinted at the flash, rubbed their eyes....

And stared at the wall. Or at what was left of the wall, because most of the wall was gone. The metal had bellied out in a six-foot hole into the storage hold beyond....

Johnny Coombs whistled. "This thing did *that*?" he whispered.

"It must have...."

"But there's no gun ever made that could do that." He walked over to the hole in the wall. "That's half-inch steel plate. There's no way to pack that kind of energy into a hand gun."

They stared at the innocent-looking weapon in Greg's hand. "Whatever it is, Dad must have put it in the gun-case."

"Yes, he must have," Johnny said.

"Well, don't you see what that means? *Dad must have found it somewhere.* Somewhere out here in the Belt ... a gun that no man could have made...."

He took the weapon, ran his finger along the gleaming barrel. "I wonder," he said, "what else Dad might have found out there."

*

Somewhere below them they heard a hatch clang shut, and even deeper in the ship generator motors began throbbing in a steady even rhythm. In the silence of the lounge they could hear their own breathing, and outside a thousand tiny sounds of the ship's activity were audible.

But now they had attention only for the odd-shaped piece of metal in Greg's hand, and for the hole that gaped in the wall.

"You think that *this* was what Dad found?" Greg said. "The Big Strike he told Johnny about?"

"It must be part of it," Tom said.

"But what is it? And where did it come from? It doesn't make sense," Greg protested.

"It doesn't make sense the way we've been looking at it," Tom said. "All we've found was some gobbledegook in Dad's private log to tell us what he found ... but it couldn't have been a vein of ore, or Tawney's men would have unearthed it. It had to be something else. Something that was so big and important that Dad didn't even dare let Johnny in on it."

"Yes, that's been the craziest part of it, to me," Johnny said. "I've done a lot of mining with your Dad. If he'd hit rich ore, he would have taken me out there to mine it with him. But he didn't. He said it was something he had to work on alone for a while, and he sent me back."

"As if he'd found something that scared him," Tom said, "or something that he didn't understand. He was *afraid* to tell anybody. And whatever he found, he managed to hide it somewhere, so that nobody would find it...."

"Then why didn't he hide this part of it, too?" Greg said.

"Maybe to be sure there was some trace left, if anything happened to him," Tom said.

They were silent for a moment. The only sound was the stertorous breathing of the unconscious guard. "Well," Greg said finally, "I have to admit it makes sense. It makes other things add up better, too. Dad was no fool, he must have known that Tawney was onto something. And Dad would never have risked his life for an ore strike. He'd either have made a deal with Tawney or let him hijack the lode, if that was all there was to it. But there's still one big question ... where did he hide what he found? And we aren't going to find the answer here." He walked over to the hole in the wall.

"Made quite a mess of it, didn't it?" Johnny said.

"Looks like it. I wonder what that thing would do to a ship's generator plant." He turned to Johnny. "We haven't much time. With this thing, we could tear this ship apart, leave them so confused they'll never know what broke loose. And if we could get that gun back to Major Briarton, he'd have to listen to us, and get the U.N. Patrol into the search...."

They had been so intent on their talking that they did not hear the footsteps in the corridor until the door swung open. It was another guard, the one who had departed with Tawney. He stopped short, blinking at his companion on the floor, and then at the gaping hole in the wall. When he saw the twins, side by side, his jaw sagged and a strangled sound came from his throat.

Then Johnny grabbed his arm, jerked him into the lounge, and slammed the hatch shut. Greg pulled the stunner from his holster and tossed it to Tom. The guard let out a roar, twisted free, and met Johnny's fist as he came around. He sagged at the knees and slid to the floor beside the other guard. "All right," Johnny said, "we've dealt the cards, now we'd better play the hand. Tom, you first."

Tom pulled the ventilator grill down, and climbed up into the shaft. Greg followed, with Johnny at his heels, pulling the grill back up into place from the inside. They waited for a moment, but there was no sound from the lounge.

"All right," Johnny said breathlessly. "Let's move."

Swiftly they started down the dark tunnel.

They did not pause, even to catch their breath, for the first twenty minutes as Tom led them swiftly and silently down through the maze of corridors and chutes that made up the ventilation system of the huge ship. Greg lost his bearing completely in the first twenty seconds; each time his brother paused at a junction of tubes, he felt a wave of panic rise up in his throat ... suppose they lost themselves in here! He heard Johnny's trousers flapping behind him, saw Tom's figure flit past another grill up ahead, and plunged doggedly on.

It was amazingly hard to move quietly. Even in stocking feet they made a soft thud with each footfall.

But there was no sign of detection, no sound of alarm. Finally they came out into a large shaft which allowed them to stand upright, and they stopped to catch their breath.

"Main tube to the living quarters," Tom said when they had caught up to him. "Joins with the lower-level tube by a series of chutes. We've actually been circumnavigating the ship ... I wanted to get as far away from that lounge compartment as possible, in case they check up on you right away."

"We can't have much time," Johnny said. "That second guard must have been coming to relieve the other, and when the first one doesn't report back, they'll smell something fishy."

*

They talked it over for a moment. Johnny had been careful to leave the hatchway into the corridor ajar before he climbed into the ventilator shaft, and then he had pulled the shaft snugly into place behind him. Anyone who came would find two unconscious guards, a burnt-out hole in the wall, and the door unlocked.

"We'll hope that he takes things at face value, and assumes we're at large in the ship somewhere, for a while at least," Johnny said. "That hole in the wall is going to set them back a couple of steps, too."

"But they'll sound the alarm, at least," Tom said.

"You bet they will! They'll have every man on the crew shaking down the ship for us. But they may not think of the ventilators until they can't find us anywhere else."

"But sooner or later they're bound to think of it."

"That's true," Johnny said. "Unless they keep seeing us in the ship. The way I figure it, this crew has been on battle stations plenty of times. They'll be able to search the whole ship in half an hour. We're just going to have to show ourselves ... at least enough to keep them searching."

"Well, what if they do think of the ventilators?" Greg said. "They'd still have a time finding us."

"Maybe, but don't underestimate Tawney. He might just mask up his crew and flood the tubes with cyanide."

They thought about that for a minute. There was no sound here but their own breathing, and the low chug-chug-chug of the pumps somewhere deep in the ship. Momentarily they expected to hear the raucous clang of the alarm bell, as some crew member or another walked into the lounge and found them gone. But so far there was no sign they had been discovered missing. "No," Johnny said finally, "if we just hide out in here, and hope for a chance at one of the scout ships, they'll find us eventually. But we've got three big advantages, if we can figure out how to use them. That fancy gun, for one. A way to get around the ship, for another ... and the fact that there's one more of us than they count on." He flipped on his pocket flash, began drawing lines on the dusty floor of the shaft. "My idea is to keep them so busy fighting little fires that they won't have a chance to worry about where the big one is."

He drew a rough outline-sketch of the organization of the ship. "This look right to you, from what you've seen?" he asked Tom.

"Pretty much," Tom said. "There are more connecting tubes."

"All the better. We want to get the generators with our little toy here first. That'll darken the ship, and put the blowers out of commission in case they think of using gas. Also, it will cut out their computers and missile-launching rigs, which might give us a chance to get a scout-ship away in one piece if we could get aboard one."

"All right, the generators are first," Tom said. "But then what? There are four hundred men on this ship. They'll have every airlock triple guarded. They'll block us for sure."

"Not when we get through, they won't," Johnny grinned. "We've got an old friend aboard who's going to help us."

"*Friend?*"

"Ever hear of panic?" Johnny said. "Just listen a minute."

Quickly then, he outlined his plan. Tom and Greg listened, watched Johnny make marks with his finger in the dust. When he finished, Greg whistled softly. "You missed your life work," he said. "You should have gone into crime."

"If I'd had a ghost to help me, I might have," Johnny said.

"It's perfect," Tom said, "if it works. But it all depends on one thing ... keeping it rolling after we start...."

For another five minutes they went over the details. Then Johnny clapped them each on the shoulder. "It's up to you two," he said. "Let's go."

They moved down the large shaft to the place where it broke into several spurs. Johnny started down the chute toward the engine rooms; Tom and Greg headed in opposite directions toward the main body of the ship. Just as they broke up, they heard a muffled metallic sound from the nearest compartment grill.

It was the *clang-clang-clang* of the orbit-ship's general alarm.

*

Crewmen stopped with food halfway to their mouths, jerked away from tables. Orders buzzed along a dozen wires, and section chiefs began reporting their battle-stations alert and ready. Finally Tawney snapped on the general public address system speaker. "Now get this," he roared. "I want every inch of this ship searched ... every corridor, every compartment. I want a special crew standing by for missile launching. I want double guards at every airlock. If they get a ship away from here, the man who lets them through had better be dead when I find him...." He broke off, clutching the speaker until his voice was under control again. "All right, move. They're armed, but there's no place they can go. Find them."

A section-chief came back over the speaker. "Dead or alive, boss?"

"Alive, you idiot! At least the Hunter brat. I'll take the other one any way you can get him."

He switched off, and waited, pacing the control cabin like a caged animal. Ten minutes later a buzzer sounded. "Hydroponics, boss. All clear."

"No sign of them?"

"Nothing."

Another buzz. "Number seven ore hold. Nothing here."

Still another buzz. "Crew's quarters. Nothing, boss."

One by one the reports came in. Fuming, Tawney checked off the sections, watched the net draw tighter throughout the ship. They were somewhere, they *had* to be....

But nobody seemed to find them.

He was buzzing for his first mate when the power went off. The lights went out, the speaker went dead in his hand. The computers sighed contentedly and stopped computing. Abruptly the emergency circuits went into operation, flooding the darkness with harsh white lights. The intercom started buzzing again.

"Engine room, boss."

"What happened down there?" Tawney roared.

The man sounded like he'd just run the mile. "Generators," he panted. "Blown out."

"Well, get somebody in there to fix them. Have a crew seal off the area...."

"Can't, boss. Fix them, I mean."

"Why not? What have we got electricians for?"

"There's nothing left to fix. The generators aren't wrecked ... they're demolished...."

"Then get the pair that did it...."

"They're not here. We've been sealed up tight. There's no way anybody could have gotten in here...."

After that, things began to get confusing.

*

For a while Merrill Tawney thought that his crew was going crazy ... and then he began to wonder if he were the one who was losing his mind.

Whatever the case, Merrill Tawney was certain of one thing. The things that were happening on his orbit-ship could not possibly be happening.

A guard in one of the outer shell storage holds called in with a disquieting report. Greg Hunter, it seemed, had just been spotted vanishing into one of the storage compartments from the main outer-shell corridor. When the guard had broken through the jammed hatchway to collar his trapped victim, there was no sign of the victim anywhere around.

At the same moment, a report came in from a guard on the opposite side of the ship. He had just spotted Greg Hunter *there*, it seemed, moving down a spur corridor. The guard had held his fire (according to Tawney's orders) and summoned help to corner the quarry ... but when help arrived, the quarry had vanished.

*

Five minutes later the Hunter boy was discovered in the Hydroponics section, busily reducing all the yeast vats to shambles with a curious weapon that seemed to eat holes in things. It ate the deck out from under the guard's feet, sending him plunging through the floor into the galley. By the time he had scrambled back again, the Hunter boy was gone, and a rapid move to seal off the region failed to turn him up again. The guard was upset; Tawney was a great deal more upset, because at the time Greg Hunter was (reportedly) playing havoc with the yeast-vats in Hydroponics he was also (reportedly) knocking guards down like ten-pins in the main corridor off the engine room while reinforcements tried to pin him down with a wide-beam stunner....

Quite suddenly emergency circuits closed and lights flashed in the control cabin, the special signal for a meteor-collision with the outer shell in No. 3 hold. Tawney signalled for the section chief frantically. "What's happening down there?"

"I can't talk," the section chief gasped. "Gotta get into a suit, we're leaking in here...."

"Well, plug up the hole!"

"The hole's four feet wide, sir!" There was a fit of coughing and the contact broke. The signals for No. 4 hold and No. 5 hold were flashing now; while the crew members in the vicinity scrambled for pressure suits someone systematically proceeded to blow holes in No. 9, No. 10 and No. 11 holds....

It was impossible. The reports came in thick and fast. Greg Hunter was in two places at once, and everywhere he went ... in both places ... there was a trail of unbelievable destruction. Bulkheads demolished, gaping holes torn in the outer shell, the air-reconditioning units smashed beyond repair.... Tawney buzzed for his first mate.

An emergency switch cut into the line, with the frantic voice of a section chief. Johnny Coombs had been spotted disappearing into the ventilator shaft in the engine sector. "Well, go in after him!" Tawney screamed. He got his first mate finally, and snarled orders into the speaker. "They're in the ventilators. Get a crew in there and stop them."

But it was dark in the ventilator shafts. No emergency lights in there. Worse, the crewmen were hearing the things that were being whispered around the ship. The ventilator shafts yawned menacingly before them; they went in reluctantly. Once in the dark maze of tunnels, identification was difficult. Two guards met each other headlong in the darkness, and put each other out of the fight in a flurry of nervous stunner-fire. While they searched more of the holds were broken open, leaking air through gaping rents in the hull....

Tawney felt the panic spreading; he tried to curb it, and it spread in spite of him. The fugitives were appearing and disappearing like wraiths. Reports back to control cabin took on a frantic note, confused and garbled. Now the second-level bulkheads were being attacked. Over a third of the compartments were leaking precious air into outer space.

When a terrified section chief came through with a report that two Greg Hunters had been spotted by the same man at the same time, and that the guards in the sector were shooting at anything that moved, including other guards, Tawney made his way to the radio cabin and put through a frantic signal to Jupiter Equilateral headquarters on Mars.

The contact took forever, even with the ship's powerful emergency boosters. By the time someone at headquarters was reading him, Tawney's report sounded confused. He was trying for the third time to explain, clearly and logically, how two men and a ghost were scuttling his orbit-ship under his very feet when one wall of the cabin vanished in a crackle of blue fire, and he found himself staring at two Greg Hunters and a grim-faced Johnny Coombs.

He made squeaky noises into the microphone and dropped it with a crash. He groped for a chair; Johnny jerked him to his feet again. "A scout-ship," he said tersely. "Clear it for launching. We want one with plenty of fuel, and we don't want a single guard anywhere near the airlock." He picked up an intercom microphone and thrust it into the little fat man's trembling hand. "Now move! And you'd better be sure they understand you, because you're coming with us."

Merrill Tawney stared first at Tom, then at Greg, and finally at the microphone. Then he moved. The orders he gave to his section chiefs were very clear and concise.

He had never argued with a ghost before, and he didn't care to start now.

*

It was over so quickly that it seemed to Tom it had just begun, and if so much had not been at stake, it might have been fun.

It had been the gun ... the remarkable gun that Roger Hunter had left as his legacy ... that had been the key. It ate through steel and aluminum alloy like putty. Whatever its power source, however it worked, by whatever means it had been built, there had been no match for it on the orbit-ship.

It had *worked* ... and that was all that mattered right then.

With it, and with the advantage of a ghost that walked like a man ... Tom Hunter, to be exact ... they had reduced the Jupiter Equilateral orbit-ship to a smoking wreck in something less than thirty minutes.

The signal came back that a scout-ship was ready, unguarded. Johnny prodded Tawney with the stunner. "You first," he said.

"But where are you taking me?"

"You'll see," Johnny said.

"It was a trick," Tawney said, glaring at Tom. "They told me they shot your ship to pieces...." .

"The ship, yes," Tom said. "Not me."

"Well ... well, that's good, that's good," Tawney said quickly. He turned to Greg. "You don't have to take me back ... the bargain is still good...."

"Move," Johnny Coombs said.

With Tawney between them, Greg and Tom marched down the corridor toward the airlock, with Johnny bringing up the rear. No one stopped them. No one even came near them. One crewman stumbled on them in the corridor; he saw Tawney with a gun in his back, and fled in terror.

They found the scout-ship, and strapped Tawney down to an accelleration bunk, binding his hands and feet so he couldn't move. Greg checked the controls while Tom and Johnny strapped down. A moment later the engines fired, and the leaking wreck of the orbit-ship fell away, dwindling and disappearing in the blackness of space.

It was a quiet journey. The red dot that was Mars grew larger every hour. One of the three stayed awake at all times to watch Tawney while the others slept. During the second rest period, Tom woke up while Greg was on duty.

"How's our prisoner doing?" Tom asked.

"No problem there, he can barely move. I almost wish he'd try something, he's too quiet."

It was true. Tawney had recovered from his shock ... but rather than grow more worried as Mars grew large on the screen, he seemed to become more cheerful by the minute. "He doesn't seem very worried, does he?" Tom said.

"No, and it doesn't quite add. We've got enough on him to get Jupiter Equilateral pushed right out of the Belt."

"I'd still feel better if we had the whole picture for the Major," Tom said. "We still don't know what Dad found, or where he hid it...."

The uneasiness grew. Tawney ignored them, staring at the image of the red planet on the viewscreen almost eagerly. Then, eight hours out of Sun Lake City a U.N. Patrol ship appeared, moving toward them swiftly. "Intercepting orbit," Greg said. "Looks like they were waiting for us."

They watched as the big ship moved in to tangential orbit, matching its speed to theirs. Then Greg snapped the communicator switch. "Sound off," he said cheerfully. "We've got a prize for you."

"Stand by, we're boarding you," the Patrol sent back. "And put your weapons aside."

Four scooters broke from the side of the Patrol ship. Greg activated the airlock. Five minutes later a man in Patrol uniform with captain's bars stepped into the control cabin, a stunner on ready in his hand. Three Patrolmen came in behind him.

The captain looked around the cabin, then saw Tawney, and took a deep breath. "Well, thank the stars you're safe at any rate. Pete, Jimmy, take the controls."

"Hold on," Greg said. "We don't need a pilot."

The Captain looked at him. "Sorry, but we're taking you in. There won't be any trouble unless you make it. You three are under arrest, and I'm authorized to make it stick if I have to. I suggest you just cooperate."

They stared at him. Then Johnny said, "What are the charges?"

"You ought to know," the Captain said. "We have a formal complaint from the main offices of Jupiter Equilateral, charging you with piracy, murder, kidnapping of a company official, and totally wrecking a company orbit ship. I don't quite see how you managed it, but we're going to find out in short order."

There was a stunned silence in the cabin, and then a sound came from the rear of the cabin.

Merrill Tawney was laughing.

They were taken to a small, drab internment room. A half hour passed and still no word from the Major. From the moment the Patrol crew had boarded them, everything had seemed like a bad dream. The shock of the arrest, the realization that the Captain had been serious when he reeled off the charges lodged against them ... they had been certain it was some kind of ill-planned joke until they saw the delegation of Jupiter Equilateral officials waiting at the port to greet Merrill Tawney like a man returned from the dead. They had watched Tawney climb into the sleek company car and drive off toward the gate, while the Captain had escorted them without a word down to the internment rooms.

The door clicked, and the Captain looked in. "All right, come along now," he said.

"Is the Major here?" Tom said.

"You'll see the Major soon enough." The Captain herded them into another room, where a clerk efficiently fingerprinted them. Then they went down a ramp to a jitney-platform, and boarded a U.N. official car. The trip into the city was slow; rush-hour traffic from the port was heavy. When they reached U.N. headquarters, there was another wait in an upper level ante-room. The Captain stood stiffly with his hands behind his back and ignored them.

"Look, this is ridiculous," Greg burst out finally. "We haven't done anything. You haven't even let us make a statement."

"Make your statement to the Major. It's his headache, not mine, I'm happy to say."

"But you let that man walk out of there scot free...."

The Captain looked at him. "If I were you," he said, "I'd stop complaining and start worrying. If I had Jupiter Equilateral at my throat, I'd worry plenty, because once they start they don't stop."

A signal light blinked, and he took them downstairs. Major Briarton was behind his desk; his eyes tired, his face grim. He dismissed the Captain, and motioned them to seats. "All right, let's have the story," he said, "and by the ten moons of Saturn it had better be convincing, because I've about had my fill of you three."

He listened without interruption as Tom told the story, with Greg and Johnny adding details from time to time. Tom told him everything, from the moment they had blasted off for Roger Hunter's claim to the moment the Patrol ship had boarded them, except for a single detail.

He didn't mention the remarkable gun from Roger Hunter's gun case. The gun was still in the spacer's pack he had slung over his shoulder; he had not mentioned it when the Patrolmen had taken their stunners away. Now as he talked, he felt a twinge of guilt in not mentioning it....

But he had a reason. Dad had died to keep that gun secret. It seemed only right to keep the secret a little longer. When he came to the part about their weapons, he simply spoke of "Dad's gun" and omitted any details.

And through the story, the Major listened intently, interrupting only occasionally, pulling at his lip and scowling.

"So we decided that the best way to convince you that we had the evidence you wanted was to bring Tawney back with us," Tom concluded.

"A brilliant maneuver," the Major said dryly. "A real stroke of genius."

"But then the Patrol ship intercepted us and told us we were under arrest. And when we landed, they let Tawney drive off without even questioning him."

"The least we could do, under the circumstances," the Major said.

"Well, I'd like to know why," Greg broke in bitterly. "Why pick on us? We've just been telling you...."

"Yes, yes, I heard every word of it," the Major sighed. "If you knew the trouble ... oh, what's the use? I've spent the last three solid hours talking myself hoarse, throwing in every bit of authority I could muster and jeopardizing my position as Coordinator here, for the sole purpose of keeping you three idiots out of jail for a few hours."

"Jail!"

"That's what I said. The brig. The place they put people when they don't behave. You three are sitting on a nice, big powder keg right now, and when it blows I don't know how much of you is going to be left."

"Do you think we're lying?" Greg said.

"Do you know what you're charged with?" the Major snapped back.

"Some sort of nonsense about piracy...."

"Plus kidnapping. Plus murder. To say nothing of totally disabling a seventeen-million-dollar orbit-ship and placing the lives of four hundred crewmen in jeopardy." The Major picked up a sheet of paper from his desk. "According to Merrill Tawney's statement, the three of you hijacked a company scout-ship that chanced to be scouting in the vicinity of your father's claim. Your attack was unprovoked and violent. Everybody on Mars knows you were convinced that Jupiter Equilateral was responsible for your father's death." He looked up. "In the absence of any evidence, I might add, although I did my best to tell you that." He rattled the report-sheet. "All right. You took the scout-ship by force, with the pilot at gunpoint, and made him home in on his orbit-ship. Then you proceeded to reduce that orbit-ship to a leaking wreck, although Tawney tried to reason with you and even offered you amnesty if you would desist. By the time the crew stopped shooting each other in the dark ... fifteen of them subsequently expired, it says here ... you had stolen another scout-ship and kidnapped Tawney for the purpose of extorting a confession out of Jupiter Equilateral, threatening him with torture if he did not comply...." The Major dropped the paper to the desk.

Johnny Coombs picked it up, looked at it owlishly, and put it back again. "Pretty large operation for three men, Major," he said.

The Major shrugged. "You were armed. That orbit-ship was registered as a commercial vessel. It had no reason to expect a surprise attack, and had no way to defend itself."

"They were armed to the teeth," Greg said disgustedly. "Why don't you send somebody out to look?"

"Oh, I could, but why waste the time and fuel? There wouldn't be any weapons aboard."

"Then how do they explain the fact that the *Scavenger* was blown to bits and Dad's orbit-ship ripped apart from top to bottom?"

"Details," the Major said. "Mere details. I'm sure that the company's lawyers can muddy the waters quite enough so that little details like that are overlooked. Particularly with a sympathetic jury and a judge that plays along."

He stood up and ran his hand through his hair. "All right, granted I'm painting the worst picture possible ... but I'm afraid that's the way it's going to be. I believe your story, don't worry about that. I know why you went out there to the Belt and I can't really blame you, I suppose. But you were asking for trouble, and that's what you got. Frankly, I am amazed that you ever returned to Mars, and how you managed to make rubble of an orbit-ship with a crew of four hundred men trying to stop you is more than I can comprehend. But you did it. All right, fine. You were justified; they attacked you, held you prisoner, threatened you. Fine. They'd have cut your throats in another few hours, perhaps. Fine. I believe you. But there's one big question that you can't answer, and unless you can no court in the Solar System will listen to you."

"What question?" Tom said.

"The question of motives," the Major replied. "You had plenty of motive for doing what Tawney says you did. But what motive did Jupiter Equilateral have, if your story is true?"

"They wanted to get what Dad found, out in the Belt."

"Ah, yes, that mysterious bonanza that Roger Hunter found. I was afraid that was what you'd say. And it's the reason that Jupiter Equilateral is going to win this fight, and you're going to lose it."

"I don't think I understand," Tom said slowly.

"I mean that I'm going to have to testify against you," the Major said. "*Because your father didn't find a thing in the Asteroid Belt*, and I happen to know it."

*

"It's been a war," the Major said later, "a dirty vicious war with no holds barred and no quarter given. Not a shooting war, of course, nothing out in the open ... but a war just the same, with the highest stakes of any war in history.

"It didn't look like a war, at first," the Major went on. "Back when the colonies were being built, nobody really believed that anything of value would come of them ... scientific outposts, perhaps, places for laboratories and observatories, not much more. The colonies were placed under United Nations control. Nobody argued about it.

"And then things began to change. There was wealth out here ... and opportunities for power. With the overpopulation at home, Earth was looking more and more to Mars and Venus for a place to move ... not tiny colonies, but places for millions of people. And as Mars grew, Jupiter Equilateral grew."

"But it was just a mining company," Tom said.

"At first it was, but then its interests began to expand. The company accumulated wealth, unbelievable wealth, and it developed many friends. Very soon it had friends back on Earth fighting for it, and the United Nations found itself fighting to stay on Mars."

"I don't see why," Tom said. "The company already has half the mining claims in the Belt...."

"They aren't interested in the mining," the Major said. "They have a much longer-range goal than that. The men behind Jupiter Equilateral are looking ahead. They know that someday Earthmen are going to have to go to the stars for colonies ... it won't be a matter of choice after a while, they'll *have* to go. Well, Jupiter Equilateral's terms are very simple. They're perfectly willing to let the United Nations control things on Earth. All they want is control of everything else. Mars, if they can drive us out. Venus too, if it ever proves up for colonies. And if they can gain control of the ships that leave our Solar System for the stars, they can build an empire, and they know it."

They were silent for a moment. Then Johnny Coombs said, "Doesn't anybody on Earth know about this?"

"There are some who know ... but they don't see the danger. They think of Jupiter Equilateral as just another big company. So far U.N. control of Mars and Venus has held up, even though the pressure on the legislators back on Earth has been getting heavier and heavier. Jupiter Equilateral won the greatest fight in its history when they limited U.N. jurisdiction to Mars, and kept us out of the Belt. And now they hope to convince the lawmakers that we're incompetent to administer the Martian colonies and keep peace out here. If they succeed, we'll be called home in nothing flat; we've had to fight just to stay."

The Major spread his hands helplessly. "Like I said, it's been a war. Our only hope was to prove that the company was using piracy and murder to gain control of the asteroids. We had to find a way to smash the picture they've been painting of themselves back on Earth as a big, benevolent organization interested only in the best for Earth colonists on the planets. We had to expose them before they had the Earth in chains ... not now, maybe not even a century from now, but sometime, years from now, when the breakthrough to the stars comes and Earthmen discover that if they want to leave Earth they have to pay toll...."

"They could never do that!" Greg protested.

"They're doing it, son. And they're winning. We have been searching desperately for a way to fight back, and that was where your father came in. He could see the handwriting, he knew what was happening. That was why he broke with the company and tried to organize a competing force before it was too late. And it was why he died in the Belt. He knew I couldn't send an agent out there without unquestionable evidence of major crime of some sort or another. But a private citizen could go out there, and if he happened to be working with the U.N. hand in glove, nobody could do anything about it."

"Then Dad was a U.N. agent?"

"Oh, not officially. There's not a word in the records. If I were forced to testify under oath, I would have to deny any connection. But unofficially, he went out there to lay a trap."

The Major told them then. It had been an incredible risk that Roger Hunter had taken, but the decision had been his. The plan was simple: to involve Jupiter Equilateral in a case of claim-jumping and piracy that would hold up in court, pressed by a man who would not be intimidated and could not be bought out. Roger Hunter had made a trip to the Belt and come back with stories ... very carefully planted in just the right ears ... of a fabulous strike. He knew that Jupiter Equilateral had jumped a hundred rich claims in the past, forcing the independent miners to agree, frightening them into silence or disposing of them with "accidents."

But this was one claim they were not going to jump. The U.N. cooperated, helping him spread the story of his Big Strike until they were certain that Jupiter Equilateral would go for the bait. Then Roger Hunter had returned to the Belt, with a U.N. Patrol ship close by in case he needed help.

"We thought it would be enough," the Major said unhappily. "We were wrong, of course. At first nothing happened ... not a sign of a company ship, nothing. Your father contacted me finally. He was ready to give up. Somehow they must have learned that it was a trap. But they had just been careful, was all. They waited until our guard was down, and then moved in fast and hit hard."

He sank down in his seat behind the desk, regarding the Hunter twins sadly. "You know the rest. Perhaps you can see now why I tried to keep you from going out there. There was no proof to uncover and no bonanza lode for you to find. There never was a bonanza lode."

The twins looked at each other, and then at the Major. "Why didn't you tell us?" Greg said.

"Would you have listened? Would telling you have kept you from going out there? There was no point to telling you, I knew you would have to find out for yourselves, however painfully. But what I'm telling you now is the truth."

"As far as it goes," Tom Hunter said. "But if this is really the truth, there's one thing that doesn't fit into the picture."

Slowly Tom pulled the gun case from his pack and set it down on the Major's desk. "It doesn't explain what Dad was doing with this."

PINPOINT IN SPACE

Tom knew now that it was the right thing to do. There was no question, after the Major's story, of what Dad had been doing out in the Belt at the time he had been killed. He had been doing a job that was more important to him than asteroid mining ... but he had found something more important than his own life, and had no chance to send word of what he had found back to Major Briarton on Mars. That had been the unforeseeable part of the trap.

But now, of course, the Major had to know.

The Mars Coordinator looked at the thing on the desk for a long moment before he reached out to touch it. The bright metal gleamed in the light, pale gray, lustrous. The Major picked it up, balanced it expertly in his hand, and a puzzled frown clouded his face. He examined it minutely.

"What is this thing?" he said.

"Suppose you tell us," Johnny Coombs said from across the room.

"It looks like a gun."

"That's what it is, all right."

"You've fired it?"

"Yes ... but I wouldn't fire it in here, if I were you," Johnny said. "You were wondering how we wrecked Tawney's orbit-ship so thoroughly. That's your answer right there." He told about the hole in the bulkhead, the way the ship's generators had melted like clay under the powerful blast of the weapon.

The Major could hardly control his excitement. "Where did you get it?" he asked, turning to Tom.

"From the space pack that you turned over to us. I didn't even look at it, until we needed a gun in a hurry. I just assumed it was Dad's revolver."

"And your father found it somewhere in the Belt," the Major said softly. He looked at the weapon again, shaking his head. "There isn't any such gun," he said finally. "These things you say it could do ... they would require energy enough to break down the cohesive forces of molecules. There isn't any way we know of to harness that kind of energy and channel it in a hand weapon. Nobody on Earth...."

He broke off and stared at them.

"That's right," Johnny said. "Nobody on Earth."

"You mean ... extraterrestrial?"

"There isn't any other answer," Johnny said. "*Look* at the thing, Major. *Feel* it. Does it feel like it was made for a human hand? It doesn't fit, it doesn't balance, you have to hold it with both hands to aim it...."

"*But where did it come from?*" the Major said. "We've never had visitors from another star system ... not in the course of recorded history. And we know that Earthmen are the only intelligent creatures in our Solar System."

"You mean that they're the only ones *now*," Tom said.

"Or any other time."

"We don't know that, for sure," Tom said.

"Look, we've explored Venus, Mars, all the major satellites. If there had ever been intelligence on any of them, we'd have known it."

"Maybe there was a planet that Earthmen haven't explored," Tom said. "Even Dad tried to tell us that. The quotation from Kepler that he scribbled down in his log ... 'Between Jupiter and Mars I will put a planet.' Why would Dad have written that? Unless he had suddenly discovered proof that there *had* been a planet there?"

"You mean this ... this gun," the Major said.

"And whatever else he found."

"But there's never been any proof of that theory ... not even a hint of proof."

"Maybe Dad found proof. There are hundreds of thousands of asteroid fragments out there in the Belt, and only a few hundred of them have ever been examined by men."

On the desk the strange weapon stared up at them. Evidence, mute evidence, and yet its very existence said more than a thousand words. It was there. It could not be denied.

And someone ... or *something* ... had made it.

Slowly the Major pulled himself to his feet. "It must have happened after his last message to me," he said. "It wasn't part of the scheme we had set up, but he made a strike just the same ... an archeological strike ... and this gun was part of it." He picked up the weapon, turned it over in his hand.

"But it was days after that last message before his signal went off, and the Patrol ship moved in."

"It makes sense," Johnny Coombs said. "He found the gun, and something more."

"Like what?"

"I wouldn't even guess," Johnny said. "A planet with a race of creatures intelligent enough and advanced enough to make a weapon like that ... it could have been anything. But whatever it was, it must have scared him. He must have known that a company ship might turn up any minute ... so he hid whatever he had found, and all he dared to leave was a hint."

"And now it's vanished," the Major said. "The big flaw in the whole idea. My Patrol ship found nothing when it searched the region. You looked, and drew a blank. The company men scoured the area." He spread his hands helplessly. "You see, it just won't hold up, not a bit of it. Even with this gun, it won't hold up. We've got to find the answer."

"It's out there somewhere," Tom said doggedly. "It's got to be."

"But *where?* Don't you see that everything hangs on that one thing? If we could prove that your father found something just before he was killed, we could tear Jupiter Equilateral's case against you into shreds. We could charge them with piracy and murder, and make it stick. We could break their power once and for all ... but until we know what Roger Hunter found, we're helpless. They'll take you three to court, and I won't be able to stop them. And if you lose that case, it may mean the end of U.N. authority on Mars."

"Then there's just one thing to do," Johnny Coombs said. "We've got to find Roger Hunter's bonanza."

*

It was almost midnight when they left the Major's office, a gloomy trio, walking silently up the ramp to the Main Concourse, heading toward the living quarters.

They had been talking with the Major for hours, going over every facet of the story, wracking their brains for the answer ... but the answer had not come.

Roger Hunter had found something, and hidden it so well that three groups of searchers had failed to discover it. After seeing the gun, the Major was convinced that there had indeed been a discovery made. But whatever that discovery had been, it was gone as if it had never existed ... as if by some sort of magic it had been turned invisible, or conjured away to another part of the Solar System.

Finally, they had given up, at least for the moment. "It has to be there," the Major had said wearily. "It hasn't vanished, or miraculously ceased to exist. We know he was working on one claim, one asteroid. There were no other asteroids in the region ... and even the ones within suicide radius have been searched."

"It's there, all right," Tom said. "We're missing something, that's all."

"But what? Asteroids have stable orbits. Nobody can just make one disappear...."

They had called it a night, finally.

Once home they found more bad news waiting. There were two messages on the recordomat. The first was an official summons to appear before the United Nations Board of Investigations at 9:00 the following morning to answer "certain charges placed against the above named persons by the Governing Board of Jupiter Equilateral Mining Industries, and by one Merrill Tawney, plaintiff, representing said Governing Board." They listened to the plastic record twice. Then Greg tossed it down the waste chute.

The other message was addressed to Greg, from the Commanding Officer of Project Star-Jump. The message was very polite and regretful; it was also very firm. The pressure of the work there, in his absence, made it necessary for the Project to suspend Greg on an indefinite leave of absence. Application for reinstatement could be made at a later date, but acceptance could not be guaranteed....

"Well, I might have expected it," Greg said, "after what the Major told us. The money for Star-Jump must have been coming from somewhere, and now we know where. The company probably figures to lay claim on any star-drive that's ever developed." He dropped the notice down the chute, and laughed. "I guess I really asked for it."

"You mean I pushed you into it," Tom said bitterly. "If I'd kept my big mouth shut at the very start of this thing, you'd have gone back to the Project and that would have been the end of it...."

*

Greg looked at him. "You big bum, do you think I really care?" He grinned. "Don't feel too guilty, Twin. We've been back to back on this one."

He pulled off his shirt and walked into the shower room. Johnny Coombs was already stretched out on the sofa, snoring softly.

Quite suddenly the room seemed hot and stuffy, oppressive. He couldn't make his thoughts come straight. There had been too much thinking, too much speculation. Tom stood up and slipped on his jacket.

He had to walk, to move about, to try to think. He slipped open the door, and started for the ramp leading to the Main Concourse.

There was an answer, somewhere.

He walked on along the steel walkways, trying to clear his mind of the doubts and questions that were plaguing him. At first he just wandered, but presently he realized that he had a destination in mind.

He went up a ramp and across the lobby of the United Nations Administration Building. He took a spur off the main corridor, and came to a doorway with a small circular staircase beyond it. At the bottom of the stairs he opened a steel door and stepped into the Map Room.

It was a small darkened amphitheater, with a curving row of seats along one wall. On either side were film viewers and micro-readers. And curving around on the far wall, like a huge parabolic mirror, was the Map.

Tom had been here many times before, and always he gasped in wonder when he saw the awesome beauty of the thing. Stepping into the Map Room was like stepping into the center of a huge cathedral. Here was the glowing, moving panorama of the Solar System spread out before him in a breath-taking three-dimensional image. Standing here before the Map it seemed as if he had suddenly become enormous and omnipotent, hanging suspended in the blackness of space and staring down at the Solar System from a vantage point a million miles away.

Once, Dad had told him, there had been a great statue in the harbor of Old New York which had been a symbol of freedom for strangers coming to that city from across the sea, and a welcome for countrymen returning home. And someday, he knew, this view of the Solar System would be waiting to greet Earthmen making their way home from distant stars. The Map was only an image, a gift from the United Nations to the colonists on

Mars, but it reproduced the Solar System in the minutest detail that astronomers could make possible.

In the center, glowing like a thing alive, was the Sun, the hub of the magnificent wheel. Around it, moving constantly in their orbits, were the planets, bright points of light on the velvet blackness of the screen. Each orbit was computed and held on the screen by the great computer in the vault below.

But there was more on the Map than the Sun and the planets, with their satellites. Tiny green lights marked the Earth-Mars and the Earth-Venus orbit-ships, moving slowly across the screen. Beyond Mars, a myriad of tiny lights projected on the screen, the asteroids. Without the magnifier Tom could identify the larger ones ... Ceres, on the opposite side of the Sun from Mars now as it moved in its orbit; smaller Juno, and Pallas, and Vesta....

For each asteroid which had been identified, and its orbit plotted, there was a pinpoint of light on the screen. For all its beauty, the Map had a very useful purpose ... the registry and identification of asteroid claims among the miners of Mars. Each asteroid registered as a claim showed up as a red pinpoint; unclaimed asteroids were white. But even with the advances of modern astronomy only a small percentage of the existing asteroids were on the map, for the vast majority had never been plotted.

Tom moved up to the Map and activated the magnifier. Carefully he focussed down on the section of the Asteroid Belt they had visited so recently. Dozens of pinpoints sprang to view, both red and white, and beneath each red light the claim-number neatly registered. Tom peered at the section, searching until he found the number of Roger Hunter's last claim.

It was quite by itself, not a part of an asteroid cluster. He stepped up the magnification, peered at it closely. There were a dozen other pinpoints, all unclaimed, within a ten-thousand-mile radius....

But near it, nothing....

No hiding place.

And then, suddenly, he knew the answer. He stared at the Map, his heart pounding in his throat. He cut the magnification, scanning a wide area. Then he widened the lens still further, and checked the coordinates at the bottom of the viewer.

He knew that he was right. He *had* to be right. But this was no wild dream, this was something that could be proved beyond any question of error.

Across the room he picked up the phone to Map Control. It buzzed interminably; then a sleepy voice answered.

"The Map," Tom managed to say. "It's recorded on time-lapse film, isn't it?"

"'Course it is," the sleepy voice said. "Observatory has to have the record. One frame every hour...."

"I've got to see some of the old film," Tom said.

"*Now?* It's three in the morning."

"I don't need the film itself, just project it for me. There's a reader here."

He gave the man the dates he wanted, Mars time. The man broke the contact, grumbling, but moments later one of the film-viewers sprang to life. The Map coordinates showed at the bottom of the screen.

Tom stared at the filmed image ... the image of a segment of the Asteroid Belt the day before Roger Hunter had died.

It was there. When he had looked at the Map, he had seen a single red pinpoint of light, Roger Hunter's asteroid, with nothing in the heavens anywhere near it.

But on the film image taken weeks before there were two points of light. One was red, with Roger Hunter's claim number beneath it. The other was white, so close to the first that even at full magnification it was barely distinguishable.

But it was there.

Tom's hands were trembling with excitement; he nearly dropped the phone receiver as he punched the buttons to ring the apartment. Greg's face appeared on the screen, puffy with sleep. "What's that? Thought you were in bed...."

"You've got to get down here," Tom said.

Greg blinked, waking up. "What's the matter? Where are you?"

"In the Map Room. Wake Johnny up and get down here. And try to get hold of the Major."

"You've found something," Greg said, excited now.

"I've found something," Tom said. "I've found where Dad hid his strike ... and I know how we can find it! We've got the answer, Greg."

THE MISSING ASTEROID

It had been a wild twelve hours since Tom Hunter's call to his brother from the Map Room in Sun Lake City. The Major had arrived first, still buttoning his shirt and wiping sleep from his eyes. Johnny and Greg came in on his heels. They had found Tom waiting for them, so excited he could hardly keep his words straight.

He told them what he had found, and they wondered why they had not thought of it from the first moment. "We knew there had to be an answer," Tom said, "some place Dad could have used for a hiding place, some place nobody would even think to look. Dad must have realized that he didn't have much time. When he saw his chance, he took it."

And it was pure, lucky chance. Tom showed them the section of the Map he had examined, with the pinpoint of light representing Roger Hunter's asteroid claim. Then the Map Control officer ... much more alert when he saw Major Briarton ... brought an armload of films up and loaded them into the projector. They stared at the screen, and saw the two pinpoints of light where one was now.

"What was the date of this?" the Major asked sharply.

"Two days before Dad died," Tom said. "There's quite a distance between them there ... but watch. One frame for every hour. Watch what happens."

He began running the film, the record taken from the Map itself, accurate as clockwork. The white dot was moving in toward the red dot at a forty-degree angle. For an instant it looked as though the two were colliding ... and then the distance between them began to widen again. Slowly, hour by hour, the white dot was moving away, off the screen altogether....

The Major looked up at Tom and slammed his fist on the chair-arm. "By the ten moons of Saturn...." he exploded, and then he was on his feet, shouting at the startled Map Control officer. "Get me Martinson down here, and fast. Call the port on a scrambled line and tell them to stand by with a ship on emergency call, with a crack interceptor pilot ready to go. Then get me the plotted orbits of every eccentric asteroid that's crossed

Mars' orbit in the last two months. And double-A security on everything ... we don't want to let Tawney get wind of this...."

Later, while they waited, they went over it to make sure that nothing was missing. "No wonder we couldn't spot it," the Major said. "We were looking for an asteroid in a standard orbit in the Belt."

"But there wasn't any," Tom said. "Dad's rock was isolated, nowhere near any others. And we were so busy thinking of the thousands of rocks in normal orbits between Mars and Jupiter that we forgot that there are a few eccentric ones that just don't travel that way."

"Like this one." The Major stared at the screen. "A long, intersecting orbit. It must swing out almost to Jupiter's orbit at one end, and come clear in to intersect Earth's orbit at the other end...."

"Which means that it cuts right through the Asteroid Belt and on out again." Tom grinned. "Dad must have seen it coming ... must have thought it was on collision course for a while. But he also must have realized that if he could hide something on its surface as it came near, it would be carried clear out of the Belt altogether in a few days' time."

"And if we can follow it up and intercept it...." The Major was on his feet, talking rapidly into the telephone. Sleep was forgotten now, nothing mattered but pinpointing a tiny bit of rock speeding through space. Within an hour the asteroid had been identified, its eccentric orbit plotted. The coordinates were taped into the computers of the waiting Patrol ship, as the preparations for launching were made.

It could not be coincidence. Somewhere on the surface of that tiny planetoid racing in toward the Sun they knew they would find Roger Hunter's secret.

*

Below them, as they watched, the jagged surface of the asteroid drew closer.

It was not round ... it was far too tiny a bit of cosmic debris to have sufficient gravity to crush down rocks and round off ragged corners. It was roughly oblong in shape, and one side was sheer smooth rock surface. The other side was rough, bristling with jutting rock. More than anything else it looked like a ragged mountain top, broken off at the peak and hurled into space by an all-powerful hand.

Slowly the scout-ship moved closer, braking with its forward jets. The pilot was expert. Carefully and surely he aligned the ship with the rock in speed and direction. In the accelleration cot Tom could feel only an occasional gentle tug as the power cut on and off.

Then the Lieutenant said, "I think we can make a landing now, Major."

"Fine. Take a scooter down first, and carry a guy line."

They unstrapped, and changed into pressure suits. In the airlock they waited until the Lieutenant had touched the scooter down. Then Major Briarton nodded, and they clamped their belts to the guy line.

One by one they leaped down toward the rock.

From a few miles out in space, the job of searching the surface had not appeared difficult. From the rock itself, things looked very different. There was no way, from the surface, to scan large areas, and the surface was so rough that they had to take constant care not to damage their boots or rip holes in their suits. There were hundreds of crevices and caves, half concealed by the loose rock that crumbled under their feet as they moved.

They spread out from the scooter for an hour of fruitless searching. Tom spent most of the time pulling his boots free of surface cracks and picking his way over heaps of jagged rock. None of them got farther than a hundred yards from the starting place. None of them found anything remarkable.

"We could spend weeks covering it this way," Greg said when they met at the scooter again. "Why don't I take the scooter and criss-cross the whole surface at about fifty feet? If I spot anything, I'll yell."

It seemed like a good idea. Greg strapped himself into the scooter's saddle, straddling the fuel tanks, using the hand jet to guide himself as he lifted lightly off the surface. He disappeared over the horizon of rock, then reappeared as he moved over the surface and back.

Tom and Johnny waited with the Major. Twenty minutes later Greg brought the tiny craft back again. "It's no good," he said. "I've scanned the whole bright-side, came as close as I dared."

"No sign of anything?" Johnny said.

"Not a thing. The dark side looks like a sheer slab, from what my lights show. If we only had some idea what we were looking for...."

"Maybe you weren't close enough," Tom said. "Why not drop each of us off to take a quarter of the bright-side and work our way in?"

The others agreed. Tom waited until the Major and Johnny had been posted; then he hopped on the scooter behind Greg and dropped off almost at the line of darkness, where the sheer slab began. All of them had hoped that there might be a sign, something that Roger Hunter might have left to mark his cache, but if there was one none of them spotted it. Tom checked with the others by the radio in his helmet, and started moving back toward the center of the bright side.

An hour later he was only halfway to the center, and he was nearly exhausted. At a dozen different spots he thought he had found a promising cleft in the rock, a place where something might have been concealed ... but exploration of the clefts proved fruitless.

And now his confidence began to fail. Supposing he had been wrong? They knew the rock had passed very close to Roger Hunter's asteroid, the astronomical records proved that. But suppose Dad had not used it as his hiding place at all? He pulled himself around another jagged rock shelf, staring down at the rough asteroid surface beyond....

At the base of the rock shelf, something glinted in the sunlight. He leaped down, and thrust his hand into a small crevice in the rock. His hand closed on a small metal object.

It was a gun. It felt well balanced, familiar in his hand ... the revolver Dad had always carried in his gun case.

He had to let them know. He was just snapping the speaker switch when he heard a growl of static in his earphones, and then Greg's voice, high-pitched and excited. "Over here! I think I've found something!"

It took ten minutes of scrambling over the treacherous surface to reach Greg. Tom saw his brother tugging at a huge chunk of granite that was wedged into a crevice in the rock. Tom got there just as the Major and Johnny topped a rise on the other side and hurried down to them.

The rock gave way, rolling aside, and Greg reached down into the crevice. Tom leaned over to help him. Between them they lifted out the thing that had been wedged down beneath the boulder.

It was a metal cylinder, four feet long, two feet wide, and bluntly tapered at either end. In the sunlight it gleamed like polished silver, but they could see a hairline break in the metal encircling the center portion.

They had found Roger Hunter's bonanza.

*

In the cabin of the scout-ship they broke the cylinder open into two perfect halves. It came apart easily, a shell of paper-thin but remarkably strong metal, protecting the tightly packed contents.

There was no question what the cylinder was, even though there was nothing inside that looked even slightly familiar at first examination. There were several hundred very tiny thin discs of metal that fit on the spindle of a small instrument that was packed with them. There were spools of film, thin as tissue but amazingly strong. Examined against the light in the cabin, the film seemed to carry no image at all ... but there was another small machine that accepted the loose end of the film, and a series of lenses that glowed brightly with no apparent source of power. There was a thick block of shiny metal covered on one side with almost invisible scratches....

A time capsule, beyond doubt. A confusing treasure, at first glance, but the idea was perfectly clear. A hard shell of metal protecting the records collected inside....

Against what? A planetary explosion? Some sort of cosmic disaster that had blown a planet and its people into the fragments that now filled the Asteroid Belt?

At the bottom of the cylinder was a small tube of metal. They examined it carefully, trying to guess what it was supposed to be. At the bottom was a tiny stud. When they pressed it, the cylinder began to expand and unfold, layer upon layer of thin glistening metallic material that spread out into a sheet that stretched halfway across the cabin.

They stared down at it. The metal seemed to have a life of its own, glowing and glinting, focussing light into pinpoints on its surface.

It was a map.

At one side, a glowing ball with a fiery corona, an unmistakeable symbol that any intelligent creature in the universe that was able to perceive it at all would recognize as a star. Around it, in clearly marked orbits, ten planets. The third planet had a single satellite, the fourth two tiny ones. The sixth eleven. The seventh planet had ten, and was encircled by glowing rings.

But the fifth planet was broken into four parts.

Beyond the tenth planet there was nothing across a vast expanse of the map ... but at the far side was another star symbol, this one a double star with four planetary bodies.

They stared at the glowing map, speechless. There could be no mistaking the meaning of the thing that lay before them, marked in symbols that could mean only one thing to any intelligence that could recognize stars and planets.

But in the center of the sheet was another symbol. It lay halfway between the two Solar Systems, in the depths of interstellar space. It was a tiny picture, a silvery sliver of light, but it too was unmistakeable.

It could be nothing else but a Starship.

*

Later, as they talked, they saw that the map had told each of them, individually, the same thing. "They had a star-drive," Tom said. "Whatever kind of creatures they were, and whatever the disaster that threatened their planet, they had a star-drive to take them out of the Solar System to another star."

"But why leave a record?" Greg wanted to know. "If nobody was here to use it...."

"Maybe for the same reason that Earthmen bury time capsules with records of their civilization," Major Briarton said. "I'd guess that the records here will tell, when they have been studied and deciphered. Perhaps there was already some sign of intelligent life developing elsewhere in the Solar System. Perhaps they hoped that some of their own people would survive. But they had a star-drive, so some of them must have escaped. And with the record here...."

"We may be able to follow them," Greg said.

"If we can decipher the record," Johnny Coombs said. "But we don't have any clue to their language."

"Did you have any trouble understanding what the map had to say?" the Major said quietly.

"No...."

"I don't think the rest will be much more difficult. They were intelligent creatures. The record will be understandable, all right." He started to fold the map back into a tube again. "Maybe Roger Hunter tried to use the film projector. We'll never know. But he must have realized that he had discovered the secret of a star-drive. He realized that the United Nations were the ones to explore it and use it, and he gave his life to keep it out of the hands of Tawney and his men...."

"A pity," a cold voice said close behind them, "that he didn't succeed, after all."

They whirled. In the hatchway to the after-cabin, Merrill Tawney was standing, with a smile on his lips and a Markheim stunner trained directly on Major Briarton's chest.

THE FINAL MOVE

"I realize I'm much earlier than you expected, Major. You did a very neat job of camouflaging your takeoff ... we were almost fooled ... and no doubt the dummy ship you sent off later got full fanfare. I suppose there will be a dozen Patrol ships converging on this spot in a few hours, expecting to surprise a Jupiter Equilateral ship making a desperate attempt to hijack your little treasure here."

The little fat man laughed cheerfully. "Unfortunately for you," he added, "we have many friends on Mars ... including a man in the Map room ... and I'm afraid your little trap isn't going to work after all."

The Major's face was gray. "How did you get here?"

"By hitch-hiking. How else? Most uncomfortable, back there, even with a pile of pressure suits for padding, but your pilot was really very skillful."

Johnny Coombs turned on the Major. "What does he mean, a trap? I don't get this...."

The Major sighed wearily. "I had to try to force his hand. Even if we found what we were looking for, we had no case that could stand up against them. We needed *proof* ... and I thought that with this as bait we could trap them. He's right about the Patrol ships ... but they won't be near for hours."

"And that will be a little late to help," Tawney said pleasantly.

The Major glared at him. "Maybe so ... but you've gone too far this time. This is an official U.N. ship. You'll never be able to go back to Mars."

"Really?" the fat man said. "And why not? Officially I'm on Mars right now, with plenty of people to swear to the fact." He chuckled. "You seem to forget that little matter of proof, Major. When your Patrol ships find a gutted ship and five corpses, they may suspect that something more than an accident was involved, but what can they prove? Nothing more than they could prove in the case of Roger Hunter's accident. Scout-ships have been known to explode before."

He ran his hand over the metal cylinder. "And as for this ... it's really a surprise. Of course when we failed to find any evidence of mining activity, we were certain that Roger Hunter's bonanza was something more than a vein of ore, but *this*! You can be certain that we will exploit the secret of a star-drive to the very fullest."

"How do you think you can get away with it?" the Major said. "Turning up with something like that right after a whole series of suspicious accidents in space?"

"Oh, we aren't as impatient as some people. We wouldn't be so foolish as to break the news now. Five years from now, maybe ten years, one of our orbit-ships will happen upon a silvery capsule on one of our asteroid claims, that's all. I wouldn't be surprised if a non-company observer might be on board at the time, maybe even a visiting Senator from Earth. For something this big, we can afford to be patient."

There was silence in the little scout-ship cabin. The end seemed inevitable. This was a desperate move on Tawney's part. He was gambling everything on it; he would not take the chance of letting any of them return to Mars or anywhere else to testify.

Greg caught Tom's eye, saw the hopelessness on his brother's face. He clenched his fists angrily at his side. If it were not for Tom, Dad's bonanza might have gone on circling the sun for centuries, maybe forever, wedged in its hiding place on the rocky surface of the eccentric asteroid.

But it had been found. Earth needed a star-drive badly; a few more years, and the need would be desperate. And if a group of power-hungry men could control a star-drive and hold it for profit, they could blackmail an entire planet for centuries, and build an empire in space that could never be broken.

He knew that it must not happen that way. Dad had died to prevent it. Now it was up to them.

*

Greg glanced quickly around the cabin, searching for some way out, something that might give them a chance. His eyes stopped on the control panel, and he sucked in his breath, his heart pounding. A possibility....

It would require a swift, sure move, and someone to help, someone with fast reflexes. It was dangerous; they might all be killed. But if his training at Star-jump was good for anything, it might work.

He caught Johnny Coombs' eye, winked cautiously. A frown creased Johnny's forehead. He shot a quick look at Tawney, then lowered his eyelid a fraction of an inch. Greg could see the muscles of his shoulders tightening.

Greg took quick stock of the cabin again. Then he took a deep breath and bellowed, "Johnny ... *duck*!"

Almost by reflex, Johnny Coombs hurled himself to the floor. Tawney swung the gun around. There was an ugly ripping sound as the stunner fired ... but Greg was moving by then. In two bounds he was at the control panel. He hooked an arm around a shock bar, and slammed the drive switch on full.

There was a roar from below as the engines fired. Greg felt a jolt of pain as the accelleration jerked at his arm. Tom and the Major were slammed back against a bulkhead, then fell in a heap on top of Johnny and the Lieutenant as the awful force of the accelleration dragged them back. Across the cabin Tawney sprawled on the floor. The stunner flew from his hand and crashed against the rear bulkhead.

On the panel Greg could see the accelleration gauge climbing swiftly ... past four g's, up to five, to six. The ship was moving wildly; there was no pilot, no course.

With all the strength he could muster Greg tightened his arm on the shock bar, lifting his other arm slowly toward the cut-off switch. He had spent many hours in the accelleration centrifuge at Star-Jump, learning to withstand and handle the enormous forces of accelleration for brief periods, but the needle was still climbing and he knew he could not hold on long. His fingers touched the control panel. He strained, inching them up toward the switch....

His fingers closed on the stud, and he pulled. The engine roar ceased. On the floor behind him Tawney moved sluggishly, trying to sit up. Blood was dripping from his nose. He was still too stunned to know what had happened.

Greg leaped across the room, caught up the stunner, and then sank to the floor panting. "All right," he said as his breath came back, "that's all. Your ship may have trouble finding us now ... but I bet our pilot can get us back to Mars."

*

When they left the Sun Lake City infirmary it was almost noon, and the red sun was gleaming down from overhead. Walking slowly, the Hunter twins moved along the surface street toward the U.N. building.

"He'll recover without any trouble," the doctor had assured them. "He caught the stunner beam in the shoulder, and it will be a while before he can use it, but Johnny Coombs will be hard to keep down."

They had promised Johnny to return later. They had had check-ups themselves. Both Tom's eyes were surrounded by purple splotches, and his broken left arm was in a sling. Greg's arms and legs were so stiff he could hardly move them. The Major and the Lieutenant had been sore but uninjured.

Now the boys walked without talking. Already a U.N. linguist was at work on the record tapes from the metal cylinder, and a mathematician was doing a preliminary survey on the math symbols on the metal block.

"I hope there's no trouble reading them," Greg said.

"There won't be. It'll take time, but the records are decipherable. And Dr. Raymond was certain that the engineering can be figured out. Earth is going to get her star-ship, all right."

"And we've got work to do."

"You mean the trial? I guess. The Major says that Jupiter Equilateral is trying to pin the whole thing on Tawney now. They won't get away with it, but it may be nasty just the same."

"Well, one thing's sure ... there'll be some changes made, with the U.N. moving out into the Belt," Greg said.

Somewhere in the distance the twins heard the rumble of engines. They stopped and watched as a great silvery cargo ship lifted from the space port and headed up into the dark blue sky. They watched it until it disappeared from sight.

They were both thinking the same thing.

An Earth-bound ship, powerful and beautiful, but limited now to the sun and nine planets, unable to reach farther out.

But someday soon a different kind of ship would rise.

Printed at Repro India Ltd.